NO MAN'S LAND

WRITINGS FROM A WORLD AT WAR

CHOSEN AND INTRODUCED
BY PETE AYRTON

A complete catalogue record for this book can be obtained
from the British Library on request

The right of Pete Ayrton to be identified as the editor of this work has been asserted
by him in accordance with the Copyright, Designs and Patents Act 1988

Selection, introduction and editorial matter © Pete Ayrton 2014
For copyright details of the selected writings see *Permissions* on pp 550–1

First published in this edition in 2015 by Serpent's Tail

First published in 2014 by Serpent's Tail,
an imprint of Profile Books Ltd
3 Holford Yard
Bevin Way
London
WC1X 9HD
www.serpentstail.com

ISBN 978 1 84668 926 0
eISBN 978 1 84765 922 4

Designed by Sue Lamble
Typeset in Bembo by MacGuru Ltd
info@macguru.org.uk

Printed and bound in Great Britain by CPI Group (UK) Ltd, Croydon CR0 4YY

1 3 5 7 9 10 8 6 4 2

This book is dedicated to Susan Sontag, who made
sure I never forgot that words have no borders

CONTENTS

CONTENTS

CONTENTS

CONTENTS

ACKNOWLEDGEMENTS

A N ENTERPRISE LIKE *NO MAN'S LAND* is a collective one. The many people who helped me have been most generous with their knowledge and time. Special thanks to Roger Little, Ruth Bush and Françoise Escholier-Achard who made possible the use of her grandfather's novel, Noel King and Garth Cartwright, Max Décharné, Ursula Owen, Giovanni Lussu for making available the new translation of his father's book, Julian Evans, Tibor Fischer, Sarah Lefanu, Maureen Freely and Professor Erol Koroglu, Edmund Fawcett, Irene Noel-Baker, Mark Thompson, Marija Mitrovic, Jeremy Beale and John Williams. To all those at Serpent's Tail and Profile who have made this book what it is - Peter Dyer, Sue Lamble, Ruthie Petrie, and Valentina Zanca. To my first editor, Peter Carson and then, John Davey, who both mixed support and criticism in the right proportions. To the translators - Peter Bush, Martin Chalmers, Izzy Finkel, Celia Hawkesworth, Malcolm Imrie, Ana Jelnikar, Cristina Viti, and Stephen Watts - who met the tightest of deadlines with a minimum of fuss. To the most helpful people at the London Library. To Helen Francis who found the rights holders and got permission to use the featured extracts. And to Sarah Martin, Carla and Oscar who lived through the roller-coaster of elation and despair as an Armenian author proved less and, then, more elusive to track down.

INTRODUCTION

I N COLLECTING MATERIAL FOR *NO MAN'S LAND*, my first priority was to feature writing from as many of the countries that took part as possible. This not from some desire to be exhaustive but because I wanted to convey that the war truly was a *world* war – so there are contributions from writers from twenty countries. The pieces in the book cover the fighting in all the theatres of the war: of course the Western Front, but also the Eastern Front, the Balkan Front, the Italian Front, Gallipoli and the War at Sea.

They also cover the experiences of the men and women left behind on the home front, of the women on the war front and of the soldiers who returned home never able to forget what they had endured. Because they come from many countries, the pieces reflect very different attitudes to the nation and very different motivations for fighting the war.

For the British, French and Germans who wrote about the war, their attitude was relatively straightforward. Whatever the historical facts, almost all of them felt loyalty to a well-defined nation which they took to be morally superior to other nations and whose war effort they supported. A small minority opposed the war but this was more because they took war of any kind to be evil than from the belief that other nations were morally equal to their own.

For combatants from other countries, the nation-state was more recent and/or more contested and they had a much more fragile commitment to nationhood and empire.

The tensions in the Italian army, for instance, reflected the fact that Italy was united only in 1861 and that the creation of Italian nationalism was a work-in-progress. In Lussu's *A Soldier on the Southern Front*, the officers went into battle with the shout 'Savoy!':

> Now that I was calm again, I could see all that was going on around me. Officers and men were falling with their arms flung wide and their rifles hurled so far in front of them that it seemed as though a battalion of dead men was advancing. Captain Bravini never stopped shouting: 'Savoy!'
>
> A subaltern of the 12th, red in the face, passed near me, clutching his rifle. He was a republican, and disliked the monarchial war-cry that we used in attack. Seeing me, he shouted: 'Long live Italy!'
>
> (*A Soldier on the Southern Front*, New York: Rizzoli, 2014, pages 121–122)

There is no doubt that the scenes of mutinous hatred described by Lussu were fuelled by the soldiers' sense of grievance at being led by an officer class whose loyalty to the Italian nation was, in their eyes, doubtful.

For those fighting in the Austro-Hungarian army, loyalty to empire was weak. In Rebreanu's *The Forest of the Hanged*, Lieutenant Bologa is a brilliant officer whose bravery will be rewarded by a Gold Medal bestowed on him by General Karg, who wants to take him with him on his next campaign to Ardeal in Romania. Apostol is not keen on going.

> 'Very well, very well,' repeated the general thoughtfully. 'Though I don't understand why you should not want to come with us. My division has a holy mission in Ardeal! A great mission. Yes! The enemy has stolen our country's soil. There the Wallachians…'
>
> Suddenly General Karg stopped short as if a ray of light had entered his brain. He again took a few steps backwards and glued his gaze on Bologa, trying to read his innermost thoughts. For

several seconds there reigned a grave-like silence in the room, while outside could be heard the grinding of cart wheels and the noisy chirping of the sparrows in a tree under the office window. Apostol unconsciously closed his eyes to protect himself from the general's scrutiny.

'You are a Romanian?' the latter jerked out abruptly, his voice almost hoarse.

(*The Forest of the Hanged*, London: George Allen & Unwin, 1930, page 100)

Bologa is prepared to fight valiantly but draws a line on going into battle against his kith and kin. Certainly, the effectiveness of the Austro-Hungarian army was undermined by its need to enlist combatants from its ethnic minorities.

The Good Soldier Švejk has a wry, sardonic attitude to the loyalty demanded by his commanding officers:

'His Imperial Majesty must be completely off his rocker by this time,' declared Švejk. 'He was never bright, but this war'll certainly finish him.'

'Of course he's off his rocker,' the soldier from the barracks asserted with conviction. 'He's so gaga he probably doesn't know there's a war on. Perhaps they're ashamed of telling him. If his signature's on the manifesto to his peoples, then it's a fraud. They must have had it printed without his knowledge, because he's not capable of thinking about anything at all.'

'He's finished,' added Švejk knowingly. 'He wets himself and they have to feed him like a little baby. Recently a chap at the pub told us that His Imperial Majesty has two wet nurses and is breast-fed three times a day.'

'If only it was all over,' sighed the soldier from the barracks, 'and they knocked us out, so that Austria at last had peace!'

And both continued with the conversation until Švejk condemned Austria forever with the words: 'A monarchy as idiotic as this ought not to exist at all...'

(*The Good Soldier Švejk*, London: Heinemann, 1973, pages 207–208)

If the patriotism of Europeans fighting varied greatly, for many of the Indians and Africans enlisted in the imperial armies it was non-existent. For some, the links were primarily monetary – they went to fight in the hope that they would come back from the wars with financial rewards and even a pension; for others there was the hope that the imperial nations would recognize the contribution made to the war effort by the soldiers from the colonies and implement political and economic reforms. As Mulk Raj Anand writes in *Across the Black Waters*:

> And once now in a while in a district arrived a hero, a man who had earned both a pension and a medal attached to it. And soon he became a legend and people came to see him, the wonder, especially as he had left an arm, a leg or an eye behind, and used a miraculous wooden substitute…
>
> Information about rewards was, therefore, the chief preoccupation of the sepoys, talking about it their main consolation in exile, the inspiration of it what spurred them on to battle. How happy would be the dear ones at home if only a ready sum could help to pay even a tenth part of the moneylenders' interest and towards the repair of the roof which had been washed out by the last monsoon before the drought!
>
> (*Across the Black Waters*, Delhi: Orient Paperbacks, 2008, page 169)

It was the same for many of the African soldiers – they were rewarded poorly and their expectations of a better life when they returned home after the war were not fulfilled. In *Mahmadou Fofana*, Raymond Escholier writes that the silver ring given by Samba Kamara's brother was

> …all that would be left to the dead man of the village he had so much hoped to see again.
>
> I must admit that to my sadness was added remorse. I felt the revolt that had found no place in the simple, docile soul of Samba Kamara. What gives us whites the right to remove a black man from the peace of his field to involve him in our quarrels, in our hatreds.

Yes, I know how the story goes: 'We are tearing these people from Barbary, we are letting them enjoy the fruits of civilisation. When the crunch comes, they must pay back their debt: we share the same course.'

(*Mahmadou Fofana*, Paris: L'Harmattan, 2013, pages 68–69)

Whatever a soldier's relationship to the army he was fighting in, the war marked a crucial period in his life – for many millions it also marked his death. Of the soldiers who survived the war and are written about in *No Man's Land*, some returned reduced by injury, others never were reconciled to the horrors they had witnessed and how the war had made them unfit for the return to civilian life. The ambulance-driver narrator in Helen Zenna Smith's *Not So Quiet: Stepdaughters of War* finds contemplation of the return unbearable:

Home, home… and I do not care.

I do not care. I am flat. Old. I am twenty-one and as old as the hills. Emotion-dry. The war has drained me dry of feeling. Something has gone from me that will never return. I do not want to go home.

I am suddenly aware that I cannot bear Mother's prattle-prattle of committees and recruiting-meetings and the war-baby of Jessie, the new maid; nor can I watch my gentle father gloating over the horrors I have seen, pumping me for good stories to retail at his club to-morrow. I cannot go home to watch a procession of maimed men in my dainty, rose-walled bedroom. It is no place for a company of broken men on parade…

(*Not So Quiet*, New York: The Feminist Press CUNY, 1989, page 169)

For some on the home front, what happened during the war was confirmation that society had to change – that other ways of organizing it were possible. Those who saw this were a minority that had to make their voice heard:

We're few; that doesn't matter. We shall be pilloried; that doesn't matter. All that matters is that we shall have striven against what our brains and our hearts recognised as evil – Oh, not only evil, but stupid and petty and beastly – and we shall have done our bit towards bringing nearer the day when militarism will be supplanted by industry, and we may hope to have an international system of legislation that'll knock out the possibility of disputes having to be settled by barbarous and unintelligent means of bloodshed.

(*Despised and Rejected*, London: GMP, 1988, page 241)

As the war went on, the minority grew and was joined by the many disillusioned soldiers who returned home determined to make sure the suffering they had endured would not be in vain. So, the post-war period was in many of the countries involved in the war a period of revolutionary fervour and/or democratic reform.

Any selection of writing on the First World War has certain criteria. To give *No Man's Land* as international a perspective as possible, translations were undertaken of works that had previously not been translated. The selection was limited to works written before 1945; this, like most criteria, is arbitrary, but I felt that the experience of the Second World War gave writers a very different perspective from which to assess the First and so marked a valid cut-off point. And priority was given to fiction and to a lesser extent memoirs – though it is clear that the boundary between them is fluid – much of the fiction about the war is autobiographical. No poetry was selected since the war poetry has already been well represented in many excellent anthologies and was relatively well known.[*]

No Man's Land begins with the declaration of war being declared in Henri Barbusse's *Under Fire* (London: Penguin, 2003, page 5):

'It's the French revolution all over again.'
'Crowned heads beware!' murmurs another.

---

[*]Where the selected piece of writing has no title I have given it one as a guide to what it is about. Other titles are provided by the authors. Some writers from the period use ellipses to indicate a pause or a change of place or tone: they do not indicate omissions (Ed.).

And a third man adds:

'Perhaps it is the war to end all wars.'

There is a pause, then a few brows shake, still pale from the wan tragedy of a night of perspiring insomnia.

'An end to war! Can that be? An end to war! The world's affliction is incurable.'

At the end is the narrator of Erich Maria Remarque's *All Quiet on the Western Front*:

But perhaps all these thoughts of mine are just melancholy and confusion, which will be blown away like dust when I am standing underneath the poplars once again, and listening to the rustle of their leaves. It cannot have vanished entirely, that tenderness that troubles our blood, the uncertainty, the worry, all the things to come, the thousand faces of the future, the music of dreams and books, the rustling and the idea of women. All this cannot have collapsed in the shelling, the despair and the army brothels.

The trees here glow bright and gold, the rowan berries are red against the leaves, white country roads run on towards the horizon, and the canteens are all buzzing like beehives with rumours of peace.

(*All Quiet on the Western Front*, London: Vintage, 1996, page 200)

In between, there is the carnage and destruction of the four years of a war that determined the history of the 20th century. The war changed all aspects of people's lives – it changed the relations between the classes, between the sexes and between races in Europe and beyond. It led to the growth of the evils that spread through Europe in the following decades: fascism, communism, anti-Semitism, and genocide. And it redrew geographical boundaries giving the victors the spoils of victory and amputating the territories of the defeated. This geographical settling of scores was fundamentally unstable – it rewarded the more powerful, it showed that might is right. And its creation of ethnic minorities all over Europe led to many of the major conflicts of the last hundred years, including, of course, the Second World War.

Editing this book has been an up-and-down journey that required much reading that chronicled the relentless brutality of mankind, but it also provided many occasions of wondrous surprise that showed the power of human beings to express solidarity and kindness in conditions of great adversity. It also enabled me to discover authors who realized they were writing on the cusp of an epochal moment in which change – in its social, political and artistic forms – was possible and who fully embraced the moment. Carlo Emilio Gadda and Mary Borden were the contemporaries of Stravinsky and Webern, Klee and Leger, Frank Lloyd Wright and Mies van der Rohe – but that is another story.

One hundred years after the beginning of the war, the celebration of the anniversary, a building block of our national identity, is contested terrain. If this anthology helps to remind us that the war was truly international, then it will have achieved its aim. I hope that reading the anthology is as rewarding an experience as it was for me to compile it.

HENRI BARBUSSE

THE VISION

from *Under Fire*

translated by Robin Buss

THE DENT DU MIDI, the Aiguille Verte and Mont Blanc stare down at the bloodless faces emerging from under the blankets lined up along the gallery of the sanatorium.

On the first floor of the palatial hospital, this terrace with its balcony of carved wood supported by a veranda is isolated in space and overhangs the world.

The fine wool blankets – red, green, havana brown or white – with emaciated faces emerging from under them, and radiant eyes, are still. Silence reigns over the chaises longues. Someone coughs. Then nothing more is heard but the turning of the pages of a book at long, regular intervals; or a murmured request and hushed reply from a bed to the one beside it; or sometimes on the balustrade, the flapping like a fan of a venturesome crow, a fugitive from the flocks that make rosaries of black pearls in the transparent void.

Silence reigns. In any case, those people, rich and independent, who have come here from all parts of the earth, struck down by the same misfortune, have lost the habit of speech. They have turned in on themselves and think about their lives and deaths.

A maid appears in the gallery. She walks softly; she is dressed in white. She is bringing newspapers which she hands around.

'That's it,' says the first one to unfold his paper. 'War has been declared.'

Expected though it was, the news causes a kind of astonishment because those who hear it sense its extreme importance.

These men are cultured and intelligent, their minds deepened by suffering and reflection, detached from things and almost from life, as distant from the rest of the human species as if they already belonged to posterity, looking far ahead towards the incomprehensible land of the living and the mad.

'Austria is committing a crime,' the Austrian says.

'France must win,' says the Englishman.

'I hope that Germany will be defeated,' says the German.

They settle back under the blankets, on their pillows, facing the mountain peaks and the sky. But despite the purity of space, the silence is filled with the news that they have just received.

'War!'

A few of those lying there break the silence, repeating the word under their breath and considering that this is perhaps the greatest event of modem times, perhaps of all time. And the annunciation even casts a kind of confused and murky veil over the clear landscape before their eyes.

The calm expanses of the valley dotted with villages pink as roses and soft pastures, the splendid outlines of the mountains, the black lace of the pine trees and the white lace of the eternal snows, are filled with the bustling of mankind.

Multitudes teem in clearly defined masses. On the fields attacks sweep forward, wave after wave, then come to a standstill; houses are gutted like men and towns like houses; villages appear in crumpled white as though they had fallen on to the earth from the sky; frightful loads of dead and wounded men alter the shape of the plains.

You can see every country where the borders are eaten away with massacres constantly tearing new soldiers from its heart, full of strength, full of blood; your gaze follows these living tributaries for the river of the dead.

North, south and west, battles rage, on all sides, in the distance. You can turn this way or that; there is not a single horizon on which there is no war.

One of the pale men watching rises on his elbow, counting and reckoning the present and future combatants: thirty million soldiers. Another man stammers, his eyes full of slaughter:

'Two armies engaged in battle are one great army committing suicide.'

'They shouldn't have done it,' says the deep, hollow voice of the first man in the row.

But another man says:

'It's the French Revolution all over again.'

'Crowned heads beware!' murmurs another.

And a third man adds:

'Perhaps it is the war to end wars.'

There is a pause, then a few brows shake, still pale from the wan tragedy of a night of perspiring insomnia.

'An end to war! Can that be? An end to war! The world's affliction is incurable.'

Someone coughs. Then the immense calm of meadows under the sun where bright cattle softly shine and black woods and green fields and blue horizons submerge the vision, quelling the glow of the fire that is consuming and breaking the old world. An infinite silence covers the murmur of the hatred and suffering of the dark teeming of the world. The speakers slip back, one by one, into themselves, preoccupied with the mystery of their lungs and the health of their bodies.

But when evening is about to fall across the valley, a storm breaks over the massif of Mont Blanc.

No one is allowed out on this dangerous evening when one can feel the last waves of wind break under the vast veranda, right beneath this port where they have taken refuge.

These men, severely smitten, eaten away by an inner wound, stare at the confusion of the elements. They watch the thunder break over the mountain, lifting up the clouds on the horizon like a sea, each clap of the storm throwing out at once into the dusk a column of fire and a column of cloud. They turn their ashen, hollow-cheeked faces to follow the eagles circling in the sky that watch the earth from on high through rings of mist.

'Stop the war!' they are saying. 'Stop the storms!'

But the watchers on the threshold of the world, free of partisan passion, free of prejudices, blindness and the shackles of tradition, also have a vague sense of the simplicity of things and of gaping possibilities...

The one at the end of the row exclaims:

'You can see things, down there, things rearing up!'

'Yes... They're like living things.'

'Sort of plants...'

'Sort of men.'

Now, in the sinister light of the storm beneath black dishevelled clouds, dragged and spread across the earth like wicked angels, they seem to see a great livid white plain extend before them. In their vision, figures rise up out of the plain, which is composed of mud and water, and clutch at the surface of the ground, blinded and crushed with mire, like survivors from some monstrous shipwreck. These men seem to them to be soldiers. The plain is vast, riven by long parallel canals and pitted with waterholes, and the shipwrecked men trying to extract themselves from it are a great multitude... But the thirty million slaves who have been thrown on top of one another by crime and error into this war of mud raise human faces in which the glimmer of an idea is forming. The future is in the hands of these slaves and one can see that the old world will be changed by the alliance that will one day be formed between those whose number and whose suffering is without end.

Henri Barbusse was born near Paris in 1873. He enlisted in the French army in 1914 and served for 17 months until, suffering from a lung condition, dysentery and exhaustion, he was invalided out of the front lines and reassigned to a desk job. Although he was a supporter of the war in 1914, Barbusse's months on the front were spent in mud, in filth, amongst the dead and with the constant terror of artillery bombardment; they completely changed his attitude to the war: 'Only on a battlefield like this, can one have a precise idea of the horror of these great massacres.' And these experiences shaped *Under*

Fire, the great war classic first published in 1916. It was an instant success; it sold 200,000 copies in its first year of publication and in 1917 won the Prix Goncourt, France's highest literary honour. Barbusse knew that the book would convey a first-hand experience of the war. But he also hoped that from the carnage would come change.

In 1918, Barbusse moved to Moscow, where he married a Russian woman and joined the Soviet Communist Party. A lifelong communist, Barbusse was involved in the setting up of the World Committee Against War and Fascism in 1933 and, with Romain Rolland, he was active in the attempts to create a proletarian literature influenced by socialist realism. Barbusse never criticized Stalinism and died in Moscow in 1935. This extract is the beginning of *Under Fire*.

MULK RAJ ANAND

MARSEILLE

from *Across the Black Waters*

'WE HAVE REACHED Marsels!'
          'Hip Hip Hurrah!'
The sepoys were shouting excitedly on deck.

Lalu got up from where he sat watching a game of cards and went to see Marseilles.

The sun was on its downward stride on the western horizon as the convoy ships went steaming up towards the coast of France, with their cargo of the first Divisions of Indian troops who had been brought to fight in Europe, a cargo stranger than any they had carried before. The cold afternoon, stirred by a chill breeze from the stormy gulf, lay quivering on the town, which sheltered beneath a few steep rocks.

'Is the war taking place there then?' a sepoy asked.

No one answered him, as most of the sepoys did not know where the war was. In fact they had not known where they were going until it was announced in the orders of the day that a message had been intercepted through the 'telephone without wires' on the ship, that the Commander-in-Chief of the British Army, Lord Kitchener, who had once been Commander-in-Chief in Hindustan, had told the House of Lords that two Divisions of the Indian Army were on their way to France. The Lords had clapped their hands, it was said, and had sent their greetings to all brave ranks of the Indian Army. The King-Emperor, too, had sent them a message, reminding them of the personal ties which bound him and his consort, Mary, to the Indians since he had visited India for the Delhi Durbar, congratulating them on their personal devotion to his throne, and assuring them how their one-voiced demand to be foremost in the conflict had touched his heart... The sepoys had been excited by these messages, the edge of their curiosity sharpened by the first authentic news which they had received of their destination. And the lives of the N.C.O.s had become unbearable answering questions, 'Where is France?' 'Is that England?' 'Where is the enemy?' 'How many miles is it from here?'... Now one of them was asking, 'Is the war there?'

Lalu felt, however, as if the naive questioner had taken the words out of his own mouth. For the rim of the sky was full of bloody contours, as if the souls of the war dead were going through the agony of being burned in their journey from hell to heaven. The battle might be raging there, though it was foolish to think so, because surely there would have been a sound of guns if the front was so near.

Lest someone should be looking at him and prying into his thoughts he began to walk away towards the prow of the ship.

'So we have come across the black waters safely,' he said to himself apprehensively, as if he really expected some calamity, the legendary fate of all those who went beyond the seas, to befall him at any moment. Truly, the black, or rather blue, water seemed uncanny, spreading for thousands of miles. It seemed as if God had spat upon the universe and the spittle had become the sea. The white flecks of the foam on the swell, where wave met wave, seemed like the froth churned out of God's angry mouth. The swish of the air as the ships tore their way across the rough sea seemed like the fury of the Almighty at the sin which the white men had committed in building their powerful engines of the Iron Age, which transported huge cities of wood and steel across vast spaces, where it was difficult to tell in which direction lay the north, the south, the east or the west.

If his father had been alive and present, he would certainly have prophesied disaster for all those who had crossed the black waters, and he would have regarded this war to which they were going as a curse laid upon the Sahibs for trying to defy nature.

'But why am I turning superstitious and thinking such thoughts?' he rebuked himself. He had always defied his father and preened himself on his schooling, and he did not realize that he had inherited many of his father's qualities, not only the enduring ones such as his short, lithe wiry frame, his love of the land, his generosity, his stubborn pride, and his humour, but also his faith and his naivete.

A few sea-gulls were coming out to meet them, and more seemed to be seated on the hills above the bay, but on closer view these proved to be houses.

It was thrilling to be going out on this adventure, he felt, 'like the pride of the beggar who suddenly finds wealth.' The smoke from the funnels of the convoy ships before, behind, and on both sides, was talking to the sky. The sea spoke the language of his soul, restless and confused while the wind went bursting with joy in the sun. And the ship was urging him forward into the unknown. He was going to *Vilayat* after all, England, the glamorous land of his dreams, where the Sahibs came from, where people wore coats and pantaloons and led active, fashionable lives – even, so it was said, the peasants and the poor Sahibs. He wondered what was his destiny.

The rocking of the boat unsteadied his steps a little and there was a strange disturbance inside him which kept welling up and choking him as if he had eaten a frog. He had prided himself on resisting sickness, when almost all the other sepoys had rolled about in their vomit, and hoped he was not going to make a fool of himself now at the end of the journey. Perhaps he had been smoking too many cigarettes, which the Government was distributing free. Or, perhaps, it was the fear of the Unknown, now that they were getting to their destination. But he had slept badly the previous night and had dreamt a weird dream about Nandpur, in which his mother was crying over the body of his dead father, and his brother, Dayal Singh, was rebuking him for running away when they most needed him. Only to him the village seemed far from here now...

'Oh Lalu! Son of a sea-cow! Let us go and get ready,' called young Subah, son of Subedar Major Arbel Singh, his round red face flushed as if he had got the direct commission which his father had been negotiating for him all the way, as the boy had been self-importantly telling everyone.

'You go, I am coming,' said Lalu evasively, to shake him off, and stood with the hordes of sepoys who leaned on the railings, watching the little tugs which had come out and were pushing and pulling the steamer from where it had slackened over the placid waters of the bay towards the wharves.

Lalu smelt the rich sunny smell which was in the air, and felt that the entrance of the harbour was a wonder such as only the heart could feel and remember.

'Boom! Zoom!' The guns thundered from somewhere on land.

'Oh, horror! The war is there!'

'To be sure!…'

'The *phrunt!*'

The sepoys burbled gravely, looking ahead of them, fascinated, in wonder and fear, intent.

But a Sikh N.C.O. said: 'Have your senses fled? These are the guns of the *Francisi* warships saluting us.'

And, indeed, the convoy ships answered back acknowledging the greetings, and the booming stopped.

Before the ship came to a standstill, a number of French officers came up on board with some British officers and shook hands with the officers of the regiment. The French Sahibs looked like the Indians with their sallow complexions, but very solemn and sad.

The sepoys looked at them and wondered. They were afraid of talking in the presence of the Sahibs and stood silent or slipped away.

The shrill crescendo of the ship's sirens shook the air with an urgent, insistent call.

Lalu was excited almost to hysteria and went down to look for Uncle Kirpu, Daddy Dhanoo or Havildar Lachman Singh, as he did not know what to do next. But the news had gone round that the sepoys would disembark here, rest for a day or two, then go by train to the front as soon as possible, for the Sarkar was anxious to avoid the disappointment which the troops might feel at not being allowed to rush and defeat the Germans at once. This relieved the tension somewhat, and soon he was hurrying to get ready to alight.

He sweated profusely as he exerted himself, and he felt a strange affection in his belly as thousands of throats on the harbour burst into an incomprehensible tumult of shouting. Then he rushed towards his bunk, losing his way going down the gangways, till he sighted Uncle Kirpu and ran up to him.

'Slowly, slowly, gentleman, Franceville is not running away,' Kirpu said, blinking his mischievous eyes, and shaking his sly, weather-beaten face in a mockery of Lalu's haste.

'Being a man of many campaigns, you feel there is nothing new,' Lalu teased.

'I don't feel peevish and shy as a virgin, as you do, son,' said Uncle Kirpu and patted Lalu on the back affectionately.

'Where is Daddy Dhanoo?' Lalu said with a pale smile.

'First on deck in full war kit! Just to set the young an example!' Kirpu said.

'Let us hurry, then, and follow his example,' Lalu said and pulled the protesting Kirpu.

As they emerged on deck, the quay seemed to be drowned in a strange and incongruous whirlpool: Pathans, Sikhs, Dogras, Gurkhas, Muhammadans in khaki, blue-jacketed French seamen and porters, and English Tommies. And there was a babble of voices, shouts, curses, salaams, and incomprehensible courtesies. He struggled into the single file which was disembarking and, before he knew where he was, stood on solid earth in the thick of the crowd, without Kirpu. The sepoys were all looking at each other embarrassedly, or talking to the *Francisis*, gesticulating and wringing their hands and turning away when they could not make themselves understood. The French carried on in their own lingo, imparting information in a tumultuous flow of words which all seemed like 'phon, phon, phon, something, something…' to the Indians.

But they were kind and polite, these *Francisis*, bowing and smiling and moving their heads, their hands, and their bodies in broad gestures, unlike the reticent Tommies.

Lalu stamped his feet to see if the impact of the earth of France was any different from the feel of Hindustan. Curiously enough, the paved hard surface of the quay, under the shadow of gigantic ships, full of cranes and masts and steel girders, seemed different somehow, new, unlike the crumbling dust of India. He swerved, and began to tap the pavement, to jump, and caper out of sheer exuberance of spirit…

The quick darting notes of the bugles tore the air, and the sepoys ran helter-skelter with their heavy trappings, and began to get into formation.

Lalu spotted Havildar Lachman Singh, rushing towards the wide gates which opened into a road from the high wall of the quay. He ran after the N.C.O. His company was already forming while he had been procrastinating to find out the exact orders. 'Fall in, son,' said Lachman Singh with a kind smile on that brave, keen face of the Dogra hillman which Lalu had always seen sweating, owing to the energy which the sergeant put into whatever he had in hand, whether it was plying a hockey stick, instructing at the gymnasium, taking out a fatigue party, or doing any other regimental duty.

As Lalu was rushing into line, warmed by the kindness of Lachman Singh, Subah shouted '*Oi,* Owl Singh!' and came and dragged him to his platoon.

'Then, what is the talk – how do you like the land of France?' Lalu asked, leaning over to Uncle Kirpu.

'This land,' said Kirpu with an amused smile, 'this land is like all the others, it came to be with the coming of life, and will go down with death.'

'How can the blind man know the splendour of the tulip!' Lalu said.

'There is one splendour in men, another in tulips,' Uncle Kirpu answered.

Lalu was too enthusiastic about the adventure to feel as Kirpu felt, but he looked at the amused unconcern in the face of the experienced soldier who accepted fate with the resignation of a mild cynic, and who smiled at everything with a gentleness born of some hurt. Then he gazed at the lined, grave, Mongoloid face of Daddy Dhanoo, who had just outlived the accidents of time, space, life, and did not speak at all, as if he had become neutral, immortal. Their behaviour was so different from Subah's blustering, and his own excited manner.

But the band struck up a tune for the route march, and the orders of the officers rang out, and the heavy tread of ammunition boots, the flashing of arms, the rustling of uniforms, transformed the air.

'*Vivonlesindu*! Something, something…' the cry rang out, above the 'lef right lef' of the N.C.O.s, from the crowd, which stood five deep under the awnings of tall, white-shuttered houses under the shadow of the harbour walls.

Lalu felt a shiver pass down his spine, and he felt shy walking as a man among men through a crowd of cheering spectators. But the cheering continued.

A Tommy cried back on behalf of the sepoys; 'Three cheers for the French – Hip hip hurrah!'

The sepoys repeated: 'Hip hip hurrah!' 'Hip hip hurrah!' Lalu scanned the faces by the cafes, the dock gates, the huge sheds and warehouses with tear-dimmed eyes. An irrational impulse was persuading him to believe that the dirty, squalid outskirts of this town were a replica of the outer fringes of Karachi Harbour. The presence of trams, motors, ships, moorings and masts encouraged the illusion. And, as he peered into the narrow, filthy lanes where women and children stood crowded in the windows and on the doorsteps, under lines of dirty washing, as he saw the small, languid unkempt Frenchmen in straw hats and with flourishing moustachios, it all seemed so like the indolent, slow-moving world of an Indian city that he felt an immediate affinity with this country.

'*Vivleshindou*! *Vivongleshindu*! *Vivelesallies*!…' the cries of the crowd became more complex as the sepoys entered a square beyond the small fort which stood on top of a hill where the warehouses ended, and where the greenish sea made an estuary, congested by hundreds of small boats painted in all the colours of the rainbow. And Lalu almost stumbled and fell out of step through the wandering of his eyes among the faces of the women who shrieked and waved their hands at the pageant of the Indian Army.

'Look out, heart squanderer,' called Subah.

'Can the blind man see the splendour of the tulip?' Lalu repeated his phrase.

As the troops turned left, and marched up the hill along the Cane-biere, the throngs multiplied on the broad pavements outside the dainty fronts of the shops, and of the beautiful high buildings decked with flowers. They were mostly women, and children, and lo and behold, as is the custom in India, they threw flowers at the sepoys while they cried: '*Vivongleshindoos! Vivangleterre! Vivelesallies! Vive…*'

Lalu could not keep his eyes off the smiling, pretty-frocked girls with breasts half showing, bright and gleaming with a happiness that he wanted to think was all for him. Such a contrast to the sedate Indian women who seemed to grow old before they were young, flabby and tired, except for a cowherd woman with breasts like pyramidal rocks!… Why even the matrons here were dressed up and not content to remain unadorned like Indian wives, who thought that there was a greater dignity in neglecting themselves after they had had a child or two!

'*Vivonleshindou!*' a thousand throats let loose a tide that flowed down the hill from the mouths of the throngs on both sides.

'What are the rape-daughters saying?' asked Kirpu, playing on the last word affectionately to take away the sting of abuse latent in the classical curse of India.

'What knows a monkey of a mirror's beauty!' said Lalu, adapting his phrase to the current description of the hillmen as monkeys.

'You don't know either,' said Kirpu.

'They are saying something about the Hindus,' said Lalu.

'What knows a peasant of the rate at which cloves are sold; he spreads a length of cloth as though he were buying two maunds of grain,' said Subah to Lalu. 'They are saying, "Long live the Indians". I can understand, because I know *Francisi*.'

'All guesswork and no certainty,' said Kirpu sceptically.

'*Vivongleshindous! Vivelangleterre! Vivonlesallies!*…' the cries throbbed dithyrambically.

'You don't know the meaning of that, do you?' said Lalu to Subah.

'*Ohe*, leave this talk of meanings, you learned owls,' said Kirpu. 'Any fool can see that they are greeting us with warmth and hospitality. Come give a shout after me, "Long live the *Francisis!*"'

'Long live the *Francisis!*' the boys shouted, and the calls were taken up, followed by roars of laughter.

Now the enthusiasm of the women in the crowd knew no bounds.

'*Vivonleshindous!*' they shouted and laughed.

'*Bolo Sri Ram Chander ki jai*!' one of the Hindu N.C.O.s shouted. And the sepoys echoed the call.

'*Allah ho Akhbar*!' someone shouted, and was echoed back by the stalwarts of the Muhammadan companies.

'*Wah Guruji ka Khalsa*! *Wah Guruji ki* Fateh!' shouted a Sikh somewhere. And the other Sikhs took up the call while someone, more full throated than the rest, added in a shrill tenor: '*Bole so Nihal, Sat Sri Akal*!'

And as a river in flood flows unchecked when once the dams of resistance have burst, so the calls of enthusiasm flowed across the tongues of the endless legion, emphasized by the stamping of determined feet, and punctuated with snatches of talk. And the long pageant, touched by the warmth of French greetings, inflamed by the exuberance of tropical hearts marched through this air, electric with the whipped-up frenzy, past churches, monuments, past rows of shuttered houses, chateaus and grassy fields, till, tired and strained with the intoxication of glory, it reached the racecourse of Parc Borely where tents had been fixed by an advance party for the troops to rest.

After a march past of various mounted English and French generals, a sudden halt was called. The general of the Lahore Division trotted his horse up to the head of the forces, adjusted a megaphone to his mouth, and shouted in a Hindustani whose broken edges gained volume from the incomprehensibility of his tone and emphasis:

'Heroes of India. After the splendid reception which you have been given by the French, and the way in which you have responded with the calls of your religions, I have no doubt that you will fulfil your duties with the bravery for which you are famous!…'

The band struck up 'God Save the King', and all ranks presented arms. After which the various regiments marched off towards the tents allotted to them.

When they had dispersed and reached their billets, and began to take off their puttees and boots, they found that their feet, unused to walking since the voyage, were badly blistered.

'Wake up, lazybones, wake up, it is time for you to say prayers,' Uncle Kirpu was shouting as he crouched in bed puffing at the end of an Egyptian cigarette.

'They must be tired,' said Daddy Dhanoo affectionately, as he wrapped the blanket round himself, shivering in the dawn, and invoking various names of God, *'Om! Hari Om! Ishwar!'*

'If we don't wake early we shall not get the ticket to heaven,' said Lalu as he stretched his body taut like a lion, yawned and rose, calling: *'Ohe,* Subah.'

'Who? What?...' Subah burst, startled out of a fitful sleep, stared at Lalu with bleary, bloodshot eyes, and then turned on his side.

'Has the bugle gone?' Lalu asked, hurrying out of his bed as though he were frightened.

'No, I was saying that you will be late for your prayers,' said Kirpu.

'Where does one say them?' Lalu asked as he started to dress. 'And does one say them seated on English commodes or crouching like black men who relieve themselves on the ground.'

'God's name is good!' Daddy Dhanoo said before Kirpu had answered. And he yawned, his big eyes closing, while the various names and appellations of the Almighty multiplied on his lips, his mouth opening like that of a tired Pekinese. This was his way of evading discussion on the topic because he had been the butt of all jokes since he had slipped off the polished edge of an English style commode on the ship.

'Om! Hari Om!' Lalu parodied him. 'May you be consigned to your own hell, and be eternally damned, Almighty Father of Fathers.' And he went out of the tent blaspheming.

Every blade of grass between the tents on the racecourse shone in the light of the rising sun, while a sharp cool breeze blew from where the blue line of the sky lost itself in the mist around the dove-coloured chateaus on the hills.

Lalu walked along, impelled by the superstition which he had practised in the village that to walk on the dew drops in the morning was good for the eyes.

He had not been out long before Subah came running after him.

A spoilt child, very conscious of his position as the son of the Indian head of the regiment, Subah wanted to go and pay his respects to his father, which usually meant that he wanted the gift of some pocket money. He persuaded Lalu to come with him by promising his friend a treat at the 'Buffet' outside the camp.

They sauntered along towards the tent of the Subedar Major, and then, seeing several important looking French and British officers gathered there, stood about discussing whether Subah should go up.

With characteristic impetuosity, however, Subah ran towards his father's tent, while Lalu stood averting his eyes for fear of the officers. Lest he be seen nosing about, he began to walk away, assuming a casual expression as if he were just 'eating the air'. Even that would be considered objectionable if he were seen by a Sahib. He hurried, because the imposing cluster of bell-topped tents spread the same fear in him as the secret, hedged-in bungalows of the Sahibs in Ferozepur cantonment, where it was an intrusion even to stare through the gates.

He hurried towards the latrines.

When he came out the camp was already alive as if it were an ordinary cantonment in India. Habitual early risers, most of the sepoys were hurrying about, unpacking luggage, polishing boots, belts and brass buttons with their spittle, washing their faces, cleaning their teeth with the chewing-sticks which they had brought from home, and gargling with thunderous noises and frightening reverberations, to the tune of hymns, chants, and the names of gods, more profuse and long winded, because the cold air went creeping into their flesh.

'As if the hissing, the sighing and the remembrance of God would keep them warm!' Lalu said to himself, feeling the incongruity of their ritual with the fashionable 'air and water of France'. He showed his face to the sun and, out of sheer light heartedness, began to jump across the strings of small tents towards his own tent.

'*Ohe*, where are you going?' Uncle Kirpu shouted.

Lalu rushed in, put on his boots quickly, adjusted his turban, and walked out again.

'The boy has gone mad!' exclaimed Kirpu to Dhanoo.

But the boy was exhilarated at being in *Vilayat*, thinking of all the wonderful shops that were in the streets through which they had passed yesterday, and the general air of elegance and exaltedness that surrounded everything.

A few Sikhs of No. 4 company stood combing their long black hair. He recalled the brutality with which the fanatics of his village had blackened his face and put him on a donkey when he had had his hair cut. The humiliation had bitten deep into him. They must look odd to the Europeans, he thought. And he wondered how many of them would have their hair cut while they were abroad or after their return to India. But the Sahibs didn't like the Sikhs to have their hair shorn, as they wanted them to preserve their own customs, even though Audley Sahib had excused him when Lance-Naik Lok Nath had reported him at Ferozepur. But for Havildar Lachman Singh and Captain Owen, the Adjutant, he would have had to go to 'quarter guard', on bread and water for a week, and his record would have been spoilt. Instead of which Lok Nath's promotion had been stopped and the Corporal had been transferred to another platoon, though that was more because Subedar Major Arbel Singh wanted to get his son, Subah, rapid promotion. The boy wondered when Lok Nath would wreak his vengeance on him...

A group of Muslim sepoys, belonging to his regiment, sat in a circle round a hookah, however, and some dark Hindu Sappers and Miners of the next regiment were jabbering in dialect as they baked chapatees within the ritualistic four lines of their kitchen, while a Jodhpur Lancer was gesticulating with his arms and his head as he explained something to a woman who – what was he doing?

Lalu stopped to listen.

The Sappers were using foul abuse. It seemed that the woman had walked into their kitchen.

'*Silvoup silvap...*' the woman said coming up to him.

Lalu just moved his head and smiled weakly.

The woman gabbled away in French.

Lalu stood dumb with humility, and was going to salute, and go away for fear an officer might see him talking to a Mem Sahib, while the Jodhpur Lancer, equally at a loss, said: 'I don't know what the sister-in-law wants.'

The French woman laughed at her own discomfiture, and then said in English 'picture', pointing at Lalu, and the Jodhpur Lancer, trying to explain with her head, her eyes, her nose, her fingers, what she wanted.

But as if the very presence of a Mem Sahib, usually so remote and unapproachable in India, had paralysed them, they stood unresponsive.

Lalu looked about furtively and scanned the cavalry horses on the right, the shouting cooks and water carriers on the left and the Baluchis and the Gurkhas who were sunning themselves ahead of him. Then he looked back towards the officers' quarters, and pointed towards them, thinking that the best thing was to send her to the Subedar Major Sahib's tent. But his gaze met Subah's, who came running along abreast of a French officer on horseback.

Lalu and the Jodhpur Lancer sprang to attention and saluted.

The officer talked in his own tongue to the woman, and then, laughing, said to Subah in English:

'The Miss wants to draw the pictures of these men.'

'Draw my picture, Mem Sahib,' Subah said coming forward.

The French woman smiled at Subah, said something to the officer, and made a gesture to the Jodhpur Lancer, Lalu and Subah, to stand together.

But Subah thrust himself forward and thumped his chest to indicate that he wanted a portrait of himself all alone.

By this time, driven by curiosity, other sepoys were gathering round.

Whereupon the French officer said in Hindustani: 'Mem Sahib would like a group.'

'Fall into the group and let all of them be in the picture,' Lalu advised Subah.

'*Han*, we also want to be in it,' said the other sepoys crowding round the woman, several rows deep, at the first touch of the pencil.

Then they all stood away, twisting their moustachios into shape and stiffening to attention as if they were going to be photographed.

The officer and the woman laughed as they talked for a moment, then the officer edged aside and the woman began to draw the picture.

'That was the interpreter sahib,' Subah said with great importance.

The French woman sketched the group. But there were any number of subjects before her now, for other sepoys from the nearby tents had gathered round. They would come and look at the woman as though she were a strange animal, because she was so homely, so informal and so unlike the white women who came to Hindustan and never condescended to greet a native. And they posed before her, proud to be sketched, their honest faces suffused with embarrassed laughter, even as they stood, stiff and motionless, their hands glued to their sides.

The woman could draw the pictures of the sitting, standing, talking, moving sepoys with a few deft strokes even before they knew they had been sketched.

And then there was much comedy, the sepoys laughing at the caricatures of each other and exclaiming wildly as they came to life on paper, happy as children to see the sketches, and insisting on signing their name in their own language on the portraits.

When the woman had made various sketches Subah began to press for a portrait of himself. But he could not communicate his wish to her in the little French which he had learnt at school. As he came up to her with a daring familiarity, Jemadar Suchet Singh, a tall, imposing officer of No. 2 company of the 69th Rifles approached to see the confusion and said:

'Get away, don't crowd round the mem sahib! Get away!'

'Come, leave the skirt, let us go,' Subah said.

'You are getting too bumptious,' shouted Suchet Singh to Subah. 'You try to be familiar with her again, and I shall have you court-martialed. Never mind whose son you are!'

After this warning the crowd of sepoys began to slink away.

'Come on, my heart-squanderer, she is beyond your reach,' said Lalu, dragging Subah away. 'And get ready to face your father because I am sure Suchet Singh will report you!...'

'Look out, son, I am to become a Jemadar soon,' Subah said to Lalu, as they hurried towards the main road. 'The Subedar Sahib told me today, so you behave if you value your life.'

'*Ohe, ja, ja*, don't try to impress me!' said Lalu.

'Oh, come, raper of your sister, we shall celebrate,' Subah said. 'You will be my friend, even when I am an officer.'

'Build the house before you make the door.'

'All right, wisdom, come, and run lest we be seen.'

'Where are we going?' Lalu asked. 'We have to get permission if we are going out of bounds.'

'You come with me,' said Subah, 'there is a stall at the end of that road. I saw it when we were marching down to camp; it seemed a wine-shop, because there were people with glasses full of red, pale and green wine before them. Come, we will walk through the camp as though we are not really going out, and then try and evade the sentry at the end of the road, or I shall tell him that I am the son of the Subedar Major Arbel Singh. Come, we shall be happy… You can live without fear of Lok Nath now, because now that I have got promotion he will remain where he is, in the mire…'

'It would be strange if the lion's offspring hasn't any claws,' said Lalu. 'It seems to me that all of us will be in the mire if you become a Jemadar, not only Lok Nath!'

'You know that my father has been invited to the officers' mess tonight where the French officers, English Sahibs, Rajahs, Maharajas and some chosen Indian officers have been invited,' Subah informed him, puffed up with pride. 'And, it is said, that Sir James Willcocks, the Commander-in-Chief of the Indian Corps is to arrive here soon, accompanied by Risaldar Khwaja Muhammad Khan, who is aide-de-camp to this general, and a friend of my father. He is a Pathan from the Yussuf Zai: he was aide-de-camp to Lord Kitchener at one time… I should like to become aide-de-camp one day…'

'You wait, son, you will become that, and more,' said Lalu with a faint mockery in his voice.

'Really, do you think?' Subah said unconscious of his friend's irony. 'Then I shall make you a Jemadar.'

'The dog eats a bellyful of food if he can get it, otherwise he just licks the saucer,' said Lalu to cut short his friend.

'Oh come, why are you always stricken even when happy?' said Subah. And, catching Lalu's hand he began to caper like a horse.

Some Sikh sepoys dressed in shorts were washing their clothes while a group of French children stood around them. One of the Sikhs brought out a flute, and began to play it to amuse them. At this some French soldiers gathered round, imagining that the flute player was going to bring out a cobra. The sepoy pretended there was a snake on the ground before him, and played around its imaginary head, deliberately swelling his cheeks with his breath till they were like two rounded balls. At this the children scattered out of fear, but came back reassured when the sepoy smiled.

One of them offered the mimicking juggler a sweet which the sepoy gulped down, rolling his eyes, and twisting his face as if he were swallowing some poison. And then there was an attempt at an exchange in the language of gesture. And, what was strange, the mime worked. And soon there was complete understanding between East and West.

Lalu, who had stood to watch this scene, responded to the hilarity by accepting a cigarette from a French soldier, which the Sikhs, whose religion taboos smoking, refused. He only wished his regiment had been transferred here as from one cantonment to another, for a sojourn during peace time. But in a war?... Now that he was in France, he felt a curious dread of the Unknown, of the things that happened in a war, even as he felt the thrill of being there.

'I am the son of Subedar Major Arbel Singh, 69th Rifles, and he has sent me to buy some cigarettes from that stall,' Subah announced to the sentry without a blush.

The sentry, a tall Baluchi, with a long crested turban, looked at him hard. 'Who is that man with you?' he asked.

'Sepoy Lai Singh, orderly to the Subedar Major Sahib Bahadur,' lied Subah.

'Go, but don't be long,' said the sentry.

The two boys passed the barrier, and made straight for the stall which stood at the crossroads.

A few French soldiers and some Tommies were standing around drinking beer. Lalu felt embarrassed, afraid, and inferior to be going to a stall where there were only white men. With the assurance cultivated through his three years at the Bishop Cotton School, Simla, Subah dragged him to the bar.

The Frenchman who owned the stall turned to them, wiping his hands on the white skirt of his apron and said, *Mussia!*. Subah pointed to some bottles which stood on the trolley. The Tommies at first stared at the two sepoys as if surprised that the Indians should have developed a predilection for drink. Then, contrary to their customary reticence in India, one of them said: 'Good eh, Blighty!'

'What, Blighty?' said Subah.

'He means *Vilayat*,' Lalu said laughing.

The French Sahib struck the knuckles of his finger against a bottle of white wine, and gesticulated. But before Subah could say anything, an English Sergeant-Major stalked up to the stall and snapped at the Tommies as well as the sepoys:

'Where the bloody hell do you reckon you are? Is this a cantonment or a bloody war?'

The soldiers stood with their heads hanging down.

'This is out of bounds,' the Sergeant Major rapped. And he leaned over to the Tommies and hissed at them angrily, snarling at the sepoys the while.

During the next few days the Indian corps began to be moved to Orleans, where, it was said, they were to be properly equipped with new machine guns, howitzers, mechanical transport, medical equipment and all the necessities that an army, trained to fight on the frontier and for policing the outposts of the Empire overseas, needed in operations in the West. They had handed over the rifles and ammunition which they had brought from India at Marseilles and fresh arms were issued to them. The sepoys adapted themselves to the new rifles, but they hoped that they would not be forced to have new machine guns, as that would entail more strenuous practice, when they were kept busy enough with packing and unpacking, and clothes drill, and they had also been given new warm clothes. It was said that this war to which they were going was unlike any other, fought with things called 'grenads' and 'mortas', and a rumour ran that the Germans had invented a gun which could shoot at range of seventy miles. But why hadn't the Sahibs thought of all these things in India? Of course, they had had to leave the cantonments in a hurry, and the Army Headquarters at Simla hadn't had enough time. But the arrangements were being pushed too fast. The officers were kind, however, patting the Gurkhas on their backs and asking them to sharpen their kukhries, telling the horsemen to value their steeds more than their lives, and encouraging the others to keep fit by wrestling exercises, as they would have to face up to the 'Huns', who were 'twice as big as the Indians in size.'... And the sepoys felt that now that they were here, they were here, and it didn't matter if they had big guns or small guns or whether they lay on mats like the beggars or slept in feather beds like the princes. Travel was good for the heart, since, contrary to the prognostications and evil forebodings of the priests, they hadn't died in crossing the black waters.

The 69th was one of the first regiments to be dispatched to Orleans.

Born in 1905, **Mulk Raj Anand** was a radical Indian writer whose work reveals a great empathy with the poor and oppressed. One part of a trilogy, *Across the Black Waters*, first published in 1939, describes the experiences of Lalu, a peasant whose family is evicted from their land and who becomes a sepoy fighting in the Indian Army in the hope that his war effort will win back lost family land. The book powerfully describes the sense of alienation felt by the Indian soldiers as they get closer to the front. In battle, they are put in the most dangerous positions on the front lines and their regiments suffer very high rates of casualty. Although they want to put on 'a good show', the soldiers in *Across the Black Waters* are also puzzled about what exactly they are doing in France and why the war is a concern of theirs. Eight hundred thousand Indian troops fought in all the theatres of war with almost 50,000 killed or missing and another 65,000 wounded. For its contribution to the war effort, India expected to be rewarded with moves towards independence. When it became obvious that this was not going to happen, support for Gandhi soared.

A life-long communist, Anand volunteered in the 1930s to fight in the Spanish Civil War. After spending the Second World War in London working for the BBC, he returned to India in 1946. Anand died in Pune in 2004.

ERNST JÜNGER

RAJPUTS

from *Kriegstagebuch 1914–1918*
(War Diary 1914–1918)

translated by Martin Chalmers

13.VI.17

This morning I had probably the most interesting war experience that
I've had so far.

Last night our company came forward from the Siegfried-Position.
My platoon was assigned to Outpost 3, I had to go with them. In the
forefield I came upon Sergeant Hackmann with some men who wanted
to carry out a patrol. I tagged along as a battlefield hanger-on. We crossed
two wire entanglements and got through between the English posts. To
the left of us there were English digging trenches, to the right of us was
an occupied piece of trench, from which came the sound of voices. We
wanted to take some prisoners, but we didn't manage it.

I returned to my outpost in a bad mood, settled down on my coat
on the steep slope and dozed. Suddenly there was rustling in the bushes
of the little wood, sentries ran away, the sound of muted whispering
could be heard. At the same time a man ran up to me: 'Lieutenant, 70
English are supposed to have appeared at the edge of the wood.' I had
four men immediately to hand, whom I positioned on the slope. Immediately after that a group of men ran across the meadow. 'Halt, who goes
there?' It was Sergeant Teilengertes trying to collect his men. I quickly
gathered everyone together, drew them up in a firing line and crossed
the meadow between slope and wood with the men. At the corner of

the wood I ordered the line to wheel right. Meanwhile furious shell and machine gun fire had begun from the English side. We ran at a march pace as far as the hill where the English trenches were, in order to gain the dead angle. Then figures appeared on the right wing. I pulled the cord on a hand grenade and threw it at the head of one of them. Unfortunately it was Sergeant Teilengertes who saved himself, thank God, by a hasty sideways leap. At the same time English hand grenades were thrown from above, while the shrapnel fire became unpleasantly intense. The men scattered and disappeared towards the slope under heavy fire, while I maintained my position with three faithful followers. Suddenly one of them nudged me: 'Lieutenant, the English!' And truly to the right a line of figures was kneeling shoulder to shoulder in two sections. As they rose, we ran away. I ran up against barbed wire treacherously stretched through the tall grass, went head over heels three times and tore my good trousers to shreds. During these events there was a tremendous noise in the wood, the rustling steps and the voices of at least 60 men were audible.

So I ran away, fell over the wire, reached the slope and I managed to collect my men and to form a line into order. However, I really had to yell at the men, I grabbed some, threw them onto their place and ordered them to remain lying where they were. The commotion in the wood grew ever louder. I roared over to the wood for what must have been five minutes, and got only strange shouts in reply. Finally I took the responsibility and ordered fire to be opened, even though my men maintained they heard German accents. The shouting in the wood increased, as my 20 rifles rattled into it. There, too, there were yellow flashes from time to time. One man was shot in the shoulder and was bound where he was. I ordered cease fire. Everyone stopped shooting and I shouted once again 'Password!' and then: '*come here, you are prisoners, hands up!*' At that a great deal of shouting over there, my men maintained it sounded like Rache! Rache! [i.e. revenge]. Suddenly a figure detached itself from the edge of the wood and came towards us. Unfortunately I shouted at him, the fellow turned round and went back. 'Shoot him down!' A salvo followed. The fellow seemed dealt with. Some time passed, then the jabbering over there rose again. 'Just let them approach!' Cries came from the edge of the wood, which sounded as if good comrades were encouraging each other to go forward together. Then a line of grey shadows appeared, advancing towards us. 'Steady fire!' The rifles banged beside me and above me, making my eardrums ring. In the middle of the field a small yellow flame still lit up from time to time, but was soon extinguished. Finally their whole left section advanced. I had one group wheel to the right and also sent these people my best wishes. Now it seemed to me that the moment for their withdrawal had come. I ordered: 'On your feet, up, march, march!' We ran towards the edge of the wood, I with some good lads far ahead of the others, and broke into the wood with a loud hurrah. Unfortunately the other fellows had not held their ground but had run away. Consequently I moved to the right along the edge of the wood into the cornfield. There I sent all of the men except 8 back to company.

While we were still standing in the cornfield we heard the English at the edge of the wood again, loud cries as well, as if the wounded were being picked up. We went round the wood and once again advanced along the break through the trees. The English had disappeared. From the meadow, where we had shot down the advancing line, we heard unfamiliar cries and moaning. We went over and saw several dead and wounded lying in the grass, who begged us for mercy. We took three of the figures hidden in the grass and dragged them with us. Now we also had living witnesses to our almost two-hour skirmish, one, however, died immediately, a bullet fired at close range had torn his skull apart. To my question: 'Quelle nation?' (They spoke French) one answered 'Rajput.' Aha so Indians! Something very special. None had been hit less than twice. One quickly shouted 'Anglais pas bon.' I quickly gave myself an English carbine with bayonet and then we made our way with the screaming prisoners to our trench, which we reached as dawn broke, welcomed by those who had remained behind, who stared in astonishment at our men. I right away drank a coffee with Kius and ate scrambled eggs, then I slept until 2 o'clock. So with 20 men we successfully fought over a hundred men, although we had orders to withdraw if approached by superior force. I must say, without wishing to praise myself, that I only achieved it through mastery of the situation, iron command of the men and through advancing with a charge against the enemy.

My losses were two wounded and one missing, but I'm certain at least 30 men were knocked out.

14.VI.17

Our action naturally caused a sensation at all the more senior levels. From the regiment I received the order to occupy the position again at night, and if the enemy were still in it to throw him out. I put together 2 patrols, one under my command, the other under Kius. We went round the wood from both sides with 45 men and met up at the slope. There was no enemy to be seen, only from the route I had taken with Hackmann's patrol did a sentry call out to us and fire a couple of shots. So I took up occupation of the place again and searched the ground, since I was naturally interested in yesterday's outcome. In the area where the section had come from the left, there were still 3 corpses in the grass, 2 Indians and a White officer with two golden stars on his epaulettes. The officer had got a bullet in the eye that had come out at the other temple. He had a massive six-barrel revolver in his left hand, while his right gripped a long wooden club that was spattered with his own blood. His helmet had been shot through. I had his epaulettes taken off, I kept one as a souvenir, likewise his cigarette case, which was not very valuable, and the shot-through helmet and the club. In his breast pocket he had a metal flask with cognac. He was lying approximately 20 yards in front of where we were standing yesterday, I had really not thought that they had come so close, at any rate these people had made a dashing attack. That he had seen us is proven by the fact that he had fired four bullets from his revolver.

My men took the things off the dead. I have always found the undressing and robbing of corpses an unpleasant business, I didn't forbid it, since it was better the men had the things than that they rot, and in war moral considerations should not be allowed to determine any action. Apart from which this feeling was not a moral but an aesthetic one. Even when one fellow wanted to pull the rings from the officer's fingers, I didn't say anything, although the repulsive laughter of this man goaded me to do so. Besides his comrades had the tact to stop him doing it. In a very small shell hole lay three helmets, a sign that our opponents would have preferred to withdraw into holes in the ground under our fire.

Also lying at the edge of the wood were gas masks, hand grenades, helmets, digging tools, ammunition pouches and other pieces of equipment that betrayed there must be corpses lying there, too. But because of the jungle-like undergrowth we were unable to search. Towards morning I withdrew to the trench and slept in my wooden shack, twice there was shellfire close by without me being able to rouse myself to get up.

18.VI.17

Yesterday evening the outpost was attacked again, this time the business didn't take such a glorious course. The commander, a Sergeant Blüm, arrived at the trench alone with a group, having left the two other groups in the lurch, but these defended themselves anyway, one man being wounded. NCO Erdelt fell down the steep slope right into a bunch of lurking Indians. He threw some hand grenades around, but was quickly held down and first of all an Indian officer struck him in the face with a wire whip. Then the Indian took his watch from him. Shoved and poked he had to march off with them and escaped again when the Indians scattered under our machine gun fire. After wandering about behind the English lines for some time he got back to our area. This time, too, the Indians must again have suffered losses, because he saw some being carried back. There were English cars waiting at the road, apparently to drive the wounded away.

There has been a truly tropical heat for the last 12 days. The overgrown fields shimmer in the brightest colours. I have been struck by one colour effect in particular, which seems as if made for the war. A green field, thick with red poppy, when darkness falls the red appears almost black and almost runs together with the darkest shades of the green.

19.VI.17

Last night I went out on patrol. I wanted to have a go at the English double outpost at the slope, if it wasn't there, push further forward and take prisoners. Without a request on my part Lieutenant Schulz and a light machine gun were assigned to me. I split up the patrol so that Schulz with the machine gun and six men went down the sunken track, I with Sergeant Teilengertes and Knigge about 40 yards to the left of it and Corporal Braun in the middle as liaison man. If a part of the patrol came under fire, the others should wheel round to attack. We went forward, bent double, expectant.

In the sunken track we suddenly heard the sound of a rifle being cocked. We lay as if rooted to the spot. Then a shot was fired. I lay behind a gorse bush and waited. Hand grenades exploded to the right. Then a general furious firing in front of us, the horrible, familiar sharp report showed that the shots were passing very close to us. I gave the order to withdraw. In mad haste we ran back. To our right infantry fire and a machine gun opened up. The bullets swarmed around us in the most unpleasant manner, that is, we heard only the sharp, brief shots, one doesn't hear a bullet fired at such close range. I didn't think I would get back in one piece. Death had come hunting. My subconscious was all the time expecting me to be hit.

To the right somewhere on the terrain a section of Indians charged with a shrill Hooray!

Once I fell and Teilengertes fell over me. In the collision I lost helmet, pistol, hand grenades. Just keep going! At last we came to the steep slope and dashed down. I came upon Schulz who told me that the impudent marksman had been chastised with hand grenades. Immediately after that two men appeared dragging along Infantryman Feldmann who had been shot twice through the legs. The others were all there. The biggest misfortune was that the fellow who was carrying the machine gun had fallen over the wounded man and left the thing lying. Notwithstanding that Schulz had ordered him to open fire, he had taken to his heels without carrying out the order.

While we were still engaged in lively debate we came under very unpleasant fire, which damned well reminded me of the night of the 12th/13th. Again there was utter confusion. I found myself quite alone on the slope with one man. Pulling himself forward with his hands the wounded man crawled up to me and moaned: 'Lieutenant, lieutenant, sir, don't leave me alone.' It was a pitiful sight, but I couldn't have the man brought back without weakening my fighting strength. So I laid the wounded man in a sentry hole, placed Infantryman Sasse beside him and made Sasse responsible. I myself gathered together the outpost squad by the wood, since the duty sergeant, being in a spot, turned to me. I positioned the men in the gun pits and wanted to run over to the wounded man again. Against my order he had been carried back by Sergeant Schnelle and his half squad. Immediately on my return I had a report handed in against the man.

I was heartily relieved when the Indians didn't come. In the wood that was behind us, we could hear shouting, it was sappers coming from the rear area who were supposed to clear a break through the wood. They abandoned their equipment and weapons and then strayed around in the forefield all night.

Only the veterans were sitting at the edge of the wood again, rifle in hand, and waiting. A tremendous stench tempted me to go into the wood. Some Indians we had killed on the first night were still lying there. I ordered the men to keep on searching and they found quite a few more. We had really messed the fellows up. The sounds of decomposition, familiar to me from Guillemont, were coming from the bodies, a wan head, resting on its hands looked ghost-like at me in the darkness. I took the gas mask from one, it was still quite warm from the warmth of the decomposition, but it didn't matter, since it was one of the older carbolic-soaked English masks.

After the shooting had completely died down, I went back with Sergeant Teilengertes.

⌒

Ernst Jünger (1895–1998) remains one of the most controversial writers of modern literature. Although he was admired on the left as well as the right, the stigma of appearing to prepare the way for Nazism still, for many, makes him unacceptable as an author of significance. If he is difficult to categorise as a conventional nationalist, he was certainly not only anti-bourgeois, in a particular dandified way, but also anti-democratic and hierarchical in his thinking. He first made his name as a writer at the age of 25 with his memoir of the Western Front, *Storm of Steel*. *War Diary 1914–1918* from which the extracts in the present volume are taken formed the basis of that memoir, but were not published in German until 2010. In them we find Jünger both discovering his voice as a writer and doing so by taking an attitude of dispassion and indifference. Yet there's also a touch of youthful immaturity to the elevation of battle as supreme human test. This nihilism, in which hatred or contempt for the enemy is absent, would not remain Jünger's attitude: it gave way in his diaries of the Second World War to something like cynical melancholy. Nevertheless the combination of boyishness and a reaching for precision and clarity of description make the *Diary* at once unique and representative of how a generation coped with the horrors of trench warfare. The extract, an encounter with Indian troops, is dated 13th and 14th June 1917 and 18th and 19th June of the same year.

D. H. LAWRENCE

THE NIGHTMARE

from *Kangaroo*

I N SEPTEMBER, ON HIS BIRTHDAY, came the third summons: On His Majesty's Service. – His Majesty's Service, God help us! Somers was bidden present himself at Derby on a certain date, to join the colours.

He replied: 'If I am turned out of my home, and forbidden to enter the area of Cornwall: if I am forced to report myself to the police wherever I go, and am treated like a criminal, you surely cannot wish me to present myself to join the colours.'

There was an interval: much correspondence with Bodmin, where they seemed to have forgotten him again. Then he received a notice that he was to present himself as ordered.

What else was there to do? – But he was growing devilish inside himself. However, he went: and Harriett accompanied him to the town. The recruiting-place was a big Sunday School – you went down a little flight of steps from the road. In a smallish ante-room like a basement he sat on a form and waited while all his papers were filed. Beside him sat a big collier, about as old as himself. And the man's face was a study of anger and devilishness growing under humiliation. After an hour's waiting, Somers was called. He stripped as usual – but this time was told to put on his jacket over his complete nakedness.

And so – he was shown into a high, long schoolroom, with various sections down one side – bits of screens where various doctor-fellows were performing – and opposite, a long writing table where clerks and old military buffers in uniform sat in power: the clerks dutifully scribbling, glad to be in a safe job, no doubt, the old military buffers staring about. Near this Judgment-Day table a fire was burning, and there was a bench where two naked men sat ignominiously waiting, trying to cover their nakedness a little with their jackets, but too much upset to care really.

'Good God!' thought Somers. 'Naked men in civilised jackets and nothing else make the most heaven-forsaken sight I have ever seen.' The big stark-naked collier was being measured: a big, gaunt, naked figure, with a gruesome sort of nudity. 'Oh God, oh God,' thought Somers, 'why do the animals none of them look like this. It doesn't look like life, like a living creature's figure. It is gruesome, with no life-meaning.'

In another section a youth of about twenty-five, stark naked too, was throwing out his chest while a chit of a doctor-fellow felt him between the legs. This naked young fellow evidently thought himself an athlete, and that he must make a good impression, so he threw his head up in a would-be noble attitude, and coughed bravely when the doctor-buffoon said cough! Like a piece of furniture waiting to be sat on, the athletic young man looked.

Across the room the military buffers looked on at the operette; – occasionally a joke, incomprehensible, at the expense of the naked, was called across from the military papas to the fellows who may have been doctors. The place was full of an indescribable tone of jeering, gibing shamelessness. Somers stood in his street jacket and thin legs and beard – a sight enough for any gods – and waited his turn. Then he took off the jacket and was cleanly naked, and stood to be measured and weighed – being moved about like a block of meat, in the atmosphere of corrosive derision.

Then he was sent to the next section for eye-tests, and jokes were called across the room. Then after a time to the next section, where he was made to hop on one foot – then on the other foot – bend over – and so on: apparently to see if he had any physical deformity. In due course to the next section where a fool of a little fellow, surely no doctor, eyed him up and down and said:

'Anything to complain of?'

'Yes,' said Somers. 'I've had pneumonia three times and been threatened with consumption.'

'Oh. Go over there then.'

So in his stalky, ignominious nakedness he was sent over to another section, where an elderly fool turned his back on him for ten minutes, before looking round and saying:

'Yes. What have you to say.'

Somers repeated.

'When did you have pneumonia –?'

Somers answered – he could hardly speak, he was in such a fury of rage and humiliation.

'What doctor said you were threatened with consumption? Give his name.' – This in a tone of sneering scepticism.

The whole room was watching and listening. Somers knew his appearance had been anticipated, and they wanted to count him out.

But he kept his head. – The elderly fellow then proceeded to listen to his heart and lungs with a stethoscope, jabbing the end of the instrument against the flesh as if he wished to make a pattern on it. Somers kept a set face. He knew what he was out against, and he just hated and despised them all.

The fellow at length threw the stethoscope aside as if he were throwing Somers aside, and went to write. Somers stood still, with a set face, and waited.

Then he was sent to the next section, and this stethoscoping doctor strolled over to the great judgment table. In the final section was a young puppy like a chemist's assistant, who made most of the jokes. Jokes were all the time passing across the room – but Somers had the faculty of becoming quite deaf to anything that might disturb his equanimity.

The chemist-assistant puppy looked him up and down with a small grin as if to say 'Law-lummy, what a sight of a human scarecrow!' Somers looked him back again, under lowered lids, and the puppy left off joking for the moment. He told Somers to take up other attitudes. Then he came forward close to him, right till their bodies almost touched, the one in a navy blue serge, holding back a little as if from the contagion of the naked one. He put his hand between Somers' legs, and pressed it upwards, under the genitals. Somers felt his eyes going black.

'Cough,' said the puppy. He coughed.

'Again,' said the puppy. He made a noise in his throat, then turned aside in disgust.

'Turn round,' said the puppy. 'Face the other way.'

Somers turned and faced the shameful monkey-faces at the long table. So, he had his back to the tall window: and the puppy stood plumb behind him.

'Put your feet apart.'

He put his feet apart.

'Bend forward – further – further –'

Somers bent forward, lower, and realised that the puppy was standing aloof behind him to look into his anus. And that this was the source of the wonderful jesting that went on all the time.

'That will do. – Get your jacket and go over there.'

Somers put on his jacket and went and sat on the form that was placed endwise at the side of the fire, facing the side of the judgment table. The big, gaunt collier was still being fooled. He apparently was not very intelligent, and didn't know what they meant when they told him to bend forward. Instead of bending with stiff knees – not knowing at all what they wanted – he crouched down, squatting on his heels as colliers do. And the doctor puppy, amid the hugest amusement, had to start him over again. So the game went on, and Somers watched them all.

The collier was terrible to him. He had a sort of Irish face with a short nose and a thin black head. This snub-nosed face had gone quite blank with a ghastly voidness, void of intelligence, bewildered and blind. It was as if the big, ugly, powerful body could not obey *words* any more. Oh God, such an ugly body – not as if it belonged to a living creature.

Somers kept himself hard and in command, face set, eyes watchful.

He felt his cup had been filled now. He watched these buffoons in this great room, as he sat there naked save for his jacket, and he felt that from his heart, from his spine went out vibrations that should annihilate them – blot them out, the *canaille*, stamp them into the mud they belonged to.

He was called at length to the table.

'What is your name?' asked one of the old parties. Somers looked at him.

'Somers,' he said, in a very low tone.

'Somers – Richard Lovatt?' – with an indescribable sneer.

Richard Lovatt realised that they had got their knife into him. So! He had his knife in them, and it would strike deeper at last.

'You describe yourself as a writer.'

He did not answer.

'A writer of what?' – with a perfect sneer.

'Books – essays –'

The old buffer went on writing. Oh yes, they intended to make him feel they had got their knife into him. They would have his beard off, too! – But would they? He stood there with his ridiculous thin legs, in his ridiculous jacket, but he did not feel a fool. Oh God no. The white composure of his face, the slight lifting of his nose, like a dog's disgust, the heavy, unshakeable watchfulness of his eyes brought even the judgment table to silence: even the puppy-doctors. It was not till he was walking out of the room, with his jacket above his thin legs, and his beard in front of him, that they lifted their heads for a final jeer.

He dressed and waited for his card. It was Saturday morning, and he was almost the last man to be examined. He *wondered* what instructions they had had about him. Oh, foul dogs. But they were very close on him now, very close. They were grinning very close behind him, like hyaenas just going to bite. Yes, they were running him to earth. They had exposed all his nakedness to gibes. And they were pining, almost whimpering to give the last grab at him, and haul him to earth – a victim. Finished!

But not yet! Oh no, not yet. Not yet, not now, nor ever. Not while life was life, should they lay hold of him. Never again. Never would he be touched again. – And because they had handled his private parts, and looked into them, their eyes should burst and their hands should wither and their hearts should rot. So he cursed them in his blood, with an unremitting curse, as he waited.

They gave him his card: C.2. – Fit for non-military service. He knew what they would like to make him do. They would like to seize him and compel him to empty latrines in some camp. They had that in mind for him. But he had other things in mind.

He went out into accursed Derby, to Harriett. She was reassured again. But he was not. He hated the Midlands now, he hated the North. People here were viler than in the South, even than in Cornwall. They had a universal desire to take life and *down* it: these horrible machine people, these iron and coal people. They wanted to set their foot absolutely on life, grind it down, and be master. Masters, as they were of their foul machines. Masters of life, as they were masters of steam-power and electric-power and above all, of money-power. Masters of money-power, with an obscene hatred of life, true, spontaneous life.

Richard Lovatt knew it. They had looked into his anus, they had put their hand under his testicles. – That athletic young fellow, he didn't seem to think he ought to mind at all. He looked on his body as a sort of piece of furniture, or a machine, to be handled and put to various uses. That was why he was athletic. Somers laughed, and thanked God for his own thin, underweight body. At least he remained himself, his own. He hoped the young athletic fellow would enjoy the uses they put him to.

Another flight. He was determined not to stop in the Derby Military Area. He would move one stage out of their grip, at least. So he and Harriett prepared to go back with their trunks to the Oxfordshire cottage, which they loved. He would not report, nor give any sign of himself. Fortunately in the village everybody was slack and friendly.

Derby had been a crisis. He would obey no more: not one more stride. If they summoned him, he would disappear: or find some means of fighting them. But no more obedience: no more presenting himself when called up. By God, no. Never while he lived, again, would he be at the disposal of society.

So they moved south – to be one step removed. They had been living in this remote cottage in the Derbyshire hills: and they must leave at half-past seven in the morning, to complete their journey in a day. It was a black morning, with a slow dawn. Somers had the trunks ready. He stood looking at the dark gulf of the valley below. Meanwhile heavy clouds sank over the bare, Derbyshire hills, and the dawn was blotted out before it came. Then broke a terrific thunderstorm, and hail lashed down with a noise like insanity. He stood at the big window over the valley, and watched. Come hail, come rain, he would go: forever.

This was his home district – but from the deepest soul he now hated it, mistrusted it even more than he hated it. As far as *life* went, he mistrusted it utterly, with a black soul. Mistrusted it and hated it, with its smoke and its money-power and its squirming millions who aren't human any more.

Ah, how lovely the South-west seemed, after it all. There was hardly any food, but neither he nor Harriett minded. They could pick up and be wonderfully happy again, gathering the little chestnuts in the woods, and the few last bilberries. Men were working harder than ever felling trees for trench-timber, denuding the land. But their brush fires were burning in the woods, and when they had gone, in the cold dusk, Somers went with a sack to pick up the unburnt faggots and the great chips of wood the axes had left golden against the felled logs. Flakes of sweet pale gold oak. He gathered them in the dusk, in a sack, along with the other poor villagers. For he was poorer even than they. – Still, it made him very happy to do these things – to see a big, glowing pile of wood-flakes in his shed – and to dig the garden, and set the rubbish burning in the late, wistful autumn – or to wander through the hazel copses, away to the real old English hamlets, that are still like Shakespeare – and like Hardy's *Woodlanders*.

Then, in November, the Armistice. It was almost too much to believe. The war was over! It *was* too much to believe. He and Harriett sat and sang German songs, in the cottage, that strange night of the Armistice, away there in the country: and she cried – and he wondered what now, now the walls would come no nearer. It had been like Edgar Allan Poe's story of the Pit and the Pendulum – where the walls come in, in, in, till the prisoner is almost squeezed. So the black walls of the war – and he had been trapped and very nearly squeezed into the pit, where the rats were. So nearly! So very nearly. And now the black walls had stopped, and he was *not* pushed into the pit, with the rats. And he knew it in his soul. – What next then?

He insisted on going back to Derbyshire. Harriett, who hated him for the move, refused to go. So he went alone: back to his sisters, and to finish the year in the house which they had paid for for him. Harriett refused to go. She stayed with Hattie in London.

At St. Pancras, as Somers left the taxi and went across the pavement to the station, he fell down: fell smack down on the pavement. He did not hurt himself. But he got up rather dazed, saying to himself, 'Is that a bad omen? Ought I not to be going back?' But again he thought of Scipio Africanus, and went on.

The cold, black December days, alone in the cottage on the cold hills – Adam Bede country, Snowfields, Dinah Morris' home. Such heavy, cold, savage, frustrated blackness. He had known it when he was a boy. – Then Harriett came – and they spent Christmas with his sister. And when January came he fell ill with the influenza, and was ill for a long time. In March the snow was up to the window-sills of their house.

'Will the winter never end?' he asked his soul. May brought the year's house-rent of the Derbyshire cottage to an end: and back they went to Oxfordshire. But now the place seemed weary to him, tame, after the black iron of the North. The walls had gone – and now he felt nowhere.

So they applied for passports – Harriett to go to Germany, himself to Italy. A lovely summer went by, a lovely autumn came. But the meaning had gone out of everything for him. He had lost his meaning. England had lost its meaning for him. The free England had died, this England of the peace was like a corpse. It was the corpse of a country to him.

In October came the passports. He saw Harriett off to Germany – said Goodbye at the Great Eastern Station, while she sat in the Harwich-Hook-of-Holland express. She had a look of almost vindictive triumph, and almost malignant love, as the train drew out. So he went back to his meaninglessness at the cottage.

Then, finding the meaninglessness too much, he gathered his little money together and in November left for Italy. Left England. England which he had loved so bitterly, bitterly – and now was leaving, alone, and with a feeling of expressionlessness in his soul. It was a cold day. There was snow on the downs like a shroud. And as he looked back from the boat, when they had left Folkestone behind and only England was there,

England looked like a grey, dreary-grey coffin sinking in the sea behind, with her dead grey cliffs and the white, worn-out cloth of snow above.

Memory of all this came on him so violently, now in the Australian night, that he trembled helplessly under the shock of it. He ought to have gone up to Jack's place for the night. But no, he could not speak to anybody. Of all the black throng in the dark Sydney streets, he was the most remote. He strayed round in a torture of fear, and then at last suddenly went to the Carlton Hotel, got a room, and went to bed, to be alone and think.

Detail for detail he thought out his experiences with the authorities, during the war, lying perfectly still and tense. Till now, he had always kept the memory at bay, afraid of it. Now it all came back, in a rush. It was like a volcanic eruption in his consciousness. For some weeks he had felt the great uneasiness in his unconscious. For some time he had known spasms of that same fear that he had known during the war: the fear of the base and malignant power of the mob-like authorities. Since he had been in Italy the fear had left him entirely. He had not even remembered it, in India. Only in the quiet of *Coo-ee*, strangely enough, it had come back in little spasms: the dread, almost the horror, of democratic society, the mob. Harriett had been feeling it too. Why? Why, in this free Australia? Why? Why should they both have been feeling this same terror and pressure that they had known during the war, why should it have come on again in Mullumbimby. – Perhaps in Mullumbimby they were suspect again, two strangers, so much alone. Perhaps the secret service was making investigations about them. Ah, canaille!

Richard faced out all his memories like a nightmare in the night, and cut clear. He felt broken off from his fellow-men. He felt broken off from the England he had belonged to. The ties were gone. He was loose like a single timber of some wrecked ship, drifting the face of the sea. Without a people, without a land. So be it. He was broken apart, apart he would remain.

The judgments of society were not valid to him. The accepted goodness of society was no longer goodness to him. In his soul he was cut off, and from his own isolated soul he would judge.

⤸

D. H. Lawrence was born in Nottinghamshire in 1880; he died in the South of France in 1930. This passage is from the autobiographical novel *Kangaroo,* an account of a visit to New South Wales of an English writer (Richard Lovat Somers) and his German wife which includes the chapter 'The Nightmare', a flashback to Lawrence's experiences in England during the war. Brutal experiences no doubt made worse by Lawrence having a German wife and the perception by the army recruiters in the Midlands that he was an intellectual trying to avoid doing his duty for King and Country:

> He hated the Midlands now, he hated the North. People here were viler than in the South, even than in Cornwall. They had a universal desire to take life and down it: these horrible machine people , these iron and coal people...

During the war, the Lawrences were accused of spying and signalling to German submarines from the Cornish coast at Zennor, where they lived. In 1917, the Lawrences were forced to leave Cornwall under the terms of the Defence of the Realm Act. This extract from 'The Nightmare' forcefully conveys the sense of crushing oppression and harassment Lawrence experienced during the war.

SIEGFRIED SASSOON

DONE ALL THAT WAS EXPECTED OF IT

from *Memoirs of an Infantry Officer*

GOING INTO LIVERPOOL WAS, for most of us, the only antidote to the daily tedium of the Depot. Liverpool usually meant the Olympic Hotel. This palatial contrast to the Camp was the chief cause of the overdrafts of Ormand and other young officers. Never having crossed the Atlantic, I did not realize that the Hotel was an American importation, but I know now that the whole thing might have been brought over from New York in the mind of a first-class passenger. Once inside the Olympic, one trod on black and white squares of synthetic rubber, and the warm interior smelt of this pseudo-luxurious flooring. Everything was white and gilt and smooth; it was, so to speak, an air-tight Paradise made of imitation marble. Its loftiness made resonance languid; one of its attractions was a swimming-bath, and the whole place seemed to have the acoustics of a swimming-bath; noise was muffled and diluted to an aqueous undertone, and even the languishing inter-mezzos of the string band throbbed and dilated as though a degree removed from ordinary audibility. Or so it seemed to the Clitherland subaltern who lounged in an ultra-padded chair eating rich cakes with his tea, after drifting from swimming-bath to hairdresser, buying a few fiction-magazines on his way. Later on the cocktail bar would claim him; and after that he would compensate himself for Clitherland with a dinner that defied digestion.

'Fivers' melted rapidly at the Olympic, and many of them were being melted by people whose share in the national effort was difficult to diagnose. In the dining-room I began to observe that some non-combatants were doing themselves pretty well out of the War. They were people whose faces lacked nobility, as they ordered lobsters and selected colossal cigars. I remember drawing Durley's attention to some such group when he dined with me among the mirrors and mock magnificence. They had concluded their spectacular feed with an ice-cream concoction, and now they were indulging in an afterthought – stout and oysters. I said that I supposed they must be profiteers. For a moment Durley regarded them with unspeculative eyes, but he made no comment; if he found them incredible, it wasn't surprising; both his brothers had been killed in action and his sense of humour had suffered in proportion. I remarked that we weren't doing so badly ourselves and replenished his champagne-glass. Durley was on sick-leave and had come to Liverpool for a night so as to see me and one or two others at the Depot. The War was very much on his mind, but we avoided discussing it during dinner. Afterwards, when we were sitting in a quiet corner, he gave me an account of the show at Delville Wood on September 3rd. Owing to his having been wounded in the throat, he spoke in a strained whisper. His narrative was something like this:

'After our first time up there – digging a trench in front of Delville Wood – we came back to Bonte Redoubt and got there soon after daylight on the 30th. That day and the next we were being shelled by long-range guns. About ten o'clock on the night of the 31st, Kinjack decided to shift camp. That took us two hours, though it was only 1,500 yards away, but it was pitch dark and pouring with rain. I'd got into "slacks" and was just settling down in a bell-tent when we got the order to move up to Montauban in double quick time. Kinjack went on ahead. You can imagine the sort of mix-up it was – the men going as fast as they could, getting strung out and losing touch in the dark, and the Adjutant galloping up and down cursing everyone; I never saw him in such a state before – you know what a quiet chap he usually is. We'd started in such a hurry that I'd got my puttees on over my "slacks"! It must have been nearly five miles, but we did it in just over the hour.

When we got there no one could say what all the "wind-up" was about; we were in reserve all next day and didn't move up to the Wood till the evening after that. We were to attack from the right-hand corner of the Wood, with the East Surreys covering our left and the Manchesters attacking Ginchy on our right. Our objective was Pint Trench, taking Bitter and Beer and clearing Ale and Vat, and also Pilsen Lane in which the Brigade thought there were some big dug-outs. When I showed the battle-plan to the Sergeant-Major, all he said was "We'll have a rough house from Ale Alley". But no one had any idea it was going to be such a schimozzle as it was!... Anyhow by 8.30 on the night of September 2nd I got C Company inside the Wood, with Perrin and his Company just in front of us. A lot of the trees were knocked to splinters and most of the undergrowth had gone, so it wasn't difficult to get about. But while we were getting into position in shell-holes and a trench through the Wood there were shells coming from every direction and Very lights going up all round the Wood, and more than once I had to get down and use my luminous compass before I could say which side was which. Young Fernby and the Battalion bombers were on my right, and I saw more of him than of Perrin during the night; he was quite cheerful; we'd been told it was going to be a decent show. The only trouble we struck that night was when a shell landed among some men in a shell-hole; two of the stretcher-bearers were crying and saying it was bloody murder.

'Next day began grey and cheerless; shells screeching overhead, the earth going up in front of the Wood, and twigs falling on my tin hat. When it got near zero, the earth was going up continuously. Boughs were coming down. You couldn't hear the shells coming – simply felt the earth quake when they arrived. There was some sort of smoke-screen but it only let the Boches know we were coming. No one seems to be able to explain exactly what happened, but the Companies on the left never had a hope. They got enfiladed from Ale Alley, so the Sergeant-Major was right about the "rough house". Edmunds was killed almost at once and his Company and B were knocked to bits as soon as they came out of the Wood. I took C along just behind Perrin and his crowd. We advanced in three rushes. It was nothing but scrambling in and out of shell-holes, with the ground all soft like potting-mould.

The broken ground and the slope of the hill saved us a bit from their fire. Bitter Trench was simply like a filled-in ditch where we crossed it. The contact-aeroplane was just over our heads all the time, firing down at the Boches. After the second rush I looked round and saw that a few of the men were hanging back a bit, and no wonder, for a lot of them were only just out from England! I wondered if I ought to go back to them, but the only thing I'd got in my head was a tag from what some instructor had told me when I was a private in the Artists' Rifles before the War. *In an attack always keep going forward!* Except for that, I couldn't think much; the noise was appalling and I've never had such a dry tongue in my life. I knew one thing, that we must keep up with the barrage. We had over 500 yards to go before the first lift and had been specially told we must follow the barrage close up. It was a sort of cinema effect; all noise and no noise. One of my runners was shot through the face from Ale Alley. I remember something like a half-brick flying over my head, and the bullets from the enfilade fire sort of smashing the air in front of my face. I saw a man just ahead topple over slowly, almost gracefully, and thought "poor little chap, that's his last Cup Tie". Anyhow, the two companies were all mixed up by the time we made the third rush, and we suddenly found ourselves looking down into Beer Trench with the Boches kneeling below us. Just on my left, Perrin, on top, and a big Boche, standing in the trench, fired at one another; down went the Boche. Then they cleared off along Vat Alley, and we blundered after them. I saw one of our chaps crumpled up, with a lot of blood on the back of his neck, and I took his rifle and bandolier and went on with Johnson, my runner. The trench had fallen in in a lot of places. They kept turning round and firing back at us. Once, when Johnson was just behind me, he fired (a cool careful shot – both elbows rested) and hit one of them slick in the face; the red jumped out of his face and up went his arms. After that they disappeared. Soon afterwards we were held up by a machine-gun firing dead on the trench where it was badly damaged, and took refuge in a big shell-hole that had broken into it. Johnson went to fetch Lewis guns and bombers. I could see four or five heads bobbing up and down a little way off so I fired at them and never hit one. The rifle I'd got was one of those "wirer's rifles" which hadn't been properly looked after, and very soon nothing happened when I pressed the trigger which had come loose somehow and wouldn't fire the charge. I reloaded and tried again, then threw the thing away and got back into the trench. There was a man kneeling with his rifle sticking up, so I thought I'd use that; but as I was turning to take it another peacetime tag came into my head – *Never deprive a man of his weapon in a post of danger!*

'The next thing I knew was when I came to and found myself remembering a tremendous blow in the throat and right shoulder and feeling speechless and paralysed. Men were moving to and fro above me. Then there was a wild yell – "They're coming back!" and I was alone. I thought "I shall be bombed to bits lying here" and just managed to get along to where a Lewis gun was firing. I fell down and Johnson came along and cut my equipment off and tied up my throat. Someone put my pistol in my side pocket, but when Johnson got me on to my legs it was too heavy and pulled me over so he threw it away. I remember him saying, "Make way; let him come," and men saying "Good luck, sir" – pretty decent of them under such conditions! Got along the trench and out at the back somehow – everything very hazy – drifting smoke and shell-holes – down the hill – thinking "I must get back to Mother" – kept falling down and getting up – Johnson always helping. Got to Battalion headquarters; R.S.M. outside; he took me very gently by the left hand and led me along, looking terribly concerned. Out in the open again at the back of the hill I knew I was safe. Fell down and couldn't get up any more. Johnson disappeared. I felt it was all over with me till I heard his voice saying, "Here he is," and the stretcher-bearers picked me up… When I was at the dressing-station they took a scrap of paper out of my pocket and read it to me. "I saved your life under heavy fire"; signed and dated. The stretcher-bearers do that sometimes, I'm told!'

He laughed huskily, his face lighting up with a gleam of his old humour…

I asked whether the attack had been considered successful. He thought not. The Manchesters had failed, and Ginchy wasn't properly taken till about a week later. 'When I was in hospital in London,' he went on, 'I talked to a son of a gun from the Brigade Staff; he'd been slightly gassed. He told me we'd done all that was expected of us; it was only a holding attack in our sector, so as to stop the Boches from firing down the hill into the backs of our men who were attacking Guillemont. They knew we hadn't a hope of getting Ale Alley.'

He had told it in a simple unemphatic way, illustrating the story with unconscious gestures – taking aim with a rifle, and so on. But the nightmare of smoke and sunlight had been in his eyes, with a sense of confusion and calamity of which I could only guess at the reality. He was the shattered survivor of a broken battalion which had 'done all that was expected of it.'

I asked about young Fernby. Durley had been in the same hospital with him at Rouen and had seen him once. 'They were trying to rouse him up a bit, as he didn't seem to recognize anybody. They knew we'd been in the same Battalion, so I was taken into his ward one night. His head was all over shrapnel wounds. I spoke to him and tried to get him to recognize me, but he didn't know who I was; he died a few hours later.'

Silence was the only comment possible; but I saw the red screens round the bed, and Durley whispering to Fernby's bandaged head and irrevocable eyes, while the nurse stood by with folded hands.

SIEGFRIED SASSOON

THAT NECESSARY FACULTY FOR TRENCH WARFARE

from Memoirs of an Infantry Officer

THE FIRST FEW DAYS were like lying in a boat. Drifting, drifting, I watched the high sunlit windows or the firelight that flickered and glowed on the ceiling when the ward was falling asleep. Outside the hospital a late spring was invading the home-service world. Trees were misty green and sometimes I could hear a blackbird singing. Even the screech and rumble of electric trams was a friendly sound; trams meant safety; the troops in the trenches thought about trams with affection. With an exquisite sense of languor and release I lifted my hand to touch the narcissuses by my bed. They were symbols of an immaculate spirit – creatures whose faces knew nothing of War's demented language.

For a week, perhaps, I could dream that for me the War was over, because I'd got a neat hole through me and the nurse with her spongings forbade me to have a bath. But I soon emerged from my mental immunity; I began to think; and my thoughts warned me that my second time out in France had altered my outlook (if such a confused condition of mind could be called an outlook). I began to feel that it was my privilege to be bitter about my war experiences; and my attitude toward civilians implied that they couldn't understand and that it was no earthly use trying to explain things to them. Visitors were, of course, benevolent and respectful; my wound was adequate evidence that I'd 'been in the thick of it', and I allowed myself to hint at heroism and its attendant horrors. But as might have been expected my behaviour varied with my various visitors; or rather it would have done so had my visitors been more various. My inconsistencies might become tedious if tabulated collectively, so I will confine myself to the following imaginary instances.

Some Senior Officer under whom I'd served: Modest, politely subordinate, strongly imbued with the 'spirit of the Regiment' and quite ready to go out again. 'Awfully nice of you to come and see me, sir.' Feeling that I ought to jump out of bed and salute, and that it would be appropriate and pleasant to introduce him to 'some of my people' (preferably of impeccable social status). Willingness to discuss active service technicalities and revive memories of shared front-line experience.

Middle-aged or elderly Male Civilian: Tendency (in response to sympathetic gratitude for services rendered to King and Country) to assume haggard facial aspect of one who had 'been through hell'. Inclination to wish that my wound was a bit worse than it actually was, and have nurses hovering round with discreet reminders that my strength mustn't be overtaxed. Inability to reveal anything crudely horrifying to civilian sensibilities. 'Oh yes, I'll be out there again by the autumn.' (Grimly wan reply to suggestions that I was now honourably qualified for a home service job.) Secret antagonism to all uncomplimentary references to the German Army.

Charming Sister of Brother Officer: Jocular, talkative, debonair, and diffidently heroic. Wishful to be wearing all possible medal ribbons on pyjama jacket. Able to furnish a bright account of her brother (if still at the front) and suppressing all unpalatable facts about the War. 'Jolly decent of you to blow in and see me.'

Hunting Friend (a few years above Military Service Age): Deprecatory about sufferings endured at the front. Tersely desirous of hearing all about last season's sport. 'By Jingo, that must have been a nailing good gallop!' Jokes about the Germans, as if throwing bombs at them was a tolerable substitute for fox-hunting. A good deal of guffawing (mitigated by remembrance that I'd got a bullet hole through my lung). Optimistic anticipations of next season's Opening Meet and an early termination of hostilities on all fronts.

Nevertheless my supposed reactions to any one of these hypothetical visitors could only be temporary. When alone with my fellow patients I was mainly disposed toward a self-pitying estrangement from everyone except the troops in the front line. (Casualties didn't count as tragic unless dead or badly maimed.)

When Aunt Evelyn came up to London to see me I felt properly touched by her reticent emotion; embitterment against civilians couldn't be applied to her. But after she had gone I resented her gentle assumption that I had done enough and could now accept a safe job. I wasn't going to be messed about like that, I told myself. Yet I knew that the War was unescapable. Sooner or later I should be sent back to the front line, which was the only place where I could be of any use. A cushy wound wasn't enough to keep me out of it. I couldn't be free from the War; even this hospital ward was full of it, and every day the oppression increased. Outwardly it was a pleasant place to be lazy in. Morning sunshine slanted through the tall windows, brightening the grey-green walls and the forty beds. Daffodils and tulips made spots of colour under three red-draped lamps which hung from the ceiling. Some officers lay humped in bed, smoking and reading newspapers; others loafed about in dressing-gowns, going to and from the washing room where they scraped the bristles from their contented faces. A raucous gramophone continually ground out popular tunes. In the morning it was rag-time – *Everybody's Doing It* and *At the Fox-Trot Ball. (Somewhere a Voice is calling, God send you back to me,* and such-like sentimental songs were reserved for the evening hours.) Before midday no one had enough energy to begin talking war shop, but after that I could always hear scraps of conversation from around the two fireplaces. My eyes were reading one of Lamb's Essays, but my mind was continually distracted by such phrases as 'Barrage lifted at the first objective', 'shelled us with heavy stuff', 'couldn't raise enough decent N.C.O.s', 'first wave got held up by machine-guns', and 'bombed them out of a sap'.

There were no serious cases in the ward, only flesh wounds and sick.

These were the lucky ones, already washed clean of squalor and misery and strain. They were lifting their faces to the sunlight, warming their legs by the fire; but there wasn't much to talk about except the War.

In the evenings they played cards at a table opposite my bed; the blinds were drawn, the electric light was on, and a huge fire glowed on walls and ceiling. Glancing irritably up from my book I criticized the faces of the card-players and those who stood watching the game. There was a lean airman in a grey dressing-gown, his narrow whimsical face puffing a cigarette below a turban-like bandage; he'd been brought down by the Germans behind Arras and had spent three days in a bombarded dug-out with Prussians, until our men drove them back and rescued him. The Prussians hadn't treated him badly, he said. His partner was a swarthy Canadian with a low beetling forehead, sneering wide-set eyes, fleshy cheeks, and a loose heavy mouth. I couldn't like that man, especially when he was boasting how he 'did in some prisoners'. Along the ward they were still talking about 'counter-attacked from the redoubt', 'permanent rank of captain', 'never drew any allowances for six weeks', 'failed to get through their wire'… I was beginning to feel the need for escape from such reminders. My brain was screwed up tight, and when people came to see me I answered their questions excitedly and said things I hadn't intended to say.

From the munition factory across the road, machinery throbbed and droned and crashed like the treading of giants; the noise got on my nerves. I was being worried by bad dreams. More than once I wasn't sure whether I was awake or asleep; the ward was half shadow and half sinking firelight, and the beds were quiet with huddled sleepers. Shapes of mutilated soldiers came crawling across the floor; the floor seemed to be littered with fragments of mangled flesh. Faces glared upward; hands clutched at neck or belly; a livid grinning face with bristly moustache peered at me above the edge of my bed; his hands clawed at the sheets. Some were like the dummy figures used to deceive snipers; others were alive and looked at me reproachfully, as though envying me the warm safety of life which they'd longed for when they shivered in the gloomy dawn, waiting for the whistles to blow and the bombardment to lift… A young English private in battle equipment pulled himself painfully towards me and fumbled in his tunic for a letter; as he reached forward to give it to me his head lolled sideways and he collapsed; there was a hole in his jaw and the blood spread across his white face like ink spilt on blotting paper…

Violently awake, I saw the ward without its phantoms. The sleepers were snoring and a nurse in grey and scarlet was coming silently along to make up the fire.

★

Although I have stated that after my first few days in hospital I 'began to think', I cannot claim that my thoughts were clear or consistent. I did, however, become definitely critical and inquiring about the War. While feeling that my infantry experience justified this, it did not occur to me that I was by no means fully informed on the subject. In fact I generalized intuitively, and was not unlike a young man who suddenly loses his belief in religion and stands up to tell the Universal Being that He doesn't exist, adding that if He does, He treats the world very unjustly. I shall have more to say later on about my antagonism to the World War; in the meantime it queered my criticism of it by continually reminding me that the Adjutant had written to tell me that my name had been 'sent in for another decoration'. I could find no fault with this hopeful notion, and when I was allowed out of hospital for the first time my vanity did not forget how nice its tunic would look with one of those (still uncommon) little silver rosettes on the M.C. ribbon, which signified a Bar; or, better still, a red and blue D.S.O.

It was May 2nd and warm weather; no one appeared to be annoyed about the War, so why should I worry? Sitting on the top of a 'bus, I glanced at the editorial paragraphs of the *Unconservative Weekly*. The omniscience of this ably written journal had become the basis of my provocative views on world affairs. I agreed with every word in it and was thus comfortably enabled to disagree with the bellicose patriotism of the *Morning Post*. The only trouble was that an article in the *Unconservative Weekly* was for me a sort of divine revelation. It told me what I'd never known but now needed to believe, and its ratiocinations and political pronouncements passed out of my head as quickly as they entered it. While I read I concurred; but if I'd been asked to restate the arguments I should have contented myself with saying 'It's what I've always felt myself, though I couldn't exactly put it into words'.

The Archbishop of Canterbury was easier to deal with. Smiling sardonically, I imbibed his 'Message to the Nation about the War and the Gospel'. 'Occasions may arise,' he wrote, 'when exceptional obligations are laid upon us. Such an emergency having now arisen, the security of the nation's food supply may largely depend upon the labour which can be devoted to the land. This being so, we are, I think, following the guidance given in the Gospel if in such a case we make a temporary departure from our rule. I have no hesitation in saying that in the need which these weeks present, men and women may with a clear conscience do field-work on Sundays.' Remembering the intense bombardment in front of Arras on Easter Sunday, I wondered whether the Archbishop had given the sanction of the Gospel for that little bit of Sabbath field-work. Unconscious that he was, presumably, pained by the War and its barbarities, I glared morosely in the direction of Lambeth Palace and muttered, 'Silly old fossil!' Soon afterwards I got off the 'bus at Piccadilly Circus and went into the restaurant where I had arranged to meet Julian Durley.

With Durley I reverted automatically to my active service self. The war which we discussed was restricted to the doings of the Flintshire Fusiliers. Old So-and-so had been wounded; poor old Somebody had been killed in the Bullecourt show; old Somebody Else was still commanding B Company. Old jokes and grotesquely amusing trench incidents were reenacted. The Western Front was the same treacherous blundering tragi-comedy which the mentality of the Army had agreed to regard as something between a crude bit of fun and an excuse for a good grumble. I suppose that the truth of the matter was that we were remaining loyal to the realities of our war experience, keeping our separate psychological secrets to ourselves, and avoiding what Durley called 'his dangerous tendency to become serious'. His face, however, retained the haunted unhappy look which it had acquired since the Delville Wood attack last autumn, and his speaking voice was still a hoarse whisper.

When I was ordering a bottle of hock we laughed because the waiter told us that the price had been reduced since 1914, as it was now an unpopular wine. The hock had its happy effect, and soon we were agreeing that the front line was the only place where one could get away from the War. Durley had been making a forlorn attempt to enter the Flying Corps, and had succeeded in being re-examined medically. The examination had started hopefully as Durley had confined himself to nods and headshakings in reply to questions. But when conversation became inevitable the doctor had very soon asked angrily, 'Why the hell don't you stop that whispering?' The verdict had been against his fractured thyroid cartilage; though, as Durley remarked, it didn't seem to him to make much difference whether you shouted or whispered when you were up in an aeroplane. 'You'll have to take some sort of office job,' I said. But he replied that he hated the idea, and then illogically advised me to stay in England as long as I could. I asserted that I was going out again as soon as I could get passed for General Service, and called for the bill as though I were thereby settling my destiny conclusively. I emerged from the restaurant without having uttered a single anti-war sentiment.

When Durley had disappeared into his aimless unattached existence, I sat in Hyde Park for an hour before going back to the hospital. What with the sunshine and the effect of the hock, I felt rather drowsy, and the columns of the *Unconservative Weekly* seemed less stimulating than usual.

On the way back to Denmark Hill I diverted my mind by observing the names on shops and business premises. I was rewarded by Pledge (pawnbroker), Money (solicitor), and Stone (builder). There was also an undertaker named Bernard Shaw. But perhaps the most significant name was Fudge (printing works). What use, I thought, were printed words against a war like this? Durley represented the only reality which I could visualize with any conviction. People who told the truth were likely to be imprisoned, and lies were at a premium... All my energy had evaporated, and it was a relief to be back in bed. After all, I thought, it's only sixteen days since I left the Second Battalion, so I've still got a right to feel moderately unwell. How luxurious it felt, to be lying there, after a cup of strong tea, with daylight diminishing, and a vague gratitude for being alive at the end of a fine day in late spring. Anyhow the War had taught me to be thankful for a roof over my head at night…

Lying awake after the lights were out in the ward, it is possible that I also thought about the Second Battalion. Someone (it must have been Dunning) had sent me some details of the show they'd been in on April 23rd. The attack had been at the place where I'd left them. A little ground had been gained and lost, and then the Germans had retreated a few hundred yards. Four officers had been killed and nine wounded. About forty other ranks killed, including several of the best N.C.O.s. It had been an episode typical of uncountable others, some of which now fill their few pages in Regimental Histories. Such stories look straightforward enough in print, twelve years later; but their reality remains hidden; even in the minds of old soldiers the harsh horror mellows and recedes.

Of this particular local attack the Second Battalion Doctor afterwards wrote: 'The occasion was but one of many when a Company or Battalion was sacrificed on a limited objective to a plan of attack ordered by Division or some higher Command with no more knowledge of the ground than might be got from a map of moderate scale.' But for me (as I lay awake and wondered whether I'd have been killed if I'd been there) April 23rd was a blurred picture of people bombing one another up and down ditches; of a Company stumbling across open ground and getting mown down by machine-guns; of the doctor out in the dark with his stretcher-bearers, getting in the wounded; and of an exhausted Battalion staggering back to rest-billets to be congratulated by a genial exculpatory Major-General, who explained that the attack had been ordered by the Corps Commander. I could visualize the Major-General all right, though I wasn't aware that he was 'blaming it on the Corps Commander'. And I knew for certain that Ralph Wilmot was now minus one of his arms, so my anti-war bitterness was enabled to concentrate itself on the fact that he wouldn't be able to play the piano again. Finally, it can safely be assumed that my entire human organism felt ultra-thankful to be falling asleep in an English hospital. Altruism is an episodic and debatable quality; the instinct for self-preservation always got the last word when an infantryman was lying awake with his thoughts.

★

With an apology for my persistent specifyings of chronology, I must relate that on May 9th I was moved on to a Railway Terminus Hotel which had been commandeered for the accommodation of convalescent officers. My longing to get away from London made me intolerant of the Great Central Hotel, which was being directed by a mind more military than therapeutic. The Commandant was a non-combatant Brigadier-General, and the convalescents grumbled a good deal about his methods, although they could usually get leave to go out in the evenings. Many of them were waiting to be invalided out of the Army, and the daily routine-orders contained incongruous elements. We were required to attend lectures on, among other things, Trench Warfare. At my first lecture I was astonished to see several officers on crutches, with legs amputated, and at least one man had lost that necessary faculty for trench warfare, his eyesight. They appeared to be accepting the absurd situation stoically; they were allowed to smoke. The Staff Officer who was drawing diagrams on a blackboard was obviously desirous of imparting information about the lesson which had been learnt from the Battle of Neuve Chapelle or some equally obsolete engagement. But I noticed several faces in the audience which showed signs of tortured nerves, and it was unlikely that their efficiency was improved by the lecturer, who concluded by reminding us of the paramount importance of obtaining offensive ascendancy in No Man's Land.

In the afternoon I had an interview with the doctor who was empowered to decide how soon I went to the country. One of the men with whom I shared a room had warned me that this uniformed doctor was a queer customer. 'The blighter seems to take a positive pleasure in tormenting people,' he remarked, adding, 'He'll probably tell you that you'll have to stay here till you're passed fit for duty.' But I had contrived to obtain a letter from the Countess of Somewhere recommending me for one of the country houses in her Organization; so I felt fairly secure. (At that period of the War people with large houses received convalescent officers as guests.)

The doctor, a youngish man dressed as a temporary Captain, began by behaving quite pleasantly. After he'd examined me and the document which outlined my insignificant medical history, he asked what I proposed to do now. I said that I was hoping to get sent to some place in the country for a few weeks. He replied that I was totally mistaken if I thought any such thing. An expression, which I can only call cruel, overspread his face. 'You'll stay here; and when you leave here, you'll find yourself back at the front in double-quick time. How d'you like that idea?' In order to encourage him, I pretended to be upset by his severity; but he seemed to recognize that I wasn't satisfactory material for his peculiar methods, and I departed without having contested the question of going to the country. I was told afterwards that officers had been known to leave this doctor's room in tears. But it must not be supposed that I regard his behaviour as an example of army brutality. I prefer to think of him as a man who craved for power over his fellow men. And though his power over the visiting patients was brief and episodic, he must have derived extraordinary (and perhaps sadistic) satisfaction from the spectacle of young officers sobbing and begging not to be sent back to the front.

I never saw the supposedly sadistic doctor again; but I hope that someone gave him a black eye, and that he afterwards satisfied his desire for power over his fellow men in a more public-spirited manner.

Next morning I handed the letter of the Countess to a slightly higher authority, with the result that I only spent three nights in the Great Central Hotel, and late on a fine Saturday afternoon I travelled down to Sussex to stay with Lord and Lady Asterisk.

〰

Siegfried Loraine Sassoon was born in Kent in 1886, the son of a merchant from a Baghdadi Jewish family and an English Gentile mother who loved Wagner's operas – hence the name Siegfried. A poet who was also a keen cricket player, Sassoon was not a political animal in these pre-war days:

France was a lady, Russia was a bear and performing in the county cricket team was much more important than either of them.

Swept up in the patriotic fervour of 1914, Sassoon enlisted and was sent to fight in France in 1915. On the front, he distinguished himself with acts of heroic bravery and in 1916 was awarded the Military Cross. *Memoirs of an Infantry Officer*, the second volume of the autobiographical George Sherston trilogy, was first published in 1930. The power of the book is manifold: there is Sassoon's growing realization of the folly of the fighting, there is his love and empathy for his fellow soldiers and there is his understated humour and ability to capture the absurdity of those in command. The book ends with the narrator, George Sherston, speaking out publicly against the war; an act of treason that could lead to his execution. He is declared suffering from shell-shock and sent to 'Slateford War Hospital'. In real life this was Craiglockhart Military Hospital where Sassoon was treated by the psychiatrist W. H. R. Rivers. At Craiglockhart, he befriended Wilfred Owen before they were both sent back to fight in France, where Owen was killed in 1918. During the war, Sassoon had become a socialist and in 1919 he became the literary editor of the left-wing *Daily Herald*. In 1931, he moved to Wiltshire, where he died in 1967.

VERA BRITTAIN

DESTINY WAS
NOT WILLING

from *Testament of Youth*

I HAD JUST GOT INTO BED on May Morning and was drifting into sleep, when the cable came from Edward to say that Geoffrey was dead.

When I had read it I got up and went down to the shore in my dressing-gown and pyjamas. All day I sat on the rocks by the sea with the cable in my hand. I hardly noticed how the beautiful morning, golden and calm as an August in Devon, turned slowly into gorgeous afternoon, but I remembered afterwards that the rocks were covered with tiny cobalt-blue irises, about the size of an English wood violet.

For hours I remained in that state of suspended physical animation when neither heat nor cold, hunger nor thirst, fatigue nor pain, appear to have any power over the body, but the mind seems exceptionally logical and clear. My emotions, however, in so far as they existed, were not logical at all, for they led me to a conviction that Geoffrey's presence was somewhere with me on the rocks.

I even felt that if I turned my head quickly I might see him behind me, standing there with his deep-set grey-blue eyes, his finely chiselled lips and the thick light-brown hair that waved a little over his high, candid forehead.

And all at once, as I gazed out to sea, the words of the 'Agony Column' advertisement, that I had cut out and sent to Roland nearly two years before, struggled back into my mind.

'Lady, *fiancé* killed, will gladly marry officer totally blinded or otherwise incapacitated by the War.'

I even remembered vaguely the letter in which I had commented on this notice at the time.

'At first sight it is a little startling. Afterwards the tragedy of it dawns on you. The lady (probably more than a girl or she would have called herself "young lady"; they always do) doubtless has no particular gift or qualification, and does not want to face the dreariness of an unoccupied and unattached old-maidenhood. But the only person she loved is dead; all men are alike to her and it is a matter of indifference whom she marries, so she thinks she may as well marry someone who really needs her. The man, she thinks, being blind or maimed for life, will not have much opportunity of falling in love with anyone, and even if he does will not be able to say so. But he will need a perpetual nurse, and she if married to him can do more for him than an ordinary nurse and will perhaps find relief for her sorrow in devoting her life to him. Hence the advertisement; I wonder if anyone will answer it? It is purely a business arrangement, with an element of self-sacrifice which redeems it from utter sordidness. Quite an idea, isn't it?'

I was still, I reflected, a girl and not yet a 'lady', and I had certainly never meant to go through life with 'no particular gift or qualification'. But – 'quite an idea, isn't it?' Was it, Geoffrey? Wasn't it? There was nothing left in life now but Edward and the wreckage of Victor – Victor who had stood by me so often in my blackest hours. If he wanted me, surely I could stand by him in his.

If he wanted me? I decided, quite suddenly, that I would go home and see. It would not, I knew, be difficult to get permission, for though the renewal of my contract was overdue and I had said that I would sign on again, I had not yet done so. Work was slack in Malta; several hospitals were closing and the rest were overstaffed. Much as I liked my hospital and loved the island, I knew that I was not really needed there any more; any one – or no one – could take my place. If I could not do anything immediate for Victor I would join up again; if I could – well, time and the extent of his injuries would decide when that should be.

That night – quiet as all nights were now that so few sick and wounded were coming from Salonika – I tried to keep my mind from thoughts and my eyes from tears by assiduously pasting photographs of Malta into a cardboard album. The scent of a vase of sweet-peas on the ward table reminded me of Roland's study on Speech Day, centuries ago. Although I had been up for a day and two nights, I felt no inclination to sleep.

I was not, as it happened, very successful in stifling thought. By one of those curious chances which occurred during the War with such poignant frequency, a mail came in that evening with a letter from Geoffrey. It had been written in pencil three days before the attack; reading it with the knowledge that he had been so soon to die, I found its simple nobility even less bearable than the shock of the cablegram.

As I took in its contents with a slow, dull pain, the silent, shadowy verandah outside the door seemed to vanish from my eyes, and I saw the April evening in France which Geoffrey's words were to paint upon my mind for ever – the battened-out line of German trenches winding away into shell-torn trees, the ant-like contingent of men marching across a derelict plain to billets in the large town outlined against the pale yellow sky, the setting sun beneath purple clouds reflected in the still water at the bottom of many 'crump-holes'. How he wished, he said, that Edward could have been with him to see this beauty if it were any other place, but though the future seemed very vague it was none the less certain. He only hoped that he would not fail at the critical moment, as he was indeed 'a horrible coward'; for his school's sake, where so often he had watched the splendours of the sunset from the school field, he would especially like to do well. 'But all this will be boring you.'

Characteristically he concluded his letter with the haunting lines that must have nerved many a reluctant young soldier to brave the death from which body and spirit shrank so pitifully.

War knows no power. Safe shall be my going…
Safe though all safety's lost; safe where men fall;
And, if these poor limbs die, safest of all.

'Rupert Brooke,' he added, 'is great and his faith also great. If destiny is willing I will write later.'

Well, I thought, destiny was not willing, and I shall not see that graceful, generous handwriting on an envelope any more. I wonder why it is that both Victor and Geoffrey were fired to such articulateness by the imminence of death, while Edward and Roland, who had the habit of self-expression, both became so curtly monosyllabic? Oh, Geoffrey, I shall never know anyone quite like you again, so true, so straight, such an unashamed idealist! It's another case of 'whom the Gods love'; the people we care for all seem too fine for this world, so we lose them... Surely, surely there must be somewhere in which the sweet intimacies begun here may be continued and the hearts broken by this War may be healed!

VERA BRITTAIN

I THANK YOU, SISTER

from *Testament of Youth*

T HE NEXT MORNING saw me begin an experience which I remember
as vividly as anything that happened in my various hospitals.

Soon after our arrival the Matron, a beautiful, stately woman who
looked unbelievably young for her South African ribbons, had questioned us all on our previous experience. I was now the owner of an
'efficiency stripe' – a length of scarlet braid which V.A.D.s were entitled
to wear on their sleeve if they had served for more than a year in military hospitals and had reached what their particular authority regarded
as a high standard of competence – and when I told the Matron of my
work in Malta, she remarked with an amused, friendly smile that I was
'quite an old soldier'. This pleasant welcome confirmed a rumour heard
in Boulogne that the hospital was very busy and every pair of practised
hands likely to count. I was glad to be once more where the work was
strenuous, but though I knew that 24 General had a special section for
prisoners, I was hardly prepared for the shock of being posted, on the
strength of my Malta experience, to the acute and alarming German
ward.

The hospital was unusually cosmopolitan, as in addition to German
prisoners it took Portuguese officers, but I can recall nothing about these
except their habit of jumping off the tram and publicly relieving themselves on the way to Le Touquet. Most of the prisoners were housed – if

the word can be justified – in large marquees, but one hut was reserved for very serious cases. In August 1917 its occupants – the heritage of Messines and the Yser – were soon to be replenished by the new battles in the Salient which have given their sombre immortality to the Menin Road and Passchendaele Ridge.

Although we still, I believe, congratulate ourselves on our impartial care of our prisoners, the marquees were often damp, and the ward was under-staffed whenever there happened to be a push – which seemed to be always – and the number of badly wounded and captured Germans became in consequence excessive. One of the things I like best to remember about the War is the nonchalance with which the Sisters and V.A.D.s in the German ward took for granted that it was they who must be overworked, rather than the prisoners neglected. At the time that I went there the ward staff had passed a self-denying ordinance with regard to half days, and only took an hour or two off when the work temporarily slackened.

Before the War I had never been in Germany and had hardly met any Germans apart from the succession of German mistresses at St Monica's, every one of whom I had hated with a provincial schoolgirl's pitiless distaste for foreigners. So it was somewhat disconcerting to be pitch-forked, all alone – since V.A.D.s went on duty half an hour before Sisters – into the midst of thirty representatives of the nation which, as I had repeatedly been told, had crucified Canadians, cut off the hands of babies, and subjected pure and stainless females to unmentionable 'atrocities'. I didn't think I had really believed all those stories, but I wasn't quite sure. I half expected that one or two of the patients would get out of bed and try to rape me, but I soon discovered that none of them were in a position to rape anybody, or indeed to do anything but cling with stupendous exertion to a life in which the scales were already weighted heavily against them.

At least a third of the men were dying; their daily dressings were not a mere matter of changing huge wads of stained gauze and wool, but of stopping haemorrhages, replacing intestines and draining and re-inserting innumerable rubber tubes. Attached to the ward was a small theatre, in which acute operations were performed all day by a medical officer with a swarthy skin and a rolling brown eye; he could speak German, and before the War had been in charge, I was told, of a German hospital in some tropical region of South America. During the first two weeks, he and I and the easy-going Charge-Sister worked together pleasantly enough. I often wonder how we were able to drink tea and eat cake in the theatre – as we did all day at frequent intervals – in that foetid stench, with the thermometer about 90 degrees in the shade, and the saturated dressings and yet more gruesome human remnants heaped on the floor. After the 'light medicals' that I had nursed in Malta, the German ward might justly have been described as a regular baptism of blood and pus.

While the operations went on I was usually left alone in the ward with the two German orderlies, Zeppel and Fritz, to dress as best I could the worst wounds that I had ever seen or imagined.

'I would have written yesterday... but I was much too busy,' runs a typical letter to my mother. 'I did not get off duty at all, and all afternoon and evening I had the entire ward to myself, as Sister was in the operating theatre from 1.30 to 8.0; we had fifteen operations. Some of the things I have to do would make your hair stand on end!'

Soon after my arrival, the first Sister-in-charge was replaced by one of the most remarkable members of the nursing profession in France or anywhere else. In an unpublished novel into which, a few weeks after leaving Etaples, I introduced a good many scenes from 24 General, I drew her portrait as that of its chief character, Hope Milroy, and it is by this name, rather than her own, that I always remember her. Sister Milroy was a highbrow in active revolt against highbrows; connected on one side with a famous family of clerics, and on the other with an equally celebrated household of actors and actresses, she had deliberately chosen a hospital training in preference to the university education for which heredity seemed to have designed her, though no one ever suffered fools less gladly than she. When she first came to the ward her furious re-organisations were devastating, and she treated the German orderlies and myself with impartial contempt. On behalf of the patients she displayed determination and efficiency but never compassion; to her they were all 'Huns', though she dressed their wounds with gentleness and skill.

'Nurse!' she would call to me in her high disdainful voice, pointing to an unfortunate patient whose wound unduly advertised itself. 'For heaven's sake get the iodoform powder and scatter it over that filthy Hun!'

The staff of 24 General described her as 'mental', not realising that she used her reputation for eccentricity and the uncompromising candour which it was supposed to excuse as a means of demanding more work from her subordinates than other Sisters were able to exact. At first I detested her dark attractiveness and sarcastic, relentless youth, but when I recognised her for what she was – by far the cleverest woman in the hospital, even if potentially the most alarming, and temperamentally as fitful as a weathercock – we became constant companions off duty. After the conscientious stupidity of so many nurses, a Sister with unlimited intelligence and deliberately limited altruism was pleasantly stimulating, though she was so incalculable, and such a baffling mixture of convention and independence, that a long spell of her society demanded a good deal of reciprocal energy.

The desire for 'heaps to do and no time to think' that I had expressed at Devonshire House was certainly being fulfilled, though I still did think occasionally, and more especially, perhaps, when I was nursing the German officers, who seemed more bitterly conscious of their position as prisoners than the men. There were about half a dozen of these officers, separated by a green curtain from the rest of the ward, and I found their punctilious manner of accepting my ministrations disconcerting long after I had grown accustomed to the other patients.

One tall, bearded captain would invariably stand to attention when I had re-bandaged his arm, click his spurred heels together, and bow with ceremonious gravity. Another badly wounded boy – a Prussian lieutenant who was being transferred to England – held out an emaciated hand to me as he lay on the stretcher waiting to go, and murmured: 'I tank you, Sister.' After barely a second's hesitation I took the pale fingers in mine, thinking how ridiculous it was that I should be holding this man's hand in friendship when perhaps, only a week or two earlier, Edward up at Ypres had been doing his best to kill him. The world was mad and we were all victims; that was the only way to look at it. These shattered, dying boys and I were paying alike for a situation that none of us had desired or done anything to bring about. Somewhere, I remembered, I had seen a poem called 'To Germany', which put into words this struggling new idea; it was written, I discovered afterwards, by Charles Hamilton Sorley, who was killed in action in 1915:

You only saw your future bigly planned,
And we, the tapering paths of our own mind,
And in each other's dearest ways we stand,
And hiss and hate. And the blind fight the blind.

'It is very strange that you should be nursing Hun prisoners,' wrote Edward from the uproar in the Salient, 'and it does show how absurd the whole thing is; I am afraid leave is out of the question for the present; I am going to be very busy as I shall almost certainly have to command the coy. in the next show... Belgium is a beastly country, at least this part of it is; it seems to breathe little-mindedness, and all the people are on the make or else spies. I will do my best to write you a decent letter soon if possible; I know I haven't done so yet since I came out – but I am feeling rather worried because I hate the thought of shouldering big responsibilities with the doubtful assistance of ex-N.C.O. subalterns. Things are much more difficult than they used to be, because nowadays you never know where you are in the line and it is neither open warfare nor trench warfare.'

A few days afterwards he was promoted, as he had expected, to be acting captain, and a letter at the end of August told me that he had just completed his course of instruction for the forthcoming 'strafe'.

'Captain B.,' he concluded, 'is now in a small dug-out with our old friend Wipers on the left front, and though he has got the wind up because he is in command of the company and may have to go up the line at any moment, all is well for the present.'

Vera Brittain was born in Newcastle-under-Lyme in 1893. She left her studies at Oxford to work as a VAD (Voluntary Aid Detachment) nurse in 1915. Her best-selling memoir, *Testament of Youth*, is an account of these wartimes experiences. Rightly seen as a classic, the book describes Brittain's falling out of love with the gung-ho enthusiasm for the war of some of her contemporaries to reach a heartfelt commitment to pacifism; in a letter written in November 1915 to Roland Leighton, her fiancé later killed in the war, she wrote:

> I have only one wish in life now and that is for the ending of the war. I wonder how much really all you have seen and done has changed you. Personally, after seeing some of the dreadful things I have seen here, I feel I shall never be the same person again, and wonder if, when the war does end, I shall have forgotten how to laugh...

Her commitment to pacifism was to last her whole life. She was a regular speaker for the League of Nations Union in the 1920s, joined the Peace Pledge Union in 1937 and during the Second World War published *Letters to Peace Lovers* which criticized the UK government for bombing urban areas in Germany. She was a founding member of the Campaign for Nuclear Disarmament (CND) in 1957.

Vera Brittain died in 1970. *Testament of Youth*, with its powerful mix of pacifism, idealism and feminism, continues to speak to successive generations.

HELEN ZENNA SMITH

LIQUID FIRE

from *Not So Quiet: Stepdaughters of War*

THE CONVOY IS LATE. We are all lined up waiting – even the five newcomers are at last toeing the line – but the long crawling length of train does not round the bend. Little groups of stretcher-bearers stand about shivering and cursing the delay. Some of them warm their hands at our radiators. Two of them are in high spirits. They have been drinking. Commandant is eyeing them. She will report them before the night is much older. It is seldom the stretcher-bearers take to drink, but one can quite understand their giving way. There are times when I would drug myself with spirits, if I could lay hands on any... Anything to shut out the horrors of these convoys. Some of the girls begin to tramp about the station yard. I am too numb to get down. I suppose I still possess feet, though I cannot feel them. The wind has dropped slightly, but it seems to get colder and colder. Oh, this cold of France. I have never experienced anything remotely resembling it. It works through one's clothing, into one's flesh and bones. It is not satisfied till it is firmly ingrained in one's internal regions, from whence it never really moves.

It has been freezing hard for over a week now. The bare trees in the road are loaded with icicles,... tall trees, ugly and gaunt and gallows-like till the whiteness veiled them – transforming them into objects of weird beauty.

Etta Potato and The Bug want me to come down. They are having a walking race with Tosh for cigarettes – the winner to collect one each from the losers. Won't I join in? I refuse,… I am too numb to move. Off they start across the snow-covered yard. Tosh wins easily. Their laughter rings out as she extorts her winnings there and then. All of a sudden their laughter ceases. They fly back to their posts. The convoy must be sighted. I crane my neck. Yes. The stretcher-bearers stop smoking and line up along the platform. Ambulance doors are opened in readiness. All is bustle. Everyone on the alert. Cogs in the great machinery. I can hear the noise of the train distinctly now,… sound travels a long way in the snow in these death-still early morning hours before the dawn. Louder and louder.

If the War goes on and on and on and I stay out here for the duration, I shall never be able to meet a train-load of casualties without the same ghastly nausea stealing over me as on that first never-to-be-forgotten night. Most of the drivers grow hardened after the first week. They fortify themselves with thoughts of how they are helping to alleviate the sufferings of wretched men, and find consolation in so thinking. But I cannot. I am not the type that breeds warriors. I am the type that should have stayed at home, that shrinks from blood and filth, and is completely devoid of pluck. In other words, I am a coward… A rank coward. I have no guts. It takes every ounce of will-power I possess to stick to my post when I see the train rounding the bend. I choke my sickness back into my throat, and grip the wheel, and tell myself it is all a horrible nightmare… soon I shall awaken in my satin-covered bed on Wimbledon Common… what I can picture with such awful vividness doesn't really exist…

I have schooled myself to stop fainting at the sight of blood. I have schooled myself not to vomit at the smell of wounds and stale blood, but view these sad bodies with professional calm I shall never be able to. I may be helping to alleviate the sufferings of wretched men, but commonsense rises up and insists that the necessity should never have arisen. I become savage at the futility. A war to end war, my mother writes. Never. In twenty years it will repeat itself. And twenty years after that. Again and again, as long as we breed women like my mother and Mrs. Evans-Mawnington. And we are breeding them. Etta Potato and The B.F. – two out of a roomful of six. Mother and Mrs. Evans-Mawnington all over again.

Oh, come with me, Mother and Mrs. Evans-Mawnington. Let me show you the exhibits straight from the battlefield. This will be something original to tell your committees, while they knit their endless miles of khaki scarves,... something to spout from the platform at your recruiting meetings. Come with me. Stand just there.

Here we have the convoy gliding into the station now, slowly, so slowly. In a minute it will disgorge its sorry cargo. My ambulance doors are open, waiting to receive. See, the train has stopped. Through the occasionally drawn blinds you will observe the trays slotted into the sides of the train. Look closely, Mother and Mrs. Evans-Mawnington, and you shall see what you shall see. Those trays each contain something that was once a whole man... the heroes who have done their bit for King and country... the heroes who marched blithely through the streets of London Town singing ' Tipperary,' while you cheered and waved your flags hysterically. They are not singing now, you will observe. Shut your ears, Mother and Mrs. Evans-Mawnington, lest their groans and heartrending cries linger as long in your memory as in the memory of the daughter you sent out to help win the War.

See the stretcher-bearers lifting the trays one by one, slotting them deftly into my ambulance. Out of the way quickly, Mother and Mrs. Evans-Mawnington – lift your silken skirts aside... a man is spewing blood, the moving has upset him, finished him... He will die on the way to hospital if he doesn't die before the ambulance is loaded. I know... All this is old history to me. Sorry this has happened. It isn't pretty to see a hero spewing up his life's blood in public, is it? Much more romantic to see him in the picture papers being awarded the V.C., even if he is minus a limb or two. A most unfortunate occurrence!

That man strapped down? That raving, blaspheming creature screaming filthy words you don't know the meaning of... words your daughter uses in everyday conversation, a habit she has contracted from vulgar contact of this kind. Oh, merely gone mad, Mother and Mrs. Evans-Mawnington. He may have seen a headless body running on and on, with blood spurting from the trunk. The crackle of the frost-stiff dead men packing the duck-boards watertight may have gradually undermined his reason. There are many things the sitters tell me on our long night rides that could have done this.

No, not shell-shock. The shell-shock cases take it more quietly as a rule, unless they are suddenly startled. Let me find you an example. Ah, the man they are bringing out now. The one staring straight ahead at nothing... twitching, twitching, twitching, each limb working in a different direction, like a Jumping Jack worked by a jerking string. Look at him, both of you. Bloody awful, isn't it, Mother and Mrs. Evans-Mawnington? That's shell-shock. If you dropped your handbag on the platform, he would start to rave as madly as the other. What? You won't try the experiment? You can't watch him? Why not? *Why not?* I have to, every night. Why the hell can't you do it for once? Damn your eyes.

Forgive me, Mother and Mrs. Evans-Mawnington. That was not the kind of language a nicely-brought-up young lady from Wimbledon Common uses. I forget myself. We will begin again.

See the man they are fitting into the bottom slot. He is coughing badly. No, not pneumonia. Not tuberculosis. Nothing so picturesque. Gently, gently, stretcher-bearers... he is about done. He is coughing up clots of pinky-green filth. Only his lungs, Mother and Mrs. Evans-Mawnington. He is coughing well to-night. That is gas. You've heard of gas, haven't you? It burns and shrivels the lungs to... to the mess you see on the ambulance floor there. He's about the age of Bertie, Mother. Not unlike Bertie, either, with his gentle brown eyes and fair curly hair. Bertie would look up pleadingly like that in between coughing up his lungs... The son you have so generously given to the War. The son you are so eager to send out to the trenches before Roy Evans-Mawnington, in case Mrs. Evans-Mawnington scores over you at the next recruiting meeting... 'I have given my only son.'

Cough, cough, little fair-haired boy. Perhaps somewhere your mother is thinking of you... boasting of the life she has so nobly given... the life you thought was your own, but which is hers to squander as she thinks fit. 'My boy is not a slacker, thank God.' Cough away, little boy, cough away. What does it matter, providing your mother doesn't have to face the shame of her son's cowardice?

These are sitters. The man they are hoisting up beside me, and the two who sit in the ambulance. Blighty cases... broken arms and trench feet... mere trifles. The smell? Disgusting, isn't it? Sweaty socks and feet swollen to twice their size... purple, blue, red... big black blisters filled with yellow matter. Quite a colour-scheme, isn't it? Have I made you vomit? I must again ask pardon. My conversation is daily growing less refined. Spew and vomit and sweat... I had forgotten these words are not used in the best drawing-rooms on Wimbledon Common.

But I am wasting time. I must go in a minute. I am nearly loaded. The stretcher they are putting on one side? Oh, a most ordinary exhibit,... the groaning man to whom the smallest jolt is red hell... a mere bellyful of shrapnel. They are holding him over till the next journey. He is not as urgent as the helpless thing there, that trunk without arms and legs, the remnants of a human being, incapable even of pleading to be put out of his misery because his jaw has been half shot away... No, don't meet his eyes, they are too alive. Something of their malevolence might remain with you all the rest of your days,... those sock-filled, committee-crowded days of yours.

Gaze on the heroes who have so nobly upheld your traditions, Mother and Mrs. Evans-Mawnington. Take a good look at them... The heroes you will sentimentalise over until peace is declared, and allow to starve for ever and ever, amen, afterwards. Don't go. Spare a glance for my last stretcher,... that gibbering, unbelievable, unbandaged thing, a wagging lump of raw flesh on a neck, that was a face a short time ago, Mother and Mrs. Evans-Mawnington. Now it might be anything... a lump of liver, raw bleeding liver, that's what it resembles more than anything else, doesn't it? We can't tell its age, but the whimpering moan sounds young, somehow. Like the fretful whimpers of a sick little child... a tortured little child... puzzled whimpers. Who is he? For all you know, Mrs. Evans-Mawnington, he is your Roy. He might be anyone at all, so why not your Roy? One shapeless lump of raw liver is like another shapeless lump of raw liver. What do you say? Why don't they cover him up with bandages? How the hell do I know? I have often wondered myself,... but they don't. Why do you turn away? That's only liquid fire. You've heard of liquid fire? Oh, yes. I remember your letter... '*I hear we've started to use liquid fire, too. That will teach those Germans. I hope we use lots and lots of it.'* Yes, you wrote that. You were glad some new fiendish torture had been invented by the chemists who are running this war. You were delighted to think some German mother's son was going to have the skin stripped from his poor face by liquid fire… Just as some equally patriotic German mother rejoiced when she first heard the sons of Englishwomen were to be burnt and tortured by the very newest war gadget out of the laboratory.

Don't go, Mother and Mrs. Evans-Mawnington,… don't go. I am loaded, but there are over thirty ambulances not filled up. Walk down the line. Don't go, unless you want me to excuse you while you retch your insides out as I so often do. There are stretchers and stretchers you haven't seen yet… Men with hopeless dying eyes who don't want to die… men with hopeless living eyes who don't want to live. Wait, wait, I have so much, so much to show you before you return to your committees and your recruiting meetings, before you add to your bag of recruits… those young recruits you enroll so proudly with your patriotic speeches, your red, white and blue rosettes, your white feathers, your insults, your lies… any bloody lie to secure a fresh victim.

What? You cannot stick it any longer? You are going? I didn't think you'd stay. But I've got to stay, haven't I?… I've got to stay. You've got me out here, and you'll keep me out here. You've got me haloed. I am one of the Splendid Young Women who are winning the War…

'Loaded. Six stretchers and three sitters!'

I am away. I slow up at the station gate. The sergeant is waiting with his pencil and list. I repeat, 'Six stretchers and three sitters.'

'Number Eight.'

He ticks off my ambulance. I pass out of the yard.

Number Eight. A lucky number! A long way out, but a good level road, comparatively few pot-holes and stone heaps.

Crawl, crawl, crawl.

Along we creep at a snail's pace… a huge dark crawling blot on the dead-white road.

Crawl, crawl, crawl.

The sitter leans back motionless. Exhausted, or asleep, after the long journey. His arm is in splints, his head bandaged, and his left foot swaddled in a clumsy trench slipper. He leans back in the darkness, his face as invisible as though a brick wall were separating us. The wind cuts like a knife. He must be numbed through, for he has no overcoat and his sleeve is ripped up. He has draped the Army blanket cloak-wise over his shoulders, leaving his legs to the mercy of the freezing night. It is snowing again. Big snowflakes that hiss as they catch the radiator. I tell the sitter he will find a cigarette and matches in the pocket of my coat nearest him. I have placed them there purposely... my bait to make him talk. I want him to talk. He does not reply. I want him to talk. If I can get a sitter to talk it helps to drown the cries from inside. I discovered that some time ago. I repeat my offer, a trifle louder this time. But he makes no reply. He is done. Too done to smoke even. No luck for me to-night.

Crawl, crawl, crawl.

How smoothly she runs, this great lumbering blot. How slowly. To look at her you'd never think it possible to run an ambulance of this size so slowly...

Crawl, crawl, crawl.

Did I hear a scream from inside? I must fix my mind on something... What? I know – my coming-out dance. My first grown-up dance frock, a shining frock of sequins and white georgette, high-waisted down to my toes... *Did I hear a scream?...* Made over a petticoat... *don't let them start screaming...* a petticoat of satin. Satin slippers to match, not tiny – my feet were always largish; so were my hands... *Was that a scream from inside?...* Such a trouble Mother had getting white gloves my size to go above the elbow... *Was it a scream?...* My hair up for the first time... *oh, God, a scream this time...* my hair up in little rolls at the back... *another scream – the madman has started, the madman has started. I was afraid of him. He'll start them all screaming...* Thirty-one little rolls like fat little sausages. A professional hairdresser came in and did them – took nearly two hours to do them while Trix and Mother watched, and Sarah came in to peep. *Don't let him start the others; don't let him start the others...* Thirty-one little sausages of hair, piled one on top of the other, and all the hair my own too, copied from a picture post card of Phyllis Dare or Lily

Elsie. Now, which one was it?... *The shell-shocked man has joined in. The madman has set the shell-shocked man howling like a mad dog...* Lily Elsie, I think it was... *What are they doing to one another in there?*

'Let me out. Let me out.'

The madman is calling that. Lily Elsie, I think it was. Lily Elsie...

'Stop screaming. You're not the only one going through bloody hell.'

A different voice that one. That must be one of the sitters... Satin slippers with buckles on the toes – little pearl buckles shaped like a crescent. Aunt Helen or Trix gave me those.

'Shut up screaming, or I'll knock hell out of you with my crutch, you bastard. Shut up screaming.'

What was that crash? They're fighting inside. They're fighting inside... Scream, scream, scream...

'I'm dying. Oh, Jesus, he's murdered me. I'm dying.'

What are they doing? Are they murdering one another in there? I ought to stop the ambulance; I ought to get out and see. I ought to stop them... I ought. A driver the other night stopped her ambulance, and a man had gone mad and was beating a helpless stretcher case about the head. But she overpowered him and strapped him down again. Tosh, that was. But Tosh is brave. I couldn't do it. I must go on...

They are all screaming now. Moaning and shrieking and howling like wild animals... All alone with an ambulance of raving men miles from anywhere in the pitch blackness,... raving madmen yelling and screaming. I shall go mad myself...

Go and see... go and see... go and see.

I will not. I cannot... my heart is pounding like a sledge-hammer. My feet and hands are frozen, but the sweat is pouring down my back in rivulets. I have looked before, and I dare not look again. What good can I do? The man who spewed blood will be lying there dead,... his glassy eyes fixed on the door of the ambulance, staring accusingly at me as I peep in,... cold dead eyes, blaming me when I am not to blame... The madman will curse me, scream vile curses at me, scream and try to tear himself from the straps that hold him down,... if he has not torn himself away already. He will try to tear himself from his straps to choke the life from me. The shell-shocked man will yammer and twitch and jerk and mouth. The man with the face like raw liver will moan… I will not go and see. I will not go and see.

Crawl, crawl, crawl.

Number Eight, where are you? Have I missed you in the monotony of this snow-covered road. I have been travelling for hours. Am I travelling too slowly? Am I being over-careful? Could I accelerate ever so slightly… cover the distance more quickly? I will do it. A fresh scream from someone as I jolt over a stone… I've hurt someone. I slow down again.

Scream, scream, scream. Three different sets of screams now – the shriek of the madman, the senseless, wolfish, monotonous howl of the shell-shock case, and now a shrill sharp yell like a bright pointed knife blade being jabbed into my brain. One, two, three, four,… staccato yells. Which one is that? Not the little fair-haired boy. He is too busy choking to death to shriek. Another one has joined in… inferno. They are striking one another again… hell let loose. Go and see, go and see…

I will not go and see. I will not go and see.

Crawl, crawl, crawl.

The sitter sleeps through it all. A pool of snow has fallen in his lap. We have missed Number Eight. I must have missed the turning in the snow. The black tree-stump on the left that leads to Number Eight… snow-obscured. I must have missed the turning in the snow.

Crawl, crawl, crawl.

The screams have died down, but a dreadful moaning takes their place. Oo-oo-oh… oo-oo-oh… dirge-like, regular, it rises above the sound of the engine and floats out into the night. Oo-oo-oh… oo-oo-oh… it is heart-breaking in its despair. I have heard a man moan like that before. The last moans of a man who will soon cease moaning for ever. Oo-oo-oh… the hopelessness, the loneliness. Tears tear at my heart… awful tears that rack me, but must not rise to my eyes, for they will freeze on my cheeks and stick my eyelids together until I cannot see to drive. Even the solace of pitying tears is denied me.

Crawl, crawl, crawl.

I have given up all hope of reaching Number Eight by now. I will go on until there is a place to turn.

Crawl, crawl, crawl.

The moans have ceased. I strain my ears. The madman is shouting again,... a hoarse vituperative monologue. I cannot catch his words. I do not want to catch his words. But I strain to catch them just the same. He will start the others again...

Crawl, crawl, crawl.

If only I could find a place to turn. The road seems to grow narrower. How many journeys shall I make to-night? Was it a big convoy? I didn't notice at the station,... I always forget to notice. Perhaps I shall have shrapnels next time... shrapnels, too exhausted from loss of blood to scream. A sitter who will talk and smoke.

...The madman is screaming again... he will start the others.

Crawl, crawl, crawl.

Is that a light? No... yes! Number Eight! The big canvas marquee gleaming dully in the darkness... the front entrance flaps already parted... white-capped nurses waiting in the doorway. They can see my lights. The orderlies are standing by... Number Eight... Number Eight... I am there at last. The tears are rolling down my cheeks... let them. Let the tears freeze my eyelids together now... let them freeze my eyelids... It doesn't matter now... nothing matters now...

HELEN ZENNA SMITH

THE BEAUTY OF MEN WHO ARE WHOLE

from *Not So Quiet: Stepdaughters of War*

I AM AFRAID OF GOING MAD... of being discovered one morning among the boulders at the foot of a rocky hillside as was The Bug the day following on the air-raid that smashed the station and the convoy train to matchwood... a night of smashings, though none so cruelly smashed as The Bug. She had lost her way and missed her footing in the darkness, said the powers-that-be. This on the brightest night in a season of moonlit nights.

An accident... So The Bug rests alongside Tosh in the bleak cemetery in the shadow of the Witch's Hand.

An accident... drivers walking about with sullen eyes, and whisperings that are not pleasant listening... and I, in the hours after the midnight convoy, sitting thinking things that are best not thought... my fingers tight against Commandant's thick, red throat, gloating in the ebbing strength of that squat, healthy body until I am sick and faint with murderous longing.

The impulse has gone... but in its place has come something worse. I am haunted now as The Bug was haunted. Whenever I close my aching red eyes a procession of men passes before me: maimed men; men with neither arms nor legs; gassed men, coughing, coughing, coughing; men with dreadful burning eyes; men with heads and faces half shot away; raw, bleeding men with the skin burned from their upturned faces;

tortured, all watching me as I lie in my flea-bag trying to sleep... an endless procession of horror that will not let me rest. I am afraid. I am afraid of madness. Are there others in this convoy fear-obsessed as I am, as The Bug was... others who will not admit it, as I will not, as The Bug did not... others who exist in a daily hell of fear? For I fear these maimed men of my imaginings as I never fear the maimed men I drive from the hospital trains to the camps. The men in the ambulances scream, but this ghostly procession is ghostly quiet. I fear them, these silent men, for I am afraid they will stay with me all my life, shutting out beauty till the day I die. And not only do I fear them, I hate them. I hate these maimed men who will not let me sleep.

Oh, the beauty of men who are whole, who have straight arms and legs, whose bodies are not cruelly gashed and torn by shrapnel, whose eyes are not horror-filled, whose faces are smooth and shapely, whose mouths smile instead of grinning painfully... oh, the beauty and wonder of men who are whole. Baynton, young and strong and clean-limbed, are his eyes serene and happy now as they were the afternoon of the concert in the prisoners' compound... or are they staring up unseeingly somewhere in No Man's Land, with that fair skin of his dyed an obscene blue by poison gas, his young body shattered and scattered and bleeding? Roy Evans-Mawnington... is he still smiling and eager-faced as on the day he was photographed in his second-lieutenant's uniform... or has the smile frozen on his incredulous lips?

Oh, the beauty of men who are whole and sane. Shall I ever know a lover who is young and strong and untouched by war, who has not gazed on what I have gazed upon? Shall I ever know a lover whose eyes reflect my image without the shadow of war rising between us? A lover in whose arms I shall forget the maimed men who pass before me in endless parade in the darkness before the dawn when I think and think and think because the procession will not let me sleep?

What is to happen to women like me when this war ends... if ever it ends. I am twenty-one years of age, yet I know nothing of life but death, fear, blood, and the sentimentality that glorifies these things in the name of patriotism. I watch my own mother stupidly, deliberately, though unthinkingly – for she is a kind woman – encourage the sons of other women to kill their brothers; I see my own father – a gentle creature who would not willingly harm a fly – applaud the latest scientist to invent a mechanical device guaranteed to crush his fellow-beings to pulp in their thousands. And my generation watches these things and marvels at the blind foolishness of it… helpless to make its immature voice heard above the insensate clamour of the old ones who cry : 'Kill, Kill, Kill!' unceasingly.

What is to happen to women like me when the killing is done and peace comes… if ever it comes? What will they expect of us, these elders who have sent us out to fight? We sheltered young women who smilingly stumbled from the chintz-covered drawing-rooms of the suburbs straight into hell?

What will they expect of us?

We, who once blushed at the public mention of childbirth, now discuss such things as casually as once we discussed the latest play; whispered stories of immorality are of far less importance than a fresh cheese in the canteen; chastity seems a mere waste of time in an area where youth is blotted out so quickly. What will they expect of us, these elders of ours, when the killing is over and we return?

Once we were not allowed out after nightfall unchaperoned; now we can drive the whole night through a deserted countryside with a man – provided he is in khaki and our orders are to drive him. Will these elders try to return us to our conventional pre-war habits? What will they say if we laugh at them, as we are bound?

I see in the years to come old men in their easy chairs fiercely reviling us for lacking the sweetness and softness of our mothers and their mothers before them; chiding us for language that is not the language of gentlewomen; accusing us of barnyard morals when we use love as a drug for forgetfulness because we have acquired the habit of taking what we can from life while we are alive to take… clearly do I see all these things. But what I do not see is pity or understanding for the war-shocked woman who sacrificed her youth on the altar of the war that was not of her making, the war made by age and fought by youth while age looked on and applauded and encored. Will they show us mercy, these arm-chair critics, once our uniforms are frayed and the romance of the war woman is no longer a romance? I see much, but this I do not see.

And the next generation... our younger brothers and sisters... young things raised in a blood-and-hate atmosphere – I see them hard and callous and cold... emotionless, unfriendly, cruelly analytical, predatory, resentful of us for stealing the limelight from their childhood, bored by the war and the men and women who fought the war, thanklessly grabbing the freedom for which we paid so dearly... all this I see as my procession of torn, dreadful-eyed men passes in the cold dark hours preceding the dawn.

And I see us a race apart, we war products... feared by the old ones and resented by the young ones... a race of men bodily maimed and of women mentally maimed.

What is to become of us when the killing is over?

★

Commandant is willing that I should go.

A rest – sick leave she calls it – but she avoids my cold glance carefully when speaking the words. She understands. I have finished with the war for good. I will take no more part in it. Why should I, who hate and fear war with all my heart, and would gladly die to end it if that were possible, work to keep it going? Etta Potato says my logic is unsound, but I am too weary to argue, too eager to be gone from the little communal bedroom where nightly marches my procession of maimed men.

I divide my kit between Etta Potato and Chutney, leaving only my uniform to travel in. My overcoat is deeply stained where Tosh's head rested... but I must wear it, for I have no other clothes. There are a few farewells; Etta Potato drives me to the station... I do not see Commandant... I am in the train at last... Etta Potato waving farewell from the platform...

My war service is ended.

I am going home.

Darkened stations... endless cold waits... soldiers in khaki... wounded soldiers in blue... V.A.D.'s... nurses... grey, uninteresting landscapes... bare trees... camps, camps, camps... tin huts, wooden huts... marching troops... desolation... cemeteries of black crosses... hospitals... and everywhere mud, mud, mud.

I am going home.

The train stops, starts again, stops; I change to another, on and on and on...

I am going home.

Why am I so calm about it?

Boulogne at last. Why do I not shout and laugh and dance? How often have I pictured this Channel crossing, my wild exhilaration, arriving under the chalk cliffs of England, the white welcoming chalk cliffs of England.

The sweetness of England... England, where grass is green and primroses in early springtime patch the earth a timid yellow... where trees in bud are ready to leaf on the first day of pale sunshine... England, England, how often have I promised to throw myself flat upon your bosom and kiss the first green blade of grass I saw because it was English grass and I had come home?

But now I am coming home... and I do not care.

I have pictured arriving at Charing Cross. Perhaps it would be raining, but it would be English rain and I would hold my face up to its drops. Father and Mother would meet me... drive me through familiar places – Piccadilly, Regent Street... as it grew dusk lights would reflect warmly on the wet, shiny pavements... London and then out through innumerable streets of toy villas towards home...

Home, home... and I do not care.

I do not care. I am flat. Old. I am twenty-one and as old as the hills. Emotion-dry. The war has drained me dry of feeling. Something has gone from me that will never return. I do not want to go home.

I am suddenly aware that I cannot bear Mother's prattle-prattle of committees and recruiting-meetings and the war-baby of Jessie, the new maid; nor can I watch my gentle father gloating over the horrors I have seen, pumping me for good stories to retail at his club to-morrow. I cannot go home to watch a procession of maimed men in my dainty, rose-walled bedroom. It is no place for a company of broken men on parade...

I cannot go home. In the morning, perhaps, but not to-night.

What has happened to me?

I am in England and I do not care.

★

'You've just come from France, haven't you?' I look up from the coffee I am drinking in the hotel lounge. He is a second-lieutenant, very spick and span in his new Sam Browne and well-cut uniform – 'Rather a nut,' The B.F. would label him. He is so immaculate I feel dirty immediately, despite my pre-dinner hot bath, my shampoo and hair-cut, my manicure and my newly-acquired powder-puff.

He smiles disarmingly. 'Awful cheek my coming over, but I embark to-morrow. First time out. Frightful novice.'

First time out. I avoid his laughing blue eyes. He is indeed a frightful novice… that is why his eyes are still laughing.

'Do let me talk to you,' he begs. 'I'm lonely and you seem lonely, too. I've been watching you all through dinner, wondering why you stayed in Folkestone instead of going straight through. Do talk to me. I'd love some tips first-hand from someone who's been out there…'

I agree to talk to him… but not of the war.

Anything but the war. My voice hardens. He notices it and his eyes are suddenly grave… but I do not want them to be grave. Let them smile while they can still smile, they will be grave soon enough. I make a stupid joke… the blue eyes dance again. Blue eyes, dancing like the sea on a breezy summer's day. There is a hop going in the ballroom… I hesitate, my uniform is almost in rags… he tells me it may be, but I look tophole, and my short hair is the sort of hair a fellow would like to rumple his fingers through if he dared… he clasps his hands together in mock penitence…

He is so gay, so audacious, this boy of my own age who is so young and brimming over with life. He invents a wild fandango, and shouts with laughter at an old lady in the corner who stares disapprovingly through lorgnettes. He is clean and young and straight and far removed from the shadow procession I watch night after night, the procession that came to me early this morning and wakened me shrieking in the presence of a compartmentful of shocked strangers. He is so gay, so full of life, this boy who is holding me closely in his arms… he could never join that ghostly parade…

Dance, dance, dance, go on dancing… press me against your breast… talk, talk, talk, go on talking… yes, daringly drop a kiss on top of my cropped head in full view of the shocked old lady with the lorgnettes… laugh, laugh, laugh, go on laughing… yes, I will drink more champagne with you, I will smile when you smile… I will press your hand when you press mine under the table… yes, I will dance with you again till I forget I have seen you at the end of the ghostly procession that has crossed the Channel with me.

He asks me to call him Robin. I tell him my name is Nell. I wish it were something more charming.

But it is charming, as charming as its owner. Oh, yes, yes, *yes*… if I shake my head again he'll kiss me in the middle of the ballroom, and the disapproving old girl with the lorgnettes will pass out completely… he loves to see me smile… Not unhappy as I was at dinner now, am I?

The last dance comes. The last chord crashes. He pulls me to him so roughly that I am left breathless for a second. 'The King' is played. He stands rigidly to attention, his eyes clouded for a moment. 'The King' finishes. I make a quick joke about Paris leave; he throws his head back and laughs. Easily and swiftly he laughs, this Robin who is straight and clean and whole.

We walk into the lounge slowly… bed now, he supposes, with a side-glance at me… hardly worth while undressing, embarking at five… filthy, unearthly hour to get a fellow out of bed…

We get into the lift without speaking… our rooms are on the same floor…

At my door he kisses me, at first gently… 'a good-night kiss'… then more ardently… how strong and beautiful he is, this Robin who has not been out to hell yet… *Dear Nell*… he kisses me again… *Dear Robin*…

Must he say good-night?… Can't he come in and talk to me after I am in bed?… I don't think him an awful rotter for suggesting it, do I?… How ingenuous he is, this Robin who kisses me so ardently, whose eyes are blue and sane… He'll be good, honestly – well, just as good as I want him to be… he kisses me again… poor Robin, poor Robin…

The luminous hands of my watch say four o'clock. It is pitch dark. I switch the bed-lamp on. He is deep in the abyss of sleep... ' Time to go, Robin.'

He awakens smiling and flushed, like a child. 'Nell...'

Then, after a while, 'You will write – promise?' I promise.

'I feel a cad, an absolute...'

No, no, no.

'I'm your first lover, aren't I? Why, Nell? Were you a bit in love with me, too?...'

I nod. A lie, but it will do. But it was not only because he was whole and strong-limbed, not only because his body was young and beautiful, not only because his laughing blue eyes reflected my image without the shadow of war rising to blot me out... but because I saw him between me and the dance orchestra ending a shadow procession of cruelly-maimed men...

Poor Robin, poor baby.

'I shall always treasure this, Nell;... you're the first girl I've loved, decently;... there have been others, but...' he stammers boyishly, embarrassed... 'When I come on leave we'll dance again, won't we?... We'll have such fun, Nell...'

I kiss him despairingly, the hot tears choking me... We will not dance again, this Robin and I; it is so pitiful; he is twenty and I am twenty-one, but he is so young...

Poor Robin, poor baby, poor baby.

He closes the bedroom door softly behind him.

~

Evadne Price, who wrote mostly under the pseudonym Helen Zenna Smith, was born either in 1901 at sea off the coast of New South Wales or, as she claimed, in 1896 in Sussex in England. *Not So Quiet: Stepdaughters of War*, first published in 1930, was based on the diaries of Winifred Young, who served during the war as an ambulance driver. Critically acclaimed on publication, the book is a powerful attack on the hypocrisy of those at home who fan the flames of nationalism totally unaware of what is really happening on the front.

'Out of the way quickly, Mother and Mrs. Evans-Mawnington – lift your silken skirts aside… Sorry this has happened. It isn't pretty to see a hero spewing up his life's blood in public, is it? Much more romantic to see him in the picture papers being awarded the V.C. even if he is minus a limb or two. A most unfortunate occurrence!

Avant-garde in style, many of the book's descriptions are like an Otto Dix painting. Evadne Price went on to become a popular romantic novelist whose best-known titles include *Society Girl!*, *Escape to Marriage* and *Air Hostess in Love*. She died in Sydney in 1985 leaving behind an unfinished autobiography, *Mother Painted Nude*.

WILLIAM BAYLEBRIDGE

THE APOCALYPSE OF PAT MCCULLOUGH: THE SERGEANT'S TALE

from *An Anzac Muster*

THE COMPANY, NOT A WHIT LESS TICKLED than their comrades had been on that delicate occasion, thought the jest a good one. Nor – like them, too – did they fail to laugh well at the discomfiture of that orderly. The result of the lad's labour, someone ventured, must in truth have been an eye-opener to Flower, to catch his eye napping in that fashion. In two words, the Crow thought his tale a success.

'Short it is,' said the Colonel, 'but' – and he here gripped his nose – '*not* sweet. And as for your moral, to hunt the beast, we should need, in an atmosphere so overcharged, a respirator indeed gas-proof.'

The Squatter, who thought the tale at least a neat one, was a little curious about the author of that couplet, that had so smartly made its point.

'What bard, then, was in action here?' he questioned. But the name of that smitten poet was unknown; and this indeed mattered little, for, as the Colonel promptly whispered him, there were, among our troops, a thousand wags who, in a like circumstance, could have passed a couplet easier than an excrement.

It was now the Sergeant's turn to give something. From his preoc-cupation, it might have been guessed that he meant to put forth, on this occasion, not the least of his powers. He sat silent; his lips were a little parted, his eyes fixed. The Colonel, after allowing him time to think out his matter, said:

'If I have hit the mark, Sergeant, we shall find profit in you. Give what you have willingly,' he continued, with a sly glance at the Crow. 'When the crow shuts his bill to, doesn't the next bird sound the better for it?'

'If my yarn's not too long, Colonel,' the Sergeant, in a doubtful tone, answered, 'I'll tell it gladly.'

The Colonel, who, in spite of his sharp hint to the Crow, was not unwilling to give time to the more discreet tellers, requested him, if it was only good, to care nothing for its length; upon which the Sergeant, without further pressing, proceeded thus.

★

The Twenty Ninth Division, doing as much as blood could, had pushed well into the containing battle at Krithia; at Lone Pine the First Brigade of Australian Infantry had done much – where so much was yet to be done – in a labour that was to put it for ever past the reach of oblivion; superb and not to be conquered, the New Zealanders, the right covering column of the main attack, had charged and secured the almost impregnable Old Number Three Post, had stormed the Turks out of the tangled and precipitous ridge at Bauchop's, and climbed to another victory on the Table Top; Damakjelik Bair was ours; the three Deres, won at a bitter price in blood and travail, were open to the two attacking columns which, even now, were advancing to the assault.

The Turks, threatened as they had hardly expected to be, shook to their marrow. They put forth their entire strength to cut us off from the crests that meant final victory. Their whole line, loud with battle, had need of them. But they had reserves; and these, in great numbers, they brought up hotly to meet this blow – a blow which, had the odds been anything but insuperable, must have meant death to all hope in them.

The men of our right attacking column, paying soon with their lives for every foot won on that implacable way, toiled up the Chailak and Sazli Beit Deres, formed a rough line up past the Table Top, and threw themselves into the confused struggle which at least led on – now towards Rhododendron Spur and the stubborn heights of Chunuk. Our remaining column, the Australians and their comrades on the left, laboured up the nerve-straining crags and across the chasms of the Aghyl Dere. They had set their great hearts on attaining the high and ultimate goal – up past Hill Q, that ruthless hill, lay Koja Chemen Tepe. This peak, dominating the whole peninsula and the waters that wash its gaunt sides, was the key to unlock the inexorable riddle: to achieve that was to make victory ours.

In this last column there was a man named McCullough; he was a Queenslander. Because he was much given to dreaming queer dreams, men called him the Prophet. But, though his fancy had run to many a new and strange thing, what one of them all had reached to the delirious dream, the nightmare of a madman, that this advance seemed?

With their blood up, with a will that looked more than human urging them on, these men struggled forward against obstacles that might surely have taken gods by the throat, and flung them aside. Stumbling, cursing, killing, now drowned in the billowing smoke and dust spread by exploding shells, or, later, advancing through a dark alive with singing lead, on, and always on, they pressed. Great masses of earth were torn away and entombed them. Men were spattered with the bowels and brains of comrades. The hungry wire raked at their flesh, and was left, if they got past it at all, dripping with their blood. Bombs and bayonets dispersed them on the shaking earth. Resolute heels ground the face of foe there and friend.

Through that bitter doing, redeemed from chaos by resolution, they still pressed on. Up the front of loose rocks, crumbling under their tense fingers, they scaled. Into unguessed chasms they were precipitated, and broken on the stones below. Unyielding thorn tore their clothes and skin off. Then came more killing, more taking and giving of pitiless steel, more blowing away of faces by rifles thrust into them from the pregnant dark.

In that high courage, that desperate devotion, did not men often embrace death with their hands empty of weapons, that they might make a way for comrades? Holding on, beating back the foe (when not tossed in pieces, like dissevered meat, to feed the rats of that hellish jungle), marking the lairs of the clustered snipers by their fire, throwing themselves prone, advancing again – through these and a thousand like experiences, onward, and always on, pressed that wonderful wave of hard-breathing and broken flesh. And ever, as they toiled forward thus, the hill in front became more steep, the pressure against them more terrible, and the power to meet it less able. But what obstacle could stay such men, who, if any throughout history have done so, in truth strove like gods?

When night had turned to the other agony of dawn, and day to night again, those for whom death was not yet still moved on – with the inviolable resolution of beings that could die but not falter. Yes, as they toiled on through those interminable agonies, it looked – in God's name it looked – like the nightmare of some madman. Lucky indeed might many think those who had been left, shapes now without meaning, in the scrub below. Had they not done with all this?

And in the shambles down there – one of those countless uncommemorated souls who, whether breath remain to them or not, are consecrated in such endeavour – lay Pat McCullough. From one labour to the eternal next he had struggled on with that marvellous company, till at length, exhausted because of the life spilt from his wounds, and constrained by a necessity to which his will meant nothing, his sight had become confused, his senses had lost their reckoning, and he had dropped into a limp heap on that inexorable track – that track watered with the blood and sweat that shall give it significance, and in the supreme degree sanctify it, to Australians for ever.

When McCullough woke, he found himself in a small depression, rough with boulders, and shut in with scrub. He stretched himself, rubbed his eyes vacantly, yawned, and sat up. The air was clear, and almost without sound; it had in it some touch of freshness that told it was yet early day. A pair of doves – to whom, plainly, nothing looked amiss – sat preening each other on a fir; and up aloft an intent hawk, as if he had sighted business in this neighbourhood, cut lessening circles against the background of pale blue.

'Strange!' thought McCullough. 'How did I get here?' He scrambled to his feet, took a few steps into the undergrowth, and discovered – for there was not much of it – that the ground about him was the summit of an insignificant hill.

In a flash all that he had been through came back to him – all that had happened before his last sleep and this awakening – that mad scramble to death or victory up the blood-sodden dere. But this? Pressing his hand to his forehead, as if to help memory, he gazed about in an effort to understand. The place looked, he thought, like the discarded pit some battery had used.

'Strange!' he repeated.

What struck him now was the weird stillness of the place. What did this mean? The roar of our guns (a sound that leapt at the ears like something palpable and alive, and with a terrific impetus), the heavy rumbling of far-off howitzers, the bursting of shells, the vicious snap of rifles, rising ever and anon dying down, the shouting of men on the Beach, the human noise set up by men cursing, or singing at their work, or crunching along on hard roads – these, with the thousand other sounds that had once travelled those hills, might never have been, so quiet was it. And then, in another flash of perception, the reason came. Deaf! Of course, he was deaf. Had he not been partially deaf, nay, and much more than that, many times before? His hearing had gone now for good. But even as he asserted this he knew that he was not deaf. A fitful breeze, from which the sun had not yet taken the salt, was blowing in from the sea, and flapping the leaves of a shrub at hand. That, beyond question, he heard. Yes, and he heard, up in the silent air, a lark singing; and were not pigeons, in the scrub below, making an audible job of their wooing?

'Surely,' he thought, 'this joke I am is still Pat McCullough, and this is Anzac; but, if that's so, my wits are out somewhere.' There was plainly need for some tough thinking; and, selecting a spot for this, he sat down to do it.

He felt his limbs, gingerly, with trepidation, as one who puts a question to Fate – half fearing the answer. As solid, they were, as a rail – the scarred but substantial flesh and bone of a soldier – and none, thank God, missing! And then it struck him that he had no clothes on: he was as bare, a glance assured him, as the back of that hand of his. In the same breath he felt a queer tickling at his belly; and, marvellously enough, when he clawed at those flies, he found that a great bunch of hair had set up the titillation.

'What's this?' he began. 'Can it be?' And then, breaking off, he stroked his chin, and burst suddenly into a laugh that was not joyous.

'A beard!' he exclaimed. 'Verily, the Prophet hath his beard!'

So grotesque did this transformation seem to McCullough that he again questioned the identity of that shape he was. Good God, had those coal-scuttles hit on the truth then? Had he died down there in the dere? And was this mystery to be explained by the transmigration of souls? Had he put off his former flesh and gone, by some dark process, into a new circumscription of earthly tissue? Good God! Well no matter – it would perhaps serve just as well.

For all that, the idea was perplexing – till it flashed on him that this point, at least, he could clear up.

He felt under his left breast. Saints and grace – the old scar was still there! A piece of shrapnel, he remembered, had knocked two teeth away on the right half of his jaw. He put his hand up, and found the gap. It was like checking off a brother, long lost, and at first doubted. He brought to mind other marks by which he could make sure of that flesh he had worn – marks that had cost the foe something – and these he went through carefully till the truth shouted at him. He *was* McCullough; and this was the skin, and the same bone, and the hair – at least some of it was – that had gone shearing with him from the Carpentaria to down below Bourke. Having settled this point, he breathed easier.

The next question to clear up was the identity of the place. Though the soil and the scrub it carried were certainly just as at Anzac, this silence – how uncanny it seemed! – was this not entirely out of keeping with the stir, and above all with the ear-shaking noises, that never gave over at that circus? It was.

McCullough got up, and made for a little spur which, as he expected, commanded the country about there. Skirting a couple of dwarfed firs, he pushed carefully through the gorse, a nasty neighbour for bare flesh, and came out on to a crumbling pinnacle, running almost sheer to the ravine below. The land beyond this ravine lay fairly flat; it was patched with crops, and carried groves of grey-leafed olive. This part he did not know well;

but that hill in the distance, that stubborn-looking lump on the skyline, might easily, he thought, be Achi Baba, a hill of many memories.

But, to McCullough, the weightiest thing in life now was to make sure. Picking his way to another spur, he again sought his answer – remembering that the point of view was new to him. He looked hard and long. Before him, now, lay a confused mass of broken hills, here thrust up into abrupt spears, there dropping away into chasms – a rough waste of savage country, leading, in a tangle of ravine, precipice, and compact jungle, to a crowning peak in the distance.

McCullough rubbed his eyes. Surely he knew that accurst landscape, and that peak! Hell and death, he ought to! But what, in the name of all things elect – what was that great, that imposing mass, stuck there on the top of it? The peak should be Koja Chemen; but the building, or whatever it was, that caught the rays of the ascending sun on its bright surface, and threw them out in a refulgence across the land – what was that? And what were these other marks – that looked so odd here – these structures (if they were indeed that) which had cropped up where, in his time, the sniper crawled? Was it Anzac, and yet not Anzac? Or was he mad? Or was this dreaming ripe?

Noting the position of the sun – an act that had its ground in habit rather than necessity – he pushed over to that side of the hill which, if the place was still what it had been, must look out to the Aegean. What he should see there would fix it. As McCullough hurried across, the life he had himself moved with at the Cove stood plain before his mind's eye. There would lie the swarm of multi-shaped barges, laden with munition for both guns and men; there the hooting pinnaces would be busy – what a fuss they made! And the longboats, lined with the wounded, would be putting out in tow to the hospital ships – coming, and waiting their turn, and going, these were there always. The blunt trawlers, the fidgety destroyers, the battle-ships, ready to comb the hills inland with their long-reaching claws – these would be there, old friends all! And the bones of wrecked shipping, things that had died bravely, these too! A few steps now, and one glance would decide it. He would soon know how his case stood; for was not that spot as well known to him as the soil he had worked on at home? Hurried forward by these thoughts, he shoved his way through the brush, and stood breathless on the hill's edge.

If McCullough had found marvels before, was there now nothing to gape at? What, by the lost in Sheol, did this mean? There, indeed there, was the Beach he had fought up in that ghostly dawn of the Twenty-fifth. He knew every foot of that. There, before him, was the first ridge – heaped, when he had seen it last, with almost its own weight of stores, and honeycombed with dug-outs. Of those stores, it is true, there was no trace whatever now, and the bareness had been cultivated in an amazing fashion; but he knew it. There, in the near distance, lay the scarps under which they had fought that bitter fight in August – last August? – or what August? The question served merely to reveal another blind spot in his brain; at once, he put it from him. And there lay those hills on the far skyline, in a country unguessed; the shape of that land, also, he knew. His eye, still in quest of a solution to this riddle of the like and the unlike, travelled back to the Beach. Running round, in the form of a boomerang, to Suvla, it was the Beach, positively, beyond doubt, where men had laughed, and cursed, and swum, and died. Ah, what soldier who had taken his baptism there could mistake it? The waves of the blue sea broke gently upon it as they did often of old. Yes, Anzac, Anzac in truth, it was; but yet not the Anzac it had been – not *his* Anzac.

He laughed like a fool; but there were tears, too, in that laughter. Not his Anzac! His Anzac? Why, mark that pretentious pier, and that hotel there – with its smug modernity – perched where the squares of the Hospital, white and friendly, had once patched the hill! A hotel it must be. But for what? For whom? The trees, to be sure, looked well. Many of them, in a blaze of gold, threw the perfect colour across the drab landscape before him. What trees were these? As if to answer his question, the breeze carried up a perfume which he sensed with a sudden wonderment of delight. Wattle! Well, that was something. The men there would at least sleep among their own trees, the trees they had slept among so often in their own land. Yes, that was much. But all these things that had so busied him, that belonged to a world as remote now as any strutting it through space, how did *they* get there?

To McCullough there was something about the whole business that was more than uncanny – it began to open pits of apprehension from which he shrank in dismay. He lived in two worlds, and as a lost soul in each. God! if he could but shake off the obsession of either, struggle back somehow, as a complete and satisfied embodiment, to one of them – no matter which! He saw what he saw; but not yet had he faith to believe in it. All the life of that place as he had known it, from the Beach to the top trenches, had disappeared. But why should it? That strip of friendly shore, where men had loafed, or lifted a speedy foot this way or that, or hauled guns and other lumber to land, or shouldered ammunition, and beef, and biscuit – that strip where mules, that kicked like machines, and wounded men on stretchers, and sergeants sawing the air, and sappers with picks, and men brooding on telegrams, or waiting their turn for water, had all, with a thousand such sights, made up an ever-changing scene in a drama which, to him, had become existence – these things that shore knew no longer. The strong squalor of a soldiers' camp had given place to this – the antithesis of all that had been there formerly. But why? How? McCullough, desperately as he tried to, could make nothing of it.

So absorbed was he in all this, so preoccupied in trying to save his wits from a collapse finally, that he did not hear the footsteps of a stranger who just now arrived, after a stiff climb, at the summit of that hill of his. The newcomer, mopping his forehead, and peering in all directions as he did so, saw someone half-hidden in the scrub.

'Seen a platoon of turkeys about here, mate?' he called out.

McCullough turned sharply. He thought his fancy must have tripped in another delusion. And yet there, looking human enough, was the shape which had doubtless addressed this question to him. He came out of the scrub, and confronted it – actually, a stout fellow, very red in the face, attired in shorts, and carrying a shot-gun.

Both men stared their surprise – McCullough, perhaps, more patently so. But the honours were even; for the hairy McCullough, clothed as his Adamic father had been, gave the newcomer a strong and a queer sensation about the spine. This gentleman held his gun ready for emergencies.

'Seen some turkeys about here, mate?' he repeated, edging off a little.

McCullough found no words to reply with. His ideas got confused again. If this fellow was looking for the enemy with a weapon no better than that in his fist, he was mad.

'They're the best table birds the boss had,' the sportsman went on, evidently confused too, and perhaps feeling himself under the necessity of saying something. 'And he'll want them soon.'

Then, as if this outlandish figure would pass well enough for a chicken-thief, he put the question a third time. 'Sure you haven't seen them?'

'I'm a stranger here,' answered McCullough, swallowing a lump which, for some reason, came into his throat.

'How'd you get here? And where's your gear?'

McCullough scratched his head.

'The truth is,' he replied, 'that's just what I've been trying to find out.'

The man with the gun, though plainly, and perhaps not unreasonably, a bit suspicious of his companion, could not question the doubt – for it was sincere enough – expressed in the face before him. Men, he knew, could lose their memories; and in such cases anything was possible – even such a mess-up as this.

'You'd better hop down to the pub,' he said at last, chancing it, 'and see what the boss'll do for you.'

'Then that building *is* one?'

'It is – the best on the Peninsula.'

The best on the Peninsula, thought McCullough. Then there must be others! He was again seized with a passionate desire to have such a solution of this mystery as would clear it up definitely; and here, as if sent for the sole purpose of yielding it, was this oracle in shorts – who was not, as he himself believed, a mere seeker of food, but an instrument of Providence.

'D'you know this place well?' McCullough questioned. The cloud of a few minutes back had already lifted magically from his spirit; and he felt a little of his old confidence again.

'Know it?' answered the sportsman, with the pride that comes of a possession undisturbed. 'I know every turn and crack, every peak and precipice, of this patch – every foot of every trench, the ground of every engagement, of every victory – every boneyard I know too. If you want the history of this battlefield, of this *glorious* battlefield,' he went on, with a flourish, 'I'm your man. That's my job. I'm a guide here.'

﹏

William Baylebridge, Australian writer and poet, is the pseudonym of Charles Blocksidge, born in Brisbane in 1883, who died in 1942. This piece, taken from *An Anzac Muster*, was published privately in London in 1921 in an edition of 100 copies. At the outbreak of the war in August 1914, Baylebridge was in England. He was not able to enlist in the Australian armed forces, but there is good evidence to suggest that he was in Egypt during the Gallipoli campaign of 1915. Baylebridge himself claimed to be doing 'special literary work' there for the British secret service. Like *The Decameron* and *The Canterbury Tales*, *An Anzac Muster* uses the device of a band of storytellers to tell their twenty-seven tales over three consecutive Saturday nights. The fabular structure of *An Anzac Muster*, written only three years after the end of the war, gives it a powerful, literary distance. 'The Apocalypse of Pat McCullough' is a surreal prediction of the sanitizing power of war tourism.

ROBIN HYDE

DAWN'S ANGEL

from *Passport to Hell*

WHEN THE TROOPS FROM THE *REDWING* were taken off on barges to Y Beach there was no more sound to disturb the morning than an occasional whiplash crack, a rifle spitting far away, or a dull thud which sounded as though a gigantic muffled hammer had been brought down on the earth. They were told in whispers that this was the concussion of a shell; but the front line, six miles distant, was still a legend to them. Everybody talked in whispers; and it was rather amusing to see the giants of Tent Eight – and stouter men than they – walking like cats on hot bricks, afraid of a shuffle of pebbles among the sands. Three miles up from Y Beach they struck Anzac Cove and a standing-up breakfast – boiling water with a pinch of tea-dust thrown in, biscuits, and bully beef.

Against them in the pale rise of the morning was something which for the New Zealanders had especial significance. The Maori Pioneer Corps, passing this way, had stopped to carve out of the yellow clay face of the Gallipoli cliffs a gigantic Maori Pa. The men now passing quietly by saw carved stockade pillars with their little lizards, ornate whorls, and leaves of carving, top-heavy idols with their huge heads lolling on their shoulders, their eyes squinting, their tongues out. The work was still fresh, and recalled to the New Zealanders their few glimpses of that old world of different fighters – the red-ochred stockades, the whare-punis, the little store-houses standing on their high stilts and daubed with crimson to keep away the night-demons; a world which now and again, behind the bush-veils and the mist-veils of the New Zealand hills, had silenced their childhood with a memory of something that fought to the death. Those native hills pitted with the brown circles of the old Maori trenches, their wounds not yet quite hidden in the green softening of grass, were not unlike the hills of Gallipoli that now slid out of the sheath of the morning mist. But where New Zealand hills hide under the grey-stemmed manuka bushes, with their pungent flower-cups brown and white or delicate peach-colour, the Gallipoli hills were covered with a little shrub of somewhat darker green, its astringent leaves bitter with a flavour of quinine.

A splendid morning sunlight began to break over the cliffs. Paddy Bridgeman and Jack Frew, Fleshy McLeod and Starkie, proceeded together. After breakfast a bugler blew the fall-in, the thin notes thrusting like an arrogant silver spear into the silence of Gallipoli. The troops were lined up above the water-tanks on the beach. Before the men were in their places, the hills above them began to flash and rattle. The fall-in woke up every sniper in the world. Four hundred men stood in line to answer the roll-call. As they stood, a man in the front rank pitched forward.

'Hullo, there's a chap fainted,' whispered Jack Frew.

Somebody turned the man over on his back. Right between his eyes there was a little blue mark, like a dot made with a slate-pencil. Death had given him no time to change the expression on his face – a boy's look of interest and curiosity. He was left lying where he fell.

The men fell into a column and marched four deep up Mule Gully under fire from machine-guns, rifles, and shells. Very few of them were old enough to be veterans of the Boer War. The way up Mule Gully was like the end of the world. Their warning of the shell's coming was a rush of air, a crash, a blinding blue flash amidst the chocolate fountain of the uptorn earth. Shrapnel burst in a dazzling hail of steel – a crash where it struck the ground, then rip – roar – and the fragments tore the sides out of skulls, cut bodies in two, dismembered men as they marched. Captain Dombey was in front of the column as the troops came in plain sight of 971, the entrenched hill of the Turks. In the harbour, British men-of-war, monitors, and destroyers began the barrage, dealing out to the Turks the death which was past the strength of the scanty British artillery. When a battleship fired a broadside at the Turk trenches, the men on shore could see her rock in a trough of smothering foam like a vast grey cradle. Those that lived, crashes and shrieks ringing in their ears as though the echo must last on for centuries, climbed blindly and helplessly up the Gully, and the cliffs pelted down death on them as they ran.

There was a tally of the men landed from the *Redwing* when they reached the top of the hill. Of about four hundred who left the troopship, less than a hundred men had come through unscathed. Some were sent straight to England, others went to the base hospitals at Lemnos and Malta, others rotted on Gallipoli. The survivors climbed into their trenches, and spent the next day chasing Turks out from the holes where an unsuccessful attack the evening before had stranded dozens of them in hostile territory.

The troops had been split up into divisions, and Starkie was properly numbered with Southland Eighth; but Paddy, McLeod, and Jack Frew were all Dunedin men, and Starkie beguiled Captain Dombey – who was half-conscious now after the terrible concussion of the shells – into letting him join up with Otago Fourth.

Silver was the first of Tent Eight's giants to go, shot clean through the head by a Turkish sniper. The sniper is the aristocrat of No Man's Land, the cold killer; and against him Starkie began to develop a murder hate, not decreased by the fact that the Turk snipers were more numerous and better than the British ones. The shell hail, even the death song of the Maxims, gives you warning to keep your head down. But the sniper isn't human. Soldiers are only men. There are times in the trenches when they forget the whole bloody, cruel gambit, stretch their legs and arms, dare to show their fool heads over a mound of earth. That's the sniper's opportunity. When the troops start to relax, from his bush-screened hole in No Man's Land he picks the play-boys off. He won't allow them their decent modicum of rest; and in consequence, where the shell gets a curse and is forgotten except by the men it cuts to pieces, the sniper starts death-feuds. Hunting snipers was a game on Gallipoli, and it wasn't played according to any known rules of sportsmanship.

The Otago trenches turned out to be holes about four feet six inches in depth, with high mud embankments screening them from the hills.

'How in blazes do you see the Turk?' grumbled Starkie.

An old hand passed him a periscope. For one moment Starkie saw the Turk all right. Then the periscope was shot out of his hands, the palms burned where the brass tube had been ripped out of them, and a howl of laughter went up along the trench at sight of the greenhorn's stupefied face. Two minutes later Charlie Saunders wanted to have a look at the Turks. He jumped up, visible above the embankment for just one moment. Then he fell back like a sack into Starkie's arms. There was no blood, just two little blue marks the size of slate-pencils. The body writhed for a moment, as if anxious to express something. Whatever it was, Charlie never got it out. His body was a corpse before his mind had stopped wondering.

In the trenches men lived like rabbits, the mud walls pitted with the little holes where they slept -- or tried to sleep. These provided earthen benches, not long enough for a grown man to lie down, but of a size sufficient for him to cram his body into shelter. At night the trenches, from above, would have presented a strange sight, like a grotto illumined by thousands of pale glow-worms. The men improvised candles, half-filling kerosene-tin lids with fat and dirt, and in the middle fashioning wicks of twisted rag soaked in grease. These fluttering little candles, evil-smelling and burning with a spluttering bluish flame, were the only trench lights after dark on Gallipoli.

In the morning the troops were issued a dixie of water to each man – about two-and-a-half cups – from which they could shave, wash, and make themselves a cup of tea. A grimy towel served months long for wiping faces and bodies. It was hot on Gallipoli.

'Aw, hell!' said Fleshy superbly. 'It's only dirty chaps that bloody well need to wash.' And he tilted the dixie to his lips.

'And it's only scrubs go shaving themselves,' added Starkie.

Thereafter, Disraeli's maxim that water is good only for washing with was disregarded in the trenches. The men drank their water issue and let hygiene go where it belongs in wartime. Not that you could call the water drinkable. There were two wells between the trenches and the beach, but both were reputed to be poisoned by the Turks – which left the New Zealand trenches with the chlorinated beach water-tanks to draw upon. The water was carted up in benzine tins, and the men drank shandies of chlorinated lime, benzine, and water. For the rest, they were issued biscuit, bully beef, cheese – they didn't know where the cheese came from, but some of them had a pretty fair idea; jam – instantly covered with swarms of black flies; blocks of black seaweed-like pipe-tobacco known as "Arf a Mo", and an amplitude of cigarettes – Red Hussars, Beeswing, Havelock, Gold Flake, Auros, and Woodbines. The boys used to get a real smoke by tying five Woodbines together and puffing them in a bundle.

There were – besides the voices of the guns – two inevitable sounds in the trenches: the yells of the muleteers, driving their stubborn little grey mokes up Mule Gully under cover of darkness; and the long-drawn-out floating cry from the Turkish trenches: 'Allah, Allah, il Allah'. The Turks – all furnished with fine leather equipment from German stores, muffled up in balaclavas, scarves, and mittens pulled over grey uniforms – came over the top with that great cry of 'Allah!' When, after dark, their wounded and dying lay out on the Gallipoli hills, all night long the same cry would rattle up to the British trenches – groans of 'Allah', from lips that would never taste the cup of life again.

On the second morning the survivors from the *Redwing* were taken out into No Man's Land as a burying-party. For this they were stripped of their uniforms, donned khaki shorts and singlets, and went armed with oiled sheets. The purpose of this they saw when they got to No Man's Land, each party breaking off under charge of an officer.

A few men found on No Man's Land were still alive. They were not always lucky. Some were stone blind and crazy with gun-flashes, others crawled near, leg or flesh wounds rotting after a night's exposure.

But the dead who waited in No Man's Land didn't look like dead, as the men who came to them now had thought of death. From a distance of a few yards, the bodies, lying in queer huddled attitudes, appeared to have something monstrously amiss with them. Then the burying-party, white-faced, realized that twenty-four hours of the Gallipoli sun had caused each body to swell enormously – until the great threatening carcases were three times the size of a man, and their skins had the bursting blackness of grapes. It was impossible to recognize features or expression in that hideously puffed and contorted blackness.

And how they had died! – some ripped to pieces by shrapnel – some of them in fragments; others having crept from the place of death to the hollow of some stunted green shrub, their arms crooked round the searching brown roots as though in a passionate, useless plea for the earth's protection against their enemies. Here and there one had found shade enough to escape some part of the disfigurement caused by the pitiless sun; and on these faces such a story was written as nobody on earth will ever dare to tell until the graves give up their dead. The Tommies from the next hill had been over in attack, and some of them lay here like the bodies of dead children, their pinched, sharp-featured little London faces white and beautifully calm. Sometimes the dead man bore only the blue seal of the bullet wound on head or breast, and the boys called that 'the mercy death'. Sometimes a man's tunic was torn open where he had clutched at it with striving hands, and revealed along his swollen body a line like a row of nails driven into his flesh – the mark of the machine-gun's killing.

The burying-party, in squads of four and five, unrolled their oiled sheets and spread them on the ground. Then they lifted or rolled on the sheets the bodies of the slain. Dissolution had overtaken many of them; and as they were lifted their heads fell back in the sunlight, showing blackened mouth and throat, gaping nostrils, as caves for the little crawling life-in-death of ants and maggots. When they were rolled on the sheets the foul air which had gathered in their grotesquely gigantic bodies came out of their throats in one appalling groan, as though in that protest the dead soldier had told all the agony and outrage of his taking-off. The stench of that deathly gas struck into the senses of the burying-party.

Some of the living and moving men – mere boys of sixteen and seventeen – sweated like horses, and tears ran down their white cheeks.

Starkie heard Paddy Bridgeman groan, 'Ah, blessed Mother of God – fine big men the one day, the next fly-blown and rotten!'

Holes were pitted in the Gallipoli hills, dug with the men's pickaxes.

Then the dead were rolled in from the oil-sheets, ten or twelve men to a grave, the faces of some lying against the boots of others in a confusion of death. The living men who dug those common graves stood retching with sickness as they shovelled earth, brown and merciful, over the faces of the dead.

The burying-party were marched back to their trenches and crawled into the dug-outs. An old hand tapped Starkie on the shoulder.

'Cup of tea, mate?'

Starkie looked at the man for a moment. Then he poured the tea into the mud of the trench. He was sick throughout the night.

In less than a month the men thought nothing of the burying-parties, and so little of the corpses on No Man's Land that money-belts were unbuckled as the rotting corpses were rolled into the pits of death.

It was only afterwards – after the War; after that outrageous libel on the normality of the human mind had been, for the time, dragged away – that every twisted limb, every blackened face waiting in those gullies, came back into memory once again, and for ever repeated the protest the tortured body uttered after its death.

In the trenches everyone was dirty and lousy – 'five hundred' and louse-catching were the major sports of Gallipoli – but the lice were objected to considerably less than the swarming black flies. Sometimes the fighting between Turk and British trenches was like a dramatic, enthralling, and hideous scene shown in a great green-and-chocolate-coloured amphitheatre. From the apex of their trenches the Otago men saw a party of Turks blown sixty or seventy feet into the air above their fortified hill, grotesque little marionette figures violently jerked skyward by the unseen hands of death.

The Turkish trenches curved in circular formation around their hill. Their aerial torpedoes came flaring over the British lines, looking like big tin canisters with six-foot tails. Little flanges kept these missiles straight, and when they struck earth there was an enormous concussion. The English lyddite shells made more row than any of the other fireworks, and Otago was supplied with Japanese lyddite shells – deadly little blackberries to be fired from the trench-mortars. But the British artillery was a very poor second compared with Johnny Turk's, and barrage was left for the most part to the ghostly grey shapes of the men-of-war riding at anchor along the coast.

They witnessed from their trenches the attack on Suvla Bay, about five miles off, across flat land broken by the cone of Chocolate Hill – a patch of brown in a green land. The Tommies attacked three times, barrage whining and splintering from both sides. The advance and retreat of the little figures was a scene in a melodrama. At the second attack, the Turks, reinforced, chased the Tommies back down the Gully. The third assault drove the Turks out of their position. The attack in all took about twenty-five minutes, and an advance of thirty yards was made by the English troops. When it was over, hundreds of corpses and wounded men – limbless, gashed and slashed and blown to pieces – lay where they had fallen. The blue flashes of the shellfire continued for a while after the main attack. The concussion rang all night long in the soldiers' ears. In the morning they helped to bury the Tommies. It didn't greatly distress them any more.

Men in the British lines were going down with dysentery; but for the most part it was only known as dysentery in the case of the officers, just as nervous breakdowns were unheard of in the ranks. The ranker got two little white number nines from King, the doctor's assistant. Number nines were used to cure the troops of headache, heartache, stomach-ache, malingering, laziness, cuts, scabies, shell-shock, and dysentery, and on the whole acted fairly well. But the bad cases hadn't a chance, the disease worked in them too quickly. If you were dying of dysentery, you were pulled out after medical parade and got your chance in the Lemnos Hospital. If you weren't dying, it was a long time before the next parade came round. The men crept away into their dug-outs and bled to death. Their mates, coming round with a drop of soup for them, found them stiffened up in the rabbit-holes, just as they had stretched themselves on the cramped earthen benches.

Night-patrol was a queer and furtive prowling in the pit of No Man's Land. Starkie made one of a patrol a little after the Tommies drove back the Turks. With ten others he was taken to a hole in the trench and down into No Man's Land. There was very little barbed wire on Gallipoli. Down in the throttle of the valley lay hundreds of Turks, many of them wounded men who had died after twenty-four hours' exposure – the burning heat of the day, and at night the chill hand of the frosts. Every face on which a light flashed bore the blackness of death upon it. There were bodies piled up in heaps, like logs brought down the waters of a mill-race to lock in some nightmare dam. The ghastliness of this place and its unburied dead became a legend in the lines. The men christened it 'Death Gully'.

By and by there were rumours of an Australian officer lying out in No Man's Land with a whole battalion's money on his back, and so dead that he certainly couldn't use it. Next morning Starkie took up Jack Frew's bet, and crept out from the lines to have a go for it. He had almost reached the little figure pointed out as the late Australian Croesus when the Turk sniper spotted him. Then began a game of cat and mouse, with Starkie for mouse. His lucky star had landed him in a fold of ground behind a rock hummock. Move backwards or forwards, and the sniper splashed dirt into his face. The sniper played marbles round his head, the little jets of soil and pebbles hitting him every now and again just to remind him that he hadn't been forgotten. The men in his own trench watched him through periscopes and yelled encouragement to him; but nobody formed a rescue-party, and Starkie didn't blame them. He lay where he was, stiff as a ramrod, from ten in the morning until after dusk. Then he crawled back to the trenches on his stomach, the vision of the gilded corpse very dim indeed. 'Money-belt? I think the Turks got it, eh?'

Rifles were wrapped in blankets in the front line and inspected every little while by querulous officers who didn't like anything about the troops' kit and appearance. Captain Smythe, after one glance at Starkie's rifle, told him he was a disgrace to Otago, no soldier, and a bloody pest. On this occasion he spoke truer than he knew. Starkie, injured, prepared to clean his rifle. Ten rounds were allowed for, and by mischance eleven had been thrust into the breech.

'Never mind, Starkie; maybe he's missed his bottle from the store-ship,' murmured Paddy encouragingly.

Starkie worked his rifle-lever, chucked out ten cartridges, shut the breech and, thinking it was empty, pulled the trigger to pull the block out. The rifle banged.

Captain Smythe, his face beautifully patterned with gravel-rash, turned again and leapt at the horrified Starkie. 'Did you try to do that? Did you try to do that?'

Starkie swore by all a soldier's gods that he hadn't done it on purpose, and Captain Smythe called him a liar. In this particular instance he was wrong. But to the end of the War, Captain Smythe maintained that Starkie had tried to shoot him.

Men from the Otago lines moved out on burial-party under Captain Hewitt, a tall and rangy disciplinarian who stood no nonsense. Some worked at gathering the dead, some at tipping the contents of the oiled sheets into the open graves. One corpse crumbled in Starkie's arms. Round the decaying body was a money-belt, and in it twenty sovereigns and a half-sovereign, in English gold. Starkie shouted his discovery to Fleshy McLeod. Something cold and round touched him behind the ear. He turned, to find Captain Hewitt's revolver nuzzling against his head.

'Don't you know that I could shoot you for looting?' asked the grim voice of the Captain.

Starkie after that followed instructions. He put the gold back into the money-belt. He got down into the grave, lifted out three of the blackened corpses, laid the soldier with the money-belt face down in the reeking, seeping soil. Then on the four bodies he piled nine more. As the last one rolled over from the oiled sheet into his arms it broke in two. For one hideous second he saw the grave, the dead men, his own body trapped in that cavern of putrefaction, just as they really were. Then Captain Hewitt saved him, shouting to him to tumble out and thank his stars he wasn't in the Imperial Army, where corpse-robbers were shot on sight.

It was tremendously important, on the way back to the trenches, that he should think of the gold in the money-belt and not of the corpses piled up above it. If you start thinking of the expression on a dead man's swollen face, you being stowed away in a rabbit-hole where the next whirling, twisting fire-cracker coming down from heaven may be your own packet, what's going to happen to you? Back in the Otago lines he told the story of the money-belt with a swagger.

'Where's he buried?' demanded Paddy.

'Hi, anyone know where a trumpet is?' Fleshy McLeod chipped in.

'What for a trumpet?'

'I want to play the Angel Gabriel and make him hop up again.'

'That one'll do no more getting up in the morning. Christ, if you'd seen the face –'

'Chuck it, Starkie! One face is the same as all the rest. What's the use of a pile of gold to him? And half of us broke…'

The last was truth. In their rabbit-warren they had nothing to do with their spare time but gamble. The slick hands gathered in every penny that came to the green-horns, and then the soldiers who had made a hit with Gippo girls were left with their last stakes – gold bangles filched from the ladies' arms as 'keepsakes'.

In the evening Fleshy McLeod tapped Starkie on the shoulder.

'Come on. I've got a new game.'

'What's its name?'

'We call it raising the dead,' said Fleshy grimly, and slid out of his corner in the trench. After a moment, Starkie passed a hand across a face dripping with sweat, and crept after him. They raised the dead.

Wherever they put the gold from the dead man's money-belt, on cards, or dice, it couldn't go wrong. Even when chance gave them an hour or two to fleece the Australians, who as gamblers made the New Zealanders look like babes in swaddling-clothes, the twenty sovereigns and the half-sovereign came home bringing little friends with them. One day a Digger asked them where they got the gold, and they were injudicious enough to blab. After that their sovereigns were ruled out of the trench gambling-schools, the boys swearing that it was haunted gold. The Fourth Brigade of Australians barred their gold as well, and from lording it over the rest with their clink of sovereigns they were driven back to the same old sixpenny throws. Between them they had chalked up a profit score of sixty pounds.

The men still used periscopes in the trenches, and it was squinting through the tube one day that Starkie spotted the Turk sniper camouflaged by the scrub in No Man's Land. None of the New Zealanders loved a sniper; and Starkie, remembering Goliath and a few more – also the way the Turk had dusted the seat of his own pants the day he went hunting the Australian gold-mine – liked him a lot less than most. The Turk sniper had made a mistake this time. He was within easy range of the Otago trench.

Starkie was cat now, and he enjoyed it. His first bullet just clipped the grass in front of the sniper's head; but the second one, before the Turk had time to break for cover, got him in the leg. The man tried to crawl away. Starkie sent little jets of soil up around him. He remembered a story which his father had told to frighten him a long time ago. A story of the Delaware way of killing a man with a small fire. This fire doesn't have to be more than six inches high, just twigs and grasses, but you light it over very close to one side of a man's head. Then you build the pile on the other side. Then lower down...

A man in the trenches cried, 'Stop it, you dirty Hun!' Other voices began to protest. Then a voice Starkie knew said from behind him, 'Give me that gun.' He slewed round to see Captain Dombey, and Captain Dombey wouldn't take no for an answer. He got the gun and stepped up on the parapet to finish off the wounded Turk sniper. Everyone knew he was one of the best rifle-shots in New Zealand.

Before his rifle had time to crack, he put a hand to his throat, said, 'God, I'm hit; get me to the dressing-station!' and tumbled back into the trench like a sack of beans.

Starkie and Captain Dombey alike had forgotten that Turk snipers often went in couples, like snakes. In the scrub of No Man's Land the sniper's mate had been waiting his chance to get a shot in. The bullet had ripped through Captain Dombey's armpit and shoulder muscles, tearing a good big hole, but not low enough to lay him out for good unless gangrene set in.

He was fifteen stone if an ounce; and though Starkie and three others bore the stretcher that took him to the dressing-station on the beach, it was a rough passage, with the bearers stumbling as they scrambled down the scrubby hills, and Captain Dombey groaning about unlimited doses of C.B. The third time the stretcher was dropped he stopped promising rewards and fairies and kept up a thin blue line of curses. Starkie told him, with reminiscent sorrow, that it wasn't as bad as C.B., or latrines, or a job in the prison barracks; but then conversation was held up where the track was blocked with a crowd of Gurkhas and Punjabis, bent on slaughtering a goat. The Gurkhas lived on the other side of Mule Gully, sweet-mannered little brown fiends who kept their faces free from whiskers by pulling every hair out of their chins with tiny tweezers.

The Punjabis were fine, big-bearded fellows, and both the gamest fighters on Gallipoli. You couldn't shove past them while they were killing meat, for if a soldier's shadow fell on their food it became unclean, and on Gallipoli nobody wasted provisions. The stretcher was set down, and the corpse and stretcher-bearers both consoled themselves with a drink and a mess of blazing curry dished up with chupattis. Meanwhile, the goat, a gingery old Nanny bleating forlornly about her home and father, was led in to the circle of black watching faces and sacrificed like Iphigenia, the silver sweep of a Gurkha knife cutting her head off in a single blow.

'Lovely ain't it?' Starkie said to Captain Dombey, his eyes fixed hungrily on the wicked curved blade of the *kukri*.

'You get to hell, and hurry me down to the dressing-station!' querulously responded the gallant captain, and the jolting progress was resumed.

Down at the dressing-station Captain Dombey first cursed them roundly in several different languages, not all known to the secretariat of the League of Nations, then lifted himself up on his good elbow and grinned at them. 'So long, boys; I'll be back in three months – and then look out!' He disappeared from their view, but kept his word. In three months to the day, the hole in his shoulder more or less satisfactorily plastered up, he was back on Gallipoli and seemed to think more of C.B. than ever.

At the water-tanks they lapped up as much as their stomachs could hold of lime, benzine, and greyish water. There was never an adequate water-ration on Gallipoli. They thieved a tin of it and started on their way home.

Captain Smythe met them with a scowl of ungenerous suspicion, Captain Dombey being his especial pal. 'Been long enough, haven't you?' he growled.

'So would you be,' retorted an exasperated bearer, 'if you was carrying an elephant on a stretcher six miles!'

For carrying the elephant they got special rations – Fray Bentos – otherwise bully beef – and Blackwell's marmalade for their bread issue, which was doled out, one loaf to eight men. The marmalade-tins were used everywhere in the trenches for making steps, walls, and floors, and some of the designs in the little earth dug-outs were really clever. Marmalade was more of a success than cheese. Such a thing as cheese that refrained from crawling was unknown in the trenches, like a pacifist louse, but they got used to it… used to anything.

〜

One of New Zealand's finest poets and writers, **Robin Hyde** was born Iris Guiver Wilkinson in Cape Town and taken to Wellington before her first birthday. Working in the 1930s as an investigative journalist, Hyde exposed the brutal conditions of New Zealand's prisons. It was during a visit to Mount Eden prison that she was introduced to Private J. D. Stark, who asked her to write a book about his experiences of the war. Hyde hesitated but in the end decided to take the risk. In a 1935 letter to John Schroder, a journalist on the New Zealand paper then called *The Sun*, she wrote:

> The book that might have been a nightmare is finished. It is a nightmare, but I think it is a book – Harder, barer and more confident – It's the story of a soldier – he exists and I know him very well. His queer racial heritage – he is half Red Indian, half Spaniard – has taken him into desperate places; prisons, battles, affairs… I wrote the book because I had to write it when I heard the story, and because it's an illustration of Walt Whitman's line – 'There is to me something profoundly affecting in large masses of men following the lead of those who do not believe in man.'*

*Quoted in D. I. B. Smith's introduction to the 1986 reprint of *Passport to Hell*, p. ix.

On its publication in 1936, the book was recognized by critics as one of the great books of the war. However, it brought Robin Hyde some fame but very little fortune. Unable to face a life of neglect and poverty, she committed suicide in London in 1939.

W. N. P. BARBELLION

BEFORE THE WAR I WAS
AN INTERESTING INVALID

from *The Journal of a Disappointed Man*

July 31

This War is so great and terrible that hyperbole is impossible. And yet my gorge rises at those fatuous journalists continually prating about this 'Greatest War of all time,' this 'Great Drama,' this 'world catastrophe unparalleled in human history,' because it is easy to see that they are really more thrilled than shocked by the immensity of the War. They indulge in a vulgar Yankee admiration for the Big Thing. Why call this shameful Filth by high sounding phrases – as if it were a tragedy from Euripides? We ought to hush it up, not brag about it, to mention it with a blush instead of spurting it out brazen-faced.

Mr Garvin, for example, positively gloats over the War each week in the *Observer*: 'Last week was one of those pivotal occasions on which destiny seems to swing' – and so on every week, you can hear him, historical glutton smacking his lips with an offensive relish.

For my part, I never seem to be in the same mind about the War twice following. Sometimes I am wonder struck and make out a list of all the amazing events I have lived to see since August 1914, and sometimes and more often I am swollen with contempt for its colossal imbecility. And sometimes I am swept away with admiration for all the heroism of the War, or by some particularly noble self-sacrifice, and think it is really all worthwhile. Then – and more frequently – I remember that this War has let loose on the world not only barbarities, butcheries and crimes, but lies, lies, lies – hypocrisies, deceits, ignoble desires for self-aggrandizement, self-preservation such as no one before ever dreamed existed in embryo in the heart of human beings.

The War rings the changes on all the emotions. It twangs all my strings in turn and occasionally all at once, so that I scarcely know how to react or what to think. You see, here am I, a compulsory spectator, and all I can do is to reflect. A Zeppelin brought down in flames that lit up all London – now that makes me want to write like Mr Garvin. But a Foreign Correspondent's eager discussion of 'Italy's aspirations in the Trentino,' how Russia insists on a large slice of Turkey, and so forth, makes me splutter. How insufferably childish to be slicing up the earth's surface! How immeasureably 'above the battle' I am at times. What a prig you will say I am when I sneer at such contemptible little devilries as the Boches' trick of sending over a little note, 'Warsaw is fallen,' into our trenches, or as ours in reply: 'Gorizia!'

' There is no difference in principle between the case of a man who loses a limb in the service of his country and that of the man who loses his reason, both have an obvious claim to the grateful recognition of the State.' – A morning paper.

A jejune comment like this makes me grin like a gargoyle! Hark to the fellow – this leader-writer over his cup of tea. But it is a lesson to show how easily and quickly we have all adapted ourselves to the War. The War is everything: it is noble, filthy, great, petty, degrading, inspiring, ridiculous, glorious, mad, bad, hopeless yet full of hope. I don't know what to think about it.

August 13
I hate elderly women who mention their legs, it makes me shudder.

I had two amusing conversations this morning, one with a jealous old man of 70 summers who, in spite of his age, is jealous – I can find no other term – of me in spite of mine, and the other with a social climber. I always tell the first of any of my little successes and regularly hand him all my memoirs as they appear, to which he as regularly protests that he reads very little now. 'Oh! never mind,' I always answer gaily, 'you take it and read it going down in the train – it will amuse you.' He submits but is always silent next time I see him – a little, admonitory silence. Or, I mention I am giving an address at——, and he says 'Oom,' and at once begins his reminiscences, which I have heard many times before, and am sometimes tempted to correct him when, his memory failing, he leaves out an essential portion of his story. Thus do crabbed age and boastful youth tantalise one another.

To the social climber I said slyly:

' You seem to move in a very distinguished entourage during your week ends.'

He smiled a little self-consciously, hesitated a moment and then said:

'Oh! I have a few nice friends, you know.'

Now I am sorry, but though I scrutinised this lickspittle and arch belly-truck rider very closely, I am quite unable to say whether that smile and unwonted diffidence meant simple pleasure at the now certain knowledge that I was duly impressed, or whether it was genuine confusion at the thought that he had perhaps been overdoing it.

Curiously enough, all bores of whatever kind make a dead set at me. I am always a ready listener and my thrusts are always gentle. Hence the pyramids! I constantly act as phlebotomist to the vanity of the young and to the anecdotage of the senile and senescent.

August 13

…I stood by his chair and looked down at him, and surveyed carefully the top of his head, neck, and collar, and with admirable restraint and calm, considered my most reasonable contempt of him. In perfect silence, we remained thus, while I looked down at a sore spot in the centre of his calvarium which he scratches occasionally, and toyed with the fine flower of my scorn… But it is a dangerous license to take. One never knows…

Equilibrium Restored

To clear away the cobwebs and to purge my soul of evil thoughts and bitter feelings, went for a walk this evening over the uplands. Among the stubble, I sat down for a while with my back against the corn pook and listened to the Partridges calling. Then wandered around the edge of this upland field with the wind in my face and a shower of delicious, fresh rain pattering down on the leaves and dry earth. Then into a wood among tall forest Beeches and a few giant Larches where I rested again and heard a Woodpecker tapping out its message aloft.

This ramble in beautiful B——shire country restored my mental and spiritual poise. I came home serene and perfectly balanced – my equilibrium was something like the just perceptible oscillation of tall Larch-tree tops on the heights of a cliff and the sea below with a just perceptible swell of a calm and perfect June day. I felt exquisite – superb. I could have walked all the way home on a tight rope.

September 2

Just recently, I have been going fairly strong. I get frequent colds and sometimes show unpleasant nerve symptoms, but I take a course of arsenic and strychnine every month or so in tabloid form, and this helps me over bad patches.

Under the beatific influence of more comfortable health, the rare flower of my ambition has raised its head once more: my brain has bubbled with projects. To wit:

(1) An investigation of the Balancers in Larval Urodeles.
(2) The Present Parlous State of Systematic Zoology (for 'Science Progress').
(3) The Anatomy of the Psocidae.

Etc.

The strength of my ambition at any given moment is the measure of my state of health. It must really be an extraordinarily tenacious thing to have hung on thro' all my recent experiences. Considerately enough this great Crab lets go of my big toe when I am sunk low in health, yet pinches devilishly hard as now when I am well.

A Bad Listener

When I begin to speak, T—— will sometimes interrupt with his loud, rasping voice. I usually submit to this from sheer lack of lung power or I may have a sore throat. But occasionally after the fifth or sixth interruption I lose my equanimity and refuse to give him ground. I keep straight on with what I intended to say, only in a louder voice; he assumes a voice louder still, but not to be denied, I pile Pelion on Ossa and finally overwhelm him in a thunder of sound. For example:

' The other day' – I begin quietly collecting my thoughts to tell the story in detail, 'I went to the—'

'Ah! you must come and see my pictures—' he breaks in; but I go on and he goes on and as I talk, I catch phrases: 'St. Peters ' or 'Michael Angelo' or 'Botticelli' in wondrous antiphon with my own 'British Museum' and 'I saw there,' 'two Syracusan,' 'tetradrachms,' until very likely I reach the end of my sentence before he does his, or perhaps his rasp drives my remarks out of my head. But that makes no difference, for rather than give in I go on improvising in a louder and louder voice when suddenly, at length made aware of the fact that I am talking too, he stops! leaving me bellowing nonsense at the top of my voice, thus: 'and I much admired these Syracusan tetradrachms, very charming indeed, I like them, the Syracusan tetradrachms I mean you know, and it will be good to go again and see them (louder) if possible and the weather keeps dry (louder) and the moon and the stars keep in their courses, if the slugs on the thorn (loudest)—' he stops, hears the last few words of my remarks, pretends to be appreciative but wonders what in Heaven's name I can have been talking about.

September 3

This is the sort of remark I like to make: Someone says to me: 'You *are* a pessimist.'

'Ah! well,' I say, looking infernally deep, 'pessimism is a good policy; it's like having your cake and eating it at the same time.'

Chorus: ' Why?'

'Because if the future turns out badly you can say, "I told you so," to your own satisfaction, and if all is well, why you share everyone else's satisfaction.'

Or I say: ' No I can't swim; and I don't want to!'

Chorus: 'Why?'
'Because it is too dangerous.'
Chorus: 'Why?'
The Infernally Wise Youth: 'For several reasons. If you are a swimmer you are likely to be oftener near water and oftener in danger than a non-swimmer. Further, as soon as you can swim even only a little, then as an honourable man, it behoves you to plunge in at once to save a drowning person, whereas, if you couldn't swim it would be merely tempting Providence.'

Isn't it sickening?

A Jolt

Yesterday the wind was taken out of my sails. Racing along with spinnaker and jib, feeling pretty fit and quite excited over some interesting ectoparasites just collected on some Tinamous, I suddenly shot into a menacing dead calm: that stiflingly still atmosphere which precedes a Typhoon. That is to say, my eye caught the title of an enormous quarto memoir in the *Trans. Roy. Soc.*, Edinburgh: The Histology of——.

I was browsing in the library at the time when this hit me like a carelessly handled gaff straight in the face. I almost ran away to my room.

★

My Pink Form just received amazes me! To be a soldier? C'est incroyable, ma foi! The possibility even is distracting! To send me a notice requesting me to prepare myself for killing men! Why I should feel no more astonished to receive a War Office injunction under dire penalties to perform miracles, to move mountains, to raise from the dead: My reply would be: 'I cannot.' I should sit still and watch the whole universe pass to its destruction rather than raise a hand to knife a fellow. This may be poor, anaemic; but there it is, a positive fact.

★

There are moments when I have awful misgivings: Is this blessed Journal worthwhile? I really don't know, and that's the harassing fact of the matter. If only I were sure of myself, if only I were capable of an impartial view! But I am too fond of myself to be able to see myself objectively. I wish I knew for certain what I am and how much I am worth. There are such possibilities about the situation: it may turn out tremendously, or else explode in a soap bubble. It is the torture of Tantalus to be so uncertain. I should be relieved to know even the worst. I would almost gladly burn my MSS. in the pleasure of having my curiosity satisfied. I go from the nadir of disappointment to the zenith of hope and back several times a week, and all the time I am additionally harassed by the perfect consciousness that it is all petty and pusillanimous to desire to be known and appreciated, that my ambition is a morbid diathesis of the mind. I am not such a fool either as not to see that there is but little satisfaction in posthumous fame, and I am not such a fool as not to realise that all fame is fleeting, and that the whole world itself is passing away.

★

I smile with sardonic amusement when I reflect how the War has changed my status. Before the War I was an interesting invalid. Now I am a lucky dog. Then, I was a star turn in tragedy; now I am drowned and ignored in an overcrowded chorus. No valetudinarian was ever more unpleasantly jostled out of his self-compassion. It is difficult to accustom myself to the new role all at once: I had begun to lose the faculty for sympathising in others' griefs. It is hard to have to realise that in all this slaughter, my own superfluous life has become negligible and scarcely anyone's concern but my own. In this colossal *sauve-qui-peut* which is developing, who can stay to consider a useless mouth? Am I not a comfortable parasite? And, God forgive me, an Egotist to boot?

The War is searching out everyone, concentrating a beam of inquisitive light upon everyone's mind and character and publishing it for all the world to see. And the consequence to many honest folk has been a keen personal disappointment. We ignoble persons had thought we were better than we really are. We scarcely anticipated that the War was going to discover for us our emotions so despicably small by comparison, or our hearts so riddled with selfish motives. In the wild race for security during these dangerous times, men and women have all been sailing so closehauled to the wind that their eyes have been glued to their own forepeaks with never a thought for others: fathers have vied with one another in procuring safe jobs for their sons, wives have been bitter and recriminating at the security of other wives' husbands. The men themselves plot constantly for staff appointments, and everyone is pulling strings who can. Bereavement has brought bitterness and immunity indifference.

And how pathetically some of us cling still to fragments of the old regime that has already passed – like ship-wrecked mariners to floating wreckage, to the manner of the conservatoire amid the thunder of all Europe being broken up, to our newspaper gossip and parish teas, to our cherished aims – wealth, fame, success – in spite of all, *ruat coelum!* Mr A. C. Benson and his trickling, comfortable Essays, Mr Shaw and his Scintillations – they are all there as before, revolving like haggard windmills in a devastated landscape! A little while ago, I read in the local newspaper which I get up from the country two columns concerning the accidental death of an old woman, while two lines were used to record the death of a townsman at the front from an aerial dart. Behold this poor rag! staggering along under the burden of the War in a passionate endeavour to preserve the old-time interest in an old woman's decease. Yet more or less we are all in the same case: I still write my Journal and play Patience of an evening, and an old lady I know still reads as before the short items of gossip in the papers, neglecting articles and leaders… We are like a nest of frightened ants when someone lifts the stone. That is the world just now.

September 5
…I was so ashamed of having to fall back upon such ignominious publications for my literary efforts that on presenting him with two copies, I told the following lie to save my face:

'They were two essays of mine left over at the beginning of the War, you know. My usual channel became blocked so I had to have recourse to these.'

'Where do you publish as a rule?' he innocently asked.

'Oh! several in the *Manchester Guardian*,' I told him out of vanity. 'But of course every respectable journal now has closed down to extra-war topics.'

I lie out of vanity. And then I confess to lying – out of vanity too. So that one way or another I am determined to make kudos out of myself. Even this last reflection is written down with an excessive appreciation of its wit and the intention that it shall raise a smile.

September 9
Still nothing to report. The anxiety is telling on us all. The nurse has another case on the 22nd.

★

I looked at myself in the mirror this morning – nude, a most revolting picture. An emaciated human being is the most unlovely thing in creation. Some time ago a smart errand boy called out 'Bovril' after me in the street.

On my way to the Station met two robust, brawny curates on the way to the daily weekday service – which is attended only by two decrepit old women in black, each with her prayer-book caught up to her breast as if she were afraid it might gallop off. That means a parson apiece – and in war time too.

↬

Bruce Frederick Cummings was born in Barnstaple, Devon, in 1889. He attempted to enlist in the Army in November 1915 but was turned down by the medical board – a letter from his doctor said that he was suffering from the disease now known as multiple sclerosis and had less than five years to live. He published his diaries in 1917 under the title *The Journal of a Disappointed Man* and chose the pseudonym W. N. P. Barbellion – the forenames 'Wilhelm', 'Nero' and 'Pilate' were for him those of the most wretched men ever to have lived. The book had been turned down by Collins, who had originally agreed to publish it, on account of its 'lack of morals'. Barbellion's voice in the diaries is delightfully self-deprecating and self-aware:

We ignoble persons had thought we were better than we really are.

We scarcely anticipated that the War was going to discover for us our emotions so despicably small by comparison, or our hearts so riddled with selfish motives.

The Journal of a Disappointed Man is a wonderful antidote to the dominant bombast and boasting. It conveys without melodrama the sense of disorientation felt by many as they saw their world cascade out of control. Cummings died in October 1919 having just finished a second volume of memoirs, 'Enjoying Life and Other Literary Remains'. As he says in the diaries, 'Death can do no more than kill you'.

THE SQUARE

from *The Forbidden Zone*

B ELOW MY WINDOW in the big bright square a struggle is going on between the machines of war and the people of the town. There are the motor cars of the army, the limousines, and the touring cars and the motor lorries and the ambulances; and there are the little bare-headed women of the town with baskets on their arms who try to push the monsters out of their way.

The motors come in and go out of the four corners of the square, and they stand panting and snorting in the middle of it. The limousines are full of smart men in uniforms with silver hair and gold braid on their round red hats. The touring cars, too, are full of uniforms, but on the faces of the young men who drive them is a look of exhaustion and excitement. The motors make a great noise and a great smell and a great dust. They come into the square, hooting and shrieking; they draw up in the square with grinding brakes. The men in them get out with a flourish of capes: they stamp on the pavement with heavy boots; they salute one another stiffly like wooden toys, then disappear into the buildings where they hold murderous conferences and make elaborate plans of massacre.

The motor cars have all gone wrong. They are queer. They are not doing what they were designed to do when they were turned out of the factories. The limousines were made to carry ladies to places of amusement: they are carrying generals to places of killing. The limousines and the touring cars and the motor lorries are all debauched; they have a depraved look; their springs sag, their wheels waver; their bodies lean to one side. The elegant limousines that carry the generals are crusted with old mud; the leather cushions of the touring cars are in tatters; the great motor lorries crouch under vast burdens. They crouch in the square ashamed, deformed, very weary; their unspeakable burdens bulge under canvas coverings. Only the snobbish ambulances with the red crosses on their sides have assurance. They have the self-assurance of amateurs.

The business of killing and the business of living go on together in the square beneath the many windows, jostling each other.

The little women of the town are busy; they are dressed in black; they have children with them. Some lead children by the hand, others are big with children yet unborn. But all the women are busy. They ignore the motors; they do not see the fine scowling generals, nor the strained excited faces in the fast touring cars, nor the provisions of war under their lumpy coverings. They do not even wonder what is in the ambulances. They are too busy. They scurry across to the shops, instinctively dodging, and come out again with bundles; they talk to each other a little without smiling; they stare in front of them; they are staring at life; they are thinking about the business of living.

On Saturdays they put up their booths on the cobble stones and hold their market. The motors have to go round another way on market days. There is no room in the square for the generals, nor for the dying men in the ambulances. The women are there. They buy and sell their saucepans and their linen and their spools of thread and their fowls and their flowers; they bargain and they chatter; they provide for their houses and their children; they give oranges to their children, and put away their coppers in their deep pockets.

As for the men on the stretchers inside the smart ambulances with the bright red crosses, they do not know about the women in the square. They cannot hear their chattering, nor see the children sucking oranges; they can see nothing and hear nothing of the life that is going on in the square; they are lying on their backs in the dark canvas bellies of the ambulances, staring at death. They do not know that on Saturday mornings their road does not lie through the big bright square because the little women of the town are busy with their market.

MARY BORDEN

THE BEACH

from *The Forbidden Zone*

THE BEACH WAS LONG AND SMOOTH and the colour of cream. The woman sitting in the sun stroked the beach with the pink palm of her hand and said to herself, 'The beach is perfect, the sun is perfect, the sea is perfect. How pretty the little waves are, curling up the beach. They are perfectly lovely. They are like a lace frill to the beach. And the sea is a perfectly heavenly blue. It is odd to think of how old the beach is and how old the sea is, and how much older that old, old fellow, the fiery sun. The face of the beach is smooth as cream and the sea to-day is a smiling infant, twinkling and dimpling, and the sun is delicious; it is burning hot, like youth itself. It is good to be alive. It is good to be young.' But she could not say this aloud so she said to the man beside her in the wheel chair:

'How many millions of years has it taken to make the beach? How many snails have left their shells behind them, do you think, to make all this fine powdery sand? A million billion?' She let the sand run through her strong white fingers and smiled, blinking in the sun and looked away from the man in the invalid chair beside her toward the horizon.

The man wriggled and hitched himself clumsily up in his chair; an ugly grimace pulled his pale face to one side. He dared not look down over the arm of his wheel chair at the bright head of the woman sitting beside him. Her hair burned in the sunlight; her cheeks were pink. He stole a timid, furtive look. Yes, she was as beautiful as a child. She was perfectly lovely. A groan escaped him, or was it only a sigh?

She looked up quickly. 'What is it, darling? Are you in pain? Are you tired? Shall we go back?' Her voice sounded in the immense quiet of the beach like a cricket chirping, but the word 'darling' went on sounding and sounding like a little hollow bell while she searched his features, trying to find his old face, the one she knew, trying to work a magic on him, remove and replace the sunken eyes, the pinched nose, the bloodless wry mouth. 'He's not a stranger,' she said to herself. 'He's not.' And she heard the faint mocking echo, 'Darling, darling,' ringing far away as if a bell-buoy out on the water were saying 'Darling, darling,' to make the little waves laugh.

'It's only my foot, my left foot. Funny, isn't it, that it goes on throbbing. They cut it off two months ago.' He jerked a hand backward. 'It's damn queer when you think of it. The old foot begins the old game, then I look down and it's not there any more, and I'm fooled again.' He laughed. His laughter was such a tiny sound in the great murmur of the morning that it might have been a sand-fly laughing. He was thinking, 'What will become of us? She is young and healthy. She is as beautiful as a child. What shall we do about it?' And looking into her eyes he saw the same question, 'What shall we do?' and looked quickly away again. So did she.

She looked past him at the row of ugly villas above the beach. Narrow houses, each like a chimney, tightly wedged together, wedges of cheap brick and plaster with battered wooden balconies. They were new and shabby and derelict. All had their shutters up. All the doors were bolted. How stuffy it must be in those deserted villas, in all those abandoned bedrooms and kitchens and parlours. Probably there were sand-shoes and bathing dresses and old towels and saucepans and blankets rotting inside them with the sand drifting in. Probably the window panes behind the shutters were broken and the mirrors cracked. Perhaps when the aeroplanes dropped bombs on the town, pictures fell down and mirrors and the china in the dark china closets cracked inside these pleasure houses. Who had built them?

'Cowards built them,' he said in his new bitter, rasping voice, the voice of a peevish, irritable sand-fly. 'Built them to make love in, to cuddle in, to sleep in, hide in. Now they're empty. The blighters have left them to rot there. Rotten, I call it, leaving the swanky plage to go to the bad like that, just because there's a war on. A little jazz now and a baccarat table would make all the difference, wouldn't it? It would cheer us up. You'd dance and I'd have a go at the tables. That's the casino over there, that big thing; that's not empty, that's crowded, but I don't advise you to go there. I don't think you'd like it. It's not your kind of a crowd. It's all right for me, but not for you. No, it wouldn't do for you – not even on a gala night.

'They've a gala night in our casino whenever there's a battle. Funny sort of place. You should watch the motors drive up then. The rush begins about ten in the evening and goes on till morning. Quite like Deauville the night of the Grand Prix. You never saw such a crowd. They all rush there from the front, you know – the way they do from the race-course – though, to be sure, it is not quite the real thing – not a really smart crowd. No, not precisely, though the wasters in Deauville weren't much to look at, were they? Still, our crowd here aren't precisely wasters. Gamblers, of course, down and outs, wrecks – all gone to pieces, parts of 'em missing, you know, tops of their heads gone, or one of their legs. When they take their places at the tables, the croupiers – that is to say, the doctors – look them over. Come closer, I'll whisper it. Some of them have no faces.'

'Darling, don't.' She covered her own face, closed her ears to his tiny voice and listened desperately with all her minute will to the large tranquil murmur of the sea. 'Darling, darling,' far out the bell-buoy was sounding.

'Bless you,' said the thin, sharp, exasperated sand-fly voice beside her. 'Little things like that don't keep us away. If we can't walk in we get carried in. All that's needed is a ticket. It's tied to you like a luggage label. It has your name on it in case you don't remember your name. You needn't have a face, but a ticket you must have to get into our casino.'

'Stop, darling – darling, stop!'

'It's a funny place. There's a skating rink. You ought to see it. You go through the baccarat rooms and the dance hall to get to it. They're all full of beds. Rows of beds under the big crystal chandeliers, rows of beds under the big gilt mirrors, and the skating rink is full of beds, too. The sun blazes down through the glass roof. It's like a hot-house in Kew Gardens. There's that dank smell of a rotting swamp, the smell of gas gangrene. Men with gas gangrene turn green, you know, like rotting plants.' He laughed. Then he was silent. He looked at her cowering in the sand, her hands covering her face, and looked away again.

He wondered why he had told her these things. He loved her. He hated her. He was afraid of her. He did not want her to be kind to him. He could never touch her again and he was tied to her. He was rotting and he was tied to her perfection. He had no power over her any more but the power of infecting her with his corruption. He could never make her happy. He could only make her suffer. His one luxury now was jealousy of her perfection, and his one delight would be to give in to the temptation to make her suffer. He could only reach her that way. It would be his revenge on the war.

He was not aware of these thoughts. He was too busy with other little false thoughts. He was saying to himself, 'I will let her go. I will send her away. Once we are at home again, I will say good-bye to her.' But he knew that he was incapable of letting her go.

He closed his eyes. He said to himself 'The smell of the sea is good, but the odour that oozes from the windows of the casino is bad. I can smell it from here. I can't get the smell of it out of my nose. It is my own smell,' and his wasted greenish face twitched in disgust.

She looked at him. 'I love him,' she said to herself. 'I love him,' she repeated. 'But can I go on loving him?' She whispered, 'Can I? I must.' She said, 'I must love him, now more than ever, but where is he?'

She looked round her as if to find the man he once had been. There were other women on the beach, women in black and old men and children with buckets and spades, people of the town. They seemed to be glad to be alive. No one seemed to be thinking of the war.

The beach was long and smooth and the colour of cream. The beach was perfect; the sun perfectly delicious; the sea was perfectly calm. The man in the wheel chair and the woman beside him were no bigger than flies on the sand. The women and children and old men were specks.

Far out on the sea there was an object; there were two objects. The people on the beach could scarcely distinguish them. They peered through the sunshine while the children rolled in the sand, and they heard the sound of a distant hammer tapping.

'They are firing out at sea,' said someone to someone.

How perfect the beach is. The sea is a perfectly heavenly blue. Behind the windows of the casino, under the great crystal chandeliers, men lie in narrow beds. They lie in queer postures with their greenish faces turned up. Their white bandages are reflected in the sombre gilt mirrors. There is no sound anywhere but the murmur of the sea and the whispering of the waves on the sand, and the tap tap of a hammer coming from a great distance across the water, and the bell-buoy that seems to say, 'Darling, darling.'

MARY BORDEN

CONSPIRACY

from *The Forbidden Zone*

I
T IS ALL CAREFULLY ARRANGED. Everything is arranged. It is arranged that men should be broken and that they should be mended. Just as you send your clothes to the laundry and mend them when they come back, so we send our men to the trenches and mend them when they come back again. You send your socks and your shirts again and again to the laundry, and you sew up the tears and clip the ravelled edges again and again just as many times as they will stand it. And then you throw them away. And we send our men to the war again and again, just as long as they will stand it; just until they are dead, and then we throw them into the ground.

It is all arranged. Ten kilometres from here along the road is the place where men are wounded. This is the place where they are mended. We have all the things here for mending, the tables and the needles, and the thread and the knives and the scissors, and many curious things that you never use for your clothes.

We bring our men up along the dusty road where the bushes grow on either side and the green trees. They come by in the mornings in companies, marching with strong legs, with firm steps. They carry their knapsacks easily. Their knapsacks and their guns and their greatcoats are not heavy for them. They wear their caps jauntily, tilted to one side. Their faces are ruddy and their eyes bright. They smile and call out with strong voices. They throw kisses to the girls in the fields.

We send our men up the broken road between bushes of barbed wire and they come back to us, one by one, two by two in ambulances, lying on stretchers. They lie on their backs on the stretchers and are pulled out of the ambulances as loaves of bread are pulled out of the oven. The stretchers slide out of the mouths of the ambulances with the men on them. The men cannot move. They are carried into a shed, unclean bundles, very heavy, covered with brown blankets.

We receive these bundles. We pull off a blanket. We observe that this is a man. He makes feeble whining sounds like an animal. He lies still; he smells bad; he smells like a corpse; he can only move his tongue; he tries to moisten his lips with his tongue.

This is the place where he is to be mended. We lift him on to a table. We peel off his clothes, his coat and his shirt and his trousers and his boots. We handle his clothes that are stiff with blood. We cut off his shirt with large scissors. We stare at the obscene sight of his innocent wounds. He allows us to do this. He is helpless to stop us. We wash off the dry blood round the edges of his wounds. He suffers us to do as we like with him. He says no word except that he is thirsty and we do not give him to drink.

We confer together over his body and he hears us. We discuss his different parts in terms that he does not understand, but he listens while we make calculations with his heart beats and the pumping breath of his lungs.

We conspire against his right to die. We experiment with his bones, his muscles, his sinews, his blood. We dig into the yawning mouths of his wounds. Helpless openings, they let us into the secret places of his body. We plunge deep into his body. We make discoveries within his body. To the shame of the havoc of his limbs we add the insult of our curiosity and the curse of our purpose, the purpose to remake him. We lay odds on his chances of escape, and we combat with death, his Saviour.

It is our business to do this. He knows and he allows us to do it. He finds himself in the operating room. He lays himself out. He bares himself to our knives. His mind is annihilated. He pours out his blood unconscious. His red blood is spilled and pours over the table on to the floor while he sleeps.

After this, while he is still asleep, we carry him into another place and put him to bed. He awakes bewildered as children do, expecting, perhaps, to find himself at home with his mother leaning over him, and he moans a little and then lies still again. He is helpless, so we do for him what he cannot do for himself, and he is grateful. He accepts his helplessness. He is obedient. We feed him, and he eats. We fatten him up, and he allows himself to be fattened. Day after day he lies there and we watch him. All day and all night he is watched. Every day his wounds are uncovered and cleaned, scraped and washed and bound up again. His body does not belong to him. It belongs to us for the moment, not for long. He knows why we tend it so carefully. He knows what we are fattening and cleaning it up for; and while we handle it he smiles.

He is only one among thousands. They are all the same. They all let us do with them what we like. They all smile as if they were grateful. When we hurt them they try not to cry out, not wishing to hurt our feelings. And often they apologise for dying. They would not die and disappoint us if they could help it. Indeed, in their helplessness they do the best they can to help us get them ready to go back again.

It is only ten kilometres up the road, the place where they go to be torn again and mangled. Listen; you can hear how well it works. There is the sound of cannon and the sound of the ambulances bringing the wounded, and the sound of the tramp of strong men going along the road to fill the empty places.

Do you hear? Do you understand? It is all arranged just as it should be.

MARY BORDEN

IN THE OPERATING ROOM

from *The Forbidden Zone*

THE OPERATING ROOM is the section of a wooden shed. Thin partitions separate it from the X-ray room on one side, and the sterilizing room on the other. Another door communicates with a corridor. There are three wounded men on three operating tables. Surgeons, nurses and orderlies are working over them. The doors keep opening and shutting. The boiler is pounding and bubbling in the sterilizing room. There is a noise of steam escaping, of feet hurrying down the corridor, of ambulances rolling past the windows, and behind all this, the rhythmic pounding of the guns bombarding at a distance of ten miles or so.

1st Patient: Mother of God! Mother of God!

2nd Patient: Softly. Softly. You hurt me. Ah! You are hurting me.

3rd Patient: I am thirsty.

1st Surgeon: Cut the dressing, Mademoiselle.

2nd Surgeon: What's his ticket say? Show it to me. What's the X-ray show?

3rd Surgeon: Abdomen. Bad pulse. I wonder now?

1st Patient: In the name of God be careful. I suffer. I suffer.

1st Surgeon: At what time were you wounded?

1st Patient: At five this morning.

1st Surgeon: Where?

1st Patient: In the arm.

1st Surgeon: Yes, yes, but in what sector?

1st Patient: In the trenches near Besanghe.

1st Surgeon: Shell or bullet?

1st Patient: Shell. Merciful God, what are you doing?

A nurse comes in from the corridor. Her apron is splashed with blood.

Nurse: There's a lung just come in. Haemorrhage. Can one of you take him?

1st Surgeon: In a few minutes. In five minutes. Now then, Mademoiselle, strap down that other arm tighter.

Nurse (in doorway) to 2nd Surgeon: There's a knee for you, doctor, and three elbows. In five minutes I'll send in the lung. (Exit.)

3rd Patient: I'm thirsty. A drink. Give me a drink.

3rd Surgeon: In a little while. You must wait a little.

2nd Patient: Mother of Jesus, not like that. Don't turn my foot like that. Not that way. Take care. Great God, take care! I can't bear it. I tell you, I can't bear it!

2nd Surgeon: There, there, don't excite yourself. You've got a nasty leg, very nasty. Smells bad. Mademoiselle, hold his leg up. It's not pretty at all, this leg.

2nd Patient: Ah, doctor, doctor. What are you doing? Aiee—.

2nd Surgeon: Be quiet. Don't move. Don't touch the wound I tell you. Idiot! Hold his leg. Keep your hands off, you animal. Hold his leg higher. Strap his hands down.

3rd Patient (feebly): I am thirsty. I die of thirst. A drink! A drink!

2nd Patient (screaming): You're killing me. Killing me! I'll die of it! Aieeeee—.

3rd Patient (softly): I am thirsty. For pity a drink.

3rd Surgeon: Have you vomited blood, old man?

3rd Patient: I don't know. A drink please, doctor.

3rd Surgeon: Does it hurt here?

3rd Patient: No, I don't think so. A drink, sister, in pity's name, a drink.

Nurse: I can't give you a drink. It would hurt you. You are wounded in the stomach.

3rd Patient: So thirsty. Just a little drink. Just a drop. Sister for pity, just a drop.

3rd Surgeon: Moisten his lips. How long ago were you wounded?

3rd Patient: I don't know. In the night. Some night.

3rd Surgeon: Last night?

3rd Patient: Perhaps last night. I don't know. I lay in the mud a long time. Please sister a drink. Just a little drink.

1st Patient: What's in that bottle? What are you doing to me?

1st Surgeon: Keep still I tell you.

1st Patient: It burns! It's burning me! No more. No more! I beg of you, doctor; I can't bear any more!

1st Surgeon: Nonsense. This won't last a minute. There's nothing the matter with you. Your wounds are nothing.

1st Patient: You say it's nothing. My God, what are you doing now? Ai—ee!

1st Surgeon: It's got to be cleaned out. There's a piece of shell, bits of coat, all manner of dirt in it.

2nd Patient: Jeanne, petite Marie, Jean, where are you? Little Jean, where are you?

2nd Surgeon: Your leg is not at all pretty, my friend. We shall have to take it off.

2nd Patient: Oh, my poor wife! I have three children, doctor. If you take my leg off what will become of them and of the farm? Great God, to suffer like this!

2nd Surgeon to 1st Surgeon: Look here a moment. It smells bad. Gangrenous. What do you think?

1st Surgeon: No good waiting.

2nd Surgeon: Well, my friend, will you have it off?

2nd Patient: If you say so, doctor. Oh, my poor wife, my poor Jeanne. What will become of you? The children are too little to work in the fields.

2nd Surgeon (to nurse): Begin with the chloroform. We're going to put you to sleep, old man. Breathe deep. Breathe through the mouth. Is my saw there? Where is my amputating saw? Who's got my saw?

3rd Patient (softly): A drink, a drink. Give me a drink.

3rd Surgeon: I can do nothing with a pulse like that. Give him serum, five hundred c.c.s and camphorated oil and strychnine. Warm him up a bit.

Door opens, nurse enters, followed by two stretcher bearers.

Nurse: Here's the lung. Are you ready for it?

1st Surgeon: In a minute. One minute. Leave him there.

The stretcher bearers put their stretcher on the floor and go out.

2nd Patient (half under chloroform): Aha! Aha! Ahead there, you son of a— Forward! Forward! What a stink! I've got him! Now I've got you. Quick, quick! Let me go! Let me go! Jeannette, quick, quick, Jeannette! I'm coming. Marie? Little Jean, where are you?

2nd Surgeon: Tighten those straps. He's strong, poor devil.

1st Patient: Is it finished?

1st Surgeon: Very nearly. Keep quite still. Now then, the dressings mademoiselle. There you are old man. Don't bandage the arm too tight, mademoiselle. Get him out now. Hi, stretcher bearers, lift up that one from the floor, will you?

3rd Surgeon: It's no use operating. Almost no pulse.

3rd Patient: For pity a drink!

3rd Surgeon: Give him a drink. It won't matter. I can do nothing.

2nd Surgeon: I shall have to amputate above the knee. Is he under?

Nurse: Almost.

3rd Patient: For pity a drink.

Nurse: There, don't lift your head; here is a drink. Drink this.

3rd Patient: It is good. Thank you, sister.

1st Surgeon: Take this man to Ward 3. Now then, mademoiselle, cut the dressings.

3rd Surgeon: I can do nothing here. Send me the next one.

3rd Patient: I cannot see. I cannot see any more. Sister, where are you?

1st Surgeon: How's your spine case of yesterday?

3rd Surgeon: Just what you would expect – paralysed from the waist down.

1st Surgeon: They say the attack is for five in the morning.

3rd Surgeon: Orders are to evacuate every possible bed to-day.

3rd Patient: It is dark. Are you there, sister?

Nurse: Yes, old man, I'm here. Shall I send for a priest, doctor?

3rd Surgeon: Too late. Poor devil. It's hopeless when they come in like that, after lying for hours in the mud. There, it's finished. Call the stretcher bearers.

1st Surgeon: Quick, a basin! God! how the blood spouts. Quick, quick, quick! Three holes in this lung.

2nd Surgeon: Take that leg away, will you? There's no room to move here.

3rd Surgeon: Take this dead man away, and bring the next abdomen. Wipe that table, mademoiselle, while I wash my hands. And you, there, mop up the floor a bit.

The doors open and shut. Stretcher bearers go out and come in. A nurse comes from the sterilizing room with a pile of nickel drums in her arms. Another nurse goes out with trays of knives and other instruments. The nurse from the corridor comes back. An officer appears at the window.

Nurse: Three knees have come in, two more abdomens, five heads.

Officer (through the window): The Médecin Inspecteur will be here in half an hour. The General is coming at two to decorate all amputés.

1st Surgeon: We'll get no lunch to-day, and I'm hungry. There, I call that a very neat amputation.

2nd Surgeon: Three holes stopped in this lung in three minutes by the clock. Pretty quick, eh?

3rd Surgeon: Give me a light, some one. My experience is that if abdomens have to wait more than six hours it's no good. You can't do anything. I hope that chap got the oysters in Amiens! Oysters sound good to me.

⤸

Mary Borden was born into a wealthy Chicago family in 1886. In England at the outbreak of the war, she used her own money to equip and staff a field hospital close to the front in which she herself served as a nurse from 1915 until the end of the war. The stories in *The Forbidden Zone* are based on her experiences in the hospital. Published in 1929, the same year as *All Quiet on the Western Front*, *The Forbidden Zone*'s graphic descriptions of wounds and amputations were too shocking for many readers – and still are. The lack of sentimentality in the precise, sparse writing makes it all the more powerful. Like the art of a pointillist painter, the power of her writing is built up word by word, sentence by sentence.

At the outbreak of the Second World War, Mary Borden set up the Hadfield-Spears Ambulance Unit, which accompanied the Free French in North Africa, Italy and France. Her book, *Journey Down a Blind Alley*, is the story of this campaign. She died in Berkshire in 1968.

EMILIO LUSSU

A REAL HERO

from *A Soldier on the Southern Front*

translated by Gregory Conti

T HE LIEUTENANT GENERAL in command of the division, held to be responsible for the unjustified abandonment of Mount Fior, was given the ax. In his stead, the division command was taken over by Lieutenant General Leone. The daily order issued by the commandant of the Third Army presented him to us as 'a soldier of proven tenacity and time-tested bravery.' I met him for the first time on Mount Spill, near the battalion command. His orderly officer told me he was the new division commander and I introduced myself.

Standing at attention, I gave him the rundown on the battalion.

'At ease,' the general told me in a decorous and authoritative tone. 'Where have you been until now in this war?'

'Always with this brigade, on the Carso.'

'Have you ever been wounded?'

'No, sir, general.'

'What, you've been on the front line for the entire war and you've never been wounded? Never?'

'Never, general. Unless we want to consider a few flesh wounds that I've had treated here in the battalion, without going to the hospital.'

'No, no, I'm talking about serious wounds, grave wounds.'

'Never, general.'

'That's very odd. How do you explain that?'

'The exact reason escapes me, general, but I'm certain that I've never been gravely wounded.'

'Have you taken part in all the combat operations of your brigade?'

'All of them.'

'The "black cats"?'

'The "black cats."'

'The "red cats"?'

'And the "red cats," general.'

'Very odd indeed. Are you perhaps timorous?'

I thought: To put a guy like this in his place it would take at least a general in command of an army corps. Since I didn't answer right away, the general, still somber, repeated the question.

'I believe not,' I replied.

'You believe or are you sure?'

'In war, you can never be sure of anything,' I replied politely, and added with the hint of a smile that was intended to be conciliatory, 'not even that you're sure.'

The general didn't smile. No, I think smiling was almost impossible for him. He was wearing a steel helmet with the neck strap fastened, which gave his face a metallic look. His mouth was invisible, and if he hadn't had a mustache you would have said he had no lips. His eyes were gray and hard, always open, like the eyes of a nocturnal bird of prey.

The general changed the subject.

'Do you love war?'

I hesitated. Should I answer this question or not? There were officers and soldiers within earshot. I decided to respond.

'I was in favor of the war, general, and at my university I was a representative of the interventionists.'

'That,' said the general in a tone that was chillingly calm, 'pertains to the past. I'm asking you about the present.'

'War is a serious thing, too serious, and it's hard to say... it's hard... Anyway, I do my duty.' And since he was staring at me dissatisfied, I added, 'All of my duty.'

'I didn't ask you,' the general said, 'if you do or do not do your duty.

In war, everyone has to do his duty, because if you don't, you risk being shot. You understand me. I asked you if you love or don't love war.'

'Love war!' I exclaimed, a bit discouraged.

The general stared at me, inexorable. His eyes had grown larger. It looked to me like they were spinning in their sockets.

'Can't you answer?' the general insisted.

'Well, I believe... certainly... I think I can say... that I have to believe...'

I was looking for a possible answer.

'Just what is it that you believe, then?'

'I believe, personally, I mean to say just for myself, generally speaking, I couldn't really affirm that I have a special predilection for war.'

'Stand at attention!'

I was already standing at attention.

'Ah, so you're for peace, are you?' Now the general's voice was tinged with surprise and disdain. 'For peace! Just like some meek little house-wife, consecrated to hearth and home, to her kitchen, her bedroom, her flowers, to her flowers, to her sweet little flowers! Is that how it is, lieutenant?'

'No, general.'

'And what kind of peace is it that you desire?'

'A peace...' And inspiration came to my aid. 'A victorious peace.'

The general seemed reassured. He asked me a few more routine questions and then asked me to accompany him on a tour of the front line.

When we were in the trench, at the highest and closest point to the enemy lines, facing Mount Fior, he asked me, 'How far is it here, between our trenches and the Austrians'?'

'About two hundred fifty meters,' I replied.

The general took a long look and said, 'Here, it's two hundred thirty meters.'

'Probably.'

'Not probably. Certainly.'

We had made a solid trench, with rocks and big clods of earth. The men could walk up and down its entire length without being seen. The lookouts observed and shot through loopholes, under cover. The general looked out from the loophole, but he wasn't satisfied. He had a pile of rocks made at the foot of the parapet and climbed upon them, his eyes behind binoculars. Standing straight up, he was uncovered from his chest to his head.

'General,' I said, 'the Austrians have some excellent snipers and it's dangerous to expose yourself like that.'

The general didn't answer me. Standing straight, he kept on looking through his binoculars. Two rifle shots rang out from the enemy line. The bullets whistled past the general. He remained impassive. Two more shots followed the first two, and one of them grazed the trench. Only then, composed and unhurried, did he come down. I looked at him up close. His face displayed arrogant indifference, but his eyes were spinning. They looked like the wheels of a race car.

The lookout who was on duty just a few steps away from him continued looking out of his loophole. But, attracted by the exceptional show, some soldiers and a corporal from the 12th Company, then on the line, had stopped in the trench, all huddled together next to the general, and they were looking at him, more distrustful than impressed. They no doubt found in the division commander's overly audacious attitude some very good reasons to ponder, with a certain amount of apprehension, their own fate. The general gazed at his onlookers with satisfaction.

'If you're not afraid,' he said, turning to the corporal, 'do what your general just did.'

'Yes, sir,' the corporal replied. And leaning his rifle against the trench wall, he climbed up on the pile of rocks.

Instinctively, I grabbed the corporal by the arm and made him come down.

'The Austrians have been alerted now,' I said, 'and they certainly won't miss on the next shot.'

With a chilling glance, the general reminded me of the difference in rank that separated me from him. I let go of the corporal's arm and didn't say another word.

'But there's nothing to it,' said the corporal, and he climbed back up on the pile.

As soon as he looked out he was greeted by a barrage of rifle fire. The Austrians, roused by his previous apparition, were waiting with their guns pointed. The corporal remained unhurt. Impassive, his arms leaning on the parapet, his chest exposed to enemy fire, he kept his eyes to the front.

'Bravo!' the general cried. 'You can get down now.'

A single shot came from the enemy trench. The corporal fell backward and landed on top of us. I bent over him. The bullet had hit him in the top of the chest, under his collarbone, going in one side and out the other. Blood was coming out of his mouth. His eyes slits, gasping for breath, he murmured, 'It's nothing, lieutenant.'

The general bent over him, too. The soldiers looked at him, hate in their eyes.

'He's a hero,' the general commented. 'A real hero.'

When he straightened up, his eyes again met mine. Just for a second. In that instant, I recalled having seen those very same eyes, cold and rotating, in the mental hospital of my hometown during a visit we'd made there with our professor of forensic medicine.

He looked for his change purse and pulled out a silver one-lira coin.

'Here,' he said to the corporal. 'You can drink a glass of wine the first chance you get.'

The wounded man shook his head in refusal and hid his hands. The general stood there with the lira in his fingers and, after a moment's hesitation, let it drop onto the corporal. Nobody picked it up.

The general continued his inspection of the line and when he got to the end of my battalion, he dispensed me from following him.

I made my way back to the battalion command. The whole line was in an uproar. The news of what had happened had already made it around the entire sector. For their part, the stretcher-bearers who had carried the corporal to the first-aid post had recounted the episode to everyone they ran into. Captain Canevacci was beside himself.

'The people in command of the Italian army are Austrians!' he exclaimed. 'Austrians in front of us, Austrians at our backs, Austrians in our midst!'

Near the battalion command I ran into Lieutenant Colonel Abbati again. That was the name of the officer from the 301st Infantry. He was supposed to go up to the front line with his battalion. He knew about the incident too. I called out to him. He didn't answer. When he got up close to me, he said, worried, 'The military art follows its course.'

He stretched out his arm to unlatch the canteen I was wearing on my belt. I rushed to offer it to him. Looking distracted, a vague look in his eyes, he took it delicately in hand. He held it up to his ear and shook it; it wasn't empty. He took out the cork and held it up to his lips to drink. But he stopped suddenly, with a look on his face of amazement and disgust, as though he'd seen the head of a snake spring forth from the mouth of the canteen.

'Coffee and water!' he exclaimed in a tone of compassion. 'Look, kid, start drinking. Otherwise you'll end up in the loony bin, too, like your general.'

EMILIO LUSSU

YOU SHOULD HAVE DONE NOTHING

from *A Soldier on the Southern Front*

translated by Gregory Conti

WE CONTINUED OUR PURSUIT the next day. After moving past Croce Sant'Antonio, the advance-guard battalion proceeded through the forest toward the grassy basin of Casara Zebio and Mount Zebio. As it advanced, it appeared more and more probable that the largest part of the enemy force had stopped in the highlands. Their resistance had become tenacious again. It was clear that the last Austrian units, in contact with our patrols, were supported by troops nearby. Given the slowness of our progress, my battalion, once we'd crossed the Val di Nos, remained inactive the whole day, waiting to be called into action.

The advance-guard 2nd Battalion received orders to stop and dig in. During the night, our battalion replaced it. When we arrived, one trench line had already been dug, hurriedly, on the outer edge of the woods. There were still some fir trees in front of us, but few and far between, as they always are on the edges of high-altitude fir woods. The terrain was still covered with bushes. Further away and higher up, several hundred meters ahead, some rocky mountain peaks loomed among the tops of the last fir trees. We could probably expect the stiffest resistance at their feet.

At dawn, Captain Canevacci and I were on the line with the 9th Company. We were waiting for the arrival of the machine-gun unit, which had stayed behind. The captain in command of the 9th was keeping watch over the terrain in front of the line with a group of sharpshooters. We were next to him, lying on the ground, behind a mound. Canevacci was looking through his binoculars.

Among the bushes, less than a hundred meters away, an enemy patrol came into view. There were seven of them, walking in single file. Convinced they were nowhere near our line, out of sight, they were proceeding parallel to our trench, walking straight up, rifles in hand, packs on their backs. They were exposed from their knees up. The captain of the 9th gestured to the sharpshooters, gave the order to fire, and the patrol crumbled to the ground.

'Bravo!' exclaimed Captain Canevacci.

One of our squads moved out of the trench on all fours. Behind them the entire line had their rifles pointed. The squad disappeared, slithering on their bellies, into the bushes. We were expecting the squad to come back in carrying the fallen, but time was going by. Our men had to advance very cautiously to avoid an ambush. Captain Canevacci was losing patience. The machine-gun unit still hadn't arrived. What if they'd gotten lost in the forest, in the middle of the other units? To keep from losing more time I went back to look for them.

I found them half a kilometer farther back, in contact with the units of the 2nd Battalion. When I saw them, a dramatic scene was being played out; General Leone, alone on his mule, was climbing up a rocky slope between the 2nd Battalion and the machine-gun unit. As the mule was moving along the edge of a steep drop, about sixty-five feet, it stumbled and the general fell to the ground. The mule, unperturbed, kept walking along the edge of the cliff. The general was still hanging on to the reins, with half of his body dangling over the precipice. With each step, the mule yanked its head from side to side, trying to shake him off. At any moment the general might fall off the cliff. There were a lot of soldiers nearby who saw him, but nobody made a move. I could see them all very clearly; some of them winked at each other, smiling.

Any minute now the mule would free itself of the general. A soldier rushed out from the ranks of the machine-gun unit and threw himself down on the ground in time to save him. Without losing his composure, as though he had trained especially for accidents of this kind, the general remounted his mule, continued on his way, and disappeared. The soldier, back on his feet, looked around, satisfied. He had saved the general.

When his comrades from the machine-gun unit reached him, I witnessed a savage assault. They mauled him furiously, pummeling him with punches. The soldier fell to the ground on his back. His comrades jumped on top of him.

'Son of a bitch! You miserable bastard!'

'Leave me alone! Help!'

Punches and kicks slammed into the poor wretch, who was powerless to defend himself.

'Here! Take that! Who paid you to be the imbecile?'

'Help!'

'Save the general! Admit that you were paid by the Austrians!'

'Leave me alone! I didn't do it on purpose. I swear I didn't do it on purpose.'

The commander of the machine-gun unit was nowhere to be seen. The beating had gone on too long. Since nobody, neither officers nor NCOs, intervened to stop it, I ran over to them.

'What's going on?' I shouted in a loud voice.

My presence surprised everyone. The aggressors dispersed. Only a couple of them remained where they were and stood at attention. I went over to the victim, held out my hand, and helped him up. By the time he was back on his feet, those few who had stayed had disappeared. I was standing there alone with the soldier. He had a black eye and a cheek covered with blood. He'd lost his helmet.

'What happened?' I asked him. 'Why did they come after you like that?'

'It's nothing, lieutenant,' he muttered under his breath.

And he turned his frightened gaze right and left, looking for his helmet, but also out of fear of being heard by his comrades.

'What do you mean, it's nothing? What about the black eye? And the blood on your face? You're half dead and it's nothing?'

Standing at attention, embarrassed, the soldier didn't respond. I insisted, but he didn't say another word.

We were both relieved of our embarrassment by the arrival of the commander of the machine gunners, Lieutenant Ottolenghi, the one who in the battle on Mount Fior, with just one gun still working, had saved the day. We were the same rank, but I was more senior. Without saying even a word to me, he went up to the soldier and yelled at him, 'You imbecile! Today you dishonored our unit.'

'But what was I supposed to do, lieutenant?'

'What were you supposed to do? You should have done what everybody else did. Nothing. You should have done nothing. And even that was too much. A dumbass like you I don't even want him in my unit. I'm going to have you thrown out.'

The soldier had found his helmet and was putting it back on his head.

'What were you supposed to do?' the lieutenant said again, with disdain. 'You wanted to do something? Well then, you should have taken your bayonet and cut the reins and made the general fall off the cliff.'

'What?' the soldier muttered. 'I should have let the general die?'

'Yes, you cretin, you should have let him die. And if he wasn't going to die, then – since you wanted to do something no matter what the cost – you should have helped him die. Go back to the unit, and if the rest of them kill you, you'll have got what you deserve.'

'Look,' I said to him after the soldier had gone, 'you'd better take things a little more seriously. In a few hours the whole brigade will know what happened.'

'Whether they know or don't know makes no difference to me. On the contrary, it's better if they do know. That way, somebody might just get the idea to take a shot at that vampire.'

He went on talking, still indignant. He stuck his hand in his pocket, pulled out a coin, tossed it into the air, and said to me, 'Heads or tails?'

I didn't answer.

'Heads!' he shouted.

It was tails.

'You're lucky,' he went on. 'Tails. If it had been heads... if it had been heads...'

'What?' I asked.

'If it had been heads… Well! Let's leave it for the next time.'

As the machine-gun unit was joining the battalion, the squad from 9th Company was coming back to the trench, dragging the bodies of the fallen patrol. Six were dead, one was still alive. Their corporal was one of the dead. From their papers we determined they were Bosnians. The two captains were satisfied. Especially Canevacci, who was hoping they could obtain some useful information by interrogating the survivor. He had him taken to the first-aid station and immediately informed the division command, where an interpreter was on staff.

The six dead men were lying on the ground, one next to the other. We contemplated them, deep in thought. Sooner or later, for us, too, the time would come. But Captain Canevacci was too pleased. He stopped next to the body of the corporal and said to him, 'Hey! My friend, if you had learned how to command a patrol you wouldn't be here right now. When you're out on patrol, the commander, first of all, has to see…'

He was interrupted by the captain of the 9th. With a finger on his mouth and a thin thread of a voice, he invited him to keep quiet. In front of us, from the same direction in which the patrol had fallen, but closer, there was a sound, like the buzzing of people having an argument. The captain looked to the front. The sharpshooters aimed their rifles. The battalion commander and I also kept quiet and made our way silently up to the line to have a look.

The sound was coming from the trunk of a big fir tree, illuminated in patches by the sunlight shining through the treetops. Two squirrels were jumping along the trunk, a few meters off the ground. Quick and nimble, they chased each other, hid, chased each other again, and hid again. Short little shrieks, like uncontainable laughter, marked their encounters each time they launched themselves with little hops from opposite sides of the trunk, the one against the other. And every time they stopped themselves in a circle of sunlight on the trunk, they stood straight up on their hind legs and, using their paws like hands, appeared to be offering each other compliments, caresses, and congratulations. The sunlight shone brightly on their white bellies and the tufts of their tails, which stood straight up like two brushes.

One of the sharpshooters looked over at the captain of the 9th and muttered,

'Shall we shoot?'

'Are you crazy?' the captain answered in surprise. 'They're so cute.'

Captain Canevacci went back over to the line of dead bodies.

'The patrol commander must see and not be seen...,' he said, continuing his sermon to the Bosnian corporal.

EMILIO LUSSU

THE AUSTRIAN OFFICER
LIT A CIGARETTE

from *A Soldier on the Southern Front*

translated by Gregory Conti

T HERE WAS NO MORE TALK of new assaults. Calm seemed to have
settled in over the valley for a good long time. On one side and
the other, positions were reinforced. The pioneers worked through the
night. The little 37mm cannon continued to pester us, still invisible.
Whole days went by without it firing a shot, then, out of the blue, it
would open fire on a loophole and wound one of our lookouts.

My battalion was still on the line and we were waiting for the relief
battalion to replace us. I wanted to be able to give precise instructions
to the commander of the unit that would be taking our place. Day and
night, I had a special observation detail on duty, in the hope that the
flash of the cannon shot or the movements of its crew might give away
its position.

The night before the change of battalions, since the observation
details hadn't produced any results, I decided to go on observation myself,
accompanied by a corporal. The corporal had gone out frequently on
patrol and had a good feel for the terrain. The moonlight was shining
through the trees and, whenever the occasional rocket whizzed by,
the sudden flash of light made it look like the forest was moving. You
couldn't always tell if it was an illusion. It might well have been men
moving around out there and not just trees that, because of the speed of

the light from the rockets passing through their limbs, looked like they were moving. The two of us had gone out from the far left end of our company, at the point where our trenches were closest to the enemy trenches. Moving on all fours, we took cover behind a bush, about ten meters beyond our line and thirty or so meters from the Austrian line. There was a slight depression between our trenches and the bush, and it crowned a rise in the terrain dominating the trench in front of it.

We were stuck there, immobile, unable to decide whether to advance farther or stay put, when there seemed to be some movement in the enemy trenches, off to our left. There were no trees in front of that part of the trench so what we were seeing couldn't have been an optical illusion. Anyway, we realized that we were in a spot from where we could see into the enemy trench, right down the line. We couldn't do that from any other point. I decided to stay there all night so we would be able to observe the enemy trench coming to life at the first light of dawn. Whether the little cannon fired or not didn't matter anymore. What was essential was maintaining that unhoped-for observation point.

The bush and the rising terrain masked our presence and protected us so well that I decided to connect them directly to our line and make them into a permanent, hidden observation point. I sent the corporal back and had him bring back a sergeant in the pioneers, whom I instructed on how to do the work. In just a few hours, a communications passage had been dug between our trench and the bush. The noise of the work was covered by the noise of the shots going off up and down our line. The passageway wasn't deep, but it was possible for a man to crawl through it, and stay covered, even during the day. The dirt from the digging was carried back into the trench, and there were no visible signs of the excavation. Small, freshly cut tree branches and bushes completed the disguise.

Hunched behind the bush, the corporal and I lay in wait all through the night without managing to make out any signs of life in the enemy trench. But dawn made our wait worthwhile. First came the vague movement of some shadows in the passageways, then, inside the trench, some soldiers appeared carrying pots. This had to be the coffee detail. The soldiers passed by, one or two at a time, without bending their heads, sure as they were that they couldn't be seen, that the trenches and the lateral crossways protected them from observation and from possible raking gunfire from our line. I'd never seen anything like it before. The Austrians were right there, up close, almost at arm's length, calm and unawares, like so many passersby on a city sidewalk. A strange feeling came over me. Not wanting to talk, I squeezed the arm of the corporal, who was on my right, to communicate my amazement to him. He, too, was intent and surprised, and I could feel the trembling that came over him from holding his breath for so long. An unknown life was suddenly showing itself to our eyes. Those indomitable trenches, against which we had launched so many futile attacks, had nevertheless ended up seeming inanimate, like dismal empty structures, uninhabited by living beings, a refuge for mysterious and terrible ghosts. Now they were showing themselves to us, in their actual lived life. The enemy, the enemy, the Austrians, the Austrians!... There is the enemy and there are the Austrians. Men and soldiers like us, made like us, in uniform like us, who were now moving, talking, making themselves coffee, exactly as, at the same time, our comrades were doing behind us. Strange. Nothing like that had ever crossed my mind. Now they were making themselves coffee. Bizarre! So why shouldn't they be making themselves coffee? Why in the world did it seem so extraordinary to me that they should make themselves coffee? And, around ten or eleven, they would have their rations, exactly like us. Did I think perhaps that the enemy could live without drinking and eating? Of course not. So what was the reason for my surprise?

They were so close to us that we could count them, one by one. In the trench, between two crossways, there was a little round space where somebody, every now and again, stopped for a minute. You could tell they were talking, but the sound of their voices didn't reach us. That space must have been in front of a shelter that was bigger than the others, because there was more movement around it. The movement stopped when an officer arrived. You could tell he was an officer from the way he was dressed. He had shoes and gaiters made of yellow leather and his uniform looked brand new. Probably he had just arrived a few days ago, maybe fresh out of a military academy. He was very young and his blond hair made him look even younger. He couldn't have been any more than seventeen. Upon his arrival, the soldiers all scattered and there was nobody left in the round space but him. The coffee distribution was about to begin. All I could see was the officer.

I had been in the war since it began. Fighting in a war for years means acquiring the habits and the mind-set of war. This big-game hunting of men by men was not much different from the other big-game hunting. I did not see a man there. All I saw was the enemy. After so much waiting, so many patrols, so much lost sleep, he was coming out into the open. The hunt had gone well. Mechanically, without a thought, without any conscious intent to do so, but just like that, just from instinct, I grabbed the corporal's rifle. He gave it up to me and I took it. If we had been on the ground, as on the other nights, flat on our bellies behind the bush, I probably would have fired immediately, without wasting a second. But I was on my knees in the newly dug ditch, and the bush was in front of me like a shield in a shooting gallery. It was as though I were on a shooting range and I had all the time I wanted to take aim. I planted my elbows firmly on the ground and started to aim.

The Austrian officer lit a cigarette. Now he was smoking. That cigarette suddenly created a relationship between us. As soon as I saw his puff of smoke I felt the need to smoke. That desire of mine reminded me that I had some cigarettes too. In an instant, my act of taking aim, which had been automatic, became deliberate. I became aware that I was aiming, and that I was aiming at someone. My index finger, pressing on the trigger, eased off. I was thinking. I had been forced to think.

Sure, I was consciously fighting in the war and I justified that morally and politically. My conscience as a man and as a citizen was not in conflict with my duty as a soldier. The war, for me, was a dire necessity, terrible surely, but one whose demands I obeyed, as one of life's many thankless but inevitable necessities. So I was fighting in the war and I had soldiers under my command. Morally, then, I was fighting twice. I had already taken part in a lot of battles. That I should shoot at an enemy officer was, therefore, in the logic of things. Even more than that, I demanded of my soldiers that they stay alert on their watch and that they shoot accurately if the enemy came into their sights. Why wouldn't

I, now, shoot at that officer? It was my duty to shoot. I felt it was my duty. If I didn't feel it was my duty, it would be monstrous for me to continue fighting in the war and to make others do so as well. No, there was no doubt; it was my duty to shoot.

And yet I wasn't shooting. My thoughts worked themselves out calmly. I wasn't at all nervous. The previous night, before leaving the trench, I had slept four or five hours; I felt fine. Behind that bush, down in the ditch, I was not threatened by any danger. I couldn't have been more relaxed in a room in my own house, in my hometown.

Maybe it was that complete calm that drove off my war-fighting spirit. In front of me was an officer, young, unconscious of the looming danger. I couldn't miss. I could have taken a thousand shots at that distance without missing even one. All I had to do was pull the trigger and he would collapse to the ground. This certainty that his life depended on my will made me hesitant. I had a man in front of me. A man!

A man!

I could make out his eyes and the features of his face. The early morning light was getting brighter and the sun was peeking out from behind the mountain tops. To shoot like this, from a few steps away, at a man… like shooting a wild boar!

I started thinking that maybe I wasn't going to shoot. I thought: Leading a hundred men, or a thousand, in an assault against another hundred, or another thousand, is one thing. Taking a man, separating him from the rest of the men, and then saying, 'There, stand still, I'm going to shoot you, I'm going to kill you,' is another. It's a totally different thing. Fighting a war is one thing, killing a man is something else. To kill a man, like that, is to murder a man.

I'm not sure up until what point my thoughts proceeded logically. What's certain is that I had lowered the rifle and I wasn't shooting. Within me two consciousnesses had formed, two individualities, one hostile to the other. I said to myself, 'Hey! You're not going to be the one to kill a man like this!'

Even I, who lived through those moments, would not be able now to give an accurate description of that psychological process. There's a jump there that, today, I can't see clearly anymore. And I still ask myself how, having reached that conclusion, I could have thought to have someone else do what I myself didn't feel I could do in good conscience. I had the rifle on the ground, sticking under the bush. The corporal was pressing up against my side. I handed him the butt of the rifle and said to him, barely whispering, 'You know… like this… one man alone… I can't shoot. You, do you want to?'

The corporal took the rifle butt in hand and responded, 'Me neither.'

We made our way back to the trench on all fours. The coffee had already been distributed and we poured some for ourselves, too.

That night, just after sundown, the relief battalion replaced us.

∾

Emilio Lussu was born in 1890 in the province of Cagliari in Sardinia. After Italy's entry into the war, he was sent to the Asiago plateau to combat the Austrian spring offensive. He captures the insanity of the campaign in *A Soldier on the Southern Front* (aka *Sardinian Brigade*). Mutiny, treason, decimation, wire-cutters that don't cut – all is grist to Lussu's startling mill. A founder of the Partito Sardo d'Azione, Lussu opposed the rise of fascism and, in 1926, he shot dead in self-defence a fascist *squadristi*. He was sentenced to five years' imprisonment on the island of Lipari, from which he escaped… to fight in the Spanish Civil War. In the Second World War, Lussu collaborated with the British Special Operations Executive, hoping to get their support for an anti-fascist uprising in Sardinia; support that did not get Foreign Office approval. A leader of the successful Sardinian resistance against the Germans, Lussu founded the left-wing Partito d'Azione in 1943. He died in Rome in 1975. *A Soldier on the Southern Front* was made into the film, *Many Wars Ago* (*Uomini contro*), by Francesco Rosi in 1970: it stars the wonderful Gian Maria Volonté.

CARLO EMILIO GADDA

THE BATTLE OF THE ISONZO

from *Journals of War & Prison*

translated by Cristina Viti

ETAILS OF THE BATTLE OF THE ISONZO and of my capture, gathered here pro memoria, in case of any accusations. (Scrupulously factual narration for personal use). – I've no ink.

11. The night between the 11th & 12th I spent on a camp bed in my sleeping-bag, brought to me by private Giudici, in the hayloft of the shack-orderly room in Košec. By my side, sleeping on the floor, was private Sassella Stefano, still not fully recovered. On the evening of the 21st, I had a haircut & a shave (barber Bricalli Gelindo from Val Malenco), washed my feet in hot water prepared by Sassella & changed into fresh underwear. I also sorted out my luggage: my case I filled with underwear, woollens etc. to take with me, leaving my beloved books, my ordnance maps & a few clothes in the large case. This I left in the hayloft of the Košec shack – but then learnt that Donadoni had put it in the cellar of same. (Large case with ordnance maps in Košec; won't say any more about it). My precious journal, relating all my hopes & passion in Turin & on the Carso (small notebook bound in black leather with *Notes* written in gold on the cover) & my rail pass, as well as the last letters, I took with me in a small wooden case.

All the letters received on the Carso were left in the large case at Košec. So on the night between the 21st & 22nd of October 1917, having eaten well for the last time, I slept happily – everything sorted, everything paid for. My good soldier Sassella by my side, and inside me the happiness of finally heading for the front line, in full trust.

12. The 22nd of October 1917 was a cloudy day that later cleared up. We bid farewell to our colleagues of the 469th & to Favia del Core, who was going on leave. The mules were loaded up with our machine guns, some crates of ammo, the rucksacks of some soldiers who were dead tired (which left us no other choice), officers' luggage & orderly room crates. The 790th (Captain Boggia) filed out ahead, followed by the 470th. We set off, as I recall, around 9 am. The 470th company left part of the ammo, officers' luggage & orderly room supplies back in Košec with Capt. Donadoni. The rucksacks that could not be loaded onto the mules were left in the troop shack with Capt. Coderoni, to be fetched on the next day. Setting up of the baggage train in Drezenca in the place mentioned.

So we started out at 9 am for Krasji Vhr: the 470th with me & Cola (Cerrato Aldo already there), plus the 790th. Our marching orders said we were going to carry out works, & that was what we believed.

Written from fresh memory, in the concentration camp, between 13.00 & 16.00 on November 7th 1917. Rastatt, 7th November 1917. I give full assurance of the accuracy of dates & facts.

23. Meanwhile our company too was stricken by a grievous fact. Before Raineri left, around 11, De Candido, the Cadore gunsmith from the 3rd (a blond from the '95 contingent, freebooterish but good-natured & brave), and private Archetti Francesco from Siliano (an island on Lake Iseo) came bolting into the tunnel, shortly after I'd left the 3rd Section & as I was conferring with Cola about the connection to be established with the 2nd. Standing outside the cave, I yelled: 'What's with this running, you idiots!' in indignation, thinking they were running for shelter under the bombing. But the poor souls were shaken by the death of their comrade Zuppini Fedele (3rd Section). We questioned them. On both their coats, especially near the hem & on the back, large blood stains & a spurt of white matter that we immediately recognized as brains.

They reported that they were standing in the gun commander's shack, Sergeant Gandola handing out tobacco (which had come with the coffee), when a grenade went off clean before their faces, striking down private Zuppini & wounding Gandola. Both the news & the look of those two shook the other soldiers & grieved us officers. Having experienced Magnaboschi & the Carso, I wasn't that upset. Gandola arrived, his face wounded in several places by small splinters & bleeding heavily – nothing serious though. After the blast the good sergeant had counted all present & jumped back into the trench to check no one else was missing. He reported that no other men had died. I had already said, let's go & see if there are any wounded. Having learnt there were none, I waited for the fire to grow a bit less violent & then with De Candido Cesare, Baccoli (a bricklayer from Brescia), Bertoldi (a gunsmith from the Veneto) & another man with a stretcher we went out under the fire to recover the body. I believe no other Italian soldier will have been so quickly & caringly brought back by his officer & his comrades.

Stone after stone we reached the shack: the corpse was lying prone, completely beheaded, his neck hanging from the edge of the fill terrace where he was stretched out. The shack only had a few small holes in the roof, the ruberoid torn in places. I judged it to have been a small calibre grenade, a 47 or 65; the fact that all present had seen the flash of the blast & the blowing away of the dead man's head excluded the possibility of it being a simple spool. The grenade had smashed with full force into the head of the poor soldier. We lifted the corpse, blood & brains dripping down the wall. The palate & teeth, with some wisps of beard & the lower jaw, were connected to the severed neck by a filament of labial mucosa. We took the corpse to Cola's cave. In the presence of the quartermaster & the Comp. Commander, I took his money & belongings, a few futile things (pipe, cards received, pocket mirror & comb) & handed them to quartermaster Dell'Orto Luigi who made a list of them. The money came to 10.30 lira & was taken by Cola to be sent to the family. The corpse was left on the stretcher, just outside the cave, under a blanket, and was to be buried in the night as soon as the fire died out. Circumstances would not allow us to see to this work of mercy.

32. Our souls were in a state of anguished doubt, gradually giving way to the horrible certainty of imprisonment. Towards the mountains, over the river, the whistles of German officers ordering their men to

advance could clearly be heard. A few more gunshots, a few brief machine gun bursts, directed I think against someone attempting to escape. We were on this side of an impassable river, with no bridges: having broken through in Plezzo & Tolmino, the Germans had regrouped over the river: they were in Caporetto: they were in Drezenca already, having come down from the Mzrli. We were exhausted in body & spirit, downcast, starving. But worst of all was the impossibility to cross the Isonzo. So Cola & I thought it useless by now to keep any hopes alive: that would have been childish. De Candido got out waving a white cloth as Raineri & I wasted the weapons of my section, taking out & scattering away breeches, firing pins & other pieces. The grief, the humiliation, the weeping inside the soul at this act which was by now inevitable. The officer who in Turin had done his best to provide the army with an excellent, fully functional unit, who had the consolation of having succeeded in that effort, now forced to throw his weapons away like that, to leave them there in the shrubs! The remaining arms supply of the 3rd Section was likewise wasted. By wasting our weapons, we carried out a final duty – though the quantity of cannons, of material, of machine guns, supplies, ammo etc. left intact was such that our act was of no use whatsoever. I also threw my revolver away, & all dropped their guns there & then; after which, in orderly single file (Cola after De Candido, then all the other soldiers & lastly I at the back), we walked down through the scrub towards the footbridge: no one left there: a desert all around: everyone had already taken the inevitable step. Below the footbridge the brutal spate of the Isonzo licked away at a heap of rifles, Fiat machine guns, belts & other stuff left behind in the rout. On the other side the German guard was watching us as we walked across, checking we had no weapons. Other armed guards were keeping watch over some prisoners rounded up in the field above, the field where we regrouped at 13.20 on October 25. We crossed the footbridge one at a time, the first ones holding on to the metal cable on the left which served as a handrail. All crossed slowly, with great caution, so as not to slip into the river: the arced shape of the bridge forced me to sit down as my hobnailed boots were slipping on the wooden plank. About halfway across I stood up & carried on upright. I crossed over with a frown on my face: numbed & lost in thought more than anything else. Among the herd huddled in front of the German guards were some who did not hide their relief at having escaped the danger. I looked at the 1st guard, who had nothing remarkable about him: upright, serious, almost frowning. In the field, on a stone, a tin of meat that some prisoner had offered a German to ingratiate himself with him; as soon as this German turned round, I lifted the tin clean away & gobbled it with much hunger & a satanic joy. It was 13.20, 25 October 1917; the German guards all armed & with bayonets; in the field we regrouped & called the roll for the last time. Then Cola & I were ordered to start off with our attendants towards Caporetto, leaving our soldiers behind. With tears in my eyes & in my heart I took my leave, shaking hands with each of them. And slowly I set off with Cola; behind us Sassella, my dear & faithful orderly, & De Candido, picked there & then by Cola as an attendant because he spoke good German. Sassella was carrying my sack, De Candido had Cola's. I was looking around, still tempted to break for the mountains; but another German troop arrived just then from the road to Caporetto. First a hideous non-com, a cross between cop & assassin, spread out his troop on the edge of the field where we were standing & port-armed his 10 or so soldiers, dead tired & back-broken with their sacks. One looked shattered & begged for a little rest: red in the face, his neck swollen with heat, he was addressing his sergeant like Christ would his torturers. The sergeant, screaming, imposed obedience: he was shaking a stick & had a revolver. Then the troop climbed up the same way as the rest of them had: the mountain must be teeming with them. After the patrol, other soldiers climbed up with their officers. They were looking at us with curiosity but, at that time, none met us with any evil acts or words. All of them wore combat helmets, wide as straw hats, with no bolt, of a special shape. One second lieutenant, bent, gaunt & bespectacled like a Jewish merchant, asked Cola in German if there were many troops up ahead. After Cola (translated by De Candido) had replied that he didn't know, he saluted & cleared off, whistling for his men to follow.

33. We carried on towards Caporetto, coming across a few straggles of people here & there. When we got to the bridge, we saw that it had collapsed into the river's gorge with two lorries. The wrecked bridge

had halted a line of lorries heading for Drezenca (!!!!!). The narrow road prevented them from reversing. The lorries looked as if raped by the violence of the blast: there were also some tractors laden with various crates. By the bridge were the corpses of two chauffeurs, face down, their clothes & flesh torn, swollen, blotched with incipient putrefaction. And planks, crates, debris. That was how I saw for the 2nd time the beautiful bridge which I had admired as I crossed it a few days earlier with intense satisfaction of sense & feeling. Down below, the Isonzo was roaring away in its deep bed. A little way ahead a few officers' cases were scattered in the road: some victuals, some wine kegs – German loot by now. At the fork, where one road leads to Caporetto & the other carries on to the left along the river, we took a moment's rest. One of our soldiers was drunkenly tapping wine from an open keg, part of the contents spilling out to stain the dust of the road a dull red. Some others were calling one another to the feast, despite the yells & threats of the German guards: all that stuff belonged to the Germans by now. So I asked Sassella to please fill my canteen with wine & took a few greedy swigs. Cola & I, deprived of the most basic things, took some vests, a uniform & some bandages from an open case: nearby was a cart laden with clothing for the troop, & another with a reserve of food. Though I could foresee what hunger we would suffer, I preferred clothes to food. Wrong decision, for the clothes ended up with Sassella & the food we could have eaten on the way. But I was brain-numbed. Unfortunately I didn't think to fill up with biscuit & food. What atrocious hunger I am suffering now. My soldier Gobbi, a fine man who had carried himself very well, gave me a coat that he'd found in the road. I took it, since everything was German loot by now, but never used it, since it stayed with Sassella together with my sack.

We carried on across the left side of Caporetto in the mellow autumn weather. Here & there houses were already being occupied by the Germans who were setting up offices etc. Some civilians were still around, scavenging. Soldiers, some German some ours, the former armed, the latter unarmed, many of them, of both sides, reeling drunk, were wandering the streets. We also came across several cars, some that had belonged to our HQ's & had already been taken & put into service by the Germans, plus some cars of German make, order carriers, motor-cyclists etc. The troop, as we were told, was already advancing full on towards Cividale, and this was a new knife wound to my heart, though I was hoping that Cadorna would be able to fill the breach & push them back to the Isonzo.

At the entrance of the town, and in the houses as well, dead mules and corpses (including, inside one house, an officer's), all asphyxi-ated: some caught in the act of taking their masks off. In the fields, pits full of grenades (one I remember was a 305) but all considered nothing like Magnaboschi, let alone the Faiti. Fact is, those grenades fell on untrained people (chauffeurs, civilians, HQ's) & they were full of asphyxiating gases, causing more panic than damage. Two cocottes oozing syphilis & coarse servility begged De Candido to recommend them to some German officers. He & Cola asked them what their fate would be & stopped to chat: I was impatient & hurried them on – we carried on. I remember the shameless, cheerfully spoken words of the smaller of the two strumpets: 'Italian or German, it's all the same to us!' At another fork in the road, where one side continues to Tolmino & the other goes to Cividale, we felt the last wish to attempt an escape. We stopped for a moment & I asked: should we break for Cividale? The others did not think that feasible: the fear of any German reprisal against the four of us, wholly unarmed, also weighed against us trying. And the guard was coming. Onwards to Tolmino, then. Me, Cola, Sassella, De Candido.

So ended our life as soldiers & good soldiers, so ended the wildest dreams, the most generous hopes of our youth: carrying inside us the image of our torn-apart homeland & the shame of the vanquished, we began the calvary of harsh prison life, of hunger, of mistreatings, of dire need, of filth. But this is part of another chapter in my wretched life, & this martyrdom is of no interest to others.

Finished writing on December 10 1917 in Rastatt.

Widely recognized as one of the most important 20th-century Italian writers, **Carlo Emilio Gadda** was born in Milan in 1893. Following some reckless business decisions on the part of his father, and the latter's death in 1909, Gadda (who had started writing at fourteen, leaving high school in 1912 with top marks for literature) agreed to study engineering with the prospect of a career that would relieve the family's economic problems. Having joined the war effort as a volunteer, he was called to the front in June 1915 and served as a lieutenant in the Alpini arm until October 1917, when he was captured during the battle of the Isonzo and interned until January 1919 in two different German camps, including Rastatt. Gadda left an extraordinary record of those years in his *Journals of War & Prison*: part personal diary, part officer's logbook, part indictment of the criminal inadequacy of the higher levels of the military hierarchy, the journals, written by Gadda between the ages of twenty-two and twenty-six, show the poised balance of deep complexity and stark simplicity that would later characterize his famous novels, including *That Awful Mess on Via Merulana* and *Acquainted with Grief*. After his return to civilian life, Gadda worked as an engineer and curated a weekly cultural programme on national radio. He devoted himself fully to writing from 1955 until his death in Rome in 1973.

PREŽIHOV VORANC

AT DOBERDOB

from *Doberdob**

translated by Ana Jelnikar and Stephen Watts

T HE BATTALION WAS PUSHING its way through the dark of night towards the fiery line that lay ahead of it to the West. – Battalion might almost be putting it too strong, for the first company of a hundred to have left the barracks hardly even knew who they were any more. Nobody could care less about the fate of the other four companies and the more the darkness crept in, the more the thought of their comrades vanished from the consciousness of each and every one of them.

The day before, the Italian army's November offensive had started on the front. And then for two days the earth thundered under the assault of thousands upon thousands of shells, which the fiery jaws on the other bank of the river Soča were incessantly spitting out towards the East. For a whole day the battalion was able to eavesdrop on this hell, until on the second day at dusk the command came: 'Forward!'

A horrific sky of heavy, blackened clouds – out of which a fine and unpleasant rain was drizzling down – hung above the Vipava valley. In the East the shimmering dawn of the Front was reflected high up beneath the sky. Tufts of bursting, birthing cloud blazed in the East from

---

* Place names are given as they feature in their respective languages – so, for instance, Doberdob and Doberdò are the same place in different languages. How to name a place was after all part of what the war was about. (Ed.)

the shelling at the Front, while on the Western side, they sank down into frightening, elongated shadows. The whole of the East was one high fiery wall that pulsed with wide flaming to the South and the North. And low on the wall's horizon – the murky, treacherous silhouettes of some mountain range that seemed at each moment about to merge into the fiery glow of the blazing wall behind and above them...

The ground was slippery, though the road was still hard and straight, so it was possible to march on. The glow of the blaze cast its light across the open fields, easing their march through the night. The fields and the banks were cut across by tongues of dark, repressive shadow that stole their way there from god knows where. It was possible to see the surroundings: trees, white houses, some village with a tall, blunted belfry. But nobody was looking at the surroundings, the eyes of everyone were pinned on the fiery wall to the East.

There towards the wall the battalion was marching...

Eyes couldn't differentiate anything; legs, of their own accord, picked the way through. Even though the wall seemed so close you could touch it with your hand, it was still some kilometres off. The path along which the battalion marched wasn't yet in range of the artillery fire.

Štefanič pinned his gaze on Barfuss, who, head lowered, was marching alongside him.

'Was it also like this in Galicia?'

Barfuss raised his head, but didn't answer right away; his gaze first took in the fiery hell before him. And only after some time did he come back in a hollow voice:

'No, there was nothing, nothing like this in Galicia...'

Before they'd departed everyone'd got a flask of rum, with the instruction that no one was to touch it before they got to the trenches. But no sooner were they on their way than the smell of rum rose into the air. And the longer the route, the stronger was the smell. Until in the end it seemed that the whole company was being accompanied by a low rum-filled cloud.

Under the fiery wall, a bright silhouette of something flat and elongated shimmered.

'What's that over there?' Palir asked.

'St. Michaels' Hill...' somebody muttered from behind.

They hadn't managed to take two further steps when the silhouette again merged with the wall into a single shooting tongue of flame, and the earth under their legs shuddered ever more fiercely.

Suddenly Demark was gripped by a gulping insight; he laughed, as if an owl had hooted, and said:

'Up there's where we're headed.'

The hundred men had been walking for some three hours, if not more. Meanwhile they'd left the main road and turned toward the left bank of the river, which, despite the rain and autumn, was barely murmuring its way towards the fiery wall. She too it seems... From then on the path became slower, but safer. The soldiers soon noticed that the main road ahead was already under artillery fire. With every step they could more clearly hear the explosions that were detonating all around the road. Occasionally a shell strayed closer to them, though none fell on their side of the river. But the wailing of iron and stones was distinctly audible through the air.

A bit further on and the company quit the valley and took a left turn towards the Karst. The path was becoming worse and worse, slippery and full of pot holes. Since it wound along the bottom of large sink-holes and along their rims, it was becoming increasingly exhausting with every step. For a good hour the soldiers held out without as much as a murmur, but because there seemed no end to the path, consternation and displeasure began to break out all round.

'What kind of a world is this?' Segal was the first to grumble. He – who for sure was carrying a double load on his back – had the right to protest.

It was all getting too much for Pekol too, even though he had the patience of Jove. But Held, furious with himself, was quick to challenge him right away:

'Ach! It was better in Karlau, wasn't it?'

And in the meantime Holcman fell down a second time on the rocks. This time his neighbours had to help him clamber back on his legs. He could hardly stand up and cursed loudly:

'I'll be damned if anyone hollers at me: heart and hand for the country... I'll smash his face...'

Amun, Štefanič and the others laughed into their hands. Palir prodded Štefanič under the armpit and whispered:

'Do you hear that?'

'I hear it alright, I hear it!'

But they were also heard by sergeant Rode, who was marching up front and who clattered back in his crass & coarse voice.

'Shut it! Who's already shat their breeches?!'

No one could counter that. The hundred were getting ever closer to the line of fire. Even though the world through which they marched was lying below the one ahead of them, they could nonetheless make out the clangour of shells shattering against the rocky plateau towards which they were moving. Shards of hard matter were clattering back and forth with a disgusting noise around the dark sinkholes and without exception brought on feelings of sickening cold.

The Karst world was treacherous. When the men thought they were within a breath of reaching the expected plateau, where the Front's fire was spewing forth, a new depression showed up in front of them, into which they had to disappear. Whereas before they had been marching along in solitary desolation, now they suddenly stumbled upon people. The pathway led through an open camp. The basin provided excellent shelter, at least from the side that bordered on the East. In the semidarkness it was possible to make out columns of carts, the horses for the most part harnessed, some laying down beneath their wooden swivels, while others calmly chewed from their nose-bags. It seemed they didn't hear the artillery fire that ra-ta-tat-tatted right above the edge of the basin, or they were so used to it that it didn't bother them anymore.

Soldier-like figures also loomed up out of the dark, but none of them so much as looked at the marching 'hundred'. The soldiers clearly had their own chores to attend to. Something snagged up at the front and the line couldn't carry on. Barfuss took advantage of the situation and turned to the dark figure standing to his right:

'And where might we be now?'

'Where – at Doberdob!' The soldier's voice was both astonished and derisive.

Barfuss was expecting to hear something entirely different. When he could see that he wouldn't get anywhere like this, he began to think:

'You're safe here from the barrage.'

'Safe, until the shit starts hitting the basin.'

The soldier disappeared into the dark. Meanwhile they started moving again up front and Rode's voice could be heard: 'Left!' and no sooner had he said that, than they had to march on. Now they found it much easier to progress. It seemed they had turned directly towards the fiery plateau. Even so their feet did not protest. They'd had enough of this wandering around in the Karst labyrinth! But instead of reaching the plateau, the line descended into another, even deeper and darker basin. This presumably was even safer than the first one, since from somewhere out of the darkness at the bottom there were some small lights shimmering. They went past a steep wall and saw two brightly-lit entrances that were only half-covered. A soldier was on watch from one of them. Palir quickly asked him:

'Have you got water?'

The soldier was a Croat and luckily could understand.

'Water? You must be joking!'

Strange and somewhat corpse-like was the sound of these words in the night. Again something had stuck, up at the front. Half the soldiers slumped down on the stony ground. The figure of one crawled up from out of the dark background. When he came right up to the line, it became apparent that his head was bandaged in white. A wounded man…

'Have you seen the hospital carts?' he asked in a barely audible, exhausted voice. He was German.

'What hospital carts?' three, four voices asked in surprise.

'But you're coming from the back-country, aren't you?'

Oh, yes, now they understood the question.

'No, we haven't seen them…'

A pause. Beside the wounded German other figures soon appeared. They were all bandaged.

'You waiting for transport?'

'Yes.'

'Are there many of you?' a voice from somewhere up ahead asked. It seemed to be Segal's.

'Many. But even more are still there at the front…'

The questioners fell silent as if on command. Their throats were tongue-tied. Only then did they notice the stench of bandaging, iodine, Lizol and something else that they hadn't smelt before and that had a deep, unpleasant odour. Like clotted blood, like rotting flesh… In the meantime their eyes became accustomed to the dark and slowly they realized that they were at the edge of the scattered stalls of the field hospital. The wounded lay in front, in the open air, even though it was drizzling. Most likely those lightly wounded who were waiting to be transported. Out at the back were some tents and through the cracks lights shimmered, and through the blurry reflection, moving figures of the hospital corps could be seen. Yes, there a canvas cover with the red cross was fluttering as well… Didn't they hear some kind of groaning too? But it was impossible to make that out clearly, since the artillery went on with its constant bombardment.

Rode's command got them on their feet again. As they were going round the depression, they could hear a commanding voice behind their backs:

'The carts won't be coming yet. Whoever's able, should go back on foot!'

The moans and cursing the command provoked soon gave way to the sound of boots clattering against the stone ground. To the right someone stepped out of the dark, vertical wall with a pocket torch. Turning to the nearby tent, he shouted:

'Major Farkaš just croaked it.'

At that a warning voice came back:

'Switch the light off, for god's sake!'

When the torch had been turned off, the same voice said:

'Right you are! Then throw him out, so there'll be space for others.'

And the bandaging quarters disappeared behind the line of soldiers. Silently each one, lost in his own thoughts, marched on. In fact nobody was thinking any more. A blunt, suffocating feeling prevailed. The soldiers only felt their exhaustion and how much they craved rest. Is there no end to the slog? Where are we pushing towards anyway? Along the path sink-holes came one after another, here and there the edges overgrown with low bushes. Who knows if these were gorge-slits made by the shells or if it was the work of nature. They stumbled across a line of mules. The animals were marching slowly but for all that very sure-footedly. One animal snorted down its nostrils and Demark's face was spattered by wet saliva. He felt it as a warm, mute greeting and didn't even bother to wipe it off… From some sink-hole came the smell of coffee with rum. That was hard to take as it aggravated the already unbearable thirst. Everyone was relieved when the intoxicating smell disappeared.

It was starting to get lighter up ahead and the racket was becoming more discernible with each step taken. Because of the downpour of artillery fire it was hard to make out each and every explosion, but it all pointed towards the fact that they were approaching the fiery belt. Exactly at the moment when everyone started instinctively to crouch down, the head of the line changed direction; and they turned first right and then left, and then began to descend again until, against all expectation, they heard Rode's voice saying:

'We have arrived?!'

At that moment they saw an elongated, dark shadow against the face of the hill. It was an ordinary, make-shift shelter, cut at an angle into the hill-face and covered with a short roof, from which wet tarpaulins hung down to the ground. The first ones to get there drew the canvas aside and from under their feet wet hay greeted them. Bed & rest? Yes, bed…

Their first impressions made them anxious. This can't be a reliable shelter! But no sooner had they thought that, than they were overcome by another thought: no cannon can be fired at this place! And then finally: high-command must know where they are putting their soldiers.

'Lie down and sleep!'

Exhausted bodies fell on the rotten hay and soon the shelter was as quiet as if it were empty. And straight after that, day started to shimmer in the East.

⌒

Prežihov Voranc* was born, son of a tenant farmer, in 1893 in the village of Podgora in the Carinthian uplands of Slovenia close to the present-day Austrian border, at the time of his birth deep within the Austro-Hungarian Empire. His writing life was framed by the First World War, where he fought on the Italo-Slovenian front line, notably the Isonzo at Doberdò; and by the rise of Slovene nationalism with the post-war collapse of the empire. His writing is marked by a rigorous but rich linguistic intensity, most clearly in his prose depictions of the poverty and class violence of the rural, farming life he was part of, and the effects of this on individual fate. Between the wars he was actively involved in the Communist Party of Yugoslavia and was imprisoned on a number of occasions. In 1944 he was arrested and interned in Sachsenhausen and Mauthausen. His best work was written in the mid to late 1930s, and it was then that his work began to be more widely known. First published in Slovenian in 1941, the novel *Doberdob* – from which the extract here is taken – is a vivid description of the savagery of war. Voranc died in 1950.

---

*He was born Lovro Kuhar, Prežihov Voranc being the nom de plume he later adopted.

WYNDHAM LEWIS

THE ROMANCE OF WAR

from *Blasting and Bombardiering*

ARRIVAL AT 'THE FRONT' for us was not unlike arrival at a big Boxing Match, or at a Blackshirt Rally at Olympia. The same sinister expectancy, but more sinister and more electric, the same restless taciturnity of stern-faced persons assembling for a sensational and bloody event, their hearts set on a knock-out. Somebody else's, of course.

We arrived at railhead at night and a battle was in progress. For a long time, as we moved slowly forward in our darkened coaches, the sound of guns had been getting louder and nearer. There was no moon or stars − all lights had been turned down for the performance. Only the unseen orchestra thundered away, before an unseen stage. We had to imagine the actors which we knew were there, crouching in their sticky labyrinths.

From the crowded carriage-windows, at last, sudden bursts of dull light could be discerned, and last of all an authentic flash had been visible, but still far away − angry and red, like a match struck and blown out again immediately.

We left the train, and finally we reached, I forget how, the fringes of this battle. We reached it unexpectedly. We were collected upon a road, I seem to think. Perhaps we were waiting for lorries to take us to billets − for we of course were not going into action then. We were not for this battle. We had no guns either. They could not be made quickly enough.

We were just the *personnel* of a battery, with no guns, who had come to stand-by, or be parcelled out as reinforcements.

With great suddenness – as we stood, very impressed as newcomers in the midst of this pandemonium – in a neighbouring field a battery of large howitzers began firing. After this particular picture I can remember nothing at all. It is so distinct everything in its neighbourhood is obliterated. I can only remember that in the air full of violent sound, very suddenly there was a flash near at hand, followed by further flashes, and I could see the gunners moving about as they loaded again. They appeared to be 11-inch guns – very big. Out of their throats had sprung a dramatic flame, they had roared, they had moved back. You could see them, lighted from their mouths, as they hurled into the air their great projectile, and sank back as they did it. In the middle of the monotonous percussion, which had never slackened for a moment, the tom-toming of interminable artillery, for miles round, going on in the darkness, it was as if someone had exclaimed in your ear, or something you had supposed inanimate had come to life, when the battery whose presence we had not suspected went into action.

So we plunged immediately into the romance of battle. But all henceforth was romance. All this culminated of course in the scenery of the battlefields, like desolate lunar panoramas. That matched the first glimpses of the Pacific, as seen by the earliest circumnavigators.

Need I say that there is nothing so romantic as war? If you are 'a romantic', you have not lived if you have not been present at a battle, of that I can assure you.

I am very sorry to have to say this. Only a care for truth compels me to avow it. I am not a romantic – though I perfectly understand romance. And I do not like war. It is under compulsion that I stress the exceedingly romantic character of all the scenes I am about to describe.

If your mind is of a romantic cast, there is nothing for it, I am afraid. The likelihood that you will get your head blown off cannot weigh with you for a moment. You must not miss a war, if one is going! You cannot afford to miss that experience.

It is commonly remarked that 'there is no romance in modern war.' That is absurd, I am sorry to have to say.

It has frequently been contended that Agincourt, or even Waterloo with its 'thin red line' and its Old Guard of Napoleonic veterans, was 'spectacular': whereas modern war is 'drab and unromantic'. Alas! that is nonsense. To say that is entirely to misunderstand the nature of romance. It is like saying that love can only be romantic when a figure as socially-eminent and beautiful as Helen of Troy is involved. That, of course, has nothing to do with it whatever! It is most unfortunate: but men are indifferent to physical beauty or obvious physical splendour, where their emotions are romantically stimulated. Yes, romance is the enemy of beauty. That hag, War, carries it every time over Helen of Troy.

The truth is, of course, that it is not what you *see*, at all, that makes an event romantic to you, but what you *feel*. And in war, as you might expect, you feel with considerable intensity.

The misunderstanding goes even deeper than that, however. Knights in armour, with plumes and lances, are not, even in the visual sense, the most *romantic* subject-matter for a romantic painter.

You only have to think a moment: the dark night, with the fearful flashing of a monstrous cannonade – all the things that do not come into the picture, which *are not seen*, in other words, but which are suggested in its darkest shadows – what could be more technically 'romantic' than that, if it is romance that we must talk about?

But even if the pictorial subject-matter were insignificant, it would still be the same thing.

Romance is partly what you see but it is much more what you feel. I mean that *you* are the romance, far more than the romantic object. By definition, romance is always inside and not outside. It is, as we say, subjective. It is the material of magic. It partakes of the action of a drug.

Place a man upon the highest passes of the Andes, and what he *sees* is always what he feels. But when *on joue sa vie*, it is not so much the grandeur of the spectacle of destruction, or the chivalrous splendour of the appointments, as the agitation in the mental field within, of the organism marked down to be destroyed, that is impressive. It is that that produces 'the light that never was on land or sea', which we describe as 'romance'. *Anything* upon which that coloration falls is at once trans-figured. And the source of light is within your own belly.

★

Of course it would be impossible to overstate the contribution of the guns to these great romantic effects. Even in such an essentially romantic context as war, they are startlingly 'romantic' accessories, and help to heighten the effect.

It is they who provide the orchestral accompaniment. It is they who plough up the ground till it looks literally 'like nothing on earth'. It is they who transform a smart little modern township, inside an hour, into a romantic ruin, worthy of the great Robert himself, or of Claude Lorrain. They are likewise the purveyors of 'shell-shock', that most dramatic of ailments. And lastly, they give the most romantic and spectacular wounds of all – a bullet-wound, even a dum-dum, is child's-play to a wound inflicted by a shell-splinter.

I have slept soundly through scores of full-dress bombardments. It is very few people who don't, in a war of positions, where bombardments are almost continuous. Through a long artillery preparation for an Attack – a hoped-for 'breakthrough', with the enemy retaliating at full blast – in the very thick of the hubbub, with things whizzing and roaring all round – I have slept for hours together as peacefully as if I were in a London garden suburb.

Rapidly one ceases to notice this orchestra. But although one forgets about it, one would miss it if it were not there. These are the kettledrums of death that you are hearing. And you would soon know the difference if they stopped.

WYNDHAM LEWIS

POLITICAL EDUCATION UNDER FIRE

from *Blasting and Bombardiering*

I DON'T THINK ARTISTS are any more important than bricklayers or stockbrokers. But I dislike the 'hearty' artist (who pretends he isn't one but a stockbroker) more than the little aesthete. I felt less inclined to immolate myself in defence of Mayfair and the 'stately homes of Old England', the more I pondered over it. I was only concerned at the idea of deserting my companions in misfortune.

When I had first attested, I was talking to Ford Madox Hueffer about Gaudier's death. I'd said it was too bad. Why should Gaudier die, and a 'Bloomsbury' live? I meant that *fate* ought to have seen to it that that didn't happen. It was absurd.

It was absurd, Ford agreed. But there it was, he seemed to think. He seemed to think *fate* was absurd. I am not sure he did not think Gaudier was absurd.

The 'Bloomsburies' were all doing war-work of 'national importance', down in some downy English county, under the wings of powerful pacifist friends; pruning trees, planting gooseberry bushes, and haymaking, doubtless in large sunbonnets. One at least of them, I will not name him, was disgustingly robust. All were of military age. All would have looked well in uniform.

One of course 'exempted' himself, and made history by his witty handling of the tribunals. That was Lytton Strachey. He went round to the tribunal with an air-cushion, which, upon arrival, he blew up, and sat down on, amid the scandalized silence of the queue of palpitating petitioners. His spidery stature was reared up bravely, but his dank beard drooped, when his name was called; and he made his famous retort. 'What,' sternly asked one of the judges, 'would you do Mr. Strachey, if you discovered a German preparing to outrage your sister?' and Strachey without hesitation replied: 'I – would – place – myself – *between* – them!'

But the 'Bloomsburies' all exempted themselves, in one way or another. Yet they had money and we hadn't; ultimately it was to keep them fat and prosperous – or thin and prosperous, which is even worse – that other people were to risk their skins. Then there were the tales of how a certain famous artist, of military age and militant bearing, would sit in the Café Royal and addressing an admiring group back from the Front, would exclaim: '*We* are the civilization for which you are fighting!'

But Ford Madox Hueffer looked at me with his watery-wise old elephant eyes – a little too crystal-gazing and claptrap, but he knew his stuff – and instructed me upon the very temporary nature of this hysteria. I was too credulous! I *believe* that he tipped me the wink. He was imparting to me I believe a counsel of commonsense.

'When this War's over,' he said, 'nobody is going to worry, six months afterwards, what you did or didn't do in the course of it. One month after it's ended, it will be forgotten. Everybody will want to forget it – it will be bad form to mention it. Within a year disbanded "heroes" will be selling matches in the gutter. No one likes the ex-soldier – if you've lost a leg, more fool you!'

'Do you think that?' I said, for he almost made my leg feel sorry for itself.

'Of course,' he answered. 'It's always been the same. After all wars that's what's happened.'

This worldly forecast was verified to the letter. There is no better propaganda against war, I think, than to broadcast such information as this (though that was not Ford's intention: he was very keen on the War). The callousness of men and women, once the fit of hysteria is over, has to be seen to be believed – if you are prone to give humanity the benefit of the doubt, and expect some 'decency' where you won't find it. They regard as positive enemies those whom a war has left broken and penniless. The 'saviours' and 'heroes' get short shrift, upon the Peace Front. No prisoners are taken there! Why, in such a 'patriot' country as France, men have, since the War, been promoted to the highest offices of State, who had been convicted of treason and 'traffic with the enemy'. Sir Roger Casement would be an O.B.E. if not a Knight of the Garter, had he not been of a romantic and suicidal turn and got himself shot.

It has been my firm intention to talk no politics in this book. I will not refer to what went on in my own mind as a result of these experiences, more than an indication, just here and there. I have spoken nowhere of the men, while I was in France. It is impossible to say anything about that. If one is not to talk politics, one has to keep one's mouth shut. All the fancy-dress nonsense of 'officers' and 'men', under the snobbish English system, is a subject distinct from war, and yet very much involved with it.

As an officer it was my unwelcome task to read great numbers of private letters. Naturally the officers would among themselves discuss with smiles the burning endearments, or the secrets of his poor little domestic economy, revealed by his letters, of this man or that. These rough and halting communings, of the most private sort, were passing through our hands every day. Yet most of the censors were, as literary artists, of not a very different clay to those who had to submit to this humiliating censorship.

My own thoughts I kept strictly to myself. I preserved my *anonymity*, in the sense in which I have already explained that principle. When I am dressed up in a military uniform I look like other people, though at other times I very easily depart from the canon, I find. One or two of my mess-mates sniffed at me suspiciously. But on the whole I was a masterpiece of conformity. – I am physically very robust. It is easy for me to go to sleep. And conformity is of course *a sleep*.

I started the war a different man to what I ended it. More than anything, it was a *political* education. I am slow to learn, but quick to understand. As day by day I sidestepped and dodged the missiles that were hurled at me, and watched other people doing so, I became a politician. I was not then the accomplished politician I am to-day. But the seeds were there.

I had no sentimental aversion to war. A violent person, who likes the taste of blood, as another does the taste of wine, likes war. I was indifferent. But this organized breakdown in our civilized manners must have a rationale, in a civilized age. You must supply the civilized man with *a reason,* much as he has to have his cocktail, flytox, and ice-water.

I, along with millions of others, was standing up to be killed. Very well: but *who* in fact was it, who was proposing to kill or maim me? I developed a certain inquisitiveness upon that point. I saw clearly that it was not my German opposite number. He, like myself, was an instrument. That we were all on a fool's errand had become plain to many of us, for, beyond a certain point, victory becomes at the best a Pyrrhic victory, and that point had been reached before Passchendaele started.

The scapegoat-on-the-spot did not appeal to me. So I had not even the consolation of 'blaming the Staff', after the manner of Mr. Sassoon – of cursing the poor little general-officers.

> *'Good morning, good morning,' the General said,*
> *As we passed him one day as we went up the line.*
> *But the lads that he spoke to are most of them dead*
> *And we're cursing his staff for incompetent swine.*
> *'He's a cheery old sport!' muttered Harry to Jack.*
> *'But he's done for them both with his plan of attack.'*

That was too easy and obvious. It amazes me that so many people should accept that as satisfactory. The incompetent general was clearly such a very secondary thing compared with the incompetent, or unscrupulous, politician, that this conventional 'grouse' against the imperfect strategy of the military gentleman directing operations in the field seemed not only unintelligent but dangerously misleading. 'Harry and Jack' were killed, not by the General, but by the people, whoever they were, responsible for the war.

Nor could I obtain much comfort from cursing my mother and father, grandmother and grandfather, as Mr. Aldington or the Sitwells did. For it was not quite certain that we were not just as big fools as our not very farsighted forebears. There was not much sense in blaming the ancestors of the community to which I belonged for the murderous nonsense in which I found myself, up to the neck, it seemed to me.

On the other hand, as it was not war *per se* that I objected to, I was not forgetful of the fact that most wars had been stupid, and had only benefited a handful of people. No one objects to being killed, if the society to which he belongs, and its institutions, are threatened, we can assume. But any intelligent man objects to being killed (or bankrupted) for *nothing*. That is insulting.

Where was I then? If you have a little politics you will say, perhaps, is *any* society worth being killed, or ruined, for? Is the Sovereign State to be taken seriously? Are any merely national institutions so valuable, so morally or intellectually valid, that we should lay down our lives for them, as a matter of course?

I could not answer that question by a mere yes or no. Naturally I can imagine a State that it would be your duty to die for. There are many principles also, which *might* find themselves incarnated in a State, which I personally consider matters of life and death. But whether the machine-age has left any State intact in such a way as to put men under a moral or emotional compulsion to die for it, is a matter I am unable to discuss. That would 'take us too far,' as the valuable cliché has it.

And too far I am not going upon those tortuous roads. This is a plain tale of mere surface events. I am not out to do more than limn the action. I am keeping out the pale cast of thought as far as possible.

⟜

Wyndham Lewis was born in Nova Scotia, Canada, in 1882. He died in London in 1957. Already an influential artist before the war, Lewis served on the Western Front from 1916 to 1918 as a battery officer. After the Third Battle of Ypres in 1917, he was appointed official war artist for both the Canadian and British governments. He wrote the autobiographical *Blasting and Bombardiering* in 1937. Like many of the modernist artists of the time, he was enamoured with the speed and noise of war. The Futurists and Marinetti wanted 'words to explode like shells, or ache like wounds' and, like them, Lewis was seduced by the 'romance of war':

> In the middle of the monotonous percussion, which had never slackened for a moment, the tom-toming of interminable artillery, for miles around, going on in the darkness, it was as if someone had exclaimed in your ear, or something you had supposed inanimate had come to life, when the battery whose presence we had not suspected went into action.

Although he was fully aware of the horrors of battle, it was the revolutionary aesthetic of war which Lewis sought to convey in his writing and painting. Warts and all, he was an artist of his time.

RICHARD ALDINGTON

CANNON-FODDER

from *Death of a Hero*

I DON'T KNOW IF GEORGE was aware of all this, because we never
discussed it. There were numbers of things you prudently didn't discuss
in those days; you never knew who might be listening and 'report'. I
myself was twice arrested, as a civilian, for wearing a cloak and looking
foreign, and for laughing in the street; I was under acute suspicion for
weeks in one battalion because I had a copy of Heine's poems and
admitted that I had been abroad; in another I was suspected of not being
myself, God knows why. That was nothing compared with the persecution endured by D. H. Lawrence, probably the greatest living English
novelist, and a man of whom – in spite of his failings – England should
be proud.

I do know that George suffered profoundly from the first day of the
War until his death at the end of it. He must have realised the awfulness
of the Cant and degradation, for he occasionally talked about the yahoos
of the world having got loose and seized control, and, by Jove! he was
right. I shan't attempt to describe the sinister degradation of English
life in the last two years of the War: for one thing, I was mostly out of
England; and for another, Lawrence has done it once and for all in the
chapter called 'The Nightmare' in his book *Kangaroo*.*

---

*See pp 32–41 in this volume.

In George's case, the suffering which was common to all decent men and women was increased and complicated and rendered more torturing by his personal problems, which somehow became related to the War. You must remember that he did not believe in the alleged causes for which the War was fought. He looked upon the War as a ghastly calamity, or a more ghastly crime. They might talk about their idealism, but it wasn't convincing. There wasn't the *élan,* the conviction, the burning idealism which carried the ragged untrained armies of the First French Republic so dramatically to Victory over the hostile coalitions of the Kings. There was always the suspicion of dupery and humbug. Therefore, he could not take part in the War with any enthusiasm or conviction. On the other hand, he saw the intolerable egotism of setting up oneself as a notable exception or courting a facile martyrdom of *rouspétance.* Going meant one more little brand in the conflagration; staying out meant that some other, probably physically weaker, brand was substituted. His conscience was troubled before he was in the Army, and equally troubled afterwards. The only consolation he felt was in the fact that you certainly had a worse and a more dangerous time in the line than out of it.

As a matter of fact, I never really 'got' George's position. He hated talking about the subject, and he had thought about it and worried about it so much that he was quite muddle-headed. It seemed to involve the whole universe, and his attempts to express his point of view would wander off into discussions about the Greek city-states or the principles of Machiavelli. He was frankly incoherent, which meant a considerable inner conflict. From the very beginning of the War he had got into the habit of worrying, and this developed with alarming rapidity. He worried about the War, about his own attitude to it, about his relations with Elizabeth and Fanny, about his military duties, about everything. Now, 'worry' is not 'caused' by an event; it is a state which seizes upon any event to 'worry' over. It is a form of neurasthenia, which may be induced in a perfectly healthy mind by shock and strain. And for months and months he just worried and drifted.

When Elizabeth decided, somewhere towards the end of 1914, that the time had come when the principles of Freedom must be put into practice in the case of herself and Reggie, and duly informed George, he acquiesced at once. Perhaps he was so sick at heart that he was indifferent; perhaps he was only loyally carrying out the agreement. What surprised me was that he did not take that opportunity of telling her about Fanny. But he was apparently quite convinced that she knew. It was therefore an additional shock when he found out that she didn't know, and a still greater shock to see how she behaved. He suffered an obnubilation of the intellect in dealing with women. He idealised them too much. When I told him with a certain amount of bitterness that Fanny was probably a trollop who talked 'freedom' as an excuse, and that Elizabeth was probably a conventional-minded woman who talked 'freedom' as in the former generation she would have talked Ruskin and Morris politico-aestheticism, he simply got angry. He said I was a fool. He said the War had induced in me a peculiar resentment against women – which was probably true. He said I did not understand either Elizabeth or Fanny – how could I possibly understand two people I had never seen and have the cheek to try to explain them to *him,* who knew them so well? He said I was far too downright, over-simplified, and *tranchant* in my judgments, and that I didn't – probably couldn't – understand the finer complexities of people's psychology. He said a great deal more, which I have forgotten. But we came as near to a quarrel as two lonely men could, when they knew they had no other companion. This was in the Officers' Training Camp in 1917, when George was already in a peculiar and exacerbated state of nerves. After that, I made no effort at any sort of ruthless directness, but just allowed him to go on talking. There was nothing else to do. He was living in a sort of double nightmare – the nightmare of the War and the nightmare of his own life. Each seemed inextricably interwoven. His personal life became intolerable because of the War, and the War became intolerable because of his own life. The strain imposed on him – or which he imposed on himself – must have been terrific. A sort of pride kept him silent. Once when it was my turn to act as commander of the other cadets, I was taking them in company drill. George was right-hand man in the front rank of No. 1 Platoon, and I glanced at him to see that he was keeping direction properly. I was startled by the expression on his face – so hard, so fixed, so despairing, so defiantly agonised. At mess – we ate at tables in sixes – he hardly ever spoke except to utter some banality in an effort to be amiable, or some veiled sarcasm which sped harmlessly over the heads of those for whom it was intended. He sneered a little too openly at the coarse, obscene talk about tarts and square-pushing, and was too obviously revolted by water-closet wit. However, he wasn't openly disliked. The others just thought him a rum bloke, and left him pretty much alone.

Probably what had distressed him most was the row between Elizabeth and Fanny. With the whole world collapsing about him, it seemed quite logical that the Triumphal Scheme for the Perfect Sex Relation should collapse too. He did not feel the peevish disgust of the reforming idealist who makes a failure. But in the general disintegration of all things he had clung very closely to those two women; too closely, of course. But they had acquired a sort of mythical and symbolical meaning for him. They resented and deplored the War, but they were admirably detached from it. For George they represented what hope of humanity he had left; in them alone civilisation seemed to survive. All the rest was blood and brutality and persecution and humbug. In them alone the thread of life remained continuous. They were two small havens of civilised existence, and alone gave him any hope for the future. They had escaped the vindictive destructiveness which so horribly possessed the spirits of all right-thinking people. Of course, they were persecuted; that was inevitable. But they remained detached, and alive. Unfortunately, they did not quite realise the strain under which he was living, and did not perceive the widening gulf which was separating the men of that generation from the women. How could they? The friends of a person with cancer haven't got cancer. They sympathise, but they aren't in the horrid category of the doomed. Even before the Elizabeth–Fanny row he was subtly drifting apart from them against his will, against his desperate efforts to remain at one with them. Over the men of that generation hung a doom which was admirably if somewhat ruthlessly expressed by a British Staff Officer in an address to subalterns in France: 'You are the War generation. You were born to fight this War, and it's got to be won – we're determined you shall win it. So far as you are concerned as individuals, it doesn't matter a tinker's damn whether you are killed or not. Most probably you will be killed, most of you. So make up your minds to it.'

That extension of the Kiplingesque or kicked-backside-of-the-Empire principle was something for which George was not prepared. He resented it, resented it bitterly, but the doom was on him as on all the young men. When 'we' had determined that they should be killed, it was impious to demur.

After the row, the gap widened, and when once George had entered the army it became complete. He still clung desperately to Elizabeth and Fanny, of course. He wrote long letters to them trying to explain himself, and they replied sympathetically. They were the only persons he wanted to see when on leave, and they met him sympathetically. But it was useless. They were gesticulating across an abyss. The women were still human beings; he was merely a unit, a murder-robot, a wisp of cannon-fodder. And he knew it. They didn't. But they felt the difference, felt it as a degradation in him, a sort of failure. Elizabeth and Fanny occasionally met after the row, and made acid-sweet remarks to each other. But on one point they were in agreement – George had degenerated terribly since joining the army, and there was no knowing to what preposterous depths of Tommydom he might fall.

'It's quite useless,' said Elizabeth; 'he's done for. He'll never be able to recover. So we may as well accept it. What was rare and beautiful in him is as much dead now as if he were lying under the ground in France.'

And Fanny agreed...

RICHARD ALDINGTON

A TIMELESS CONFUSION

from *Death of a Hero*

FOR WINTERBOURNE THE BATTLE was a timeless confusion, a chaos of noise, fatigue, anxiety, and horror. He did not know how many days and nights it lasted, lost completely the sequence of events, found great gaps in his conscious memory. He did know that he was profoundly affected by it, that it made a cut in his life and personality. You couldn't say there was anything melodramatically startling, no hair going grey in a night, or never smiling again. He looked unaltered; he behaved in exactly the same way. But, in fact, he was a little mad. We talk of shell-shock, but who wasn't shell-shocked, more or less? The change in him was psychological, and showed itself in two ways. He was left with an anxiety complex, a sense of fear he had never experienced, the necessity to use great and greater efforts to force himself to face artillery, anything explosive. Curiously enough, he scarcely minded machine-gun fire, which was really more deadly, and completely disregarded rifle-fire. And he was also left with a profound and cynical discouragement, a shrinking horror of the human race...

A timeless confusion. The runners scattered outside their billet and made for the officers' cellar through the falling shells, dodging from one broken house or shell-hole to another. Winterbourne, not yet unnerved, calmly walked straight across and arrived first. Evans took him aside:

'We're going up as a company, with orders to support and co-operate with the Infantry. Try to nab me a rifle and bayonet before we go over.'

'Very good, sir.'

Outside was an open box of S.A.A., and they each drew two extra bandoliers of cartridges, which they slung around their necks.

They moved off in sections, filing along the village filled with fresh debris and ruins re-ruined. It was snowing. They came on two freshly-killed horses. Their close-cropped necks were bent under them, with great glassy eyeballs starting with agony. A little further on was a smashed limber with the driver dead beside it.

In the trench they passed a batch of about forty German unarmed, in steel helmets. They looked green-pale and were trembling. They shrank against the side of the trench as the English soldiers passed, but not a word was said to them.

The snowstorm and the smoke drifting back from the barrage made the air as murky as a November fog in London. They saw little, did not know where they were going, what they were doing or why. They lined a trench and waited. Nothing happened. They saw nothing but wire and snowflakes and drifting smoke, heard only the roar of the guns and the now sharper rattle of machine-guns. Shells dropped around them. Evans was looking through his glasses, and cursing the lack of visibility. Winterbourne stood beside him, with his rifle still slung on his left shoulder.

They waited. Then Major Thorpe's runner came with a message. Apparently he had mistaken a map reference and brought them to the wrong place.

They plodged off through the mud, and lined another trench. They waited.

Winterbourne found himself following Evans across what had been No Man's Land for months. He noticed a skeleton in British uniform, caught sprawling in the German wire. The skull still wore a sodden cap and not a steel helmet. They passed the bodies of British soldiers killed that morning. Their faces were strangely pale, their limbs oddly bulging with strange fractures. One had vomited blood.

They were in the German trenches, with many dead bodies in field grey. Winterbourne and Evans went down into a German dug-out. Nobody was there, but it was littered with straw, torn paper, portable cookers, oddments of forgotten equipment, and cigars. There were French tables and chairs with human excrement on them.

They went on. A little knot of Germans came toward them holding up their shaking hands. They took no notice of them, but let them pass through.

The barrage continued. Their first casualty was caused by their own shells dropping short.

★

Major Thorpe sent Winterbourne and another man with a written duplicate message to Battalion Headquarters. They went back over the top, trying to run. It was impossible. Their hearts beat too fast, and their throats were parched. They went blindly at a jog-trot, slower in fact than a brisk walk. They seemed to be tossed violently by the bursting shells. The acrid smoke was choking. A heavy roared down beside Winterbourne and made him stagger with its concussion. He could not control the resultant shaking of his flesh. His teeth chattered very slightly as he clenched them desperately. They got back to familiar land and finally to Southampton Row. It was a long way to Battalion Headquarters. The men in the orderly-room eagerly questioned them about the battle, but they knew less than they did.

Winterbourne asked for water and drank thirstily. He and the other runner were dazed and incoherent. They were given another written message, and elaborate directions which they promptly forgot.

The drum-fire had died down to an ordinary heavy bombardment as they started back. Already it was late afternoon. They wandered for hours in unfamiliar trenches before they found the Company.

★

They slept that night in a large German dug-out, swarming with rats. Winterbourne in his sleep felt them jump on his chest and face.

★

The drum-fire began again next morning. Again they lined a trench and advanced through smoke over torn wire and shell-tormented ground. Prisoners passed through. At night they struggled for hours, carrying down wounded men in stretchers through the mud and clamour. Major Thorpe was mortally wounded and his runner killed; Hume and his runner were killed; Franklin was wounded; Pemberton was killed; Sergeant Perkins was killed; the stretcher-bearers were killed. Men seemed to drop away continually.

★

Three days later Evans and Thompson led back forty-five men to the old billets in the ruined village. The attack on their part of the front had failed. Further south a considerable advance had been made and several thousand prisoners taken, but the German line was unbroken and stronger than ever in its new positions. Therefore that also was a failure.

Winterbourne and Henderson were the only two runners left; and since Evans was in command, Winterbourne was now company runner. The two men sat on their packs in the cellar without a word. Both shook very slightly but continuously with fatigue and shock. Outside the vicious heavies crashed eternally. They started wildly to their feet as a terrific smash overhead brought down what was left of the house above them and crashed into the duplicate cellar next door. A moment later there was another enormous crash and one end of the cellar broke in with falling bricks and a cloud of dust. They rushed out by the steps at the other end, and were sent reeling and choking by another huge black explosion.

They stumbled across to another cellar occupied by what was left of a section, and asked to sleep there since their own cellar was wrecked. Six of them and a corporal sat in silence by the light of a candle, dully listening to the crash of shells.

★

In a lull they heard a strange noise outside the cellar, first like wheels and then like a human voice calling for help. No one moved. The voice called again. The Corporal spoke:

'Who's going up?'

'Mucked if I am,' said somebody; 'I've 'ad enough.'

Winterbourne and Henderson simultaneously struggled to their feet. The change from candle-light to darkness blinded them as they peered out from the ruined doorway. They could just see a confused dark mass. The voice came again:

'Help! for Christ's sake come and help!'

A transport limber had been smashed by a shell. The wounded horses had dragged it along and fallen outside the cellar entrance. One man had both legs cut short at the knees. He was still alive, but evidently dying. They left him, lifted down the other man and carried him into the cellar. A large shell splinter had smashed his right knee. He was conscious, but weak. They got out his field-dressing and iodine and dripped iodine on the wound. At the pain of burning disinfectant the man turned deadly pale and nearly fainted. Winterbourne found that his hands and clothes were smeared with blood.

Then came the problem of getting the man away to a dressing-station. The Corporal and the four men refused to budge. The shells were crashing continuously outside. Winterbourne started out to get a stretcher and the new stretcher-bearer, groping his way through the darkness. Outside their billet he tripped and fell into a deep shell-hole, just as a heavy exploded with terrific force at his side. But for the fall he must have been blown to pieces. He scrambled to his feet, breathless and shaken, and tumbled down the cellar stairs. He noticed scared faces looking at him in the candle-light. He explained what had happened. The stretcher-bearer jumped up, got his stretcher and satchel of dress-ings, and they started back. Every shell which exploded near seemed to shake Winterbourne's flesh from his bones.

He was dazed and half-frantic with the physical shock of concussion after concussion. When he got back in the cellar he collapsed into a kind of stupor. The stretcher-bearer dressed the man's wound, and then looked at Winterbourne, felt his pulse, gave him a sip of rum and told him to lie still. He tried to explain that he must help carry the wounded man, and struggled to get to his feet. The stretcher-bearer pushed him back:

'You lie still, mate; you've done enough for to-day.'

⌣

> To my astonishment, my publisher informed me that certain words, phrases, sentences, and even passages, are at present taboo in England. I have recorded nothing which I have not observed in human life, said nothing I do not believe to be true... At my request the publishers are removing what they believe would be considered objectionable, and are placing asterisks to show where omissions have been made... In my opinion it is better for the book to appear mutilated than for me to say what I don't believe.

This disclaimer appeared in the first edition of **Richard Aldington**'s *Death of a Hero*, which was published in 1929. An autobiographical novel, it describes the life and death of George Winterbourne, a young artist. The book's descriptions of London life are brilliantly acerbic, but it is the descriptions of the fighting on the Front which make the book so memorable. Not surprisingly, writing that so caustically depicts the indifference and cant of those in charge of the war back home was received with great hostility and convinced Aldington that he had made the right decision to go into self-imposed exile in France the year before publication. *Lawrence of Arabia: A Biographical Inquiry*, his controversial biography of T. E. Lawrence published in 1955, brought Aldington further animosity. He died in France in 1962, at the age of 70. His obituary in the London *Times* described him as 'an angry young man of the generation before they became fashionable' and who 'remained something of an angry old man to the end'.

A. T. FITZROY

BEETHOVEN AND BACH

from *Despised and Rejected*

ENNIS AND ANTOINETTE exchanged a look of amusement and again, as previously in the crowd, she felt conscious of a delicious feeling of security. It was good to be with him, and to be enjoying these people with him. Outside, the strange bodiless legs passed and passed; the cries of the newspaper boys echoed down the stone passage; and inside, the atmosphere became smokier and smokier, and bits of *risqué* stories became mingled with political arguments, theatrical jargon with the orders for meals; and the mournful lilt of the Irish voices was a queer contrast to the high-pitched shrieks and giggles of the flappers. And it was all very delightful and unconventional and unlike Cadogan Gardens. And Dennis was being nice to her. And she was very happy.

The door to the street banged, and quick footsteps came down the stairs. A voice, youthful and eager, was heard asking: 'Is Mr. Barnaby in there?'

Dennis started. Was it hallucination again that made him believe it was Alan's voice, the same hallucination that only a few days ago had made him believe that it was Alan's figure he had seen in the crowd? He had suffered from so much of this kind of hallucination at one time…

'Yes, we're all here, Rutherford, come in,' cried Barnaby. Antoinette glanced at Dennis's face. And had no need to be told that already her precarious hold on happiness was threatened.

'This is the man I was telling you about, Dennis, I wanted you to meet—'

Alan cut him short. 'We met ages ago. I've still got one of his hand-kerchiefs in my possession. Do you remember tying up my gory wound for me, Dennis?'

'I remember,' said Dennis, and Alan grinned at Conn and Pegeen, flung off his hat, and seated himself between Everard and Barnaby.

'What about your tribunal?' asked the journalist.

'The local tribunal has already passed me for Combatant Service,' replied Alan, 'but I'm appealing again at the House of Commons next week. And then – good-bye to freedom for me, I suppose! But I'll tell 'em a few home-truths before I'm locked up. Beefy, sanctimonious old men, sitting there to tell me it's my duty to go out and take my share in murdering peasant-boys and students and labourers… And the same sort of old men on their side, egging *them* on to fight us, with just the same platitudes about duty and honour and self-defence, saying that we declared war first, just as we say they sprung the war on us! And the capitalists of all countries coining money out of bloodshed… Do they want the war to stop, those government contractors, making their millions by supplying munitions or boots or food for the armies?'

Dennis watched him through narrowed eyes. He had not altered much. He was eighteen months older, that was all. But there was the same quick impatience in phrase and gesture, the same vivid look.

He went on: 'The only way to stop the war – not only this war, but all future wars, is by opposing conscription. You're all for the good cause here, I suppose?'

Barnaby answered for the company in general: 'Yes, they're all appealing on different grounds. Everard, I forget what yours are?'

'I've not had the honour of being called up yet,' the actor replied evasively.

'And yours, Crispin?'

By a series of grunts, Crispin made it known that he did not intend to fight against the nation that had produced Beethoven and Bach.

'I'd like to appeal on every ground there is!' Oswald cried excitably, 'one can't do enough to keep the horror from going on.'

'I'm appealing on racial and personal grounds,' declared Benny, 'I won't be made to fight the Jews of other countries, even to avenge Brave Little Belgium, or prove myself a true patriot!'

Oswald began:

'"Breathes there a man with soul so dead

Who never to himself has said—"'

'I've said "This is my own, my native land" at least half a dozen times in half a dozen different lands,' Benny interrupted, 'I have relatives scattered about in allied, enemy and neutral countries alike. And how can a man fight for any particular country, when he's got an aunt in every port?'

'And England talks of defending the honour of small nations,' murmured Conn, 'has she forgotten Ireland at her very door, Ireland that she's oppressed and ground under her heel these many years? Let her recognise Ireland as an equal and raise her up from the thraldom of a vassal before she takes Belgium's name in vain to hide her desire for gain.'

'Well, at least you're free from the necessity of appealing,' said Barnaby, 'they'll never dare introduce conscription into Ireland. It'll mean revolution if they do.'

'And may I be the first to fly the *Sinn Féin* flag in the streets of Dublin that day!'

'What about you, Dennis?' said Alan.

'Humanitarian grounds.'

'Good!' For a second their eyes met, and then parted again. There was chaos in Dennis's mind. Alan's personality had lost none of its potent spell… and there was Antoinette beside him… and he longing and longing to have the boy all to himself… And he knew that all his energies must go to the concealment of that desire. He leant back in his chair and listened to Alan's voice – and was aware that Antoinette's gaze rested always on himself.

'Conscription has got to be fought,' Alan repeated, 'without conscription, Germany could never have gone to war. And the people have got to be made to see reason, those who say that we must go on with the war "for the sake of the men who have fallen." What sense is there in that? Because we have wasted a million good lives already, why should we throw another million on to the same refuse-heap? "To make their sacrifice worth while!" As if anything could make their sacrifice in such an iniquitous cause worth while! "They died gladly for their country" – it's all cant, cruel sickening cant to make the people at home see the war through rose-coloured spectacles. If they saw it without the spectacles, they wouldn't be so willing to go on paying for the continuation of it. "We must fight until the whole of Germany is crushed" – is the whole of Germany to blame for this war, any more than the whole of England? Blame it on the German High Command, if you like, and on the Prussian Junkers and their kind, but not on the people – people as straight and decent as ours, only maddened by this artificially worked-up hatred, this dizzy vision of world-power and world-empire. But in Germany, just as in every other country, there are people who don't let themselves be dazzled by that vision, and who are ready to work for the overthrow of governments that can organise wholesale butchery as a means by which to extend dominion.'

'The pity of it is, that we're so few,' said Benny, 'such a small and unpopular minority.'

Alan returned impatiently: 'We're not out for laurels.'

'No, it's more likely to be the broad arrow,' said Oswald.

'Let it be the broad arrow, then! It'll be the badge of freedom of the future, badge of honour for those who have struggled against the tide of public opinion. The militarists' hatred of us is much more bloodthirsty than their hatred of the Germans; we are the cowards and the traitors who are deliberately delaying victory. "If we don't give Germany a knock-out blow now, the war will start all over again for the next generation" – you hear the ignorant and the thoughtless reiterating that catch-phrase like a lot of parrots. The war all over again – that's exactly what they will have if they do win their complete military victory. When the "knock-out blow" has been dealt, they'll have to go on keeping big armies and building big ships, to consolidate their position as top-dog. And as long as we have big armies and navies, we shall always have wars. The pretty toys have to be used – they can't be kept for show… People call us "Pro-Germans" – it's laughable. If I'd been in Germany or anywhere else, I'd have fought just as hard against being turned into a cog in the infernal machinery of war. It's the whole system of militarism I'm up against, not the individual wrongs of one country or another. No civilised industrial population of any country wants war. Miners in Cornwall and Lancashire or Galicia and Siberia; poor devils sweating in our factories and in *their* factories; railwaymen, schoolmasters, farmers – what do they want with war? Nothing… until the idea is drilled into them by those in power. The people who want war and believe that war is good, should be allowed to make a private picnic of it. The government officials and cabinet ministers and war profiteers on both sides; the people who say they'd rather lose all their sons, than that they shouldn't go out and fight—'

'The khaki-clad females who say they wish they were men, so that they could kill a few Huns themselves,' Dennis put in.

'Yes, if only that small handful who started the war, and are continuing it, could finish it up amongst themselves, without implicating the masses!'

'Without the masses, there would be no war,' said Barnaby.

'Exactly!' cried Alan, 'without the masses, there *could* be no war, and that is the solution of it all, and the end and the aim of socialism – to free the masses from the tyranny of governments that can drive them like cattle to be slaughtered in this crazy campaign of greed and hatred. Look at the wonderfully organised man-power of all the nations, with all the woman-power behind it; look at the scientific miracles and the ceaseless labour and energy that go to the production of big guns, submarines, aeroplanes, poison-gas; think of all this employed in the cause of destruction… And think of the heroism and self-sacrifice of those who really "die gladly" for a mistaken ideal; and the tremendous flame of patriotism that's burning in the hearts of all the peoples alike: if all these tangible and intangible splendours could have been used in the furtherance, instead of in the destruction of civilisation!

'And you're expected to take your share in the destruction, without asking if it's right or wrong. All honour to the men who, when war broke out, almost as a matter of course left their homes and their loves and their careers, because they thought it was the only decent thing to do… And all blame to the old men at home, and to the narrow-minded women and unimaginative girls who made it appear the only decent thing! We're convinced that it isn't, and *we must stand firm,* cost what it may! We're few: that doesn't matter. We shall be pilloried: that doesn't matter. All that matters is that we shall have striven against what our brains and our hearts recognised as evil – Oh, not only evil, but stupid and petty and beastly – and that we shall have done our bit towards bringing nearer the day when militarism will be supplanted by industry, and we may hope to have an international system of legislation that'll knock out the possibility of disputes having to be settled by the barbarous and unintelligent means of bloodshed.'

'Unintelligent, good Lord, yes!' cried Barnaby, 'the whole thing is unintelligent, even from the militarist point of view. There are thousands of men being forced to fight, who are physically and mentally unfit to be of the least use in battle, but whose brains might have given us scientific inventions that would have benefited humanity, works of art, books, music… No, they won't let them stop at home and do what they *can* do, but must send them out to do incompetently things against which their whole nature rises in revolt. From the general utility standpoint: in which capacity is the artist of more value to the nation? As a creator of a work that may live, or as a mass of shattered nerves, totally incapable either of fulfilling the requirements of the army or of carrying out his own ideas?'

'Oh, how much does the general public care about art or the artist these days?' exclaimed Dennis.

'They may not care now,' rejoined Barnaby, 'but it's the sacred duty of everyone who's got the gift of creation to try and keep it intact. When the war is over we shall be grateful to those who through the long night of destruction have kept alight the torch of art and intellect. That's rendering a greater service to mankind than putting your life at the disposal of the war-machine.'

'And the sight of all those war-shrines makes me sick!' cried Alan. '"*Greater love hath no man*—" How dare they profane the words? It's not that a man is merely "laying down his life for his friends," but trying to do some other man in at the same time. How does that fit in with "*Thou shalt not kill*"?'

An unobtrusive-looking spectacled man, who all this while had sat silent at the corner table which Crispin had vacated, looked over at the group. 'It does not fit in, and it never will, but the Church has become untrue to herself, as those who serve her have become untrue, perverting her words until they seem to serve the ends of the State.'

Alan asked eagerly: 'Are you appealing on religious grounds, then?'

The man replied, 'Yes. And I daresay I'll get partial exemption. Non-Combatant Service. The despicable compromise that some men can make with their conscience. "*Thou shalt not kill*" – they think they're obeying the letter of the law if they don't bear arms and go to the fighting-line; but they're scarcely obeying the spirit when they accept work in munition-factories, or otherwise help to release men to be killed in their place.'

'Yes, I'm up against people of that sort, as much as I'm up against rabid militarists,' said Alan; 'they are the cowards and shirkers who deserve all the onus heaped upon the community of pacifists and socialists as a whole. Men whose conscience won't let them kill, but who haven't the courage to back their opinions – I've no use for them. Passive pacifism won't do any good. What we want is active pacifism, fearless and unashamed, ready to join hands with the workers of all other countries; to stand firm against their immoral, gain-seeking governments; and ready to suffer the utmost penalty of their idiotic and benighted law.'

Crispin rose from his chair. 'You b-bloody pacifists make as much noise as b-bloody militarists. One c-can't hearoneselfthink…' And on this cryptic utterance he made his exit.

The cloud of smoke became denser and more dense. Roy Radford and the flappers had long since departed, and the remaining company, having abandoned their separate tables, formed one collective straggling group. Through the smoke, Antoinette watched them; O'Farrell's fine sensitive features and visionary eyes shadowed by a thatch of wild auburn hair; Barnaby's rough-hewn head and hunched shoulders; Everard's sleek good looks; Harry Hope's chubbiness; Benny Joseph's dark eyes and Semitic profile; the nondescript appearance of the religious 'objector' who had joined in the conversation; Oswald's thin pale face and jerkiness of movement; Pegeen's tilted nose, and the cigarette stuck impertinently in one corner of her mouth… Picturesque enough,

NO MAN'S LAND

the whole group, only now Antoinette dared not glance at that slim boy with his dark flaming eyes, nor at Dennis... not since she had seen that look on his face when Alan had entered.

Barnaby was saying: 'From every possible point of view, whether from religion, art, socialism or humanity, war is a disgrace to any civilised nation. Personally, I'm out of the running, altogether, but I envy you fit men for having the chance to do your bit in the cause of peace.' Antoinette got up to go, wondering if Dennis would accompany her as usual. He followed her up the stairs, but it was evidently his intention to return to the others when he had said good-bye to her.

At the top of the stairs she faced him.

'Is that – is that the boy we saw the other night?'

'Yes.'

'It's the one you told me about?'

'Yes...'

'You're still in love with him...?'

And again: 'Yes...'

With one hand she was clutching the wooden balustrade. He saw her knuckles whiten under the strain, as she said in a dead, unemotional voice: 'D-do you want me to back out altogether?'

'My dear, it's for you to say.'

He could not bring himself to make a quick, clean end to the situation then and there. He was too dazed and bewildered to think. He only knew that he could not speak the word that would hurt her so much, not now, although her head was defiantly raised, her eyes downcast, as if she were determined that nothing should be visible to him of the pain he might choose to inflict.

'It's for you to say.'

She relaxed the tenseness of her attitude, and seemed suddenly to go limp. 'Oh, I don't know what to say...' The situation had come upon them both as a shock. Neither of them felt capable of coping with it at the moment, and in the doorway...

'Meet me down here one day, and we'll talk it all out,' he whispered hurriedly.

She nodded and turned away.

· 204 ·

◡

Rose Allatini was born in Vienna in 1890. Her first novel, *Happy Ever After*, was published by Mills and Boon in 1914. Throughout her life in England, she published under many pseudonyms, including A. T. Fitzroy. *Despised and Rejected*, from which this extract is taken, was published in May 1918 and immediately caused controversy on account of its political and sexual content. The government seized unsold copies and Allatini and the publisher C. W. Daniel were arrested and prosecuted. The book was banned in October 1918 under DORA (the Defence of the Realm Act) as 'likely to prejudice the recruiting, training, and discipline of persons in his Majesty's Forces'. The banning shocked Daniel, who claimed he had published the book for its pacifist message but added:

> Personally, I would rather the book were burnt that I should be party to lending support to the depravity of either the homo-sexual or the contra-sexual types...

The book was rediscovered and reprinted in the 1970s. Rose Allatini married Cyril Scott the composer in 1921 and lived with him and their two children until the end of the Second World War. She then moved to Rye to live with Melanie Mills, another writer of romances with numerous pseudonyms. She died in 1980.

WILLIAM FAULKNER

CREVASSE

from *These 13*

THE PARTY GOES ON, skirting the edge of the barrage weaving down into shell craters old and new, crawling out again. Two men half drag, half carry between them a third, while two others carry the three rifles. The third man's head is bound in a bloody rag; he stumbles his aimless legs along, his head lolling, sweat channeling slowly down his mud-crusted face.

The barrage stretches on and on across the plain, distant, impenetrable. Occasionally a small wind comes up from nowhere and thins the dun smoke momentarily upon clumps of bitten poplars. The party enters and crosses a field which a month ago was sown to wheat and where yet wheatspears thrust and cling stubbornly in the churned soil, among scraps of metal and seething hunks of cloth.

It crosses the field and comes to a canal bordered with tree stumps sheared roughly at a symmetrical five-foot level. The men flop and drink of the contaminated water and fill their water bottles. The two bearers let the wounded man slip to earth; he hangs lax on the canal bank with both arms in the water and his head too, had not the others held him up. One of them raises water in his helmet, but the wounded man cannot swallow. So they set him upright and the other holds the helmet brim to his lips and refills the helmet and pours the water on the wounded man's head, sopping the bandage. Then he takes a filthy rag from his pocket and dries the wounded man's face with clumsy gentleness.

The captain, the subaltern and the sergeant, still standing, are poring over a soiled map. Beyond the canal the ground rises gradually; the canal cutting reveals the chalk formation of the land in pallid strata. The captain puts the map away and the sergeant speaks the men to their feet, not loud. The two bearers raise the wounded man and they follow the canal bank, coming after a while to a bridge formed by a water-logged barge hull lashed bow and stern to either bank, and so pass over. Here they halt again while once more the captain and the subaltern consult the map.

Gunfire comes across the pale spring noon like a prolonged clashing of hail on an endless metal roof. As they go on the chalky soil rises gradually underfoot. The ground is dryly rough, shaling, and the going is harder still for the two who carry the wounded man. But when they would stop the wounded man struggles and wrenches free and staggers on alone, his hands at his head, and stumbles, falling. The bearers catch and raise him and hold him muttering between them and wrenching his arms. He is muttering '…bonnet…' and he frees his hands and tugs again at his bandage. The commotion passes forward. The captain looks back and stops; the party halts also, unbidden, and lowers rifles.

'A's pickin at's bandage, sir-r,' one of the bearers tells the captain. They let the man sit down between them; the captain kneels beside him.

'…bonnet… bonnet,' the man mutters. The captain loosens the bandage. The sergeant extends a water bottle and the captain wets the bandage and lays his hand on the man's brow. The others stand about, looking on with a kind of sober, detached interest. The captain rises. The bearers raise the wounded man again. The sergeant speaks them into motion.

They gain the crest of the ridge. The ridge slopes westward into a plateau slightly rolling. Southward, beneath its dun pall, the barrage still rages; westward and northward about the shining empty plain smoke rises lazily here and there above clumps of trees. But this is the smoke of burning things, burning wood and not powder, and the two officers gaze from beneath their hands, the men halting again without order and lowering arms.

'Gad, sir,' the subaltern says suddenly in a high, thin voice; 'it's houses burning! They're retreating! Beasts! Beasts!'

''Tis possible,' the captain says, gazing beneath his hand. 'We can get around that barrage now. Should be a road just yonder.' He strides on again.

'For-rard,' the sergeant says, in that tone not loud. The men slope arms once more with unquestioning docility.

The ridge is covered with a tough, gorselike grass. Insects buzz in it, zip from beneath their feet and fall to slatting again beneath the shimmering noon. The wounded man is babbling again. At intervals they pause and give him water and wet the bandage again, then two others exchange with the bearers and they hurry the man on and close up again.

The head of the line stops; the men jolt prodding into one another like a train of freight cars stopping. At the captain's feet lies a broad shallow depression in which grows a sparse, dead-looking grass like clumps of bayonets thrust up out of the earth. It is too big to have been made by a small shell, and too shallow to have been made by a big one. It bears no traces of having been made by anything at all, and they look quietly down into it. 'Queer,' the subaltern says. 'What do you fancy could have made it?'

The captain does not answer. He turns. They circle the depression, looking down into it quietly as they pass it. But they have no more than passed it when they come upon another one, perhaps not quite so large. 'I didn't know they had anything that could make that,' the subaltern says. Again the captain does not answer. They circle this one also and keep on along the crest of the ridge. On the other hand the ridge sheers sharply downward stratum by stratum of pallid eroded chalk.

A shallow ravine gashes its crumbling yawn abruptly across their path. The captain changes direction again, paralleling the ravine, until shortly afterward the ravine turns at right angles and goes on in the direction of their march. The floor of the ravine is in shadow; the captain leads the way down the shelving wall, into the shade. They lower the wounded man carefully and go on.

After a time the ravine opens. They find that they have debouched into another of those shallow depressions. This one is not so clearly defined, though, and the opposite wall of it is nicked by what is apparently another depression, like two overlapping disks. They cross the first depression, while more of the dead-looking grass bayonets saber their legs dryly, and pass through the gap into the next depression.

This one is like a miniature valley between miniature cliffs. Overhead they can see only the drowsy and empty bowl of the sky, with a few faint smoke smudges to the northwest. The sound of the barrage is now remote and far away: a vibration in earth felt rather than heard. There are no recent shell craters or marks here at all. It is as though they had strayed suddenly into a region, a world where the war had not reached, where nothing had reached, where no life is, and silence itself is dead. They give the wounded man water and go on.

The valley, the depression, strays vaguely before them. They can see that it is a series of overlapping, vaguely circular basins formed by no apparent or deducible agency. Pallid grass bayonets saber at their legs, and after a time they are again among old healed scars of trees to which there cling sparse leaves neither green nor dead, as if they too had been overtaken and caught by a hiatus in time, gossiping dryly among themselves though there is no wind. The floor of the valley is not level. It in itself descends into vague depressions, rises again as vaguely between its shelving walls. In the center of these smaller depressions whitish knobs of chalk thrust up through the thin topsoil. The ground has a resilient quality, like walking on cork; feet make no sound. 'Jolly walking,' the subaltern says. Though his voice is not raised, it fills the small valley with the abruptness of a thunderclap, filling the silence, the words seeming to hang about them as though silence here had been so long undisturbed that it had forgot its purpose; as one they look quietly and soberly about, at the shelving walls, the stubborn ghosts of trees, the bland, hushed sky. 'Topping hole-up for embusqué birds and such,' the subaltern says.

'Ay,' the captain says. His word in turn hangs sluggishly and fades. The men at the rear close up, the movement passing forward, the men looking quietly and soberly about. 'But no birds here,' the subaltern says. 'No insects even.'

'Ay,' the captain says. The word fades, the silence comes down again, sunny, profoundly still. The subaltern pauses and stirs something with his foot. The men halt also, and the subaltern and the captain, without touching it, examine the half-buried and moldering rifle. The wounded man is babbling again.

'What is it, sir?' the subaltern says. 'Looks like one of those things the Canadians had. A Ross. Right?'

'French,' the captain says; '1914.'

'Oh,' the subaltern says. He turns the rifle aside with his toe. The bayonet is still attached to the barrel, but the stock has long since rotted away. They go on, across the uneven ground, among the chalky knobs thrusting up through the soil. Light, the wan and drowsy sunlight, is laked in the valley, stagnant, bodiless, without heat. The saberlike grass thrusts sparsely and rigidly upward. They look about again at the shaling walls, then the ones at the head of the party watch the subaltern pause and prod with his stick at one of the chalky knobs and turn presently upward its earth-stained eyesockets and its unbottomed grin.

'Forward,' the captain says sharply. The party moves; the men look quietly and curiously at the skull as they pass. They go on, among the other whitish knobs like marbles studded at random in the shallow soil.

'All in the same position, do you notice, sir?' the subaltern says, his voice chattily cheerful; 'all upright. Queer way to bury chaps: sitting down. Shallow, too.'

'Ay,' the captain says. The wounded man babbles steadily. The two bearers stop with him, but the others crowd on after the officers, passing the two bearers and the wounded man. 'Dinna stop to gi's sup water,' one of the bearers says. 'A'll drink walkin'.' They take up the wounded man again and hurry him on while one of them tries to hold the neck of a water bottle to the wounded man's mouth, clattering it against his teeth and spilling the water down the front of his tunic. The captain looks back.

'What's this?' he says sharply. The men crowd up. Their eyes are wide, sober; he looks about at the quiet, intent faces. 'What's the matter back there, Sergeant?'

'Wind-up,' the subaltern says. He looks about at the eroded walls, the whitish knobs thrusting quietly out of the earth. 'Feel it myself,' he says. He laughs, his laughter a little thin, ceasing. 'Let's get out of here, sir,' he says. 'Let's get into the sun again.'

'You are in the sun here,' the captain says. 'Ease off there, men. Stop crowding. We'll be out soon. We'll find the road and get past the barrage and make contact again.' He turns and goes on. The party gets into motion again.

Then they all stop as one, in the attitudes of walking, in an utter suspension, and stare at one another. Again the earth moves under their feet. A man screams, high, like a woman or a horse; as the firm earth shifts for a third time beneath them the officers whirl and see beyond the down-plunging man a gaping hole with dry dust still crumbling about the edges before the orifice crumbles again beneath a second man. Then a crack springs like a sword slash beneath them all; the earth breaks under their feet and tilts like jagged squares of pale fudge, framing a black yawn out of which, like a silent explosion, bursts the unmistakable smell of rotted flesh. While they scramble and leap (in silence now; there has been no sound since the first man screamed) from one cake to another, the cakes tilt and slide until the whole floor of the valley rushes slowly under them and plunges them downward into darkness. A grave rumbling rises into the sunlight on a blast of decay and of faint dust which hangs and drifts in the faint air about the black orifice.

The captain feels himself plunging down a sheer and shifting wall of moving earth, of sounds of terror and of struggling in the ink dark. Someone else screams. The scream ceases; he hears the voice of the wounded man coming thin and reiterant out of the plunging bowels of decay: 'A'm no dead! A'm no dead!' and ceasing abruptly, as if a hand had been laid on his mouth.

Then the moving cliff down which the captain plunges slopes gradually off and shoots him, uninjured, onto a hard floor, where he lies for a time on his back while across his face the lightward- and airward-seeking blast of death and dissolution rushes. He has fetched up against something; it tumbles down upon him lightly, with a muffled clatter as if it had come to pieces.

Then he begins to see the light, the jagged shape of the cavern mouth high overhead, and then the sergeant is bending over him with a pocket torch. 'McKie?' the captain says. For reply the sergeant turns the flash upon his own face. 'Where's Mr. McKie?' the captain says.

'A's gone, sir-r,' the sergeant says in a husky whisper. The captain sits up.

'How many are left?'

'Fourteen, sir-r,' the sergeant whispers.

'Fourteen. Twelve missing. We'll have to dig fast.' He gets to his feet. The faint light from above falls coldly upon the heaped avalanche, upon the thirteen helmets and the white bandage of the wounded man huddled about the foot of the cliff. 'Where are we?'

For answer the sergeant moves the torch. It streaks laterally into the darkness, along a wall, a tunnel, into yawning blackness, the walls faceted with pale glints of chalk. About the tunnel, sitting or leaning upright against the walls, are skeletons in dark tunics and bagging Zouave trousers, their moldering arms beside them; the captain recognizes them as Senegalese troops of the May fighting of 1915, surprised and killed by gas probably in the attitudes in which they had taken refuge in the chalk caverns. He takes the torch from the sergeant.

'We'll see if there's anyone else,' he says. 'Have out the trenching tools.' He flashes the light upon the precipice. It rises into gloom, darkness, then into the faint rumor of daylight overhead. With the sergeant behind him he climbs the shifting heap, the earth sighing beneath him and shaling downward. The injured man begins to wail again, 'A'm no dead! A'm no dead!' until his voice goes into a high sustained screaming. Someone lays a hand over his mouth. His voice is muffled, then it becomes laughter on a rising note, becomes screaming again, is choked again.

The captain and the sergeant mount as high as they dare, prodding at the earth while the earth shifts beneath them in long hushed sighs. At the foot of the precipice the men huddle, their faces lifted faint, white, and patient into the light. The captain sweeps the torch up and down the cliff. There is nothing, no arm, no hand, in sight. The air is clearing slowly. 'We'll get on,' the captain says.

'Ay, sir-r,' the sergeant says.

In both directions the cavern fades into darkness, plumbless and profound, filled with the quiet skeletons sitting and leaning against the walls, their arms beside them.

'The cave-in threw us forward,' the captain says.

'Ay, sir-r,' the sergeant whispers.

'Speak out,' the captain says. 'It's but a bit of a cave. If men got into it, we can get out.'

'Ay, sir-r,' the sergeant whispers.

'If it threw us forward, the entrance will be yonder.'

'Ay, sir-r,' the sergeant whispers.

The captain flashes the torch ahead. The men rise and huddle quietly behind him, the wounded man among them. He whimpers. The cavern goes on, unrolling its glinted walls out of the darkness; the sitting shapes grin quietly into the light as they pass. The air grows heavier; soon they are trotting, gasping, then the air grows lighter and the torch sweeps up another slope of earth, closing the tunnel. The men halt and huddle. The captain mounts the slope. He snaps off the light and crawls slowly along the crest of the slide, where it joins the ceiling of the cavern, sniffing. The light flashes on again. 'Two men with trenching tools,' he says.

Two men mount to him. He shows them the fissure through which air seeps in small, steady breaths. They begin to dig, furiously, hurling the dirt back. Presently they are relieved by two others; presently the fissure becomes a tunnel and four men can work at once. The air becomes fresher. They burrow furiously, with whimpering cries like dogs. The wounded man, hearing them perhaps, catching the excitement perhaps, begins to laugh again, meaningless and high. Then the man at the head of the tunnel bursts through. Light rushes in around him like water; he burrows madly; in silhouette they see his wallowing buttocks lunge from sight and a burst of daylight surges in.

The others leave the wounded man and surge up the slope, fighting and snarling at the opening. The sergeant springs after them and beats them away from the opening with a trenching spade, cursing in his hoarse whisper.

'Let them go, Sergeant,' the captain says. The sergeant desists. He stands aside and watches the men scramble into the tunnel. Then he descends, and he and the captain help the wounded man up the slope. At the mouth of the tunnel the wounded man rebels.

'A'm no dead! A'm no dead!' he wails, struggling. By cajolery and force they thrust him, still wailing and struggling, into the tunnel, where he becomes docile again and scuttles through.

'Out with you, Sergeant,' the captain says.

'After you, sir-r,' the sergeant whispers.

'Out wi ye, man!' the captain says. The sergeant enters the tunnel. The captain follows. He emerges onto the outer slope of the avalanche which had closed the cave, at the foot of which the fourteen men are kneeling in a group. On his hands and knees like a beast, the captain breathes, his breath making a hoarse sound. 'Soon it will be summer,' he thinks, dragging the air into his lungs faster than he can empty them to respire again. 'Soon it will be summer, and the long days.' At the foot of the slope the fourteen men kneel. The one in the center has a Bible in his hand, from which he is intoning monotonously. Above his voice the wounded man's gibberish rises, meaningless and unemphatic and sustained.

William Faulkner was born in New Albany, Mississippi, in 1897. He enlisted in the Royal Air Force in Canada in July 1918 but the war ended before he completed his training. *Crevasse*, the story included here, was first published in 1931 in *These* 13, Faulkner's first collection of short stories. In 1926, Faulkner had published his first novel, *Soldier's Pay*, a powerful account of a wounded aviator's return home to a small town in Georgia at the end of the war. His writings on the war already show Faulkner's brilliance at setting a scene and capturing a mood through dialogue. One of the great writers of the 20th century, Faulkner was awarded the Nobel Prize for Literature in 1949. Winning the prize brought him worldwide recognition and put Yoknapatawpha County, his fictional rendering of Lafayette County where he grew up, on the literary map. Faulkner died in Byhalia, Mississipi, in 1962.

FREDERIC MANNING

CUSHY AVEC MADEMOISELLE

from *Her Privates We*

> But thy speaking of my tongue, and I thine, most truly-falsely, must
> needs be granted to be much at one.
>
> Shakespeare

BOURNE NEVER SLEPT MUCH: as soon as he put out his cigarette and rolled himself up in his blankets, he would sleep like a log for an hour or two perhaps, and then so lightly that the least sound would wake him. It was a legend among the other men, that nobody ever woke, during the night, without finding Bourne sitting up and smoking a cigarette. Company guard didn't bother him in the least. It was a cushy guard, without formality; and he liked the solitude and emptiness of the night. One bathed one's soul in that silence, as in a deep, cold pool. Earth seemed to breathe, even if it were only with his own breathing, giving consciousness a kind of rhythm, which was neither of sound nor of motion, but might become either at any moment. The slagheaps, huge against the luminous sky, might have been watchtowers in Babylon, or pyramids in Egypt; night with its enchantments, changing even this flat and unlovely land into a place haunted by fantastic imaginings. Morning gave again to life, its sordid realities. He got himself some tea at the cooker, yarned to Abbot while he drank it, and was washed and shaved before the rest of his hut were fully awake.

The battalion fell in on the road, at about twenty minutes past nine; and five minutes later the commanding officer and the adjutant rode down the line of men; perhaps less with the object of making a cursory inspection, than for the purpose of advertising the fact, that they had both been awarded the Military Cross for their services on the Somme.

'Wonder they 'ave the front to put 'em up,' said Martlow, unimpressed. Major Shadwell and Captain Malet had no distinctions.

'I don't want no medals meself,' added Martlow, disinterestedly.

Bourne was struck by the adjutant's horsemanship; when the grey he rode trotted, you saw plenty of daylight between his seat and the saddle; and the exaggerated action made it seem as if, instead of the horse carrying the adjutant, the adjutant were really propelling the horse. However, he brought to the business the same serious attention which he gave to less arduous duties at other times. The men were forbidden to drink from their water-bottles on the march until permission were given. They moved off, and, by ten o'clock, were marching through Noeux-les-Mines again; and presently word was passed along that they were going to Bruay. There was no doubt about it this time: Captain Malet had told Sergeant-Major Robinson, and the men swung forward cheerfully, in spite of dust and heat, opening out a bit, so that the air could move freely between them. On the whole their march discipline was pretty good. They arrived at their new billets at about one o'clock.

Bruay was built on two sides of a valley, and their billets were naturally in the poorer part of the town; in one of the uniform streets which always seem to lay stress on the monotony of modern industrial life. It was a quarter given up to miners. The street, in which A Company had billets, was only about a hundred yards long, led nowhere, and ended abruptly, as though the builders had suddenly tired of their senseless repetition. But it was all very clean; dull and dingy, but clean. Some of the houses were empty, and Bourne, Shem, and Martlow, with the rest of their section, were in one of these empty houses. The town, however, was for the most part earlier than the days when towns came to be planned. You could see that the wisdom of cattle, which in such matters is greater than the wisdom of man, had determined the course of many of its sinuous streets, as they picked their way to and from their grazing, guided only by the feel of the ground beneath them, and the gradients with which they were confronted. So the town still possessed a little charm and character. It had its *Place,* its sides all very unequal, and all of it on the slope. Even the direction of the slope was diagonally across it, and not merely from side to side or end to end. Perhaps the cattle had determined that too, for the poor fool man has long since lost his nature. Houses in the older parts of the town, though modest and discreet, still contrived to have a little air of distinction and individuality. They refused to be confounded with each other. They ignored that silly assumption that men are equal. They believed in private property.

It was obviously the intention of authority that the men should be given an opportunity to have a bon time. They were to be paid at two o'clock, and then were free to amuse themselves.

'You're comin' out with me tonight,' said Martlow to Bourne decisively.

'Very well,' said Bourne, dumping his pack on the floor of the room they occupied, and opening the window. They were upstairs; and he looked out and down, into the street. There were five or six corporals, and lance-corporals, standing just outside; and both Corporal Green-street and Lance-Corporal Jakes spotted him immediately, and shouted for him to come. He went, a little reluctantly, wondering what they wanted.

'You're the man we was lookin' for,' said Corporal Greenstreet. 'The sergeants are runnin' a sergeants' mess for the couple of days we'll be 'ere; an' we don't see why we can't run a corporals' mess.'

'Well, run one, Corporal,' said Bourne distinterestedly. 'There's nothing in King's Regs. against it, so far as I know.'

'Well, we can't run it ourselves. That's where you come in, you know the lingo a bit, an' you always seem able to get round the old women. A corporal don't get a sergeant's pay, you know, but we want to do it as well as we can. There'll be eight of us; Jakes, Evans, an' Marshall are in billets 'ere, an' we could 'ave the mess 'ere, if she'd do the cookin'. You 'ave a talk to 'er.'

'This is all very well,' said Bourne reasonably; 'but now we're in a decent town I want to have a good time myself. I've just told Martlow I should go out with him tonight.'

'Well, I've got 'im down for company guard tonight.'

'Have you, Corporal? Well, you just take him off company guard, or there's absolutely nothing doing. Every time we arrange to go out on a bit of a spree together, he, or Shem, or myself are put on company guard. I was on last night.'

'Well, Sergeant-Major Robinson told me to put you on guard last night, 'e said it would do you good, you were gettin' a bit fresh.'

'I guessed that,' said Bourne. 'He didn't want to be nasty, of course, but he thought he would give me a reminder. I don't mind taking my share of guards. But, if you put one of us on, you might just as well put us all on together, and make a family party of it. I don't mind helping you to run a mess, but I want to have a good time, too.'

'Well, you muck in with us,' said Corporal Greenstreet.

'An' you needn't put anythin' in the kitty,' added Lance-Corporal Jakes.

'Oh, thanks all the same, but I like to pay my own way,' said Bourne coolly. 'I don't mind going in and asking madame what can be done in the matter; and then, if we can come to some arrangement, I shall see about buying the grub; but before things go any further, it has got to be clearly understood that neither Shem, nor Martlow, is on any guard tonight. We three are going out on a spree together. I shall muck in with you tomorrow night.'

'That's all right,' said Corporal Greenstreet hastily. 'I'll get some other bugger for the bloody guard, if there is a guard. I've 'ad no orders yet.'

'It's just as well to take the possibility into consideration,' said Bourne; 'but mind you, you would do it just as well on your own, without me.'

'Come on. You parlez-vous to the old woman,' said Corporal Greenstreet, and hurried him through the house into the forefront of the battle, which was the kitchen. Madame was a very neat and competent-looking woman, and she faced Bourne with her two daughters acting as supports immediately behind her. Bourne got through the preliminary *politesses* with a certain amount of credit. She had already understood that the corporals required her assistance in some way, but they had failed apparently to make matters clear.

'Qu'est-ce que ces messieurs désirent?' she inquired of Bourne, coming to the point with admirable promptitude, and when he explained matters they launched into a discussion on ways and means. Then Bourne turned to Corporal Greenstreet.

'I suppose it is pukka that we stay here two nights, is it?'

'That's accordin' to present plans. Of course you can't be certain of anything in the bloody army. Does it make any differ to 'er?'

'Not much,' said Bourne. 'You can have grilled fillet of steak with fried onions, and chips and beans, or you can have a couple of chickens. I am wondering what sort of sweet you can have.'

'Could we 'ave a suet puddin' wi' treacle?'

'No, I don't think so,' said Bourne reflectively. 'I don't think the French use suet much in cooking, and anyway I don't know the French for suet, if they do. *Suif* is lard, I think. Could you pinch a tin of pozzy out of stores? Then you might have a sweet omelette with jam in it. Perhaps it would be better to buy some decent jam, you don't want plum and apple, do you? Only I want to make the money go as far as possible. I like those little red currants in syrup which used to come from Bar-le-Duc.'

'Get 'em. I don't care a fuck where they come from. We don't want any bloody plum an' apple when we can get better. An' don't you worry about the money, not in reason anyway. They've only let us come 'ere for a couple of days to 'ave a bon time before they send us up into the shit again. Might just as well get all we can, while we can.'

Bourne turned to Madame again, and asked her if she would do the marketing for them, and the upshot of it was that they both agreed to go together. Bourne turned to Corporal Greenstreet and asked him about money.

'Will it do if we all put twenty francs into the kitty to start with?'

'I don't think I shall want so much: give me ten each, and if that isn't enough, then you can each give me up to another ten. I am going to let her buy the wine because she knows somebody in the trade, and says she can get us good sound wine, which you don't get in estaminets, fairly cheap.'

'Dinner's up, Corporal,' said Corporal Marshall, putting his head in the door; and thanking Madame, they left to get their meal rather hurriedly.

'Where've you bin?' said Martlow indignantly to Bourne, and Shem burst out laughing at the way in which the question was put.

'What the bloody 'ell is 'e laughin' at?' said Martlow, his face all in a pucker.

'I have been doing my best to get you off company guard tonight.'

'Me!' exclaimed Martlow. 'Me, on bloody company guard tonight, an' the only cushy town we've been in! It's a bugger, ain't it? D'you mean to say they 'ad me on bloody guard?'

'Well, I have taken on the job of rationing officer to the corporals' mess, on condition they find someone else in your place: that is if they should mount a guard tonight; they may give it a miss. It isn't a bad stew today, is it? Seems to me a long time since we had any fresh meat, except for a few weevils in the biscuits. As soon as I have had dinner, I shall go off with Corporal Greenstreet, and make the other corporals ante up. Then I shall be back in time to get my pay; and afterwards I shall go out and do the marketing with Madame. When we have had tea, the three of us had better hop it to the other side of the town right away, in case they come along and pinch us for any fatigues. There's a cinema, up there. And look here, Martlow, you're not going to pay for everything tonight, see? We shall have to make the most of our opportunity to have a bon time, as it may be our last chance. I hate the thought of dying young.'

'Well, I'll stan' the supper,' said Martlow reasonably. 'I've got about three weeks' pay, an' me mother sent me a ten-bob note. I wish she wouldn't send me any money, as she wants all she gets, but there's no stoppin' 'er.'

'Shem can pay for the drinks afterwards. Of course, he has got money. To be a Jew and not to have money would be an unmitigated misfortune. Enough to make one deny the existence of Providence. He never will offer to pay unless you make him. He wouldn't think it prudent. But all the same, if you are broke to the wide, Shem will come down quite handsomely; he doesn't mind making a big splash then, as it looks like a justification of his past thrift. Shem and I understand each other pretty well, only he thinks I'm a bloody fool.'

'I don't think you're a bloody fool,' said Shem indulgently; 'but I think I could make a great deal more use of your brains than you do.'

'Shem thinks he is a practical man,' said Bourne, 'and a cynic, and a materialist; and would you believe it, Martlow, he had a cushy job in the Pay Office, to which all his racial talent gave him every claim, and he was wearing khaki, and he had learnt how to present arms with a fountain-pen: the most perfect funk-hole in Blighty, and he chucks the whole bloody show to come soldiering! Here you are, clean out my dixie, like a good kid, and my knife and fork. I must chase after these corporals. I wouldn't trust any of them round the corner with a three-penny bit; not unless I were a sergeant.'

He found Corporal Greenstreet ready, and they set off together; the corporal had collected all the money except from Corporal Farman and Lance-Corporal Eames.

'What about Corporal Whitfield?' Bourne asked him.

''e's no bloody good,' said Greenstreet. ''e never will join in with us in anything. Do you know, 'e gets at least one big parcel out from 'ome every week, an' I've never seen 'im give away a bite yet. In any case, 'e's no good to us. 'e's a Rechabite.'

'What the hell is that?' inquired Bourne, somewhat startled.

'I don't know. It's some kind o' sex or other, I think. They don't drink, an' they don't smoke either; but you ought to see the bugger eat. 'e's no bloody good to us.'

'I don't know anything about him,' Bourne explained.

'No, an' you don't want to,' said Greenstreet earnestly. 'I'm in the same billets as I was last time, but I 'aven't 'ad time to look in on 'em yet. An old maid owns the 'ouse, an' she 'as an 'ousekeeper: cook-'ousekeeper, I should say. They're very decent to all us. Respectable people, you know; I should say the old girl 'ad quite a bit o' rattle to 'er. Lives comfortable anyway. Likes you to be quiet an' wipe your feet on the mat. You know.'

The house was in one of the streets leading off the *Place*; and it had a gate at the side giving access to a small yard, with a garden, half flowers, half vegetables; there was a tree bright with early red apples, and a pollarded plane with marvellously contorted branches and leaves already yellowing. Corporal Farman was just coming out of the door, as they entered the gate, and he handed over his ten francs cheerfully. He and Corporal Greenstreet were perhaps the two best-looking men in the battalion, fair-haired, blue-eyed and gay-complexioned. The *ménagère*, recognizing the latter, waved a welcome to him from the doorway.

'She's been askin' about you, Corporal.'

'Bonjour, Monsieur Greenstreet,' she cried, rolling each 'r' in her throat.

'Bongjour, madame, be there in 'arf a tick. I'll meet you up at the company office, Corporal, and show you the billets. Bourne's runnin' the show.'

Farman waved a hand, and departed on his own business. Corporal Greenstreet and Bourne went into the house, after using the door-mat rather ostentatiously; but even so the *ménagère* looked a little suspiciously at Bourne.

'Vous n'avez pas un logement chez nous, monsieur,' she said firmly.

'C'est vrai, madame; mais j'attends les ordres de monsieur le caporal.'

He spoke deliberately, with a little coldness in his manner, *de haut en bas,* as it were, and after a further penetrating glance in his direction, she ignored him for the moment. Corporal Greenstreet left his pack in a room off the kitchen, but one step higher and with a wooden floor instead of tiled; then he returned, and the woman opened on him rapidly, expressing her pleasure at seeing him, and her further gratification at seeing him so obviously in good health. He did not understand one word of what she said, but the pleasure and recognition in her face flattered him agreeably.

'Ah, oui, madame,' he said with a gallant effort.

'Mais vous n'avez pas compris, monsieur.'

'Ah, oui, compris, madame. Glad to be back, compris? Cushy avec mademoiselle.'

The expression on the face of the *ménagère* passed very rapidly from astonishment to indignation, and from indignation to wrath. Before Corporal Greenstreet realized what was about to happen, she had swung a muscular arm, and landed a terrific box on his ear, almost knocking him into a scuttle containing split wood and briquettes for the stove. Bourne, thinking with a rapidity only outstripped by her precipitate action, decided that the Hindustani 'cushy' and the French 'coucher' must have been derived from the same root in Sanskrit. He interposed heroically between the fury and her victim, who without any hesitation had adopted the role of a non-combatant in trying circumstances.

'Mais madame, madame,' he protested, struggling to overcome his mirth. 'Vous vous méprenez. "Cushy" est un mot d'argot militaire qui veut dire doux, confortable, tout ce qu'il y a de plus commode. Monsieur le caporal ne veut pas dire autre chose. Il veut vous faire un petit compliment. Calmez-vous. Rassurez-vous, madame. Je vous assure que monsieur a des manières tres correctes, tres convenables. Il est un jeune homme bien élevé. Il n'a pour vous, ainsi que pour mademoiselle, que des sentiments tres respectueux.'

Bourne's French was only sufficient, when circumstances allowed him an economical use of it; and these were enough to make him a bankrupt even in English. Madame was now moving about her kitchen with the fine frenzy of a prima donna in one of the more ecstatic moments of grand opera. Every emotion has its appropriate rhythm, and she achieved what was proper to her own spontaneously, through sheer natural genius. Perhaps she was too great an artist to allow Bourne's words to have their full effect at once. She could not plunge from this sublimity to an immediate bathos. Innocence in adversity was the expression patent on the corporal's face, and perhaps the sight of it brought into her mind some mitigating element of doubt; which she resisted at first as though it were a mere feminine weakness.

'Nous nous retirons, madame, pour vous donner le temps de calmer vos nerfs,' said Bourne, with some severity. 'Nous regrettons infiniment ce malentendu. Monsieur le caporal vous fera ses excuses quand vous serez plus à même d'accepter ses explications. Permettez, madame. Je suis vraiment désolé.'

He swept the corporal out of the house, and into the street, and finding a secluded corner, collapsed.

'What the fuckin' 'ell is't all about?' the awed but exasperated corporal inquired. 'I go into th' 'ouse, an' only get as far as 'ow d'you do, when she 'ands me out this bloody packet. You'll get a thick ear yourself, if you don't stop laffin'.'

Bourne, when he had recovered sufficiently, explained that the housekeeper had understood him to express his intention of going to bed with her mistress.

'What! D'you mean it? Why, the old girl's about sixty!' Bourne whistled the air of *Mademoiselle from Armentieres*, leaving the corporal to draw his own conclusions from it.

'Look 'ere,' said Corporal Greenstreet, with sudden ferocity. 'If you tell any o' them other buggers what 'as 'appened I'll…'

'Oh, don't be a bloody fool,' said Bourne, suddenly firing up too. 'If there's one thing that fills me with contempt, it is being asked not to tell. Do you think I have got no more sense than a kid or an old woman? You would look well with that tin can tied to your tail, wouldn't you? We had better get moving. They will have started to pay out by now.'

'Wish to God I knew a bit o' French,' said the corporal earnestly.

'I wish to God you wouldn't mix the little you do know with Hindustani,' said Bourne.

The whole company were in the street, waiting to be paid: they formed in little groups, and men would pass from one group to another, or two groups would merge together, or one would suddenly split up completely, distributing its members among the others. Their movements were restless, impatient, and apparently without object. Corporal Greenstreet, finding Lance-Corporal Eames, collected his subscription to the mess, and then handed over the whole eighty francs to Bourne. Presently a couple of men brought a table and an army blanket out of one of the houses. The table was placed on the footpath parallel to the street, and the blanket was spread over it. One of the men went back into the house and returned with two chairs, followed by Quartermaster-Sergeant James, who detailed the same two men as witnesses. Almost immediately afterwards Captain Malet appeared with a new subaltern, a Mr Finch, who was not yet twenty, though he had already been in action with another battalion, and had been slightly wounded. The quartermaster-sergeant called the company, now grouped in a semi-circle in front of the table, to attention, saluted, and Captain Malet, acknowledging the salute, told them to stand easy.

There was a moment's pause; and then one of the witnesses brought a third chair for the quartermaster-sergeant, who sat on Captain Malet's left. The three then proceeded to count the notes and arrange them in bundles, while the men in front shifted from one foot to another, and whispered to each other. The sergeant-major, who had been to the orderly-room, returned and saluted Captain Malet. He was the first man to be paid, and then the quartermaster-sergeant, and Sergeant Gallion and Sergeant Tozer. The others were paid in alphabetical order; and as each man's name was called he came forward, saluted, and was ordered to take off his cap, so that the officer could see whether his hair had been properly cut. Men had a strong objection to their hair being cropped close. They had been inclined to compromise by having it machined at the back and sides, and leaving on the crown of the head a growth like Absalom's, concealing it under the cap. In the case of a head wound, this thick hair, matted with dried blood, which always became gluey, made the dressing of the wound much more difficult for the doctor and his orderlies, delaying other equally urgent cases. In consequence, all men were ordered to remove their caps before receiving their pay, and if a man's hair were not cropped it was only credited to him; and there were formal difficulties in the way of any attempt to recover arrears.

Bourne had always liked his hair very short. He objected to growing a moustache, which collected bits of carrot and meat from the eternal stew. He thought it inconsistent in the Army Council to make men grow hair in one place and shave it in another, as though they were French poodles. He had once, when they were discussing the matter in the tent, told the men that they should be made to shave all over, as then they would not provide so many nurseries for lice. They thought the suggestion indecent.

'Don't be a bloody fool,' Minton had objected. 'Fancy a man 'avin' to let 'is trousers down before 'e gets 'is pay!'

'But the commanding-officer wants to put us all in kilts,' Bourne had replied in a reasonable tone; and Major Blessington's avowed preference for a kilted regiment had always been a ground of resentment.

His name being early on the list, and his head almost shaven, he was soon free; and he left immediately to take Madame marketing. She had insisted that he should be present, so that he would know exactly how much everything cost. After Corporal Greenstreet's involuntary collision with the housekeeper, Bourne had become a little anxious as to the possibility of any misunderstanding with this other, more tractable but equally muscular, lady with whom he had to deal. However, when he presented himself in her kitchen, he found that she had changed her mind, and had decided that the elder of her two daughters should take her place. She explained that she had other work to do in the house.

The daughter was waiting, demurely clothed in black, which perhaps enhanced her complexion, but seemed in any case to be the uniform dress of nubile maidens in France. She carried a large basket, but wore no hat, content with the incomparable sleekness of her black hair, which was rolled up just above the nape of her neck. It was something about her neck, the back of her small head, and the way her little ears were set, flat against her bright hair, which attracted Bourne's appraising eyes. She knew, because she put up a hand, to smooth or to caress it; and a question came into her eyes quickly, and was gone again, like a rabbit appearing and disappearing in the mouth of a burrow. Apart from the firm but delicate modelling of the back of her head and neck, and her rather large eyes, at once curious and timid, she had little beauty. Her forehead was low and rather narrow, her nose flattish, and her mouth too large, with broad lips, scarcely curving even when she smiled. She had good small teeth.

Bourne had always treated women, with a little air of ceremony, whatever kind of women they might be. The case of the girl at Noeux-les-Mines was exceptional, but she was of the type who try to stimulate desire as by an irritant, and he had too sensitive a skin. All the same he had reproached himself a little on her account, for after all it was her vocation in life. Now, he professed that he was entirely in the hands of Madame; he did not think it necessary that he should go, but if she wished it, it would be a great pleasure to accompany Mademoiselle. Madame was flattered by his confidence, but thought it right that he should go; perhaps she had less confidence in him than he in her; or was it only that she was interested where he was indifferent? He followed the girl out into the street. The greater part of the company were still waiting to draw their pay; and, as Bourne and the girl passed behind them, the men turned curiously to look at the pair.

''ullo, Bourne! Goin' square-pushin'?' one of his acquaintances asked him with a grin.

Bourne only looked at him, and moved a little closer to the girl, a combative feeling rising in him. After all, if the girl were not beautiful, she had poise and character. She ignored all those eyes, which were filled with desire, and furtive innuendo, and provocative challenge; as though indifferent to the tribute which all men pay, one way or another, to the mystery she embodied. With women of her race, it was still a mystery. It gave her the air of saying that she could choose for herself as she pleased, her own will being all that mattered. Even Captain Malet, as Bourne passed on the other side of the street with a correct if perfunctory salute, glanced up at them with a fleeting interest.

'So that's the way he spends his money, is it?' he murmured, half to himself and half to the quartermaster-sergeant; though the two witnesses, all ears and attention, naturally overheard him.

As soon as they had turned the corner she spoke to Bourne, opening out quite frankly. She had two brothers, who had been at the front, but were now working in a mine. They were apparently on a kind of indefinite leave, but were liable to be recalled at any moment to the colours. Then, others, who had also earned a rest from trench life, would take their place. *C'est dure, la guerre.* But all the same she felt about it as did so many of them, to whom war seemed as natural and as inevitable as a flood or an earthquake. Bourne had noticed very much the same feeling among peasants close to the line. They would plough, sow, and wait for their harvest, taking the chance that battle might flow like lava over their fields, very much as they took the chance of a wet season or of a drought. If the worst happened, then the ruin of their crops might seem mere wanton mischief on the part of a few irresponsible generals; and whether it were a German or a British army which ravaged their fields and shattered their homesteads, did not affect their point of view very materially. On the whole, however, their pessimism was equal to the occasion.

'C'est la guerre,' they would say, with resignation that was almost apathy: for all sensible people know that war is one of the blind forces of nature, which can neither be foreseen nor controlled. Their attitude, in all its simplicity, was sane. There is nothing in war which is not in human nature; but the violence and passions of men become, in the aggregate, an impersonal and incalculable force, a blind and irrational movement of the collective will, which one cannot control, which one cannot understand, which one can only endure as these peasants, in their bitterness and resignation, endured it. *C'est la guerre.*

The demure little person hurrying beside him with her basket realized that the war made life more precarious, chiefly because it resulted in a scarcity of provisions, and a rise, if only a restricted rise, in prices. There was something always a little disconcerting to the soldier in the prudence, foresight, and practical sense of the civilian mind. It is impossible to reconcile the point of view, which argues that everything is so scarce, with that opposed point of view, which argues that time is so short. She was amazed at his extravagance, as she bought under his supervision chickens and beef and eggs and potatoes and onions, and then four bottles of wine. Salad and beans her mother's garden could provide; but as an afterthought, when buying the red currants in syrup, he bought some cream cheese. Then, their shopping completed, they turned back. She touched him lightly on the arm once, and asked him why he had no stripes on his sleeve.

'Je suis simple soldat, moi,' he explained awkwardly.

'Mais pourquoi…?' And then, noticing his expression, she turned away from the subject with what was no more than the shadow of a shrug. Women must be always stimulating some man's ambition. He followed her movement, as she half turned away from him, almost with suffering in his eyes. He wanted to kiss that adorable neck, just where the black hair was lifted from it, leaving uncaught a frail mesh that was almost golden in the light. Then that pathetic face, almost monkey-like, with its lustrous velvet eyes, turned to him; and touching his sleeve again, she told him that he could, if he would, do her a great service, but it must be kept a profound secret. He asked her what it was, startled a little by her manner. She had a friend, an English soldier who had been billeted on them for ten days, not very long ago, and she gave the name of his regiment. He had written to her three letters, and she had written to him, but he knew no French, and she only knew a few words of English. She had promised him that she would learn, so that she might write to him in his own language. Would Bourne help her? The hand, a little red and shiny from work, fluttered on his sleeve. Would Bourne translate his letters to her, and help her to write him a letter in English? Bourne, amazed, tried to picture the man to himself, as though his mind were a kind of crystal in which he might expect to see visions, as a moment before he had been dreaming dreams. It baffled him.

'Restez, monsieur, restez un moment,' she said, placing her basket on the footpath; and then, putting a hand into her blouse, and hunching her shoulders a little as she forced it slightly but perceptibly between her breasts and corset, she drew out a letter, an authentic letter stamped with the postmark of the field service post-office B.E.F., and with the name of the officer who had censored it scrawled across the lower left-hand corner of the envelope. She gave it to him.

'Lisez, monsieur. Je serai très contente si vous voulez bien la lire. Vous êtes si gentil, et je n'aime que lui.'

It was a simple letter. There was no self-consciousness intervening between the writer and the emotion which he tried to put into words, though he had been conscious enough of the censorship, and perhaps of other things intervening between them. Her hand fluttered again on Bourne's sleeve, as she coaxed him to translate it for her; and he did his best, his French halting more than ever, as he studied the handwriting, thinking it might give him some notion of the writer. The script was clear, rather large, commonplace enough: one might say that he was possibly a clerk. Everything was well, that went without saying; they were having a quiet spell; the village where they had their rest-billets had been evacuated by its inhabitants, except for a few old people; the war could not last much longer, for the Hun must know that he could not win now; and then came the three sentences which said all he could say: 'I shall go back and find you some day. I wish we were together again so that I could smell your hair. I love you always, my dearest.'

There were signs of haste in the handwriting, as though he had found some difficulty at that point in opening his heart.

'C'est tout?'

'Je ne puis pas traduire ce qu'il y a de plus important, mademoiselle: les choses qu'il n'a pas voulu écrire.'

'Comme vous avez le coeur bon, monsieur! Mais vraiment, il était comme ça. Il aimait flairer dans mes cheveux tout comme un petit chien.'

She tucked the letter away into that place of secrets, and lifted her hand again, to caress the beloved hair. Suddenly he became acutely jealous of this other man. He stooped, and picked up her basket.

'Ah, mais non, monsieur!' she protested. 'C'est pas permis qu'un soldat anglais porte un panier dans les rues. C'est absolument défendu. Je le sais bien. Il m'a dit toujours, que c'était defendu.'

'Had he?' thought Bourne, and tightened his grip on the handle of it.

'Je porterai le panier, mademoiselle,' he said quietly.

'Mais pourquoi…?' she asked anxiously.

'Parcequ'apparemment, mademoiselle, c'est mon métier,' he said with an ironic appreciation of the fact. She looked at him with troubled eyes.

'Vous voulez bien m'aider à écrire cette petite lettre, monsieur?'

'Mademoiselle, je ferai tout ce que je puis pour vous servir.'

She suddenly relapsed into anxious silence.

‿

Born in Sydney in 1882, **Frederic Manning** settled in the UK in 1903. When the war broke out, he was keen to enlist and enrolled in the King's Shropshire Light Infantry as a private with the number 19022 – who was credited with the authorship of *Her Privates We* when it was published in an expurgated version in 1930. The book had been published anonymously in 1929 in a limited edition of 500 with the title *The Middle Parts of Fortune*. Praised highly by Ernest Hemingway, T. E. Lawrence and Ezra Pound, the book conveys, with robust language and gallows humour, the life of soldiers as opposed to officers. In his introduction to the Serpent's Tail edition of the book, William Boyd writes:

> It is the unremitting honesty of *Her Privates We* that stays in the mind; its refusal to idealise the serving soldier and military life; the absolute determination to present the war in all its boredom, misery and uncertainty; its refusal to glorify or romanticise; the candour that makes a soldier say about the civilians back home, 'They don't give a fuck what 'appens to us 'uns.' We know now that all this was true – but we needed Frederic Manning to bear fictional witness for us, to make it truer.

Manning died in 1935 in Hampstead.

STRATIS MYRIVILIS

ANIMALS

from *Life in the Tomb*

translated by Peter Bien

A NIMALS in wartime.

All day today I have been thinking of nothing else. It's fine and dandy for the humans involved in war. People have 'interests,' ideologies, whims, megalomanias and enthusiasms – just what the doctor ordered for cooking up a truly first-class conflict. And once the war is declared, we have our tricks for saving ourselves once we see that the affair is likely to be a little more than we bargained for. Dugouts and 'going sick,' for example, not to mention desertions.

But what about the animals? What about the poor innocent beasts mobilized by us to wage war at our sides?

Do you know what I think? I think that even if the human race succeeds one day in driving out the devil which makes it erupt in periodic fits of mass murder, it will still have cause to hang its head in shame for the remainder of its existence. Why? For one reason only: because it dragged innocent beasts along to its wars. On reflection, I feel that the day will come when this is considered one of the blackest marks in human history.

Our division carried numerous donkeys along with it when it left the island. An entire ammunition train, in fact. The entry in our official documents speaks of 'an ammunition train of mules,' but if truth be told, the unit has nothing but donkeys. Getting these animals on shipboard caused them considerable suffering, as did getting them off again at Salonika. The angrily groaning cranes seized them and lifted them aloft in strong slings. This drove them wild. Their fright was depicted with astonishing vividness in their frantic eyes. They kicked into the void, brayed, rolled their eyeballs. The horror impressed wrinkles on their hides. After this, they traversed all of Macedonia with us, laden with munitions. By this time they had their own accounts to settle with the Germans, Turks and Bulgarians. When we occupied the trenches their park was established behind our lines at Koupa, a village devastated by artillery-fire and inhabited only by a few French bakers. There, at Koupa, in a beautiful ravine, our division's 'ammunition train of mules' put down its stakes.

The animals were allowed to rest for a few days to recuperate from the prolonged journey, which had left them stunned with fatigue. They caught their breath again. Indeed, they discovered grass in abundance, ate, and began to feel like their old selves. Invigorated, they suddenly noticed that springtime had covered the earth with its resplendence, and that Love was prodding all things, from grubs to flowers, to join in the age-old festival of reproduction. Obedient, filled like all animals with innocence and unknowing, the donkeys heeded the great summons and answered 'Present!' with their amorous trumpet-call. Their ravine droned with jarring epithalamiums; the brayings reverberated through the various defiles until this amorous trumpeting reached all the way to the Peristeri ridges. At this point an airplane took off with a roar from somewhere opposite us. It flew to the ravine and circled it once or twice. As for the donkeys, they did not change their tune. The plane then headed home amidst the enthusiastic reception provided for it by our anti-aircraft batteries whose shells, bursting in the sky, surrounded it with an ever-multiplying flock of little white lambs.

Donkeys do not even know that planes exist. In any case, these particular donkeys were so corporeally absorbed in the joy of living that they had no time left to notice anything else.

Shortly afterwards a series of piercing whistles and sonorous bangs set the ravine howling with pain. It was a genuine slaughter of the innocents. The beasts were massacred on the tender grass, disemboweled amidst the orgasmic intoxication of their genital pleasure. They expired like humans, sighing. Falling to the ground, they gave up the ghost little by little, bending their necks to gaze mournfully at their entrails swaying like red snakes between their legs. Comprehending nothing, they moved their large heads up and down, shuddered; dilated their quivering nostrils; spread their broad lips and uncovered their teeth; drew themselves along the ground on shattered legs. In the end they died, watering the flowers with their blood, their huge eyes filled with perplexity and suffering. One animal with a broken spine dragged its body for a distance of about fifteen meters supported by its front legs only. Then its knees buckled, it turned its head toward its large wound, and gasped with protracted death-throes until it passed on.

One of the drivers started to run like mad as soon as the bombardment commenced. Though in a daze, he had enough presence of mind to keep a tight hold on his donkey's bridle, and he still had it firmly in his grip when he arrived at the dugout occupied by the French bakers. Here, amidst general jeering from our Gallic allies, he finally realized that all he had been pulling behind him was the donkey's head, scythed off at the neck.

The animal was still holding a clump of daisies between its clenched teeth, the yellow petals speckled with blood.

STRATIS MYRIVILIS

ANCHORITES OF LUST

from *Life in the Tomb*

translated by Peter Bien

NVESTIGATING THE WALLS of the dugout today, I encountered a recess whose opening was covered by a triangular stone. It is practically a cupboard, a diminutive one. Inside, I found two cigars which had been forgotten, some additional quinine (what huge amounts our Gallic allies seem to require) and a thin book in French.

A book! How many months since I had set eyes upon one! Snatching this specimen up avidly, I discovered it to be a pornographic pamphlet meant for young adolescents, the kind which, using the pretense of 'science,' informs the teenager about the ugliest perversions of the sexual instinct, complete with outlandish details. The booklet made me realize that French soldiers, and indeed all soldiers of the world's nationalities – including the Greeks – dedicate the long and interminable days in the trench to smut. Millions of men everywhere, underground, sitting there in the dirt: filthy, stinking, covered with whiskers and lice…, and they babble about women!

Although I am extremely ashamed to admit the pleasure I experienced in finding this booklet, I have read it over and over with a glee which seems insatiable. At first I deceived myself, concluding that the mere possession of a book – of the 'printed word' which my spirit had been deprived of for so long – explained my avidity. Now, however, I see my mistake very clearly. No, it was not the hunger for books which caused me to cry out with gluttonous joy when I swooped down, hastily clutched this rotten bone thrown to me by fortune, and began to suck at it as though it were a delicacy; it was another hunger, the craving for female flesh. This lust is inflamed here by our obscene talk. It is a passion which grows from deprivation by consuming its own flesh, an unsatisfied instinct whose embers, as soon as they begin to settle inside the tormented body, are blown again into sky-high flames by the aroused imagination. Not only the officers but the N.C.O.s as well – whoever is privileged to visit the dugouts in the French sector on the next hill – have brought back piles of colored pictures from Parisian magazines and have pinned them on their walls. Before sleeping or eating, and each time they wake up, they cross themselves (half in jest, half seriously) and plant huge, copious kisses on the nude women in the pictures: on their breasts, their legs, their bellies – prolonged, juicy kisses. This is supposed to be a joke, yet they close their eyes voluptuously while they execute this 'joke.' As for me, I have often caught myself discovering a thousand and one excuses to be assigned some duty connected with the sergeant-major's dugout, the chief reason being that I want to loiter there (without seeming to) and waste my time in front of these shameless pictures – one in particular!

The men here wrestle beneath Death's shadow; they crawl on the ground like snakes, a convulsive grimace of doleful pleasure on their faces. Everyone is aware of this unliftable shadow as it settles over the trench, expands invisibly into the very air we breathe and thence into our lungs. It is cast by a cloud which hovers motionlessly above us, cutting us off from divine sunlight and hurling down its threats upon us. Death is omnipresent; he touches everything, wraps everything in his acrid essence, bequeathes to everything a special appearance and a symbolic meaning. His taste is uninterruptedly on our lips. We all are his vassals, all of us, living in his kingdom on sufferance. At any moment he may blow his chilling breath into our lairs. Then, the limbs of all these young bodies panting with sexual frenzy will instantaneously stretch out stiff and yellow. The human form will remain frozen in the ultimate posture of 'attention' which it assumes when Death's trumpet sounds the ultimate roll-call – fingers rigid, jaws hanging loose, eyes glazed. And then, finally, our bodies will be relieved of every lustful desire, for ever and ever.

So get it while you can

STRATIS MYRIVILIS

HOW ZAFIRIOU DIED

from *Life in the Tomb*

translated by Peter Bien

A LONG WITH MY RATIONS TODAY, Dimitratos brought me a piece of
news from the company which has kept me in a state of turmoil
ever since. From the disconnected fragments he let fly, I realized from
the start that he had something to tell me. As soon as he had put down
the mess tin, my wine, and the plate of meat (you see, we don't eat too
badly here in the rest-camp) he emitted a hypocritical sigh:

'Ah, my friend, the world is full of surprises.'

'What surprises, for instance?'

'Mmm, nothing. It's not the best of subjects for mealtime. Eat first;
we'll have the leisure to talk afterwards. Ask the girl to make me a cup
of coffee if you don't mind and give me your cigarettes to keep me busy
in the meantime.'

He dropped the bomb as soon as I had finished.

'They found Sergeant Zafiriou!'

'They caught him?'

'Heaven help us, no! First and foremost, he didn't have to be caught
– he was absolutely stationary. Second, in the state he was in, no one had
the nerve to set hands on him.'

'So he's dead, is he? Get it over with; you're driving me crazy!'

'As you like. It's a rather… um… *filthy* story. He didn't come to a good
end, this "Hellene". Have you ever considered the worst possible way

a man could die? No? Well then, listen. You know we have a common latrine at the regimental encampment – a large ditch with some long, wide planks placed over it from one edge to the other, like bridges. The boys pull down their skivvies and squat there in rows with their left foot on one plank and their right on another. Groaning away, they evacuate their whole gut along with the salted Australian buffalo the French toss us to eat – you'd think we were wild beasts in a circus. When we pitched camp we found a French regiment cursing up hill and down dale as they pulled up stakes and put their kits together for up top – for the trenches. So we inherited some nice things from that regiment: its kitchens, artillery, a lumber dump, quite a few barrels of vegetable fat, a couple of sleeping-dens infected with scabies, and last but not least a colossal ditch like the one I was telling you about. Nearly full… Well we, our bellies flat as tambourines from the rations in the line, no sooner do we pitch camp than we set the dixies bubbling and dive into the chow. So it didn't take us more than a day or two, praise the Lord, before we filled that ditch right up to the top with shit. Then comes an order: we were supposed to get a working-party to remove the planks from the old ditch and throw them over the new one which had been dug alongside it. The same working-party was to stuff the abandoned latrine solid with stones and dirt. Stones! That was fine in theory, but in practice they'd have to be hauled from a considerable distance in wheelbarrows, since Ordnance Stores wouldn't allot a single cart. So the men of the working-party got going. They sprinkled the ditch with dirt only, and the hell with the rest.

'"Did you stuff it full?" they were asked when they returned.

'"Yes."

'"Really full?"

'"Solid!"

'A lousy pack of lies… Well, Zafiriou the "Hellene" gets up one night to take a piss. Maybe he was a little tipsy – who knows? We'd had a ration of cognac distributed to us that evening. Maybe he was just groggy because his sleep had been interrupted. In any case, instead of going to the new latrine, he heads straight for the old one. This looked like firm ground because of the dirt they'd thrown over it. He makes a bee-line for it with that regulation marching-step he used even for going to the jakes, and braaaaf! down he goes, almost to the bottom. He fought down there, he struggled, tried to jump out, but no use. The poor devil just sank deeper and deeper until he suffocated and kicked the bucket. The doctor says he died from asphyxia. Your fine hero gave up the ghost gorged with shit.'

'What you're doing is cheap and vulgar, Dimitratos.'

'Take it easy, friend. What doesn't become cheap and vulgar as soon as you tell it the way it really is?'

'Zafiriou was a genuine hero. He proved it in the trenches. You should show some respect...'

'A hero by pre-arrangement, just like all the others who make war their profession. And what about me? I'm a hero too, aren't I? I even have the War Cross, now that we're on the subject. But never mind; that's another story... After all, as soon as we fished your genuine hero out of the latrine with a net, Balafaras of course must have sent one of those "lovely letters" to Mytilene – typewritten. You know, the ones the men have learned by heart, offering the parents "congratulations [Is there any reason for congratulations that you know of?] for the glorious death of your son, who, having demonstrated incomparable gallantry worthy of the best Hellenic traditions, was killed on such-and-such a date, bravely fighting for Faith and Fatherland, against the foe." As soon as you decide to tell the truth, all this becomes cheap and vulgar. Just imagine, for instance, if he'd written: "Zafiriou died gallantly wrestling with allied Franco-hellenic shit. Unfortunately, he was unable to cry 'Long live the Fatherland' at the moment of his glorious demise, because... er... he happened to have a mouthful"!'

STRATIS MYRIVILIS

ALIMBERIS CONQUERS HIS FEAR OF SHELLS

from *Life in the Tomb*

translated by Peter Bien

FOR THE PAST TWO WEEKS they've been preparing us for the great undertaking. Our entire division, reinforced by two non-divisional regiments of reservists, is going to charge the enemy in order to capture one of their large fortified garrisons. The organization needed for this colossal slaughter – needed until the very moment we receive the signal for it to begin – is proceeding with a system so scientifically refined, down to its last insignificant detail, that it boggles the mind. Every conquest of the human brain in engineering, the sciences, psychology, even in art, has become an instrument to aid, as much as it can, the complete extermination of the human beings across the way, men who are lying in wait just as we are, wrapped in their mud.

Satanic engines, murderous vapors enclosed in tubes and shells: they poison the air, expunge the vision from one's eyes, raise suppurated pustules on the lungs. Flame which lays waste whatever it finds before it except tanned leather. Flame which re-ignites automatically by itself after it has been dipped in water and drawn out again into the air. Short, plump torpedoes pregnant with terrible explosive matter. A smaller type which we launch in a kind of tiny trench mortar, using compressed air instead of gunpowder and wick. Incendiary bombs which spill thousands of burning grains out of their bellies when they burst, grains which hop about on their own like devils and can therefore kindle a great number of fires. Thermite bombs capable of developing sufficient heat to melt the breech and barrel of a large-bore cannon, fusing them into a doughish lump of undifferentiated metal. (Once we ignited one inside a steel helmet, which melted and turned to ash in a minute, as though made of cardboard.) Complicated pumps whose nozzles sprinkle fire and death. Masks resembling those worn by sponge-divers. Straps, rubber belts, respirators, chemical apparatuses, electronic mechanisms with microphones that overhear secrets and betray them. Magnificent flares which will ignite like multicolored constellations over thousands of innocent men when they are writhing on the ground, their lungs smashed and their living intestines wriggling between blood-stained clots of mud like flayed serpents.

But of all these repulsive inventions, the one which sends the ugliest chill up my spine is the trench knife. This simple, plain knife with its wide blade is used by the 'liquidators': soldiers who stay behind in a conquered trench in order to 'mop it up' while the waves of the assault move forward. What this means is that they slaughter all of the enemy who have remained hidden in dark corners or in the abandoned dugouts, whether from fear or cunning – slaughter them coolly and deliberately, by hand, at close range, like lambs. These liquidators or 'mop-up men' (doesn't their ironic name remind you of municipal street-cleaners or of peaceful bank-clerks?) must put every last one of the laggards to the knife, one by one. If you want to 'cleanse' a dugout you start by tossing in a couple of hand-grenades, or you spray it with the flame-thrower. If you have a gas bomb on you, so much the better. This is the burning of the hornet's nest. You heave one inside and all who are hiding there dart through the entrance, stumbling from suffocation and inflamed eyes. The liquidators are waiting for them outside. They slaughter them and then proceed to the next dugout.

All this is being instructed by means of lectures, illustrations, realistic mock-ups, and very enlightening theory.

Last night the captain gathered the whole company together in the large anti-bombardment bunker. He told us that he didn't want a single coward to be found among our ranks during the attack. One and one only, he said, was enough to spread panic, causing the failure of an opera-tion and the useless deaths of countless comrades. This we all found very reasonable in every respect. Afterwards, however, he rested his eyes on us and, smiling in a kindly manner, issued a request. If there was anyone among us who knew himself to be 'faint-hearted,' would he please not hesitate to say so frankly. What mattered was that he declare himself *now.*

This made all of us feel rather strange. The great bunker where we had assembled is a complete gallery burrowed six meters beneath the surface. We gather here whenever the enemy begins an all-out bombard-ment, because the other dugouts cannot withstand the 'big boys' for very long whereas this place is an entire fortress. The timbers lining its walls and roof are whole tree-trunks, its ingress a veritable labyrinth; there is a layer of soil five meters thick above it and armor plating inside. Big as it is, however, it holds all two hundred of us only with difficulty. Whenever we remain inside for more than a few hours at a time, the air grows noxious. If the sentries at the door had allowed it, many would have slipped outside during the bombardments to fill their lungs with 'clean', cool air at the risk of losing their lives…

The atmosphere this time was just the same, gathered as we were once more in the great bunker, the cannons howling across the way. During a long interval we did not talk; we just listened to the bursting shells as they barked in the air. The captain's voice had sounded so calm amid all this uproar in the background that it made one feel almost safe just to be near him. With that ingratiating smile on his rosy lips, he promenaded his gaze upon us and waited to discover whether or not there really was a 'faint-hearted' man in our company.

We all understood perfectly well, yet no one possessed the courage to open his heart and utter the truth. Looking straight ahead because of our embarrassment yet filled with a certain curiosity, we waited. As soon as the slightest murmur or noise was heard, however, we turned with a mass movement and searched about in order to discover who was ready to confess his 'faint-heartedness'. The unshaven faces gleamed as white as plaster beneath the illumination of the acetylene lamp, a secret fever burning in their sunken eyes. I felt an inner urge to push my way through the crowd and station myself at the captain's side so that I could

face all of my comrades and say to them: 'Listen, every one of you –
does this mean that there isn't a single brave man among us? We're two
hundred strong here. The captain is looking for one coward; I'm looking
for one man of courage – a man brave enough to confess that he is afraid
to die. Nobody? Well then, every last one of us is faint-hearted, we're a
lot of cowardly and good-for-nothing liars.'

At the same time, however, I felt that not even I myself possessed
such inner courage. Indeed, I wouldn't have been at all surprised if my
lips were being sealed by the War Cross, my tongue being tied in knots
by my second stripe.

Meanwhile, a voice did speak out. It came from the rear of the
gallery during those difficult moments we were all experiencing.

'Sir, if you please…'

A rustling, a stirring. The mass of soldiers squeezed itself together
even tighter than before and opened an aisle down which came a short
private with curly hair and squarish shoulders. Vasilios Athanasios Alimberis. Speaking slowly, and searching for the proper expressions, he made
the following declaration:

'I respectfully inform you, Captain, that I am faint-hearted, and I
earnestly request that I may be left behind when the attack takes place.'

'Do you mean to say you're afraid?'

The captain asked this in a tone of near-astonishment, as though
actually insulted that such a declaration should be heard in his company.
Alimberis answered, more boldly now, a confessional tone entering his
heavy, boorish speech:

'That's what I mean, Captain. Yes, afraid. I'm a carpenter, just a
simple carpenter, you understand. I'm still single, because I have my old
mother and four sisters to support – a hopeless business to be sure. I
haven't even been able to marry off the oldest yet. They sold our little
farm, the only thing our father left us when he died, and for the time
being they're eating up the proceeds. I've got them on my mind day
and night; I can't think of anything else. Tell me, what will become of
five women with no means of support, if the war lasts much longer?…
In my whole life I've never quarreled with a single soul. I don't have
the courage to kill. Every time I hear a shell, I feel like I'm giving up

the ghost. I shiver; you'd think I was freezing. I might faint at the sight of blood. But work – nothing but the best. Give me all you like; I'm at your service, with pleasure! I can run a lathe. Hand me some wood and I'll turn you out the most ingenious things you've ever seen, absolutely first class... Please forgive me, Captain, for making bold to tell you all this. You see, I've spoken as in the confessional. We all know you to be a man of good heart. That's why I said to myself, Let's tell him the whole truth, seeing that he's ordered us to, and he'll forgive me.'

Vasilios Athanasios Alimberis spoke these words and then fell silent. He had remained at rigid attention the whole time, motionless except for his fluttering eyelids. Behind his coarse pronunciation I felt that I heard the muted, tender tones of another voice which had died. Yes, what I heard was the painful lamentation of Gighandis – the only difference being that he, lacking Alimberis's extreme simplicity and possessing an ego whose multifarious weaknesses had been cultivated to an incredible degree, would never have yielded up the unpardonable truth about himself to so many people.

No one knew what would happen next. Alimberis remained at attention. His innocent eyes, fixed directly upon the captain, were awaiting some response which assuredly would be crucial for his life. All the rest of us were awaiting that response too, since very likely it would have repercussions for others as well. Outside, the cannonade was still bellowing away maniacally. The captain grimaced, deep in thought. His hands were behind his back and he was thinking – but he certainly was not thinking pleasant thoughts. Ugly wrinkles creased his ruddy features and a flash of harsh cruelty passed across his eyes as he slowly lifted his gaze from Alimberis's feet and paraded it gradually up his entire body until it halted inside the carpenter's eyes. This stare into the eyes lasted just a moment. Then the captain smiled courteously (Alimberis returned the smile, mirror-like), motioned the soldier to stand at ease, and commanded: 'Sergeant Pavlelis!'

'Here, Captain.'

'You will accompany the second patrol when it leaves. You will take four men from your platoon and convey Private Alimberis through the exit *boyau* to the second row of barbed wire. There you will bind him to the steel post which stands to the right of the entanglement's ingress, where he shall remain – in order to grow accustomed to shellfire – until I send someone to bring him back.' (Then, as though by way of explanation:) 'It's just a question of habituation, this. Getting it out of one's system, that's all. Then you're not afraid any more.'

The captain's very first words had turned Alimberis pale as wax. Now he held out his hands and cast terrified glances first at the captain, then at Sergeant Pavlelis, after which he began to stammer rapidly and in great confusion, his eyes filled with tears:

'You couldn't do that. Captain, Sir... I respectfully inform you... no, you wouldn't do that to me, Sir... you'll take pity.'

'But it's not anything you need be frightened about, as you seem to think,' said the captain. 'You won't get the slightest scratch, I assure you. The place is hidden behind some bushes, quite aside from the fact that our friends happen to be pounding us on the left flank just now. I'm trying to help you get it out of your system, don't you see? Tomorrow, never fear, you'll come back to us a real champ. Greece has lots of good carpenters. Well, now they've all got to become good soldiers... And there's no call, if you please, for snivelling and tears. Men at war, Private Alimberis, do not cry!'

Alimberis wiped his eyes with his huge hands and answered:

'I'm crying for myself, Captain, and I'm crying for five women too...'

Late that night, Sergeant Pavlelis presented himself at the captain's dugout, his hand raised in salute.

'Your orders have been carried out, Sir.'

'My orders?'

'Concerning Private Alimberis. We bound him to the post at the ingress to the second row of barbed wire, just as you commanded.'

'How did he behave? Did he offer any resistance?'

'None at all. He just kept pleading with us, blubbering away. He said he'd die if we left him alone out there in the darkness with all those rockets. I felt sorry for him, to tell you the truth. Every shell that passes overhead makes him jump clear out of his skin.'

★

Who knows what tragedy unfolded out there at the ingress to the second row of barbed wire, during the night. The darkness was so thick, probably even God himself was unable to witness it.

Two men went out at dawn to bring Alimberis back. They found him completely calm. His arms, bound at the elbows behind the post, were bloody from the rope and the barbed wire. He was leaning back against the post, his head resting on his left shoulder. When they released him he sat down on the ground and studied his hands, first the palms then the backs. Next, he commenced to cut off his buttons one by one and to pull out the threads ever so slowly with his fingernails, whistling softly all the while He performed this task with the utmost care. The soldiers, who still had not understood, kept telling him: 'Let's get a move on before daylight comes and you get us in trouble. You can do your mending in your dugout. Looks like they've really made a man out of you at last.' Alimberis seemed not to hear. Bending down in the half-darkness, they saw him close at hand, clearly, and only then did they understand. They grasped him beneath the armpits. With one in front dragging and the other in back pushing, they got him into the exit *boyau* and brought him from there to the trench. He whistled the whole way. Afterwards, he continued to whistle, always unraveling his clothes. When he finally gave this up his lips remained puckered in the same position, as though still whistling. Today, he was sent to the hospital. To arrive there you have to negotiate an exposed pass, a section which the enemy bombards if even so much as an ant attempts to cross it. With great difficulty they got him to crouch over and make a run for it. The shells that raced shrieking over his head were unable to instil either fear or interest into his tormented spirit, which had already died. It had been taken out there to the exit at the second row of barbed wire one terrible night during the bombardment, and killed. Why? Because he had dared to let this spirit reveal its true condition.

I feel no love for my captain any longer. I can only pity him – or can I?

STRATIS MYRIVILIS

GAS

from *Life in the Tomb*

translated by Peter Bien

FROM ALL APPEARANCES they've caught wind across the way of the great undertaking which we are organizing in our front lines and in the supply stations behind us. For three days now, enemy planes have been operating over our positions with admirable bravery and daring. In all the raids the sky fills with little cotton-like clouds which sprout everywhere and follow behind each enemy aircraft like a flock of lambs. These are the shells from our anti-aircraft batteries bursting high in the blue sky. Occasionally, one of the metallic war-birds is brought down. Three mornings ago a lone German bomber engaged seven allied fighters above our lines. It escaped intact after downing an English plane, which fell from the top of the sky, howling as it descended (as though in pain) and trailing a comet of pitch-black smoke behind it. The pilot's body worked loose and fell straight downward like some kind of black thing, whereas the airplane kept burning and weeping until it crashed a mile away. On another day two German planes came and trained their sights on a huge observation-balloon which hovered in the air like a colossal yellow kidney, permanently moored to a small humpish mountain. A bullet found it, igniting the hydrogen inside, and the observer who was in its basket plunged to the ground out of a majestic fire whose flaming tongue licked the heavens, fluttered for a moment like a sheet of gold, and then abruptly died out. The observer was a young French major. He lived for a short time, and with his last breaths he begged his Command to tell his brother, who was serving in France, not to remain in the forces any longer but to go and stay with their mother. Of her four sons, this brother was the only one left.

★

The offensive is now the one great topic of conversation in the trenches. Apparently the hour is approaching. And apparently the enemy are fully expecting us. These last few days their artillery batteries have been literally maniacal in their attempt to eradicate our trenches – especially in the mornings, when the whole universe seems to be falling apart. The men have come to display a melancholy fatalism when they discuss the impending events. Everyone knows that he is bound to play a part, like it or not.

Two days ago, at dawn, the Bulgarians started bombarding us with time-fire projectiles and asphyxiant gas, combined. It was our first opportunity to experience the latter weapon in actual use. True, we had heard of it previously as a kind of legend, thanks to the theoretical lectures delivered to us before we buried ourselves in the trenches. Since then, our gasmasks had been an almost senseless luxury, indeed a troublesome one, since their containers, suspended awkwardly from our belts at the end of a cord, bang relentlessly against our thighs and make noise as they strike our rifles.

About a dozen friends were gathered in my dugout telling stories when the initial gas bombs landed, making a special type of hollow sound. We took them at first for common shells which had plunged into some boggish area and failed to explode. Several of the men even shouted out the customary mock – 'New fuse needed! Take aim, boys!' – and then returned to their storytelling as if nothing had happened.

Afterwards we caught a whiff of some scent in the air. It was an extremely light and pleasant aroma resembling bitter-almond. The concentration soon increased, however, and before long the air was acrid, pungently sour, poisoned. In an instant the trench hummed with sudden stirrings. A pandemonium of cries, the stupefied confusion of shrieks and commands.

'Gas! Gas!' shouted the N.C.O.s maniacally. 'Masks everyone! Your masks!'

But practically none of us had his mask ready to hand. Those who chanced to be visiting in someone else's dugout at that moment, far from their kits, had an especially bad time of it. What followed was a tragedy of mass confusion. Most of the men attempted to flee my dugout. It's a deep one, you see, and thus more and more of the gas – which is heavier than air – kept settling inside and filling it. But how could anyone stick even his nose out into the trench? It was guaranteed suicide. The sky out there was raining lead and steel, the time fuses just waiting for each man to scamper out of his dugout so that they could smash him head-on; the 'bonbonnières' were bursting at a fixed height over our lines and scattering a thick hail of lead upon anyone who dared emerge. So all the men retreated back into the shelter. Climbing over one another like drunkards or lunatics, they dug their fists into eyes that were smarting horribly and flooding with tears as though sprinkled with red pepper. Their noses and mouths (which were locked tight) they thrust so deeply beneath blankets that they were in danger of suffocating. A painful clawing in the throat and nose made everyone bellow with a harsh cough while the mud-covered hands kept furiously rubbing enflamed eyes. It was a sight whose unspeakable bestiality I could never have imagined before I actually saw it. In my own case, I had managed to find my mask in time, searching blindly with eyes squeezed tight. Soon, I was staring through its clouded lenses, overcome by the unheard-of horror and listening to the agony of my tormented comrades all of whom were rolling about in one frenzied mass of pale, blinded, mud-besplattered humanity, rolling about and bellowing as though in the last throes of rabies. Howling, they bit into their greatcoats and blankets. Their heads groped about and knocked against each other inside this skein of tangled bodies, like the heads of newly-born puppies when their eyes are still sealed and they search in chaos, using the sensitivity to touch possessed by their naked snouts. I was glued against the shelter's partition-wall pressing my palms tightly against the mask and overcome to such a degree by fear and pain that I could give no assistance whatsoever to anyone. If an enemy soldier had entered our dugout at that point, one single enemy soldier, he would have been able to polish us all off without the slightest difficulty. We would have sat there and allowed him to slaughter us just as we were, with our blinded eyes, powerless to defend our lives, and weeping like little girls. Several might even have thanked him profusely for delivering them from this torment.

Fortunately, it did not last very long. Even better, a furious wind began to blow immediately afterward, a wind which went right inside us, reviving us as it raced refreshingly through our flaming lungs like a fountain of life. It rinsed the infection out of the trench's air and carried away the lethal vapor. Places where the gas bombs exploded are still unapproachable. Most of the shells, however, we buried. To fumigate the dugouts we burned solidified alcohol inside them.

Although the horror did not last very long, hordes of men were sent to the hospitals: blinded, vomiting, coughing until racked with convulsions, grimacing horribly and spitting blood, viscera festering, eyes swollen shut: pasted together by yellowish discharges and resembling two wounds beginning to scab. In our trench six men died, among them George Dimitratos, who suffocated within ten minutes. When I went to see him I failed to recognize him at first. His face was bloated, his lips so swollen that the hairs of his mustache were standing erect, like porcupine quills. He seemed to be holding a mouthful of water between his distended cheeks, prior to spitting it out at us in jest. In short, the Jack-of-all-trades will not be court-martialed after all. Nor shall we hear him ever again telling any of those cynical jokes of his. May God have pity on his children, so that he may repose in eternal peace. Amen.

The rest of us have acquired an uninterrupted watering of the eyes as our souvenir from this bombardment. Strong light irritates us now and we seek out dim corners like people infected with rabies. In addition, there have been repercussions in our stomachs, which balk at accepting nourishment. The chief sentiment which this weapon has left in us is rage – an impotent rage for having undergone humiliation, and especially a humiliation caused by such an unmanly means of waging war. All such means are so contrary to the traditions of Greek gallantry that they are almost incomprehensible to us. The men have been going into the trench and spitting toward the Bulgarian line.

'Cheats! Frauds! Charlatans!… Phthou!'

⤙

Stratis Myrivilis is the pseudonym of Efstratios Stamatopoulos, who was born on the Greek island of Lesbos in 1890. After enlisting to fight in the first Balkan War against Turkey in 1912, he returned home injured. In the First World War, Myrivilis fought in the army of Elefterios Venizelos' breakaway government on the Macedonian front. *Life in the Tomb*, his novel of his wartime experiences, was published in serialised form in the weekly newspaper *Kambana* in 1923/24. It was published in book form in Athens in 1930 and is seen as the novel that founded modern Greek literature. A journalist and broadcaster, Myrivilis opposed the German occupation during the Second World War and was until 1951 director of the Greek National Broadcasting Institute. He died in Athens in 1969.

In *Life in the Tomb*, Myrivilis uses an ironic, mocking and humorous voice to attack his many targets. He was never one to beat about the bush, and his message comes across loud and clear – put a foot wrong and you end up in the shit.

RAYMOND ESCHOLIER

SHEEP

from *Mahmadou Fofana*

translated by Malcolm Imrie

In memory of Major Mazand
  In these flowery meadows
  Watered by the Seine,
  Seek the one who leads you,
  My dear little sheep.

Mme Antoinette de Lafon de Boisguérin Deshoulières (c. 1634–1694)

I

Dinner had just finished. Warrant officer Bourriol stretched out his hand to the flask draped in a blue cloth that still stood on the table:

'Be generous with it!' he advised.

And yet the draught he poured himself scarcely filled two-thirds of his quarter-litre tin mug, which long use had coated with a thick, dark patina.

It is true, though, that this was just the post-*digestif* which, as everyone knows, follows the coffee, the after-coffee snifter, and the *digestif* itself.

Nevertheless, don't imagine that warrant officer Bourriol nurtured any special love for army-issue *gnole*.* On the contrary, he claimed that he had never drunk such a treacherous concoction. Back in France, no

---

*A very rough brandy (*trans.*).

SHEEP

one had ever persuaded him to touch even a drop of the stuff. But, as
Bourriol put it, you've got to drink something, and where are you going
to find anything better in this Balkan village in the back of beyond?

For all this was happening at Grechowatz, in the non-commissioned
officers' mess of the 196th battalion of the *Tirailleurs sénégalais*.

After the woeful hours of the victorious attack in Dobropol* and
the terrible suffering of the pursuit that followed (oh, those dark days in
Eğri Palanka, where breakfast was a biscuit and dinner a potato found
in a field!), Bourriol and his pals were enjoying a wonderful feeling of
peace and comfort in this rustic village of Old Serbia.

In the centre of the large, low room with whitewashed walls and a
floor covered with wooden pallets for lounging or sleeping, the wood-
fired stove snored softly; pipe smoke was starting to obscure the ceiling.
Bourriol warmed his stained mug in his hands and every now and then
took another swig of the caustic beverage that seemed like a mixture
of tobacco juice and paregoric elixir. No one said a word, basking in a
glow of well-being.

Little Sergeant Barbotin, the most fidgety of them all, broke this
blissful silence:

'Hey, Pitit!' he shouted suddenly at tirailleur Tiani Bigo, who was
busy tidying up the food locker... 'Pitit! Is my belly good enough to
eat?'

And tirailleur Tiani Bigo, nicknamed Pitit on account of his diminutive stature, baby face and gazelle-like eyes, tirailleur Tiani Bigo diligently
recited:

'No, sergeant, it's gone off!'

---

*Dobropol, now Dobro Pole in the Republic of Macedonia, was the site of a decisive battle
on 15 September 1918 at the end of the long Serbian campaign. French and Serbian troops
defeated the Bulgarians who had occupied the town since 1915 and who as a result signed an
armistice and withdrew from the war. Eğri Palanka (then in Bulgaria) is now Kriva Palanka
(in Macedonia). The story of the missing sheep that follows here takes place in towns and
villages around the Serbia/Bulgaria border, so that Tsaribrod, where the sheep were collected,
then in Bulgaria, is now Dimitrovgrad in Serbia, and Zaïtchar, where they were eventually
delivered, is now Zaječar in Serbia. Pirot, where the sheep went missing, is still Pirot and still
in Serbia. And, despite an awful lot of historical cartographical research, I still have no idea
where Grechowatz was, or is! (*trans.*)

You will not be surprised to learn that such a witty joke originally met with considerable success. But its frequent repetition ever since by Sergeant Barbotin, its inventor, had robbed it of much of its humour. On this particular day, the mirth that it produced was nothing out of the ordinary. It was not enough to drag Bourriol away from his dreams; he was dozing now, beside his empty mug, off in some sort of nirvana.

Standing by the window, chief warrant officer Fouillepot did not move either, and continued to gaze out through the little square panes, and between the wooden arches of the balcony, on to the orchard in front of the house which spread out the yellowing carpet of its damp grass and the gnarled trunks of its quince trees whose branches now bore only a few rare, golden-brown leaves.

Still, someone asked:

'How about a round of manille?'

'I vote for auction manille,' said Bourriol. 'That's the best version.'

The chief warrant officer shrugged.

'Pah! Rubbish! The king of all games is 4-hand piquet. But if it makes you happy, I'll play auction manille.'

★

Sergeant Rossignol was starting to shuffle the cards when the door opened to admit tirailleur John. The latter took a few steps on to the floor of beaten earth, corrected his position, saluted, looked round for the chief warrant officer and, having found him, said:

'Warrant officer, sir, the captain he ask for you straight away.'

And John stood still, hands on the seams of his trousers, his saffron-coloured face embellished with strange peacock blue tattoos, glowing with self-importance.

'So the captain's asking for me, is he? You tell him,' exclaimed Fouillepot, 'you tell him he's getting on my bloody nerves!'

John lowered his head under a torrent of curses... Isn't it always the same people who get called? We ever going to get a moment's peace in this shit job? When are they going to stop f–... fooling around?

★

While Fouillepot was swearing and demanding his boots, his belt and his puttees, Sergeant Barbotin struck up a conversation with tirailleur John:

'So, John, you are still happy English?'

The yellowish-skinned tirailleur narrowed his eyes a little.

'Yes, sergeant, me Senegal English! Senegal English only make Senegal war. Not make France war! Senegal English make France war, that not good way.'*

Thus *tirailleur* John expressed the bitterness in his soul. He considered himself the victim of a great injustice, something outrageously unfair.

A citizen of Fataba, in Sierra Leone, on one ill-starred day in 1915 he had crossed the border to go to Goundiou, in French Guinea. Had he not been assured that there he would find excellent kola nuts at an amazingly good price?

He had set off with no misgivings. It would be a very short trip. He would be back in Fataba within three days at the outside. But alas! John was forgetting that the door of our dwelling opens on to infinity and he who fancies that he knows where he is going when he crosses that threshold has taken leave of his senses.

No sooner had John entered Goundiou than he was brought to a halt by a large gathering. In the middle of a circle, helped by an interpreter, a white officer was berating a native who, as John quickly understood, was the village head:

'I must have five volunteers!' shouted the officer. And the unfortunate Samba Dialo, Goundiou's headman, replied with despairing gestures. Let the lieutenant look around him, search the village; he would only find old men, women, and children!

---

*John, like most of the other *tirailleurs sénégalais* in this novel (who despite the name given to them in the French army did not only come from Senegal but also from other French colonies in West Africa and sometimes other parts of Africa too), speaks a very simplified French adaptation of the Bambara language which was used as a kind of Esperanto in the army, and given the rather racist name *petit-nègre*. My English version is partly based on a guide for white French officers published in 1916 called *Le français tel que le parlent nos tirailleurs sénégalais* (*trans.*).

Then suddenly the officer, who had just noticed John, exclaimed, 'And what about this one?' The village head rubbed his eyes, thought he was dreaming. Who was this tall stranger with broad shoulders, in the flower of robust youth?

'This man', declared Samba Dialo, 'this man is not from Goundiou, which does not prevent him from being an ideal volunteer.'

This was indeed the lieutenant's opinion, too. And so it was that John found himself promoted straight away to the honourable position of volunteer soldier for the duration of the war in the glorious corps of *tirailleurs sénégalais*.

When he grasped what was going on, John cried out in dismay:

'Me Senegal English! Senegal English not...'

'That'll do! What's your name?'

'My name John, me Senegal English...'

'That's quite enough. You're repeating yourself! But John isn't a Soussou name. Don't you have another?'

'My name John. Mister Bulwer always call me like that. Me his boy.'

'Yes, fine. Now stop babbling!'

After that, John had never seen Fataba again, but he had gone on a long journey across the rolling sea. He had come to know Marseille, Saint-Raphaël and the army camp Gallieni in neighbouring Fréjus, along with the beaches of Valescure and the pine woods of Boulouris; and then he had visited Champagne, and the Somme, before returning to the sea again, with its golden isles,* and its floating mines, and its underwater torpedoes, and finally disembarking at ancient Thessaloniki.

But he had still refused to give any other name than John. And in fact no one had bothered too much about this little detail and he had been registered under the name of John, as he wanted.

As for sending him back to his home, the question had never even been considered, and yet has it not been proven that someone who bears the name of John can only be English Senegalese?

So by what law was John made into a volunteer? His complaints

---

*'golden isles' here probably refers specifically to the little Île d'Or just off the coast at Saint-Raphaël and to the four Îles d'Hyères, also known as the Îles d'Or, just to the west (*trans.*).

about this matter are endless: 'French not bad but me Senegal English! Senegal English not…'

'Come on, John, give it a rest!'

Chief warrant officer Fouillepot is ready to leave. John follows him.

Outside, neither says a word as they walk along the rough surface of the village's only street, past thatched barns and houses with wooden balconies, with a bitter wind blowing the fine autumn rain into their faces.

John continues to meditate on the cruel twist of fate that has taken him away from Fataba, while Fouillepot worries about what the captain might want of him. 'What stupid scheme have they come up with now?' he asks himself.

[The captain's 'stupid scheme' turns out to be to order Fouillepot to take a squad of men headed by corporal Mahmadou Fofana, the novel's eponymous hero, to collect a flock of 407 sheep, destined for feeding the troops, in nearby Tsaribrod and take them to a centre in Zaïtchar, some 120 kilometres away. The last time something similar was attempted, a third of the sheep 'disappeared' en route, so Fouillepot is given strict instructions to ensure that he does not lose any.

We rejoin the story some way into the journey when they have reached the town of Pirot, where they are given a warm welcome by the inhabitants and where Fouillepot is given an especially warm welcome by a young Serbian widow named Militza. The 'reverie' from which he is about to get a rude awakening is of the night he has just spent with her.]

★

When Fouillepot emerged from his reverie, he was in the courtyard of the barracks. His first thought was for the sheep, and he headed towards the stables. He had only just opened the gate when the two guards Zangué Diarra and Balisé loomed up, looking threatening. They were already pulling out their machetes when they recognised their leader.

Come on now! Nothing bad could have happened. It would be a waste of time to count the sheep again before setting off.

Nonetheless, once the sun was up Fouillepot did check the number just to put his mind at rest.

Oh! What a terrible shock! There were only three hundred and ninety-two. Fifteen sheep were missing! Oh, dear God!

They searched the stable. Right at the back, under a flight of steps, there was a little door covered in dust and spiders' webs that no one had noticed before. It was still half-open. That is where they had got out! Now what?

Fouillepot went off to explain the situation to Major Stoïanovitch. This old warrior expressed no surprise, then, elaborating his thoughts, let it be known that during the occupation the town had been infested by a great number of Bulgarians, Levantines, thieves and hoodlums who had not yet been entirely purged, but nonetheless he would clean this Augean Stable or his name wasn't Stoïanovitch! As for those who had stolen the sheep he would find them and have them beaten to death. How could these good and courageous allies have been so treacherously robbed in the town of Pirot! This was something he would never get over!

In his agitation he was stamping his foot on the ground and lashing his high, polished boots with his riding whip.

'Yes, sir,' continued Fouillepot. 'But what am I going to do now?'

'Ah, my friend! All you can do is continue with your journey.'

'Well, that's it!' muttered the chief warrant officer. 'Now I'm for it! Ah, the swine!'

And off he went, lost in dark thoughts.

★

He cheered himself up by giving the tirailleurs a piece of his mind:

'Listen to me, you bunch of rotten, good-for-nothing bastards! Joking's over. You take it from me! I'll show you that courts martial weren't invented for dogs!'

Then he singled out Fofana, declaring that whoever had made him a corporal had taken stupidity to new limits and would have done better – a hundred times better – if he'd given the red wool stripes to the most half-witted pack mule of the battalion.

They passed through Pirot, heads bowed. As they went over the bridge on the Nischava, Fouillepot looked up for a moment. Among the little columns of smoke rising from the rooftops, he looked for one in particular. He thought he'd found it. It was there, last night, that... A little tenderness crept into his soul. But it quickly vanished, and the next moment he was brooding bitterly again.

Occasionally he would revive, just long enough to stamp his heel on invisible enemies or issue more dire threats.

'*Amagni!*'* spat Kouroué Taraoré in disgust.

The tirailleurs were in great distress. Would they now have to endure long days of fear and foreboding? The last stage of the journey had been so nice, so easy! And this next one should have been even better.

How simple it would have been just to wander along peacefully in the gentle warmth of this golden autumn day telling tall stories or singing soothing laments. Instead of which they had the formidable fury of chief warrant officer Fouillepot hanging over their heads! *Amagni!*

Crestfallen, Mahmadou Fofana walked on, his face fixed in thought.

★

They had left the straight and level main road to follow a hilly, winding country lane through freshly planted fields or stubble, through vineyards and pastures. The countryside was deserted. Here and there, a ploughman could be seen leading his team of huge buffaloes, or some shepherd with his flock.

Meanwhile Fofana was still deep in thought. Then all of a sudden he jumped, and smacked his forehead. Tirailleurs Mesi Mara and Kouroué were walking nearby in grim silence. He waved them over and conferred with them in a low voice for a few moments. All at once they grasped what he was saying and started roaring with laughter, slapping their thighs.

Fouillepot glared at them like a tiger and started cursing again.

'Listen to me, you, you've got some bloody nerve to laugh after what has happened, but God help me you won't be laughing long, I can promise you that!'

Fofana dared to interrupt him:

'Chief warrant officer, sir, not bad laugh! We soon find the sheep again.'

**Amagni is the general word for 'bad' in Bambara (*trans.*).

'What did you say? "We will find the sheep"?'

'You taking the piss out of me by any chance?'

Mahmadou spoke with authority, politely and firmly:

'Chief warrant officer, sir. You same time our mother and father: no one think of taking piss out of you. I only say what is sure. This day we will find sheep taken from us by those do "very bad things".'

The chief warrant officer knows that Fofana does not tend to speak idly and that he has more than one trick up his sleeve. Yet what he is saying is a bit too much to be true. Find the sheep again? If they were still in Pirot, such a thing might just be possible, but here?

Still, Fouillepot is intrigued. He waits with curiosity to see what will happen next.

Mahmadou Fofana, who only a short while ago showed no interest in the outside world, now scans the landscape attentively. The tirailleurs watch what he's doing surreptitiously and occasionally chuckle to themselves. Only Fouillepot remains puzzled. The country lane is little more than a track. Their convoy has to trek up some tough slopes, then scuttle down steep inclines. And there's nothing, still nothing, to be seen!

But now the squad reaches the top of a hill looking down on a narrow valley. A couple of hundred paces below the hilltop, a shepherd is grazing his sheep. Fofana says a few winged words to his men and makes a request to Fouillepot:

'Chief warrant officer, sir, if you say nothing it will be good!'

Then he leaves the group and approaches the shepherd. The latter stares in utter astonishment at the black herdsmen in blue helmets leading such a huge flock along the path. He is a man with a bushy grey beard. His leather sandals are held on with laces wound round the narrow legs of coarse, wool trousers – true Gallic britches. With his sheepskin jerkin and thick brown serge cap, he resembles a shepherd from an old Nativity scene.

With a sweeping gesture, Fofana invites him to come over. At first the Serb is a little hesitant. Then he decides to come and meet the black man. The latter starts by trying to reassure him:

'*Serbo dobro! Aïdé, Belgrad! Serbo dobro!*'

Then he shows him his pipe and makes a sign to suggest that he doesn't have anything to light it with. The other man eventually understands. He hunts in his pocket and pulls out an old flint and wick lighter which he prepares to strike. The corporal asks him to wait, looks for his tobacco pouch and starts filling his pipe, slowly and carefully.

Whatever he does, this damned shepherd had better not turn round! And so, to be sure he doesn't, Fofana starts waving his arms about:

'*Pirot dobro!*'

★

Pirot is such a beautiful town!... The man does his best to imitate him approvingly, indicating that he knows the town and pointing out the direction in which it lies with his arm.

Ah! *Pirot dobro!*

Meanwhile, the tirailleurs carry on shepherding their flock. They have now gone past the Serb and Fofana.

The latter keeps a furtive eye on their progress. Suddenly his face lights up. Driven quickly off the track, Fouillepot's sheep are heading for the Serb's flock, who glance up at the newcomers and then return to grazing. The two flocks are now very close to each other.

'Ah! *Pirot dobro! Serbo dobro!*'

Mahmadou indicates to the shepherd that now is the right moment to strike his lighter then takes the long, smouldering wick in his hand, lights his pipe, and happily puffs away on it. Smiling broadly, he offers his pouch. The Serb accepts a pinch of tobacco which he puts in his mouth.

'*Aïdé Belgrad!... Dobro dan!*'

Fofana shakes the shepherd's hand and walks off.

★

Then the Serb turns round and stands stupefied. Where have his sheep gone? On the open slope running down to the little brook, all he can see is one flock, one single flock that the Blacks are hurriedly driving off without looking back.

He cannot believe his eyes, but what has happened is all too clear! They are taking his sheep! There is a lump in his throat, he wants to shout but he's choked with fear… Then he rushes after them and in a few seconds catches up with Fouillepot, who is bringing up the rear:

'*Gospodine! Gospodine!*'

The Serb gesticulates helplessly. His sheep are there. He raises his open hands five times in succession. He had fifty sheep! But the chief warrant officer shrugs his shoulders, shakes his head. What does he want? He doesn't understand! And he urges the column to speed up. Come on, let's go! Be off with you! We're in a hurry!

★

After a few minutes they come to a wooden bridge under which flows a trickle of clear water. On either side meadows of short grass spread their green carpet. It is a spot which seems to invite you to call a halt, take a break. And besides, it is time for lunch. Fouillepot orders them to stop. Only then does he give some attention to the supplicant Serb whose complaints have intensified.

The chief warrant officer, who now seems to have grasped the reason, explains to him in his turn that his flock consists of four hundred and seven animals. Like the Serb, he uses lots of gestures, then with his finger he traces the numbers in the dust of the track.

'Corporal Mahmadou Fofana,' he orders in a ringing voice, 'make gap in hedge by track with your machete!'

The order is executed in the twinkling of an eye.

'Corporal Mahmadou Fofana, make sheep go through gap!'

With a mischievous grin, the corporal passes the order down to the men.

'One, two, three, four…' begins Fouillepot, and carries on counting the sheep one by one as they go through the gap in the hedge.

'407!' shouts the chief warrant officer. 'No more! Stop there! Hell! Are we honest or are we not? And as for you, *Serbo dobro*, old pal, take back your property, take away your flock!'

★

The Serb, who has followed every stage of the operation with great anxiety, feels a surge of joy when Fouillepot indicates, with a magnanimous gesture, that he may leave with the little flock that remains on the track.

But alas! The poor devil quickly realises that the numbers don't add up. He starts complaining again, waving his arms about, counting on his fingers. He had fifty sheep, not thirty-five.

So Fouillepot softens his tone:

'Listen, my old Serbski pal, I really feel for you. I can imagine myself in your place. Obviously, it is all very distressing, and, oh, if it was just up to me… but that's my problem, I'm all heart. So, no, that's the situation, I'm afraid. Nothing I can do. I have to hang on to my four hundred and seven sheep. I haven't kept any more than that. So…?'

★

…So, we do not know how things would have turned out had Mahmadou Fofana not intervened. Mahmadou, who has observed the scene with keen interest, feels how perfectly satisfied Fouillepot would be if only this troublemaker would disappear.

And so the corporal moves purposefully towards the Serb's little flock and pretends to start driving it down on to the pasture with the other one.

The unfortunate shepherd can sense catastrophe looming. Ah, what good does it do to protest, to stand up for yourself? With rapid strides he rejoins his flock and scurries off with them, not looking back, as if behind him stands some celestial archangel brandishing a fiery sword ready to turn him into a statue of stone or salt.

'Bon voyage!' Fouillepot calls out, seeing him vanish into the distance.

A faint smile lingers on his lips. And then, as if someone was listening who would take it as a mark of his absolute honesty and sincerity, he declares:

'He's a good one, that, with his sheep! Is it my fault if he's lost them? What the hell does he want me to do about it? I'm not God, am I? I'm not God!'

Raymond Escholier was born in Paris in 1882; he died in Nîmes in 1971. He enlisted in 1914 and fought at the Marne and at Verdun, which he reported on for *L'Echo de Paris*. In 1917, he joined the *Tirailleurs Sénégalais* and fought on the Macedonian front in the battles of Kravitza and Vetremick against the Bulgarians. His novel *Mahmadou Fofana* is based on real soldiers Escholier fought alongside. In his war diaries, he wrote: 'By which right, in the name of the so-called benefits of civilisation that we bring them, do we ask Africans to give up their lives for values that have nothing to do with them?' Not surprisingly, the African soldiers portrayed in the book are well aware how random their route to the front has been. The *Tirailleurs Sénégalais* fought heroically in the First World War on the Western Front, in the Dardanelles, in Morocco, as well as on the Macedonian front. Their casualty rates were extremely high – 30,000 killed out of a total of 200,000 troops. They also fought with great valour in the Second World War and were then used by the French to help repress nationalist uprisings in Algeria, Morocco and Indochina. The last unit of the *Tirailleurs* was disbanded in 1964. Unavailable for many years, *Mahmadou Fofana* has recently been republished and rediscovered in France.

ROBERT MUSIL

THE BLACKBIRD

from *Posthumous Papers of a Living Author*

translated by Peter Wortsman

PLEASE BE ASSURED then that my reason is still the equal of your enlightened mind.

Then, two years later, I found myself in a tight fix, at the dead angle of a battle in the south Tyrol, a line that wound its way from the bloody trenches of the Cima di Vezzena all the way to Lake Caldonazzo. There, like a wave of sunshine, the battle line dove deep into the valley, skirting two hills with beautiful names, and surfaced again on the other side, only to lose itself in the stillness of the mountains.

It was October; the thinly-manned trenches were covered with leaves, the lake shimmered a silent blue, the hills lay there like huge withered wreaths; like funeral wreaths, I often thought to myself without even a shudder of fear. Halting and divided, the valley spilled around them; but beyond the edge of our occupied zone, it fled such sweet diffusion and drove like the blast of a trombone: brown, broad and heroic out into the hostile distance.

At night, we pushed ahead to an advanced position, so prone now in the valley that they could have wiped us out with an avalanche of stones from above; but instead, they slowly roasted us on steady artillery fire. The morning after such a night all our faces had a strange expression that took hours to wear off. Our eyes were enlarged, and our heads tilted every which way on the multitude of shoulders, like a lawn that had just been trampled on. Yet on every one of those nights I poked my head up over the edge of the trench many times, and cautiously turned to look back over my shoulder like a lover: and I saw the Brenta Mountains light blue, as if formed out of stiff-pleated glass, silhouetted against the night sky. And on such nights the stars were like silver foil cutouts glimmering, fat as glazed cookies; and the sky stayed blue all night; and the thin virginal moon crescent lay on her back, now silvery, now golden, basking in the splendor. You must try to imagine just how beautiful it was: for such beauty exists only in the face of danger. And then sometimes I could stand it no longer, and giddy with joy and longing, I crept out for a little nightcrawl around, all the way to the golden-green blackness of the trees, so enchantingly colorful and black, the like of which you've never seen.

But things were different during the day; the atmosphere was so easygoing that you could have gone horseback riding around the main camp. It's only when you have the time to sit back and think and to feel terror that you first learn the true meaning of danger. Every day claims its victims, a regular weekly average of so-and-so many out of a hundred, and already the divisional general staff officers are predicting the results as impersonally as an insurance company. You do it too, by the way. Instinctively you know the odds and feel insured, although not exactly under the best of terms. It is a function of the curious calm that you feel, living under constant crossfire. Let me add the following, though, so that you don't paint a false picture of my circumstances. It does indeed happen that you suddenly feel driven to search for a particular familiar face, one that you remember seeing several days ago; but it's not there anymore. A face like that can upset you more than it should, and hang for a long time in the air like a candle's afterglow. And so your fear of death has diminished, though you are far more susceptible to all sorts of strange upsets. It is as if the fear of one's demise, which evidently lies on top of man forever like a stone, were suddenly to have been rolled back, and in the uncertain proximity of death an unaccountable inner freedom blossoms forth.

Once during that time an enemy plane appeared in the sky over our quiet encampment. This did not happen often, for the mountains with their narrow gaps between fortified peaks could only be hazarded at high altitudes. We stood at that very moment on the summit of one of those funereal hills, and all of a sudden a machine-gun barrage spotted the sky with little white clouds of shrapnel, like a nimble powder puff. It was a cheerful sight, almost endearing. And to top it off, the sun shone through the tricolored wings of the plane as it flew high overhead, as though through a stained-glass church window, or through colored crepe paper. The only missing ingredient was some music by Mozart. I couldn't help thinking, by the way, that we stood around like a crowd of spectators at the races, placing our bets. And one of us even said: Better take cover! But nobody it seems was in the mood to dive like a field mouse into a hole. At that instant I heard a distant ringing drawing closer to my ecstatically upturned face. Of course, it could also have happened the other way around, that I first heard the ringing and only then became conscious of the impending danger; but I knew immediately: It's an aerial dart. These were pointed iron rods no thicker than a pencil lead that planes dropped from above in those days. And if they struck you in the skull, they came out through the soles of your feet, but they didn't hit very often, and so were soon discarded. And though this was my first aerial dart – bombs and machine-gun fire sound altogether different – I knew right away what it was. I was excited, and a second later I already felt that strange, unlikely intuition: It's going to hit!

And do you know what it was like? Not like a frightening foreboding, but rather like an unexpected stroke of good luck! I was surprised at first that I should be the only one to hear its ringing. Then I thought the sound would disappear again. But it didn't disappear. It came ever closer, and though still far away, it grew proportionally louder. Cautiously I looked at the other faces, but no one else was aware of its approach. And at that moment when I became convinced that I alone heard that subtle singing, something rose up out of me to meet it: a ray of life, equally infinite to that death ray descending from above. I'm not making this up, I'm trying to put it as plainly as I can. I believe I've held to a sober physical description so far, though I know of course that to a certain extent it's like in a dream where it seems as though you're speaking clearly, while the words come out all garbled.

It lasted a long time, during which I alone heard the sound coming closer. It was a shrill, singing, solitary, high-pitched tone, like the ringing rim of a glass, but there was something unreal about it. You've never heard anything like it before, I said to myself. And this tone was directed at me; I stood in communion with it and had not the least little doubt that something decisive was about to happen to me. I had no thoughts of the kind that are supposed to come at death's door, but all my thoughts were rather focused on the future; I can only say that I was certain that in the next second I would feel God's proximity close up to my body – which, after all, is saying quite a bit for someone who hasn't believed in God since the age of eight.

Meanwhile, the sound from above became ever more tangible; it swelled and loomed dangerously close. I asked myself several times whether I should warn the others; but let it strike me or another, I wouldn't say a word! Maybe there was a devilish vanity in this illusion that high above the battlefield a voice sang just for me. Maybe God is nothing more than the vain illusion of us poor beggars who puff ourselves up in the pinch and brag of rich relations up above. I don't know. But the fact remains that the sky soon started ringing for the others too; I noticed traces of uneasiness flash across their faces, and I tell you – not one of them let a word slip either! I looked again at those faces: fellows, for whom nothing would have been more unlikely than to think such thoughts, stood there, without knowing it, like a group of disciples waiting for a message from on high. And suddenly the singing became an earthly sound, ten, a hundred feet above us and it died. He – it – was here. Right here in our midst, but closer to me, something that had gone silent and been swallowed up by the earth, had exploded into an unreal hush.

My heart beat quickly and quietly; I couldn't have lost consciousness for even a second; not the least fraction of a second was missing from my life. But then I noticed everyone staring at me. I hadn't budged an inch but my body had been violently thrust to the side, having executed a deep, one hundred-and-eighty degree bow. I felt as though I were just waking from a trance, and had no idea how long I'd been unconscious. No one spoke to me at first; then, finally, someone said: 'An aerial dart!'

And everyone tried to find it, but it was buried deep in the ground. At that instant a hot rush of gratitude swept through me, and I believe that my whole body turned red. And if at that very moment someone had said that God had entered my body, I wouldn't have laughed. But I wouldn't have believed it either – not even that a splinter of His being was in me. And yet whenever I think back to that incident, I feel an overwhelming desire to experience something like it again even more vividly!

↬

One of the greatest German-language writers of his time, **Robert Musil** was born in Klagenfurt in Austria-Hungary in 1880 and died in Geneva in 1942, in flight from the Third Reich. From 1930 onwards, Musil worked on his master-piece *The Man without Qualities*, which remained unfinished at his death. This piece was included in his *Posthumous Papers of a Living Author*, published in 1936 and banned by the Nazis in 1939. Musil was always searching for a way in his writing to fuse the imaginative and the philosophical. Writing about the *Posthumous Papers*, Musil worried that

> To publish nothing but little tales and observations amidst a thundering, groaning world, to speak of incidentals when there are so many vital issues: to vent one's anger at phenomena that lie far off the beaten track: this may doubtless appear as weakness to some.

In fact, what he achieves in *The Blackbird* is something very special – to make universal his personal experiences of the war in the South Tyrol. In the face of death, he has a near-religious epiphany. All Musil's writings reflect his attempt to find a literary form to express the cataclysmic events of the first half of the 20th century that marked the lives of millions including his own.

LIVIU REBREANU

TO THE ROMANIAN FRONT

from *The Forest of the Hanged*

translated by A. V. Wise

FOR SEVERAL NIGHTS the search-light did not appear. Apostol Bologa, on the look-out at the observation post in the infantry trenches, waited for it with strained expectancy, bent on satisfying Klapka. In the stillness of the nights, broken only at rare intervals by stray rifle shots, he had plenty of leisure to weigh, as was his custom, his new creed, for he was convinced that nothing but that which could endure keen scrutiny of the mind was worthy to dwell eternally in the soul of man. And he rejoiced, feeling his spiritual regeneration, no matter how he viewed it, send a warm glow through his heart, whereas his old 'conception', for which he had risked his life for twenty-seven months, had always been as unkind to him as a stepmother. He now told himself that life acted only through the heart, and that without the heart the brain would be nothing but a mass of dead cells. But he was ashamed to think that it had required two years of war for him to reach the point from which he had started, against the advice of Doamna Bologa, of the Protopop, and of everyone else except Marta. Round his neck he wore a locket which contained a mesh of blond hair and the picture of a charming little head. She had given him these when he had been home on leave and had whispered to him: 'My hero!' She also called him that in her letters.

'It's all Marta's fault,' he tried to tell himself secretly as an excuse in face of his rebuking conscience. But he pulled himself up and put away such cowardice. 'Marta never urged me by a single word to enlist. It was only my wretched jealousy which counted on the uniform and the glamour to win over her frivolousness. So that I alone am to blame, and I must face my conscience.'

The past seemed dead to him, and he took care not to dig it up again. He was more preoccupied with the future, which dawned for him like a dazzling morn after a stormy night. He did not yet perceive it clearly, but the fog which veiled it from his sight had rosy tints. His heart was full of comfort.

'From to-day a new life begins!' he kept on thinking joyfully. 'At last I have found the right road. Gone are hesitations and doubts! Henceforth, forward!'

A wild desire to live filled his breast. In the morning, when he came away from the observation post, he stretched himself on his plank bed and quickly fell asleep and dreamt of happiness.

Late one afternoon he again met Klapka by the battery. Bologa, remembering how worried the captain had been that last night, was surprised to see him serene and smiling, with a look of almost challenging equanimity in his eyes. After they had inspected together guns and men, they went down into the command post, where a candle-end was burning.

'I've had no luck, sir,' said Apostol hesitatingly. 'It didn't appear...'

'What?' asked Klapka. 'Oh, yes... the... oh, well, let that search-light go to the devil, Bologa!' he added indifferently.

The lieutenant kept a worried silence, staring into the captain's eyes, in which, only a few days ago, he had seen reflected the Forest of the Hanged. But Klapka proceeded serenely:

'A man with a troubled conscience takes fright at every shadow. That's what I did, too, with regard to our colonel. I took him for a man-eater, whereas he is a very decent fellow. Ah! of course, I haven't told you! He has been to my dug-out every day, about four times a day. You can imagine in what a blue funk I was. I felt sure he wanted to make an end of me. Finally, yesterday, out of sheer fright, I told him straight out why I had been transferred over here, vowing, of course, that I was innocent, that... He listened to me and at last, without the least hint of censure, you understand, he said: "Yes, I know, that's the way misfortunes befall mankind." And that was all! Then we talked about Vienna, about musical comedies, about Americans – in short, chatted like comrades! In fact, I even think that he has taken rather a liking to me, for this morning he came again to inspect – a so-called inspection. Instead, he gave me a definite proof of trust. A decided proof! In absolute confidence he told me a great official secret. So that henceforth I have no fear, my mind is at rest…'

The captain's high spirits and serenity annoyed Bologa. Censoriously he interrupted him.

'Of what importance is an official secret to us? Trust and suspicion are equally troublesome!'

'No, no!' exclaimed the captain with warmth. 'Do not let us exaggerate. There are decent people everywhere, in every race. Why exaggerate? Well, the colonel is a man who cares nothing for his rank, we must acknowledge that! Besides, the secret does affect us also, because there is some talk of changing the division. There is a tired-out division on its way from Italy to take our place.'

'And are we to go back to the Italian front?' asked Bologa.

'No, not to the Italian front,' answered Klapka quickly, with some pride. 'To the Romanian front.'

As he was uttering the last word he remembered that the lieutenant was a Romanian, but it was too late to do anything but utter the word in a lower key. Bologa paled, and as if he had not caught the words, repeated mechanically:

'To the Rom…' Something seemed to clutch at his throat and he could get no further. He remained with his mouth open, staring idiotically at the captain, who, realizing how imprudent he had been, was murmuring inanely:

'Forgive me, friend. I had forgotten that you… I am a…'

But Apostol's brain was only just beginning to grasp the meaning of the words which had given him so sharp and poignant a shock, as if he had received a dagger-thrust. He leapt to his feet and walked backwards and forwards, wringing his hands and whispering desperately:

'Impossible, impossible, impossible!…'

Klapka, nonplussed, tried to console him by saying, without conviction:

'Calm yourself, Bologa; what the hell... When all is said and done one cannot live without compromise, without sacrifices and...'

Suddenly Apostol Bologa stopped in front of him, his face white, his eyes dull, and the captain's words dried in his throat.

'Anything else, anything else, but this – this cannot be,' burst from Bologa in burning tones. 'That would be... a... a...'

The walls of the dug-out turned his efforts to find a word into a long-drawn-out echo, which made Klapka seize him by the arm and bid him speak lower. And Apostol, as if he had understood, became embarrassed, dropped his eyes, and ended in a mutter:

'A... a... crime...'

'So it is, but what are we to do?' said the captain in a smothered voice, his eyes fixed on the entrance. 'I understand and share your perturbation, but you others have at least the consolation of knowing that there are kinsmen in the other camp fighting for your salvation, whereas we can hope for nothing from anywhere! For us, the only means of proving our patriotism is to die on the gallows!' Bologa, overcome, had dropped into a chair. Klapka, thinking that he had calmed down, went on speaking with more confidence.

'War is, in any circumstances, a colossal crime, but a still greater crime is the Austrian war. When people of the same blood take up arms, whether they are in the right or not, they all know that success will be for the good of the race and consequently each man can die with the conviction that he has sacrificed himself for the good cause of all. But in our case cruel masters have sent their slaves to die whilst strengthening their chains! Well then? In the midst of this turmoil of crime what can the small crime like the one that is crushing your soul matter? Who cares here about our souls?'

'Which means that...?' Bologa, who had begun to listen, queried impatiently.

'That you are to go where we shall all go,' said Klapka gravely, with painful resignation. 'That you are to go and do what we shall all do, and that you are to seal hermetically all the inlets to your soul until peace comes or until the world will be destroyed, or until your turn to die will come and put an end to all your torment!'

Apostol started and answered protestingly:

'But if I don't want to die? I don't want to, I no longer want to! Now I want to live, I no longer want to die!'

Klapka was silent for a moment, and then said with a smile that tried to hide his embarrassment:

'I know I am hardly the person to talk to you of death. Through fear of death or love of life – perhaps it is the same thing – I am a coward… Yes, yes, I acknowledge and confess that I am capable of swallowing any shame, any humiliation. Nevertheless, I have told myself many a time, yes, even as I am I have said to myself that the dead are happiest, because they at least have finished with suffering. I like you, Bologa, and had I not found you here I should not have had so much confidence in myself. But you see, even we, whose souls have been drawn so close together by our common suffering, even we must share our anguish in a foreign tongue! How, then, can we help envying those that are dead, Bologa?'

The lieutenant was no longer listening to his words. Klapka's calm increased his agitation. And all of a sudden he asked with a glimmer of hope in his eyes:

'Do you think that it is a certainty?'

The captain, after a slight hesitation, answered resolutely, as if he wished to cure him by drastic means: 'Unfortunately there is no doubt about it, my dear fellow. The other division has already left Italy. Tomorrow or after tomorrow it will arrive. In a week's time it will have taken our place, and a few days later we shall be in Ardeal, on the Ro…'

Bologa's eyes scorched him. He broke off abruptly and lowered his eyes, staring at his muddy boots and nervously jerking his knees, while Apostol walked up and down like a caged wolf, breathing heavily, his temples burning. Two minutes later, with a new determination, the lieutenant again halted in front of Klapka.

'Sir, I beg of you… I implore you, save me… You can save me… I cannot go to that front…'

Klapka raised his eyes and looked at him. He did not understand what Bologa wanted him to do. The latter continued frenziedly:

'A means of salvation must be found! Transfer me to a regiment which is staying here; or send me back to Italy, wherever you like, only not there! I'll fight as I have fought until to-day, I swear I will! I'll… I have three medals for bravery; all three won with… But there I cannot go! There I feel sure that I shall die… And I don't want to die! I must live!'

He fell on the bed, his face in his hands, convulsed by sobs. The captain was deeply moved and felt that if he tried to speak he, too, would weep. In the dark dug-out Apostol's sobs made the air heavy, and the smoky light on the table threw uneasy shadows on the walls. Presently, when the lieutenant's sobs had ceased, Klapka said:

'Do you feel better now? Well, then, we can talk as man to man and soldier to soldier! The truth is that in war-time one must not think, one must just fight… Anyway, that's what a general said in a speech at head-quarters the other day. But this thing we must consider very carefully and without hurry, otherwise… If you stop to think you will see that I am powerless. I cannot propose anything because I am stigmatized: a Czech – that is to say, a traitor… It was for people like us that the idea of putting machine-guns behind the lines was invented, so that they should sharpen our desire for glory in case there should be any hesitation. If I dared to suggest your name for transfer we should both be suspected immediately – immediately! A Czech with a record like mine to take the part of a Romanian? You can imagine the to-do there would be, the… Only the general could save you, if he were human and had a heart. But do you really think that out here there are people that are human? Do you really believe that…?'

Bologa, who had sat up and was listening surlily, clung to one word and exclaimed:

'I'll go and see the general!'

Klapka became cold with fear, as if the general himself had caught him plotting, and said in a whisper:

'Calm yourself, Bologa! Please! Don't you know General Karg? Why, he has been your C.O. for nearly a year – Karg! A dog, a… He would be quite capable of court-martialling you straight away instead of giving you any answer at all…'

'Consequently I am to leave without even trying to protect myself or to prevent a crime?' burst out Apostol again, but this time furiously and grinding his teeth.

'Listen to my advice, friend,' answered the captain quietly. 'I am older than you and have suffered much during my life. War has no other philosophy but luck. Trust to luck! Death has whistled in your ears in all keys during the last two years, and yet luck has protected you. Perhaps Fate loves you! Don't rub her up the wrong way, don't tempt her… Leave her alone.'

'How certain I am that a terrible danger is awaiting me over there!' murmured Bologa, shuddering and feeling all at once fearfully depressed. 'Never have I had so strong a presentiment.'

'To-day there are dangers everywhere,' said Klapka, keeping a tight hold on himself. 'In the air, at the front, at home, in the whole world. The earth itself, it seems to me, is passing through a danger zone. What can we do? Luck is every man's shield, that's a fact! Take my advice… You'll see, before long you'll tell me I was right. But without passion, without haste! Calmly, calmly!'

He rose slowly, put on his helmet, ready to go.

'Rather than go there, I'll desert to the Russians!' then came in a whisper from Bologa, as he looked straightly at the captain.

'That's easily said,' answered Klapka calmly, as if he had been waiting for these very words from the lieutenant. 'But if you don't succeed you know what awaits you! Only the other day I told you the tale of those three. They also spoke as you are doing – even more boldly. And yet, to-day they are probably still in the Forest of the Hanged to terrify others!'

'I don't worry about that,' said Bologa confidently. 'If I am caught I'll shoot myself and finish quickly! No matter what happens, I won't die by the rope, I promise you!'

'They also promised me that, friend, but circumstances proved stronger than their resolution. That's why I bid you take care, don't play with Fate! There are thousands, nay, tens of thousands in your position, and Fate looks after them as she thinks fit.'

Klapka pressed his hand warmly, and the next minute Apostol

Bologa found himself alone, rooted to the spot, with eyes staring into vacancy, haunted by apparitions. When he came out of his trance he felt so weak that he threw himself on the bed. On the table, in the improvised candlestick, the light began to flicker quickly, grew less bright, and suddenly went out. The darkness startled Bologa, but his feverish lips whispered bravely:

'It is impossible! It must not happen!'

LIVIU REBREANU

'WE'LL SEE WHAT
YOU DO THERE...'

from *The Forest of the Hanged*

translated by A. V. Wise

TOWARDS MIDDAY, whilst Bologa was still asleep, a shrill buzzing at the head of his bed startled him and made him jump to his feet, under the impression that the dug-out was being blown up. The adjutant was roaring into the telephone:

'Lieutenant Bologa? Hallo! Himself speaking? Oh, is it you, old chap? Colonel's orders you are to leave immediately and report yourself to his Excellency. His Excellency wishes to see you. Very urgent! Of course, you'll call on us on your way, for the colonel also wants to speak to you. At the same time I want to congratulate you! You've saved the honour of the whole division. The colonel phoned to headquarters right away during the night. The fourth one is on the way, Bologa, bravo!'

An hour later Apostol was in a motor-car, sitting next to a staff captain whom he had met at the command post of the regiment and who had offered to take him to headquarters, as he himself was just due to leave. On the way the captain told him that the destruction of the search-light deserved a special reward – all his comrades, including the colonel, had told him so. Bologa listened thoughtfully and silently. Several times his eyes travelled down to his breast, where the three medals for bravery shone, and he remembered his emotion when the first one had been pinned on. How he had longed for it, and how small he had felt until he had received it! It had seemed to him as if he were the only one who had none, and he had felt unhappy and dishonoured. He had hurled himself where lurked the greatest danger, where death reaped oftenest, without fear, with no other thought in his mind but that medal! And when the colonel had pinned it on his breast in the presence of the troops, his heart had wept tears of joy. Not until then had he thought himself worthy to live.

In the courtyard of the divisional headquarters he met Lieutenant Gross, who, being a sapper, constantly had work to do at headquarters. Gross greeted him with an ironical grimace.

'Bravo, philosopher! You've killed a few more people for a bit of tin.'

'Listen, Gross,' answered Bologa, suddenly annoyed, 'when you cease to carry out orders, then you may make imputations against others! Until then, be a little more modest, please!'

'I execute orders, it is true,' said the sapper, still in a bantering tone. 'I commit or help barbarities, but with nausea, friend! Not with enthusiasm, like others! I do not seek to distinguish myself!'

'It would be better if you practised what you preached,' murmured Bologa, looking him straight in the eye. 'To talk is easy, but...'

'Well, we'll see what you'll do tomorrow or the day after on the Romanian front,' interrupted Gross with a sour smile. 'We'll see what you'll do there...'

'I'll never go there!' said Bologa with a start and flushing deeply.

Gross was about to say something else, but just then there appeared on the doorstep a smart sergeant, who called importantly:

'Lieutenant Bologa! Please to come in, his Excellency is expecting you, sir.'

A few seconds later Apostol Bologa was standing stiffly before General Karg, who was short and squat, with an ugly, harsh face, darkened by a bristling moustache and pierced by round eyes whose gaze, darting from under very thick, frowning eyebrows, made one think of two venomous daggers.

The lieutenant's heart contracted when he saw him rise heavily from the table laden with bundles of paper and maps. The recollection flashed through him that each time he had set eyes on the general he had felt a strange fear, as if he were in face of a merciless enemy or of a terrible and unexpected danger which he could not avoid.

The general, with chin uplifted, held out his hand and said heartily:

'Well done, Bologa! Your action has been reported to me, and I wished particularly to congratulate you in person. Yes, I wished... absolutely...'

His voice was rasping and penetrating, and he seemed to be scolding even when he joked.

Apostol bowed slightly, pressing the general's hand. Then he gave him a detailed account, using short, dry, military sentences, of how he had destroyed the search-light. While he was speaking, however, he noticed that the general's nostrils had hair growing out of them, and he thought that very probably he snored horribly at night; also he remembered that he had not seen him since the execution of the Czech. Karg listened to his account attentively, now and again nodding and darting pleased looks at him. Then, when Bologa had finished, he slapped him amicably on the back, murmuring:

'I have proposed you for the Gold Medal. You may be sure you will get it. We need soldiers like you, and they deserve all distinctions. Well done, Bologa! I am proud to have the honour of commanding brave officers such as you.'

The general stopped, racking his mind to find one or two more suitable words to say. But he could not think of anything else, and, after a short pause, repeated more mildly:

'I am proud... very proud...' and again he stretched out his hand, ready to dismiss him. Then Bologa, completely self-possessed, his voice clear, and looking straight into the general's grey eyes, said:

'Excellency, I beg you to give me leave to make a request!'

General Karg, unpleasantly surprised that the lieutenant, especially after he had shown him such marked favour, should dare to speak without being addressed and to ask a favour without first having put his name down at orderly hour in the hierarchical manner required by the regulations, took two steps backward with knitted brow. Nevertheless, wishing to show every indulgence to a good soldier, he answered in a friendly tone:

'Yes, yes, I am listening. A good soldier... naturally... willingly...'

At that moment Bologa felt clearly that his audacity was vain and useless, and he hesitated. Beads of perspiration broke out on his forehead. To gain time and to regain his composure he coughed and bent his head.

Then, his self-confidence reasserting itself, he fixed his eyes resolutely on the general's face and said, speaking rapidly and jerkily:

'Excellency, I know – I have heard – that in a few days' time our division is leaving here to go somewhere else, to another front...'

'Quite correct,' answered the general wonderingly as he saw that Bologa faltered.

'Then, Excellency,' continued the lieutenant abruptly, as if the interruption had given him renewed courage, 'then I would ask you to allow me to stay behind here... Or, if this is not possible, to send me to the Italian front...'

The general stared at him perplexedly and twirled his moustache nervously. Then he said:

'Very well. Although I am sorry to lose you. An excellent officer, brave... But as you are so keen on this... However, I think that here would be better than in Italy...'

'I don't mind going there, Excellency. I was at Doberdò for a few months, and on the whole I should prefer it...'

Bologa's face was now lit up with joy and hope. He could no longer control his emotion. He sighed deeply with relief.

'Very well, very well,' repeated the general thoughtfully. 'Though I don't understand why you should not want to come with us. My division has a holy mission in Ardeal! A great mission. Yes! The enemy has stolen our country's soil. There the Wallachians...'

Suddenly General Karg stopped short as if a ray of light had entered his brain. He again took a few steps backwards and glued his gaze on Bologa, trying to read his innermost thoughts. For several seconds there reigned a grave-like silence in the room, while outside could be heard the grinding of cart wheels and the noisy chirping of the sparrows in a tree under the office window. Apostol unconsciously closed his eyes to protect himself from the general's scrutiny.

'You are a Romanian?' the latter jerked out abruptly, his voice almost hoarse.

'Yes, Excellency,' answered the lieutenant quickly.

'Romanian!' repeated the general, surprised and irritated, in a tone as if expecting a denial.

'Romanian!' repeated Bologa more firmly, drawing himself up and puffing out his chest slightly.

'Yes, very well, of course…' stammered Karg presently, suspicious and scrutinizing. 'Yes, certainly… But then your request surprises me… very much… It would seem to me that you differentiate between the enemies of your country?'

Apostol Bologa met the flashing eyes of the general with a calmness which made him marvel at himself. He felt determined and unshaken, as he always did when violently attacked. Now he wished obstinately to convince the enemy, though he realized very well that his efforts would be fruitless. He found himself talking calmly, without the slightest trace of emotion or hesitation; he might have been arguing with a friendly comrade.

'Excellency, for twenty-seven months I have fought in such a way that I can look anyone in the face unashamed. I have never shirked my duty. My whole heart and soul was in my work. To-day, however, I find myself in a morally impossible situation.'

The general shuddered as if a sword had been thrust into his breast. His eyes flashed and glinted like steel. He rushed at Bologa with raised and bent arm, ready to knock him down, roaring:

'What is that? Morally impossible situation? What sort of talk is that? How dare you? I know nothing of such nonsense, which is intended purely and simply to conceal the cowardliness of men without patriotic feelings. I know nothing about it, do you understand? I don't want to know anything about it!'

Apostol tried to protest, but the general cut him short, purple with fury.

'I don't allow you to speak, do you understand? Each word of yours deserves a shot! The thoughts concealed behind your words are criminal! Do you understand? Criminal! Oh… oh…! So that's what your bravery amounts to? Behold what sort of a person I've recommended for the Gold Medal! A fine thing! Gold Medal! Shots – not medals!'

He glared at him with dislike and contempt and then abruptly turned his back on him, smothering an oath between his teeth and tugging at his moustache with his right hand, a small, plump hand, laden with rings, like the hand of a woman.

Bologa remained serene, unmoved, persisting in the idea that he must convince him. The fury of the general did him good and gave him courage. When he thought that the latter had calmed down a little, he said again, in the same clear voice:

'I asked a favour of your Excellency in the belief that you would kindly try to understand my spiritual state. That is why I have taken the liberty of speaking to you as man to man.'

The general, who had paused by the window, cursing and muttering, turned sharply on the lieutenant and answered with more restraint:

'I do not listen to such requests, nor do I hold conversation with such people! Do you understand? As it is, I have talked too much with you! You ingrate!'

He did not hold out his hand this time, but looked him up and down with disgust, and then sat down at the table and began turning over some of the papers on it. Bologa saluted and went out quietly, confidently, as if after an intensely pleasant interview. The general stared after him, shook his head, surveyed attentively the closed door, and suddenly, again filled with rage, banged his fist violently on the spread-out map. Just then the adjutant sidled into the office, alarmed and filled with curiosity.

'Note down Lieutenant Bologa,' mumbled General Karg, addressing the amazed adjutant. 'He is dangerous and... It wouldn't surprise me to hear some fine day that he had deserted to the enemy. What men! What an army!'

The adjutant bowed, put some documents on the table and made haste to disappear on tiptoe, without noise, for fear the general should unload his fury on his own head.

In the middle of the courtyard Apostol Bologa gazed around him as if this were the first time he had been there in his life. The enclosure was large, with a wooden paling on the street side. The new plank

door which had been let into it was now open. There were a few
carts in a file at the back, near the stables, and the motor-car in which
he had come stood there abandoned, its doors gaping. The stone
house, roofed with old tiles and as immense as a barracks, was pitted
with shrapnel dating from the period when the war had passed over
the village and when a shell had actually exploded in the little front
garden, tearing from its roots the twin of the tree in which a pair of
noisy sparrows were now quarrelling. The sky had cleared and filled
the atmosphere with a blue more tender than usual. The sun smiled in
the west, yellow and frail as the face of a gay old man, and the light of
it kissed the earth like a beneficent dew, diffusing joy and awakening
hope everywhere.

Apostol stood a while with his eyes turned towards the sun, drinking
in thirstily the smiling light. He felt relieved, as if he had just eased by
a spell of passionate weeping a long-standing ache. His thoughts no
longer oppressed him but bent docilely to his will, and had he wished
he could have strung them nicely, like glass beads, on a thread.

He left the courtyard. In the street, opposite the mess-room, he saw
a lorry loaded with equipment, ready to leave for the front. He jumped
on. He wanted to get back as soon as possible to his battery. He was in
a hurry...

Born in 1885 in Tarlisue, Transylvania, then part of Austro-Hungary, **Liviu Rebreanu** lived from 1909 in Bucharest. During the war, he was a reporter for the Romanian left-wing daily *Adevarul*. In 1920, he published *Ion*, a book about the harsh lives of the peasants of Transylvania before the war, which is the first great Romanian novel. *The Forest of the Hanged* was published in 1922. Based on the life of Rebreanu's brother Emil, it tells the story of Apostol Bologa, the son of a Romanian lawyer who becomes a decorated officer and in a court-martial even votes in favour of the death sentence for a Czech officer who has deserted. Sent to fight against his countrymen in the Carpathians, Apostol walks towards the Romanian lines. Caught and tried for desertion, he, like the Czech officer he helped condemn, is hung. Surreal and bitter, *The Forest of the Hanged* forcefully conveys what the war was like for the many ethnic minority members conscripted to fight against their fellow countrymen. Rebreanu died in Valea Mare, Romania, in 1944.

JAROSLAV HAŠEK

ŠVEJK GOES TO THE WAR

from *The Good Soldier Švejk*

translated by Cecil Parrott

AT THE TIME WHEN THE FORESTS on the river Raab in Galicia saw the Austrian armies fleeing across the river and when down in Serbia one after the other of the Austrian divisions were taken with their pants down and got the walloping they had long deserved, the Austrian Ministry of War suddenly remembered Švejk. Why, even he might help to get the Monarchy out of the mess.

When they brought Švejk the order to report within a week for a medical examination on Střelecký Ostrov, he happened to be lying in bed, stricken once more by rheumatism.

Mrs Muller was making coffee for him in the kitchen.

'Mrs Muller,' Švejk called softly from his room, 'Mrs Muller, come here for a moment.'

When the charwoman stood by his bed, Švejk repeated in the same soft voice: 'Sit down, Mrs Muller.'

There was something mysterious and solemn in his voice.

When she had sat down, Švejk drew himself up in bed and announced: 'I'm going to the war!'

'Holy Mother!' shrieked Mrs Muller. 'What ever are you going to do there?'

'Fight,' answered Švejk in sepulchral tones. 'Things are going very badly for Austria. Up above they're already creeping on us at Cracow and down below on Hungary. They're crushing us like a steam-roller on all sides and that's why they're calling me up. I read you yesterday from the newspaper, didn't I, that dark clouds were enveloping our dear fatherland.'

'But you can't move.'

'That doesn't matter, Mrs Muller, I shall go to the war in a bathchair. You know that confectioner round the corner? Well, he has just the right kind of bathchair. Years ago he used to push his lame and wicked old grandfather about in it in the fresh air. Mrs Muller, you're going to push me to the war in that bathchair.'

Mrs Muller burst into tears: 'Oh dear, sir, shouldn't I run for the doctor?'

'You'll not run anywhere, Mrs Muller. Except for my legs I'm completely sound cannon-fodder, and at a time when things are going badly for Austria every cripple must be at his post. Just go on making the coffee.'

And while Mrs Muller, tear-stained and distraught, poured coffee through the strainer, the good soldier Švejk started singing in bed:

'General Windischgrätz as the cock did crow
Unfurled his banner and charged the foe.
Rataplan, rataplan, rataplan.

Charged the foe and brandished his sword
Calling to Mary, Mother of the Lord.
Rataplan, rataplan, rataplan.'

The panic-stricken Mrs Muller under the impact of this awe inspiring war-song forgot about the coffee and trembling in every limb listened in horror as the good soldier Švejk continued to sing in bed:

'With Mary Mother and bridges four,
Piedmont, strengthen your posts for war.
Rataplan, rataplan, rataplan.

At Solferino there was battle and slaughter,

Piles of corpses and blood like water.
Rataplan, rataplan, rataplan.

Arms and legs flying in the air,
For the brave 18th were fighting there.
Rataplan, rataplan, rataplan.

Boys of the 18th, don't lose heart!
There's money behind in the baggage cart.
Rataplan, rataplan, rataplan.'

'For God's sake, sir, please!' came the piteous voice from the kitchen, but Švejk was already ending his war-song:

'Money in the cart and wenches in the van!
What a life for a military man!
Rataplan, rataplan, rataplan.'

Mrs Muller burst out of the door and rushed for the doctor. She returned in an hour's time, while Švejk had slumbered off.

And so he was woken up by a corpulent gentleman who laid his hand on his forehead for a moment and said:

'Don't be afraid. I am Dr Pávek from Vinohrady – let me feel your pulse – put this thermometer under your armpit. Good – now show me your tongue – a bit more – keep it out – what did your father and mother die of?'

And so at a time when it was Vienna's earnest desire that all the peoples of Austria-Hungary should offer the finest examples of loyalty and devotion, Dr Pávek prescribed Švejk bromide against his patriotic enthusiasm and recommended the brave and good soldier not to think about the war:

'Lie straight and keep quiet. I'll come again tomorrow.'

When he came the next day, he asked Mrs Muller in the kitchen how the patient was.

'He's worse, doctor,' she answered with genuine grief. 'In the night he was singing, if you'll pardon the expression, the Austrian national anthem, when the rheumatism suddenly took him.'

Dr Pávek felt obliged to react to this new manifestation of loyalty on the part of his patient by prescribing a larger dose of bromide.

The third day Mrs Muller informed him that Švejk had got even worse.

'In the afternoon he sent for a map of the battlefield, doctor, and in the night he was seized by a mad hallucination that Austria was going to win.'

'And he takes his powders strictly according to the prescription?'

'Oh, no, doctor, he hasn't even sent for them yet.' Dr Pávek went away after having called down a storm of reproaches on Švejk's head and assured him that he would never again come to cure anybody who refused his professional help and bromide.

Only two days remained before Švejk would have to appear before the call-up board.

During this time Švejk made the necessary preparations. First he sent Mrs Muller to buy an army cap and next he sent her to borrow the bathchair from the confectioner round the corner – that same one in which the confectioner once used to wheel about in the fresh air his lame and wicked old grandfather. Then he remembered he needed crutches. Fortunately the confectioner still kept the crutches too as a family relic of his old grandfather.

Now he only needed the recruit's bunch of flowers for his button-hole. Mrs Muller got these for him too. During these last two days she got noticeably thinner and wept from morning to night.

And so on that memorable day there appeared on the Prague streets a moving example of loyalty. An old woman pushing before her a bath-chair, in which there sat a man in an army cap with a finely polished Imperial badge and waving his crutches. And in his button-hole there shone the gay flowers of a recruit.

And this man, waving his crutches again and again, shouted out to the streets of Prague: 'To Belgrade, to Belgrade!'

He was followed by a crowd of people which steadily grew from the small group that had gathered in front of the house from which he had gone out to war.

Švejk could see that the policemen standing at some of the cross-roads saluted him.

At Wenceslas Square the crowd around Švejk's bathchair had grown several hundreds and at the corner of Krakovská Street they beat up a student in a German cap who had shouted out to Švejk:

'*Heil! Nieder mit den Serben!*'*

At the corner of Vodičkova Street mounted police rode in and dispersed the crowd.

When Švejk showed the district police inspector that he had it in black and white that he must that day appear before the call-up board, the latter was a trifle disappointed; and in order to reduce disturbances to a minimum he had Švejk and his bathchair escorted by two mounted police all the way to the Střelecký Ostrov.

---

*'Down with the Serbs.'

The following article about this episode appeared in the *Prague Official News*:

A CRIPPLE'S PATRIOTISM

Yesterday afternoon the passers-by in the main streets of Prague were witnesses of a scene which was an eloquent testimony to the fact that in these great and solemn hours the sons of our nation can furnish the finest examples of loyalty and devotion to the throne of the aged monarch. We might well have been back in the times of the ancient Greeks and Romans, when Mucius Scaevola had himself led off to battle, regardless of his burnt arm. The most sacred feelings and sympathies were nobly demonstrated yesterday by a cripple on crutches who was pushed in an invalid chair by his aged mother. This son of the Czech people, spontaneously and regardless of his infirmity, had himself driven off to war to sacrifice his life and possessions for his emperor. And if his call: 'To Belgrade!' found such a lively echo on the streets of Prague, it only goes to prove what model examples of love for the fatherland and the Imperial House are proffered by the people of Prague.

The *Prager Tagblatt* wrote in the same strain, ending its article by saying that the cripple volunteer was escorted by a crowd of Germans who protected him with their bodies from lynching by the Czech agents of the Entente.

Bohemie published the same report and urged that the patriotic cripple should be fittingly rewarded. It announced that at its offices it was ready to receive gifts from German citizens for the unknown hero.

If in the eyes of these three journals the Czech lands could not have produced a nobler citizen, this was not the opinion of the gentlemen at the call-up board – certainly not of the chief army doctor Bautze, an utterly ruthless man who saw in everything a criminal attempt to evade military service, the front, bullets, and shrapnel.

This German's stock remark was widely famous: 'The whole Czech people are nothing but a pack of malingerers.' During the ten weeks of his activities, of 11,000 civilians he cleaned out 10,999 malingerers, and he would certainly have got the eleven thousandth by the throat, if it had not happened that just when he shouted 'About turn!' the unfortunate man was carried off by a stroke.

'Take away that malingerer!' said Bautze, when he had ascertained that the man was dead.

And on that memorable day it was Švejk who stood before him. Like the others he was stark naked and chastely hid his nudity behind the crutches on which he supported himself.

'That's really a remarkable fig-leaf,' said Bautze in German. 'There were no fig-leaves like that in paradise.'

'Certified as totally unfit for service on grounds of idiocy,' observed the sergeant-major, looking at the official documents.

'And what else is wrong with you?' asked Bautze.

'Humbly report, sir, I'm a rheumatic, but I will serve His Imperial Majesty to my last drop of blood,' said Švejk modestly. 'I have swollen knees.'

Bautze gave the good soldier Švejk a blood-curdling look and roared out in German: 'You're a malingerer!' Turning to the sergeant-major he said with icy calm: 'Clap the bastard into gaol at once!'

Two soldiers with bayonets took Švejk off to the garrison gaol.

Švejk walked on his crutches and observed with horror that his rheumatism was beginning to disappear.

Mrs Muller was still waiting for Švejk with the bathchair above on the bridge but when she saw him under bayoneted escort she burst into tears and ran away from the bathchair, never to return to it again.

And the good soldier Švejk walked along unassumingly under the escort of the armed protectors of the state.

Their bayonets shone in the light of the sun and at Malá Strana before the monument of Radetzky, Švejk turned to the crowd which had followed them and called out:

'To Belgrade! To Belgrade!'

And Marshal Radetzky looked dreamily down from his monument at the good soldier Švejk, as, limping on his old crutches, he slowly disappeared into the distance with his recruit's flowers in his button-hole. Meanwhile a solemn-looking gentleman informed the crowd around that it was a 'dissenter' they were leading off.

Original illustrations by Josef Lada.

JAROSLAV HAŠEK

FROM HATVAN TOWARDS
THE GALICIAN FRONTIER

from *The Good Soldier Švejk*

translated by Cecil Parrott

ŠVEJK GOT CAUTIOUSLY INTO HIS VAN and lying down on his greatcoat
and pack said to the quartermaster sergeant-major and the others:

'Once upon a time a man got sozzled and asked not to be disturbed…'

After these words he rolled over on his side and began to snore. The
gases which he emitted by belching soon filled the whole compartment,
so that Jurajda, inhaling the atmosphere through his nostrils, declared:
'God! It certainly reeks of cognac here.'

Marek, who after all his tribulations had finally attained the rank of
battalion historian, was sitting at a folding table.

He was engaged in writing up in advance the heroic deeds of the
battalion, and it was obvious that he derived great pleasure from his look
into the future.

Vaněk watched with interest how the volunteer was busily writing
and laughing heartily in the process. Then he got up and leant over his
shoulder. Marek started to explain to him: 'You know, it's enormous
fun writing a history of the battalion in advance. The main thing is to
proceed systematically. In everything there must be system.'

'A systematic system,' observed Vaněk with a more or less
contemptuous smile.

'Oh, yes,' the volunteer said nonchalantly, 'a systemized systematic system of writing the battalion's history. We can't march off straight away with a magnificent victory. Everything must go gradually according to a definite plan. Our battalion cannot win this world war all at once. *Nihil nisi bene.* The main thing for a conscientious historian like me is first to draw up a plan of our victories. For example, here I describe how our battalion – this will perhaps be in two months' time – nearly crosses the Russian frontier, which is very strongly defended by, let's say, the Don regiments of the enemy, while a number of enemy divisions surround our positions. At first sight it looks as if it's all up with our battalion and that the enemy will make sausage-meat of us. But at this very moment Captain Ságner gives the following order to our battalion: "It is not the Lord's will that we should perish here. Let's flee." And so our battalion starts to flee, but when the enemy division, which has encircled us, sees that we are actually running after them, they begin to retreat in panic and fall into the hands of our army's reserve without firing a shot. It is at this point really where the whole history of our battalion begins. From unimportant events, to speak like a prophet, Mr Vaněk, far-reaching things develop. Our battalion goes from victory to victory. It will be interesting to read how it attacks the enemy when he is asleep. For this we obviously need the style of the *Illustrated War News,* which was published by Vilímek during the Russo-Japanese war. Well, as I said, our battalion attacks the camp of the enemy while he is asleep. Each man of us seeks out an enemy and with all his force thrusts a bayonet into his chest. The finely sharpened bayonet goes through him like a knife through butter. Only here and there a rib cracks. The sleeping enemy jerk convulsively in their death spasms. For a moment they roll and goggle their eyes, but they are eyes which no longer see anything. Then they give the death rattle and their bodies stiffen. Bloody saliva appears on their lips, and with this it's all over and victory is on the side of our battalion. Or it will be even better in, say, three months' time, when our battalion captures the Tsar of Russia. But we'll talk about that later, Mr Vaněk. Meanwhile I must prepare in advance small episodes which testify to the battalion's unexampled heroism. I'll have to think out an entirely new war terminology for it. I've already invented one new term. I intend to write about the self-sacrificing resolution of our men, who are riddled through and through with splinters of shrapnel. As a result of an explosion of an enemy mine one of our sergeants, shall we say, of the 12th or 13th company, has his head blown off.

'By the way,' he said, hitting himself on the head, 'I nearly forgot, sergeant-major, or if we're to talk on civilian terms, Mr Vaněk, that you must get me a list of all the officers and N.C.O.s. Give me the name of a sergeant-major of the 12th company. – Houska? Good. Houska now will have his head blown off by that mine. His head flies off, but his body still marches one or two steps forwards, takes aim and shoots down an enemy plane. It's quite obvious that in the future these victories and their repercussions will have to be celebrated within the family circle at Schönbrunn. Austria has very many battalions, but there is only one battalion like ours, which distinguishes itself so much that in its honour a small intimate family celebration is held in the Imperial Household. I visualize it in the following way, as you can see in my notes: the family of the Archduchess Marie Valerie moves from Wallsee to Schönbrunn for this celebration: the function is a purely private one and takes place in the hall next to the Monarch's bedroom, which is lit with white candles, because, as is well known, they do not like electric bulbs at the court in case there should be a short circuit, to which the old monarch has strong objections. The ceremony in honour and praise of our battalion starts at six o'clock in the evening. At this moment His Majesty's grand-children are brought into the hall, which is actually part of the suite of the late Empress. Now it's a question as to who will be present besides the Imperial Family. The Monarch's general adjutant, Count Paar, must and will be there, and because during such family and intimate receptions someone occasionally feels faint (by which of course I don't mean that Count Paar himself should vomit), the presence of the personal doctor, the Counsellor of the Court, Dr Kerzl, will be required. For the sake of decency, to ensure that the court footmen shouldn't permit themselves any liberties with the ladies-in-waiting present at the reception, the Marshal of the Court, Baron Lederer, the Chamberlain, Count Bellegarde, and the principal Lady-in-Waiting, Countess Bombelles, will appear. The latter fulfils the same role among the ladies-in-waiting as madame does in the Prague brothel, U Šuhů. As soon as these exalted gentry are assembled the Emperor is informed and appears accompanied by his grandchildren. He sits down at a table and proposes a toast in honour of our march battalion. After him the Archduchess Marie Valerie makes a speech in which she pays a special compliment to you, quartermaster sergeant-major. Of course, according to my notes our battalion will suffer heavy and severe losses, because a battalion without dead is no battalion at all. I shall still have to prepare a new article about our fallen. The history of a battalion should not consist merely of dry facts about victories, of which I have already recorded in advance some forty-two. You, for example, Mr Vaněk, will fall by a small stream, and Baloun, who's staring at us here in such an extraordinary fashion, will die an entirely different death. It will not be by bullet, shrapnel or shell. He will be strangled by a lassoo, thrown down from an enemy plane at the very moment when he is wolfing his lieutenant's dinner.'

Baloun stepped back, waved his hands despairingly and remarked dejectedly: 'I'm sorry, you know, but I can't help my nature! Even when I was in regular service I used to turn up some three times for mess in the kitchen until they put me in gaol for it. Once I had boiled rib of beef for dinner three times and because of that I was in quod for a month. May God's will be done!'

'Don't be afraid, Baloun,' the volunteer consoled him. 'In the history of the battalion there'll be no mention of the fact that you perished when you were guzzling grub on the way from the officers' mess to the trenches. You'll be mentioned together with all the men of our battalion who fell for the glory of our Empire, as for instance Quartermaster Sergeant-Major Vaněk.'

'What kind of death are you preparing for me, Marek?'

'Don't rush me, please, sergeant-major. It doesn't go as quickly as all that.'

The volunteer thought for a moment: 'You're from Kralupy, aren't you? Then write home to Kralupy that you are going to be missing without a trace, but write cautiously. Or would you prefer to be seriously wounded and remain lying beyond the barbed-wire entanglements? You could lie beautifully like that with a broken leg the whole day. In the night the enemy lights up our positions with his searchlights and notices you; he thinks you're spying and begins to riddle you with shells and shrapnel. You have performed a tremendous service for the army, because the enemy has had to expend on you as large a quantity of munitions as would have been needed for a whole battalion. After all these explosions your bits float freely in the air over you and, penetrating it with their rotations, sing a paean of glorious victory. In short everybody will have his turn, everyone of our battalion will distinguish himself so that the glorious pages of our history will overflow with victories – although I really would much prefer them not to overflow, but I can't help it. Everything must be carried out thoroughly so that some memory of us will remain until, say, in the month of September there will be really nothing left whatsoever of our battalion, except these glorious pages of history which will carry a message to the hearts of all Austrians, making it plain to them that all those who will never see their homes again fought equally valiantly. And I've already written the end, you know, Mr Vaněk – the obituary notice. Honour to the memory of the fallen! Their love for the Monarchy is the most sacred love of all, for death was its climax. Let their names be pronounced with honour, as for instance the name of Vaněk. Those who felt deepest of all the loss of their breadwinners may proudly wipe away their tears. Those who fell were the heroes of our battalion.'

Chodounský and Jurajda were listening with great interest to the volunteer's exposition of the forthcoming history of the battalion.

'Come closer, gentlemen,' said the volunteer, turning the pages of his notes. 'Here is page 15. "The telephonist, Chodounský, fell 3 September together with the battalion cook, Jurajda." Now listen further to my notes: "Exemplary heroism. The former, at the sacrifice of his life, protects the telephone wires in his cover when left at his telephone for three days without relief. The latter, observing the danger threatening from an enemy encirclement of our flank, throws himself at the foe with a cauldron of boiling soup, scattering terror and scaldings in his ranks." That's a splendid death for both of them, isn't it? One torn to pieces by a mine, the other asphyxiated by poison gas which they put under his nose, when he had nothing to defend himself with. Both perish with the cry: "Long live our battalion commander!" The High Command can do nothing else but daily express its gratitude in the form of the order that all other units of our army should know of the courage of our battalion and follow our example. I can read you an extract from the army order which will be read out in all units of the army and which is very like the order of the Archduke Karl, when he stood with his army in 1805 before Padua and got a frightful drubbing the day after. Listen to what people will read about our battalion as a heroic unit, which is a glowing example for all armies. " ... I hope that the whole army will follow the example of the above-named battalion, and in particular adopt its spirit of self-confidence and self-reliance, its unshakeable invincibility in danger and its qualities of heroism, love and confidence in its superior officers. These virtues, in which the battalion excels, will lead it on to glorious deeds for the victory and blest happiness of our Empire. May all follow its example!'"

From the place where Švejk lay a yawn resounded and he could be heard talking in his sleep: 'Yes, you're right, Mrs Muller, people are all alike. In Kralupy there lived a Mr Jaros who manufactured pumps and he was like the watchmaker Lejhanz from Pardubice, as like as pins. And Lejhanz again was strikingly like Piskora of Jičín, and four together resembled an unknown suicide whom they found hanged and completely decomposed in a lake near Jindřichův Hradec, just underneath the railway line, where he probably threw himself under the train.' There resounded another yawn and it was followed by: 'And then they sentenced all the others to a huge fine, and tomorrow, Mrs Muller, please make me some noodles with poppy-seed.' Švejk turned over on the other side and went on snoring, while between Jurajda and the volunteer a debate started about what would happen in the future.

~

Jaroslav Hašek was born in Prague (then within Austria-Hungary) in 1883. His life was even more eventful than that of Švejk, the hero of the darkly funny *The Good Soldier Švejk*. Hašek was a lifelong anarchist who fought in the war, was captured by the Russians in 1915, sent to a prisoner-of-war camp and in 1916 was recruited into the Czechoslovak Brigade to fight the Austro-Hungarian army. Hašek disagreed with the decision of the brigade to go to the Western Front and in October 1918 he joined the Soviet Red Army. He returned to Prague in 1920 and had completed the first three volumes of *The Good Soldier Švejk* by the time of his death in 1923 in Lipnice, Czechoslovakia. With a life like that he could have written many more volumes! Widely translated, the book appeals to audiences the world over because of the character of Švejk, who undermines the authority of the powerful with subtle irony and apparent obedience: the dialogue is a festival of surreal non-sequiturs. The drawings that are an essential part of the book's appeal are by Hašek's friend Josef Lada. In all Lada made over 900 drawings for the illustrated edition of the book, which was published in 1924 in the Czech daily *České Slovo*.

MIROSLAV KRLEŽA

HUT 5B

from *The Croatian God Mars*

translated by Celia Hawkesworth

C OUNT MAXIMILIAN AXELRODE, Commander of the Sovereign Military Order of Malta, had become a Johannieter Chevalier de
Justice, in gala uniform with a silver cross, in his fourteenth year. Instead
of having the sixteen noble and chivalrous forebears in the line of his
respected father, and his respected mother, a noblewoman of high birth,
required for the rank of high dignitary of the high Order of Malta,
Count Maximilian Axelrode numbered in his lineage twenty-eight
plumes and helmets, beneath which blue blood pulsed, so when the
Great Priorate of the Sovereign Order of Malta sent to His Majesty's
office priceless letters patent sealed with gold for the supreme 'Impri-
matur', it was a great occasion, such as rarely occur on this earth.

Throughout his entire life, Count Maximilian Axelrode had only
one idea: to draw his sword for his proud Maltese motto 'Pro Fide', wrap
himself in his black cape that fell in heavy folds and hasten to his death,
head held high and proud. So, when he travelled to Jerusalem for the
first time he had wept bitterly with grief onto the marble of Santa Maria
Latina, because he had not been granted the immense good fortune of
scattering his noble bones here, eight hundred years previously, with
the great Godfrey of Bouillon, or if not that, then at least of being born
three hundred years later, when the cannons thundered on Rhodes
and Malta. But no! He had fallen onto the globe in a cowardly, stupid

age, when the noble Villiers de l'Isle-Adam family had become socialist agitators of some kind, inciting the rabble on the First of May, and when the greatest military event was reduced to a manoeuvre where there was blind firing, but limited, because some Minister of Finance and some 'crass' parliamentarians had brayed that the army was too costly. 'Ugh, this idiotic age of steam locomotives, when everything is hamstrung by rails and so-called democracy, and when the noble Knights of Malta met in hotels, wearing burghers' bowler hats, and duels were banned by law!'

Count Maximilian Axelrode had grieved in this sterile way for a whole sixty-three years when he awoke one morning and thought he must be dreaming. His lackey handed him a dispatch from the Priorate of the High Order, informing him that mobilisation had been declared and that, following its high tradition, the Order of Malta would at last raise its banner in the name of its great motto 'Pro Fide' and somewhere on the imperial military stage erect tents and organise a hospital. And so Count Maximilian Axelrode became the head of a big Maltese hospital, consisting of forty-two large wooden huts, with its own electricity generator, whole companies of Red Cross nurses, and so on and so forth. The armies shifted a hundred kilometres east, and then two hundred kilometres west, and then again east, from one season of war to the next, as war decrees, and so Count Axelrode travelled with his Maltese circus from east to west, from Stanislavov to Krakow and back for three whole years, and now it was August 1916, the sun was blazing at forty-nine Celsius and the situation was serious and tense.

The hospital, with fifteen hundred patients, was full and there was every chance that the Russians were going to cut the railway line to left and right, and that the noble count, the Maltese Grand Master, would be in Moscow in two weeks' time. At noon a dispatch arrived, stating that the Russians had indeed moved the front line northwards, between two stations, but the hospital should stay where it was, because a counter-offensive was underway. That, the fact that the Russians had cut the line in the north, meant that all the transports began to move south and that resulted, naturally enough, in a crash (seventy-two dead, many injured), and all the convoys were left without provisions, so the wounded were crying out, for the fifth day now, with no water and they were being fed (oh, don't laugh, it's true!) with peppermint drops for the prevention of intestinal worms and people all along the line were out of their minds, and so Count Axelrode had to take in, on top of his full complement, another five hundred patients. That day happened to be the hottest day of the whole summer, when the sun was formally crushing the earth with its fiery mass, and it seemed as though someone had thrown a burning millstone onto the white wooden huts and everything had caught fire. The boards bent and cracked with the drought, and the whitewash from the walls peeled like old men's skin and the green bindweed and flowers in the decorative round beds had all withered, everything was rotten, decayed, trampled.

The new group of five hundred wounded soldiers included Vidović, a student whose lungs had been shot through and he was bleeding. Although there is nowhere a man can get as filthy as at the front, when they placed Vidović in the large steam bath, appallingly grimy, like all patients carried in transports of wounded soldiers in cattle trucks in the month of August, he was still capable of being disgusted.

And if you were to take such a pathetic, nervous figure as Vidović out of a certain relatively European way of life and put him into that steam bath, it is very likely that such a man would develop cramps and start to vomit. But, after everything that had happened to him that day and the day before, after the fire the previous night at the station, when petrol cans had exploded one after the other, and after those peppermint drops for the prevention of intestinal worms, when twelve hundred throats were crying out for water, and there was none, and after that pig wagon, Vidović did not vomit in the steam of the bathroom, but everything revolted him.

Ugh! How disgusting and frightful it was! The concrete bath swirled with stinking yellow water and grey-green foaming soap, with bloody bandages and cotton wool floating in it. Suppurating, nauseating cotton wool. The water steamed and stank of mud and clay, the steam showers hissed, and in the thick steam, black shadows could be made out running to and fro in the mist, and all their faces were swollen and bloody, and a generator throbbed somewhere, and it was midday in August. Here a man was dying under a shower on a glass table, there another was wailing, ventilators hummed like invisible insects, while Russians in khaki kerchiefs carried in new wounded material like sacks, and the nurses and wounded men and doctors all shouted and ran around, demented.

They washed Vidović in that dirty, bloody hell and took him into Hut 5B, which looked inside like the guts of a great barge. With cruel protestant pedantry, it contained sixty precisely arranged beds, one body on each, with a label above each body, with information about that body's state. The barge was divided into three groups. The first were the broken bones. (Bones protruded like splinters. The men lay silent by day. It was only at night that their cries were heard, as from Golgotha.) The second were amputees. (Arm or leg, or leg and arm. The wounds were not bandaged, but left to dry under gauze like cured meat.) The third group, to the left of the door, were the 'transients'. Those transients were only passing through Hut 5B. They travelled from the bathroom to the morgue. And when someone was placed in the third group, Hut 5B knew the state of play.

When they brought the injured Vidović into the hut and laid him on bed number eight, a Hungarian, a great hulk of a man from the first group (broken bones) spat contemptuously and traced a cross in the air with his finger:

'*No hát, Istenem!** This one could have gone straight to the morgue.'

'There's a new number eight! Hey!'

'Number eight! Number eight!'

The news spread through the hut and many heads were raised, to see this new number eight. It was true! They had all been fundamentally mangled and bloodied by life! But, even if a man had lost a leg, it wasn't as though he was number eight! He was number twenty-one! Or fifteen!

'I've lost an arm! Yes! And my bones are broken! Yes! But I'm alive! Dear God! I'm still alive! And when the Russians come in with a black coffin and shove the new number eight into it, I'll fill my pipe, watch the insects sticking to the fly-paper and drink milk! That's some kind of life, after all! That's not what's in store for number eight!'

---

*'Ah well, my God!'

For four days now number eight had kept changing. It was only that morning that the Russian prisoners had taken out one of theirs, a Russian colleague. His intestines had been ripped open and he had yelled for two days and nights. Before the Russian there had been a kindly Viennese man and now there was Vidović.

On bed number seven, to the left of Vidović, there was a Mongol, a Siberian with a bullet in his head, who had been screaming in his death throes for three days now. He kept shouting something, all sharp consonants, but no one understood anything, and they all kept thinking he was done for, but then he would start tossing and writhing, so that a ribbon of burning red blood seeped through the bandage on his head. In bed number nine, to the right, a young Slovak was dying, his throat shot through. His windpipe had been severed and he breathed through a glass cannula, so that foaming saliva, pus and lymph could be clearly heard gurgling in the little tube.

And so Hut 5B began to bet on Vidović's head, that he wouldn't make it through the night.

'I know our doctor. If he doesn't get a man under the knife at once, then it's curtains!'

'That's not true! He wouldn't have left him till tomorrow, if that was true! He's still young!'

'That Viennese "blade" was eating rice and laughing! But we went straight to the cutting table.'

'So what? Is it worth a bottle of red? Dead before morning?'

'Done! A bottle of red!'

★

And so the August night fell.

Big stars appeared, huge and brilliant, while the great blue firmament, like a crystal dish, enclosed the whole valley with Axelrode's Maltese hospital, and thousands upon thousands of tons of incandescent gases pressed down on Hut 5B, and there was not a breath of wind, not the slightest quiver. The flies in the hut had now fallen asleep and were no longer buzzing, and somewhere in the middle of that perverse ship, crammed with human flesh, a green lamp was burning and everything was floating in the half dark. Dark, dark, half-dark and pain, inexpressible pain, hidden during the day, now breathed out through every pore and throbbed with every heartbeat. Now every slightest splinter of even the tiniest shattered bone could be felt, convulsions shook the nerves, spewing sounds out of the depths of a man, like lava from a volcano. Men clenched their teeth, shivering in sweat, foaming and biting their tongues and lips, and suddenly their whole lower jaw stretched away, their faces were distorted in a bestial grimace and their voices cried from the depths of their innards, as from the mouth of a well.

'*Mamma mia, mamma mia*,' pleaded someone at the end of the room in Italian.

'*Gospodi, Gospodi, Gospodi*,'* groaned a Russian with a bullet in his intestines, then quiet again, green quiet, half-darkness.

Worn out from loss of blood, Vidović had slept the whole afternoon, but now he woke, and did not know where he was or what had happened, or how he had ended up here. He heard human voices, groaning, but his raging wounds had eased and the fever seemed to have been extinguished, and, with great effort, the tormented Vidović found a slightly cooler spot on his pillow. His burning lids closed again, and a dense, weighty silence poured over them, while his thirst had somehow evaporated, and the hut was already beginning to dissolve and fade into an agreeable blackness, when it was rent once again by an animal cry of pure pain, which suddenly shattered the whole edifice of sleep built with such difficulty somewhere on the cooler edge of the pillow, and the whole thing collapsed in a single instant.

And so it went on, the whole night, over and over again.

'Oh! Just five minutes! Just five minutes' sleep!'

It must have been towards dawn, for clear light was penetrating through the green gauze. Outside guards were shouting, while the bindweed climbing up the ropes seemed to tremble in a morning breeze. Moths circled round the lamp, their wings fluttering.

'What time is it?'

There's no time! There's nothing! Only pain.

---

*'Lord, Lord, Lord!'

'*Mamma mia! mamma mia! Gospodi! Gospodi!*'
'Ah, if I could only sleep for a minute! A second!'
'*Gospodi!*'

★

On the second morning the situation began to change ominously. In the early dawn, the Russians had broken through in the south and so cut off the last remaining imperial and royal railway link, and the trains had begun to turn back, and the order was given to the engineers, and locomotives started exploding into pieces, like toys. Everything was stranded. Artillery, the wounded, magazines, the great divisional stoves with their sooty chimneys, pontoons, horses, the whole lot; all that could be heard was the dull thunder of wrecked engines being blown up. And the whole morning troops marched, so the patients of the Maltese hospital from A, C and D huts (the lightly injured, who did not travel on stretchers, but could just about hobble) looked happily out through the barbed wire at the horror of the retreat, to where later in the day men would collapse onto the roads with sunstroke, and, believe it or not, in spite of everything, they felt good. They were there, under the Red Cross, and no one was chasing them anywhere, and if the Russians came, they would carry them off again somewhere far away, into Russian hospitals and camps where there would be no war, and they would survive and so for them, in all probability, the war would end this very morning. And that was the only thought the wounded men had in their heads.

Count Maximilian Axelrode, Chief of the Maltese Hospital, dispatched the fashionable female personnel (two or three baronesses and a general's wife) in cars, while he himself decided to stay with his Maltese flag here, in harm's way, to the bitter end. The bell on the morgue rang, and Count Axelrode walked, in his black uniform with its Maltese cross, through the huts, as he did every morning, looking at the naked yellow corpses that the Russians carried in their coffins; the Russians carried the corpses and saluted the Count, doffing their caps and bowing to the ground.

'Who would have thought that things in the whole hospital could have slipped so far in just twelve hours!

'Yes! It's true! Yesterday was an exceptionally nerve-racking day. The damned sun shrivelled everyone's brains, and what with the alarming news, and the dispatches, and the blown-up locomotives, all of that affected the "ambiance"! Then this new transport, it has completely ruined the domestic order of the hospital, both the kitchens and the nursing stations. Yes! This transport too! But today, when the troops are passing by outside, and when it can all be seen as on a chess board, when you can see the figures falling, it's all increasingly clear and it all looks increasingly destructive. Would that medical corporal have dared, even yesterday at this time, to drink brandy from a large bottle in front of His Excellency. Today, he had seen the Count coming, but he had gone on calmly drinking, as though none of it had anything to do with him. And why are many of the patients pulling such mocking faces? And why are the Russians singing?' (That was the Russian prisoners holding a service in their hut, because that day was an Orthodox holy day.) 'See! No one is watering the flowerbeds today, although that is particularly stressed in the hospital rules! And there's no one anywhere!'

The Count was completely isolated in that rabble. He stood alone, like a shadow, himself shaken, and could not find the energy to put things back in order, and he did not know what to do. He was unable to contact Headquarters, he did not know the orders, and the general's staff had hurtled past here in their cars, a few minutes previously, and had not stopped! So the Count called the divisional chiefs into his hut for a consultation, to reach a decision as to what was to be done.

Some favoured the idea that fifty per cent of the personnel should remain and the other fifty per cent should leave; others did not agree, while still others were not in favour of either idea, but some third option, and this wrangling went on so long that in the end nothing was decided, 'until further notice'.

That 'further notice' arrived, however, at around five pm, when it became unequivocally clear that the hospital would find itself, that very night, between the lines; for it seemed that on this section of the front the Russians were not engaging in battle with our troops. And if the planned large-scale counter-offensive, announced forty-eight hours previously, did not succeed (which was highly likely), then on

the following day at the same hour the future of the Maltese Hospital
would in all probability be decided by the Medical Officer of some
Russian division.

It was therefore resolved that Count Axelrode, with the surgeons
and most valuable materials, and fifty per cent of the personnel, should
retreat this very night to a farmstead, some fifteen kilometres to the
west, that he should make contact from there with a larger group, and
send a written complaint that he and his hospital had been forgotten;
as though he were a needle, when he was not a needle, but a Maltese
hospital with fifteen hundred wounded patients.

The last substantial infantry formations had passed by, and heavy
gunfire could be heard drawing near. By then patients had torn out the
barbed wire fence, and were sitting by the ditches on the road, talking
to people who had come from the battle about 'Him'. And 'He' was
Brusilov. 'He' was Russian.

'Where is "He"?'

'Is "He" here?'

'What is "He" doing?'

'When is "He" coming?'

'"He's" on his way.'

'"He" won't stop till Vienna.'

'"He's" coming.'

But the troops were tired and thirsty, and everyone said something
different, no one knew anything, but 'He' was definitely coming.

Evening fell and searchlights began to weave over the sky, and heavy
guns thundered in the distance, and the last companies of soldiers had
passed. But there was no sign of 'Him'. 'He' had stopped for some
unknown reason and, strangely, he had stopped like an interrupted
breath. Three kilometres in front of the hospital muddy water spilled
through a grove of willows, under clearly visible, burning bridges. And
over on the other side, there was calm, no one was there. In that mysterious time, when no one knew anything, not where 'He' was or what
'He' was doing, the whole Maltese hospital felt as though it was hanging
in the air between Vienna and Moscow, and it was very likely that it was
closer to Moscow than Vienna – that was when someone had the bright

idea of stealing the first bottle of brandy from the store, because who knew what the next day would bring?

There was brandy and red burgundy and Hungarian Villány wines and champagne in the store room, and an hour later the whole Maltese hospital was blind drunk, and wine was flowing through the huts, and full bottles of beer were being broken, because who wants to drink beer! Intoxicated by the shining illusion that they would be leaving the very next day for their countryside in the Urals, on the Volga, the Russian prisoners began to dance through the huts, and when a Hungarian doctor fired a revolver in an attempt to control the alcohol with gunpowder, a whole small battle and exchange of fire ensued, and the Hungarian doctor gave up and retreated, disappearing somewhere with the nurses in the darkness. Two German nurses, sister Frieda and sister Marianna (whose fiancé had fallen at Verdun and who was forever reading *Ullstein*), were discovered in their rooms and raped and after that everything fell apart, and the crowd began to drink freedom, increasingly intensely and deeply, becoming drunk on that illusion to the point of madness, and everything became like a drunken dream. Each rocket that shot up, minute by minute, from the forest opposite, was greeted by these drunken wounded soldiers, in their shirtsleeves, with bottles in their hands, with wild whoops and whistles, and everyone lost control, as at a country fair.

They carried wine in buckets into Hut 5B, to those poor wounded folk, and the ones with broken bones and those with their legs sawn off, the stumps drying under gauze like cured meat, they all got drunk as lords, and some Hungarians started playing Twenty-One on Vidović's bed.

'Dealer, hit!' 'Hit, dealer!' came their cries, and the cards were shuffled, and they drank, and all their faces looked like the masks of Chinese pirates, grimacing and contorted, bristling with hollow teeth, and grinning: 'Hit, one!' One fool climbed onto the roof of the hut and began dancing and the plaster started to crack and it looked as though the ceiling would come down and everything collapse. And from Hut C came the sound of a harmonica, a ocarina and *gusle* – that was where the men from the Srem district were, and singing rang out, with a lot of 'mama and papa' too, and the wanton, wild scherzo vibrated, clearly audible over there in Hut 5B, where Vidović lay, bullet-riddled and in despair, with just one thought in his head: 'Are they going to operate? If they had only taken this all out of me today, I would not be bleeding! Where are they? Why don't they operate? What's going on?'

'Hit! One! Hit! Dealer!'

'*Mert arról én nem tehetek, hogy nagyon nagyon szeretlek,* * *taralala lalalala.*' One of the amputees sang the Budapest couplet, putting the organza cover for his amputated leg on his head like a hat and bowing coquettishly to left and right. And an Italian sang the Irredenta, his tenor voice sobbing with emotion – *amor, amor, amor!* People sang, drank, spilled brandy, and the scabby patients began to throw brooms through the huts, yelling, and everything howled like a menagerie, and it seemed as though all those huts, like wounded, grimy, blind hens, would start jumping up and down on their one amputated, bandaged leg, to and fro, to the rhythm of the heavy gun music, that was thundering from the railway station increasingly powerful, increasingly loud.

Hände waschen vor dem Essen,
Nach dem Stuhlgang nicht vergessen.†

The Tyroleans began yodeling in chorus, from the sign that hung in Austrian hospitals in the three so-called state languages. Not to be outdone, the Hungarians sang their own Hungarian verse after that:

Egyél igyál de mindig elóbb mosdjál!‡

And the third verse:

Peri ruke svagda prije jela,

---

*'I am good for nothing, if I love you so much.'
†'Wash your hands before all ingestion,/and wash after each bodily motion.'
‡'Eat, drink, and always wash your hands before eating!'

Peri poslije ispražnjenja tijela.*

But no one sang that third verse in the Croatian of the home-guardsmen, they simply mocked it, as though it were something African. One short-sighted Styrian infantryman (whose spectacle lenses enlarged his eyes, so that they bulged green like glass marbles) was ready to explode with laughter. He had a cough that sputtered and rasped, he went purple in the face, choking, while he twisted his tongue in order to read that famous Croatian song: *'Peri ruke svagda prije jela, peri poslije ispražnjenja tijela'.*

'Haha! Ist das aber wirklich dumm! Ist das dumm, dieses "peri"! Was ist das, du – dieses – peri?'†

'"Vazistas!" "Vazistas!" Stupid dolt. *Nichts! Nichts!* You tell him, Štef, what he's asking! You've been to Graz! Hey, there! Schnapps!'

And they drank, and grinned, squabbled, sang, yelled: Babylon! Someone had learned in a camp for Italian prisoners: *'Porca Madonna, io parlo italiano!'* so they shouted this to the Italians, waving to them, *'Porca Madonna, porca, porca, porca'*, while someone mocked the Romanians with a quote from the infectious diseases hospital for typhoid patients: *'Nueste permis ascipi per podele! Haha! Sci rumunjesci!'*‡

'Dear brothers! Please! Be quiet! I'm in pain! I'm in terrible pain,' shouted Vidović, but his voice was faint, and he just croaked, and blood gushed through his teeth.

'Te! Mi az? Pain? Mindig ez a pain? Mi az pain?'§

'That's like, when you feel pain, my friend,' a bullet-ridden man explained to the Hungarian. 'You know, when you're wounded, then you feel pain! Or you bump into something! And you feel pain!'

'Woonded? Bumb? Pain? Haha, pain! Pain!'

'And mama and papa...'

And the heavy gunfire was coming closer, as though someone was chopping wood underneath the hut.

---

*'Always wash your hands before eating/and wash after each emptying of the body.'
†'Ha! Ha! How stupid is that! How stupid is that "peri"! Hey you, what is that "peri"?'
‡'Spitting on the ground is forbidden! Ha! Ha! You understand Romanian!'
§'Hey, what is "pain"? Always "pain". What is "pain"?'

★

The major counter-offensive, announced forty-eight hours earlier, was a success and at dawn the Russians were repulsed at a stroke, in an attack from two directions. Some fifteen infantry battalions and several batteries were captured, and at half-past nine in the morning Count Maximilian Axelrode returned to the hospital, accompanied by Baroness Liechtenstein.

First there was an investigation into the rape of the German nurses (sexually abused by some Hungarians), around half-past twelve seven Russians were shot, before which they had dug their own graves, and some three hundred and fifty malingerers (men with trachoma, scabies, venereal disease, light grazing and bruising, and all inmates of Huts A 2, 3, 4 and 5, apart from those with a temperature over 38°C) were thrown into the battle, and by half-past ten a sober Johanniter Maltese order prevailed once again over the hospital.

In order to establish the authority of the imperial flag and discipline, which appeared to have been so compromised the previous night, Count Axelrode ordered that the great victory should be celebrated in the hospital with a torch-lit rally and procession. All patients (without exception) would march past the black and yellow flag, and those who were bed-ridden would be carried by the Russians on stretchers, but all would process. And that is how it was.

All the huts were arranged into companies and each soldier was handed a burning torch, and the procession was led by a mess-officer, who had never sat on a horse in his life, but he clinked his spurs and organised the crowd like a theatre director. A procession of several hundred people in bloody grey kerchiefs gathered, each holding a green or red torch, and against the ash-blue moisture of the dusk, all the strong colours stood out and it looked like a ghostly vision.

The procession moved off.

The grandsons of the long dead, fallen at the Viennese barricades in forty-eight, the sons of Garibaldi's flag-bearers, Hussites, God's warriors, Jelačić's frontiersmen, Hungarian supporters of Kossuth, all crippled, lame, mutilated, bandaged, amputees, on crutches, in wheel-chairs, on stretchers, pushed and shoved, while up there flew the large black and yellow flag, with Count Alexrode beneath it in his black uniform with the Maltese cross, and behind him the nurses with their red crosses and the doctors, and they all sang in unison: *Gott erhalte!** The men walked quietly, their heads bowed, as though ashamed, still bleary from the previous night, carrying their yellow torches like candles at a funeral, while a horn-player climbed onto the roof of a hut, droning the trumpet call for the arrival of a general. When they brought Vidović back from that shameful march-past to Hut 5B, he was racked by a raging fever.

Everything had turned bad the previous night, and now everyone in the whole hut, animated by alcohol, felt their wounds to an extreme degree. The Siberian in bed seven had been drunk that night and in the morning he was dead, but it was only in the afternoon that he was carried out of the hut, and everything smelled terrible, because of the great quantity of blood. The Slovak with the cannula in number nine was still suffering and his rasping breath could still be heard. And a Russian was shouting horribly down there, among the Hungarians. The night before he had wanted to dance, and now he was yelling like a lunatic.

'*As atya úr istennét, ennek a Ruszkinak! Ruszki!*'†

'Shut it! You, Russian! Why are you shouting?'

'I'm in pain, and I'm not shouting!'

'I want to sleep! Damn your bloody mother!'

'Shut it, Russian!'

'Shh! Quiet! Sshh! Sshh!'

Vidović lay listening to the hut quarrelling and felt the end coming.

'So why in fact was I born, and what purpose did it have? To be born into such an absurd "café-concert" civilization, where there is no pity and where everything is an operetta! And what a shameful death! How deeply shameful! I wanted to experience life, I wanted to live! And what happened? Hospitals, nothing but hospitals! Could anyone in the

---

*'Gott erhalte Franz den Kaiser' (God Save Emperor Franz), originally written as an anthem to Franz II.

†'For God's sake, that Russian! That Russki!'

wide world make sense of this hospital? Nothing but hospitals! For two years now I've done nothing but travel through hospitals. Decorative city hospitals with high-class courtesans! Monasteries, where consumptives die! They inject them with serum, which no one believes in. And huts! Filthy, smelly, lousy wooden huts like this! Ah, how disgusting it all is! Ugh!'

And, in need of some kind of action, to rouse himself, jump up, run, to shout at the top of his voice, Vidović tried to sit up, but he could not. He was pinioned. Pain overwhelmed the rebellion of his nerves and he was lost in mists and began to groan loudly.

'Ssshh! Ssshh!' complained the hut, hissing in the darkness.

And pain began ever more tightly to grip the countless bloody, shattered limbs scattered through the whole of Hut 5B. Pain began to take on supernatural forms and people started calling on their god. The Good Lord was summoned as the last resort, as appeals are addressed to the Court Chancellery when all else has failed.

A Hungarian called on his *Isten** to help him! For his *Isten* to come in his wide horseman's breeches and down two or three bottles of red Bull's Blood, and play a tune on a *gusle*, and to let him die once and for all or be resurrected. Carrying on like this was unbearable!

'*Gospodi! Gospodi! Gospodi!!*' cried a Russian, pale, translucent as a Byzantine icon, praying to the Russian Lord God in a boyar's fur coat, sitting on a golden throne in the Kremlin, and the Russian shouted, shouted so that his voice was heard as far as Mother Moscow, shouted, put his palms together and cried like a baby! *Gospodi! Gospodi!*

And Vidović shuddered and it seemed to him that *Isten* had come to the Hungarian and sat down on his bed and poured wine for him from a flask, and the Hungarian was drinking ever more eagerly and the *gusle* scraped, ah, how good it was to drink wine offered to one, to the sound of a *gusle*! It was good! It helped one sleep! And the Russian Lord God, He too was walking through the hut, with His rich entourage, and icons flared and the bells of the Holy Mother pealed and that old gentleman with a white beard and silken fur coat, He rummaged in the Russian's

---

*St Stephen.

innards and removed that bloody bullet from the Russian and it felt better, ah, it was better, thank you, Lord, it is better!

'Hey! They all have their gods! They each have a god! The man from Fiume as well ("*Mamma mia! Mamma mia!*"), he too has his cardinals and popes and Roman flags, and the Russian and the Hungarian, they all have their gods, but who do I have? I'm in pain too! I've been shot just like them! But I have no one!'

And Vidović was hurting so badly that he raised his arms and stretched them out to someone, but his hands hung in the air, and he felt a terrible emptiness, and his throat caught and he sobbed out loud.

'Oh yes! I've seen Christ hanging outside our inns! The true Croatian Christ, all his thirty-three ribs broken, his chest pierced, and bleeding from innumerable wounds! But I never believed in him! A wooden Christ like that on a muddy road, awash with manure; where not a single drunkard passes without cursing him; that kind of wooden Croatian god, naked, pitiful, whose left leg is missing, oh, a god with a soldier's cap, he, he – and I'm supposed to pray to him, to ask him to help me…'

Lieb' Vaterland, magst ruhig sein,
Wir wollen alle Mütter sein –
Treu steht und fest die Wacht am Rhein.*

'What's this? Have I gone mad? Who am I praying to? It's hurting! I'm praying! What are those voices?'

From outside, through the green gauze above Vidović's head, a yellow light was seeping in and women's voices in a minor key could be heard, softly chanting lines of verse. And the clinking of crystal glasses could be heard! Soft tinkling, soft voices, but clear: '*Lieb' Vaterland, magst ruhig sein…*'

Right beside Hut 5B was an arbour, where the doctors and ladies from the Red Cross often dined. And this evening, the formal dinner

---

*Dear Fatherland, be calm,/We all wish to be mothers –/The guard on the Rhine true and firm.

was attended, exceptionally, also by Count Axelrode, to celebrate the victory with his staff.

Intoxicated by the magnificent event of the victory (when it had seemed as though the dice had fallen badly, and then everything had turned round so wonderfully), and lulled by the patriotic melody of the ladies ready to conceive for the sake of war and warfare, Count Maximilian Axelrode, Commander of the Maltese Order, stood and raised his glass, to toast the victory. He spoke exaltedly, about the victories of His Majesty, with the Maltese banner, undefeated and sovereign, at his side.

'My ladies! Luogotenente Father Giovanni Battista Ceschi a Santa Croce, who experienced with his own eyes the Jacobin attack on this holy Maltese cross of ours, which I have the honour of representing here, that noble knight wrote in his chronicle, my ladies, that when the Holy Father comes to divide the good from the evil, above the extinguished sun, then black Maltese cloaks will stand guard in the divine shade…'

Vidović heard the clink of glasses in the arbour and recognised the voice of the commander and remembered his mask that evening in the torch-lit procession.

'I've gone mad! I was ready to pray! Oh! And, outside they're singing! It's true! Celebrating their victory! And that Maltese knight is talking…'

'What's up with number nine? He's torn the cannula out of his throat! He's bleeding! Nurse!'

'Sshh! Sshh!'

'But number nine is bleeding! Nurse!'

'There's no one anywhere! Where's the nurse? Number nine…'

Outside in the arbour, the other side of the whitewashed boards, glasses clinked, while, in his death throes, number nine had pulled out his cannula, and his blood was draining away. Number nine was breathing heavily, croaking, like a pig whose throat has been slit, and then ever more quietly…

Vidović wanted to cry out, but he could not make a sound. It was clear that they ought to light a candle for number nine.

'They should light a candle! For the peace of his soul!' He just kept repeating that incessantly, his eyes fixed on the pool of black blood on bed nine. He wanted to howl, with all his might, but could only splutter, rasping.

'Hush! For God's sake!'

'*Az apád istennét! Csönd!*'*

'Hush!'

'Number nine is dead! Number nine is dead! And those gentlemen out there are singing and clinking glasses! Father Giovanni Battista a Santa Croce! If I could just set eyes on him! Just see the Chevalier de Malte...'

And in the exultation of his last effort, which was in fact the final spasm of death, Vidović raised himself up like a ghost and tore the gauze from above his head! Now there was a bright square and in the bright green illuminated spot among the leaves of the arbour he could see white ladies with red crosses, tipsy, smiling, loud, the future mothers of future butchers.

'Aaagh,' Vidović wanted to yell, and a bright thought flashed through his mind, that he ought to hurl his porcelain pot of filth onto that white tablecloth and soil everything – soil it – so that a terrible great stain would be left on that white tablecloth, and they would all shout: a stain – a stain.

To carry out that last pathetic wish, Vidović reached down for his pot, and felt, as he was falling, his hands sinking into that terrible slimy matter – and everything drowned in the blood that spurted from him in a torrent.

⁓

Born in Zagreb, then Austro-Hungary, in 1893, **Miroslav Krleža** is regarded by many as the finest Croatian writer of the 20th century. A member of the Communist Party of Yugoslavia from 1918, Krleža was a prominent figure in the cultural life of both Croatia and the whole of Yugoslavia, contributing decisively in the first years of communist Yugoslavia to the rejection of Socialist

---

*Hungarian oath: On your father's god! Shut up!

Realism in favour of freedom of artistic expression. In the First World War, he served in the Austro-Hungarian army on the Eastern Front. After the war he quickly established himself as a major modernist writer, with a series of striking expressionist plays and novels. His collection of short stories about the First World War, *Hrvatski bog Mars* (The Croatian God Mars), which includes *Hut 5B*, was published in 1922; it is a powerful condemnation of the treatment of Croatian soldiers sent to the battlefields. A recurring theme of many of his works is the abuse of power by the ruling elites in the Austro-Hungarian Empire, typifying what he saw as the hypocrisy and criminal origins of their wealth. Krleža established several influential literary and political reviews. In 1950 he founded the Yugoslav Institute for Lexicography, now the Miroslav Krleža Lexicographical Institute, holding the position as its head until his death in Zagreb in 1981.

MILOŠ CRNJANSKI

MY GOOD GALICIAN FORESTS

from *Diary about Čarnojević*
translated by Celia Hawkesworth

A LL NIGHT LONG, the battalion dragged itself through wet fields and stubble. Cigarettes flickered in the darkness. We came slowly to a halt. We were aware, to right and left, of hordes dragging themselves through the night and the fields. The artillery clanged, clinked and swore. We passed through white, empty houses, trampled gardens, and found everywhere nothing but cucumbers, heaps of cucumbers in water. We slept on low hills piled on top of each other; men were joining us from all directions. The first dawn mists were forming; in the chill twilight we hauled ourselves to the foot of a hillock and began digging ourselves in. I did not. I needed sleep, weary of the whole thing.

We dug ourselves into a wet potato field and finally a lovely August dawn broke. Behind us, from a little copse someone sang, all night, to an accordion, something sad, in Czech. Everything was quiet and subdued in the mist. Above us the pink clouds were playing hide-and-seek. The earth too was becoming slowly, steadily pink. Then something burst, flared like furious barking behind us. They were shooting a few yards over our heads. Someone swore and fell into the ditch. 'Take cover!' he shouted and everyone burrowed into the trench. Straw was dragged in, God alone knows from where, and after that there were chewing and sniggering sounds from the ditches, while the mortar fire criss-crossed alarmingly over our heads. It began deep and low. Beside me lay a shop assistant from Bela Crkva, Radulović, a good lad. He said there'd be a counter-attack. I said nothing and bowed my head. Behind me I could hear the guy who for months had been reciting 'The Dream of the Holy Virgin' every morning, and I bowed my head again and began to eat bread, sprinkling it with sugar. I could hear people behind us beside the mortars shouting orders and numbers and, softly, painfully, I coughed and I coughed. Somewhere to the left of us I saw people in a miserable village making their way out.

Woo-oosh, the first sign of the Russians. 'Behind us ...' I heard someone whisper. Then the earth high above us shook and horses began charging down the hill. Up there the clouds were still playing hide-and-seek and all that could be heard was a sound like heavy, overloaded trains clanking through the air. The Russians scattered shrapnel over the potato field. Then there was nothing again. Far behind the hill, machine guns crackled hideously. At around ten o'clock a soldier arrived. He read out our orders. He mentioned Königgraetz and Custozza. We buckled our bags. 'Don't forget the sugar,' I heard my companion whisper. Bent double, we dragged ourselves through the trenches towards the village. The mortars went wild. Up on the hill men were running with sticks in their hands. Bullets raked them. One of them spun round. We ran slowly through the village. In front of the houses stood filthy women and many, many ragged, filthy children. One of them ran along beside us for a long time, begging me, wanting what – I've no idea. A handsome little Jew, swarthy. Beside the last houses, in a plum orchard, the leaves trembled under a hail of bullets. We entered ever more deeply into the trenches. The wounded were sitting, bloody, dirty, shivering, they were cold. A corpse lay face down in a pool of blood. He had been stripped naked. 'See, didn't I tell you to watch your back,' said my friend. In the hollows, people sat, lay, fired guns. On another small hill, opposite, in a fog of smoke and soil spraying and spinning all around us, the Russian wires could be made out. Someone shouted something to me ironically in Hungarian from a hole, swearing dreadfully. To our right, men of the 33rd Batallion swarmed out of the trenches like ants and charged, with terrible cries, shouts and wails. We dragged ourselves through the barbed wire. Someone cursed our mothers in German and called us dogs. I leaped up.

All the air around me shook as though it was full of bullets. I fell into some rye. The earth whirled and gushed upwards in front of me. I ran like a lunatic. We slithered down into a marsh. Someone fell beside me into the mud and I heard him whisper: 'So, this is Zlota Lipa.' In the grass in front of me lay some boots, and to my right I saw bodies, grimacing, with their legs comically twisted and with hard, strangely hard, knees. Up ahead of us bounded masses of Russians in yellow cloaks; they looked comical and fat. They ran into the forest. We lay down again. To our left a village was burning, its terrible smoke unable to rise from the earth. We started running again. There was horrific slaughter in the forest. Right in front of us. People ran up out of breath, terrified – trying to escape. We dug ourselves in right on the edge of the forest. I lay and breathed, breathed rapidly; blood was trickling slowly out of my nose. Wiii–iiish… a bullet whistled past my head and sank into the earth. It was all utter confusion. People were firing from the left and the right. I pressed my cheek into the soil and breathed, breathed. My breath shook my whole body.

Afterwards, we got up again and pushed on into those dense forests. I slept everywhere, but the dawns woke me. The dawns, the dawns are wonderful. Young, golden forests, my good Galician forests. Through the forests we slowly approached Podkamien. In the Russian trenches there were foot rags and bloody shirts, shattered rifles, bodies – a hideous hotch-potch. My men, who two or three days earlier had been singing, lay in front of those trenches with smashed skulls. Lousy, unwashed, weak, yellow, stinking men; some still alive, expiring with crazed expressions. One of our men recognised his brother lying among them and started shaking and yelling horribly. The battalion trudged and staggered ever deeper into the forests…

★

In those days in Vienna people danced the tango, and we, lads from the Banat, wore silk socks. Yes, student life was no longer what it once was in Heidelberg; there were all sorts now. The days passed. I studied. I mostly sat where people talked about the movements of the poor, enthusiastic masses. I liked that. The red blood spilt in the streets. We used to sit, a few Poles and Jews and I, listening to the history of the Russian soul; it had reached us like a dense fog from the East. And I knew that some great storm had to come to sweep away that hidebound life without guts or pain. Books, whole hills of books lay scattered through the room; outside was the fateful spring about which no one yet knew what it was to bring. And we wore silk socks and spent whole days in the street and in cafés. We wanted to save the world – we, Slav students. Who knows? Perhaps one day there will be a very different art, an art that does not say either what it intends or what its statements might mean. Perhaps speech, and writing, and denotation – that this is death, this love, and this spring, this music – will disappear. Who knows? Ah, I remember: in those days I used to sign my letters 'Poor Yorick', and my mother ran round the neighbourhood all day asking what Yorick was. That's how we lived before the war. Ah, I was young and I had such fine, slender, white shoulders and wings.

★

Radulović brought me rolls. We caressed some filthy women and bought chocolates everywhere. We brought bags full of food from Złoczew. There were several Ruthenians hanged in the square. We caught three heavy shells on the main road. There were quite a few casualties by then. We had got used to it.

The forests were increasingly lovely; golden, red, young forests. An unnamed sorrow had settled on my heart. At night I was racked by fever, I kept coughing but carried on, bent double. No one beat me any more. And the young, red and faded forests, with their warm, sweet mist protected us, safeguarded us and that mist seeped into our souls for ever – for a whole lifetime.

'Ping, ping' – we heard bullets hit the trees. We fixed our bayonets. It was nearly midday. No one had any idea where the Russians were or where we were going. Scrub and brambles scratched us. We came out of the forest; we crossed several stubble fields to a small hill. A few of us were moving ahead of the others. When we reached the top, a valley was spread below us. Suddenly there were explosions around us to the right and left. I was spattered with earth and rolled into some potato trenches. I pressed my face into the soil and breathed, breathed. Behind us the forest screeched and shook horribly under the showers of shrapnel. Someone beside me cried out and started singing. I raised my head. Behind his ear, his head was covered in blood, his mouth was full of blood and he was choking. He straightened and sat up, sang, and spoke of his wife and children, he called me by my name and looked at me, looked only at me. I thrust my head into the earth and said nothing. The sun was blazing. People were running and shouting around me. I fell asleep. Sleep always overwhelmed me, as soon as I lay down. I woke. Mist, evening mist was again falling onto us. Behind the forest two cars sped past. We got up quietly. We made our way down one by one back into the forest. And when darkness fell, we began to walk through the forest again. People smoked and laughed. My group was singing softly. I was used to that as well. We trudged on, and on, again. Beside the batteries, set up along the edge of the wet forests, the terrible, dark forests. It had been raining for three days. The Russian trench on the hill, completely sodden, gave no sign of life. They must have retreated somewhere – into underground trenches. The forests steamed, full of clouds. For three days now, we had been lying squeezed into a ditch, one on top of the other. That is where we had dug ourselves in under the worst of the fire.

I was shaken by fever. That day a teacher from Sombor had deserted, and people punched me in the chest and slapped me. I looked around me blearily, humming and whistling all day. And again you could hear men talking of celebrations and roasts, of fights in alehouses, of women, and reading 'The Dream of the Holy Virgin'. Three Slovaks struggled all day to cook something over a candle. We spread tent fabric over the trench, but it leaked. We sat, and lay, in mud. No, it had been hard, marching through Srem and the burnt Posavina; it was horrible too near Rača in the water: all those slaps, curses; but this, this was madness in a sea of mud. Everything soaked, constant rain, destroyed houses, the water we drank was muddy, the bread was full of mud. He had lain in the mud in front of us all night, it was only now that we noticed him. We dragged him into the trench. He lay rigid, filthy, stinking. In his right-hand pocket he had some bread and in the left thirteen forints and twenty-six kreitzers. We would have to write a card. People knew where he was from. His name was Lalić. The majority proposed that the money should not be given to the officer, but kept and drunk. They said: that's what he'd have told us to do, if he could, he liked buying drinks for people.

In the afternoon, the mortars began again. The Russian trench disappeared in clouds of yellow earth and mud that shot into the air. We emerged slowly from the ditch and began running. Most went calmly, slowly, no one any longer had the strength to run. We walked calmly. There was a cry, all around us the earth boomed, spurted, men keeled over, shrieked. I went on, stumbling under my pack: racked by fever. I felt someone walking beside me. We were both exhausted. The earth burst open, shooting upwards. I saw the yellow cloaks of Russians leaping out of the trenches. The barbed wire and soil in front of their trench churned under the pounding of the mortars. I reached the wires. A man somersaulted in front of me, bent double and hopping. A shell had passed through him from head to foot. 'Let's go,' said Radulović, standing up. Someone ran past us. I saw blood pouring from my nose onto my chest. Others ran past us holding spades in front of their heads. They leapt into the trench, yelling, running, with terrible cries, onto the bayonets. I did not lie down, I kept going slowly on. Any minute now I'll be killed, one of these big, yellow, fat Russians, jumping about in front of me like lunatics, is definitely going to kill me. The blood was coursing from my nose now. I lay down. The reserve rolled over me into the trench. People were lying everywhere, grimacing in the mud. I do not know why every wounded man was half-naked, but how they screamed, oh, how doggedly they screamed. I lay like that, with no strength.

I lay on a cart and saw only the hunched back of the man who was driving and kept encouraging the nags with clicking noises. The cart could hardly move through the mud. He looked round often, squinting under his fur hat. There was someone else lying beside me. We skirted deserted villages. Here and there we saw a few wretched, hideously poor, ragged Jews. Fine Russian churches, wet forests that steamed. Mud, a vast sea of mud. Dogs scampered through the villages. Dogs and pathetic, filthy, crushed Jewish women. Little girls of twelve or ten offered themselves. Everywhere were carts, mangy horses and interminable, muddy roads. Wounded men lay on the roads. In the afternoon cars came for us. And a weak sun, a good sun, poured over the houses and roads. I lay down on a blanket, racked by coughing, leaving red drops of blood on my dirty handkerchief. And I fell asleep right there. We stopped in a courtyard. There were lanterns swaying round us, as they lifted us, one by one, and carried us into a building. And in the morning, they took us, yellow and half-dead to the baths; we came out through another door full of laughter. I went over to a window and saw below me a small white village, full of streams and mills.

In a green coat and a cap with no brim, I dragged myself, like a strange shadow, smiling, along the streams where the watermills sang. Oh, they sang, they sang to me; they knew where I came from, and I had a smile on my face. How narrow the lanes were. Old women looked at us sadly and pityingly. And the sun? Oh that wan sun, I shall never forget it. Something warm and passionate trembled on my hands. Oh, it was life, young life, playing billiards so skilfully in an unknown café in that town, not I.

★

Who are you? Who are you, with your warm, yellow eyes in the evening mist? Am I not still too sick and frail to touch you? How blurred and gentle your Polish language is! Why are you so good to me, when that's not your trade. Why do you look at me so sweetly? The folds of your blouse brush my head, that burns and aches, fever shakes me. Who are you, wonderful, beautiful, passionate, among the mirrors and glasses in the twilight of the café? Ah, no, it is not here that I want you to be; I want to go outside, I want you to go outside. Look, have you seen these springs; ah, come and hear how charmingly they murmur, how tenderly they splash. I'm almost sorry I didn't die, but that's what autumn does to you. That weak sun pouring over the clean, white houses. What do those forests want of me; over there, behind the hills, they're calling to me, they're laughing cheerfully with me. Why do I touch the walls so tenderly? Where am I going? I have no one in this little town, I don't know the way. Who loves me? Why are these old people looking at me like that?

Look, a cake shop. Let's go in! Little girls sit, arranged with small-town elegance; my fingers fumble. Little knives, light, silver, are you ashamed of my hands? Ah, yes, they are caked with mud, which will not come off, and my crooked, cracked nails frighten you. And the slightly easy girls, the slightly bad girls giggled, and I smiled too. Oh, what do I know, what should I think about all of this. The earth danced – why don't we dance? Autumn has danced with me – come on, let's dance. I chose one. This one. Who's laughing at me? She was called Lusja. She laughed a lot, at everything, her gloves were slightly torn. And I began to beg her comically and good-naturedly. I forgot desire and just looked at those warm, I knew in advance, warm lips. Her companions, full of laughter, left us alone. We walked beside the mills. She was afraid that someone would see her. 'If I hadn't seen from your badge that you're a student, I wouldn't have let you accompany me. Do you think I'm shameless?' Oh, what did I think? I was full of laughter. She was just sad that I was ill, she thought I'd been wounded. She didn't like the fact that I'm so wild. She said that with her more could be achieved by delicacy.

That evening, I recall, the sky was strange. Autumn skies are always strange. I found her in front of the hospital, waiting for me. With trembling hands she showed me her key, she could stay out until midnight. We set off through the streets, where russet leaves were swirling. She asked me whether Serbs had churches and pinched me passionately. She wanted to be driven somewhere; an old hackney carriage took us. She lay across my chest and loosened her hair, such lovely blond hair, with none of that heavy, intoxicating aroma of black hair in the darkness. Streetlights meandered around us. Under the yellow, gold woods on the hill, the carriage swayed and jolted. The sky was filled with stars. At that time, somewhere far away to the south, old women were praying for me. And somewhere far away to the north, my companions were lying dirty, louse-ridden and hungry in the mud, shivering with cold and waiting for a shell to destroy them.

'Das Hundsregiment', as we were known.

We reached the wood and continued on foot. She pressed against me fearfully. Some time before, a girl had been murdered by soldiers. We entered a forest that was dark, with red treetops. Leaves fell onto us, and pink moonlight spilled over the trees, moving us to tears, to a painful tenderness; I kissed her, as though I had no one else in the whole world. Crazed, troubled, breathing heavily, she whispered bitterly about how horrible everything was, how everyone was after her, how men were all scoundrels. Her mother tormented her all day long, but she wanted to stay respectable. The little town was glowing below us in the pink moonlight and the Prussian frontier, with its white markers, encircled us. Her white undergarments were scented. That naïve attention, that foresight touched me and I told her so. She was offended. In the dark I could just make out her head, but her arms were infinitely sweet; her only fear was that I would think badly of her. In the distance the little town lay white, its small white houses like children's toys. Suddenly she gave a soft cry. A bird was startled and knocked into a tree. She wailed painfully and glanced behind her into the forest. In the moonlight she was terribly pale and beautiful. Down below in the little town military music was playing.

༄

Miloš Crnjanski was born in Csongrád, Hungary, in 1893. A controversial figure in Tito's Yugoslavia because of his perceived 'bourgeois' views, Crnjanski served in the diplomatic service, ending his career in Berlin and Rome, from where he was evacuated to London in 1941, living there as an émigré until his return to Belgrade in 1965. At the outbreak of the First World War, Crnjanski, a Serb, was drafted into the Austro-Hungarian army and sent to the Galician front, where he was wounded in 1915. He spent most of the war in hospital in Vienna. After the war, he stayed on to study art history and philosophy. Best known for his lyrical 'diary' about the First World War, *Dnevnik o Čarnojeviću* (*Diary about Čarnojević*), published in 1921, and his novel *Migrations* (English translation, 1994), Crnjanski infuses his works with a sense of nostalgia and lost illusion. He interprets Serbian destiny as tragically influenced by foreign powers. Valued as a stylist and for the elegiac tone of his two most important works, Crnjanski remained outside the literary life of Belgrade during his years of exile. In 1971, he published *Roman o Londonu* (*A Novel about London*), a bitter account of the life of the émigré. He died in Belgrade in 1977.

VIKTOR SHKLOVSKY

THE DEMOCRATIC PRINCIPLE
OF DISCUSSION

from *A Sentimental Journey*

translated by Richard Sheldon

LATER ON, I REALIZED that all these groups meant nothing in the army
– neither the small-time ones nor the other kind. Moral authority
was held by the Petersburg Soviet, not by any of the parties. Everyone
recognized the Soviet, believed in it, followed it.

True, it was standing still; consequently, everyone who followed it
had gone on past.

We didn't stay long in Czernowitz. Filonenko gave his first public
address here and we had our first falling-out. He arrived at the army
committee and gave the troops a briefing in which he touched mainly on
external policies and painted a glowing picture of the relations between
the Allies and revolutionary Russia. It was so irresponsible and, in fact, so
detrimental even from a practical standpoint – because you can't fool a man
forever – that I sent him a note pointing out the folly of such statements.
Then he abruptly changed the subject and launched a frenzied attack on
the bourgeoisie and on the idea of not being able to get along without
them. All this was done very vividly and clearly; it struck the committee
as a revelation – a complete clarification of the issue. But the committee
at this moment was not concerned primarily with information.

Everyone knew that there would be an offensive and the representatives of the units sent around a questionnaire asking if their men

were willing to fight. The answers were lacking in assurance. I remember one especially: 'I don't know whether the field committees will fight, but the regimental committee will fight.' But this was not the important thing. The men were complaining because the units were under strength, because each company was only forty strong, and because these forty men were barefoot and sick. Only the representative of the so-called 'Savage Division', made up of mountaineers, answered with conviction: 'We will fight anytime and against anyone.' Kornilov cleared things up. His words amounted to this – that despite the units' being under strength, we had a fivefold advantage over the enemy at the point of the proposed attack and that our military objectives could be attained on the basis of the actual strength of the units. But some divisions were only nine hundred strong!

The apprehensions of the soldiers – that they would be assigned military objectives based not on the actual number of troops, but on the regulation strength of the unit – were not unfounded. I knew a case under the old regime when an infantry regiment (the Semyonovsky) was replaced at the front by a dismounted cavalry regiment about one-fifth its size.

One other general complaint was heard in all the speeches of the delegates and to this complaint, of course, Kornilov could say nothing – this was the complaint about being completely cut off from any signs of life. I already knew the front a little and I could imagine the anguish of the man in the trenches, where nothing was visible, not even the enemy – only snow in winter, blades of grass in summer.

At one session, a very detailed report was given about the strength of the army and its weapon supply. The only thing not designated was the point for the breakthrough, but everyone knew it would be Stanislau.

It was strange to hear the plan for the offensive discussed in such detail: at the meeting, more than a hundred men talked about roads, about the number of weapons. The democratic principle of discussion was carried here to the absurd, but we managed eventually to extend and elaborate this absurd. At Stanislau, right before the offensive, all members of the company committees representing the shock troops – the Nineteenth Corps – were gathered together and at this gathering they were still discussing the question: to attack or not to attack. This is not to mention the meetings right in the trenches – sometimes held a few dozen steps from the enemy. But that didn't seem strange to me then. I don't think that even Kornilov clearly understood the hopelessness of the situation. He was first and foremost a military man. A general charging into the fray with a revolver. He viewed the army as a good driver views his automobile. The most important thing to the driver is that the car runs, not who rides in it. Kornilov needed the army to fight. He was surprised at the strange methods used by the revolution to prepare the offensive. He still wanted to believe that it was possible to fight that way – just as a driver, trying a new fuel, very much wants the car to run as well as it does with gasoline and can get carried away with the idea of using carbide or turpentine.

This wasn't the first time I had met Kornilov. I had seen him during the April days when the Petersburg regiments were demonstrating aginst Milyukov. At that time he had called up to order some armored cars from our division. We had already unanimously resolved to place ourselves directly under the command of the Soviet. Therefore the resolution was 'not to consider it under any circumstances.' When I went to convey the news to him, Kornilov spoke very softly, obviously not understanding at all how it was that he, a commander, had no troops and wondering who needed him as a commander. He found it unpleasant to see me in the army; later he reconciled himself to me, but began to take me for a madman.

The army committee firmly believed in Kornilov at that moment. When he appeared after giving a report to the officers, he was welcomed enthusiastically. But no one liked 'Kornilov's men'. That's what they called the men of the first 'Death Battalion', which was being formed in Czernowitz of volunteers – for the most part, men from the service units and company clerks who had decided to see some action.

I can testify that this battalion fought no worse than the best of the old regiments. But these shock battalions, already sewing the skull and crossbones on their sleeves, hurt the unity of the army and made the highly mistrustful soldiers fear that now certain special units were being created to act as policemen. The most loyal committee members were against the shock troops. They got on the soldiers' nerves; it was said of them that they received a big salary and had special privileges. I was unconditionally against the shock battalions, because to make them up, men with energy and enthusiasm, men of relatively high intelligence, were taken out of the regiment. What drove them from the regiments was the grief of seeing the army already beginning to decay. But they were even more needed in these regiments, like salt in corned beef.

On the committee, 'Kornilov's men' were violently attacked; they justified themselves rather peevishly.

By the way, I remember the women's battalions. This idea was undoubtedly hatched on the home front and thought up expressly as an insult to the front.

I wandered around Czernowitz. A clean little town resembling Kiev. We ate very well there – in the European style, which is cleaner than ours. The soldiers hadn't pillaged the town; in the apartment where I bunked there were even some pillows, rugs and silver things around. The apartment was of the usual, rather plush, old-gentry type. The streetcars were running; people weren't hanging onto them and they paid for the ride. Reinforcements were leaving town for the front, although hardly any troops ever arrived from the rear; and when they did arrive, they badly demoralized the regiments. As far as the condition of the garrison went, the town was, all in all, not bad. But none of this depended on conscious will, which could not exist among men who had not yet truly gone through the revolution; in other words, all hung precariously on good intentions.

Filonenko and his secretary Vonsky, a cheerful, sturdy and, in his own way, good guy, very energetic and resourceful, remained in Czernowitz. Anardovich and I left for the front, where the offensive was supposed to begin at any moment. And so, for the fourth time, my automobile drove through the fields of Galicia with their Polish cemeteries, where the crosses are melodramatically huge in the Polish style, the Jewish painted tombstones overgrown with dry grass, the marble statues battered by the wind and rain. At the crossroads, the dear, blue, orthodox crucifixes of Galicia, with saints fastened to the diagonals of the crosses. With sharp turns, the road kept going along the same narrow but smooth way.

Sometimes we drove past clumps of trees; then the measured knock of the car was echoed in the trees by a sound that resembled the sound of a whip cracking through the leaves. We arrived at some dark little town. This was the headquarters of the corps which was assigned to make the breakthrough.

It was the Twelfth Corps. We were greeted by the chief of staff, who was dead-tired (it was night). He looked as if he had been working for a week, had not slept for a week and had a toothache besides. He didn't have a toothache, but he must have felt like a man with paralyzed legs ordered to jump or a man with frozen fingers ordered to pick up silver coins off a stone floor. He began to talk hopelessly about how the regiments refused to dig parallels – a parallel is a trench dug in front of the main trench and joined to it by a passageway; its purpose is to get closer to the enemy in order to minimize losses during an attack. Some vagabond regiment had just made its appearance in this area – without officers or transport, with only its field kitchen. It had detached itself from a nearby army and was homeward bound – and the offensive only a few days off. While he talked, in the next room, dimly lit with a kerosene lamp, telegraph machines feebly clicked and threw off blue sparks; narrow paper ribbons slowly crept out of the machines.

From headquarters, we waded through dark, deep mud over to see the commander of the corps, General Cheremisov. Cheremisov resembled Kornilov, also short with a yellow Mongolian face and slanted eyes, but somehow rounder, less dried up. He seemed smarter and more talented than Kornilov. He had been in this area during the previous offensive as chief of staff and had a really superb knowledge of Galicia and Bukovina. He instinctively liked the revolution and war because of the wide opportunities they gave him. Cheremisov was not afraid of the soldiers: I know for a fact that when one company decided to kill him and set up a mortar in front of his house, he came out to see what all the noise was and very calmly pointed out to the soldiers that it was improper to use the mortar in this position, since the explosion of the shell would destroy the neighboring houses. The soldiers agreed and took away the mortar. Cheremisov was not very put out, but he did indicate one thing that was certainly true: what upset the soldiers most of all was the clamor in the newspapers – the loud cries from the home front, 'Attack! Attack!' At the moment in question, this is how things stood: in the area of Stanislau, we had concentrated up to seven hundred heavy guns; the buildup of this sector of the front had begun. Troops were being withdrawn from the sectors of the front previously assigned to them and new units were being poured in to take their places. Then came the first hitch. The Eleventh Division, which was in good condition, didn't want to go to the front, not because it was against the offensive – I hardly ever ran across direct repudiations of the war – but because it had been taken from another sector of the front; moreover, it had been promised a rest. The Sixty-first Division, I think (I don't remember the exact number; I know that it included the Kinburg Infantry Regiment), didn't want to dig parallels; some other division also wanted this and didn't want that. And the enemy in front of us had almost nothing – some barbed wire, machine guns and almost empty trenches. We decided to go without delay to Stanislau. We went at night. It was still a long way to the town, which was right in the line of trenches. But the front was already outlined by the uninter-rupted flights of rockets, which the Germans burned in fear of a night attack. The cannons weren't firing, or at least we didn't hear them. The car noiselessly pursued the road, left it behind and rushed straight for those blue fires. We passed some quietly running, heavy vehicles of the ordnance depot, carrying shells. The stream of vehicles kept getting thicker, becoming solid as we drew nearer to the town. The drivers, tired from the lateness of the hour, sat silently on the jolting, heavy wagons; the horses pulled silently at the traces.

We reached the town. Stayed at a hotel – the Astoria, I think. The town of Stanislau had changed hands several times. The Russians and the Austrians had taken it from the right and from the left, then from the front and from the rear. This was already the third time I had entered it during the war and each time by a different road. It had been a pros-perous town; the houses were still intact; the shooting had damaged them very little. The outlying area, as well as the gasworks, had suffered most of all. But this is not surprising: some of the small houses on the outskirts stood a few steps from the trenches. People were living in these houses. Our lines began just on the other side of the Bistritsa River. Everyone said this was an awkward disposition of the troops. It had been done this way so that that the dispatch could say: 'Our troops have crossed the Bistritsa.' The town was overflowing with troops.

The headquarters of nearly all the divisions of the Twelfth Corps, which at that time constituted nearly a whole army in itself, were crowded into the town. The members of the headquarters operations section lived in the hotel where I was staying. In the courtyard was a gun battery, on the roof an artillery observation point; below, in a Polish café doing a lively business, sat the officers; and in the air hung a two-colored haze, brown and bluish, from the shell-bursts of the Austrian shrapnel. At night you could hear the boom of our heavy guns; they resounded right in your ear, reflecting off the walls of the courtyard with a hollow sound – the same sound you make when you throw a large ball with all your strength against a stone floor.

Stanislau was the only place at the front where I had occasion to sleep on a bed – with real blankets and sheets. I didn't stay long in Stanislau this time. I was summoned to the Aleksandropol Regiment, which occupied a rather unusual position.

The enemy forces stood facing our troops on a round, wooded fountain called Kosmachka. Our regiment was encamped on another mountain. Between us and the German troops was a distance of not less than two miles. There wasn't really a war going on here. Planks had been thrown over the trenches and the trenches themselves were half filled up. The men had fraternized long and assiduously; the soldiers had been getting together in the villages situated between the lines and here they had set up an exclusive, neutral brothel. Even some of the officers took part in the fraternization – among them a brave and capable man, bearer of the Cross of St. George and apparently once a student – one Captain Chinarov. I think that Chinarov was fundamentally an honest man, but he was so incredibly muddled that when we occupied the village of Rosulna, the inhabitants informed us that Chinarov had repeatedly driven to Austrian headquarters, where he went on sprees with the officers and accompanied them on trips behind the Austrian lines.

When we took Rosulna, we found in the Austrian headquarters building a German manual on fraternization, published by German headquarters on very good paper – in Leipzig, I think.

Chinarov had been arrested by Kornilov and was in the guardhouse with a certain second lieutenant K., who later turned out to be an *agent provocateur* from Kazan.

I tried to get Chinarov out, because our conceptions of the freedom of speech and action belonging to each individual citizen were fantastically broad then. I didn't get Chinarov out. His regiment wanted him back, so I set off to calm the men down.

I drove a long time, apparently through the little town of Nadworna. You could already begin to feel the Carpathians. The road was paved with slabs of wood. Over it was placed something on the order of triumphal arches decorated with fir boughs – a technique of camouflaging roads borrowed from the Austrians. First we stopped by corps headquarters (the Sixteenth Corps); here a perplexed General Stogov met us. He understood nothing. 'All these Bolsheviks, Mensheviks,' he complained to me, 'I've come to consider you all – excuse the expression – traitors.' He didn't hurt my feelings. It was very hard for him. His corps consisted entirely of reserve divisions, with six or seven hundred men in each, brought together out of several regiments during the regrouping, when the divisions had shifted from four battalions to three.

These hastily assembled units, with no traditions, with the commanders quarreling among themselves, were, of course, very bad. General Stogov was very fond of 'his men' and it pained him that the soldiers were in such bad shape. He had no influence with the soldiers, though they knew and appreciated him.

After seeing Stogov, I went to division headquarters. There too everything was complete confusion. Although everyone knew that no military objective had been assigned to this corps, still it was strange to see troops in such a state; it was impossible to count on them even for simple garrison duty in the villages abandoned by the enemy.

I went to the regiment. I assembled the soldiers without organizing a rally, so as not to heat up the atmosphere, and simply talked to them in an ordinary voice. I said that Chinarov would be tried and that I couldn't return him to them. The soldiers obviously thought very highly of him and lost no time in giving me some false testimony about him.

But anyway the regiment quieted down a little simply from having unburdened themselves to an outsider. Later this regiment gave Filonenko and the army committee a lot of trouble. Finally it was disbanded.

From the Aleksandropol Regiment, I returned to Stanislau. There I was asked to go to the Kinburg Regiment. Things were also very bad in that regiment, which was stationed about a mile from Stanislau. These troops were in a battle zone and were refusing to dig parallels – consequently they were not preparing for the offensive. I set off again. This time it wasn't a trip but an automobile race the whole length of our positions. The Germans could see the road and kept it under fire. They were hitting all around the car, but it looked possible to get through and we got through.

We crossed the Bistritsa River and soon reached the regiment's position. We assembled the soldiers, using a dugout for the speakers' platform. One soldier said to me, 'I don't want to die.' With desperate energy, I spoke about the right of the revolution to our lives. I didn't despise words then, as I do now. Comrade Anardovich told me that my impassioned speech had made his hair stand on end. The audience was deciding the question of its own death, an immediate death, and the necessity of ordering men to renounce themselves, the silence of this sad crowd of thousands and the vague uneasiness caused by the proximity of the enemy stretched nerves to the breaking point.

After I got through, a short, very dirty soldier spoke – all decked out in his uniform. His talk was simple and to the point, about the most elementary things. From his words, I realized that he was among the half-dozen men who had decided the previous night to work up ahead of our trenches.

Later on, after the rally, I went up and started to talk to him. He turned out to be a Jew, an artist who had returned from abroad to enlist. This was almost saintliness. Neither the soldier in a service unit, nor the infantry officer, nor the commissar, nor any man who has an extra pair of boots and underwear can comprehend all the anguish of the common soldier, all the heaviness of his burden.

This Jewish intellectual carried the weight of the earth in his boots.

Then Anardovich spoke. He spoke convincingly; he was intoxicated through and through by the spirit of the Soviet; he was happy, not knowing how difficult and complicated our situation was. His convictions made him simple and convincing. All the commonplaces of all the speeches given at the Soviet were included in his hour-long speech. The revolution had engraved its norms on his soul. He was like an Orthodox Christian.

Afterwards we went down some dark narrow streets and again talked, this time to a dark, invisible crowd of men with shovels who didn't know whether to go or not to go.

We convinced the Kinburg Regiment.

We were spending the night somewhere at regimental headquarters. That same night, sleepy and rumpled like a soldier's overcoat, we drove on to talk to the Malmyzh Regiment.

More conversations. Here I encountered something new. A group of soldiers announced with a happy smile: 'Don't talk to us; we don't understand anything; we're deaf as Mordvinians.' Afterwards, I guess, we went to the Urzhum Regiment. The hardest thing was having to appear everywhere as exponents of pure reason and at the same time operate in the places where conditions were the most serious.

The Urzhum Regiment – or whatever this regiment was called – was living in the trenches. The men wandered around in the narrow crevice of the trench. Two huge gray heaps of earth inclined toward each other; between them, seated in a hole, the men wearily bided their time. The regiment extended out over nearly half a mile. The men in the trenches were making themselves at home. Some were cooking rice kasha in their small field mess-tins; others were digging themselves a hole for the night.

When you stuck your head out of the trench, what you saw was blades of grass, what you heard was the occasional leisurely whistle of bullets.

Making the rounds, I talked to the soldiers; they sort of huddled together.

Along the bottom of the trench, a narrow little stream ran under the boards you walked on.

We followed its course. As the terrain descended, the walls got damper, the soldiers gloomier.

Finally the trench broke off. We came out in a swamp. Only a low wall made of bags of dirt and sod separated us from the enemy.

A company consisting almost entirely of Ukrainians was sitting there. It was impossible to stand – dangerous. The wall was too low.

We felt the utter confusion of these men. It seemed to me that they had been sitting that way the whole war.

I started to talk to them about the Ukraine. I had thought that this was a major and important question. At least the people in Kiev could talk of nothing else. They stopped me:

'Don't bother us with that!'

For these troops, the whole question of an independent or a dependent Ukraine did not exist. They hastened to inform me that they were for the commune. What they meant by that, I don't know. Perhaps only communal pastures. The soldiers were talkative; they were evidently overjoyed to talk to someone new, but they didn't know they had to argue if they wanted the answer that would instantly banish all their doubts.

The ability to ask questions is an important ability. A noncommissioned officer, obviously popular with his company, stood among the sitting soldiers like a chairman and asked me:

'Our boys are upset. Is it true that Kerensky's a Socialist Democrat instead of a Socialist Revolutionary? That's why they're upset.'

I answered his question. Although my answer did seem to dispel his doubts, he wasn't satisfied with its brevity.

It seemed to me that the soldiers would listen to such a noncom, who didn't understand anything himself and who couldn't be understood, and then they would say 'So what' and go their own ways.

I went over to the officers' meeting. 'Our regiment is in poor shape,' said the officers, 'bad, unreliable.'

So it seemed to me. But what could be done?

They look at your hands and wait for a miracle. But I performed no miracle – I left for Stanislau.

Back to the same town. Polish, secretly hostile. Clean, pillaged. They told me that I had to go to the Eleventh Division. There, things were still worse. This fresh, recently replenished division didn't want to stay in the trenches. Sitting in trenches is generally difficult, but here it was worse than usual. I took off. Everything went wrong on the road. The tires blew out, the rims flew off, the complete breakdown of the car seemed imminent, though the driver clearly was trying to get us there no matter what. We made it. First of all, if I'm not mistaken, to headquarters of the Forty-first Yakut Regiment – a small Galician hut, rather clean and brightly colored inside. The commander of the regiment reported that his men categorically refused to fight. We called a rally. A cart was placed in the middle of a field; felled birches and maples were put around it; next to it, still unfaded, a red-and-gold banner. Heat. The sun beat down. High in the air, a German plane watched closely as the Russians got ready for the offensive. Anardovich spoke first – the usual speech, along the lines of *Izvestia*. He spoke without a cap; the sun glared on his shaved head. Someone in the crowd said, 'That's right!' His neighbors jabbed him and he shut up. The regiments knew nothing about freedom of speech; they regarded themselves as a single voting entity. Those who opposed the majority were beaten up. In the Malmyzh Regiment a telegraph operator was beaten so unmercifully for a speech urging continuation of the war that he crawled away on all fours.

I spoke after Anardovich finished. I have the strange habit of always smiling when I talk. This irritates a crowd, especially when it's in a menacing mood. 'Laugh, you toothless wonder!' Then a soldier got up; he spoke badly, but was no demagogue. His arguments went like this: 'In the first place, why not let the Germans alone? Once you stir them up, they'll be hard to handle. In the second place, why not let the Eleventh Division alone? We just got out of the trenches and were promised a rest before moving out. The general even said, "Congratulations, comrades, on getting a rest."' We talked and got nowhere. We went to the next regiment. The same thing. The regiments stood fast and said they weren't going anywhere. We stopped by division headquarters. The company was staying at a large, fairly clean farmhouse. There we found the division commander, who felt guilty though he didn't know of what – also the chaplain, some staff members and some who were apparently members of the Simferopol Soviet. They had come to the front with presents for the troops and were astonished that all this was nothing like what they had expected. They too had been talking about the offensive and the troops had nearly beaten them to death. We joined this coalition and sadly ate dinner.

It was raining and we had left our overcoats back at the regiment. But the division had to be mobilized at all costs. The words 'at all costs' were running through my brain so furiously that later on, in Persia, I felt that 'Atallcosts' was one word and 'Atallcos' a city in Kurdistan. We left to mobilize the division. Filonenko was summoned. Even before his arrival, we found out that the machine-gun, grenadier and engineer companies were in favor of carrying out the order, that they had even formed a separate camp and were keeping watch over the rest of the infantry. I should say that all the trained units of the army were for the offensive and, above all, for maintaining order and discipline. City people are more unselfish, but they have more imagination and can't conceive of an 'Eleventh Division' or a 'Fifth Company' as something autonomous. But what we needed was a division, not separate outfits. We assembled, via the regimental committee, all the leaders who disagreed with us. We told them that it was impossible to sit still and rot: we had to fight or disperse. The life of everyone who spoke was at stake. We promised to hold an inquest to find out why the Eleventh Division had been deceived – lured to the trenches with the promise of a rest. We all parted with broken hearts, very unhappy with each other. But, still, the Eleventh Division did 'move out'.

The first to get under way were the machine gunners, who moved out pulling their machine guns behind them, ready for the attack. That night a machine-gun company deserted from the regiment; the rest went after them to Stanislau, where they all remained, keeping each other guarded. But still the division had been mobilized. I bring in this story with such detail to show how problems of moderate difficulty were solved.

We arrived at Stanislau ahead of the Eleventh Division.

Here, in a movie theater, Filonenko organized a huge meeting of the delegates from all the regimental and company committees of the

Twelfth Corps – the shock troops. It was unanimously decided to attack. Battle committees were chosen to assist the commanders; the rest of the committee members were to fight in the ranks. It may very well be that all the men who voted for this were mistaken, but their sacrifice was based on an honest mistake. They decided on death if it would only tear the noose of war from the neck of the revolution. While we were having troubles with the Twelfth Corps, things in the nearby corps were also a mess. News came that the Glukhov Regiment of the Seventy-ninth Division – I've forgotten its number, but I'll never forget its name – was in complete disarray. The officers had scattered; the regimental committee had been changed three times and no longer had the confidence of the soldiers; the committee members had been forbidden to talk in the barracks, so they had to hold their meetings on the street. In another regiment of the same division, the soldiers had mercilessly beaten the chairman of the regimental committee, Doctor Shur, an old member of the Bund; provocation by the police sent to the front was assumed. The beaten doctor had been placed under arrest. Filonenko went to rescue him, which he succeeded in doing without artillery or cavalry. Three of us went to the Glukhov Regiment – Filonenko, Anardovich and I – leaving Tsipkevich to organize the corps for the offensive. Tsipkevich was a superb organizer, having formerly worked in a workers' brigade, then in the Nikolaevsky ship-building yards and finally in the Eighth Army, where the committee members revered him.

His method of operation was as follows. In the evening the corps commander informed him of our army's objectives for the next day. That night Tsipkevich would assign sectors of the front to the committee members and send them off; the next day they would telegraph the results. They paid special attention to our troop movements and the flow of matériel. And while Tsipkevich was using his revolutionary methods to unsnarl bottlenecks on the railroad, we went to the Glukhov Regiment.

The Glukhov Regiment stood on our left flank in the Carpathians, not far from Kirlya-Baba. Even during the reign of Nicholas, this regiment had deserted their positions two or three times – or so they boasted. They were camped in a dismal, rainy, godforsaken place with no roads.

The road kept climbing higher and higher; at times we could see below us villages and hills descending gradually into the valley.

Finally we came to the burned remains of two small towns, divided by a shallow but swift river. Dangling from the railroad bridge over the river was a tiny locomotive. The retreating troops had pushed it off the bridge and it still hung there. These little towns are called Kuty and Wiznitz; they stand right at the gates of the Carpathians. Farther on, the road went along a river, as is generally the case in the Carpathians. On the opposite side, a train was rolling slowly along the narrow-gauge tracks. An agonizing road. Steep inclines, log surfaces – the only thing able to withstand the rains of the Carpathians – all this combined to make our trip terribly difficult. Beside the road were slopes covered with the dark fur of gloomy spruce trees and occasionally an almost vertical field: it seemed that a man and horse could climb and plow such a steep slope only on all fours – and then only by clinging to the rocks with their teeth. From time to time we encountered old mountaineers in their short, bright-colored sheepskin coats, with black umbrellas in their hands. Squads of girls were repairing the road; they smiled readily at the car. It was raining; every few minutes, it would not exactly clear but sort of turn gray and the rain would stop. Halfway there, the car gave out completely; the tires were torn to shreds. It was dark. We forded the river and spent the night in a mountaineer's cabin. It looked like Peer Gynt's abode. In the morning we patched the tires somehow, stuffing one of them with moss. We finally arrived at the regiment. Headquarters was deserted. Some second lieutenant met us – a suspicious-looking type. No doubt he had conducted a campaign against the officers and committees and had joined up with the Muravyovs, as I would now say; then when everything started shaking and falling apart, he got cold feet. Now he had just one ambition – to go on leave. The regiment was unbearable. Its noncommissioned officers had almost all run off to join the shock troops. It had no bottom and no top.

The committee tried to talk us out of a rally, but we decided to call one anyway. There was a rostrum in the middle of the meadow. The soldiers assembled; an orchestra showed up. When the orchestra played the 'Marseillaise,' they all saluted. We got the impression that these men still had something – the regiment hadn't completely turned into mush. Life in the trenches over such a long period had worn the men down; many used sticks and walked with the practiced steps of blind men: they were suffering from ophthalmia. Worn out, cut off from Russia, they had formed their own republic. The machine-gun detachment was once again the exception. We conducted the rally. They listened restlessly, interrupting with shouts:

'Beat him up; he's a bourgeois dog; he's got pockets in his field shirt,' or 'How much are you getting from the bourgeois dogs?' I succeeded in finishing my speech, but while Filonenko was talking, a crowd under the leadership of a certain Lomakin ran up to the rostrum and grabbed us. They didn't beat us up, but shoved against us with shouts of 'Come to stir us up, huh!' One soldier took off his boot and kept spinning around, showing his foot and shouting, 'Our feet! The trenches have rotted our feet!' They had already decided to hang us – as simple as that – to hang us by the neck, but at this point Anardovich rescued us all. He began with a terrible string of mother curses. The soldiers were so taken aback that they calmed down. To him, a revolutionary for fifteen years, this mob seemed like a herd of swine gone berserk. He wasn't sorry for them or afraid. It's hard for me to reproduce his speech; I only know that, among other things, he said, 'And even with a noose around my neck, I'll tell you you're scum.' It worked. They put us on their shoulders and carried us to the car. But as we drove off, they threw several rocks at us.

Ultimately Anardovich got the regiment under control. He went by himself, ordered them to hand over their rifles, divided them into companies, separated out seventy men and sent them under guard (one Cossack) to Kornilov's battalion, where they said they were 'reinforcements' and where they fought no worse than anyone else. The rest went with him.

They turned out no worse than the other regiments. All this, of course, came to no avail: we were trying to keep the individual regiments from disintegrating, but this disintegration was a rational process, like all that exists, and was taking place all over Russia.

∽

Viktor Shklovsky was born in St Petersburg in 1893; like many of the writers in *No Man's Land,* he was involved in the crucial moments of 20-century history. During the war he volunteered for the Russian Army, participated in the February Revolution of 1917 and was wounded on the South-western Front. He then served in the Russian Expeditionary Corps in Persia. In 1918, he opposed Bolshevism and took part in an anti-Bolshevik plot led by the Socialist-Revolutionary Party. Protected by Maxim Gorky, Shklovsky was pardoned but in 1922 the political tide once more turned and he fled to Berlin. Here in 1923 he published *A Sentimental Journey* in homage to *A Sentimental Journey through France and Italy* by Laurence Sterne, one of his heroes. The same year Shklovsky was allowed to return to the Soviet Union, where he lived until his death in Moscow in 1984. *A Sentimental Journey*, his memoirs of the period 1917–22, is an impressionistic account that captures the revolutionary tide sweeping through Europe and Asia in those years. The chaos is there but also the generosity of spirit and the refusal of all forms of authority – not the best basis on which to run an army!

GABRIEL CHEVALLIER

I WAS AFRAID

from *Fear*

translated by Malcolm Imrie

W̲E FIRST MADE REAL CONTACT when I asked for some books. When people like to read, they can readily find common ground. Preferences lead to debate, and give a rapid measure of each other's opinions. On my bedside table I soon had Rabelais, Montesquieu, Voltaire, Diderot, Jules Vallès, Stendhal naturally, some Maeterlinck, Octave Mirbeau, and Anatole France, etc., all suspect authors for the young daughters of the bourgeoisie. And I rejected, as conventional and insipid, the writers whom they'd been fed.

Once I'd won over one nurse she'd bring along another one, and so it went. The conversations began and I was surrounded and bombarded with questions. They asked me about the war: 'What did you do at the front?'

'Nothing worth reporting if you're hoping for feats of prowess.'

'You fought well?'

'I really have no idea. What do you mean by "fought"?'

'But you were in the trenches... Did you kill any Germans?'

'Not that I know of.'

'But you saw them right in front of you?'

'Never.'

'How can that be? At the front line?'

'Yes, at the front line I never saw a living, armed German before me.

I only saw dead Germans: the job had been done. I think I preferred it that way... Anyway, I can't tell you what I'd have done faced with some big, fierce Prussian, and how it would have turned out as regards national honour... There are actions you don't plan in advance, or only plan pointlessly.'

'So what have you actually done in the war?'

'What I was ordered to do, no more no less. I am afraid there's nothing very glorious in it, and none of the efforts I was compelled to make were in the least prejudicial to the enemy. I am rather afraid that I may have usurped the place I have here and the care you are bestowing on me.'

'Oh, you *do* get on my nerves! That's not an answer. I asked you what you *did*!'

'Yes?... Well, all right, what did I do? I marched day and night without knowing where I was going. I did exercises, I had inspections, I dug trenches, I carried barbed wire, I carried sandbags, I did look-out duty. I was hungry and had nothing to eat, thirsty and had nothing to drink, was tired without being able to sleep, was cold without being able to get warm, and had lice without always being able to scratch... Will that do?'

'That's all?'

'Yes, that's all... Or rather, no, that's nothing. Would you like to know the chief occupation in war, the only one that matters: I WAS AFRAID.'

I must have said something really disgusting, something obscene. They gave a little indignant shriek and ran off. I saw the revulsion on their faces. From the looks they exchanged I could guess their thoughts: 'What? A coward! How can this man be French!' Mademoiselle Bergniol (twenty-one, a colonel's daughter, with all the fervour of a Child of Mary, but with wide hips that would predispose her to maternity) asked me insolently:

'So, you are *afraid*, Dartemont?'

A very unpleasant word to have thrown at you, in public, by a young woman, and quite an attractive one at that. Ever since the world began, thousands and thousands of men have got themselves killed because of that word on women's lips... But it isn't a matter of making these girls happy by trumpeting out a few appealing lies like a war correspondent narrating daring deeds. It's a matter of telling the truth, not just mine but ours, theirs, those who are still there, the poor bastards. I took a moment to let the word, with all its obsolete shame, sink in, and accepted it. I answered her slowly, looking her in the face:

'Indeed, mademoiselle, I am afraid. Still, I am in good company.'

'Are you claiming that others were also afraid?'

'Yes.'

'It is the first time I have ever heard such a thing and I must say I find it hard to accept. When you're afraid, you run away.'

Nègre, who wasn't asked, comes to my rescue spontaneously, with this sententious statement:

'The man who flees has one inestimable advantage over the most heroic corpse: he can still run!'

His support is disastrous. I can feel that our situation is getting seriously out of hand and sense a collective rage rising up in these women, like the one that possessed the mobs in 1914. I quickly intervene:

'Calm down, no one runs away in war. You can't...'

'Ah-ha! You *can't*... but what if you could?'

They are looking at me. I scan their faces.

'If you could?... *Everyone would take to their heels!*'

Nègre can no longer restrain himself:

'Yes, everyone, no exceptions. French, German, Austrian, Belgian, Japanese, Turkish, African... the lot... If you could? I tell you it'd be like a great offensive in reverse, a bloody great Charleroi, every direction, every country, every language... Faster, forward! The lot, I'm telling you, the whole lot!'

Mademoiselle Bergniol, standing between our beds like a gendarme at a crossroads, tries to put a stop to this rout.

'And the officers?' she snaps. 'Generals were seen charging at the head of their divisions!'

'Yes, so it's said... They marched with the troops once to show off, to play to the gallery – or simply because they didn't know what would happen, just as we didn't the first time. Once but not twice! When you've tasted machine-gun fire on open ground once, you're not going to go there again for the fun of it... You can bet that if generals had to go over the top, they wouldn't launch attacks so lightly. But then they discovered defence in depth, those aggressive old chaps! That was the finest discovery of the General Staff!'

'Oh, this is quite dreadful talk!' says Mademoiselle Bergniol, pale with fury.

It is painful to watch her and we get the feeling it might be wise to change the subject. Then Nègre turns the tables:

'Don't get all het up, mademoiselle, we're exaggerating. We have all *done our duty courageously*. It's not so bad now that we are starting to get *covered trenches* with all the modern conveniences. There's still no gas for cooking but we already have gas for the throat. We have running water every day that it rains, eiderdowns sprinkled with stars at night, and when our rations don't arrive, we don't mind at all: we eat the Boche!'

He asks the whole ward:

'Be honest, lads, hasn't the war been fun?'

'It hasn't half been fun!'

'An absolute scream!'

'Hey, Nègre, what does Poculotte have to say?'

'The General told me: "I know why I see such sadness in your eyes, little soldier of France... Take courage, we will all soon be back to our pig-stickers. Ah, I know how you love your bayonet, little soldier!"'

'Yay, hoorah for the bayonet! Long live *Rosalie*!'

'Long live Poculotte!'

'Thank you, my children, thank you. Soldiers, you will always know I am behind you at the hour of battle, and you will always see me in front of you, boots polished and brass shining, on the parade ground. We are together, in life, in death!'

'Yes, yes!'

'Soldiers, I will send you against machine guns, and will you destroy them?'

'The machine guns don't exist!'

'Soldiers, I will send you against artillery and will you silence those guns?'

'We'll shut their mouths for good!'

'Soldiers, I will throw you against the Imperial Guards and will you crush the Imperial Guards?'

'We'll crush them into meatballs, into pasties!'

'Soldiers, will nothing stop you?'

'Nothing, General!'

'Soldiers, soldiers, I can feel your impatience, sense how your generous blood is boiling. Soldiers, soon I won't be able to hold you back. Soldiers, I can see it, you want an offensive!'

'Yes, yes, an offensive, now! Forward! Forward!'

The whole room is now gripped by warlike delirium. People are imitating the rattle of machine guns, the whistle of shells, explosions. Roars and shouts of hatred and triumph evoke the frenzy of an attack. Projectiles are thrown, bedside tables shaken, and everyone joins in the furious fun. The nurses rush to calm it down and stop the noise disturbing patients in other wards.

Nègre has pulled the blankets off his thigh and stuck his leg in the air. He has put a képi on his foot and is waving it around to imitate a capering, conquering general at the head of his army.

★

Looking very serious, Mademoiselle Bergniol comes to my bedside: 'Dartemont, I have been thinking about what happened yesterday and I fear I may have offended you…'

'Please don't apologise, mademoiselle. I have been thinking about it, too, and I should not have spoken to you as I did. I've come to realise that in this war it is just not possible for people at the front and people at the rear to see eye to eye.'

'Still, you don't really believe what you said, do you?'

'I really do believe it, as do many others.'

'But there is still such a thing as duty, they must have taught you that.'

'I've been taught a great many things – like you – and I'm aware that one has to choose between them. War is nothing but a monstrous absurdity and nothing good or great will come from it.'

'Dartemont, think of your country!'

'My country? Another concept to which you attach from a distance a rather vague ideal. You want to know what "my country" really is? Nothing more or less than a gathering of shareholders, a form of property, bourgeois mentality, and vanity. Think about all the people in your country whom you wouldn't go near, and you'll see that the ties that are supposed to bind us all together don't go very deep... I can assure you that none of the men I saw fall around me died thinking of his country, with "the satisfaction of having done his duty". I don't believe that many people went off to fight in this war with the idea of sacrifice in their heads, as real patriots should have done.'

'This is demoralising talk!'

'What's really demoralising is the situation in which we soldiers are put. When I thought of dying, I saw death as a bitter mockery, since I was going to lose my life for a mistake, someone else's mistake.'

'That must have been terrible!'

'Oh, it's quite possible to die without being a mug. In the end I wasn't so afraid of dying. A bullet in the heart or the head... My worst fear was mutilation and the long drawn out agony that we witnessed.'

'But... what about liberty?'

'I carry my liberty with me. It is in my thoughts, in my head. Shakespeare is one of my countries, Goethe another. You can change the badge that I wear, but you can't change the way I think. It is through my intellect that I can escape the roles, intrusions and obligations with which every civilisation, every community would burden me. I make myself my own homeland through my affinities, my choices, my ideas, and no one can take it away from me – I may even be able to enlarge it. I don't spend my life in the company of crowds but of individuals. If I could pick fifty individuals from each nation, then perhaps I could put together a society I'd be happy with. My first possession is myself; better to send it into exile than to lose it, to change a few habits rather than terminate my role as a human being. We only have one homeland: the world.'

'But don't you think, Dartemont, that this feeling of fear you talked about yesterday has helped make you lose all your ideals?'

'That word fear shocked you, didn't it? It's not a word you'll find in histories of France, and that won't change. But I'm sure now that it will have its place in our history, as in all others. In my case I reckon convictions will overcome fear, rather than fear overcoming convictions. I think I'd die quite well for something I believed in passionately. But fear isn't something to be ashamed of: it is a natural revulsion of the body to something for which it wasn't made. Not many people avoid it. Soldiers know what they're talking about because they have often overcome this revulsion, because they've managed to hide it from those around them who were feeling it too. I knew men who believed I was brave by nature, because I had hidden what I was going through. For even when our bodies are wriggling in the mud like slugs and our mind is screaming in distress, we still sometimes want to put on a show of bravery, by some incomprehensible contradiction. What has made us so exhausted is precisely that struggle between mental discipline and flesh in revolt, the exposed, whimpering flesh that we have to beat into submission so we can get up again… Conscious courage, mademoiselle, starts with fear.'

Such are our most frequent topics of conversation. They lead us, inevitably, to define our notion of happiness, our ambitions, the goals of humanity, the summits of thought, even god and religion. We re-examine the old laws of humanity, laws created for interchangeable minds, for the whole flock of bleating minds. We discuss every article of her own morality, the morality which has guided the endless procession of little souls down through the ages, indistinct little souls which twinkled like glow-worms in the darkness of the world, and were extinguished after one night of life. Today we offer our own feeble light, which isn't even enough for us.

Through my questions, I lead the nurses into traps of logic, and ensnare them in syllogisms that completely undermine their principles. They struggle like flies in a spider's web, but refuse to surrender to the mathematical rigour of reason. They are led by the sentiments that a long passage of generations, ruled by dogma, has incorporated into the very substance of their being – sentiments that they have got from a line of women, housewives and mothers, who were alive in their early years and then crushed by domestic drudgery, worn out by the daily round, who crossed themselves with holy water to exorcise any thoughts they might have.

They are surprised to learn that duty, as they understand it, can be opposed to other duties, that there are seditious ideas vaster and more elevated than theirs, and which could be more beneficial to humanity.

Nonetheless, Mademoiselle Bergniol declared:

'No son of mine will be brought up to think like you.'

'I know that, mademoiselle. You could bear flaming torches as well as babies, but you'll only give your son the guttering candle that you were given; its wax is dripping and burning your fingers. It is candles like that which have set the world ablaze instead of illuminating it. Blind men's candles, and you can be sure that tomorrow they'll relight the braziers that will consume the sons of your loins. And their pain will be nothing but ash, and at the moment their sacrifice is consummated, they will know this and will curse you. With your principles, if the occasion presents itself, then you in turn will be inhuman mothers.'

'Do you deny that there are heroes, then, Dartemont?'

'The action of a hero is a paroxysm and we don't know what causes it. At the height of fear, you can see men becoming brave; it is a terrifying kind of bravery because you know that it's hopeless. Pure heroes are as rare as geniuses. And if in order to get one hero you have to blow ten thousand men to pieces, then we can do without heroes. You should remember that you would probably be unable to carry out the mission you give us. You can only be sure of how calmly you'll face death when you're facing it.'

When Mademoiselle Bergniol has gone, Nègre, who was following our conversation, shared his opinion:

'The delicate little dears! What they need is a hero in their beds, a real live hero with a bloody face, to make them squeal with pleasure!'

'They don't know…'

'They don't know anything, I agree. When all's said and done, women – and I've known plenty of them – are females, stupid and cruel. Behind all their airs and graces, they are just wombs. What will they have done during the war? They'll have egged on men to go and get their heads blown off. And the men who will have disembowelled lots of the enemy will receive their reward: the love of a charming, right-thinking young woman. What sweet little bitches!'

While he's talking I am watching the women going about their duties. Mademoiselle Bergniol is energetic in a methodical way, busying herself with studied cheerfulness: she seems transformed by the sense of duty that she upholds. Mademoiselle Heuze is a big girl, homely and rather awkward, but the shape of her large mouth gives her a kindly appearance. Mademoiselle Reignier is full of goodwill, clumsy, a bit daft, and already too fat; in a few years she'll make 'a good, plump mother' without a trace of ill-nature. With Madame Bard, her nonchalance and the way she swings her strong hips suggests desire; with the rather sultry gaze of a woman lacking a husband, her eyes linger on our bodies, a little covetously, perhaps. I avoid the attentions of grey-haired Madame Sabord, a fussy woman with dry fingers whose touch is unpleasant. Mademoiselles Barthe and Doré, one blonde the other brunette, both with bruised eyes, are almost inseparable, wrapping their arms round each other's waists, whispering confidences which make them burst into shrill laughter, like giggles, in a way men find irritating. There is some-thing a bit too voluptuous in their sisterly embraces. Mademoiselle Odet offers everyone her sad smile, her veiled words and the ardour of her feverish eyes. She is too pale, too thin; her frail shoulders already bent beneath the weight of life at its start. You can see she will not have the strength to bear this life for long. We are grateful to her for sharing this short future with all of us, for caring for us when she needs someone to care for her, and the least we can do is to give a smile of encouragement in return for her smile, so full of self-denial.

I know nothing of them apart from these impressions and that's enough for me. I don't try to understand what brought them here. I am simply thankful that they are here, gliding gracefully around the ward, filling it with flowers and their various charms. I'm thankful, too, that they have lost that little edge of bourgeois arrogance they had at the start, when they spoke to us as if they were addressing their staff. I even allow myself the forbidden pleasure of catching them unawares with the ghost of a blush on their cheeks which they hide by turning away, or of suddenly looking deep into their eyes and finding the trace of some illicit emotional agitation which makes their hearts beat differently. But I stop myself on the threshold of this disquiet, like a gentleman at the door of a boudoir.

And above all I am delighted that we have become such good friends, that these young ladies (it's the young ones who display the most curiosity) spare me an hour of their time every day. The clamour of war is silenced by the murmur of their voices. Their words may not always be true, may be empty, but they are kind and gentle, and this pulls me back into life outside the battle zone – though it strikes me every now and then that my return here is unlikely to be permanent.

*

Every now and then the door of the ward silently opens, and a dark shadow appears beside one of the beds, mumbling unctuous words over the occupant. It's the hospital chaplain, the former head of the Saint-Gilbert school.

Now, I respect all faiths (and occasionally envy them) but I am always surprised at the furtive approach of some of these people, at their unconvincing smiles. If they are truly performing a holy and noble ministry then why do they behave like touts, and give the impression that they are soliciting your soul with a 'psst!' from the end of some dark alleyway. This particular chaplain is of the type that seem to impose themselves on you by calculating your faults. Under their embarrassing gaze I suddenly feel like a monster of depravity, and I'm always waiting for them to say: 'Come, my son, and confide in me all your filthy little sins…' Father Ravel took a particular interest in me in the beginning, and I suppose that the nurses, knowing my religious background, must have told him about me. In the period just after I arrived he would visit me every day and asked me to come and see him as soon as I could walk. I put this off as long as I could.

But he managed to drag a promise out of me, in a way that I find unfair. On the evening after my operation, seeing me weak and no more capable of resistance than a dying man, he persisted at great length and, still lost in the fog of chloroform, I said yes. Afterwards he kept reminding me of this promise and repeating: 'I am waiting for you', in a reproving tone that made it seem like I was the one acting in bad faith.

He did this so much that last week I eventually followed him out of the ward. He took me to his room and sat himself down in the chair beside the prie-dieu, where penitents kneel before Christ. But I've known that old trick with the furniture for a long time. So instead of kneeling on the prie-dieu, I sat on it. Once he had recovered from his astonishment, he questioned me, rather clumsily.

'So, my dear son, what do you have to tell me?'

'I don't have anything to tell you, sir.'

I realised that I should not expect any sophisticated conversation from him and that the only reason he'd brought me there was to catch me off guard and steal my sins. For him, every soul must be healed by absolution, rather in the way that some doctors use purges for every illness. I let him go on. He reminded me of my Christian childhood, and asked:

'Do you not want to come back to God? Do you not have sins to repent?'

'I don't have sins any more. The greatest sin, in the eyes of the Church and the eyes of men, is to kill your brother. And today the Church is ordering me to kill my brothers.'

'They are the enemies of our nation.'

'They are nonetheless the children of the same God. And God, the father, presides over the fratricidal struggle of his own children, and the victories on both sides. He's just as happy whichever army sings the *Te Deum*. And you, one of the just, you pray to him to ruin and annihilate other just men. How do you expect me to make sense of that?'

'Evil comes from men, not from God.'

'So God is powerless?'

'His plans are beyond our comprehension.'

'We have that saying in the army, too: "Don't try to understand." It's the logic of a corporal.'

'I implore you, my child, for it is written: "Pride is the beginning of all sin: He that holdeth it, shall be filled with maledictions, and it shall ruin him in the end."'

'Yes, I know: "Beati pauperes spiritu". It's a form of blasphemy, since He created us in his image and likeness!'

He got up and showed me the door. We did not exchange another word. Instead of the affliction at the sight of this lost sheep that should have been in his eyes, all I could see was a glint of hatred, the fury of a man who had been defeated and whose pride (yes, he too!) was wounded. I wondered how this fury could relate to the divine...

Still, I would have liked it if this priest had given me a few words of hope, indicated a possibility of belief, explained things to me. Alas, God's poor ministers are just as much in the dark as we are. You must believe like old women believe, the ones that look like witches, who mumble to themselves in churches under the nose of cheap, plaster saints. As soon as you start to use your reason, to look for a rainbow, you always run up against the great excuse, mystery. You will be advised to light some candles, put coins in the box, say a few rosaries, and make yourself stupid.

If the Son of God exists, it is at the moment when he bares his heart, while so many hearts are bleeding – that heart so full of love for man. Was it all to no purpose, had his Father sacrificed him pointlessly? The God of infinite mercy cannot be the God of the plains of Artois. The good God, the just God, could not have allowed such bloody carnage to be carried out in His name, could not have wanted such destruction of bodies and minds to further his glory.

God? Come off it, the heavens are empty, as empty as a corpse. There's nothing in the sky but shells and all the other murderous devices made by men...

This war has killed God, too.

★

The nurses leave the ward between noon and two o'clock, after our lunch. To avoid the embarrassment of relieving ourselves in their presence, we have regulated our bodily functions so that – unless it's unavoidable – they are only exercised in that period. The only job of the male army nurse who covers for them is to remove the bedpans. Those waiting for him to come look at the ceiling and smoke energetically to dispel the odour. Once the big rush is over and we no longer risk catching cold, we open the windows. Winter sunlight pours into the ward and we let it trickle between our hands, pale with idleness, so that they acquire a faint flush of pink.

Someone had given this male nurse the cruel surname of Caca. I know this name upsets him, know it because I knew André Charlet before the war, at university, where he was one of the star students, bursting with curiosity and ideas. In student reviews he published some brilliant sonnets, which represented life as a vast field of conquests, a heavenly forest full of surprises, into which ventured great explorers who brought back amazing fruit with unfamiliar tastes, women of savage beauty, and a thousand barbaric objects of refined savagery. When the mobilisation began he was one of the first to join up and he was severely wounded the following year.

Now I found him here, broken, drained, and dirty. A few months of war had brought about this metamorphosis, given him this agitated manner, emaciated body and yellow skin. It has left him with the mad terror that you can see behind his eyes. So that he could stay in the hospital he accepted this job and the disgusting duties that go with it. By being Caca, he gets to spend an extra three months in hospital, through some military decision or other allowing medical staff to take on temporary assistants. If he hadn't done this he would most likely have joined the auxiliaries unless he'd been declared unfit for service altogether. But he doesn't want to go before a panel except as a last resort for he isn't convinced that his health has been sufficiently ruined to exempt him from returning to front-line duty. He is alone in doubting it; we believe he is likely to die from tuberculosis, more infallible than shells.

I try to win him round, recalling our adolescent years together, our friends, our happiness, our former ambitions. But I cannot interest him. He smiles weakly and says: 'It's all over!'

'And what about poetry, old pal?' I reply.

He shrugs his shoulders: 'Poetry is like glory!', then leaves because someone is calling him. A moment later he returns with steaming bedpan, turns his head away in utter disgust, and sneers: 'There you are, poetry!'

Among his memories of the war, this one is truly appalling:

'It was in the eastern zone, end of August. Our battalion attacks with bayonets. You have no idea how idiotic those first assaults were, what a massacre. What distinguished that period without a doubt was the incompetence of our leaders – and they were sometimes victims themselves. They had been taught that battles were decided by the infantry, and cold steel. They didn't have the faintest idea about the effects of modern weaponry, of artillery and machine guns, and their big hobby horse was Napoleonic strategy – nothing new since Marengo! We were under attack and instead of establishing solid positions, we were scattered across the plains, unprotected, wearing uniforms straight out of a circus and then ordered to charge at forests, from 500 metres. The Boche picked us off like rabbits and then, once they'd done all the damage they could, they fled when we got close enough for hand-to-hand fighting. Finally on that particular day, having lost half our men, we managed to drive them out. But the bastards had a diabolical idea. There was a strong wind blowing against us and they set fire to the cornfields from which we were chasing them… What I saw there was a vision of hell! Four hundred wounded men, lying still on the ground, suddenly bitten and revived by the flames, four hundred turned into human torches, trying to run on broken limbs, waving their arms and screaming like the damned. Their hair went straight up in flames, like tongues of fire on the head of the Holy Ghost, and the cartridges they had in their belts exploded. We were struck dumb, unable to think of taking cover, as we watched four hundred of our comrades sizzling and twisting and rolling in this inferno, swept by machine- gun fire, unable to reach them. I saw one stand up as the wave of fire approached him and shoot his neighbours to spare them this horrible death. And then several of them, about to be engulfed by the flames, began screaming to us: "Shoot us, pals, shoot us!" and maybe some of us had that terrible courage… And Ypres! The night battles at Ypres. You didn't know who you were killing, who was killing you. Our colonel had told us: "Treat prisoners well, my children, but *don't take any*." The people we were facing had surely been given the same instructions.'

～

Gabriel Chevallier was born in Lyon, France, in 1895. He is best known as the author of *Clochemerle*. *Fear* is an autobiographical novel about his experiences in the war. It was published in 1930 and withdrawn with the author's consent in 1939 at the onset of the Second World War. The book was republished in French in the 1950s to critical acclaim and first published in English in 2011. As Chevallier writes in his preface to the 1951 edition:

> The great novelty of this book, whose title was intended as a challenge, is that the narrator declared: I am afraid. In all the 'war books' I had read, fear was indeed sometimes mentioned, but it was other people's fear. The authors themselves were always phlegmatic characters who were so busy jotting down their impressions that they calmly greeted incoming shells with a happy smile.
>
> The author of the present book believed that it would be dishonest to speak of his comrades' fear without mentioning his. That is why he decided to admit, indeed to proclaim, his own fear...

After the worldwide success of *Clochemerle*, Chevallier wrote two sequels, *Clochemerle Babylon* and *Clochemerle les Bains*, and in 1948, he published *Mascarade*, a collection of stories that include 'Crapouillot', a darkly funny First World War story of a general who 'needs deaths' to make his statistics competitive. He died in Cannes in 1969.

JULES ROMAINS

JERPHANION WRITES
TO HIS WIFE

from *The Prelude to Verdun*

translated by Warre B. Wells

I LOVE YOU, ODETTE DARLING, I love you, my precious wife. You are always in my mind. It is sheer agony for me to be separated from you. I am writing now as though we were talking face to face. I am writing in order to give myself the illusion of your presence.

Even here, in mid-winter, we could be so happy, dear child, you and I together. Through my attic window I can see the spread of sky above the plain. In spite of the season it is very blue, incredibly blue, like the sky in some southern land. Here and there its brightness is framed in bunches of white cloud such as one sees in summer. And the distant view has nothing in it of January. There seems as much green in it as brown and grey. I can see lovely long roofs, great simple masses, and roads, and the grassy verges where they twist and turn. To make it into a background of quiet happiness against which we two could spend long hours loving and sauntering, all that is necessary is to wipe out of the landscape the figures of all these poor fellows in faded blue who move about like so many great heavy ants.

The plain in which this village lies hidden is completely pastoral, with nothing military about it at all. An hour after the last man in blue has vanished, it will look once more exactly like one of Millet's pictures. Even the village has a curious beauty of its own. It is the one I told you of in my previous letters. To think that we've been here a month already! It's all so good that it's really rather frightening. I keep on wondering what horrible thing is going to happen next. But I do my best to enjoy the moment. The great thing is just to go on living.

The village rather reminds me of the places in the Beauce that we used to visit in the car. (Dear car! I often think of it. Do you remember how we used to bump along those village streets?) A group of large, squat farms, neither too crowded nor too far apart. Huge walls with only a few windows. Plenty of big square buildings. Great roofs with their slopes set at right angles. In the middle of the village is a large open space with a pond surrounded by a wall – there's even a balustrade on one side – which serves as a drinking-place for animals. They reach it by a gentle slope which leads straight down into the greenish-grey water.

Oh, I can tell you the name of the village. Until now I've always concealed it because instructions on that subject have again been renewed. But what possible harm can it do? We are so far from the front! Besides, no one but you is going to read this letter.

It is called Grandes-Loges. Perhaps you can find it on a road-map (about twelve kilometres south of Mourmelon-le-Grand). I like the name. It is as old and solid as a farmer's clothes-press. I can imagine us staying here, you and I, with some rich peasant uncle and his stableful of animals. He would put us up for a month during the winter. We should have good solid meals, washed down with the local wine (which is no more nor less than Champagne!), and we would go for long walks in the plain. When night fell we would make love for hours together in our room – it would be a bit cold (but there would be a feather bed with plenty of thick blankets and a huge eiderdown).

There are two battalions of the 151st regiment here. The second battalion is at Bouy – a few kilometres away – with the regimental details. That makes it all the quieter for us.

I have got for my company an enormous loft, which is over a stable, and so quite dry. My own quarters are in a real room belonging to a building near by. It must formerly have belonged to one of the farm-hands. It's got a great rough floor, a beamed roof, and a tiny window through which I can see the plain and the blue sky I have told you of.

For once, Cotin – the fellow who obsesses and terrifies my mind like a problem that is at once insoluble and quite uninteresting – has had what might be called a good idea. He has made the men gather, from the neighbouring wood, logs and branches of pine and fir, even ivy and mistletoe, and has shown them how to build little cabins, rustic huts, dotted about anyhow, in the huge, healthy loft, which is about as hospitable as a desert and as cold as a railway station. This has given the men no end of fun. Some of them have been extraordinarily ingenious in building and adorning their little hide-outs. One of them has even built a miniature house, with two floors, an outside staircase, and a balcony. It looks charming. Each of these small constructions is inhabited by a squad, a half-squad, or sometimes by still smaller groups, just as the men want to arrange. They pay one another visits. Quite apart from occupying their minds, they keep warmer this way and get a sense of greater intimacy. The whole thing looks rather like a model of a charcoal-burners' camp in a booth at the Lyons fair. It is all very cheerful.

But the most marvellous thing of all, the thing that really makes this place seem like paradise, is that we don't hear a single gun – or not what you would call hearing – not one. I wonder whether you can under-stand, can realize exactly what that means. Not only does a stray shell never come our way, but even by straining our ears we can hear nothing that even remotely resembles the sound of a gun firing or the burst of a shell. For instance, since I started this letter I've heard the sound of voices, the clatter of mess-tins, the noise of wheels on the road – even, though you'll hardly believe it, the clucking of a hen that's just laid an egg – but not the remotest suspicion of boom-boo-oo-oom, boom!...

It makes one want to cry, to tremble, with the sheer wonder of it. Oh, my dear darling! For all your sensitive understanding, I don't suppose you can begin to realize what it means for all us poor wretches to live beneath a blue winter sky, with white clouds, unsmirched by even the faintest whisper of gunfire.

There is very little for us to do. We are spared the awful drill in the bare fields with which they used to poison our periods of rest. For the last few days they have been sending us to a point rather farther to the north to dig trenches, machine-gun emplacements, communications, and to set up a lot of wire. The only trouble about that is the distance we have to cover, and the uncomfortable thought: 'They must be worried, to organize positions so far to the rear.' But, as I said before, it's no good meeting trouble half-way. We'll do as much digging as they want if only we can stay a bit longer at Grandes-Loges.

Odette darling! When next you write tell me something of the quays of the Seine near where we live, between the Halle-aux-Vins and the Pont National. How I'd love to be walking with you by the river and watching the Métro viaduct, graceful as a leaping goat, and the Bercy reservoirs beyond! I'd like to plunge with you into the narrow lanes of Picpus. The days are already lengthening. When it's clear and not too cold, the evening light seems to hang suspended just a second or so longer than one expects, and for the two or three minutes before darkness falls, there is a feeling of spring in the air.

Here, where we are, the thought of spring is not wholly a mockery. The heart soars, and then suddenly awakes to all the horror of what it is missing, what it has lost. Who will give me back this day as it might have been if only I could have spent it with you, our evening together, the walk we might have taken, the silent laughter with which you would have turned to me when I took you in my arms as we climbed the slope of one of those Picpus alleys? Who will give me back the happiest years of my life – even if I live to know others just as happy? Who will compensate me for these long months of exile? Poor us, dear, darling wife, who have not even had the consolation of finding life empty, who would have been contented with modest treasures which we could have enjoyed without harming anybody. Sometimes I think I have discovered the secret of this monstrous tragedy in which we have been caught. There are not enough people in the world who value living for its own sake, not enough who can find in the peace of every day the most wondrous miracle of all. Most men and women are tormented by miserable little worries and demand the dramatic as a dog devoured by fleas demands a violent counter-irritant and jumps into the fire to find it. I would go even so far as to say that many human beings ought never to have been born at all and spend most of their lives trying to correct that elementary mistake. The pity is that they should have to involve us in their attempt to get back to the primordial chaos.

⊷

Jules Romains was born Louis Henri Jean Farigoule in the Loire valley in 1885. He moved to Paris to study and had his first success in 1925 with the play *Dr Knock*, a brilliant satire on doctors and the 'science' of medicine. In 1932, he started writing the *Men of Good Will*, which contained fourteen volumes when Romains finished it in 1946. The extract is taken from *The Prelude to Verdun*, which powerfully captures the eerie atmosphere of battle. The series is an attempt to portray the whole of French society from October 1908 to October 1933. A reflection of Romains' spiritual beliefs, it presents the changes that occurred over this 25-year period as being the achievement of collectives – villages, factories and schools – and not of individuals.

Men of Good Will celebrates over a quarter-century the friendship of the writer Jallez and the politician Jerphanion. One of Romains' many achievements is to convey the poignancy of the everyday pleasures of life lost to those on the front.

JEAN GIONO

JULIA REMEMBERS

from *To the Slaughterhouse*

translated by Norman Glass

'IT'LL BE A FINE CLEAR NIGHT,' Julia said. 'You can tell from the air, and you can see Saint Victor's.'

The alpine wind had swept the twilight free of clouds and the edges of the sky stood out sharp as a scythe. Where the sun set, the hump of Lure with its smoking collieries rose up in celestial green lovely as meadow dew.

'Where are you going?' the father asked.

'To feed the animals.'

As usual on windy days, night descended abruptly, complete with bright stars in the broad milky way.

Julia groped her way along the shed wall for the door. I wonder if it'll be like the last time, she thought. And that was all she needed to excite her. She lifted the wooden latch. Yes, it was just like the last time and it would always be the same. Every time she'd come to this door she'd be greeted by the smell of fresh hay, that smell that made her heart beat like water brimming over the edge of a fountain. That smell of hay and horses. A smell of solid life which scraped her skin like a stone. The last time, she remembered, she'd dropped the pitchfork, and when she bent down to pick it up the smell rose up so strongly she got gooseflesh. Her body wanted to burst into flowers. She felt she was being carried away by the leaves and the wind. No use in fighting against it. She remembered her marriage night, everybody tipsy with wine, and the new linen against her skin, and the corset which squeezed her in the right places, and then Joseph kissing her with his mouth wide open as though he was biting into a slice of melon...

Julia climbed the ladder and got piles of hay ready. The smell made her giddy. The stack was like a huge flower opening at every thrust. She watched the forkfuls steaming in the lantern-light.

She returned to the kitchen, shaking her legs at the door to let the hay dust drop from under her dress. Madeleine was knitting, or making a skirt perhaps. It was hard to tell which, because she was sitting almost completely in the shadow. Jerome was sleeping, his mouth closed tight. The clock was ticking. Not a cheerful sight! Sometimes you need to... Ah! it was hard to be away from men. Julia sniffed her hands heavy with the smell of horses.

'Hello, Madeleine,' she said.

Up in her room Julia lit the candle and moved it away in case the heat cracked the glass face of the clock. Just underneath the clock there was the remains of a photograph of her and Joseph at their wedding. Those white gloves were so uncomfortable! Joseph had orange blossom in his button-hole. Oh, the monster!

Julia undid her corset and pulled up the lace of her slip. She bent down to take off her shoes. Her breasts were heavy. The shoelace was caught in a knot. She'd better sit down. Her cold bare arms rubbed against her naked breasts which felt so much warmer.

She peeled off her stockings as though skinning a rabbit. She had to take them off inside out because the sweat had stuck them to her foot. She hung them over the back of the chair to dry. She looked at her bare feet, enjoying the sensation of wiggling her toes. The hay dust got into everything. Stockings, the corners of shoes, and made everything sticky. She wiped her feet and rubbed a swollen vein on the foot which hurt when she moved her big toe. She stood up and went to the small square mirror to arrange her hair.

Walking across the stone slabs with her bare feet, she felt she was stepping through a dew-drenched meadow. The smell of horses still clung to her hands. She let down her black hair, heavy as wet wool. She didn't bother to use a comb, she twisted her hair with her hands. Whatever she did, she felt her breasts. If she bent down, she was conscious of their weight, if she lifted up her arms, they pulled at her flesh like string. Joseph always had that living smell, like a horse's smell, that smell of work and strength which filled your nose when he undressed. A smell of leather and sweaty hair, like the smell of those big summer salads when you crush garlic and mix it with vinegar and mustard powder in the salad bowl.

She took off her skirt and petticoat at the same time and stepped out of the pile of clothes. She gave her hips a brisk rubbing. This hay gets all over you, she thought. She might have been covered with fleas. She hurried to be completely naked in order to feel the tart night round her skin. She'd walk arm in arm with the cold wind, looking up at the stars, she'd feel her body and brains cleaned and freshened by the alpine wind. She took off her blouse, then blew out the candle and went to the window. She rubbed her breasts all over with a duster, she might have been cleaning little melons. And it's true, with the veins and the nipple hard as the end of a stalk, they really were like little melons crackling between her fingers.

The wind flew high in the night like an immense bird. At the end of August there was always a smell of corn in the sheafs, corn abandoned by men, and the smell of roasting on the threshing-floors. The wind dropped and the night grew hot. Her whole body breathed and tingled and she could hear her blood beating in the night which pressed upon her. She had two creases in her hips going down to her belly, her flat, smooth belly. The clock ticked on. Her breasts were still now, like solid hillside stones. Joseph used to say, 'They're winter turnips. Show me your winter turnips. Give me your winter turnips!' Joseph! Her heart was sour with longing for that old smell of man and work. Julia went to uncover the bed, so used to Joseph that his place was carved out in it. There might be a phantom lying under the white sheet. She drew back the sheet to shake away the imprint, but it refused to move. She put on her clean night-shirt and stretched out in Joseph's place. Just before she fell asleep, Julia sniffed the horse smell on her fingers, then she stuck her hand between her thighs.

JEAN GIONO

THE SALT OF THE EARTH

from *To the Slaughterhouse*

translated by Norman Glass

MADELEINE WIPED HER HANDS QUICKLY on the dishcloth. Her body shook when she thought about the rendezvous whistle. She was about to leave when her father came in. 'Come here,' he said, 'come and read this letter. Give Julia a call.'

Through the window, in the spring air, she could see the blue tops of the mountains above the almond trees, and down there, under the oaks, Oliver would be whistling.

'Oh, it's always the same…' Madeleine muttered.

'What's that?' Jerome asked.

'Nothing. Give me the letter.' She closed the window and took her brother's letter.

'Julia!' the father called.

Julia's big healthy body took up all the doorway. Her thighs were plump under her skirt. She ran a hand through her hair, black and shining like oil at the bottom of an earthenware jar.

'We've got a letter from Joseph,' Jerome said. 'Read loudly, Madeleine.' Leaning on his stick, he turned his good ear towards her. Julia looked out of the window, towards the spring, the mountains, and the almond blossoms.

'"Dear wife and father…"'

'What's the date?'

'March 22nd... "Dear wife and father. Here's some good news for you. When I got the parcel we were on the march and you know my feet don't take too kindly to the road, so I waited. Thank you for the meat pie. Please send me some lard because I need it as usual to rub my feet. I can't walk for an hour without getting blisters. It's not so bad now that I've got the slippers, I put them on as soon as we arrive. But they let the water in. I was glad to get a card the other day from cousin Maria and hear she's taking life in her stride. I wanted to reply, but she scribbled the address and I can't make it out. If she's changed her farm, she'll come to Chauranes for sure. I know her. Be sure you don't lend her my old plough. That's what she's after. And as for getting anything back from her!..."'

'Wait a minute,' the father said. 'Come to think about it, Julia, how is that old plough?'

'It's hung up by the hook and the handles,' she said. 'I had a look at it. The wood's straight. It hasn't warped and it's nearly a month now since I poured on the remains of the oil.'

'That's good, because we have to think about using it. Maria's at Saint-Firmin, isn't she?'

'Yes, at Chauvinières near Saint-Firmin.'

'Read on...'

'"Life isn't much fun here, but there's nothing we can do about it. Let's hope we'll all soon be home. It was snowing a while ago, now it's raining. Don't forget the lard. Dear wife, I was at a farm where they've found a use for pig manure. I saw them putting it on the little plants. But it burns them up, I told them. They told me no, because it's the piss which burns, so they make a drain for the piss to run down and then they can use the dung. The ground isn't bad at all, it's been taken over from the landowners. Remember the fellow I told you about who came from Perpignan where he worked in a shoe factory, well, he got killed yesterday, but it was his own fault. They've told me that we may be going to the real fighting. I can't tell you where it is, but you must have read about it in the papers. Don't worry. It isn't even certain yet. Anyhow, we don't have any choice. Oh, I've got something else to tell you. A fellow from Valensole who's got relations at Colon told me that Bonnet's son had been killed. Tell his mother how sorry I am. Also I want to tell you what dolts you are for missing the Casimir farm. It was up for sale so you should have bought it, even if it wasn't ready yet for planting. I'll look after that myself when I get back. And how are things with Casimir? You told me his son, Oliver, is going to the front, so this time don't miss the opportunity. Those young ones always want to play the hero. Even if he doesn't get killed, there's only the grandfather and the mother and they might want to sell the land at the foot of the hill. That would be fine for us. Father, keep an eye on what's happening there. Soon as Oliver leaves, look the ground over. I don't seem to have anything more to say. A kiss for my sister, Madeleine. Don't forget what I've told you. I'm thinking about it. I kiss my dear wife and father. Joseph."'

Julia sighed. She took the letter from Madeleine, folded it and put it in her pocket.

'He's right,' the father said. 'We haven't been very smart. I'll go have a look at Gardette's place this evening. It's Oliver's last…'

Julia interrupted him with a glance. 'The man from the town hall is already on the fields,' she said.

'Who did he want?' the father asked, scarcely opening his lips.

'Not us,' Julia said. 'He was opposite the door and when he saw me come out, he signalled to me to say no.'

'So who did he want?'

'It's Arthur, Arthur Buissonnades.'

'Arthur!' the father exclaimed. 'That tall fellow? Felicity's husband? The one who was so good at plucking grapes? The one who helped us the year of the storm? Is that the fellow?'

'That's the one,' Julia said. 'Felicity's alone with the child.'

'Give me my stick,' the old man said. 'I'm going there. A woman can't stay alone on a beautiful day like this with all that on her mind. What wretched times we live in!' He took his stick, went out and banged the door. Madeleine pressed her face to the window and watched her father. He hurried as fast as he could along the Buissonnades' road.

'Too many have died,' Julia said. 'Too many. It doesn't seem possible. Arthur! You remember, Madeleine?'

Madeleine's tears streaked down the window.

'And we're all involved, you know,' Julia said. 'Madeleine, that's something we don't think about often enough.' She went back to the cattle-shed.

The window felt cold against Madeleine's forehead. The glass was misty with her tears. She could no longer see the green corn, the almond blossoms and the swallows. Arthur! He was never that close to us, but that doesn't make it any easier to bear. A handsome man he was and so well built! And how he could laugh! The whole world was heavy with mist. If she opened the window everything would be clear again. She'd feel the fresh wind. She'd see tulips and watch the almond blossoms falling. God pardons us for not always thinking about death.

JEAN GIONO

NEWS FROM JOSEPH

from *To the Slaughterhouse*

translated by Norman Glass

WHERE COULD SHE HIDE, where could she hide? Wherever she ran, things rose up against her. Her feet no longer recognized the threshing-floor, or the courtyard, or the path that led to the fountain, nor that fragment of meadow, nothing. Everything capsized around her. She stumbled against the stones and her skirt got tangled in her legs. Where could she hide herself?

She couldn't bear to see old Jerome as he looked at his hand; nor the sight of his earthy face furrowed by old age and ancient sorrows, his old man's mossy, earthy face all wet with big white tears; those trembling lips, that fallen chin which he couldn't lift to close his jaws, and the saliva and tears, and the moaning of a man at the end of his days. If that was all! But no. Through his tears he stared at his big right hand. It was deformed.

No. She had buried her head in her apron and wept with him, but suddenly she could stand it no more. Go away? No. Hide herself, get into some little corner like an animal, writhe on the ground, roll up into a hole in the earth and stay there. Stay there, huddled up, with her flesh, her tears, her sorrow.

Julia pushed open the stable door. The old horse turned its head and looked at the woman. It wasn't feeding time.

'Move over,' Julia said.

She slid against the horse, went to the back of the stable and lay down in the straw under the trough, in the warmth, reassured by the horse's shadow, comforted by its smell and heat. The horse jangled its chain and gently tapped its hoof in the straw. So, just like that, they'd cut off Joseph's arm! His right one. It's done. There's nothing more to do, that's how it is. She'd got the news in a letter. The arm! The hand and all. They cut off his arm! Is it possible? How did they do it? Why did they do it? He must have suffered! Oh, Joseph, my poor love! And now there's nothing more on your right side? No more arm? That explained the long silence. That was why they hadn't heard from him for over three weeks. It was as though he'd been rubbed out with an eraser. No more Joseph! Lost in the wind. And that was when they'd cut off his arm. Where? At the elbow? Is there a stump or has it all been levelled off? Oh, my poor love!

'Oh, Bijou,' Julia called to the horse. The old horse lowered its head towards her and sniffed her, spraying its heavy breath over her through the two jets of its nostrils. 'You, you're happy!'

The horse's large, kind eyes were green and red. It had spent all its life looking down at the earth and up at the trees. Its eyes were brimming with sweet and ancient things.

She had been happy too. There was the dance-hall down in the village, which they used to decorate every Sunday with box-tree and oak branches. And Jerome came down from the hills with his accordion on a shoulder-strap, and young Mercier came down also with his brightly polished cornet. From one o'clock onwards the benches used to be packed with girls. But Julia went to stand behind the houses, at the edge of the apple trees from where you could see the road. She watched Madeleine arriving in her blue dress, her face red from the bright sun, but there was always a lovely blue air about her from the reflection in her eyes. 'He's coming,' Julia used to say. 'He's put on that handsome hat.' Then she ran across the orchard towards the hall. She just had time to sit down with the others, on the edge of the bench near the door, when he appeared, Joseph, standing in the doorway, almost filling it with his broad shoulders, and his big black hat tilted to the left of his head. The horse rubbed its forehead against Julia's shoulders.

'Oh, Bijou, yes, my beauty!'

She had loved Joseph at once with the whole of herself, without holding anything back. She was smitten by him, by the way he swung his shoulders when he walked, by his solidity, the health glowing in his reddish-brown eyes. Jerome played the accordion, young Mercier said: 'One, two,' then put his cornet to his mouth. And Joseph took her in his big arms.

'Oh, my love, my poor love!'

His arm! They've cut off that arm. The one he put around me. Warm and firm around me when we waltzed! That was the hand that he touched me with the first time, there, on the cheeks, on the eyes, on the mouth. We were in the hay-shed at seven o'clock. We looked up through the sky-light at the night, violet like a plum. The smell of crushed hay when we sat down!

And all that happiness made me giddy as we nestled together and we were drunk with joy that ran through our bodies to our finger-tips. That was the hand he touched me with the first time. On my cheek. He touched the round of my cheek. Then my mouth and eyes. That was the hand he knew me with afterwards…

'Oh, Joseph, oh, my poor love!'

And now there's only half of you left. You won't be touching me any longer with that hand, will you? It was a clever hand, darting around like a little animal, hot and hard, and no stranger to any part of me. Never again, will you? Why? Tell me. I haven't had that hand for very long. So, you'll have to learn to touch me with the other hand, won't you?

She was sitting in the straw. The old horse lowered its head again, stuck out its tongue and tried to lick Julia's cheek, but the bridle was too short.

'Julia!' a man's voice called. It was Jerome.

'Yes,' Julia said. She came out from under the trough.

'I was looking for you. I was afraid. I saw you running away so wildly. Be reasonable, try to…'

They stood and faced each other in silence. Tears streamed down their faces.

'Oh,' Jerome cried out, lifting up his arms, 'the right hand has gone from the plough. Oh, my son!'

JEAN GIONO

JOSEPH'S LEFT HAND

from *To the Slaughterhouse*

translated by Norman Glass

T HERE WERE THREE PRECISE LITTLE BLOWS on the door below, then the
noise of somebody moving back into the straw of the threshing-
floor to look up at the window. Julia listened, holding her breath. Joseph
was asleep, lying beside her. He had arrived in the five o'clock mail-
coach. He was nailed to her by the hook of his thin thigh. Julia gently
took hold of that thigh at the top, by the thick part, unhooked it, and
slipped out of bed. She stood up. Joseph remained deep in sleep.

Julia opened the door. As recently as yesterday she used a whole
piece of lard on the hinges. She went down the stairs on her heels,
because anybody on the look-out would have heard the noise of her
toe-nails on the stone.

There were splinters of broken glass on the kitchen floor. Joseph
had thrown a bottle at Madeleine's head. Fortunately the little one had
ducked. She had run towards the door, at which he had grabbed the
jug in his hand, as though about to throw that at her too. There's some
strength in his left hand.

There was another small knock on the door. Julia touched the frame
of the doorway with the palms of her hands. She touched the lock, but
not the key; instead she went higher and only opened the peep-hole.
Outside the night was clear. The man was there with his face stuck
against the small window.

'Julia!' With his low voice, he breathed into the room the tart sweat of August.

'Yes,' Julia said softly.

'It's three days now. Come!'

'No, I've got my man.'

'What man?'

'My own.'

The big face no more than skin and bone, with a head like a beast's, eyes like stars, and the large ravenous mouth wounded by more than hunger.

'Do you want some bread?'

'You!'

'Tobacco?'

'You, Julia, come on, I need you, I'm alone, alone! Only once. Just once more. Come, Julia!'

There was silence for a moment. The man's big body trembled against the wood of the door.

'No,' Julia said, 'it's no.'

The man breathed heavily into Julia's face. His breath smelled of raw grass and tobacco.

'I'll give you some bread, if you want, and some cartridges.'

'I don't give a fuck for your bread.'

An owl hooted.

'And I don't give a fuck for you.'

He spat into the peep-hole. Julia closed the little shutter and put up the bar. The man leaned with all his weight against the door. She listened to the cracking of his bones and his heavy, weary breathing, like an animal's. He went away. Julia wiped her forehead with the back of her hand. The man's spittle was running down to her lips.

Joseph was asleep. He didn't wake up, he didn't turn round. The hook of his thigh was still there, in the air, waiting for the woman's flesh. Julia climbed gently into the bed. She checked to see if Joseph was well covered, over there, on the right side which he couldn't look after alone any longer. She stretched out under the hook of thigh. She drew her night shirt up like a cushion under her chin. She took Joseph's left hand and spread out his fingers. She put one of her breasts in the full of that left hand and, softly, she stayed there, under that hand, breathing and living.

～

Jean Giono was born in 1895 in Manosque in the South of France, where he died in 1970. He fought in the war and the horrors he experienced on the front turned him into a lifelong pacifist. In the 1930s, he produced his great pacifist works, including *To the Slaughterhouse* (*Le Grand Troupeau*), written in 1931, *Refus d'obéissance* (1937) and *Lettre aux paysans sur la pauvreté et la paix* (1938). With like-minded pacifists, Giono met in the village of Contadour in Haute-Provence from 1935 to 1939; their writings were published yearly as the 'Cahiers de Contadour'. The French title of *To the Slaughterhouse*, *Le Grand Troupeau*, refers to both men and animals. The novel starts the day after a group of soldiers leave for the front, with a great herd of sheep passing through the village where there is no one to look after them. Giono powerfully conveys how the balance of the rural community is disrupted by the removal of the men – the crops are not cared for and the women pine for their lost companions and lovers. Giono lived all his life in the Haute-Provence: *The Man who Planted Trees* (1953) brought him fame and is an ecological classic. Giono's insistence on the need for an equilibrium between mankind, animals and nature is readily understood by today's readers.

LOUIS-FERDINAND CÉLINE

IN TEN THOUSAND YEARS, THIS WAR WILL BE UTTERLY FORGOTTEN

from *Journey to the End of the Night*

translated by Ralph Manheim

THERE WAS QUITE A COMMOTION. Some people said: 'That young fellow's an anarchist, they'll shoot him, the sooner the better... Can't let the grass grow under our feet with a war on!...' But there were others, more patient, who thought I was just syphilitic and sincerely insane, they consequently wanted me to be locked up until the war was over or at least for several months, because they, who claimed to be sane and in their right minds, wanted to take care of me while they carried on the war all by themselves. Which proves that if you want people to think you're normal there's nothing like having a lot of nerve. If you've got plenty of nerve, you're all set, because then you're entitled to do practically anything at all, you've got the majority on your side, and it's the majority who decide what's crazy and what isn't.

Even so my diagnosis was very doubtful. So the authorities decided to put me under observation for a while. My little friend Lola had permission to visit me now and then, and so did my mother. That was all.

We, the befogged wounded, were lodged in a secondary school at Issy-les-Moulineaux, especially rigged to take in soldiers like me, whose patriotism was either impaired or dangerously sick, and get us by cajolery or force to confess. The treatment wasn't really bad, but we felt we were being watched every minute of the day by the staff of silent male nurses endowed with enormous ears.

After a varying period of observation, we'd be quietly sent away and assigned to an insane asylum, the front or, not infrequently, the firing squad.

Among the comrades assembled in that suspect institution, I always wondered while listening to them talking in whispers in the mess hall, which ones might be on the point of becoming ghosts.

In her little cottage near the gate dwelt the concierge, who sold us barley sugar and oranges as well as the wherewithal for sewing on buttons. She also sold us pleasure. For non-coms the price of pleasure was ten francs. Everybody could have it. But watch your step, because men tend to get too confiding on such occasions. An expansive moment could cost you dearly. Whatever was confided to her she repeated in detail to the Chief Medical Officer, and it went into your court-martial record. It seemed reliably established that she'd had a corporal of Spahis, a youngster still in his teens, shot for his confidences, as well as a reservist in the corps of engineers, who had swallowed nails to put his stomach out of commission, and a hysteric, who had described his method of staging a paralytic seizure at the front... One evening, to sound me out, she offered me the identification papers of a father of six, who was dead, so she told me, saying they might help me to a rear-echelon assignment. In short, she was a snake. In bed, though, she was superb, we came back again and again, and the pleasure she purveyed was real. She may have been a slut, but at least she was a real one. To give royal pleasure they've got to be. In the kitchens of love, after all, vice is like the pepper in a good sauce; it brings out the flavour, it's indispensable.

The school buildings opened out on a big terrace, golden in summer, surrounded by trees, with a magnificent panoramic view of Paris. It was there that our visitors waited for us on Thursdays, including Lola, as regular as clockwork, bringing cakes, advice and cigarettes.

We saw our doctors every morning. They questioned us amiably enough, but we never knew exactly what they were thinking. Under their affable smiles as they walked among us, they carried our death sentences.

The mealy-mouthed atmosphere reduced some of the patients under observation, more emotional than the rest, to such a state of exasperation that at night, instead of sleeping, they paced the ward from end to end, loudly protesting against their own anguish, convulsed between hope and despair, as on a dangerous mountain spur. For days and days they suffered, and then suddenly one night they'd go to pieces, run to the Chief Medical Officer, and confess everything. They'd never be seen again. I wasn't easy in my mind myself. But when you're weak, the best way to fortify yourself is to strip the people you fear of the last bit of prestige you're still inclined to give them. Learn to consider them as they are, worse than they are in fact and from every point of view. That will release you, set you free, protect you more than you can possibly imagine. It will give you another self. There will be two of you.

That will strip their words and deeds of the obscene mystical fascination that weakens you and makes you waste your time. From then on you'll find their act no more amusing, no more relevant to your inner progress than that of the lowliest pig.

Beside me, in the next bed, there was a corporal, a volunteer like me. Up until August he had been a teacher at a secondary school in Touraine, teaching history and geography, so he told me. After a few months on the front lines this teacher had turned out to be a champion thief. Nothing could stop him from stealing canned goods from the regimental supply train, the quartermaster trucks, the company stores and anywhere else he could find them.

So he'd landed there with the rest of us, while presumably awaiting court martial. But since his family persisted in trying to prove that he had been stupefied and demoralized by shell shock, the prosecution deferred his trial from month to month. He didn't talk to me very much. He spent hours combing his beard, but when he spoke to me it was almost always about the same thing, about the method he had discovered for not getting his wife with any more children. Was he really insane? At a time when the world is upside down and it's thought insane to ask why you're being murdered, it obviously requires no great effort to pass for a lunatic. Of course your act has got to be convincing, but when it comes to keeping out of the big slaughterhouse some people's imaginations become magnificently fertile.

Everything that's important goes on in the darkness, no doubt about it. We never know anyone's real inside story.

This teacher's name was Princhard. What can the man have dreamt up to save his carotids, lungs and optic nerves? That was the crucial question, the question we men should have asked one another if we'd wanted to be strictly human and rational. Far from it, we staggered along in a world of idealistic absurdities, hemmed in by insane, bellicose platitudes. Like smoke-maddened rats we tried to escape from the burning ship, but we had no general plan, no faith in one another. Dazed by the war, we had developed a different kind of madness: fear. The heads and tails of the war.

In the midst of the general delirium, this Princhard took a certain liking to me, though he distrusted me of course.

In the place and situation we were in, friendship and trust were out of the question. No one revealed any more than he thought useful for his survival, since everything or practically everything was sure to be repeated by some attentive stool pigeon.

From time to time one of us would disappear. That meant the case against him was ready and the court martial would send him to a military tribunal, the penal colonies, the front or, if he was very lucky, the insane asylum in Clamart.

More dubious warriors kept arriving, from every branch of service, some very young, some almost old, some terrified, some ranting and swaggering. Their wives and parents came to see them, and their children too, staring wide-eyed, on Thursdays.

They all wept buckets in the visiting room, especially in the evening. All the helplessness of a world at war wept when the visits were over and the women and children left, dragging their feet in the bleak, gas-lit corridor. A herd of snivelling riff-raff – that's what they were – disgusting.

To Lola it was still an adventure, coming to see me in that prison, as you might have called it. We two didn't cry. Where would we have got our tears from?

'Is it true that you've gone mad, Ferdinand?' she asked me one Thursday.

'It's true!' I admitted.

'But they'll treat you here?'

'There's no treatment for fear, Lola.'

'Is it as bad as all that?'

'It's worse, Lola. My fear is so bad that if I die a natural death later on, I especially don't want to be cremated! I want them to leave me in the ground, quietly rotting in the graveyard, ready to come back to life... Maybe... how do we know? But if they burned me to ashes, Lola, don't you see, it would be over, really over... A skeleton, after all, is still something like a man... It's more likely to come back to life than ashes... Reduced to ashes, you're finished!... What do you think?... Naturally the war...'

'Oh, Ferdinand! Then you're an absolute coward! You're as loath-some as a rat...'

'Yes, an absolute coward, Lola, I reject the war and everything in it... I don't deplore it... I don't resign myself to it... I don't weep about it... I just plain reject it and all its fighting men, I don't want anything to do with them or it. Even if there were nine hundred and ninety-five million of them and I were all alone, they'd still be wrong and I'd be right. Because I'm the one who knows what I want: I don't want to die.'

'But it's not possible to reject the war, Ferdinand! Only crazy people and cowards reject the war when their country is in danger...'

'If that's the case, hurrah for the crazy people! Look, Lola, do you remember a single name, for instance, of any of the soldiers killed in the Hundred Years War?... Did you ever try to find out who any of them were?... No! You see? You never tried. As far as you're concerned they're as anonymous, as indifferent, as the last atom of that paperweight, as your morning bowel movement... Get it into your head, Lola, that they died for nothing! For absolutely nothing, the idiots! I say it and I'll say it again! I've proved it! The one thing that counts is life! In ten thousand years, I'll bet you, this war, remarkable as it may seem to us at present, will be utterly forgotten... Maybe here and there in the world a handful of scholars will argue about its causes or the dates of the principal hecatombs that made it famous… Up until now those are the only things about men that other men have thought worth remembering after a few centuries, a few years, or even a few hours… I don't believe in the future, Lola…'

When she heard me flaunting my shameful state like that, she lost all sympathy for me… Once and for all she put me down as contemptible.

She decided to leave me without further ado. It was too much. When I left her that evening at the hospital gate, she didn't kiss me.

Evidently the thought that a condemned man might have no vocation for death was too much for her. When I asked her how our fritters were doing, she did not reply.

On my return to the dormitory, I found Princhard at the window with a crowd of soldiers around him. He was trying out a pair of dark glasses in the gaslight. The idea, he explained, had come to him last summer at the seashore, and since it was summer now, he was planning to wear them next day in the park. That park was enormous and exceedingly well policed by squads of vigilant orderlies. The next day Princhard insisted on my going for a walk on the terrace with him to try out his beautiful glasses. A blazing afternoon beat down on him, defended by his opaque lenses. I noticed that his nose was almost transparent at the nostrils and that he was breathing hard.

'My friend,' he confided, 'time is passing and it's not on my side… My conscience is immune to remorse, I have been relieved, thank God, of those fears… It's not crimes that count in this world… people stopped counting them long ago… What counts is blunders… And I believe I've made one… that's absolutely irremediable…'

'Stealing canned goods?'

'Yes, just imagine, I thought I was being so clever! My idea was to abstract myself from the battle and return, disgraced but still alive, to peace, as one returns, exhausted, to the surface of the sea after a long dive… I almost succeeded… but this war, undoubtedly, has been going on too long… So long that cannon fodder disgusting enough to disgust the Nation is no longer conceivable… She has begun to accept every offering, regardless of where it comes from, every variety of meat… The Nation has become infinitely indulgent in its choice of martyrs! Today there's no such thing as a soldier unworthy to bear arms and, above all, to die under arms and by arms... They're going, latest news, to make a hero out of me!... How imperious the homicidal madness must have become if they're willing to pardon – no, to forget! – the theft of a tin of meat! True, we have got into the habit of admiring colossal bandits, whose opulence is revered by the entire world, yet whose existence, once we stop to examine it, proves to be one long crime repeated ad infinitum, but those same bandits are heaped with glory, honours and power, their crimes are hallowed by the law of the land, whereas, as far back in history as the eye can see – and history, as you know, is my business – everything conspires to show that a venial theft, especially of inglorious foodstuffs, such as bread crusts, ham or cheese, unfailingly subjects its perpetrator to irreparable opprobrium, the categorical condemnation of the community, major punishment, automatic dishonour and inexpiable shame, and this for two reasons, first because the perpetrator of such an offence is usually poor, which in itself connotes basic unworthiness, and secondly because his act implies, as it were, a tacit reproach to the community. A poor man's theft is seen as a malicious attempt at individual redress, you understand?... Where would we be? Note accordingly that in all countries the penalties for petty theft are extremely severe, not only as a means of defending society, but also as a stern admonition to the unfortunate to know their place, stick to their caste, and behave themselves, joyfully resigned to go on dying of hunger and misery down through the centuries for ever and ever... Until today, however, petty thieves enjoyed one advantage in the Republic: they were denied the honour of bearing patriotic arms. But that's all over now, tomorrow I, a thief, will resume my place in the army... Such are the orders... It has been decided in high places to forgive and forget what they call my "momentary madness", and this, listen carefully, in consideration of what they call "the honour of my family". What solicitude! I ask you, comrade, is it my family that's going to serve as a strainer and sorting house for mixed French and German bullets?... It'll just be me, won't it? And when I'm dead, is the honour of my family going to bring me back to life?... I can see how it will be with my family when these warlike scenes have passed... as everything passes… I can see my family on fine Sundays… joyfully gambolling on the lawns of a new summer… while three feet under papa, that's me, dripping with worms and infinitely more disgusting than a kilo of turds on Bastille Day, will be rotting stupendously with all my deluded flesh… To fertilize the fields of the anonymous ploughman – that is the true future of the true soldier! Ah, comrade! This world, I assure you, is only a vast device for kidding the world! You are young. Let these minutes of wisdom be as years to you! Listen well, comrade, and don't fail to recognize and understand the telltale sign, which glares from all the murderous hypocrisies of our society: "Compassion with the fate, the condition of the poor…" I tell you, little men, life's mugs, beaten, fleeced to the bone, sweated from time immemorial, I warn you that when the princes of this world start loving you, it means they're going to grind you up into battle sausage… That's the sign… It's infallible. It starts with affection. Louis XIV at least, and don't forget it, didn't give a hoot in hell about his beloved people. Louis XV ditto. He wiped his arsehole with them. True, we didn't live well in those days, the poor have never lived well, but the kings didn't flay them with the obstinacy, the persistence you meet with in today's tyrants. There's no rest, I tell you, for the little man, except in the contempt of the great, whose only motive for thinking of the common people is self-interest, when it isn't sadism… It's the philosophers, another point to look out for while we're at it, who first started giving the people ideas… when all they'd known up until then was the catechism! They began, so they proclaimed, to educate the people… Ah! What truths they had to reveal! Beautiful! Brilliant! Unprecedented truths! And the people were dazzled! "That's it!" they said. "That's the stuff! Let's go and die for it!" The people are always dying to die! That's the way they are! "Long live Diderot!" they yelled. And "Long live Voltaire!" They, at least, were first-class philosophers! And long live Carnot, too, who was so good at organizing victories! And long live everybody! Those guys at least don't let the beloved people moulder in ignorance and fetishism! They show the people the roads of Freedom! Emancipation! Things went fast after that! First teach everybody to read the papers! That's the way to salvation! Hurry hurry! No more illiterates! We don't need them any more! Nothing but citizen-soldiers! Who vote! Who read! And who fight! And who march! And send kisses from the front! In no time the people were good and ripe. The enthusiasm of the liberated has to be good for something, doesn't it? Danton wasn't eloquent for the hell of it. With a few phrases, so rousing that we can still hear them today, he had the people mobilized before you could say fiddlesticks! That was when the first battalions of emancipated maniacs marched off! The first voting, flag-waving suckers that Dumouriez led away to get themselves drilled full of holes in Flanders! As for Dumouriez himself, who had come too late to these new-fangled idealistic pastimes, he discovered that he was more interested in money and deserted. He was our last mercenary… The gratis soldier was something really new… So new that when Goethe arrived in Valmy, Goethe or not, he was flabbergasted. At the sight of those ragged, impassioned cohorts, who had come of their own free will to get themselves disembowelled by the King of Prussia in defence of a patriotic fiction no one had ever heard of, Goethe realized that he still had much to learn. "This day," he declaimed grandiloquently as befitted the habits of his genius, "marks the beginning of a new era!" He could say that again! The system proved successful and pretty soon they were mass-producing heroes, and in the end, the system was so well perfected that they cost practically nothing. Everyone was delighted. Bismarck, the two Napoleons, Barrès, Elsa the Horsewoman. The religion of the flag promptly replaced the cult of heaven, an old cloud which had already been deflated by the Reformation and reduced to a network of episcopal money boxes. In olden times the fanatical fashion was: "Long live Jesus! Burn the heretics!" But heretics, after all, were few and voluntary… Whereas today vast hordes of men are fired with aim and purpose by cries of: "Hang the limp turnips! The juiceless lemons! The innocent readers! By the millions, eyes right!" If anybody doesn't want to fight or murder, stinking pacifists, grab 'em, tear 'em to pieces! Kill them in thirteen juicy ways! For a starter, to teach them how to live, rip their guts out of their bodies, their eyes out of their sockets, and the years out of their filthy slobbering lives! Let whole legions of them perish, turn into smidgens, bleed, smoulder in acid – and all that to make the Nation more beloved, more fair, and more joyful! And if in their midst there are any foul creatures who refuse to understand these sublime truths, they can just go and bury themselves right with the others, no, not quite, their place will be at the far end of the cemetery, under the shameful epitaphs of cowards without an ideal, for those contemptible slugs will have forfeited the glorious right to a small patch of the shadow of the municipal monument erected by the lowest bidder in the central avenue to commemorate the reputable dead, and also the right to hear so much as a distant echo of the Minister's speech next Sunday, when he comes around to urinate at the Prefecture and sound off over the graves after lunch…'

But from the end of the garden someone was calling Princhard. The head physician had sent his orderly to get him on the double.

'Coming,' Princhard cried. He had barely time enough to hand me the draft of the speech he had been trying out on me. A ham if there ever was one.

I never saw Princhard again. He had the same trouble as all intellectuals – he was ineffectual. He knew too many things, and they confused him. He needed all sorts of gimmicks to steam him up, help him make up his mind.

It's been a long time since that night when he went away, when I think about it. But I remember it well. Suddenly the houses at the end of our park stood out sharply, as things do before the night takes hold of them. The trees grew larger in the twilight and shot up to the sky to meet the night.

I never made any attempt to get in touch with Princhard, to find out if he had really 'disappeared', as they kept saying. But it's best if he disappeared.

⌐

Louis-Ferdinand Céline was born near Paris in 1894 and died in Meudon in 1961. The virulently anti-Semitic views expressed in his writings in the 1930s and later have always made it difficult to offer a balanced assessment of Céline's literary genius. The fact remains that *Journey to the End of the Night* is one of the great novels to feature the First World War. Although less than a quarter of the book takes place in wartime, the disgust, hatred and bile that the narrator Bardamau, Céline's fictional alter ego, feels for the war colours the whole book. Céline found an appropriate, fragmented style to convey the irrational convulsions of the war. Bardamau is afraid and prepared to admit his fear:

> 'Oh, Ferdinand! Then you're an absolute coward! You're as loathsome as a rat...'
>
> 'Yes an absolute coward, Lola. I reject the war and everything in it... I don't deplore it... I don't resign myself to it... I don't weep about it... I just plain reject it and all its fighting men...'

Journey to the End of the Night, which covers (French) imperialism in Africa and the horror of the car assembly lines of Detroit as well as the war itself, is truly international in its scope but never loses sight of how it is individuals that the system crushes. The book has an extraordinary ability to go from the personal to the political and back again. Maybe not someone you would want to go out drinking with, but Céline sure can write!

ISAAC BABEL

PAPA MARESCOT'S FAMILY

from *On the Field of Honour*

translated by Peter Constantine

W E OCCUPY A VILLAGE that we have taken from the enemy. It is a tiny Picardy village, lovely and modest. Our company has been bivouacked in the cemetery. Surrounding us are smashed crucifixes and fragments of statues and tombstones wrecked by the sledgehammer of an unknown defiler. Rotting corpses have spilled out of coffins shattered by shells. A picture worthy of you, Michelangelo!

A soldier has no time for mysticism. A field of skulls has been dug up into trenches. War is war. We're still alive. If it is our lot to increase the population in this chilly little hole, we should at least make these decaying corpses dance a jig to the tune of our machine guns.

A shell had blown off the cover of one of the vaults. This so I could have a shelter, no doubt about it. I made myself comfortable in that hole, *que voulez-vous, on loge ou on peut.**

So – it's a wonderful, bright spring morning. I am lying on corpses, looking at the fresh grass, thinking of Hamlet. He wasn't that bad a philosopher, the poor prince. Skulls spoke to him in human words. Nowadays, that kind of skill would really come in handy for a lieutenant of the French army.

---

*What do you expect, one holes up where one can.

'Lieutenant, there's some civilian here who wants to see you!' a corporal calls out to me.

What the hell does a civilian want in these nether regions?

A character enters. A shabby, shrivelled little old man. He is wearing his Sunday best. His frock coat is bespattered with mud. A half-empty sack dangles from his cowering shoulders.

There must be a frozen potato in it – every time he moves, something rattles in the sack.

'*Eh bien,* what do you want?'

'My name, you see, is Monsieur Marescot,' the civilian whispers, and bows. 'That is why I've come…'

'So?'

'I would like to bury Madame Marescot and the rest of my family, Monsieur Lieutenant.'

'What?'

'My name, you see, is Papa Marescot.' The old man lifts his hat from his gray forehead. 'Perhaps you have heard of me, Monsieur Lieutenant!'

Papa Marescot? I have heard this name before. Of course I have heard it. This is the story: Three days ago, at the beginning of our occupation, all non-enemy civilians had been issued the order to evacuate. Some left, others stayed. Those who stayed hid in cellars. But their courage was no match for the bombardment – the stone defense proved hopeless. Many were killed. A whole family had been crushed beneath the debris of a cellar. It was the Marescot family. Their name had stuck in my mind, a true French name. They had been a family of four, the father, mother, and two daughters. Only the father survived.

'You poor man! So you are Marescot? This is so sad. Why did you have to go into that damned cellar, why?'

The corporal interrupted me.

'It looks like they're starting up again, Lieutenant!'

That was to be expected. The Germans had noticed the movement in our trenches. The volley came from the right flank, then it moved farther left. I grabbed Papa Marescot by the collar and pulled him down. My boys ducked their heads and sat quietly under cover, no one as much as sticking his nose out.

Papa Marescot sat pale and shivering in his Sunday best. A five-inch kitten was meowing nearby.

'What can I do for you, Papa? This is no time to beat about the bush! As you can see, we're at each other's throats here!'

'*Mon lieutenant*, I've told you everything. I would like to bury my family.'

'Fine, I'll send the men to collect the bodies.'

'I have the bodies with me, Monsieur Lieutenant!'

'What?'

He pointed to the sack. In it were the meager remains of Papa Marescot's family.

I shuddered with horror.

'Very well, Papa, I will have my men bury them.'

He looked at me as if I had just uttered the greatest idiocy.

'When this hellish din has died down,' I continued, 'we shall dig an excellent grave for them. Rest assured, *père Maresco*, we will take care of everything.'

'But I have a family vault.'

'Splendid, where is it?'

'But… but …'

'But what?'

'But we're sitting in it as we speak, *mon lieutenant*.'

◡

Isaac Babel was born in 1894 in Odessa, the inspiration for many of his best short stories. Schooled by private tutors because there was a quota for Jewish pupils at state schools, he grew up speaking fluent French, the language in which he first wrote. In 1915, he moved to Petrograd. At that time he was much influenced by French writers and 'Papa Marescot's Family', one of the first stories Babel wrote in Russian, shows clearly the influence of Maupassant. According to one of his stories, Babel fought on the Romanian front until the end of 1917. He returned to Petrograd in 1918 and worked as a reporter on Gorky's newspaper *Novaya zhizn*. As the Russian Revolution hardened,

Babel became more and more disillusioned. A trip in 1930 to the Ukraine enabled him to see at first hand the effects of the forced collectivization of the peasantry. His response was to become 'a master of a new literary genre, the genre of silence'. But this wisdom came too late. His works were deemed to be 'off message', and not even Maxim Gorky, his patron, could save him. As part of Stalin's Great Purge, Babel was arrested in 1939. After 'confessing' to being a Trotskyist terrorist and foreign spy, he was executed in January 1940.

DALTON TRUMBO

A DATE WITH THE SHELL

from *Johnny Got His Gun*

H E HAD LOST ALL TRACK OF TIME. All his work to trap it all his counting
and calculation of it might just as well never have happened. He
had lost track of everything except the tapping. The instant he awakened
he began to tap and he continued until the moment when drowsiness
overcame him. Even as he fell asleep the last portion of his energy and
thought went into the tapping so that it seemed he dreamed of tapping.
Because he tapped while he was awake and dreamed of tapping while
he was asleep his old difficulty in distinguishing between wakefulness
and sleep sprang up again. He was never quite positive that he was not
dreaming when awake and tapping when asleep. He had lost time so
utterly that he had no idea how long the tapping had been going on.
Maybe only weeks maybe a month perhaps even a year. The one sense
that remained to him out of the original five had been completely
hypnotized by the tapping and as for thinking he didn't even pretend
to any more. He didn't speculate about the new night nurses in their
comings and goings. He didn't listen for vibrations against the floor. He
didn't think of the past and he didn't consider the future. He only lay
and tapped his message over and over again to people on the outside
who didn't understand.

The day nurse tried hard to soothe him but she did it only as if
she were trying to calm an irritable patient. She did it in such a way

that he knew he would never break through as long as he had her. It never seemed to occur to her that there was a mind an intelligence working behind the rhythm of his head against the pillow. She was simply watching over an incurably sick patient trying to make his sickness as comfortable as possible. She never thought that to be dumb was a sickness and that he had found the cure for it that he was trying to tell her he was well he was not dumb any longer he was a man who could talk. She gave him hot baths. She shifted the position of his bed. She adjusted the pillow in back of his head now higher now lower. When she moved it higher the increased angle bent his head forward. After tapping for a time in this position he could feel pain shooting all the way down his spine and across his back. But he kept right on tapping.

She got to massaging him and he liked that she had such a brisk gentle touch to her fingers but he kept on tapping. And then one day he felt a change in the touch of her fingers. They were not gentle and brisk any longer. He felt the change through the tips of her fingers through the tenderness of her touch he felt pity and hesitancy and a great gathering love that was neither him for her nor her for him but rather a kind of love that took in all living things and tried to make them a little more comfortable a little less unhappy a little more nearly like others of their kind.

He felt the change through the tips of her fingers and a sharp little twinge of disgust went through him but in spite of the disgust he was responding to the touch responding to the mercy in her heart that caused her to touch him so. Her hands sought out the far parts of his body. They inflamed his nerves with a kind of false passion that fled in little tremors along the surface of his skin. Even while he was thinking oh my god it's come to this here is the reason she thinks I'm tapping goddam her god bless her what shall I do? – even while he was thinking it he fell in with her rhythm he strained to her touch his heart pounded to a faster tempo and he forgot everything in the world except the motion and the sudden pumping of his blood...

There was a girl named Ruby and she for him was the first. It was when he was in the eighth maybe the ninth grade. Ruby lived down in Teller Addition on the other side of the tracks. Ruby was younger than he maybe only in the sixth or seventh grade but she was a great big girl an Italian and very fat. All the boys in town somehow began with Ruby because she never embarrassed them. She came right to the point and that was that although once in a while you had to tell her she was pretty. But no other nonsense and if a guy didn't have any experience why Ruby never laughed at him and never told on him she just went right ahead and gave it to him.

The guys liked to talk about Ruby when there wasn't anything better to talk about. They liked to laugh about her in such talks and say oh no I never see Ruby any more I manage to get around I'm finding something new every day. But that was all talk because they were really very young guys and Ruby was the first and only girl they knew they were too shy with other girls with nice girls. They soon grew ashamed of Ruby and when they went down they would always feel a little dirty and a little disgusted. They came away blaming Ruby somehow for making them feel that way. By the time they got to the tenth grade none of them would ever speak to Ruby and finally she disappeared. She just wasn't around any more and they were all kind of glad they didn't have to meet her on the street.

There was Laurette down at Stumpy Telsa's place. Stumpy Telsa had a house in Shale City. She had five or six girls there and the finest pair of Boston bulls in town. The guys when they were young when they were maybe fourteen or fifteen used to wonder a great deal about Stumpy Telsa's place. For them it was the most wonderful the most exciting the most mysterious house in Shale City. They would hear stories from older guys of what went on down there. They could never quite decide whether they were for it or against it but they were always interested.

One night three of them went down through the alley in back of Stumpy Telsa's and crept through the back yard and tried to peek in through the kitchen door. There was a colored cook there making sandwiches and she saw them and let out a howl. Stumpy Telsa came swinging into the kitchen on her peg leg and grabbed a butcher knife and came out into the back yard. They all ran like hell with Stumpy Telsa yelling after them that she knew who they were and she was going right inside and phone their folks. But it was a bluff. Stumpy hadn't seen their faces and she didn't telephone anybody.

Later on when they were seventeen or eighteen and practically ready to get out of high school he and Bill Harper decided the hell with talking about the place all the time so they went down to Stumpy Telsa's one night to find out for themselves. They walked right into the front room and nobody pulled a knife on them or anything. It was about eight o'clock and evidently things weren't very busy because Stumpy came into the parlor and talked to them and wasn't sore at all. They were too embarrassed to say anything to Stumpy about why they came and Stumpy didn't say anything to them about it either so it turned out to be just a visit. Stumpy called upstairs to the girls for a couple of them to come down and sit in the parlor and she told the colored woman to make up a plate of sandwiches. Then she went away. Alone in the parlor they could hear the two girls coming down from upstairs and they knew that now they were going to find out whether all the things they had heard about such places were true. Some guys said that the girls came right smack into the parlor stark naked and other guys said they'd never let you see them naked they always wore a kimono or something. Nothing they hated said these guys so much as a man who wanted to see them without any clothes at all. So they sat with their hearts in their throats and waited and watched.

But when the girls came down they were fully dressed. They were dressed better than most of the girls in Shale City and they were prettier than most of them too. They came in and sat down and they talked just like anybody else would talk. One of them seemed to like Bill Harper the best and the other one seemed to like him. The one who liked him talked about books all the time. Had he read this had he read that and he hadn't read any of them and he got to feeling pretty much like a dummy. After about a half hour of munching sandwiches and talking about books Stumpy Telsa came in all beaming and smiling and told them it was time to go home. So they got up and shook hands with the two girls and went away.

That night they took a long walk through the town discussing all the things they had heard about Stumpy Telsa's place and deciding they were either lies or else they were the kind of guys that women didn't like in that way. That was bad maybe they'd be failures with women all their lives maybe there was something they didn't have. They decided not to tell anybody about their visit because they felt they were much more disgraced than if things had turned out differently.

Later on he got to thinking about the girl who talked books and after thinking about it for a long while he went down to see her again. Her name was Laurette and she seemed glad to see him. She told him if he wanted to see her always to be sure he made it before nine o'clock because after that time things were generally pretty busy. He did come again and several times more and always they sat in the parlor and always they talked. He got to thinking maybe I'm in love with Laurette now wouldn't that be a fine thing me falling in love with her and how would I break the news to my mother and father? And on the other hand he would think why is it that all we do is talk what does she think I am? All during the winter of that year and on through the spring he went down to see Laurette once maybe twice sometimes even three times a month. And each time he went down just before he knocked on the door he would pull himself together and he would say to himself Joe Bonham be a man this time. But Laurette was so nice he couldn't figure out how a fellow started things like that without seeming kind of dirty. So he never did.

When he graduated from high school he got a pair of gold cuff links through the mail and all they had with them was a card that had the initial L written on it. He had a hell of a time explaining to his folks who sent him the links but he prized them very highly and he decided that tomorrow night after graduation he would go down to Stumpy Telsa's. Now that Laurette had told him in a kind of roundabout way that she loved him things would be different. So about nine o'clock on the big night he went down to Stumpy Telsa's still hunting for some pleasant and polite way to express the thing that was in his mind. He knocked on the door and Stumpy Telsa invited him in and when he asked for Laurette she told him Laurette wasn't there. Where had she gone? She had gone to Estes Park. Every year said Stumpy Telsa she takes three months off up there. All winter long she buys new clothes and she saves her money and for three months she lives at the best hotel in Estes Park. She goes out with guys and she dances and she dearly loves to have the guys fall in love with her and when they fall for her she is always nice to them but she is never too nice. She is never as nice as they want her to be. She is a smart girl that Laurette said Stumpy Telsa she eats her cake and she has it too. And on top of that she saves her money and she has a nice little bankroll. Why don't you get a job in some other town and then come around in the fall after Laurette is rested up and talk things over with her? Maybe you and Laurette would be very happy. But by the time fall came he was working in a bakery fifteen hundred miles away and he never saw Laurette again.

There was a girl named Bonnie. She clapped him on the back one day while he was sitting in Louie's drug store near the bakery having a coke. She slapped him on the back and she said to him you're Joe Bonham ain't you Joe Bonham from Shale City? Well I'm Bonnie Flannigan we used to go to school together Jesus it's good to see somebody from god's country. He looked at her and he couldn't remember her at all. Oh yes he said I remember you. She nodded and said you were ahead of me in school and you never would give me a tumble how are you and why don't you come over to see me sometime? I live in the bungalow court just three doors from the bakery. You work in the bakery I know. I see some of the guys once in a while sweet guys all of them they told me you were there.

He looked at her and he could tell she was younger than him and he could tell what she was. He felt a little pain in his stomach because girls like that might come from New York or Chicago or St. Louis or Cincinnati they might come from Denver or Salt Lake or Boise Idaho or Seattle but they never came from Shale City because Shale City was home.

He went over to see her. She wasn't a small girl and she wasn't a very cute girl but she was awfully good natured and she was busy with plans for the future and she was full of life. I been married three times already said Bonnie I been married three times and all my husbands said I looked just like Evelyn Nesbitt Thaw. Do you think I look like Evelyn Nesbitt Thaw?

In the mornings around five or six o'clock sometimes they would go over to Main Street for breakfast over in the bright cheap shiny white tiled restaurants where you could get anything for a dime. They would go there and the place would be filled with sleepy sailors wondering what to do now that it was morning and Bonnie would know them all. She would slap them on the shoulders as they walked toward their booth and she would call them by name. Hi Pete well if it ain't old Slimy hi Dick well if it ain't old George. When they got to the booth and ordered their ham and eggs she would say to him Joe if you're a smart guy you'll stick with me. You want to go through school huh? Joe you stick with me. I'll send you through school. I make the fleet and I know all these guys and I know where their pocketbooks are and I'm smart and careful I never even had clap you stick with me Joe and we'll wear diamonds. See that guy over there? He always says I look just like Evelyn Nesbitt Thaw do you think I look like Evelyn Nesbitt Thaw dearie?

There was a girl named Lucky. She was the Statue of Liberty and Aunt Jemima and the girl-you-left-behind to about a half a million doughboys in Paris. They had a regular American house in Paris and when they were on leave there when they were away from the trenches and the killing all the guys went to the American house and talked to American girls and drank American whiskey and were happy.

Lucky was the best one of the bunch the nicest and about the smartest. She would receive him in her room and she would be stark naked with a great red scar where somebody had yanked her appendix. He would come into her room pretty tired at the end of a night and maybe a little drunk and he would lie down on her bed and put his hands behind his head and watch Lucky. The minute she saw him she would smile and go over to her dresser and out of the top drawer she would bring a doily. She was always crocheting on that doily. She would sit at the foot of the bed all brightness and gossip and friendliness and crochet the doily and talk to him.

Lucky had a son. He was six maybe seven years old and Lucky was keeping him in a school on Long Island. She was going to raise him to be a polo player because polo players got around and they met all the best people and nothing was too good for Lucky's son he was such a cute little bastard. Figuring out the house percentage and towel expenses and medical care Lucky still made herself from a hundred and fifty to two hundred dollars a week at two dollars apiece. But of course we live it up we got to dress up to our positions it costs lots in clothes I can tell you but a girl's got to look smart.

Lucky had been in the San Francisco earthquake. She must have been sixteen or seventeen then and that would make her almost thirty now. When the earthquake hit San Francisco Lucky was on the fourth floor of a hotel on Market Street. I was entertaining a gentleman friend and when I first felt that thing hit I said to myself Lucky I said that's an earthquake and you ain't going to be caught dead with no son-of-a-bitch on top of you. So I pushed him off and I run right down into the street stark naked and you should of seen the guys stare.

To talk with Lucky to be with Lucky to lie with Lucky was like finding peace in a heathen country it was like breathing the air of a place you love when you're sick and dying for a breath of it. To see her smile to hear her bright chatter to watch her bony little fingers fly as they worked the crochet needle with the night noises of Paris a foreign city just outside the window was enough to make anybody feel better and less lonely.

Paris was a strange city a foreign city a dying city a lively city. It had too much life and too much death and too many ghosts and behind the bars of the cafes too many dead soldiers. Have a drink. Oh Paris is a woman's town with flowers in her hair. No doubt about it Paris was a wonderful town a woman's town but it was also a man's town. Ten thousand doughboys tommies poilus on leave ten thousand a hundred thousand of them. A few days boys a few days and then you go back and each time you go back the chances are more against you than they were the last time. Remember that there is a law of averages so come on dearie turn a trick five francs ten francs two dollars oh boy what's that an American voice? me for her. What the hell a song in the parlor and a swig of cheap cognac and let's go because out there in the east the place they call the western front there is a little old guy keeps a book and figures averages all day long and all night long he never makes a mistake. Flor da lee. Flor da lee. God save the king. Come on up honeybunch lonesome wanta try something new parley vous fransays? A gallon of red wine like water and sourdough bread and maybe please god I find an American girl who don't talk heathen languages. Jig-jig hell that's not what I want. I want something loud because there is a voice I want to drown out. It's a voice that doesn't make any sound but I can't get away from it.

Somewhere it is being prepared. Somewhere deep in the heart of Germany the shell is being made. Some German girl is polishing it right now polishing it and cleaning it and fitting the charge into it. It glistens in the factory light and it has a number and the number is mine. I have a date with the shell. We shall meet soon.

Motor lorries rumbling through the street gathering guys up outside gathering up the late ones saying come on buddy time's up down to the station and jump on the old box car. Because you're going back. Back to the little old guy who figures out there the guy who figures all day long and all night long and never makes a mistake. The stars and stripes forever ta-da da-de-um da-de-ah. Try it kid it's good some guys say it's got dope in it don't believe a thing they tell you. Some guys say it dries you out. It's called absinthe let it filter down in your glass it's swell. Parley vous parley vous yes sir no sir lonesome honey where's that American voice? god I'd like to find her. Where's Jack where's Bill where's John gone all gone. Gone west. Taps. Ten thousand dollars for the folks back home. Ten thousand simoleons Jesus. I know a house on Rue Blondel black and white all nations. Americans? Sure anything you want oh god that isn't what I want what I want's a long long way off but I'll take whatever you got. It's a long way to Tipperary. Lights out.

Nearer nearer. Some top-heavy canvas-covered German truck is plunging toward France right now. In it are shells and among the shells the one with my number. It's coming toward the west through the Rhine valley I always wanted to see it through the Black forest I always wanted to see it through the deep deep night coming toward France the shell I shall meet. It's coming nearer and nearer nothing can stop it not even the hand of god for I have a time set and it has a time set and we shall meet when the time comes.

America expects every man to do his duty France expects every man to do his duty England expects every man to do his duty every doughboy and tommy and poilu and what the hell did they call the Italians? anyhow they're expected to do their duty too. Lafayette we come and so in Flanders fields the poppies blow between the crosses row on row check off the rows for the little old guy with the book the little old guy who figures all day long and all night long and never makes a mistake. Oui oui parley vous jig-jig? Sure jig-jig what the hell five francs ten francs who says two dollars two good old American dollars and a glass of corn whiskey? My god this cognac I always thought it was a swell drink I heard so much about it it's terrible give me corn and what do you think of the prohibitionists? Four million of us gone four million votes I suppose we don't count they'll ruin us yet let's go out and hunt corn good old American corn. Darling honey deary sweet tired lonesome wanta friend take a table take a chair take a bed only don't take too long there's lots of guys Paris is full of them so don't take too long.

Hidden beneath some gentle rolling hill that is like a woman's breast on the solid flesh of the land hidden under the hill in some unknown ammunition dump is my shell. It is ready. Hurry boy hurry doughboy don't be late finish whatever you have to do you haven't much time left.

Sing a rag-time jig-jig sing a rag-time mam'selle sing a hot time in the old town tonight. Sing a Joan of Arc and a flor da lee sing a mademoiselle from Armentieres. Sing a Lafayette parley vous fransays. Get up and jump jump mighty fast make the smoke whirl in the air smash the chairs smash the windows tear down the house goddam it move boy move girl put cognac in your joints and turn the lights out and beat the drums and get out of the trenches by christmas and see Paris by night and turn a trick for five francs and oui-oui parley vous hunky-dory corn in my belly and a little old guy with a book who figures all day long and all night long and he figures faster and faster faster and quicker harder and stronger and faster faster faster.

It will come with a rush and a roar and a shudder. It will come howling and laughing and shrieking and moaning. It will come so fast you can't help yourself you will stretch out your arms to embrace it. You will feel it before it comes and you will tense yourself for acceptance and the earth which is your eternal bed will tremble at the moment of your union.

Silence.

What's this what's this oh my god can a man ever get lower can a man ever be less?

Weariness and gasping convulsive exhaustion. All life dead all life wasted and becoming nothing less than nothing only the germ of nothing. A kind of sickness that comes from shame. A weakness like dying weakness and faintness and a prayer. God give me rest take me away hide me let me die oh god how weary how much already dead how much gone and going oh god hide me and give me peace.

⤶

Dalton Trumbo was born in Montrose, Colorado, in 1905 and died in Los Angeles in 1976. He was one of the highest-paid screenwriters of his time. One of the Hollywood Ten, Trumbo was blacklisted in 1947 after he refused to testify before HUAC (House Un-American Activities Committee) during the Committee's investigation of communist influence in Hollywood.

Trumbo wrote *Johnny Got His Gun* in 1938; it won a National Book Award in 1939. A powerful anti-war novel, the book provided a rallying-point for opposition to US entry to the Second World War. After the German invasion of the Soviet Union in June 1941, Trumbo, as a fellow traveller of the Communist Party, and his publisher, who both supported US entry into the war, decided to suspend publication of the book until the end of the war. A film version directed by Trumbo won the Jury Prize at the 1971 Cannes Festival. A series of flashbacks, the book is a startling mix of domestic scenes and scenes of mad carnage. It ends with a call for class war – 'we will have the hymns and we will have the guns and we will use them and we will win': the journey on the way has been a staccato blast of emotion and passion.

WILLA CATHER

MANGER, AIMER, PAYER

from *One of Ours*

W HEN THE SURVIVORS OF COMPANY B are old men, and are telling
over their good days, they will say to each other, 'Oh, that week
we spent at Beaufort!' They will close their eyes and see a little village
on a low ridge, lost in the forest, overgrown with oak and chestnut and
black walnut... buried in autumn colour, the streets drifted deep in
autumn leaves, great branches interlacing over the roofs of the houses,
wells of cool water that tastes of moss and tree roots. Up and down those
streets they will see figures passing; themselves, young and brown and
clean-limbed; and comrades, long dead, but still alive in that far-away
village. How they will wish they could tramp again, nights on days in
the mud and rain, to drag sore feet into their old billets at Beaufort! To
sink into those wide feather beds and sleep the round of the clock while
the old women washed and dried their clothes for them; to eat rabbit
stew and *pommes frites* in the garden, – rabbit stew made with red wine
and chestnuts. Oh, the days that are no more!

As soon as Captain Maxey and the wounded men had been started
on their long journey to the rear, carried by the prisoners, the whole
company turned in and slept for twelve hours – all but Sergeant Hicks,
who sat in the house off the square, beside the body of his chum.

The next day the Americans came to life as if they were new men,
just created in a new world. And the people of the town came to life...

excitement, change, something to look forward to at last! A new flag, *le drapeau étoilé*, floated along with the tricolour in the square. At sunset the soldiers stood in formation behind it and sang 'The Star Spangled Banner' with uncovered heads. The old people watched them from the doorways. The Americans were the first to bring 'Madelon' to Beaufort. The fact that the village had never heard this song, that the children stood round begging for it, '*Chantez-vous la Madelon!*' made the soldiers realize how far and how long out of the world these villagers had been. The German occupation was like a deafness which nothing pierced but their own arrogant martial airs.

Before Claude was out of bed after his first long sleep, a runner arrived from Colonel Scott, notifying him that he was in charge of the Company until further orders. The German prisoners had buried their own dead and dug graves for the Americans before they were sent off to the rear. Claude and David were billeted at the edge of the town, with the woman who had given Captain Maxey his first information, when they marched in yesterday morning. Their hostess told them, at their mid-day breakfast, that the old dame who was shot in the square, and the little girl, were to be buried this afternoon. Claude decided that the Americans might as well have their funeral at the same time. He thought he would ask the priest to say a prayer at the graves, and he and David set off through the brilliant, rustling autumn sunshine to find the Curé's house. It was next the church, with a high-walled garden behind it. Over the bell-pull in the outer wall was a card on which was written, '*Tirez fort.*'

The priest himself came out to them, an old man who seemed weak like his doorbell. He stood in his black cap, holding his hands against his breast to keep them from shaking, and looked very old indeed, – broken, hopeless, as if he were sick of this world and done with it. Nowhere in France had Claude seen a face so sad as his. Yes, he would say a prayer. It was better to have Christian burial, and they were far from home, poor fellows! David asked him whether the German rule had been very oppressive, but the old man did not answer clearly, and his hands began to shake so uncontrollably over his cassock that they went away to spare him embarrassment.

'He seems a little gone in the head, don't you think?' Claude remarked.

'I suppose the war has used him up. How can he celebrate mass when his hands quiver so?' As they crossed the church steps, David touched Claude's arm and pointed into the square. 'Look, every doughboy has a girl already! Some of them have trotted out fatigue caps! I supposed they'd thrown them all away!'

Those who had no caps stood with their helmets under their arms, in attitudes of exaggerated gallantry, talking to the women, – who seemed all to have errands abroad. Some of them let the boys carry their baskets. One soldier was giving a delighted little girl a ride on his back.

After the funeral every man in the Company found some sympathetic woman to talk to about his fallen comrades. All the garden flowers and bead wreaths in Beaufort had been carried out and put on the American graves. When the squad fired over them and the bugle sounded, the girls and their mothers wept. Poor Willy Katz, for instance, could never have had such a funeral in South Omaha.

The next night the soldiers began teaching the girls to dance the 'Pas Seul' and the 'Fausse Trot.' They had found an old violin in the town; and Oscar, the Swede, scraped away on it. They danced every evening. Claude saw that a good deal was going on, and he lectured his men at parade. But he realized that he might as well scold at the sparrows. Here was a village with several hundred women, and only the grandmothers had husbands. All the men were in the army; hadn't even been home on leave since the Germans first took the place. The girls had been shut up for four years with young men who incessantly coveted them, and whom they must constantly outwit. The situation had been intolerable – and prolonged. The Americans found themselves in the position of Adam in the garden.

'Did you know, sir,' said Bert Fuller breathlessly as he overtook Claude in the street after parade, 'that these lovely girls had to go out in the fields and work, raising things for those dirty pigs to eat? Yes, sir, had to work in the fields, under German sentinels; marched out in the morning and back at night like convicts! It's sure up to us to give them a good time now.'

One couldn't walk out of an evening without meeting loitering couples in the dusky streets and lanes. The boys had lost all their bashfulness about trying to speak French. They declared they could get along in France with three verbs, and all, happily, in the first conjugation: *manger, aimer, payer*, – quite enough! They called Beaufort 'our town,' and they were called 'our Americans.' They were going to come back after the war, and marry the girls, and put in waterworks!

'*Chez-moi*, sir!' Bill Gates called to Claude, saluting with a bloody hand, as he stood skinning rabbits before the door of his billet. 'Bunny casualties are heavy in town this week!'

'You know, Wheeler,' David remarked one morning as they were shaving, 'I think Maxey would come back here on one leg if he knew about these excursions into the forest after mushrooms.'

'Maybe.'

'Aren't you going to put a stop to them?'

'Not I!' Claude jerked, setting the corners of his mouth grimly. 'If the girls, or their people, make complaint to me, I'll interfere. Not otherwise. I've thought the matter over.'

'Oh, the girls—' David laughed softly. 'Well, it's something to acquire a taste for mushrooms. They don't get them at home, do they?'

★

When, after eight days, the Americans had orders to march, there was mourning in every house. On their last night in town, the officers received pressing invitations to the dance in the square. Claude went for a few moments, and looked on. David was dancing every dance, but Hicks was nowhere to be seen. The poor fellow had been out of everything. Claude went over to the church to see whether he might be moping in the graveyard.

There, as he walked about, Claude stopped to look at a grave that stood off by itself, under a privet hedge, with withered leaves and a little French flag on it. The old woman with whom they stayed had told them the story of this grave.

The Curé's niece was buried there. She was the prettiest girl in Beaufort, it seemed, and she had a love affair with a German officer and disgraced the town. He was a young Bavarian, quartered with this same old woman who told them the story, and she said he was a nice boy, handsome and gentle, and used to sit up half the night in the garden with his head in his hands – homesick, lovesick. He was always after this Marie Louise; never pressed her, but was always there, grew up out of the ground under her feet, the old woman said. The girl hated Germans, like all the rest, and flouted him. He was sent to the front. Then he came back, sick and almost deaf, after one of the slaughters at Verdun, and stayed a long while. That spring a story got about that some woman met him at night in the German graveyard. They had taken the land behind the church for their cemetery, and it joined the wall of the Curé's garden. When the women went out into the fields to plant the crops, Marie Louise used to slip away from the others and meet her Bavarian in the forest. The girls were sure of it now; and they treated her with disdain. But nobody was brave enough to say anything to the Curé. One day, when she was with her Bavarian in the wood, she snatched up his revolver from the ground and shot herself. She was a Frenchwoman at heart, their hostess said.

'And the Bavarian?' Claude asked David later. The story had become so complicated he could not follow it.

'He justified her, and promptly. He took the same pistol and shot himself through the temples. His orderly, stationed at the edge of the thicket to keep watch, heard the first shot and ran toward them. He saw the officer take up the smoking pistol and turn it on himself. But the Kommandant couldn't believe that one of his officers had so much feeling. He held an *enquête,* dragged the girl's mother and uncle into court, and tried to establish that they were in conspiracy with her to seduce and murder a German officer. The orderly was made to tell the whole story; how and where they began to meet. Though he wasn't very delicate about the details he divulged, he stuck to his statement that he saw Lieutenant Muller shoot himself with his own hand, and the Kommandant failed to prove his case. The old Curé had known nothing of all this until he heard it aired in the military court. Marie Louise had lived in his house since she was a child, and was like his daughter. He had a stroke or something, and has been like this ever since. The girl's friends forgave her, and when she was buried off alone by the hedge, they began to take flowers to her grave. The Kommandant put up an *affiche* on the hedge, forbidding any one to decorate the grave. Apparently, nothing during the German occupation stirred up more feeling than poor Marie Louise.'

It would stir anybody, Claude reflected. There was her lonely little grave, the shadow of the privet hedge falling across it. There, at the foot of the Curé's garden, was the German cemetery, with heavy cement crosses, – some of them with long inscriptions; lines from their poets, and couplets from old hymns. Lieutenant Muller was there somewhere, probably. Strange, how their story stood out in a world of suffering. That was a kind of misery he hadn't happened to think of before; but the same thing must have occurred again and again in the occupied territory. He would never forget the Curé's hands, his dim, suffering eyes.

Claude recognized David crossing the pavement in front of the church, and went back to meet him.

'Hello! I mistook you for Hicks at first. I thought he might be out here.' David sat down on the steps and lit a cigarette.

'So did I. I came out to look for him.'

'Oh, I expect he's found some shoulder to cry on. Do you realize, Claude, you and I are the only men in the Company who haven't got engaged? Some of the married men have got engaged twice. It's a good thing we're pulling out, or we'd have banns and a bunch of christenings to look after.'

'All the same,' murmured Claude, 'I like the women of this country, as far as I've seen them.' While they sat smoking in silence, his mind went back to the quiet scene he had watched on the steps of that other church, on his first night in France; the country girl in the moonlight, bending over her sick soldier.

When they walked back across the square, over the crackling leaves, the dance was breaking up. Oscar was playing 'Home, Sweet Home,' for the last waltz.

'*Le dernier baiser*,' said David. 'Well, tomorrow we'll be gone, and the chances are we won't come back this way.'

Willa Cather was born in Virginia in 1873 and died in New York in 1947. This piece is taken from *One of Ours*, which was published in 1922 and won the Pulitzer Prize the following year. When Willa was ten, the family moved to Nebraska, and it was there that she found the themes that were to inspire her best work, including the *Prairie Trilogy* – *O Pioneers*, *The Song of the Lark* and *My Antonia* – and *One of Ours*. This last is the story of Charles Wheeler, a Nebraska man, who enlists when the USA joins the war and finds a meaning to his life on the battlefields of Europe: it is here that he feels for the first time that he matters. *One of Ours* contains powerful battle scenes but also scenes that show great sympathy for those who remained behind on the home front, whose lives were overwhelmed by the consequences of the fighting.

IRENE RATHBONE

WHO DIES IF ENGLAND LIVES?

from *We that Were Young*

T HAT EVENING AFTER SUPPER Joan went straight to her room, and sat
for a long time in her kimono by the open window. There wasn't a
breath of air.

She had been kept so hard at it for the past few weeks that she had
scarcely been beyond the hospital grounds; in her rare off hours she had
felt too bone-weary to do anything but lie reading in the rest-room or on
the grass outside. The last time she had seen Pamela – some time in June
– the girl had been like a dancing fairy over her engagement. Joan could
see her now, standing in a patch of sunlight in Lady Butler's little drawing-
room, exclaiming jubilantly: 'I'm done for, Joan! I'm completely done
for!' and contrasted that radiant creature with the tight-lipped figure of
this afternoon – the gold in her all turned to iron, the song to silence.

What was the use of winning the war, Joan cried to herself in sudden
despair, if none of the men who won it were to live? The papers were
for ever quoting 'Who dies if England lives?' But after all what was
England? The old men who sat at home, and in clubs, and gloatingly
discussed the war? The bustling business men who thought they ran it?
The women with aching hearts? Or the young manhood of the nation
– that part of the nation that should be working, mating, begetting, but
which now was being cut down? There was no question – the last. And
in a year or two there'd be no 'England.'

She thought of Colin, Philip, and other friends, not seen for so long, and now in hourly danger. Colin's letters had been very scrappy of late. She thought of a second cousin of hers, killed in the fighting round La Boiselle. She thought of her cousin Jack lying badly wounded at Boulogne. The waste, the waste of it all!

Sighing, she drew her writing-pad towards her. Might as well do something. Better to write than to think.

Write to Jack. Write to Betty to go and look up Jack in hospital. Write, too, to Barbara Frewen, who had recently gone over there to nurse. She read through again Barbara's last two letters.

The first was written from Sussex, early in July. 'We really do seem to be getting a move on at last, and the guns for the past ten days have been perfectly appalling – booming incessantly, day and night. It has been like one huge throb through all the air. The windows rattle all the time, and even the china on the washstands. One daren't think what it must be like out there.'

The second was from No. 14 Stationary, Wimereux, and had come last week. 'Most extraordinary luck getting here, for I never even asked for France. The hospital is right on the sea, as you know. We work in tents and huts which are delightfully airy and bright. Of course it's within easy reach of Betty and all of them, and I've already paid several visits to the Alexandra, and also to the dear old Connaught (which, my dear, does not look so nice as in our day!). Yesterday I spent a heavenly afternoon in the woods at Hardelot, and how I thought of you! I could just see you there sitting on the ramparts, surrounded with poetry-books! I am much more at peace in my mind now that I am nursing, but also I shall never like the work so much. That time with the Y.M.C.A. was a beautiful time, all so sunny and romantic somehow. But it was a very easy life, we could do practically what we liked, and we felt – didn't we? – that it was too pleasant. How is your friend, that boy whom I sent you out for a walk with from Ostrohove? My Sam is somewhere behind the lines at the moment, thank heaven – at one of those instruction schools. He hopes to come up and see me at Boulogne before long.'

Yes, it was all sunny and romantic! thought Joan, looking back on those days, already so long ago. She envied Barbara being in dear

Boulogne again – even though it was as a V.A.D., and not as a Y.M. worker.

It was nearly midnight when she finished writing to her various friends (the letter to Pamela was the most exhausting of all); and when, dazed with fatigue, she dropped into bed, the last thing that her sleepy eyes beheld was her apron, with its red cross, hanging over the back of the chair. Symbol of servitude. For how many months, for how many years, would she, and her kind, be wearing uniform?

★

Miss Leather was right. Joan never heard another word from Matron about the Richardson business; and her early indignation died down as she realised that Matron had no more meant the insulting things she had said to her than a sergeant-major meant the things he roared out when he strafed a Tommy. She had employed a drastic form of utterance to express disapprobation of a small lapse, and that was all there was to it.

And so, when the time came, Joan signed her death-warrant (as the V.A.D.s called it) without let or hindrance, and thankfully bound herself to serve at the 1st London for the next six months, at a salary of £20 a year.

But that the spirit of the hospital – as far as the regular staff went – was an unimaginative and flinty one was shown a few weeks later by an event which shook the whole community.

Working with Phipps in Sister Grundle's ward was a girl called O'Reilly – a good-natured creature, a little slow and vague, but willing. Somehow or other, in spite of the warm weather, O'Reilly had managed to catch a very bad cold. She took no notice of it at first, but after a time it went on to her chest, and she had prolonged fits of coughing. As the cough kept her awake for hours at night, and was a source of intense irritation to Sister Grundle by day, O'Reilly suggested that she had perhaps better 'go sick.' Sister Grundle glared at her opprobriously, for a moment, over a gigantic bosom, then took her temperature, saw that it was a few points above normal, and, more to be rid of her than for any humanitarian reason, dispatched her to Matron.

Matron received her in the stony manner which was characteristic of her, and laid a couple of fingers on the girl's pulse.

'There's nothing the matter with you at all, Nurse,' she snapped. 'Many people have a slight cough without making a fuss of this sort. What you want is a little hard work. You V.A.D.s are far too easily sorry for yourselves. Go back to your ward.'

And back O'Reilly went, swearing to herself that nothing in heaven or earth would induce her ever to report sick again.

'And she's getting worse and worse,' declared Phipps to the others at night. 'Soon she'll scarcely be able to crawl round the ward. She refuses to take her own temperature – says it would be useless. I keep pressing aspirins and cough lozenges on her, but—'

There came a point when O'Reilly's condition could no longer be ignored. Having almost collapsed one morning, she was sent to the sick-room at the top of the main building and put instantly to bed. It was found that she had bronchial pneumonia. From then onwards she received the best attention which the hospital could provide. But by then it was too late.

Everyone went about, as it were, on tip-toe. 'How is O'Reilly?' would be asked in frightened whispers – even by those who had only known the girl by sight. Guarded reports came from the sick-room. Nothing could be definitely ascertained. At mealtimes Matron's face was scanned by hundreds of young eyes, but it preserved its nutshell impenetrability.

Then it was rumoured that O'Reilly had become unconscious; then that her people had been sent for; then that she was a little better and was being kept alive on oxygen and brandy.

By the time that her parents had been able to get over from Ireland the girl was dead.

O'Reilly had not been a particularly popular or a particularly significant member of the community of the 1st London, but thenceforward she became a symbol and a martyr. For days feeling ran high among those who knew the facts about her; but Phipps's fury of indignation against Matron was mingled with remorse that she herself had not been able to do more to help the girl.

Outwardly, of course, the higher authorities proceeded on their way as before, but their attitude to V.A.D.s as malingerers underwent a profound change. In dying poor O'Reilly had done more for her companions than ever she had done by living.

★

The stifling August days wore through, and now that work was less of a nightmare, Joan, in her off hours, used to take a bus and go into London.

She saw Pamela twice, but was unable to dissuade her friend from the munitions scheme; and when, soon afterwards, Pamela left Bruton Street and went to work in some awful factory out at Willesden, Joan realised that henceforward meetings would be impossible.

On ordinary days it was not worth while to go as far as Hampstead, but on her 'half-day' a week (from 2 p.m. to 10 p.m.) it was very pleasant to be at home, to lie curled on the old chintz-covered sofa in the drawing room, to chat to Aunt Florence, to hear news of relations, and of how Jimmy was getting on in the country where he was 'cramming' with three friends. Not so pleasant to trek back after dinner (a little tug at the heart) by tube and bus to dreary Camberwell – allowing just enough time to arrive at the hostel before Sister Ansdell locked up for the night.

Sometimes, instead of going home, Joan would divide her 'half-day' between different friends – tea-ing at one house, dining at another; or else go to a matinee with an officer on leave, or to dinner with him at a restaurant. Swift delightful patches of another sort of life, taking the smell of lysol and of wounds from the nostrils.

These London expeditions of Joan's earned her, from her roommates, the reputation of living 'a double life.' One of them, especially, a kindly individual called Gower with a long nose and a pronounced cockney accent, thought her almost paralysingly energetic. Gower herself seldom went beyond the hospital grounds.

'You'll come to a bad end, Seddon,' she used to say to Joan through the curtains of her cubicle at night. 'Can't live the double life, you know – end by wearing yourself out!' (she pronounced it 'ay-out').

'Out on the tiles again, Seddon?' she would call, as Joan came in, by the skin of her teeth, at ten o'clock from a 'half-day.' And Joan would laugh at the stock joke, and keep up the fiction of secret dissipations.

★

September sailed in on the calm glory of a full moon.

On the second night, at about twelve o'clock, Joan was awakened from fathom-deep sleep by the murmur of voices in the bedroom. Reluctantly she opened an eye, and saw, outlined against the window, the heads of the three other V.A.D.s. But what struck through her half-consciousness as an odd fact was that their heads were silhouetted against crimson. Was it morning, she wondered vaguely, or was there a fire?

'Get up, Seddon – air raid!' she heard Gower's voice somewhere in the darkness.

'Air raid?' grunted Joan.

'Yes – Zeppelin! You'll probably see it if you go to the window. Slip on your shoes and your coat, and you'd better put a few 'air-pins in your pocket – you never know.'

Gower spoke in matter-of-fact tones, but Joan couldn't for the life of her see the necessity for putting hair-pins into her coat pocket. She knew she was excessively sleepy, and not in a condition to reason about anything – but hairpins? She saw a vision of herself with Gower, Sister Ansdell, and the rest, wandering about outside, screwing up their hair in an attempt at decency while dodging German bombs. Then she dropped off.

Voices broke in on her again. 'There it is! There it is!' This time she roused herself fully, scrambled out of bed, and went to the window. An extraordinary spectacle met her eyes. Far up in a murky pink sky gleamed a small silver cigar, and near it hovered, dancingly, a fire-fly. For a moment these two objects kept at an equal distance from one another, then merged, and there was a burst of flames. A roar, as from the whole of London, went up; and the flaming cigar sank through the sky and disappeared beyond the trees.

The whole thing had been so unexpected, so eerie, and Joan had been so far from wide awake that she could never clearly remember afterwards what she had imagined, and what she had really seen and heard.

For instance, why had the sky appeared red against the window-panes when first she woke – for that was surely before the Zeppelin caught fire? And that dull terrifying roar – had it actually come from the throats of thousands of London onlookers miles away, or only from a few folk on Denmark Hill? All was confused. But printed vividly on her brain for ever was the picture of that small silver cigar and the dancing fire-fly.

Later she learnt – as did all the world – that the German military air-ship, S.L. 11, had been attacked by Lieut. Leaf Robinson, and had fallen, a burning mass, near Cuffley, Middlesex. It was considered that London had been saved by the young man's deed, and he was awarded the V.C.

'Can't 'elp being sorry for them pore burnt Germans,' remarked one of the charwomen, who scrubbed the ward-floor, to Joan. 'Mothers' sons every one of 'em. And coming by night all that way from their 'omes too, up in the air.'

This was so concise an expression of the haunting thoughts which Joan had been trying to hold at bay that she shuddered. It could not have been better put: 'Mothers' sons every one of 'em.' An instant's imagination as to what that Zeppelin crew must have been feeling as their machine caught fire would have checked the roar which had greeted its destruction.

And apart from this, although it was true that Robinson had done a very gallant thing, was there not, Joan asked herself, something distasteful in the frantic eagerness with which he had been praised and decorated? – something that savoured of smug self-congratulation on the part of the city at its escape? Every day, in the skies of France, deeds as gallant were being performed and going unrewarded; every day the stolid soldiers in the trenches were unostentatiously 'saving London.' But for once the civilian population had really felt itself to be in danger, had actually seen itself defended, and had gone mad with gratitude.

Irene Rathbone was born in 1892. Before the war she pursued a theatrical career and was a dedicated suffragist. During the war, she worked as a nurse in hospitals in England and as a VAD (Volunteer Aid Detachment) nurse in France. Written in 1930, *We that Were Young* is an autobiographical novel that reflects those experiences and poignantly conveys how for a whole generation the war was a time of tragedy but also of exhilarating change:

> 'How you must have cursed the war,' murmured Molly.
>
> 'We did – we did. But looking back, now, I think we loved it too. Oh, it's so difficult to explain… It was our war, you see. And although it was every-dayish at the time, and we were so sickened with it, it seems now to have a sort of ghastly glamour.'

But as more and more injured and maimed soldiers pass through the rest camps, the exhilaration of the women gives way to a powerful sense of injustice. After the publication of *We that Were Young*, Rathbone became more radical – she was a committed pacifist, an anti-fascist and a supporter of Republican Spain. *They Call it Peace*, written in 1936, reflects these views. Irene Rathbone died in Oxford in 1980.

ROSE MACAULAY

EVENING AT VIOLETTE

from *Non-Combatants and Others*

After supper Kate got out the good coffee cups, and they waited for the Vinneys. Kate was rather pink, and wore a severe blouse, in which she looked plain; it was a mortification she thought she ought to practise when the Vinneys came. Evie was skilfully altering a hat. Alix made a pen-and-ink sketch of her as she bent over it.

Mrs Frampton knitted a sock. The *Evening Thrill* came in, and Kate opened it, for Mrs Frampton liked to hear tit-bits of news while she worked.

'Stories impossible to doubt,' read Kate, in her prim, precise voice, 'reach us continually of atrocities practised by the enemy...' She read several, unsuitable for these pages. Mrs Frampton clicked horror with her tongue. The papers she took in were rich in such stories. As it was impossible to doubt them, she did not try. Possibly they gave life a certain dreadful savour.

'To think of the march of civilisation, and this still going on,' Mrs Frampton commented. 'I'm sure any one would think they'd be ashamed.'

Kate said, with playful acidity – (Kate had reached what with many is a playful age), 'Thank you, Alix. Thank you ever so much, Alix, for getting between me and the lamp.' Alix moved, her attempt foiled.

Kate read next the letter of a private soldier at the front. 'The Boches are all cowards. They can't stand against our boys. They fly like rabbits when we charge with the bayonet. You should hear them squeal, like so many pigs. There's not a German private in the army that wants to fight. The officers have to keep flogging them on the whole time.'

'Poor things, I'm sure one can't but be sorry for them,' said Mrs Frampton. 'Knit two and make one, purl two, slip one, pass the slipped one over, drop four and knit six.' (Or anyhow, something of that sort, for she had got to the heel, as one unfortunately at last must.)

'It's wonderful how long the war goes on, since all the Germans are like that,' said Kate, without conscious irony, as she took up her own knitting. Hers was a body-belt. 'I believe this new wool is different from the last. Somewhat stringier, it seems. Brown will have to take it back, if it is.'

'I say, just fancy,' said Evie, 'those sequin tunics at B & H's have come down to seven and eleven three. I think I could rise to that, even in war time.'

The war mainly affected Evie by reducing the demand for hats, and consequently lowering the salary she received at the exclusive and lady-like milliner's where she worked.

As she spoke she caught sight of her threequarter likeness as etched by Alix.

'Goodness gracious,' she commented. 'You've made me look anything on earth! I mayn't be much, but I hope I'm not that sort of freak.'

'It's very good,' said Alix complacently. 'Rather particularly good. I shall take it to the School on Monday and show it to Mr Bendish.'

'It may be good,' said Evie, 'since you say so. All I say is, it isn't me. It's more like some wild woman out of a caravan. Don't you go telling people it's me, or they'll be coming to shut me up. There's the bell; that's them.'

The Vinney party arrived. It consisted of Mr Vincent Vinney, a bright young solicitor of twenty-eight; his lately acquired wife, a pretty girl who laughed when he was witty, which was often; his young brother Sidney, a stout, merry youth of nineteen, a bank clerk; and their cousin Miss Simon, the fat girl in the sailor blouse, which was, it seemed, her evening toilette also. (In case some should blame the Vinney brothers for not taking an active part in the war, it may be remarked that the elder supported a wife and the younger a mother, that they represented a class which, for several good reasons, produces fewer soldiers than any other, and that they both belonged to the Clerks' Drill Corps, and wore several flags on their bicycles. And young Mrs Vinney belonged to a Voluntary Aid Detachment, not at present in working.)

They came in with the latest news. The British had been driven back out of a thousand yards of trench they had taken. They hadn't enough ammunition.

'Well,' said Mrs Frampton, knitting, and really more interested in her heel than in the fortunes of war, 'it's all very dreadful to think of. But I suppose we must leave it in the hands of the Almighty, who always moves in a mysterious way.'

(Mrs Frampton had been brought up evangelically, and so mentioned the Almighty more casually than Kate, who was High, thought fit.)

'Well, what I say is,' said young Mrs Vinney, who was of a cheerful habit, 'it's not a bit of use being depressed by the news, because no one can ever tell if it's true or not. It's all from that Bureau, and we all know what they are. Why, they said there weren't any Russians in England, when every one knew there were crowds, and they always say the Zepp. raids don't do any damage to factories and arsenals, and every one knows they do. They don't seem to mind *what* they say.'

'Well, for my part,' Evie said, 'I don't see why we shouldn't all be as chirpy as we can. We can't *help* by being glum, can we?'

'That's just it,' said Mrs Vinney. 'Now, there's the theatre. Of course, you know, Vin and I wouldn't go to anything really *festive* just now, like the *Girl on the Garden Wall,* but I'm not ashamed to say we did go to the *Man Who Stayed Behind.*'

'Why wouldn't you go to anything really festive?' Alix asked, curious as to the psychology of this position.

Mrs Vinney looked round for sympathy.

'Why, what a question! It's not the moment, of course. One wouldn't *like* to. You wouldn't, would you?'

'Oh, me. I'd go to anything I thought would amuse me.'

'Well,' Mrs Vinney decided, 'I suppose you and I aren't a bit alike. I just couldn't, and there it is. I dare say it's all my silliness. But with the men out there in such danger, and laying down their lives the way they're doing… well, I *couldn't* sit and look at the *Girl on the Garden Wall,* not if I had a stall free. The way I see it is, the men are fighting for us women, and where should we be but for them, and the least we can do is not to forget all about them, seeing gay musical plays. The way I'm made, I suppose, and I don't pretend to judge for others.'

'It's all a question of taste and feeling,' Kate pronounced absently, more interested in a new stitch she was introducing into her body-belt.

The fat dark girl, Miss Simon, came in on the mention of women. It was her subject.

'Women's work in war time is every bit as important as men's, that's what I say; only they don't get the glory.'

Mrs Vinney giggled and looked at the others.

'Now Rachel's off again. She's a caution when she gets on the woman question. She spent most of her time in Holloway in the old days, didn't you, dear?'

'She thinks she ought to have the vote,' Sid Vinney explained to Alix in a whisper. Alix, who had hitherto moved in circles where every one thought, as a matter of course, that they ought to have the vote, disappointed him by her lack of spontaneous mirth.

Miss Simon was inquiring, undeterred by these comments, 'Who keeps the country at home going while the men are at the war? Who brings up the families? Who nurses the soldiers? What do women get out of a war, ever?'

'The salvation of their country, Miss Simon,' said Mrs Frampton, 'won for them by brave men.'

'After all,' said Sid, 'the women can't *fight,* you know. They can't *fight* for their country.'

Miss Simon regarded him with scorn.

'How much are you fighting for your country, I'd like to know?'

'One for you, Sid,' said Evie cheerily, ignoring Sid's aggrieved, 'Well, you know I can't leave mother.'

'And fighting isn't everything,' Miss Simon went on, 'and war time isn't everything. There's women's work in peace time. What about Octavia Wills that did so much for housing? Wasn't *she* helping her country? And, for war work, what price Florence Nightingale? What would the country have done without *her*, and what did she get out of all she did?'

Mrs Frampton, who had not read the life of that strong-minded person, but cherished a mid-Victorian vision of a lady with a lamp, sounder in the heart than in the head, said, 'She kept her place as a woman, Miss Simon.'

Evie, who was not listening much, finding the subject tedious, put in vaguely, 'After all, when it comes to fighting, we are left in the lurch, aren't we?'

Sid said, 'Oh dear no, Miss Evie. What price Christabel and Co.? They ought to have had the iron cross all round, the militants ought. They did more to earn it than the Huns ever did.'

'Cheap sarcasm,' said Miss Simon, 'is no argument. And I don't blame any woman for using what means she's got. There are times when a woman's got to forget herself.'

Kate said, 'I don't think a woman's ever got to forget herself,' and there was a murmur of applause. Alix giggled. She wondered if social evenings at Violette were often like this.

'You don't understand,' said the roundfaced girl helplessly. '*You* may be all right, in your station of life, but you've got to look at other women – the poor. We've got to do something about the poor. The vote would help us.'

'There have always,' said Mrs Frampton, 'been the poor, and there always will be.'

'That's just why,' suggested Alix, momentarily joining in, 'it might be worth while to do something about them.' Miss Simon looked at her in sudden gratitude; she had a misplaced and soon-quenched hope that this seemingly indifferent and amused girl might prove an ally.

Kate said, placidly, 'Well, they say that if you were to take a lot of men and women and give them all the same money, they'd all be quite different again to-morrow...'

Mrs Frampton added that she went by the Bible. 'The poor ye shall have always with you.'

'Mrs Frampton, it doesn't say that. And even if it did, well, it's as Miss

Sandomir says, it's all the more reason for thinking about them. Anyhow, you can't take the Bible that way; it's nothing to *do* with it.'

'It's the plain word of God, and that's sufficient for me,' said Mrs Frampton repressively.

Vincent Vinney, tired of the poor, who are indeed exhausting, regarded in the mass as a subject for contemplation, brought the discussion back to women.

'What I'd like to know is, where is a woman to get her knowledge from, if she's to help in public affairs? A man can pick up things at his work and his club, but a woman working in the house all day has no time even to read the papers. And if she did, her husband wouldn't like her to start having opinions, perhaps different to his. There are far too many divorces and separations already because husbands and wives go different ways, and it would be worse than ever. Eh, Flossie?'

Mrs Frampton said, 'We heard of a woman only last month who went out to a public meeting – something about foreign politics, I think it was – and her baby fell on to the fire and was burnt to a cinder, poor little love.'

'Well, she might just as likely have been going out shopping.'

'But she wasn't,' said Kate conclusively.

'I don't think,' said Mrs Frampton, 'that a woman desires any more than her home and her husband and children, if she's a proper woman.'

Evie's contribution was, 'Well, I must say I do prefer men to girls, and I don't mind saying so.'

Sid's was, 'I heard of a man whose wife took to talking about politics, and he hung his coat to one peg in her wardrobe and his trousers to another, and he said, "Now, Eliza, which will you wear?"'

It was apparently the combination of this anecdote and Evie's remark before it that broke Miss Simon down. She suddenly collapsed into indignant tears. Every one was uncomfortable. Mrs Frampton said kindly, 'Come, come, my dear, it's only talk. It isn't worth crying about, I'm sure, with so many real troubles in the world just now.'

'You won't see,' sobbed Miss Simon, who looked particularly plain when crying. 'You none of you see. Except her,' – she indicated Alix – 'and she won't talk; she only smiles to herself at all of us. You tell silly tales, and you say silly things, and you think you've scored but you haven't. It isn't *argument,* that you like men more than women or women more than men. And that man married to Eliza was an idiot, and not a bit funny or clever, and you all think he scored over her.'

'Well, really,' said Sid, and grinned sheepishly at the others.

Kate had fetched a glass of water. 'Drink some,' she said kindly. 'It'll make you feel better.' But Miss Simon pushed it aside and mopped her eyes and blew her nose and pulled herself together.

★

'Fancy crying before every one,' thought Evie. 'And just from being in a passion about getting the worst of it in talk. She is a specimen.'

'The boys shouldn't draw Rachel on to make such a silly of herself,' thought young Mrs Vinney.

'Poor girl, she must have been working too hard, she's quite hysterical,' thought Mrs Frampton.

'Having her staying with them must draw Vin and Floss very close together,' thought Kate, who had loved Vin long before Floss met him.

'We shan't have any more fun out of this evening; we'll go home,' thought Vincent, and glanced at his wife.

'What a difference between one girl and another,' thought Sid, and gazed at Evie.

'I wonder if many people are like these,' thought Alix, speculating. Were discussions at Violette, discussions in all the thousands of Violettes, always like this? Not argument, not ideas, not facts. Merely statements, quotations rather, of hackneyed and outworn sentiments, prejudices second-hand, yet indomitable, unassailable, undying, and the relation of stories, without relevance or force, and (but this much more rarely, surely) a burst of bitterness and emotion to wind it all up. Curious. Rachel Simon, like the rest, was stupid and ignorant, her brain a chaos of half-assimilated, inaccurate facts (she said Wills when she meant Hill) and crude sentiments. She seemed to belong, oddly, to an outworn age (the late eighties, was it? Alix wasn't old enough to know). But Alix was sorry for her, remembering the look in her face when they had each in turn dealt her a finishing blow. Alix rather wished Evie hadn't made that idiotic remark about men and girls; wished Mrs Frampton hadn't talked of proper women; wished Kate hadn't said 'But she wasn't'; even wished she herself had joined in a little. Only it was all too inane.

★

To change the subject Vincent Vinney said they had collared another German baker spy down in Camberwell.

'These bakers,' said Mrs Frampton, 'do seem to be dreadful people. We've left off taking our Hovis loaf, since they found that wireless in Camberwell the other day.'

'You can't be too careful, can you?' said Mrs Vinney. 'For my part I'd like to see every German in England shut up in gaol for a life-sentence. But we must be trotting, Mrs Frampton, or we shall miss our beauty-sleep. Good-night; we've enjoyed the evening awfully. Oh, Evie, I've got those blouse patterns from Harrod's; can you come round to-morrow afternoon and help me choose? Come early and stay to tea. You too, Kate, won't you? You are a girl; you never come when I ask you.'

Kate looked uncomfortable, and helped Miss Simon (now composed, but looking plainer than ever with her red eyes and nose) into her coat. To see the Vinneys together by their own fireside was rather more than Kate could bear, though she had a good deal of stolid outward endurance. Her hands shook as she handled the ugly green coat. She wanted to avoid shaking hands with the Vinneys, but she could not. The familiar physical thrill ran through her at Vincent's hearty clasp, and left her limp.

'I'm afraid it's commencing to rain,' said Kate.

'Good-night all,' said Mrs Frampton. 'We've had quite a little discussion, haven't we? I'm sure one ought to talk things out sometimes, it improves the mind. Now I do hope you won't all get wet. You must take our umbrellas.'

∽

Rose Macaulay was born in Rugby in 1881. At the beginning of the war, she worked in the British Government Propaganda Department. In May 1915

Macaulay went to work as a Volunteer Aid Detachment (VAD) nurse at a military convalescent hospital near Cambridge. *Non-Combatants and Others*, from which this extract is taken, was published in 1916 and is an autobiographical account of her time spent as a VAD nurse. Dedicated to 'my brother and other combatants' the book is a critical portrayal of a middle England self-glorifying in its recognition of the bravery and sacrifice of its soldiers. During the war relations between women and men changed. The women, many of whom lost loved ones at the front, reacted to the cynicism and indifference that prevailed at home. They put their energy and enthusiasm into the campaign for the vote, for equality and for peace. After the war Rose Macaulay became a sponsor of the Peace Pledge Union, touring the country and using, whenever possible, the BBC to get the pacifist message across. During the Blitz, her London apartment was totally destroyed and she had to rebuild her life and library from scratch. Her best-known novel, *The Towers of Trebizond*, was published in 1956. Rose Macaulay died in 1958.

JOSEP PLA

VERITABLE EQUINE
ITEMS OF DENTISTRY

from *The Grey Notebook*

translated by Peter Bush

6 JULY. The war is about to end. Germany is responding like a cornered animal. Thousands of Americans are landing in Bordeaux. All the arrogance of the early years of the war has evaporated like a puff of smoke. The Germanophiles have shut up. The Kaiser's boasting now begins to look absurd and grotesquely flamboyant. The war will end in a matter of weeks…

Mossèn Così bumps into Grandmother Marieta in the street. Mossèn Così, the parish sacristan, cultivates a plot of land he rents from Grandmother Marieta. He says: 'Just you see, Mrs. Marieta, just you see! England will win again! We had such high hopes and all dashed to the ground! The Protestants are going to win again, the simpletons who believe in a free conscience… What will ever become of us, Mrs. Marieta? The future looks very black, very black indeed… We would have been so happy with the order the Germans would have established! Now, to be frank, I don't know whether I will be able to pay you your rent…'

'What was that?' Grandmother Marieta asks quickly and energetically. 'Are you saying you won't pay me my rent because England will win the war? What kind of excuse is that, Mossèn Emili? Have you gone mad? If you don't pay the rent by St. Michael's day, I assure you I will send you packing… Whatever *has* got into you?'

Reactionaries in our country have always and will always be Germanophiles. Their *bête noire* will always be England. And that is because of what Mossèn Così was saying a moment ago, because England embodies the spirit of free conscience. This is the perennial complaint. Those who claim the preferences of these people are incoherent because Germany is as Protestant as England have got it wrong. There is no incoherence whatsoever, quite the contrary: they grasped the issue perfectly… They know that Protestantism in Germany is quite innocuous. Let's be absolutely clear: German Protestantism counts for nothing when compared with the German military spirit of authoritarianism and subordination. And it is this spirit of Germany that fascinates them. They know that German Protestantism has no punch and literally counts for zero in comparison to this military spirit. And they are quite right. Germany is a country where authority is all-important, even though it is Protestant. England is *the* country of free conscience, even if it has such a poor army. Mossèn Così knows what he is talking about.

★

6 August. In Canadell there is a young lady who is so distinguished and posh that she calls a barometer a 'baarrometer'. On the other hand, fishermen call a thermometer a 'tarmometer'.

After reading Carles Riba's wonderful translation of *The Odyssey*, what one most misses, in the air along this coast, is the smell of grilled meat, hecatombs of oxen and calves spread on the pagan strands in the era of Homer. This scent makes you daydream. The smell of pinecones is very pleasant. The smell of shellfish is intense rather than substantial. The southwesterly wafts a briny smell. What we lack is the strong, manly smell of legs of beef being grilled. This country would be complete, would be sensational with this additional aroma.

I observe three or four fourteen- or fifteen-year-olds making holes in the walls of the wooden beach huts with their catapults so they can watch the ladies undressing when it is time for a swim. It is always amusing to compare perennial schoolboy tales with the touchstone of reality.

In my adolescent days we too made holes in beach hut walls.

However, it is evident that these lads work in a much more discreet, coordinated fashion. While one is twisting his catapult, two or three others provide a screen so nobody can suspect what he is about to do. In my day we were much more blasé. We made our holes out in the open and made no attempt to camouflage or keep secret what we were doing. No doubt about it: on this point, we won the day.

Because of the war there are a number of families in El Canadell who would normally live in France and Germany. They've taken refuge there while they wait for the war to end. These families have spent their lives doing business together, have always been acquainted and are related, be it closely or distantly. Now war has come between them. They have quarreled and spend their time scowling or grimacing at each other. When they meet on the beach or anywhere else, they create a spectacle, the amusing spectacle a head-on meeting of Marshal Hindenberg and General Foch would generate. They go rigid and defiant and only refrain from trading insults or coming to blows because too many people are around.

From one day to the next, Xènius now flourishes the idea of the moral unity of Europe. It is an admirable, sublime idea, but the situation in El Canadell shows how that moral unity has splintered. It is sad to have to acknowledge that the importance we accord to the most sublime, rapturous principles depends on circumstance. Man is no rational animal. He is a sensual beast.

★

22 *August*. Yesterday was a bad day. A light easterly wind (or wind from the eastern plains). Intermittent rain. Holidaymakers at a loss. Their houses are too small to withstand a cloudburst. The fishermen keep their clogs on all day. The novel phenomenon of clogs echoing along streets. Today people have returned to their espadrilles. Everything has dried out. A lively wind from the north and blue sky, and it's as if everything has resurrected anew. The chill in the air has gone. At any rate, the breeze is lighter, less invasive and the sultriness has gone too. The gentle wind is so pleasant it is like a splash of cool water on the cheek.

Hermós is fixing a trawl line in the shadow from a boat hauled up on the sand. I go over when he calls. He takes off his skipper's cap to reveal a sizeable whitish-yellow bald patch. Small, separate drops of sweat run down his pate. His face is ferocious and hairy with an anthropoid's flared nostrils and flabby lips.

'So he says the war is coming to an end?' he comments, knocking a fishhook on the rim of the boatside.

'Who does?'

'A gentleman wearing shoes, in the café…'

'Good heavens!'

After a long pause he declares: 'Anyway, it's bad news.'

'It's bad news to say the war is coming to an end?'

'Yes, wars produce fish.'

'Come on!'

'I'm telling you! The voice of experience. I've had a new net made for catching argentines. I'm about to dye it. If the war ends, you can say goodbye to the argentines. You won't see one for love or money… Fish like noise, buzz, cannon fire, disasters…'

Sometimes, contact with humanity can be depressing.

Hermós said this with eyes that saddened as he spoke: his eyes believed what he was saying. My depression deepened. I never know what to say in these circumstances.

Fishermen like to sing – particularly songs with a lyric the mouth can relish to tunes rocked by the roll of the waves.

A fisherman from Calella who is fond of singing says to me: 'I'd much rather be able to play the guitar than have a fancy mausoleum…'

When he speaks of his companion who he thinks is singing out of tune, he says: 'When he sings it's like a fire crackling…'

★

3 September. The war has lasted over four years – four years and one month to be precise. The number of dead, the amount of suffering, the volume of destruction and devastation the war has produced is beyond words. The arguments between Francophiles and Germanophiles have evaporated. It is impossible to sustain such tension for four years. People simply think about making money… and tomorrow is another day. If war wasn't ingrained with the arrant idiocy of cosmic phenomena, if war was triggered by the convergence of forthright, determined wills, it would shape and demonstrate human pettiness more clearly than any other act or argument – more than if a million tons of rocks were to crash on our backs. Human pettiness is indescribable. It makes absolutely no difference whether people do or don't think – whether they do or don't believe.

Watching how war impacts on certain individuals is an exercise in the observation of absurdity. A large number of *nouveaux riches* have had gold, silver or porcelain teeth and molars fitted – whole sets of teeth. Some have naturally horsy features. Others tend to create a similar effect by having huge teeth or dentures fitted that are quite out of proportion with the human mouth – veritable equine items of dentistry. In years to come, when these characters hear the name of Verdun, they will think: 'Ah, Verdun, Verdun, oh right, that was when they fitted me with those teeth that proved to be so heavy I had to have them out…'

Only a few days ago Mr. C. was telling me with candid glee: 'Well, surely you wouldn't want to deny this? We made a nice little pile out of this war… And you'll never guess what I told my good lady… You know, I told her: "Emília, we should have a water closet installed". "Are you really sure, Artur, are you sure…?" my wife replied. I felt she was being excessively cautious. A few words did the trick: I summoned the plumber, and he installed the W.C. in next to no time. You realize we couldn't go on like as before, not for a single day more. It has quite transformed our life, do you see?'

★

4 September. I bump into Marià Vinyas from Sant Feliu de Guíxols on carrer de Cavallers. He is perhaps the best performer of Chopin in these parts. Tall, elegant, urbane, smart and incisive, he still bears traces of style from the era of modernism. Like his close friend, Cambó, he wears his collar too high and too stiff. He tends to hold his back rather stiff to boot. Nonetheless, Vinyas is extremely witty and contemporary ways haven't dimmed this excellent side of him.

We talk about Juli Garreta, the composer of *sardanas*.

'You know, we are good friends. A delightful man. We began playing together. He is a man who knows nothing much with any precision or detail but endlessly fresh, dynamic music pours from him. He is a miracle of infallible spontaneity and the best musician we have at the moment and I think his best is yet to come. He is very fond of rain. When it rains, he *enjoys* it like a lunatic. He was telling me yesterday that what he would most like would be a house in a barren waste, an isolated farmstead, so he could repair there on rainy days – repair there in order to see and hear the rain...'

Vinyas pauses and adds: 'Last week he went to Roses on some business or other. He saw a local girl, probably a fishwife, beautiful, buxom and brimming with energy. He thought he'd seen a Greek marble statue and wrote a *sardana*. On his return to Sant Feliu he asked Rafael Pitxot to give it a Greek name, a dedication to a young woman. Pitxot laughed and said: "Call it 'Nydia'". Now, I do believe "Nydia" is the best *sardana* ever written in this country. It is truly wondrous...'

I reluctantly bid farewell to Vinyas. We friends that live in the Ampurdan are close neighbours but never meet. It is inexplicable, most peculiar. If we had more frequent contact, perhaps we would waste less time.

In the café, Joan B. Coromina says: 'The perennial, if not the only problem with easel painting is this: is it or isn't it a good likeness? A painting is either realism or trash.'

Coromina makes this judgment as a result of his – very understandable – fascination for the paintings by the old artist, Gimeno, who continues to paint – in a famished, feverish state – the solitary fastnesses of Fornells. His opinion is possibly too judgmental. I think there is much more one could say...

We Francophiles are all smiles. At last we are beginning to throw off our obsession with Germany and this makes us feel lighter hearted. It is like being weaned off margarine.

I take my temperature day in day out. Despite all the pressures and pitfalls, I realize that I tend to be rather passive and don't feel a genuine yearning to possess the things of this life. Perhaps it's more than simply timidity; it's probably a fundamental, constitutional, somatic predisposition. I am totally convinced I will always be what they call an unhappy man.

★

4 October. Gori speaks as forcefully as ever in the café. Red-cheeked and apoplectic, he says: 'If this war did anything, it brought one big change: it replaced long underpants; today, humanity can breathe. We used to wear wool in winter and cotton in summer, tied round the ankle with ribbons... We wore a warrior's underpants... Now things have shortened and the air circulates in spaces that were traditionally thought closed. It implies, in terms of dress, a huge revolution, an ineffable revolution...'

A countryman drinking coffee at the adjacent table whispers in my ear: 'This gentleman speaks of revolution. Perhaps he is aware of a fresh development?'

'No, sir, not at all! Mr. Gori is simply talking about short underpants...'

'Oh! That's what I thought, nothing really new has happened...'

★

5 November. The newspapers are full of grim news. Half of Europe is collapsing, like a submerged building that's falling apart. Russia, Austria, Germany... My feelings lead me from the side that's collapsing. My reason doesn't!

★

6 November. Before supper, a long conversation with my father about the new map in Europe and the huge upsurge of socialism. My father, who'd thought for as long as it was possible that Germany was going to win the war, because – in his view – it was best for the onward march of progress, is hugely shaken. Nonetheless, curiously enough, we speak perfectly calmly. Personally, this sudden advance by the poor has made an enormous impact on me: an inextricable mixture of satisfaction and fear.

★

10 November. Sunday. I meet Mrs. Carme Girbal (Mr. Esteve Casadevall's sister-in-law) on carrer de Cavallers, who is going about her duties. She seems like a little old lady preserved in a glass-case. She is exquisitely dressed. Her pale pink face and pure white hair are like something out of a miniature. Her presence catches me opposite the oranges on her orange trees that gleam in the patches of sun in her bright, perfect, orderly kitchen garden. She speaks with antique grace. She says: 'I am on my way to a meeting of the Daughters of Mary... I am in such a hurry. We must discuss the triduum of the Puríssima... We are still without a preacher... We have never been in such a situation! What a world, Most Holy Virgin! What an undertaking!'

In Germany, everyone is abdicating.

★

13 November. The war is over. We had become so accustomed to the war it beggars belief. Now war will break out here. People have jumped and danced. Federals have besported themselves. Francophile liberals have contained themselves. Fear of the poor grows by the day. At any rate, such an important, historical event, like the armistice, as seen from a small town seventy kilometres from the French frontier, is of little consequence.

★

30 December. The daily newspapers. In the course of the war, people read two journalists in particular: 'Gaziel', Agustí Calvet, who was *La Vanguardia*'s Paris correspondent, and Domínguez Rodiño, sent by the same paper, on the suggestion of Don Àngel Guimerà, to Berlin. These two men came to be immensely popular and when they went into a shirt-maker's for made-to-measure shirts they were always on the house. Calvet was a Frenchified man from the Ampurdan, clever, subtle, with the sarcasm of an academician, who wrote magnificent chronicles. When there is a war, the ideal journalist is non-bellicose.

Now the war is over, the writers of ideological articles have re-appeared and the articles by Jaume Brossa in *La Publicitat* are much read. Brossa – from the photos I have seen – is a man with a beard, from the days of Modernism. He has a 'mug', destined for the police archives. He is an ultra-liberal, that is, an anarchist.

Always sensitive to what Xènius calls 'the pulse of our times', Gori was talking about this writing today and said: 'It is a real pity there have to be two kinds of liberals: conservative liberals and anarchist liberals. It demonstrates, nevertheless, that they are separated by a different degree of tension in temperament rather than by ideas. Brossa belongs to the second category. In barbers' shops he is thought to be a difficult author. In fact he is puerile. To everyone's great surprise, he comes out emphatically against the Russian Revolution and against the German Revolution, that is now in full swing. A revolution is but a sudden change of leaders. In Russia, the revolution is far-reaching: the leaders have been totally changed. In Germany the revolution is simply a process that will return to the same starting point – exactly. Every rapid change in personnel implies the establishing of a new conception of the world – implies revolution. The shifting of power from the aristocracy to the bourgeoisie implies a revolution. The shifting of power from the bourgeoisie to the workers is a revolution. The shifting of power from one bourgeois group to another is not a revolution. In such situations, shades of political freedom are at stake. In the previous case, political freedom will count for little; the establishing of economic equality will be the decisive factor.

'Brossa's problems have to do with political freedom. He is as radical as you like, but he is a man who stopped at the French Revolution. For him, there can only be freedom with democracy, namely human equality before the law. For socialists, on the contrary, there can only be freedom if there is equality before the bread cupboard, and that cupboard lays down the law. Brossa is, then, an anachronism. In Russia he would be thought a trite sniveler, quick to tears.

'As far as I am concerned, Brossa's position is extremely powerful and irrefutable. How is it possible to establish economic equality without an iron dictatorship? At this point socialists equivocate and deceive people. Why don't they come out and say they are going to establish a dictatorship, and then we will immediately be enlightened?

'Besides, Brossa's position is human. He experienced the great era of the bourgeoisie, of expansion, of a door open to human pretensions. He is terrified by the destruction of commerce, the origin of economic unequality, or the destruction of everything that makes life comfortable. He thinks life isn't worth living if you have to spend your day queueing outside the bakery. I quite agree. The mere thought horrifies me.'

'The man who has money and does business,' says Coromina in the café, 'is like the individual who is sweating from every pore and stands next to the fireplace…'

'That was before, in the heyday of the rentiers,' retorts Frigola. 'Those of us who now live on our income receive less and less and one reduction follows another. The process of capital evaporation is very swift. I have calculated that if you want to maintain the rate of return on your accumulated capital, you must add by half the income you earn every three months.'

Not a day passes when I don't think about the room in the farmhouse attics that faces the rising sun and the south. When can I go and live there? I often wonder. But at the same time I am ashamed and horrified to see that I am only just twenty-one and am already such a pathetic coward and conservative.

⌒

Josep Pla (1897–1981) is one of the finest Catalan writers of the last century. *The Grey Notebook*, a diary that apparently covers the years 1918 and 1919, records events from earlier on when he was at school in Girona as well as life in the family home and cafés in Llofriu and Palafrugell on the Costa Brava. It is a witty portrait of his times which shows a man who was equally at ease with local fishermen and farmers in Calella de Palafrugell as with the writers and intellectuals such as Eugeni d'Ors (Xènius) he met at the Athenaeum in Barcelona. Catalan industry boomed during the First World War thanks to Spain's neutrality, and Pla focuses ironically on the gold teeth and water closets it brought to those who prospered and lamented the war's end. After completing his law degree he found work as a foreign correspondent and worked throughout Europe in the 1920s. In 1924, he faced a military trial for an article he wrote criticizing dictator Primo de Rivera. In the 1930s, he was a journalist in Madrid, where his articles described political life in the Second Republic while he consorted with Adi Enberg, a Norwegian woman who spied for the Fascists. *The Grey Notebook* shows him as a liberal who was not in favour of the power of the Catholic Church and as a student who experienced poverty and hated the sons of the rich who filled the university but weren't interested in learning. It is the creation of a supreme storyteller.

A. P. HERBERT

ONE OF THE BRAVEST
MEN I EVER KNEW

from *The Secret Battle*

THAT EVENING I SAT IN C COMPANY MESS for an hour and talked with
them about the trial. They were very sad and upset at this thing
happening in the regiment, but they were reasonable and generous,
not like those D Company pups, Wallace and the other. For they were
older men, and had nearly all been out a long time. Only one of them
annoyed me, a fellow in the thirties, making a good income in the City,
who had only joined up just before he had to under the Derby scheme,
and had been out a month. This fellow was very strong on 'the honour
of the regiment'; and seemed to think it desirable for that 'honour' that
Harry should be shot. Though how the honour of the regiment would
be thereby advanced, or what right he had to speak for it, I could not
discover.

But the others were sensible, balanced men, and as perplexed and
troubled as I. I had been thinking over a thing that Harry had said in his
talk with me – 'If I did have the wind-up I've never had cold feet.' It is
a pity one cannot avoid these horrible terms, but one cannot. I take it
that 'wind-up' – whatever the origin of that extraordinary expression
may be – signifies simply 'fear.' 'Cold feet' also signifies fear, but, as I
understand it, has an added implication in it of *base yielding* to that fear.
I told them about this distinction of Harry's, and asked them what they
thought.

'That's it,' said Smith, 'that's just the damned shame of the whole thing. There are lots of men who are simply terrified the whole time they're out, but just go on sticking it by sheer guts — will-power, or whatever you like — that's having the wind-up, and you can't prevent it. It just depends how *you*'re made. I suppose there really are some people who don't feel fear at all — that fellow Drake, for example — though I'm not sure that there are many. Anyhow, if there are any they don't deserve much credit though they do get the V.C.'s. Then there are the people who feel fear like the rest of us and don't make any effort to resist it, don't join up or come out, and when they have to, go back after three months with a blighty one, and get a job, and stay there.'

'And when they are here wangle out of all the dirty jobs,' put in Foster.

'Well, they're the people with "cold feet" if you like,' Smith went on, 'and as you say, Penrose has never been like that. Fellows like him keep on coming out time after time, getting worse wind-up every time, but simply kicking themselves out until they come out once too often, and stop one, or break up suddenly like Penrose, and—'

'And the question is — ought any man like that to be shot?' asked Foster.

'Ought any one who *volunteers* to fight for his country be shot?' said another.

'Damn it, yes,' said Constable; he was a square, hard-looking old boy, a promoted N.C.O., and a very useful officer. 'You must have some sort of standard — or where would the army be?'

'I don't know,' said Foster, 'look at the Australians — they don't have a death-penalty, and I reckon they're as good as us.'

'Yes, my son, perhaps that's the reason' — this was old Constable again — 'the average Australian is naturally a sight stouter-hearted than the average Englishman — they don't need it.'

'Then why the hell do they punish Englishmen worse than Australians, if they can't even be *expected* to do so well?' retorted Foster; but this piece of dialectics was lost on Constable.

'Anyhow, I don't see that it need be such an absolute standard,' Smith began again, thoughtfully; he was a thoughtful young fellow. 'They don't expect everybody to have equally strong arms or equally good brains; and if a chap's legs or arms aren't strong enough for him to go on living in the trenches they take him out of it (if he's lucky). But every man's expected to have equally strong nerves in all circumstances, and to *go on having them* till he goes under; and when he goes under they don't consider how far his nerves, or guts, or whatever you call it, were as good as other people's. Even if he had nerves like a chicken to begin with he's expected to behave as a man with nerves like a lion or a Drake would do...'

'A man with nerves like a chicken is a damned fool to go into the infantry at all,' put in Williams – 'the honour of the regiment' person.

'Yes, but he may have had a will-power like a lion, and simply made himself do it.'

'You'd be all right, Smith,' somebody said, 'if you didn't use such long words; what the hell do you mean by an absolute standard?'

'Sorry, George, I forgot you were so ignorant. What I mean is this. Take a case like Penrose's: All they ask is, was he seen running the wrong way, or not going the right way? If the answer is Yes – the punishment is death, *et cetera, et cetera*. To begin with, as I said, they don't consider whether he was *capable* physically or mentally – I don't know which it is – of doing the right thing. And then there are lots of other things which *we* know make one man more "windy" than another, or windier to-day than he was yesterday – things like being a married man, or having boils, or a bad cold, or being just physically weak, so that you get so exhausted you haven't got any strength left to resist your fears (I've had that feeling myself) – none of those things are considered *at all* at a court-martial – and I think they ought to be.'

'Well, what do you want,' Foster asked, 'a kind of periodical Wind-up Examination?'

'That's the kind of thing, I suppose. It *is* a medical question, really. Only the doctors don't seem to recognize – or else they aren't allowed to – any stage between absolute shell-shock, with your legs flying in all directions, and just ordinary skrim-shanking.'

'But damn it, man,' Constable exploded, 'look at the skrim-shanking you'll get if you have that sort of thing. You'd have all the mothers' darlings in the kingdom saying they'd had enough when they got to the Base.'

'Perhaps – no, I think that's silly. I don't know what it is that gives you bad wind-up after a long time out here, nerves or imagination or emotion or what, but it seems to me the doctors ought to be able to test when a man's really had enough; just as they tell whether a man's knee or a man's heart are really bad or not. You'd have to take his record into account, of course…'

'And you'd have to make it a compulsory test,' said Smith, 'because nowadays no one's going to go into a Board and say, "Look here, doctor, I've been out so long and I can't stand any more." They'd send you out in the next draft!'

'Compulsory both ways,' added Foster: 'when they'd decided he'd done enough, and wasn't *safe* any longer, he oughtn't to be *allowed* to do any more – because he's dangerous to himself and everybody else.'*

'As a matter of fact,' said Williams, 'that's what usually does happen, doesn't it? When a chap gets down and out like that after a decent spell of it, he usually gets a job at home – instructor at the Depot, or something.'

'Yes, and then you get a fellow with the devil of a conscience like Penrose – and you have a nasty mess like this.'

'And what about the men?' asked Constable. 'Are you going to have the same thing for them?'

'Certainly – only, thank God, there are not so many of them who need it. All that chat you read about the "wonderful fatalism" of the British soldier is so much bunkum. It simply means that most of them are not cursed with an imagination, and so don't worry about what's coming.'

'That's true; you don't see many fatalists in the middle of a big strafe.'

'Of course there *are* lots of them who *are* made like Penrose, and with a record like his, something—'

---

*It is only fair to say that, long after the supposed date of this conversation, a system of sending 'war-weary' soldiers home for six months at a time was instituted, though I doubt if Foster would have been satisfied with that.

'And it's damned lucky for the British Army there are not more of them,' put in Constable.

'Certainly, but it's damned unlucky for them to be in the British Army – in the infantry, anyhow.'

'And what does that matter?'

'Oh, well, you can take that line if you like – but it's a bit Prussian, isn't it?'

'Prussia's winning this dirty war, anyhow, at present.'

So the talk rambled on, and we got no further, only most of us were in troubled agreement that something – perhaps many things – were wrong about the System, if this young volunteer, after long fighting and suffering, was indeed to be shot like a traitor in the cold dawn.

Nine times out of ten, as Williams had said, we knew that it would not have happened, simply because nine men out of ten surrender in time. But ought the tenth case to be even remotely possible? That was our doubt.

What exactly was wrong we could not pretend to say. It was not our business. But if this was the best the old men could do, we felt that we could help them a little. I give you this scrap of conversation only to show the kind of feeling there was in the regiment – because that is the surest test of the rightness of these things.

They were still at it when I left. And as I went out wearily into the cold drizzle I heard Foster summing up his views with: 'Well, the whole thing's damned awful. They've recommended him to mercy, haven't they? and I hope to God he gets it.'

★

But he got no mercy. The sentence was confirmed by the higher authorities.

I cannot pretend to *know* what happened, but from some experience of the military hierarchy I can imagine. I can see those papers, wrapped up in the blue form, with all the right information beautifully inscribed in the right spaces, very neat and precise, carefully sealed in the long envelopes, and sent wandering up through the rarefied atmosphere of the Higher Formations. Very early they halt, at the Brigadier, or perhaps the Divisional General, some one who thinks of himself as a man of 'blood and iron'. He looks upon the papers. He reads the evidence – very carefully. At the end he sees 'Recommended to Mercy.' – 'All very well, but we must make an example sometimes. Where's that confidential memo we had the other day? That's it, yes. "Officer who fails in his duty must be treated with the same severity as would be awarded to private in the same circumstances." Quite right too. Shan't approve recommendation to mercy. Just write on it, "See no reason why sentence should not be carried out" and I'll sign it. – Or, more simply perhaps: "Mercy! mercy be damned! must make an example. I won't have any cold feet in my Command".' And so the Blue Form goes climbing on, burdened now with that fatal endorsement, labouring over ridge after ridge, and on each successive height the atmosphere becomes more rarefied (though the population is more numerous). And at long last it comes to some Olympian peak – I know not where – beyond which it may not go, where the air is so chill and the population so dense, that it is almost impossible to breathe. Yet here, I make no doubt, they look at the Blue Form very carefully and gravely, as becomes the High Gods. But in the end they shake their heads, a little sadly, maybe, and say, 'Ah, General B—— does not approve recommendation to mercy. He's the man on the spot, he ought to know. *Must* support *him*. Sentence confirmed.'

Then the Blue Form climbs sadly down to the depths again, to the low regions where men feel fear…

The thing was done seven mornings later, in a little orchard behind the Casquettes' farm.

The Padre told me he stood up to them very bravely and quietly. Only he whispered to him, 'For God's sake make them be quick.' That is the worst torment of the soldier from beginning to end – the waiting…

★

After three months I had some leave and visited Mrs. Harry. I had to. But I shall not distress you with an account of that interview. I will not even pretend that she was 'brave.' How could she be? Only, when I had explained things to her, as Harry had asked, she said: 'Somehow, that does make it easier for me – and I only wish – I wish you could tell everybody – what you have told me.'

And again I say, that is all I have tried to do. This book is not an attack on any person, on the death penalty, or on anything else, though if it makes people think about these things, so much the better. I think I believe in the death penalty – I don't know. But I did not believe in Harry being shot.

That is the gist of it; that my friend Harry was shot for cowardice – and he was one of the bravest men I ever knew.

꘍

A. P. Herbert was born in Surrey in 1890 and went to Oxford in 1910. At the outbreak of the war, he joined the Royal Naval Volunteer Reserve and was sent to Gallipoli in 1915. Injured in Gallipoli, he rejoined his division in France which served in the last phases of the Battle of the Somme. Again wounded, Herbert returned home and started writing *The Secret Battle*. The novel, in part autobiographical, tells the story of Henry Penrose, a sensitive officer who buckles under the pressure of repeated front-line campaigns and is executed after a court-martial. Based on the true story of Sub-Lieutenant Edwin Dyett's trial for desertion, the book was praised by Lloyd George and Winston Churchill, who wrote that it was 'one of those cries of pain wrung from the fighting troops... like the poems of Siegfried Sassoon it should be read in each generation, so that men and women may rest under no illusions about what war means.' First published in 1919, it was not a commercial success and turned Herbert away from writing serious literature. He is best known for his *Misleading Cases in the Common Law*, satirical pieces on various aspects of the legal and judicial system that first appeared in *Punch*. Extremely funny, the pieces also expressed his desire for law reform. Herbert died in London in 1971.

VAHAN TOTOVENTS

INFIDELS AND CURS

from *Scenes from an Armenian Childhood*

translated by Mischa Kudian

W E HAD TURKISH NEIGHBOURS, too.

Shemsy was the son of this Turkish family. We were about the same age and had grown up together. We had done so like two brothers: we would give each other small knuckle-bones with which we used to play games; we would offer each other sweetmeats from our homes; we would go swimming together; together, we would tease his sister, who was two years older than him; and we would cry together.

Sanié, his sister, was like a fairy: she was so light she seemed to be made of air; her colouring was white and golden, in spite of her brother's dark skin, black hair and eyebrows, and inky eyes.

There was a big acacia-tree in their garden. I used to liken her so much to the whiteness of that tree.

Sanié used to speak through her nose a little – having fallen as a child and hurt herself – but I was very fond of the twang in her voice; so much so that I wished all girls would speak that way.

But it was not the same with Shemsy. He would constantly make fun of the nasal tone in her speech; and she would approach me with great warmth, sensing that the defect which was the cause of his mockery used to please me, and she would let me touch her freely all over with my hands.

And she would laugh.

And the blue stream which flowed from heaven would babble away…

★

Sometimes Shemsy and I would fight together. We would do so without any particular cause.

He would suddenly call me: 'Infidel!' And I would immediately retaliate with: 'Cur!'

We had learnt these words from our homes and schools. All Turks used to call Armenians 'infidels', and all Armenians used to call Turks 'curs'.

When Turks visited my father, he would receive them with hospitality. But after they had gone, parting with friendly and respectful greetings, my father would grunt: 'Curs!'

And, of course, when my father had received similar hospitality from them, the Turks would grunt: 'Infidel!' after he had left.

The 'giavour' and the 'eet' – Turkish for 'infidel' and 'cur' – could not live together.

If any Turk called me an 'infidel', I would automatically retaliate with 'cur', except for Sanié.

Sanié was the acacia-blossom which scented the cool air of the nights in springtime.

When an Armenian or a group of them were taken to prison in chains, they would hang down their heads as they went by, whilst the Turks would stand in the streets and laugh at them with delight.

And when a Turkish coffin was taken by, the Armenians would look skywards and murmur: 'Thank Thee, O Lord!' They would be pleased that there was one Turk less.

I did not understand why this should have been so, but, without questioning it, my hatred for the 'curs' grew more intense inside me, as it did with Shemsy towards the 'infidels'.

Sanié disappeared behind latticed windows: a grim cloud had covered the silvery moon, and I was not able to unravel the mysteries of the scented, the intoxicating, the blossoming stranger; the deep hidden folds, the lines, the velvety expanses remained concealed from me; I was not able to dominate that field of marble in its entirety…

Sanié would go past our front door, enveloped in the violet cloud of her long veil; and my eyes would penetrate through this veil to wander in the hidden starry regions of an unknown world...

★

Every morning and every evening, an eye would peer through a latticed window; a hand would stretch out and throw a flower at my feet.

The house where this latticed window was belonged to a Turkish mullah, and it was a few doors beyond ours. On Fridays – being the Mohammedan day of worship – the mullah would not greet any Christians, nor would he reply when they greeted him.

But on Fridays, as on other days, the same hand, delicate as a jasmine in the morning, would stretch out, throw a flower, and withdraw.

Through the latticed window would be heard her gentle laugh and suppressed scream of delight.

It was the mullah's third wife, a youthful girl, imprisoned inside a cage.

A longing would be set ablaze within me. I would develop an urge to see her, to speak to her.

I would pick up the flower she had thrown down. I would take it home, and smell it incessantly. An unfamiliar tremor, a shudder filled with ecstasy would flow from that flower into my soul.

The mullah was over sixty years of age, with a bent back and yellow, evil eyes. He used to shave his prominent cheek-bones, trim his beard to a rounded shape, and dye it with henna.

Every time he went out of the house he would give strict orders to the other two women to keep guard over Bahrié and not to allow her to go near a window; not a fly was to enter the house!

But Bahrié, fired by the spring, found ways not only of approaching the window but of sliding her hand out, throwing a flower, and sighing.

'Come into the garden tomorrow; the old witches will be out,' I heard her say from behind the window one day.

That voice chirruped in my ears, and it awakened within me... woman.

I heard her and went on my way, but she seemed to have struck at my heart and dragged it inside through the closely-latticed meshes of the window.

I moved away, but her voice continued to ring in my soul, louder and louder.

I stopped in the shadow of a tree. The sun had woven a pattern of flowers on the ground, and I could see Bahrié in that pattern. The wind whispered in the leaves – it was Bahrié saying:

'Come into the garden tomorrow…'

At night I stood on the roof: the branches of the acacia-tree are bent down; the moon is immediately above our roof. I can see Bahrié's face on it, with large, black eyes; her hair, cut short, is strewn across her forehead. She is smiling.

In the morning, I climbed on to our garden wall and jumped down into our neighbour's garden. My clothes were moistened by the morning dew. I had to cross three gardens before I came to Bahrié's.

I stood on her garden wall. I was shivering, but it seemed to me that I could have flown into the air.

Bahrié saw me. She ran down.

I am inside, under the blossoming pomegranate-tree. A little beyond, a lilac-tree is hiding me. Bahrié appears. She stops. She is panting, shivering, with her hand on her swollen breast. I embrace her. I become drunk with her scent; my lips are aflame…

'Let's go,' she whispers. 'Let's go inside!'

The mullah had gone to the old town by night with his two other wives – in connexion with some hereditary lawsuit. They had locked the front door on Bahrié, and there was no way of her leaving the house.

Bahrié took me by the hand and led me inside, into the bedroom.

She threw her arms round me; she cried; she laughed; she kissed me. The bed was not yet made, she had only just flown out of it. I embraced the fresh, youthful girl, and we rolled on to the bed. A woman's scent is intoxicating…

I was set aflame by a woman for the first time in my life…

I was surrounded by a sense of fear and the first happiness.

Everything was in song; every object cried out with ecstasy:

'Bahrié!'

She is lying there motionless. Silently, within a few minutes, she is living the joy of centuries.

'Go quickly, go!'

She begins to cry.

'They will be back in the evening,' she adds.

Her tears mingle with the azure drops of her happiness.

She seems to be seeing the old man, with his yellow eyes.

She accompanies me to the blossoming pomegranate-tree. I pick a red flower and put it on her bosom. I take her hand and kiss it...

I climb the wall; I can hear the sound of her crying and her gasp of happiness. She stands under the dark-green shelter of the lilac-tree, casting a longing look.

I jump down into the next garden and part for ever from the first woman.

★

The following day, I met Veronica – Christina's cousin. Veronica was an ethereal being, as feathery as a fawn; she had pale-chestnut eyes and the complexion of a rose. I used to bare my soul to her every time we met; but on this occasion it was covered with a pink veil of shame. I could not look into her eyes. I took hold of her hand, kissed it, and cried. I wanted to confess, but I could not expose my soul to her, instead I stood firmly before its sealed doors.

'Is your mother ill?' Veronica inquired innocently.

'No, she isn't.'

She could not possibly have guessed the truth. She was probably roaming in the blue hills of innocence. No doubt some bewitching, enchanting song of nature was also whispering within her bosom, but she was far from suspecting my sin. Veronica could never, never have imagined that a woman, a blossoming woman had displayed the hidden treasures of her body before me without shame.

We go to the bottom of the garden together, crushing flowers under our feet. The fruit is hanging from the trees. I decide to confess my sin when we reach the mulberry-tree; but once we are there, Veronica begins to run about and cry: 'Catch me!' I run after her, but I am reluctant to catch her quickly. In the end, I do. And our lips cling to each other through some unknown urge. All the leaves seem to applaud, and the fruit seems to sing, whilst the garden vibrates like a cymbal.

'Veronica!' a voice is heard to say quietly.

We turn round. It is Christina. We go to her. She is shaking with all her body. She can hardly breathe:

'Benon is coming.'

'Let him,' says Veronica, and lifting up her arms she picks a fruit. Her bosom seems to want to fly skywards with emotion.

Benon was Veronica's brother and my school-friend. Christina was not shaking because of him, but because of our kiss.

Benon arrives. Together we climb the mulberry-tree. Its fruit has been scorched by the sun; it has dried and sweetened it.

The turquoise of the sky crumbled on to Veronica's head, too. The deadly, parching winds blew from the desert and covered her body under the sands…

Only the morning star shed a few tears upon her, after which, evening fell with blood-stained eyes…

★

It is morning. The sky is grey and dark. But the snow has fallen all night and the countryside seems to be covered with lilies.

I have come out of the house to run to school, with my satchel on my back. The dogs are there to greet my morning.

I can see men walking with hurried steps, silently, their minds preoccupied. A woman is standing at the corner of the first street. There is a silence as deep as a chasm in her eyes.

A general stillness reigns everywhere, as if the snow were the gigantic shroud of a coffin. Instinctively, I sense that there is something amiss in the air, which fills me with awe – a fear which grows with every step I take.

Someone draws a curtain mysteriously from behind a window, as if they do not want the daylight to penetrate inside. Another opens a front door, looks up and down the street with frightened eyes, and shuts it.

I meet Krikor Agha, who is normally a man with slow movements, but he is hurrying.

'Where are you going?' he asks.

'To school,' I reply.

He wants to say something, but he clasps his hands together and continues on his way. This leisurely man is running like an ox, as if fleeing from some impending danger.

A group of people, cowered, but with hurried steps, are coming away from the square of the town. I want to ask them something, but none of them lifts up his head. They go past hurriedly.

The shops are shut: it is neither Sunday nor Friday. There are one or two half-opened ones here and there. I look inside through the shutters.

The people there are sitting curled up in corners, without uttering a word; they are merely smoking.

No one speaks to me – no one. Each one looks at me, and smiles painfully.

The nearer I approach the square, the more profound the silence becomes.

A woman emerges; her hair is uncombed and she is almost in her night-attire; she takes hold of a ten-year-old child by the shoulder and hastily drags him inside. The door shuts.

I reach the square.

In the middle of the square, in the overall whiteness of the snow, there is a black mass. Four soldiers with gleaming bayonets stand round this black mass. One by one the huddled-up and terrified men approach it; they look; they shut their eyes and hurry past silently.

I go near.

I see a body without a head!

The blood has congealed on the snow and turned black… The head is lying on one side, as if asleep.

I look back again: the body without a head has its arms thrust into the snow…

I am rooted to the ground – petrified! My feet refuse to move.

One of the soldiers orders:

'Go away!'

I go away.

In the twilight of the morning, the Sultan's tyranny had cut off the heads of two revolutionaries.

The other was in the upper square of the town.

For the first time, I see the picture, the horrifying picture of the cruel tyranny.

My childhood soul is saddened.

I want to go back home, but a noise rises from another part of the square. A crowd gathers. I too run there.

'It's Fouad Bey, Fouad Bey!'

Fouad Bey is a handsome Turk, with dreamy, tawny eyes and a wide forehead. He is young, slightly built, but virile. He is dressed in Circassian clothes, and walks slowly and proudly. He is one of the Turkish revolutionaries, exiled from Constantinople, who had raised his voice in protest against the beheading of the two revolutionaries.

He climbs the stone steps of one of the shops and speaks to the crowd gathered before him. His eyes are no longer dreamy; they have assumed a look of fierceness, sublimely savage. With his fur cap in hand, his tawny hair is scattered across his wide forehead. I can hardly catch and understand a few words here and there. The faithful soldiers of tyranny arrive and surround Fouad Bey. They push him about and tie up his hands and drag him away.

Horrified and frightened, the crowd disperses.

The silence descends once more, heavy and deep.

I return home. The curtains of all the windows are drawn.

I go in.

No one speaks.

I throw my arms round my mother.

She strokes my head silently.

The silence chokes me.

I want to scream, but I am chained by the very silence. The whole town has turned into a cemetery.

Every now and then a pounding is heard in my heart. It echoes dully, and dies down.

A head cut off... Do they not only cut off sheep's heads?

Who had done it?

'Ahmed Tchavoush! Ahmed Tchavoush!…' they whisper.

To my eyes, Ahmed Tchavoush becomes that fabulous monster about which I had heard so much, but which I had never seen and could not visualize.

★

One rainy night the headmaster of our school, Hagop Simonian, was stabbed to death under the thorny tree in front of his house.

In the morning, the news spread like lightning: the Turks had stabbed Hagop Simonian to death. The Turks, the curs…!

The more the news spread, the deeper the hatred grew and frothed.

There had already been some clashes between the Armenians and the Turks in some of the streets. As the latter had gone by the Armenians had insulted them, their religion, and Mohammed, and fighting had broken out.

Meetings were held at the premises of the Armenian Prelacy. They had wanted to send a telegram to the Patriarch in Constantinople to protest against the murder which had taken place. The town was surrounded by troops and at every street-corner stood armed policemen, who would not allow people to go about, arresting those who were already out in the streets.

But they only arrested the Armenians. To evade this, many of them bound white scarves round their fezes and went out that way. Seeing the white scarves, the soldiers took them for mullahs and let them pass. By the evening the town was filled with 'mullahs'.

This state of affairs continued for three days and turned into a grim nightmare. The body remained in the house, surrounded by relatives.

There was no way of burying it.

The funeral took place at the end of the three days, and those who had been arrested were released in order to take part in it. Several thousand people were present at the funeral. They had even come from distant villages. The burial took place without any disturbances. Everyone had sobered down. They hung their heads almost as if in shame.

Why?

It had been revealed that Hagop Simonian's murderer had not been a Turk, after all, but a young Armenian. Furthermore, he had been one of the headmaster's pupils, who had finished school two years earlier and had become a teacher.

Why had this Hagop killed Hagop Simonian?

The murderer's name was also Hagop.

There was a pretty young girl who was related to the headmaster and with whom the murderer had fallen in love.

The girl's parents had sought the headmaster's opinion about his pupil, in order to make a final decision about the girl's future.

'He is a mad, stupid boy!' the headmaster had replied.

To persuade their daughter the parents had told her what their relative had said, as he was one of the most intellectual people in the town. In her turn the girl had disclosed the headmaster's views to Hagop, to explain the difficulties which weighed down against her marrying him.

And so the mad and stupid Hagop had waylaid the headmaster in the middle of the night and had stabbed him there and then.

Not a single Turk had taken the slightest part in this murder. Ashamed, the Armenians kept quiet about it, but the Turks tried not to forget it.

★

A month after this incident, the wife of one of the fiercest Turks in the town, Ahmed Tchavoush by name, was found strangled in her own bed.

Ahmed Tchavoush was a town-crier, with a hoarse, stentorian voice.

Whenever there was an occasion for the Government to make an announcement they would call Ahmed Tchavoush, and they would enjoin him with the task. Suddenly, his voice would be heard to ring out: '…all defaulters will be hanged…' His declarations always ended with the pronouncement of this supreme punishment.

And suddenly, in the dead of night, Ahmed Tchavoush's voice was heard in our district: 'The Armenians have strangled my wife and have escaped!' A violent bellowing followed these words; it was as if a wild animal was wailing. The voice came from his roof. He had gone up there and, marching up and down along the edge, with his upraised hands shaking in the air, he was roaring: 'The Armenians have strangled my wife and have escaped!'

Everyone sat up in their beds in the middle of the night, awakened from their sleep and terrified, they crossed themselves and remained silent, waiting for whatever disaster might follow in the morning.

But the disaster did not wait until the morning; it came in the middle of the night.

Ahmed Tchavoush's house was filled with policemen and Turks.

The Armenians had entered Ahmed Tchavoush's house. They had tied him up, gagged him with cotton wool, and when he had tried to free himself, they had beaten him up, had strangled his wife in bed and had run away – this was the story Ahmed Tchavoush told the police and the Turks.

Even the Armenians believed this story, taking it for an act of revenge. It was Tchavoush who, some months earlier, had cut off the heads of two Armenian revolutionaries in public with a butcher's yataghan. He was the only man to have agreed to act as executioner. After this horrible deed, he had scooped up some of the blood with the palm of his hand, rubbed it into his beard, and had knelt down a few paces away from the severed heads and prayed to Allah.

The arrests began in the middle of the night and lasted until the morning. The prison was filled with Armenians. On the way there, they were beaten, wounded, spat at, and insulted.

On the evening of the incident, Tchavoush had told his wife that he was going to the village, which he often visited. He had gone to the market-place to hire a horse. There he had been promised one; but having waited in vain until late at night he had returned home, and had found his wife in the arms of a Turkish youth. Enraged, Tchavoush had strangled the young man and had thrown him into the well. Then he had strangled his wife and, leaving her in bed, had climbed up to the roof and had begun to roar: 'The Armenians have murdered my wife and have escaped!'

This was what had really happened.

They brought out the Turkish youth's body from the well, and arrested Ahmed Tchavoush. The young Turk's parents were wealthy and influential. They pursued the case closely, and had Ahmed Tchavoush exiled to Konia and forbidden to return.

The arrested Armenians were not all released together, but one at a time, in gradual stages. Even the last one, on the very last day, was cross-examined in connexion with Ahmed Tchavoush.

★

A Turk had gone to an Armenian shopkeeper, and after choosing some material, he had asked the price.

'Ten kouroush an arsheen,' the shopkeeper had replied.

'Make it five,' the Turk had suggested.

'I can't; it cost me eight, in the first place.'

The Turk had demanded that he sold it for five. The Armenian had refused. The Turk had left full of hatred, gnashing his teeth together.

A day or two had gone by, and an uproar had broken out in the street – the Turks were beating up an Armenian.

It was the shopkeeper who had refused to sell the material at five kouroush an arsheen. The Turk had met him again in the street, and had asked:

'Well, will you sell it at five kouroush, you infidel?'

'No!'

And the Turk had started to shout:

'Help! Help! He insulted my religion! I was walking by quietly and he insulted Mohammed and our holy religion!'

And so the crowd had set upon the Armenian and had broken his nose and cut his lip. Whilst at every blow the shopkeeper had shouted:

'I'll give it away for nothing, but I will not sell it at five kouroush an arsheen! You can take it!'

No one had bothered to ask why the man who was being beaten should be shouting these words, or what connexion they had with the holy religion.

★

Dikran, the goldsmith, had a vineyard near the slaughterhouse of the town. I had gone to the vineyard of a relative of ours, which was next to the goldsmith's.

At noon, a Turk, carrying a basket, entered Dikran's vineyard and asked him for some grapes. The latter did not want to give him any, but his mother intervened:

'I should; he is a cur; he would only create trouble.'

So Dikran gave him some, but without filling the basket. The Turk demanded that he filled it completely.

'It would be too heavy to carry,' said Dikran, playfully hinting that he did not want to give any more.

The Turk insisted on having a full basket. The mother intervened again, but Dikran was furious and refused.

'You have enough there, and I gave it to you for nothing!' Dikran exclaimed. The Turk demanded again. They started fighting.

Dikran was a thin, delicate man; whilst the Turk was well built and strong. Dikran had the worst of the fight; he was thoroughly beaten and even lost a tooth. No one intercepted.

'He is a cur, he would go and create a thousand and one mischiefs!' they all said and allowed him to be beaten.

Five days later, Dikran was summoned to court.

I went to the trial to see what would happen, in spite of my mother's orders to keep away from such places.

The Turk appeared in court with a white handkerchief tied across his forehead. Dikran was supposed to have struck him on the forehead with a stone and broken it. Dikran was condemned to two months' imprisonment, and he was beaten as they took him to prison; whilst in court Dikran begged them only to remove the handkerchief and see for themselves if there was a wound there.

But they refused to listen to him: there was the government doctor's report, and that was enough!

When they had taken Dikran to prison and we had come out of court, I saw with my own eyes how, once he was in the street, the Turk untied his handkerchief without the slightest compunction, and put it in his pocket. There was not a sign of a wound, not even the trace of a scratch on his forehead.

★

One day, in broad daylight, a terrible piece of news went round: an

Armenian barber had cut the throat of a Turk whom he had been shaving!

The news spread like lightning. Everyone tried to shut their shops immediately and go home. Within fifteen minutes the shopping area of the town looked as it did on Sundays – deserted.

What had happened?

The barber had been shaving the Turk, when an Armenian acquaintance had come in and whispered in his ear:

'What are you doing here? The Turks and the Armenians are fighting outside!'

This had been simply meant to be a joke.

The barber had thought for a minute: they had already started outside, and here before him was a ready-made opportunity. So he had taken advantage of it, and then he had hurried out, razor in hand, to join in the fray. When he had discovered that everything was quiet outside, the prospect of the consequences had horrified him. He had jumped on to a horse and had fled out of town.

That evening the barber's wife was taken to prison, was beaten, and persistently questioned:

'Where's your husband hiding?'

★

The Ottoman Constitution was declared.

There was an outburst of greetings, kisses, embraces; an overflow of affection and of brotherhood.

The prison gates were opened, and out came the political prisoners, amongst whom were also my two teachers.

A celebration of freedom took place in front of the government house. Out came the Turkish revolutionaries and spoke about the Constitution.

It was the first time that I had seen Turkish revolutionaries. How was it possible for a Turk to become a revolutionary? That was what I had heard and believed.

I was on my way back from that celebration, tired, covered in dust, thirsty, and full of joy.

I met Shemsy in the street.

We had not greeted each other for a long time. He had called my father an 'infidel', and I had called his a 'cur'. We had often called each other by these names before and had made it up, but on that occasion we had directed them at each other's parents.

I, in particular, had been painfully hurt, because at the time when Shemsy had insulted my father, he was turning to dust in the cemetery…

Shemsy looked at me out of the corner of his eyes.

So did I.

I smiled.

He did the same.

I do not know how, but our feet moved towards one another and our arms embraced each other.

Shemsy dragged me to their home. The house seemed so strange to me – I had not been there for a long time. He led me in, ignoring the custom of segregating the womenfolk in their home. I kissed his mother's hand. I turned and saw Sanié, who stood there smiling. Our hands went forward in the way they do when one's heart wants to applaud.

It was a very long time since I had last seen Sanié without her violet veil.

She had lost a little, a very little, of her ethereal qualities, but she had become more full-blooded.

When I gripped her hand firmly, she blushed, her lips trembled and, turning to her mother, she whispered something. There was so much femininity in her whisper that, at once, I visualized her swimming in the pond, and the icy water quivering with the sunny warmth of her body.

★

The kisses and embraces did not help in any way, because barely a few days later 'wise' Armenians whispered into the ears of others:

'Don't be deceived!'

'Wise' Turks also whispered:

'Beware, the Armenians want to rule our country and abolish our religion!'

The clock seemed to have been put back.

★

When we were children, we used to play a game called 'Armenians and Turks'. It was a simple game: there would be a mass of stones in the centre, called the 'fortress'. The children would divide into two teams, to occupy the 'fortress'. One of the teams would be called 'The Armenians' and the other, 'The Turks'.

'The Turks are going in, boys!'

'The Armenians are getting near the fortress! Attack them!'

It was looked upon as an innocent game.

And it continued so until the First World War. The same game was played during that war, with the exception that, this time, the sides were taken by real Armenians and real Turks and they were playing on real soil, roused by an immeasurable hatred.

No one, absolutely no one, ever told us not to play this game. Whenever we did the grown-ups, men with moustaches, men famed for their learning and for their seriousness, would watch us and smile. And they would usually be delighted when the 'Turks' were defeated. The passions would become so heated that the 'Armenians' would call the 'Turks' during play by those insulting names which they did at other times.

We would always be faced with one difficulty at the beginning of the game: no one would want to be a 'Turk'. We would be forced to draw lots. Anyone who drew 'Armenian' would be enormously delighted, whilst those who drew 'Turk' would be upset, reluctantly taking part in the game, simply to obey the rules of children's games.

It was in this spirit that we grew up.

And future generations will tell a strange tale:

'Once upon a time, there was a small and ancient nation, which lived in the lands extending from Lake Van to the Mediterranean Sea and from Baghdad to Byzantium. This ancient nation was made up of farmers, poor craftsmen, intellectuals, merchants, landlords, bankers, high government officials, dustmen, servants, slaves and so on. These people were ardently loved by their wealthy compatriots beyond the limits of their country. They were likewise ardently loved by ministers of Western countries, because of their black and beautiful eyes and because they spread culture throughout the dark East.

'Moved by their ardent love, the wealthy compatriots and the Western ministers pushed these people into fighting their neighbours – neighbours who differed from them in religion, in blood and in culture, and who possessed swords and armour, an army, a navy, and superior numbers.

'And once upon a time, there was a great war. The whole world was enveloped by the smoke of gunpowder, and there flowed rivers of blood. The ministers and the wealthy compatriots shouted into these people's ears: "The hour of freedom has come! Strike your neighbour! Strike his crescent with your cross!" The black and beautiful eyes of this ancient nation sparkled with the desire of freedom. An unequal fight began; they struck; and were struck. And of these ancient people there remained a mere fragment, in memory of a nightmare.

'Whereupon, with supreme and sublime cynicism, the ministers and the wealthy compatriots laughed at the bones and the ashes…

'And three apples fell from heaven: one for the story-teller, one for the listener, and one for the eavesdropper…'

Vahan Totovents was an Armenian writer born in Mezre (modern Turkey), a small town on the Euphrates, in 1889. He served as a volunteer on the Caucasian front during the war. He went to war to see his country liberated.

> I saw instead its total destruction, and torrents of my countrymen's blood. I saw human suffering of such depth that there can be nothing deeper in this world. I saw nights gorged with blood. I saw men crazed with hunger; I saw bloodthirsty mobs attacking innocent men, women and children, and I heard the howls of their innocent victims.

After the war, he went to live in Yerevan in Soviet Armenia. In the 1930s he was accused of producing works lacking in proletarian content and exiled to Siberia. Little is known of his last years in exile. Totovents died in 1937. This extract is taken from his *Scenes from an Armenian Childhood*, written and first published in 1930 (filmed as *A Piece of Sky* by Henrik Malyan in 1980).The touch is light but the message is clear: children's games are not innocent.

ÖMER SEYFETTIN

WHY DIDN'T HE GET RICH?

translated by Izzy Finkel

'A few pages from the diary of a teacher.'

7th of January

THEY SAY THAT A NATION without a history is a happy one. I'll add that a person without recollections is a happy one, too. Since I taught history for five years, I found it necessary to cast my eye over a fair number of books. No sooner had I left school than I ordered the works of the historians Rambaud and Lavisse. The commerce in used books to which I'd gradually become accustomed since then had filled up my library quite a bit. Now I suddenly find myself having read all of these books. It did not escape my notice; this thing we call history is the bearer of misfortunes! It makes no mention of felicities, or else it skims past them superficially. Even in the most joyful and most fortunate of periods it is expert at discovering some calamity, perfidy, anguish, or poison! This sorrowful tendency within the record of man that is history is found also in man himself. Each misfortune, affliction or grief leaves a deep mark like a scar on our souls. Our delights and our joys, our happy days melt away and are forgotten with the very weightlessness of a dream. Just this morning, in the corner of my drawer I found a notebook I had begun to scribble in ten years ago. I looked over what I had written. There was nothing there to afford me peace of mind!

I had recorded at length how my darling mother who died of cancer gradually ebbed away, and how we'd suffered terrible burdens as the poor thing was dragged off beyond redemption, moaning and wailing into perdition… What terrible remedy is time! Now I cannot feel one scintilla of those burdens. Then I went abroad! There were but two lines about this! Then I got married! There is no mention of that at all. I had a child. I hadn't written about that either. Involuntarily I sniffed in these pages, which for some reason had yellowed without ever seeing the sun. The bitter, narcotic smell of an ailing autumn! From these old leaves, amongst these old books, from these old forgotten notebooks, ah! The smell of mourning.

★

Yes, if only I had not had such memories to write about. How empty are the eventless, regular, self-same days! But how free from pain… After the war broke out this emptiness, that is to say this contentment and peace, abruptly broke apart. I must have abandoned my habit, because for two years I didn't set down any of the things I'd experienced. To be living happily in the world of beliefs, in the world of opinions, to be living happily in the pursuit of knowledge, that spiritual pleasure which resembles no other delicacy – and suddenly to be thrust into the darkness of want! To crawl along a desert of famine without hope, under a maelstrom of hunger, and to witness those close to you meet their slow, uncomplaining deaths! How miserable I was that day! Whatever my wife had had, we sold. Not a linen bath towel remained. Our bedding, our bedsteads, the library my father had left me, even the pram of my poor child, my poor Orhan, went off to be pawned when its turn came. My monthly salary was fifteen lira… We even pawned the house that my mother had given me, the house that had guaranteed me an income of six lira. The bread rations we ate, the cracked wheat with olive oil we got from the school! I am in awe of my wife's fortitude. She managed to take care of both the house and the child. She is endlessly darning socks. She takes apart the old ones. She dresses me and her child.

–If only the fighting would stop! All this will be forgotten, she says.

But I do not see that this crisis has any hope of ending soon. What will become of us? From time to time I consider going abroad. But those coming from the outside say that their hunger is worse even than ours. Remembering the terror of tomorrow turns my mind upside down. I'm struck dumb. I still can't think of what to say. I can't collect my thoughts on paper.

★

14th of January

I ought not to have begun to write again in this inauspicious book! Yesterday Orhan fell ill. Our neighbour the doctor who came round to treat him as a favour told us to feed him only milk. Milk... A measure of it is half a lira! I piled all the books I own onto the back of a street porter. I sold them. Off they went. Sixty lira's worth of cash came into my hands. I bought charcoal with twenty of it. The cold was wretched.

★

30th of January

Turning it over in my mind, I realise that a life like this is no longer livable. That evening, when I was having my boots polished, I asked the shoe-shine boy how many pennies he received from his master each month.

–Twenty lira! he said. A gypsy child of sixteen! I'm the thirty-one-year-old scion of an ancient family! I was brought up in the most comfortable fashion. How can I, with a wife and with a child, get by on fifteen liras a month? A challenge? It's not even possible! For two years we've been selling and scrimping, topping that up with the fifteen liras to ward off death. But it can't go on like this. In a month's time I won't have anything left to sell. I need to find a job. Teaching would fail to feed not just a man but a chicken.

★

16th of February

I had been looking for work for fifteen days. At last I found something from a bookseller, translation for ten kurush a page. I can't describe how happy it made me… Each section brings in one hundred and sixty kurush. I get thirty lira for a three-hundred-page book.

★

7th of April

I have got into the habit of doing a regular ten pages of translation a night, for which four hours will suffice. And so it goes… It seems as if our life is improving. Orhan can drink his milk. Semiha and I will be able to acquire a pair of ration boots each. The fact is that working every night without break has ruined my eyesight. But we found a solution to this. Last week I bought some glasses from the eye doctor.

★

2nd of May

Yesterday I chanced upon a friend of mine, Shem, in Cenyo… The boy had bunked off from when we were in secondary school. I used to see him from time to time. He had become a businessman.

−I've got seventy-five thousand lira! he said, in just two months…

−You're joking, I laughed.

−You're welcome to ask any bank you want.

−But then how can that be?

−It's pretty easy if you can find your 'angle of approach'!

An ambition was stirring inside me. Seventy-five thousand lira in two months… I remembered how I'd sweated for one single lira. Four hours every night by the light of a carbide lamp I'd bought from the Germans in the interests of economy. The man opposite me was quite stretched as if to burst from health. Jewels studded his plump fingers.

−So what's this 'angle of approach' business then?

−It's easier than tapping up Topal!*

---

*Topal Pasha was the military's chief of logistics, and a symbol of mismanagement during the war years.

—Who's this Topal?

—Come on… Where have you been? You've really no idea who Topal is? Good God! Whoever gets a piece of him becomes a million-aire! Today, all of Turkey is in his hands! Seventy five thousand million lira jumps into action at his behest.

He began at great length to explain the virtues, the talents and the capabilities of the chief of procurement. I listened in amazement. At last I explained that I knew not a soul in the War Ministry. He felt for me.

However:

—Don't be so crestfallen, he said, there's no need to tap up Topal directly. It's enough that you tap up a man of his man…

—Well then, I'm tapping you up! I said, laughing.

—Not so fast! he said, erupting into a cackle. There's seven shirts' separation between him and my man. But I do need someone I can trust to do a job. And I can slip about eighty lira into your pocket from the deal.

Eighty lira a day… I couldn't believe my ears. Any more and I would have planted kisses all over the hands of this nouveau riche. A weight was coming off my shoulders. The promise of riches suddenly over-comes a man, like a hit of ether.

—Come and see me the day after tomorrow! I'm on the second floor of the Ömer Abid building, he said.

I'm going to go to see him tomorrow. He will ensure I earn some cash. Income without capital! I would never have dared imagine it! I'm going to become swiftly rich, like so many of those others. Farewell to this penury! This decrepit black wooden house! Farewell, bedbug colony! I'm so excited that I'm rolling up my trousers before I have reached the stream. I haven't been able to continue with translation for two days! Dare I take these paper scraps to bookseller Acem and say, 'Stuff your translations! Keep your money. May God do with you what he will!'? Semiha is suspicious of my state of mind.

—Something's the matter with you, something's the matter with you! she stands there saying. She asks why I'm not translating. I tell her my head hurts. Let them wait for me as long as they want at the school tomorrow! With what unknowable self-importance the poor director of assistant teachers will count up the hours of my absence, trying to collect enough to dock my pay. Gormless fellow.

★

15th of September

We returned from Büyükada* two days ago, and today we moved into our apartment. I've managed to get this place for 750 a year. How very wonderful it is... A bathroom, heating, electric heating – it has it all. Six bedrooms, two salons. I spent exactly five thousand furnishing it. I'm going to put together my library again. Yes, this happy state breezes past like a dream. I can't even remember how I spent this summer... I haven't even officially left my post yet. I've left a proxy in my stead. I got a certificate from the doctor stating that I'm ill. I give my stand-in an extra ten lira to top up the wages I'm passing on. If I leave the school, there's a risk I'll be called up for military service. It sneaks up on you all of a sudden, and business can't rescue you. Shem got me 3000 lira in kickbacks in the first month. The truth is I am very grateful to him. He has turned me into a man. We deal in flour. There's nothing very lucrative about that. So we dabble in a bit of cereal as well. We hoard some sugar and the like. I smiled to myself as I read over the things I wrote only four months ago. I'll be damned! How did I put up with such squalor! Sweating in an airless school room for five hours, for half a lira a day! And what's more, to consider so explicit a degree of servitude to be a virtue! Thankfully I've abandoned the virtue of master worship. It is true that the milieu in which I now find myself is a bit coarse. In fact it displays not a whit of sophistication... Everyone's longing, philosophy, and intention is but this: Making money! No room for abstracts! No place for dreams! Market rigging gives enough food for thought! Avarice is the greatest asset... I daresay that in the space of a year I'll have overtaken Shem. Ah, why was there no one to guide me by the hand at the beginning of the war? We still count amongst the poorest

---

*An island just off Istanbul in the Sea of Marmara where many wealthy Istanbul residents spent, and still spend, their summers.

today. They say there are men now who've earned ten million lira over the last two years. The Americans should get involved! When I was still in teaching, a friend of mine had me read a book. I remember its French name: *L'Alphabet des Richesses*! The man starts with one dollar on the way to getting rich. To make his million, he labours day and night for thirty years. Here if you're shrewd, you can make that million in liras without breaking into a sweat. All it takes is a little arrangement with Topal! If you could get the Balkan trains, the Anatolian line, to work for you for just a month…

I no longer hope to fill this notebook. When a man is rich, he hates to write just as much as he hates to read. Nevertheless I won't throw it out, so that it remains as a remembrance. Indeed to forget one's former poverty would not be very dignified. I will put it away in my library.

My Semiha…

How exacting she is! She simply can't decide how the dining room should go. She's been going at it all morning with the decorator from Psalti. Let me go and see what they're up to.

★

2nd of February 1917

Six months on, my poor true notebook! How eagerly I take you into my hands; I'm in a painful turmoil. I can't but speak of it, I'm like a criminal whose sin is poised in his mouth because it won't fit into his heart. The other day I was invited to Cerrapasha for dinner at the house of one of the nouveau riche. They played us string music *à la Turca*. We ate and drank until midnight. I could not sleep. I left my house early in the morning. The cold was vicious. I could not find a carriage. I went down the hill to Aksaray. Again, there were no carriages. I looked up from the corner of the Valide Mosque where I used to attend Friday prayers with my dad when I was small. It seemed the echo of something forgotten… The whole of it a ruin… I could see the Tulip Mosque, the back of the Hasan-pasha Building. I was awash with regret. I walked along slowly. We lived on the street that went down from Laleli to Yenikapi in a big house with a garden, cellars and a pool. That was twenty-five or twenty-six years ago…

We had a neighbour opposite. Mrs Guzin. Her daughters' voices were so thick... Just like a bugle. Remembering the days of my childhood on this morning transported me back to childhood itself; to have found the plot of land where we had lived amid the fire-scorched earth! What was I to do! Nothing! I wondered if the pool still remained. I stepped in amongst the ruins. There was nobody around. Broken halves of chimneys and hearths were sleeping in the degradation of an unmarked grave. Within the limits of the house I had been looking for this debris was all the denser. I looked and saw four bedraggled people wandering around. They were bending to look inside the hearths. I was curious. What did they hope to find? I followed. I reached them and asked what they searched for.

–We're looking for corpses! they said.

–The corpses of what?

The short, old fellow with the hoary beard gave a reply.

–The corpses of people.

–The corpses of people, you say?

–Yes...

He paused, understanding me to be surprised. He looked at me from head to toe. Then he shook his head.

–Well, well, well! he said. So you, Sir, don't have any idea about this either? We're with the municipality. We come here every day to collect those who die of hunger. We put them into that cart over there. We take them away, we bury them.

–So there are those who die of hunger... I said, turning to ice. It was as if my heart had stopped. I had been cut off at the knees. The old man opened his mouth. How poor Muslims have been broken by hunger in the last few years, he began to wail with the fever of a mournful preacher who has been thrown into the fire. He railed about those who were forced to sell and eat everything out from under their feet and over their heads, about how in the end those poor souls without no one to cling to had fallen into the ramshackle pits which lay all around them like helpless, lonely, hungry, thirsty, shivering dogs.

–If these traitors don't stop this unholy scourge, there will be no more Muslims left in the world! he said.

– Who are these traitors? I asked.

—But who should they be? They are those who feed the people sand and call it bread! Those whose food is of the ground and not from it! They strip away at the destitute to enrich themselves. Those flying past in their automobiles!

– …

Then he stood for a moment. His friends were not as agitated as he was. He lifted hands and head up to the sky:

—When we will see these people hanged, oh God?! he cried, taking a deep, painful and dark breath. I let out not a sound. Yes, it was we who were killing people with hunger! Those showing us the way, those helping us out, those stealing alongside us! In Kagithane Shem and I had discovered a rich 'lode of flour'. For three months, we had been selling the fine dust we found there to the central food distribution centre. There they pool it all together quite knowingly and add some chaff and send it out to the bakeries. I followed after the men searching for the dead as if I had been magnetised. They had found two so far. I looked. I was poisoned to the core. The corpses were half-naked. Their leather skin had dried on the bone. There was no meat on them at all. One was a woman. Her blond hair had matted. So much had I chewed at my lips that I felt warm drops of blood start to drip down my chin. I felt that the corpse's cavernous blue eyes were looking straight at me. It was as if I'd snapped. I lost it. I began to run like a madman. I don't know how I reached Beyazit, but there I hailed a cab. I got home. I passed out. The doctor and everyone turned up. When I came to, I told Semiha what I'd seen. She was deeply distressed and burst into tears. Now I'm confined to my bed. I've become a fanatical anarchist. I'm going to kill this Topal, this man whose armed gang is causing this nation to die of hunger, and I'm going to kill all those in league with this low-life. Yes, the government intend to ruin this nation! I no longer hold any doubts about it! Who ever doubts this is a donkey! Topal, the whole rotten syndicate, that treacherous, son-of-a-dog evil organisation, they have wrapped themselves around this nation like a seven-headed monster! They sap at our blood, our marrow, our bones. I must put an end to him. Killing just one of them is more noble than killing a thousand enemy soldiers in the trenches – indeed far more noble…

★

19th of March

I did not kill them. If it lives through this, the nation shall put an end to them! It will string them up on the gallows! Killing them is not the due of any one man! The traitors have the power of a seven-headed, nine-souled dragon! It is a fearful organisation! But I did kill myself! I killed the profiteer in me... I sold every last thing I had.

All the money I had got through killing my nation with hunger I distributed to the soup kitchens, to the poor houses and to the community. I did everything anonymously. We left the apartment and all its trappings. Semiha and I took our little Orhan with us, and we rented a teeny-tiny house in Üsküdar's Chavushdere, on the Asian side of the Bosphorus. Now we're so very happy... Thank goodness I never left my post at the school! I've started teaching lessons again. My friends think I'm bankrupt. I went to Acem again. He likes my translations! Now he's prepared to give me twelve kurush a page! In the evenings, I dictate and Semiha writes it down. I'm able to earn fifty lira a month. For a tightly-managed household, this is more than enough... But the last ten months are always in my mind, like a terrible nightmare. I cannot forget it. I cannot forget those I killed from hunger. I can't forget the stare of the women's corpse as it lay amid the scorched earth. I can't forget that for ten months I've been living off blood, tears and pus, that I've been living at the expense of the innocents piled up having died from lack of milk and sugar. A dark shadow haunts my soul at every moment. You too were involved in bloody robbery. You too, you too. Constant rows of gallows appears before my eyes. If I were to hang from one of these! I do not think that the stinging pain in my conscience will be extinguished. Even after I die, I am sure this torment will turn me in my grave!...

〜

Ömer Seyfettin was born in Gönen in 1884 and died in Istanbul in 1920. He was a fervent nationalist, and his work is much praised for simplifying the

Turkish language by eliminating the Persian and Arabic words and phrases that were common at the time. The son of a military official, he spent his early life travelling around the coast of the Marmara Sea. He graduated from a military veterinary academy in 1896, and fought in the 1903 conflicts in Macedonia. Captured and made prisoner of war in the Balkan War of 1913, he did not fight in the First World War but his literary output during the war was prodigious. The Turkish forces were engaged on four different territorial fronts as well as in internal battle with their Ottoman sovereigns, who would eventually be supplanted by the military politicians with whom Seyfettin shared his reformist vision. 'Why didn't he get rich?', first published in *Büyük Mecmua*, issue 3, 20 March 1919, is not a tale of heroism, but of corruption and inequality. Seyfettin was disillusioned by the war and by the poverty he saw around him. An important thing to remember about the Turkish experience of the Great War is that it was not the first terrible war fought in the last years of the empire, and it would not be the last. The Turkish War of Independence of 1918–19 was aimed at pushing back the colonial advances of the victorious allies. In the republic that emerged from the war Ömer Seyfettin's stories are still taught, and his language is now its language.

JAMES HANLEY

I SURRENDER, CAMERADE

from *The German Prisoner*

'ELSTON!'

'Yes.'

'Oh! you're awake. I say, we must have slept a hell of a time. My watch has stopped too. This blasted fog hasn't risen yet, either. We'd better move.'

'What's that you say?'

'What's up now? Got the bloody shakes again?' asked O'Garra.

'Listen,' said Elston.

Somewhere ahead they could hear the movement of some form or other.

'Let's find out,' said O'Garra, and jumped to his feet.

'No need now,' said Elston. 'Here it comes. Look!'

They both looked up at once. Right on top of them stood a young German soldier. His hands were stuck high in the air. He was weaponless. His clothes hung in shreds and his face was covered with mud. He looked tired and utterly weary. He said in a plaintive kind of voice:

'Camerade. Camerade.'

'Camerade, you bastard,' said Elston, 'keep your hands up there.'

And O'Garra asked: 'Who are you? Where do you come from? Can you speak English? Open your soddin' mouth!'

'Camerade. Camerade.'

'You speak English, Camerade?'

'Yes… a little.'

'Your name,' demanded Elston. 'What regiment are you? Where are we now? No tricks. If you do anything, you'll get your bottom kicked. Now then – where have you come from, and what the hell do you want?'

'My name it is Otto Reiburg. My home it is München. I am Bavarian. I surrender, Camerade.'

'That's all,' growled Elston.

'I am lost, is it,' replied the German.

He was a youth, about eighteen years of age, tall, with a form as graceful as a young sapling, in spite of the ill-fitting uniform and unkempt appearance. His hair, which stuck out in great tufts from beneath his forage cap, was as fair as ripe corn. He had blue eyes, and finely moulded features.

'So are we,' said Elston. 'We are lost too. Is it foggy where you came from? It looks to me as if we'll never get out of this hole, only by stirring ourselves together and making a bolt for it.'

'That's impossible,' said O'Garra. 'True, we can move. But what use is that? And perhaps this sod is leading us into a trap. Why not finish the bugger off, anyhow?'

The two men looked at the young German, and smiled. But the youth seemed to have sensed something sinister in that smile. He began to move off. Elston immediately jumped up. Catching the young German by the shoulder he flung him to the bottom of the hole, saying:

'If you try that on again I'll cut the bollocks out of you. Why should you not suffer as well as us? Do you understand what I am saying? Shit on you,' and he spat savagely into the German's face.

From the position the youth was lying in, it was impossible for either of the men to see that he was weeping. Indeed, had Elston seen it, he would undoubtedly have killed him. There was something terrible stirring in this weasel's blood. He knew not what it was. But there was a strange and powerful force possessing him, and it was going to use him as its instrument. He felt a power growing in him. There was something repugnant, something revolting in those eyes, in their leer, and in the curled lips. Was it that in that moment itself, all the rottenness that was his life had suddenly shot up as filth from a sewer, leaving him helpless in everything but the act he was going to commit? O'Garra was watching Elston. He too seemed to have sensed this something terrible.

His gaze wandered from Elston to the young German. No word was spoken. The silence was intense. Horrible. These three men, who but an hour ago seemed to be charged for action, eager and vital, looked as helpless as children now. Was it that this fog surrounding them had pierced its way into their hearts and souls? Or was it that something in their very nature had suffered collapse?

One could not say that they sat, or merely lay; they just sprawled; each terribly conscious of the other's presence, and in that presence detecting something sinister; something that leered; that goaded and pricked. Each seemed to have lost his faculty of speech. The fog had hemmed them in. Nor could any of them realize their position, where they were, the possibility of establishing contact with other human beings. What was this something that had so hurled them together?

O'Garra looked across to Elston.

'Elston! Elston! What are we going to do? We must get out of this. Besides, the place stinks. Perhaps we are on very old ground. Rotten ground; mashy muddy ground. Christ, the place must be full of these mangy dead.'

Elston did not answer. And suddenly O'Garra fell upon him, beating him in the face, and screaming out at the top of his voice:

'Hey. Hey. You lousy son of a bitch. What's your game? Are you trying to make me as rotten as yourself, as cowardly, as lousy? It's you and not this bloody Jerry who is responsible for this. Do you hear me? Do you hear me? Jesus Christ Almighty, why don't you answer? Answer. Answer.'

The young German cowered in the bottom of the hole, trembling like a leaf. Terror had seized him. His face seemed to take on different colours, now white, now red, now grey, as if Death were already in the offing. Saliva trickled down his chin.

These changes of colour in the face seemed to pass across it like gusts of wind. Gusts of fear, terror, despair. Once only he glanced up at the now distorted features of the half-crazy Irishman, and made as if to cry out. Once again O'Garra spoke to Elston. Then it was that the Englishman opened his eyes, looked across at his mate, and shouted:

'O'Garra! O'Garra. Oh, where the funkin' hell are you, O'Garra?'

He stared hard at the Irishman, who, though his lips barely moved, yet uttered sounds:

'In a bloody madhouse. In a shit hole. Can't you smell the rotten dead? Can you hear? Can you hear? You louse, you bloody rat. Pretending to be asleep and all the while your blasted owl's eyes have been glaring at me. Ugh! Ugh!'

'Camerade.'

A sigh came from the youth lying at the bottom of the hole. It was almost flute-like, having a liquidity of tone.

'Ah! *uck you,' growled O'Garra. 'You're as much to blame as anybody. Yes. Yes. As much to blame as anybody. Who in the name of Jesus asked you to come here? Haven't I that bastard there to look after? The coward. Didn't I have to drag him across the ground during the advance? Yes. YOU. YOU. YOU,' and O'Garra commenced to kick the prisoner in the face until it resembled a piece of raw beef. The prisoner moaned. As soon as O'Garra saw the stream of blood gush forth from the German's mouth, he burst into tears. Elston, too, seemed to have been stirred into action by this furious onslaught on the youth. He kicked the German in the midriff, making him scream like a stuck pig. It was this scream that loosed all the springs of action in the Manchester man. It cut him to the heart, this scream. Impotency and futility seemed as ghouls leering at him, goading him, maddening him.

He started to kick the youth in the face too. But now no further sound came from that inert heap. The Englishman dragged himself across to O'Garra. But the Irishman pushed him off.

'Get away. I hate you. Hate you. HIM. Everybody. Hate all. Go away. AWAY.'

'By Jesus I will then,' shouted Elston. 'Think I'm a bloody fool to sit here with two madmen. I'm going. Don't know where I'll land. But anything is better than this. It's worse than hell.'

He rose to his feet and commenced to climb out of the hole. He

looked ahead. Fog. And behind. Fog. Everywhere fog. No sound. No
stir. He made a step forward when O'Garra leaped up and dragged him
back. Some reason seemed to have returned to him, for he said:

'Don't go. Stay here. Listen. This state of affairs cannot go on for ever.
The fog will lift. Are you listening, and not telling yourself that I am
mad? I am not mad. Do you understand? Do you understand? Tell me!'

'Is it day or night, or has day and night vanished?' asked Elston.

'It might well be that the whole bloody universe has been hurled
into space. The bugger of it is, my watch has stopped. Sit down here. I
want to talk. Do you see now? I want to talk. It's this terrible bloody
silence that kills me. Listen now. Can you hear anything? No. You can't.
But you can hear me speak. Hear that *ucker – moaning down there.
They are human sounds. And human sounds are everything now. They
can save us. So we must talk. All the while. Without resting, without
ceasing. Understand? Whilst we are conscious that we are alive, all is
well. Do you see now? Do you see now?'

'I thought the bloody Jerry was dead,' muttered Elston. 'Dead, my
arse. Come! What'll we talk about? Anything. Everything.'

And suddenly Elston laughed, showing his teeth, which were like
a horse's!

'Remember that crazy house down in Fricourt? Remember that?
Just as we started to enter the God-forsaken place, he began to bomb
and shell it.'

'Remember? We both went out in the evening, souveniring. Went
into that little white house at the back of the hotel. Remember that?'

'Well!'

'Remember young Dollan mounting that old woman? Looked like
a bloody witch. I still remember her nearly bald head.'

'Well!'

'And you chucked young Dollan off, and got into bed with her
yourself.'

'Was it a long time ago? In this war, d'you mean?'

'Yes. Are you tapped, or what? Course it was in this bloody war.
What the funkin' hell are you thinkin' of, you loony?'

For the first time since they had found themselves in this position, they both laughed. And suddenly Elston looked up into his companion's face, laughed again, and said softly:

'Well, by Christ, d'you know that laugh has made me want to do something.'

'Do something?' queried O'Garra.

'Yes,' replied Elston, and standing over the prisoner in the hole, he pissed all over him. Likewise O'Garra, who began to laugh in a shrill sort of way.

There is a peculiar power about rottenness, in that it feeds on itself, borrows from itself, and its tendency is always downward. That very action had seized the polluted imagination of the Irishman. He was helpless. Rottenness called to him; called to him from the pesty frame of Elston. After the action they both laughed again, but this time louder.

'Hell!' exclaimed O'Garra. 'After that I feel relieved. Refreshed. Don't feel tired. Don't feel anything particularly. How do you feel?' he asked.

'The same,' replied Elston. 'But I wish to Christ this soddin' fog would lift.'

This desire, this hope that the fog would lift was something burning in the heart, a ceaseless yearning, the restlessness of waters washing against the floodgates of the soul. It fired their minds. It became something organic in the brain. Below them the figure stirred slightly.

'*Ah!— Ah!—*'

'The *ucker hasn't kicked the bucket yet,' said Elston. He leaned over and rested his two hands on O'Garra's knees. 'D'you know when I came to examine things; that time I thought you were asleep you know, and you weren't; well I thought hard, and I came to certain conclusions. One of them was this. See that lump of shit in the hole; that Jerry I mean? You do. Well now, he's the cause of everything. Everything. Everything. Don't you think so yourself?'

'Yes I do,' said the Irishman. 'That's damn funny, you know. Here is what I thought. I said to myself: "That bastard lying there is the cause of all this." And piece by piece and thread by thread I gathered up all the inconveniences. All the actions, rebuffs, threats, fatigues, cold nights, lice, toothaches, forced absence from women, nights in trenches up to your knees in mud. Burial parties, mopping-up parties, dead horses, heaps of stale shite, heads, balls, brains, everywhere. All those things. I made the case against him. Now I ask you. Why should he live?'

'Yes,' shouted Elston. 'You're right. Why should he? He is the cause of it all. Only for this bloody German we might not have been here. I know where I should have been anyhow. Only for him the fog might have lifted. We might have got back to our own crowd. Yes. Yes. Only for him. Well, there would not have been any barrage, any attack, and bloody war in fact.'

'Can't you see it for yourself now? Consider. Here we are, an Englishman, and an Irishman, both sitting here like soft fools. See! And we're not the only ones perhaps. One has to consider everything. Even the wife at home. All the other fellows. All the madness, confusion. Through Germans. And here's one of them.'

'*Ah!*—'

Elston glared down into the gargoyle of a face now visible to them both, the terrible eyes flaring up at the almost invisible sky.

'Water— *Ah!*—'

A veritable torrent of words fell from Elston's lips.

'Make the funkin' fog rise and we'll give you anything. Everything. Make the blasted war stop, now, right away. Make all this mud and shite vanish. Will you? You bastards started it. Will you now? See! We are both going mad. We are going to *kill* ourselves.'

'Kill me—'

'Go and shite. But for the likes of you we wouldn't be here.'

'Water—'

In that moment O'Garra was seized by another fit of madness. Wildly, like some terror-stricken and trapped animal, he looked up and around.

'Fog. Yes fog. FOG. FOG. FOG. FOG. FOG. Jesus sufferin' Christ. FOG. FOG. FOG. HA, HA, HA, HA, HA. In your eyes, in your mouth, on your chest, in your heart. FOG. FOG. Oh hell, we're all going crazy. FOG. FOG.'

'*There you are!*' screamed Elston into the German's ear, for suddenly seized with panic by the terrific outburst from O'Garra he had fallen headlong into the hole. The eyes seemed to roll in his head, as he

screamed: 'There you are. Can you hear it? You. Can you hear it? You
★ucker from München, with your fair hair, and your lovely face that we
bashed in for you. Can you hear it? We're trapped here. Through you.
Through you and your bloody lot. If only you hadn't come. You baby.
You soft stupid little runt. Hey! Hey! Can you hear me?'

The two men now fell upon the prisoner, and with peculiar movements of the hands began to mangle the body. They worried it like
mad dogs. The fog had brought about a nearness, that was now driving
them to distraction. Elston, on making contact with the youth's soft
skin, became almost demented. The velvety touch of the flesh infuri-
ated him. Perhaps it was because Nature had hewn him differently. Had
denied him the young German's grace of body, the fair hair, the fine
clear eyes that seemed to reflect all the beauty and music and rhythm of
the Rhine. Maddened him. O'Garra shouted out:

'PULL his bloody trousers down.'

With a wild movement Elston tore down the prisoner's trousers.

In complete silence O'Garra pulled out his bayonet and stuck it up
the youth's anus. The German screamed.

Elston laughed and said: 'I'd like to back-scuttle the bugger.'

'Go ahead,' shouted O'Garra.

'I tell you what,' said Elston. 'Let's stick this horse-hair up his penis.'

So they stuck the horse-hair up his penis. Both laughed shrilly. A
strange silence followed.

'Kill the bugger!' screamed O'Garra.

Suddenly, as if instinctively, both men fell away from the prisoner,
who rolled over, emitting a single sigh – *Ah…* His face was buried in
the soft mud.

'Elston.'

'Well,' was the reply.

'Oh Jesus! Listen. Has the fog risen yet? I have my eyes tight closed.
I am afraid.'

'What are you afraid of? Tell me that. There's buggerall here now.
This fellow is dead. Feel his bum. Any part you like. Dead. Dead.'

'I am afraid of myself. Listen. I have something to ask you. Will you
agree with me now to walk out of it? We can't land in a worse place.'

'My *arse* on you,' growled Elston. 'Where can we walk? You can't see a finger ahead of you. I tell you what. Let's worry each other to death. Isn't that better than this moaning, this sitting here like soft shits. That time I fell asleep I did it in my pants. It made me get mad with that bugger down there.'

'A thing like that,' O'Garra laughed once again.

'Listen,' roared Elston. 'I tell you we can't move. D'you hear? Do you? Shall I tell you why?

'It's not because there is no ground on which to walk. No. Not that. It's just that we can't move. We're stuck. Stuck fast. Though we have legs, we can't walk. We have both been seized by something, I can't even cry out. I am losing strength. I don't want to do anything. Nothing at all. Everything is useless. Nothing more to do. Let's end it. Let's worry each other like mad dogs. I had the tooth-ache an hour ago. I wish it would come back. I want something to worry me. Worry me.'

'Listen! Did you hear that?'

'Well, it's a shell. What did you think it was? A bloody butterfly?'

'It means,' said O'Garra, 'that something is happening, and where something is happening we are safe. Let's go. Now. Now.'

'Are you sure it was a shell?'

'Sure. There's another,' said O'Garra.

'It's your imagination,' said Elston laughing. 'Imagination.'

'Imagination. Well, by Christ. I never thought of that. Imagination. By God, that's it.'

They sat facing each other. Elston leaned forward until his eyes were on a level with those of the Irishman. Then, speaking slowly, he said:

'Just now you said something. D'you know what it was?'

'Yes. Yes. Let's get out of it before we are destroyed.'

'But we're destroyed already,' said Elston, smiling. 'Listen.'

'Don't you remember what you said a moment ago?' continued Elston. 'You don't. Then there's no mistake about it, you are crazy. Why, you soft shite, didn't you say we had better talk, talk, talk? About anything. Everything. Nothing. Let us then. What'll we talk about?'

'Nothing. But I know what we must do. Yes, by Jesus I know. D'you remember you said these Germans were the cause of the war? And you kicked that fellow's arse? Well, let's destroy him. Let's bury him.'

'He's dead, you mad bugger. Didn't we kill him before? Didn't I say I felt like back-scuttling him? I knew all along you were crazy. Ugh.'

'Not buried. He's not buried,' shouted O'Garra. 'Are you deaf? Mad yourself, are you?'

The fog was slowly rising, but they were wholly unconscious of its doing so. They were blind. The universe was blotted out. They were conscious only of each other's presence, of that dead heap at the bottom of the hole. Conscious of each other's nearness. Each seemed to have become something gigantic. The one saw the other as a barrier, a wall blotting out everything. They could feel and smell each other. There was something infinite in those moments that held them back from each other's throats.

'Not deaf, but mad like yourself, you big shithouse. Can't you see that something has happened? I don't mean outside, but inside this funkin' fog, savvy?'

'Let's bury this thing. UGH. Everything I look at becomes him. Everything him. If we don't destroy him, he'll destroy us, even though he's dead.'

'Let's dance on the bugger and bury him forever.'

'Yes, that's it,' shouted O'Garra. 'I knew an owld woman named Donaghue whose dog took poison. She danced on the body.'

And both men began to jump up and down upon the corpse. And with each movement, their rage, their hatred seemed to increase. Out of sight, out of mind. Already this mangled body was beginning to disappear beneath the mud. Within their very beings there seemed to burst into flame, all the conglomerated hates, fears, despairs, hopes, horrors. It leaped to the brain for O'Garra screamed out:

'I hate this thing so much now I want to shit on it!'

'O'Garra.'

'Look. It's going down, down. Disappearing. Look,' shouted Elston. 'Elston.'

'Let's kill each other. Oh sufferin' Jesus—'

'You went mad long ago but I did not know that—'

'Elston,' called O'Garra.

'There's no way out is there?'

'*Uck you. NO.'

'Now.'

'The fog is still thick.'

'Now.'

The bodies hurled against each other, and in that moment it seemed as if this madness had set their minds afire.

Suddenly there was a low whine, whilst they struggled in the hole, all unconscious of the fact that the fog had risen. There was a terrific explosion, a cloud of mud, smoke, and earthy fragments, and when it cleared the tortured features of O'Garra were to be seen. His eyes had been gouged out, whilst beneath his powerful frame lay the remains of Elston. For a moment only they were visible, then slowly they disappeared beneath the sea of mud which oozed over them like the restless tide of an everlasting night.

∽

James Hanley was born in Liverpool in 1897. He went to sea at the age of 17. He jumped ship in New Brunswick in 1916 and enlisted in the Canadian Expeditionary Force, which was part of the Canadian contingent that contributed to the crucial victories of Passchendaele and Vimy. In 1931, he published privately *The German Prisoner* with an introduction by Richard Aldington, who wrote:

> Gentlemen! Here are your defenders, ladies! Here are the results of your charming white feathers. If you were not ashamed to send men into the war, why should you blush to read what they said in it? Your safety, and indeed the almost more important safety of your incomes, were assured by them. Though the world will little note nor long remember what they did there, perhaps it will not hurt you to know a little of what they said and suffered.

Not surprisingly, this short novel, which features the brutality of two working-class soldiers (one from Belfast, one from Manchester) towards a German prisoner, proved too controversial for audiences of the time and was reprinted only in 1967. It is less shocking to a contemporary audience used to the news from Guantanamo and Iraq. Also in 1931, Boriswood Press published Hanley's novel *Boy*, a powerful tale of sadism inflicted on a boy who becomes a slave at sea: the book was banned for obscenity in 1935 and not republished until 1990 with an introduction by Anthony Burgess. Hanley continued to write until his death in London in 1985. As his work becomes more available, he is now beginning to get the recognition denied him during his lifetime.

THEODOR PLIEVIER

MUTINY!

from *The Kaiser's Coolies*
translated by Martin Chalmers

T HE SHIP'S DOCTOR of His Majesty's Auxiliary Cruiser 'Wolf' has put on his full dress uniform and requested to see the commander.

The commander receives him standing.

The quarterdeck is packed with prisoners. Hundreds, in rags, a dull grey mass, thrown together from every race. Only at meal times is there movement in the crowd. Otherwise they squat next to each other, like a society of great brooding birds, stare into the air or over the eternally blue ocean.

The doctor reports:

'The state of health of the prisoners is even more worrying, but the same typical symptoms are present on the mess deck: cardiac dilatation, muscular atrophy, trapped nerve pain. Many are losing their teeth. All beds in the sick bay are occupied. A further hundred men should be admitted to the sick bay, thirty can no longer stand. A couple collapse every day. All are suspected of having scurvy. If the voyage is not brought to an end within a few weeks, the whole crew is facing death!'

That was in the Indian Ocean.

Since then we have sunk more ships, rounded the Cape of Good Hope and crossed the Atlantic Ocean from south to north. For the second time we are lying off the Denmark Strait, this time off the western channel.

The distance we have covered is equivalent to circling the globe three times and we have sunk 300,000 tons of shipping. All that is behind us. Our holds are stacked up to the hatches with precious cargo. The engines are overtaxed; the ship's hull has sprung a leak because of repeatedly going alongside and unloading the captured steamers. We're taking on 840 metric hundredweight of water every hour. The bilge pumps cope with the inflow of water.*

The wind is blowing from the north and throwing fields of broken ice at us. In front, at the sides, under the keel, ice everywhere. Vast herds of great grey pieces. The hull echoes under the hard blows. Now and then the dammed-up sea hurls a piece on deck. It then moves back and forth like a freight car being shunted on a swaying track, crushing superstructure and emplacements. A torpedo bay is gone. Number II windlass is smashed to pieces.

The blocks of ice are wedged in and dumped overboard again, making use of the ship's motion. Cables, crowbars, other hand tools! One hundred and fifty pairs of arms and legs! And we've got nothing on our bones, are drained of strength by scurvy, when we bend down we're already wet with weakness. A prisoner jumps overboard, Captain Tominaga of the sunken Japanese steamer 'Hitachi Maru'.

The Denmark Strait is blocked.

The ice forces us south. Finally we find our way into the North Sea between Iceland and the Shetland Islands and reach the Norwegian coast without catching sight of one of the English patrol boats.

We sail on within the three-mile zone, at night pass the lights of fishermen lying by their nets – Skagerrak, Jutland, the Little Belt!

We drop anchor in Kiel Bay. After 444 days at sea.

Sent out on our voyage to sink and drown! The death notices have already been written and sent to relatives by the Admiralty Staff. But now we have returned and put in to Kiel. A hospital ship takes off the sick, another the prisoners. Twenty-six of our men are in prison in Bombay for murder and piracy. The four victims of our own guns lie in the Indian Ocean.

*The voyage of the 'Wolf' was certainly an epic one, but the tonnage actually sunk owing to its actions seems to have been about 110,000 tons (trans.).

The rest of us have fallen in on deck.

The commander of the Baltic Station, a white-bearded admiral, inspects the ranks and puts 'affable' questions, always the same ones: 'What is your name?' – 'How old are you?' – 'What is your position?' – 'Geulen, Sir!' – 'Twenty-five, sir!' – 'Seaman, sir!'

A welcoming telegram from the German Emperor is read out and the order 'Pour le mérite' placed around the commander's neck. Then the Iron Crosses are distributed.

Two days later:

The Iron Crosses have been taken away from us again, the 'Pour le mérite' from the commander. The admiral has come on board again, this time with a captain from the 'Propaganda Office for Raising War Morale in the Hinterland'. A film camera! Close-ups: of the commander, of the pack of dachshunds, of the crew.

The cameraman turns the handle. The admiral awards the confiscated Iron Crosses for the second time, puts the same idiotic questions, reads the same telegram from the Emperor, places the 'Pour le mérite' round the commander's neck again. A big cinema show! The nation's highest military honour has become a prop. The commander who is not allowed to marry his wife because she is an actress is himself forced to take the part of an actor. All the other officers including the admiral and head of the Baltic Station make up the extras. The crews of the warships in harbour, the jetties populated on orders provide the big and cheap background. We roar hurrah half a hundred times until we're hoarse and grin as we do so: propaganda to raise war morale in Germany!

Sixteen hundred feet of film for the hinterland and the military hospitals. The captured cargo to the value of 40 million marks, raw rubber, copper, human hair, rice, coffee, tea, tinned meat, delicacies, spirits is not intended for the hinterland and the military hospitals. The Kiel Officers' Mess is interested in the cargo, sends out a number of barges in a kind of surprise attack and wants to begin the unloading. But as commander of a ship operating alone the commandant is not subordinate to any unit and has sole right of disposal. On his instruction the prize goods are taken off in the open harbour of Lübeck beyond the control of the naval authorities.

We are loaded with decorations. The Kings of Saxony, of Bavaria, of Württemberg, the Free Hanseatic Cities send medals on board by the box load. The officers are promoted. The commandant gets his fourth gold stripe: means a salary rise of 800 marks a month. The Artillery Officer his second stripe, 400 marks a month.

We remain coolies, on a daily wage of 50 pfennigs. The prize money due to us gets stuck somewhere in the maze of bureaucratic procedure. The soldiers' wives of Lübeck, who take us into their beds, wear night-shirts of coarse cloth, wash themselves with soap lacking oils or fat; they don't even have enough money to buy the rationed ersatz foodstuffs. We steal as much of the cargo as we can, split with customs and police, sell to the black marketeers and middlemen who have turned up. A retired senior naval officer resident in the town writes to the Admiralty Staff: '...the celebrated crew of His Majesty's Ship "Wolf" – no heroes, but robbers and thieves! Making off with state property! Should all, right down to the youngest sailor, be court-martialled!'

But we're loaded onto the train, transported to Berlin, march through the Brandenburg Gate, flanked on either side by a guard of honour. The city commandant gives a speech. The Empress waves her hand when we are allowed to march past her. Women from 'patriotic associations' hand out flowers. The city hosts a lunch for us, the Kempinski restaurant a supper. At the Zirkus Busch, in the theatre foyers, at the Zoo we are almost crushed by vast crowds of patriotic ladies. The directors of this show have their offices in the War Ministry. The march past of the crew of the auxiliary cruiser is just one item in the generals' programme against increasing war weariness.

*

We've had eight weeks convalescent leave. Twenty per cent are left behind in hospitals, in gonorrhoea wards or prison cells. The remainder of the crew of His Majesty's Ship 'Wolf' returns to Wilhelmshaven.

Personnel Office: 'Fall in with kitbags! In ranks wheel to the right! Break step, march!'

Onto ships on forward position!

Onto minesweepers!

After a privateering expedition across the North Atlantic and the sinking of eighteen merchant steamers Count zu Dohna-Schlodien has been appointed aide-de-camp to His Majesty. After an unparalleled voyage across five oceans, after laying mines outside important harbours and sinking 300,000 tons of enemy shipping the middle-class commander of the auxiliary cruiser 'Wolf' has been made minesweeper in chief of the North Sea.

C-Boat 212.

The boat is like a cardboard box and as flat as one. When we leave harbour with the other boats, then the crews of the proper ships know what's happening: 'The crab louse squadron is putting to sea.'

Before fleet movements the crab louse squadron each time clears a passage through the mine-infested waters of the North Sea. Two boats always trail the search device, which consists of a cable with a blade, behind them. The wire cable catches on the mine and separates it from its anchoring. The mines drifting on the surface are then dealt with by rifle fire. The silly thing is that we drag the cable behind us and have to sail over the minefields in front.

There are eighteen of us on board.

When the device is out, we crouch in the stern, the stoker off-watch, the deck crew, also the commander, a deputy helmsman, whom we call 'Sea Duster'. We sit on the railing, ready to jump overboard. That way we at least stand a chance of saving our arses, the stokers and the man at the helm next to none.

On the last trip out '110' blew up. We fished out eleven men. At Cuxhaven they got a new kitbag, after that a new boat. The kitbags are stored packed and ready at barracks. The missing men are replaced by a couple from the fleet and one pardoned from prison.

The summer has passed.

One leave, three detentions! We have a new boat now. 'C 212' blew up with the stokers' watch, the deck officer and cook. Since then we're allowed to call our commander 'Sea Duster' even when he's around.

The system is going to pieces.

The Emperor gives a speech, in Essen, to 1500 starving factory workers: 'My dear friends of the Krupp factories…'

New troops being sent up to the front have written on their railway carriages: 'Cattle for slaughter for Wilhelm & Sons'. – His Majesty's Ship 'Nürnberg' on forward duty in the North Sea: In the mess they're all drunk. The Engineer Officer has his bare backside smeared with mustard and sticks it out the window. The lieutenants declare: 'It's our latest searchlight!' – There are still wild parties in the messes of the naval officers with musicians playing every evening. – Ten death sentences, 181 years penal servitude, 180 years imprisonment have been imposed on the men of the fleet. And the apparatus of the courts-martial goes on working.

28th October 1918!

Quartermaster-General Ludendorff has taken his leave. The newly installed civilian government has offered the Entente an armistice. The whole of the German High Seas Fleet has been concentrated in Wilhelmshaven and in safe anchorages.

The minesweeper flotillas have orders to go fishing for mines, the squadron chiefs have received sealed operational commands: 'Forces of the High Seas Fleet are to go into action to attack and defeat the English fleet!'

Squadrons I, II, III, IV! Stoke all boilers! The ships raise steam, black balls of smoke ascend into the starless sky.

Anchors are to be raised at 10 p.m.

His Majesty's Ship 'Thüringen' blacked-out. Not one ray of light coming from it. Nothing is to be seen of the next ship anchored in line. A call through the damp air: "Thüringen" ahoy!' A boat emerges from the fog, a steam launch, then another, a third, a fourth. The first launch ties up by the jack ladder. The rest sail on to the other ships. The officers are coming on board again, from the officers' mess ashore.

On the 'Thüringen', at the top of the jack ladder, a bunch of sailors, off-duty stokers, critical expressions: 'They're all pissed out of their minds again!'

The men sit in the casemates under their strung up hammocks. Electric light, steel walls, steel ceilings. No one lies down to sleep. Four and half years of war! The military collapse is here! Doesn't matter: It means peace.

But in the bowels of the ship, in bunkers and boiler rooms forces are at work. Coal is being brought up, fires stoked, the boilers, curling smoke, turbines fill with trembling atmospheres.

Why have the minesweepers left harbour?

Why is the fleet lying at anchor in Schillig Roads?

Why is steam being raised?

There's something in the air!

The sailors and stokers roam from one casemate to the next, run over the decks, lurk around the bridge, under cover of darkness crowd as far as the quarterdeck.

Things are getting very lively in the mess. By now the gentlemen feel so hot that they've pulled open the skylight. A gramophone is playing, there's singing.

Champagne corks, glasses, babble of voices!

The gramophone stops playing, abruptly. A kick has hurled it to the floor. Those of the officers who can still stand have jumped to their feet. The stewards fill the glasses once again.

The sailors at the skylight looked down onto the officers. They forget all caution, and their eyes are transfixed. They soak up every one of the words spoken below.

There stands Lieutenant-Commander Rudloff, glass in hand: 'We'll fire our last two thousand shells at the English and then go down gloriously! Better an end with honour, than a life in shame!'

'Better ten years of war than such a peace!' – 'Lawyers, people in trade, newspaper scribblers, they want to rule our country now!' – 'We don't give a shit about the government! The fleet, the fleet commander has complete freedom of action!'

Pale faces, voices hoarse with excitement.

'The "Thüringen" must die! Comrades, gentlemen! It is a matter of our honour, this glass…'

'To the last battle of the German Fleet!'

'To the last voyage!'

'To the last two thousand shells!'

The sailors draw back from the skylight. They run through the casemates, through the seamen's decks, stokers' decks, shouting out what they've heard. Everywhere groups cluster. Those already sleeping are pulled from their hammocks.

The same on the 'Helgoland', 'Ostfriesland', 'Oldenburg'.

On the other ships, too, the signs have been observed, minesweepers putting to sea, steam in all boilers, the shouting in the officers' messes. Same old wartime tune: Victory or death! Crews of thousands of men all share the same feeling: Do something! Enough is enough! Or they lie waiting in the half-light of the casemates as if struck down.

The new fleet flagship SMS 'Baden', the biggest and most modern of the battleships, 15 inch guns, 56,000 shaft horse power! The 'Baden' is lying at anchor by the quay in the inner harbour. The crews are sleeping. Suddenly a cry goes up. 'Every man for himself! The officers are going to blow up the ammunitions rooms!' It spreads through the casemates, hysterical, alarming: 'Officers... ammunition... Every man...' The one thousand five hundred seamen pour through the armoured hatches, crowd over the deck, clamber ashore.

A catastrophic mood on all the ships!

SMS 'Thüringen', ten in the evening.

Bosuns' pipes shrill. Commands are sung out.

'Cutter detachment weigh anchor!'

'Mount naval sentries!'

The cutter detachment climbs up to the forecastle, makes its way to the capstan. Handles are turned. The capstan wheezes as the steam pours in. Link by link the heavy anchor is heaved through the hawsehole onto the ship. The bridge, occupied by officers, is invisible in the darkness, only the fat balls of smoke rising from the funnels.

A mob of sailors storms up onto the forecastle. They haven't waited, half-dressed, some barefoot: 'Boys, lads!' – 'This is crazy' – 'Hands off the capstan!' – 'We're not sailing any more!' – 'They can sail by themselves! Let them go down without us!'

A petty officer, a lieutenant, officers! Revolver muzzles raised threateningly! The men of the cutter detachment obey compulsion and the discipline drilled into them over the years. The chain rumbles and squeals, grows shorter. The anchor is hanging free, bangs heavily against the armoured side of the ship.

The funnels spew sparks.

The silhouette of a ship sails past.

Another one! The fleet is on the move.

The night is ripped apart. A cry – a single man cries out. The echo, anger and despair bursts from hundreds of throats! The top deck of the 'Thüringen' is thick with sailors. At that moment the other anchor drops; a couple of the men have let it fall. The chain rumbles through the hawsehole and immobilises the ship once again. Now the stokers are here as well. The stokers extinguish the furnaces.

The trails of smoke have been torn off, white steam pours from the funnels.

The masses are in motion.

They crowd through the casemates, into the forward battery, lash down the anchor chain, shut off the petty officers' quarters which lie below the seamen's deck and wedge the hatch covers shut. They cut the vangs and cutter checks, no boat can be lowered now. Officers who come down from the bridge are showered with everything possible, with washbasins, boots, lumps of lime scale from the boilers. Arms! Fists! The portrait of the 'Victor of Skagerrak'* is broken in pieces. Lamps are smashed, rifles, bullets distributed. Munition for the medium guns demanded.

The casemates thunder:

'Peace must come!'

'We must have freedom!'

'The aristocrats! The racketeers! The Imperial Navy: Down with them! Down with them!'

A searchlight! Morse signals!

His Majesty's Ship 'Helgoland' replies:

'Comrades, keep it up! We're doing the same!'

'Thüringen' remains anchored in Schillig Roads.

'Helgoland' remains in Schillig Roads.

The fleet, the cruisers and battleship squadrons, raises anchor. In the white cones of the searchlights the commanders have succeeded

---

*In German the Battle of Jutland is known as the Skagerrak Battle (*trans.*).

in dispersing the crowds of sailors on the decks and in securing the capstans. For the last time the naval officers appeal to a sense of duty, speculate on the gullibility of their crews: 'No, we're not sailing out to fight the British! We're only going out to sweep mines! There are still ninety U-boats at sea. They don't know the channel through the mine-fields. We have to bring them in!'

The fleet proceeds in a long line ahead.

Slowly! The stokers are keeping the steam low.

Twelve to fourteen nautical miles are sufficient to sweep mines and to bring in the U-boats. On leaving the Jade Estuary a wind rises. The foggy sky breaks, damply gleaming stars. The ships move in the heavy rhythm of the ocean. A change of course! The weather shifts to the other side. One can feel it right down to the casemates!

Course northwest!

Towards England!

Orders that don't come from the bridge. 'Out of your hammocks! Up to the forward battery! All men to the forward battery!'

There one of the men stands on the chain locker:

'The course is northwest! An attack! There are maps of the east coast of England on the navigation officer's table. On the flying bridge the signals are clear for full steam! They've lied to us, as they always do! Four and half years of war! Now the end is here! Their careers are finished, their glorious unemployed existence! They're afraid of the future and would rather take their own lives!

'This attack is suicide. We're supposed to be part of it. We're supposed to sacrifice ourselves for it!'

The ship rolls over the ocean swell.

Half a thousand men are by the chain locker in the forward battery. The punishment for mutiny is death! One group has settled down by one of the medium guns, they try to overcome their agitation by singing: 'I want to see home again...'

A speaker, a second, a third.

Now the Chief Mate is here.

'But only one man at a time can talk to me, or two at most. – I'm from south Germany, eighteen years with the Navy. – I don't want to die – Something has been thrown at me. That's not right – Comrades! Comrades!'

'Liar.'

'He wants to get killed!'

'Get him! Hit him!'

Light bulbs are smashed.

The forward battery is plunged into darkness.

Stamping of feet! The pushing and shoving of many bodies.

'Bloody cowards, stop that singing!' – 'The stokers, where are the stokers?' – 'Down to the boiler rooms. Damp the fires!' – 'Put out the searchlights!'

'Lights out!'

'Fires out!'

For a moment searchlights illuminate the men pouring out of the armoured decks and the crowds moving over the decks. Then the cones of light waver away into the sky and are extinguished.

Radio signal from the fleet commander:

'Operation is to be carried out unconditionally.'

Reply: 'Operation cannot be carried out!'

A siren wails.

Between decks. Entries to the stokeholds, groups of sailors! Fleeing engineering officers! Lumps of coal are flung. Non-commissioned officers defend the posts.

Wheels! Hand grips! Counterweights!

Extinguishers are pulled.

Furnace hatches torn open!

The alarm bell, telephone!

A last effort by the commanders:

'Clear for action! General quarters!'

The ploy doesn't work any more. In the boiler rooms the columns of steam rise like wild giant jungle trees. In the light of the fading flames struggling knots of bodies. Engineers, leading seamen are pushed aside by the mass.

The last boiler falls out.

The ship is immobile.

One after the other! One ship after another leaves the line and comes to a clumsy stop on the waves. The rudderless drifting vessels are like dead, very bloated carcasses.

The fleet attack is broken off.

The fleet staff moves from the battleship 'Baden' to the mastless and engineless office ship 'Kaiser Wilhelm II' in the inner harbour.

Fog on the Jade Estuary, on the Kiel Canal and on Kiel Bay. The surfaces of the sea look like dilute milk. Gulls flutter in the wake of the slowly moving ships, shriek and scrap over the slops thrown overboard, disappear swiftly in the airflow. The squadrons have separated, are returning to their home ports, to Wilhelmshaven, Cuxhaven, Brunsbüttel, Kiel.

Office ship 'Kaiser Wilhelm II'.

The staff officers are hanging on the telephone lines. Typewriters are rattling away. Orderlies are chasing back and forward. Letter telegrams! Wireless telegram messages: 'The naval prisons Fort Schaar, Gökerstrasse, Heppens are to be cleared as far as possible! – To accommodate a larger number of men the steamer "Frankfurt" of Norddeutsche Lloyd has been located. Solitary confinement is out of the question! – The members of the courts-martial… the clerks of court with typewriters to board the "Schwaben"! Embarkation under special orders! – A company of marines at war strength to embark on two harbour steamers to arrest the mutineers! – Should the men not willingly obey the command to come to the forecastle, a torpedo boat is to fire shells into the forward battery. In case of emergency a U-boat should take up position close to the "Thüringen"!'

A lieutenant-commander, the submarine commander Spiess, has finally found Fleet Staff, he reports to the Chief of Staff, Admiral von Trotha, putting 'U-135' at his disposal.

The chief of staff has already packed his cases.

Not to set sail: for four weeks now he has had an order to report to Imperial Army Headquarters and considers this moment, at which the Fleet is completely falling apart, as suitable for departing as quickly as possible. He never got to Imperial Army Headquarters!

'Are you sure of your crew?'

'Aye, aye, Admiral!'

Admiral von Trotha informs the submarine commander of the task. 'Putting to sea and ensuring that the mutineers of "Thüringen" and "Helgoland" can be arrested!' – 'Putting to sea', 'ensuring', the First Lieutenant doesn't like the terminology. What seems to be meant is torpedoing and blowing up their own ships of the line. He asks for a written order.

The Admiral replies.

'There is none at present.'

The submarine commander understands the situation: He is to act at his own risk, as so often before! The higher authorities don't want to take any responsibility! He doesn't get a clear order from the Fleet Commander either, a brief greeting, a bow, and he's standing outside again. Half an hour later the 'U-135' moves out into the fog in the wake of the steamer loaded with marines.

Three hundred men of the 'Thüringen' are detained. The same number from the 'Helgoland'!

The fleet returns. Battle cruisers, battleships, destroyers, in no order, in packs like fleeing animals.

A battleship, turrets, superstructure!

From the flagpole waves the war flag.

The crew, windbreakers, work trousers, sea boots, unwashed, stubble, thin and with leaden limbs, four and a half years of war and blockade in their faces, a grey flood pouring over the decks.

A reserve officer who doesn't read the signs: 'Lads, does it have to come to this – in 1914 I worked my passage over – from New York as a trimmer in the engine room...'

Poles! Hand tools! Bayonets!

The cells are wrecked.

The prisoners stream up to the light.

The reserve officer is overwhelmed. The crew rolls towards the stern like an avalanche. No resistance, the officers have barricaded themselves into the armoured deck. Fourteen hundred sailors and stokers, above their heads flutters the war flag, black on a white field, the Iron Cross in the left corner.

The knots of the flag halyard are not loosened. A thicket of arms and outstretched hands.

The halyard breaks.

The war flag sinks down.

A pair of arms raises a mop, a swab, used to wipe the decks, old and frayed by the sweat of countless coolies condemned to the work as punishment.

'The mop – tie it on!'

'Done – all men! Raise the flag!'

The tow swab rises into the air, remains hanging above. On the gaff on which in four and half years of war and since the founding of the Navy the symbol of the Empire has waved!

And on the other ships: The flags come down. Swabs, coal sacks, red flags go up.

Five thousand naval officers who have sworn an oath to the flag! At lavish celebrations with full champagne glasses in their hands they have repeated countless times that they are prepared to lay down their lives for flag and Emperor.

Five thousand admirals, captains, officers!

Only three defend their flag.

On SMS 'König' the commander, the First Officer and the adjutant, a twenty-year-old lieutenant. Pistol in hand the three stand on the afterdeck, abandoned by all the rest. A sailor falls under their shots. Then they're engulfed, a grey tidal wave breaks over them, clubs, shots! Bodies! Arms! Legs!

Commander and First Officer fall to the deck wounded.

The adjutant lies there dead.

The Emperor's flag sinks!

The red flag is raised!

All other ships give up without a fight.

The naval bases ashore give up without a fight.

The Imperial Navy Department in Berlin – Permanent Secretary, admirals, captains, lieutenant-commanders, several hundred officers armed with daggers, pistols, hand grenades, machine guns, supported by a company of riflemen at war strength, loyal to the Emperor: this fortress capitulates to an NCO and six men.

And the Supreme War Lord, Wilhelm II, Imperator Rex!?

After he has fled across the border in a car, his adjutant, Lieutenant-Colonel Niemann, asks him why he didn't seek death at the head of his troops. The Emperor replies:

'The time for heroic gestures is over!'

⇛

Even by the standards of German writers in the first half of the 20th century, **Theodor Plievier** led a life that was rich in drama and incident. Born in 1892 into a working-class family in Berlin, Plievier left home early, spending years as a vagabond and casual labourer in various European and South American countries. In between he went to sea. In 1914 he was more or less press-ganged into the German Imperial Navy. He was present at the Battle of Jutland and saw long service in the auxiliary cruiser SMS *Wolf*, raiding Allied shipping in the Atlantic and Indian Oceans, before playing a leading role in the mutinies which were the prelude to the fall of the government of the Reich in 1918. Plievier's first big success as an author was with *The Kaiser's Coolies* (1931), which deals with his wartime experience at sea. In 1933, the book was one of those symbolically burned by the Nazis. Although he had been politically active as an anarchist in the 1920s, Plievier and his wife sought shelter in the Soviet Union. Several times ordered to move to different locations in Russia, they were lucky to escape arrest. After the Nazi attack on the Soviet Union, Plievier was allowed to read captured correspondence and to interview German prisoners of war. This led to the writing of his great Second World War trilogy *Stalingrad*, *Moscow* and *Berlin*. In 1945 Plievier went to the Soviet Zone of Occupation in Germany but moved to West Germany in 1947. He died in Switzerland in 1955.

ARNOLD ZWEIG

SNOW

from *The Case of Sergeant Grischa*

translated by Eric Sutton

SNOW ON WESTERN RUSSIA! Somewhere above the forests lay the pivot of the storm. Round it, like the spokes and rim of a mighty crystal wheel, whirled legions of white flakes above the silent earth. The air was rent in pieces by the frenzied gusts. The storm swooped down, lashing and shrieking, upon tree-tops, hedges, and roofs – on all that stood up before it, and across the stretching plains that cowered beneath the blast. Myriads of flakes had begun to melt, but the cold laid hold upon them, and in a few hours the slush was covered with a solid and enduring robe of winter. The world was changing her face; it was becoming white, and black, and grey. The forests between Brest-Litovsk and Mervinsk were seething and howling with the storm. Flakes fell in the rivers and were drowned, but elsewhere they conquered. They swept over that vast land, falling thick and heavy among the tree-tops; the pine-needles were soon matted with their covering of snow, and in a few hours they would strain like sails beneath the storm. The stout sixty-year-old pines creaked in the wind like masts; they shuddered, bent, and swayed, but their roots held fast. The good months were over and the bad time had come again... The beasts crouched in their lairs and hearkened to the onslaught of winter: badgers and hamsters, who are always careful to keep a well-filled larder; foxes, bold and fearless – the snow does not spoil their hunting; but the hares with quivering ears and the rabbits would come off badly in the next few weeks. Mother lynx with her now strong and healthy brood sniffed fearlessly at the icy wind; once again there would be chances of pulling down young deer whose long legs had got caught in the undergrowth. In the plantations, where the old trees had been cut down, the roe-deer lay huddled side by side, and the stag, his eyes mournful with presage of the lean months to come, raised his steaming nostrils to the sky, and laid back his branching antlers. Winter had come upon the world. The men out yonder in the interminable trenches and dug-outs that war had made, watched drearily and grimly the beginning of yet another winter of war, drew gloves over their numbed fingers, piled wood into their stoves, and stamped savagely through the slush that squelched about their feet. 'We shall be home for Christmas,' said they, and they knew that they were lying; while above their heads the spirit of the snow danced a wild dance over the desolate places and the forests, and strove with all his might to entangle the branches of the trees together, and strew the ground with heaps, drifts, and swathes of snow.

From Brest-Litovsk there stretched over the land a network of black lines in all directions: wires, flexible and coated with rubber, soaked in protective solution, and covered with twisted thread. Like thin black nerves, they coiled over the earth in shallow ditches, just beneath the surface, or traversed the air on tall poles. They accompanied the telegraph wires along all the railway lines; they crossed the forests on straight paths decreed for them. The telephone wires of the army hung high above the earth in the forest tree-tops; their course was marked on the map and the line was carefully secured wherever necessary. In the summer no one paid any attention to them, but in the winter they paid dearly for this neglect. The forests, where the wind-spirit waved his snowy hands, took little heed of these black rubber-coated wires. Suddenly the tree-tops and the branches would break under their great burden of snow, and bring the wire down with them. Sometimes it caught in the fork of a branch a little lower down, stretched taut like the string of a violin; and a wire, that had been laid loosely across the trees, now had to stand a strain and the contraction of the cold. If only it were made of copper which is so tough and classic! But for a long time past steel wire had been used for all the army telephones, except for the Imperial Section between Mitau and the Palace at Berlin which was of pure copper; so the wire, in obedience to the laws of physics, broke. It stood the tension stubbornly for a while and then snapped; one of the parted ends whistled through the air and curled round a branch like a lasso, tangled among the slender birch twigs; the other sprang back, caught in the undergrowth, and lay there in loose folds; in a few hours it was buried beneath half a yard of snow. At the edge of the forest, snow-drifts a yard high were heaped up before nightfall; the wind was the master-mason of this wall. Roaring and exulting he laid his snow-bricks against trunks, undergrowth, and tree-tops; the swirling air, like a solid thing, served him both as trowel and as mortar. To the right or left of the railway lines, according to the direction of the wind, there rose silently or in tumult, slanting dunes of snow, which could engulph a man up to his chin. Twilight fell, and winter howled and laughed and moaned.

Throughout the land, in corrugated-iron hutments, the timber houses of the country, and cabins of tarred pasteboard, were scattered the signallers, the telegraph-companies, repair-parties, and labour-companies. They knew there would be plenty for them to do next day, so they sat listening to the spirit of the snow as he clapped his hands and drummed and beat upon their walls, and they watched the cracks which had let in so many draughts, getting gradually blocked up, so that a genial warmth began to spread about the room. There were some pleasant trips before them in the morning, but they would not think about that now. This evening they would play *skat* under the lamp or sleep in their bunks. It would do no harm to grease their boots again, oil the soles, and hold their puttees up against the light to see if there were any holes in them.

Snow upon Mervinsk… The city, on the slope of its low hill, was protected from the weather, and some distance from the centre of this whirling storm. But at nights the street grew full of snow. Winter had begun. It was now time to see whether there was wood enough stacked up in the courtyards, so that at least they might keep warm. The Jewish and Polish cab-drivers were polishing up their little Russian street-sleighs. Over the open spaces on the outskirts of the town, between railway buildings, platforms, hutments, store-houses, and over the town itself, blew an icy wind with flurries of snow, a faint image of the storm that roared and revelled in the forest. But no one minded the windy tournament in the sheltered streets of the town that was their home. This time the snow was falling heavily. It had begun the day before, and now it was lying two feet deep. Electric light had been newly installed, and a sturdy little dynamo made the wires hum with throbbing life. Would the snow bring them down? – that was what everyone was thinking about. If they held, they held. If they broke, offices, hutments, and prisons would be plunged in darkness till they were repaired.

★

When, early in the morning after Lychow's departure, an order was received from the Kommandantur that the prisoner Bjuscheff was not to leave his cell that day, the corporal on duty whistled through his teeth and merely said:

'So soon?'

Daylight was slow in coming. When they crowded into the yard for parade, some rubbed their eyes and thought the snow looked very comfortable, others hoped for a little snowballing. But the sergeant-major detailed the men for duty and kept them busy supervising the gangs of civilians who were sweeping away the snow; after which, quite casually and without any explanation, he gave the order about Grischa; and so Grischa was allowed to snore in peace.

He slept on in happy ignorance, and as the day was dark, he slept till late into the morning, and the guard were not disposed to wake him. As compared with Lychow, he was but a mole, he could not know what was happening in the kingdom of the gods, how his protector had gone on leave, though he had left Winfried with full authority to represent him in the matter. When Grischa at last awoke about midday, much refreshed by his sleep, but hungry and chilled to the bone, he had a somewhat uncanny feeling. The sense of time, which never entirely forsakes a man, told him that several hours of the day had already gone. He was amazed that nobody had opened the door, that he had not been called for parade or for breakfast. Under his bed was a secret and forbidden store of cigarettes, bread, all sorts of odds and ends, and a little money. The stove would want stoking up to-day, he thought; he felt terribly cold. Unfortunately he had given Max's bottle of schnapps to Babka. He had, however, such profound confidence in his friend the General, that he merely thought some detail of the daily routine had gone wrong; he never guessed that his own life was at stake. He drew his stool up to the window: a thick cushion of white snow lay along the narrow projecting ledge in front of it. Snow lay everywhere. Grischa's heart rejoiced. Snow meant home: snow meant Vologda, and the little sledge in which Grischa raced over the steppes drawn by his grandfather's solitary dog. Snow was an infinite playground: snow was so clean that a boy might eat it, snow was so soft that a boy might roll in it; it was warm and it was cold. A snowfall in Mervinsk might well have surprised him; but it merely gave him intense pleasure. For in his home at Vologda, towards the end of October, the great snowstorms had already begun to sweep over the long-since frozen steppe, and with the snow came sledges in which men travelled all the faster to their friends. 'This snow,' said Grischa to himself with a smile, 'is blowing in the Germans' faces.' As he was hungry, he lit a cigarette and smoked with tolerable contentment though he was shivering with cold. He unfolded his cloak which had served him as a pillow, and put it on. 'Ah, that's better,' he thought with satisfaction, 'now I don't mind what happens.' And something did happen. He had not smoked a third part of his yellow cigarette when a guard hammered on the cell door.

'Russky,' said a voice, 'you're smoking. Don't let anyone catch you; I don't mind, but if anyone comes I'll let you know.'

'Come in, open the door, comrade,' said Grischa, astonished. 'What's happening in Mervinsk?'

'You may well ask,' said the other.

'It's snowing,' said Grischa, by way of a reply.

'You may say that,' said the other.

'Is there no work to-day? Is it a holiday?'

'You may say that too,' answered the voice, gruffly. It was Arthur Polanke of the Landwehr, from the Choriner Strasse, Berlin N., who was talking to the prisoner. 'Yes, it's a holiday. To-day's Reformation Day; but that means nothing to you, you're little better than a heathen.'

'It's all so quiet,' said Grischa. 'I shouldn't mind a bit of breakfast.'

'Of course it's quiet when the company's away on duty; but you can have some coffee, though if I were you I should wait till twelve o'clock. It won't be long; it's nearly half-past eleven now.'

'Company away on duty?' said Grischa in astonishment. 'Then why have I been in bed so long?'

The man outside was silent. He seemed to be reflecting for a moment whether he should speak; then he said in a low voice:

'I'll tell you. The old man went on leave yesterday.'

'Who?' asked Grischa innocently. 'Brett-schneider?'

'Lord, no, he's there all right. I meant your old man, Lychow. And we've had orders that you're not to be let out of your cell. It's a summer cell too, so they must have their knife into you again. And as your case isn't settled and you haven't got into any more trouble, you may explain it if you can, because I can't.'

Grischa listened, and laboriously reproduced these words and images in the terms of his own thoughts; then with a short laugh he said:

'Beasts! They're revenging themselves while the General's away. Afterwards they'll say it was a mistake, or somebody's orders.'

As the prisoner could not see him, the guard grinned ominously and muttered: 'I'm glad you take it like that. Now I'll open your cell, and you can clean it – that'll let some warmth into it. There's no work this afternoon, the stoves will all be going strong, and if the corporal on duty will look the other way, we'll leave the door open all the afternoon, so that you'll at least have company, and it will be nice and warm for you.'

And Grischa thanked him.

And when the dried vegetables and tinned beef were brought round at midday, Grischa's mess-tin was filled very full, and he thoroughly enjoyed his dinner.

Then he left his cell, which they had actually forgotten to lock, and went into the guardroom, where the men of the Landwehr were just lighting their pipes, and the barrack orderly was carrying off the empty mess-tins to wash them out with warm water and wood-shavings. When Grischa came in some of them glanced up from the cards which had been just dealt, others from their letters, or their books, and then turned back to what they were doing, with rather too noticeable an unconcern. Grischa filled a pannikin with hot water from the great iron cauldron on the stove, and was about to go and empty his mess-tin in the common trough outside – that invaluable trough that provided food for three pigs. And as Lychow lived near by, the men might rely on the fact that these animals would be fattened up for ham and bacon, and not wasted as mere pork, as happened to so many pigs behind the lines; strict orders were given that these valuable animals should have free access to the kitchen refuse. But when he had got to the door, Corporal Hermann Sacht walked up to Grischa and said:

'Half a minute, Russky; you go and wash that out in your bucket.'

'But what about the pigs?' Grischa answered with a smile.

'We won't bother about the pigs to-day, old man,' said the corporal very gravely. 'You mustn't be seen outside. You're to exercise in the yard from two to three, with the others; you'd better curl up in your bunk.'

From this, and from the strange deathly stillness that followed the corporal's words, Grischa understood. He stood motionless, his mouth and eyes grew a little pale, as he looked at the man who was almost his friend.

'Now you know what's up,' said the corporal contemptuously; but the contempt was not for Grischa.

'Yes,' said Grischa, 'I do.' He cleared his throat sharply, and then, stiffly and with measured steps he crossed the room, followed by the looks of all that sat there, and passed along the dark passage to his cell; it was one of the first, on the right hand, against the outer wall. Hermann Sacht watched him go, and then went after him.

'Leave the door of your cell open, Russky, you must keep warm, and if you want to smoke – well, we're smoking, and no one will notice you.'

And Grischa thanked him.

About this time the snowstorm burst in full force over Mervinsk. The cell was full of smouldering twilight. Grischa stretched himself out on the bed, with his hands under his head, and covered by his two blankets. He reflected that a mattress, stuffed with wood shavings, did not give much warmth in winter. At first the shrill icy blasts of wind whistled through the window-frames, cleaving the tobacco smoke into whirling clouds, but in a few minutes that same wind had blocked up every crack with snow, and the air in the stone-paved cell gradually grew warmer.

'Now it is finished,' thought Grischa, 'and I must go.'

Only a few minutes before, he had felt himself secure, sheltered by a protecting hand, and now the certainty of death was upon him, swift and inevitable, death while his limbs were strong and wholesome, and he turned over on his bed as if he felt the walls of his coffin against his body, and all were at an end. A bitter taste mounted to his palate from his throat, and he thought: 'Well, I shan't be sorry when it's finished; now, at least, my troubles will be over.'

He sank back in utter exhaustion and despair, his mouth opened suddenly and as the pipe dropped from his hand he fell into a deep sleep, though, indeed, his heavy meal and the oncoming darkness had as much to do with it as the numbness at his heart. Men who have known something of life, and have had to bear a hand in tasks that they have hated, have no great need of telegrams and official instructions in order to grasp what is going on. Grischa, who was to be shot, and the company who were presumably to shoot him, alike knew what was to happen, even before Schieffenzahn, far away at Brest, had taken down the telephone receiver to send a certain order on its way along the wire.

Shortly before two o'clock Hermann Sacht, who had passed quietly by the open cell, said in astonishment to the corporal on duty:

'Russky's asleep; do you think we'd better leave him alone?'

'I don't mind,' said the corporal, 'but orders are orders; he must go out for exercise.'

'Yes, his health is very precious,' said Hermann Sacht, in grim irony, as he snapped the padlock on the cell door, 'but perhaps he would like to have another look at the snow coming down, and hear the doves cooing up in the roof, and the sparrows fluttering through the drill-shed, which is the only place you get a breath of air in this sort of weather. Who do you think will have to do him in?'

'We shall, of course; it's our job.'

'That's right enough,' said Hermann Sacht, with a laugh, as he slung his rifle over his shoulder, 'he'll be shot with the rifles he's cleaned himself.'

'Oh, well, he'll be sure there'll be no dirt on the bullets,' said the other, nodding. 'And we'll have our cartridge-cases to remember the Russky by, until we throw them away.'

'Perhaps it would be a good thing to dig his grave soon; if we wait till the ground freezes it will take twice as long.'

'And perhaps there'll be one of those coffins left which he and the little Jew sweated at for so long.'

'Of course there will,' said one of the company, looking up from his game of draughts; 'there are at least five in reserve and two extra big ones. He'd certainly fit one of those.'

'Two minutes to two,' said the other with a whistle of surprise as he glanced at his watch. 'Wake him up, and a pleasant afternoon to you.'

★

Under the drill-shed, which was well enough suited for parades and physical exercises, though it was hardly large enough for drilling, the wind blew wafts of snow, tiny icy crystals, or gusts of frozen rain, right under the roof almost to the inner wall. Little spectral eddies of dust arose from the ground, twisting like dervishes till they dropped and gave up their transient ghosts. The sparrows chirped busily in every corner, pecked about for seeds, or sat, puffed out like little balls, upon the rafters. From their safe, warm lodging in the roof came the contented cooing of the doves.

'It's hardly weather for a walk even here,' thought Hermann Sacht as he stamped about patiently by the side of Grischa whose hands were thrust deep in his overcoat pockets. His woolly, khaki-coloured overcoat (one of those which Sluschin & Co. did so well over), and his German boots which did not match, kept him warm. He tramped along, inside the row of wooden roof supports, from one end to the other of the shed, ninety-three paces in all, and back again. And Hermann Sacht saw that he was thinking. But he was not exactly thinking: as he walked up and down, he watched the snow in the air, his eyes wandered over the dust on the ground, the wooden beams, the nails, the nests in their several corners, the dark nooks where the beams joined the rafters, the spiders' webs, and the fluffy little sparrows; and he listened to the cooing of the doves and the creaking of his guard's leather belt. As he took all these things in, he asked himself:

'Will these things last?'

The keen air did him good. 'How long,' thought he, 'shall I breathe this air?' He must try to understand how the air entered his lungs: man is blown out like a ball. He frowned, and stared steadily before him as he tried to imagine what it would be like when a man could no longer blow out this ball. After about twenty minutes he turned to Hermann Sacht, who, so as not to disturb his prisoner, was walking quietly up and down in the opposite direction; but his cloak was much thinner, he was pitiably cold, and he was burdened with a rifle weighing nine pounds, not to speak of a supply of cartridges.

'Shall we go in?'

It was not really a question, but a kind of friendly command. Grischa was changed, though he had not noticed it. In a tone of voice that he had not used since his escape, and with the quiet assurance of a seasoned soldier, he had suggested what he knew was best for him.

Hermann Sacht looked at him doubtfully. 'This sort of breeze takes a bit of getting used to; and you've got the right to a full hour, Russky.'

Grischa nodded. 'I know,' he said, 'but we'd better go in all the same.'

'If you weren't a decent sort,' said Hermann Sacht, with a sigh of relief, as they hurried back to the building, keeping close to the wall and carefully avoiding the storm-swept yard, 'you might have kept me hopping about here for a good forty minutes, though I want to pack up a parcel and write a letter with it. But you are a decent sort,' he reflected, as his eyes wandered over his prisoner, apparently seeking some solution; 'a really decent sort, and yet everything goes wrong with you.'

'Oh, what does it matter whether I'm a decent sort or not,' said Grischa, in a voice that showed his complete indifference to such distinctions. 'When did the sentence or the order come through?'

'Sentence?' said Hermann Sacht, as they walked through the covered passage which connected the main building and the second yard, or drill-ground, with the guardroom. 'You've made a mistake. It hasn't come through, nor yet an order. Nothing has happened at all.'

'Then how do you know that they are going to…'

'Oh come, old boy,' said Hermann Sacht, meaningly, 'it's pretty clear, isn't it? They've had their knife into you for a long time, and have made up their minds to carry the sentence out, and as soon as the General has turned his back, they lock you up. That's as plain as your face. If the Divisional Office ask for you this morning the people here will say you're ill, or they'll have the cheek to say straight out: "Nothing doing." Meanwhile they'll telephone to Schieffenzahn. "Lychow's away," they'll say, "shall we do it now?" What more do they want? I may be wrong, but we're both old soldiers; we've been a long time in this line of business. And, O Lord—' he suddenly stopped. 'Here's the War going on for another winter.'

These last words were uttered in so hopeless a tone, that Grischa realized that here was a man who envied him – who would certainly sooner live than die, but if he had to die, would rather be killed now than next spring.

'True, comrade,' he said, 'the grave is dark but at least it's quiet,' and a wan smile flickered round the corners of their dark unshaven lips and their despairing eyes.

⌒

Arnold Zweig was born in Glogau, Silesia (now Glogow, Poland) in 1887, the son of a Jewish saddler. At the outbreak of the war, he enlisted in the German Army. He was first sent to the Western Front (he fought at Verdun) and then served at the Army Headquarters on the Eastern Front, where he came into contact with the Jews of eastern Europe. In 1920, he published *The Face of East European Jewry*, written in an attempt to convince German Jews to empathize with their eastern European brethren. A committed Socialist Zionist, Zweig went in 1923 to Berlin to edit the *Judische Rundschau* newspaper. He began Freudian therapy and started a revealing correspondence with Freud: in a letter he told Freud: 'I personally owe to your psychological therapy the restoration of my whole personality.' In 1927, Zweig published *The Case of Sergeant Grischa*, now a classic of war literature. Based on an actual case, it is the story of the mistaken identity of a Russian sergeant who is caught, tried and executed as a deserter from the German Army. A powerful satire on bureaucracy, the book is unusual in its sympathetic portrayal of the relationship between guards and prisoners. Witnessing in 1933 the burning of his books by the Nazis, Zweig remarked that the crowd 'would have stared as happily into the flames if live humans were burning'. A year later, he went into voluntary exile; first in Czechoslovakia, later in Palestine, where he became disillusioned with Zionism. In 1948, he returned to the GDR. Zweig died in East Berlin in 1968.

EDLEF KÖPPEN

CAVALRY CHARGE

from *Military Communiqué*

translated by Martin Chalmers

CURTAIN UP!
       Curtain up, Fricke turns away from the binocular periscope, his hand grabs Reisiger's collar: 'Cavalry!'

Cavalry. The enemy is attacking with cavalry. Cavalry appears out of the hollow. Grey, gleaming bubbles approach: Steel helmets, a line, from Loos to the slagheap. There approach horses' heads, a nodding line, brown and black and white, from Loos to the slagheap. It comes brown and black and white, closely crowded bulk, squeezed forward without a gap from Loos to the slagheap.

It grows out of the hollow, pushed up, hastening, cavalry bounding up in unbroken rank! Up, and in full view now. And stands, pausing incomprehensibly slowly between hail and rain and thunder of the German infantry, of the German batteries.

Fricke at the binoculars: 'There's a second line coming!'

Before the naked eye the same again. Out of the hollow, behind the slow mass of pushing horse bodies, once again horses and riders. From Loos to the slagheap.

'Lieutenant!' Aufricht has put down the telephone, is staring beside Reisiger.

Fricke: 'Let them, let them, they have to come closer.'

He says it hoarsely, strangely, bawling. – 'They have to come closer.' Reisiger's knees are shaking: 'There!'

As yet no artillery round falls in the waiting, the rising phalanx of horsemen.

And Reisiger, his arm suddenly under the lieutenant's arm: 'They're charging!'

They're charging. The first wave briefly rises. Sinks back. Rises. Down. Up, down, up, down, up. Trotting. Behind it the second rank, up, down, up, trotting, two ranks simultaneously, close together, trotting. And trotting. And, at one bound, the whole front jumps forward, horses' legs lengthening their stride, hooves stretching into the air, and up and stretched, and down and gallop, and their stomachs on the ground, heads forward, full gallop! Nearer, two rows, towards the trenches. And the riders, lances still at shoulder-height, and now couched, nearer, full gallop.

There an animal falls, there one goes down on its front legs, there one rears up, there a rider rolls off, there one is dragged along by the stirrup.

Full gallop forward.

There a gap tears open, four horses wide, in the first rank. There six, eight, nine topple sideward and twitch in a struggling heap. Unchecked, irreversible, unstoppable living force, gallop. Closer, nearer, closer. Over the top of the English infantry positions, further, closer, nearer. – The three observing from the chimney panting. Their eyes back and forward, first rank, second rank, back and forward, riders, horses, first rank, second rank nearer, nearer, gallop.

And—

Open fire between the lines!

How many telephones buzz at this moment?

How many voices shout: 'Cavalry between the trenches'?

How many commands, hard, metallic in tone, call a halt, reduce range, bring the barrage back just in front of the German positions as a curtain of leaping flames.

'Cavalry between the trenches!' Each leap means coming closer by three yards. Closer, gallop—

And that's where it comes to a stop.

The Germans forget everything, out of holes and trenches, up out of cover, standing and firing, gaze burning in horses' eyes, in horsemen's eyes, blood-red flickering pupils looking straight at them. In their sights – Fire! Light machine-guns, heavy machine-guns, Fire! Field artillery, Fire!

And all of it biting greedily, biting into the dully groaning thick mass of the thundering cavalry charge.

The three on the factory chimney, command gasped out, hoarsely passed on, and now hanging over the edge.

This drama on the most tremendous scale! The first rank, the second rank, no longer separate now, embroiled, already in trouble, already only one rank, already too close to the intended movement. And there's a sawing and stamping and crushing and wallowing and biting in.

Machine-guns in among the kicking horses' legs, the jagged stumps scuff over the ground, shrapnel bursts at their chests, shells below their stomachs, bundled sulphur-yellow tongues of flame, columns of brown smoke, jets of blood and entrails as thick as an arm, limbs and rumps of animals and men hurled up. All that as far as the massif stretches, from Loos to the slagheap.

The whole now collapses into squares, gaps between them. The squares now ponderously pressing forward, break, pile up in a mass, detach themselves, so that everywhere something jumps up, up, sinks down, thrashes about, lies. All that: crushed horses, crushed riders from Loos to the slagheap.

And still no end. One group tries to turn the horses' heads around, away, back! And there something dashes away. And there something crawls with fluttering movements.

Fricke, shrilly: 'There, Reisiger – they want to break away, there—' And even more shrilly: 'Battery rapid fire, a hundred yards forward!' How many commands have raced down the telephone lines? Rapid fire! Let no one get away!

Rapid fire. How can even one rider escape?

Madness is quick, the final fear, the most terrifying terror. Not one horse turns. Even the dead still presses only forward.

All the batteries and every rifle remain right in front of their noses.

Hundreds crash down again and again, hundreds try to scramble up again and again. All batteries, all rifles against it.

Even the dead is torn to pieces again and again, again and again.

Hands are raised out of the tenacious, blood-streaming rampart; faces, unrecognisable, rise, gestures flutter.

Standing, in the open, the German infantry brings to bear its coups de grâce. Until everything suffocates inertly in the bloody pulp.

And the English infantry behind that, in their trench, separated from the Germans only by this steaming rampart? Have they had to look on, destruction of their people, death of their brothers down to the last man? Have they fled?

The three on the chimney, greedy for more hits: 'Where is the English infantry?'

The telephone buzzes. Aufricht picks up. 'Our infantry will mount an attack on the lost positions in four minutes. All batteries heavy barrage.'

Fricke, calmly: 'Increase the range, old target!'

How many wires give the same order at the same moment? – All the artillery of the section puts down a heavy barrage on the English infantry.

Fricke: 'How many minutes left?'

Aufricht: 'The attack begins in one minute.'

The English trenches are ploughed by the annihilatory barrage. And now the German infantry jumps up, forward, certain, wades through the bloody swamp, up to their waists in slippery corpses.

Is the enemy firing?

Some raise their rifles to their cheek, no more than one every ten yards, and are cut to pieces by shells. No machine-guns, artillery quite tentative, only shrapnel and the rounds much too high to hold the attacker.

And the Germans, as their artillery, precise to the second, lifts the curtain of fire, safely down into the trenches, into the old position.

Whatever raises its arms is cut down with the bayonet. With hand grenades whatever tries to come up the steps of the dugouts in surprise. 'The operation,' say the telephone lines in the Loos–slagheap section, 'has been carried out in accordance with orders.' The three on the chimney are relieved around midday. The firing position and the streets of Lens are quiet.

Today 1/96 artillery regiment has fired for four hours without itself being hit once.

★

...but to break through without rest day and night, across the second and third lines into the open ground... These conditions ensure success...

⌣

The posthumous literary reputation of **Edlef Köppen** (1893–1939) depends essentially on one book, *Heeresbericht*, published in 1930. There was an English translation as early as 1931 under the title 'Higher Command' – though an accurate rendering of the German title would be 'Military Communiqué'. In the novel Köppen describes the experience of Adolf Reisiger, a volunteer and junior officer in an artillery unit who serves, largely on the Western Front, from October 1914 to the end of the war. Köppen's own wartime career was broadly similar to that, except that in September 1918 he was confined in a mental asylum for disobeying orders. *Heeresbericht* is, on the one hand, a description of human survival amidst the immense technological expenditure of modern warfare and, on the other, an account of increasing disillusion in the face of the slaughter on the Western Front and elsewhere. The chapters which describe the combat situations, the competing artillery barrages and the hospital stays are interrupted by documentary quotations, montages of extracts from newspaper reports, army dispatches, government declarations, wartime advertising and theatre programmes. After the war Köppen suffered ill health, having been several times wounded in action. He found a professional home, however, in the new medium of radio and helped develop the radio play as a form. His pacifist views and his novel cost him his job when the Nazis came to power in 1933. He got by writing reviews and scripts under a pseudonym, but died in 1939 due to the long-term effect of a war wound.

JOSEPH ROTH

DAD

MY ~~SON~~ IS DEAD!

from *The Radetzky March*

translated by Michael Hofmann

T HAT VERY NIGHT, the Jäger battalion marched to the north-eastern frontier at Woloczyska. It began raining, gently at first, then harder and harder, until the white dusty roads were turned to silvery grey mud. The mud smacked together over the boots of the soldiers, and spattered the spotless uniforms of the officers marching to their regulation deaths. Their long sabres got in their way, the magnificent, long-haired pompoms dangling from their black and yellow sashes were now tangled, wet and mired by thousands of little spots of mud. At daybreak, the battalion reached its destination, joined up with a couple of other infantry regiments, and fell into extended order. They waited like that for two days, and there was nothing to be seen of the war. Sometimes they heard isolated, distant shots from somewhere to the right of them. There were little frontier skirmishes between cavalry units. From time to time they caught glimpses of wounded revenue officers, and occasionally a dead border guard. Medical orderlies removed the casualties, dead or wounded, under the eyes of the waiting troops. The war refused to start. It hung fire, as occasionally thunderstorms will hang fire for days before breaking out.

On the third day came the command to withdraw, and the battalion got into marching order. Officers and men alike were disappointed. A rumour spread that two miles east of them, an entire regiment of dragoons had been pulverized, and that enemy Cossacks had already broken through into the interior. The troops marched westward in grim silence. They soon realized that this was an unplanned retreat, because at the crossroads and in the villages and small towns on their route, they encountered a confused mixture of all sorts of forces. The high command issued contradictory orders. Most of these were to do with the evacuation of towns and villages, and the treatment of pro-Russian Ukrainians, Orthodox priests and spies. Hastily formed courts martial handed down hasty judgments. Secret informants supplied unverifiable reports on peasants, priests, teachers, photographers, civil servants. There was no time. They were in a hurry to retreat, but also in a hurry to punish the traitors. And while ambulances, baggage columns, field guns, dragoons, uhlans and infantrymen met up in various configurations under the incessant rain on the softened roads, while couriers galloped this way and that, while the inhabitants of the little towns fled west in endless hordes, surrounded by the white terror, laden with chequered white and red feather beds, grey sacks, brown chairs and tables, and blue oil lamps – while all this went on, in the little church squares of the villages and hamlets, the shots of hastily assembled firing squads executed the hasty death sentences, and ominous drum rolls accompanied the monotonous judgments of the courts martial, and the wives of the slain lay screaming for mercy in front of the muddied boots of the officers, and flickering red and silver flames shot out of huts and barns, sheds and outbuildings. The Austrian army's war began with punishments, with courts martial. For many days the real or supposed traitors were left dangling on trees in the church squares, as an example to the living. But far and wide, the living had fled. Fires burned round the hanging corpses, and the leaves caught, and the fire was stronger than the continuous, drizzling rain that ushered in a bloody autumn. The old bark of the ancient trees slowly turned to charcoal, and tiny, silver, smouldering sparks darted out between the little ridges of it, like fiery worms, and licked at the leaves; the green foliage shrivelled up and turned red, then black, then grey; the ropes loosened, and the corpses fell to the ground, with blackened faces and bodies untouched.

One day, they stopped in the village of Krutyny. They had got there in the afternoon and were due to leave the next morning, before daybreak, on their westward route. That day, the rain had let up, and a late September sun spun a kindly, silvery light over the wide, still unharvested fields, the living bread that would never be eaten. An Indian summer drifted slowly through the air. Even the crows and ravens were quiet, deceived by the brief peace of the day, and hence without hope of any carrion. The troops had been in the same clothes for eight days now. Their boots were sodden, their feet swollen, their knees stiff, their calves sore, their backs too locked to bend. They found billets in some huts, tried to pull dry clothes out of their kit-bags and wash in the few wells. It was a clear, calm night, but for the noise of abandoned dogs howling with fear and hunger in the isolated farmyards; the Lieutenant was unable to sleep. He left the hut where he was billeted. He walked down the long village street, towards the church tower which pointed its Orthodox double cross at the stars. The church, with its shingle roof, stood in the middle of a small graveyard, ringed by crooked wooden crosses that seemed to dance in the night. Outside the wide, grey, open gates of the graveyard three bodies were hanging, a bearded priest flanked by two young peasants in sand-coloured jackets with coarsely woven straw shoes on their motionless feet. The priest's black cowl reached down to his shoes. Occasionally, the night wind caused his feet to brush against his priestly robe like the clapper of a bell, but without making any noise.

Lieutenant Trotta went up to the hanged men. He looked at their swollen faces. He thought he could recognize in the three of them various of his men. They were the faces of people with whom he dealt on a daily basis. The broad black beard of the priest reminded him of Onufri's beard. That was what Onufri had looked like, the last time he'd seen him. And who knows, maybe this hanged priest was Onufri's brother. Lieutenant Trotta looked around. He listened. There were no human sounds to be heard. In the bell tower of the church, there was the rustle of bats. The abandoned dogs barked in the abandoned farms. The Lieutenant drew his sabre, and one after the other, cut down the three hanged men. Then he shouldered one body after the other and carried them to the graveyard. With his shining sabre, he began to loosen the soil on the paths between the graves until he thought he'd made enough space for three bodies. He laid them in the hole, all together, scraped the earth over them, with sabre and scabbard, trampled it down with his feet and trod it firm. Then he made the sign of the cross. Not since the final mass in the cadet school of Mahrisch- Weisskirchen had he made the sign of the cross. He wanted to say a Lord's Prayer as well, but he only moved his lips soundlessly. Some unknown night bird screamed. The bats rustled. The dogs howled.

The following morning, they were on the march again before sun-up. The world was swathed in the silvery fogs of an autumn morning. Before long, though, the sun came through, glowing like high summer. They became thirsty. They were marching across a sandy, abandoned plain. From time to time they had the illusion of hearing the sound of running water. A few soldiers ran in the direction of the sound, only to turn back soon enough. No streams, no ponds, no wells. They passed through a couple of villages, but their wells were choked with the corpses of shootings and summary justice. The corpses, some of them bent double, dangled over the wooden rims of the wells. The soldiers didn't bother to look into the depths. They rejoined the company. They marched on.

Their thirst grew. Noon approached. They heard shots, and flung themselves to the ground. The enemy had presumably overtaken them. They crawled forward on their hands and knees. Ahead of them, they could see already, the road widened. There was the gleam of an abandoned railway station. The tracks began there. At a trot, the battalion reached the security of the station; for a few miles from there, they would be covered by the railway embankments. The enemy, perhaps a swift sotnia of Cossacks, might be just alongside them, on the other side of the embankment. Depressed and silent, they marched along between the embankments. Suddenly a man cried: 'Water!' And a moment later, they had all seen the well on the embankment slope, next to a watchman's hut. 'Halt!' ordered Major Zoglauer. 'Halt!' the other officers ordered. But the thirsty men could not be stopped. One by one to begin with, then in groups, the men charged up the slope; shots rang out, and the men fell. The enemy cavalry the other side of the embankment shot at the thirsty men, and more and more thirsty men ran towards the fatal well. By the time the second platoon of the second company approached the well, there were already more than a dozen bodies on the green slope.

'Platoon halt!' ordered Lieutenant Trotta. He stood aside and said: 'I'll get you water! No one move! Wait here! Get me a bucket!' He was brought a couple of waterproof canvas buckets from the machine gun section. He took one in each hand. And he walked up the slope, towards the well. Bullets whistled around him, clattered at his feet, flew past his ears and his legs and over his head. He leaned over the well. On the other side of the slope he saw two rows of Cossacks firing at him. He wasn't afraid. It never occurred to him that he, like the others, might be shot. He could hear the bullets before they were shot, and, at the same time, the first drumming bars of the Radetzky March. He stood on the balcony of his father's house. The army band was playing below. Now Nechwal raised the black ebony baton with the silver head. Now Trotta dipped the second of his buckets into the well. Now the cymbals clashed. Now he pulled the bucket up. With a brimming bucket in either hand, with bullets fizzing around him, he put out his left foot to begin the descent. He took two steps. Now it was only his head that wasn't covered by the slope.

And now a bullet struck his skull. He took another step and fell. The buckets toppled and swayed and emptied themselves over him. Warm blood poured from his head on to the cool earth of the embankment. From down below the Ukrainian peasants in his platoon chorused: 'Praise be to Christ Jesus!'

For ever and ever, amen! he wanted to say. They were the only words of Ruthenian that he knew. But his lips could no longer move. His mouth gaped open. His white teeth grimaced against the blue autumn sky. His tongue slowly went blue, he could feel his body cool. And then he died.

That was the end of Lieutenant Carl Joseph, Baron von Trotta.

So simple and so inappropriate for literary treatment in the primers of the K-and-K elementary schools of Austria was the death of the grandson of the hero of Solferino. Lieutenant Trotta died, not with sword in hand, but with a couple of buckets of water. Old Trotta read the letter a couple of times, and let his hands sink. The letter fell from his hands, and fluttered down on to the burgundy carpet. Herr von Trotta did not remove his pince-nez. His head trembled, and the wobbly pince-nez, with its oval glasses, fluttered like a glass butterfly on the old man's nose. Two heavy, crystal tears fell simultaneously from Herr von Trotta's eyes, smeared the glasses of his spectacles, and ran on down into his whiskers. His body remained still, only his head trembled back and forth and from side to side, and all the time the glass wings of his pince-nez were aflutter. The District Commissioner sat at his desk like that for an hour or more. Then he stood up, and walked through into his house, quite normally. He took his black suit out of his wardrobe, his black tie and his black crepe mourning ribbons that he had worn on his hat and sleeve following his father's death. He changed, not looking in the mirror as he did. His head was still trembling. He did his best to tame his unruly head. But, the harder the District Commissioner tried, the more his head trembled. His pince-nez still sat fluttering on his nose. At last, the District Commissioner gave up all his endeavours, and simply allowed his skull to tremble. In his black suit, with his black mourning ribbon on his sleeve, he went into Fraulein Hirschwitz, remained standing in the doorway, and said: 'My dear, my son is dead!' He quickly shut the door, went into his office, from one room to the next, stuck his trembling head in all the doors and announced everywhere: 'My son is dead, Herr Suchandsuch! My son is dead, Herr Suchandsuch!' Then he took his hat and cane, and went out on the street. All the passers-by greeted him, and were bemused by his trembling head. The District Commissioner would stop the occasional one of them and say: 'My son is dead!' And he didn't wait for the other to show consternation and sympathy, but walked straight on, to Dr Skovronnek. Dr Skovronnek, now in the uniform of a colonel in the army Medical Corps, was spending his mornings in the garrison hospital and his afternoons, as before, in the café. He rose when the District Commissioner walked in, saw the old man's trembling, and looked at his unsteady head and fluttering pince-nez. 'My son is dead!' repeated Herr von Trotta. Skovronnek kept his friend's hand for a long time, for minutes. Both remained standing there, hand in hand. The District Commissioner sat down, Skovronnek moved the chess board on to an adjacent table. When the waiter came up, the District Commissioner said: 'My son is dead!' And the waiter bowed very low, and brought him a cognac.

'Another, please!' ordered the District Commissioner. At last, he removed his pince-nez. He remembered that the notification of his death was still lying on the carpet in the office, and he got up and returned to his residence. Dr Skovronnek followed him. Herr von Trotta appeared unaware of it. But nor was he at all surprised when, without knocking, Skovronnek opened the office door, walked in, and stopped. 'This is the letter!' said the District Commissioner.

The old Herr von Trotta did not sleep that night or on many of the following nights. His head continued to tremble and shake, even when it was resting on pillows. Sometimes the District Commissioner would have dreams of his son. Lieutenant Trotta would stand in front of his father, with his officer's cap filled with water, and say: 'Drink, Father, you're thirsty!' The dream recurred more and more frequently. And eventually the District Commissioner learned to summon his son every night, and some nights Carl Joseph came to him more than once. In consequence, Herr von Trotta began to long for night and bedtime, the day made him impatient. And when spring came, and the days grew longer, the District Commissioner would darken his room in the mornings and evenings, and so seek to prolong the nights artificially.

His head would not stop shaking. And he himself and everyone else gradually became used to the continual shaking.

The war seemed not to concern Herr von Trotta very much. He would only pick up a newspaper in order to conceal his trembling head behind it. There was never any discussion of victories and defeats between himself and Dr Skovronnek. Usually they just played chess, and in complete silence. But sometimes one would say to the other: 'Do you remember the game we played two years ago? You were just as careless then as you are now.' It was as though they were talking about events that had transpired decades before.

A long time had passed since the news of the death, the seasons had relieved one another in accordance with the old and immutable laws of nature, though mankind barely felt them under the red veil of war, and, of all men the District Commissioner felt them perhaps the least. His head was still trembling like a large, though light fruit on the end of a thin stem. Lieutenant Trotta had long since rotted away, or been eaten by the ravens who circled that day over the deadly railway embankment, but old Herr von Trotta continued to feel as though he'd learned of his death only yesterday. And he kept the letter from Major Zoglauer, now also deceased, in his inside pocket; every day he read it and it retained its terrible freshness and novelty, just like a funeral mound that is kept and tended by grieving hands. What did Herr von Trotta care about the hundred thousand dead who had since followed his son? What did he care about the hasty and confused decisions taken by the people above him, that were issued on a weekly basis? And what did he care about the end of the world, which he could now see approaching with even greater clarity than once the prophetic Chojnicki could? His son was dead. His job was over. His world had ended.

↬

Joseph Roth was born in 1894 in the Galician town of Brody, then part of the Austro-Hungarian Empire. He died in Paris in 1939. In 1914, Roth went to Vienna to study philosophy and in 1916 he volunteered to fight in the Imperial Army on the Eastern Front. The war and the collapse of the Austro-Hungarian Empire were key events in Roth's life and the major themes of his writing. His best-known work is *The Radetzky March*, from which this extract is taken. In his fiction and journalism, Roth deals with the major events of his time – the migration of millions of displaced persons, the rise of National Socialism and the dangers of appeasement. 'It must be understood – let me say loud and clear – the European mind is capitulating. It is capitulating out of weakness, out of sloth, out of apathy, out of lack of imagination…' *The Radetzky March* is very much a book that announces the end of empire. At the end of the book, Lieutenant Trotta dies, his father dies and the Emperor dies. Dr Skovronnek is still alive but without a chess partner:

It occurred to him that it was afternoon, the hour for their chess game was approaching. Now he didn't have a partner any more; nevertheless, he decided to go to the café. As they left the cemetery, the burgomaster invited him to ride in his carriage. Dr Skovronnek climbed in.

'I would have liked to say in my address,' said the burgomaster, 'that Herr von Trotta couldn't have outlived the Emperor. Don't you agree, doctor?'

'I don't know,' replied Dr Skovronnek, 'I don't think either of them could outlive Austria.'

No one does 'elegiac' like Roth.

JOHN GALSWORTHY

THE GIBBET

from *Forsytes, Pendyces and Others*

CAN'T DESCRIBE THE STREET I turned into then – it was like no street I have ever been in, so long, so narrow, so regular, yet somehow so unsubstantial that one had sometimes a feeling that walking at the grey houses on either side one would pass through them. I must have gone miles down it without meeting even the shadow of a human being, when just as it was growing dusk I saw a young man come silently out as I supposed of a door, though none was opened. I can describe neither his dress nor figure. Like the street, he looked unsubstantial, and left on me an impression as of hunger. Yes, the expression on his shadowy face haunted me; it was so like that of a starving man before whom someone has set a meal down, then snatched it away. And now out of every house on either side young men like him started forth in that mysterious manner, all with that hungry look on their almost invisible faces. They seemed to gaze at me as I passed as if they were looking for someone, till, peering at one of them, I said:

'What do you want – whom do you want?'

He gave me no answer, and by now it was so dark that I could not see his face at all – none of their faces, and only had the feeling of being hungrily watched as I went along, it seemed for ever, without getting to any turning out of that interminable street. At last in desperation I doubled in my tracks and began walking back in the direction whence

I had come. A lamplighter must have been following me, for now every lamp was lighted, giving a faint glittering greenish glare, as might lumps of phosphorescent matter hung up in the dark. The hungry phantom-like young men had vanished, and I was wondering where they could have gone when I saw – some distance ahead – a sort of greyish whirl-pool stretching across the street, under one of those lamps that flickered like a marsh light. A noise was coming from that swirl or whatever it was, for it seemed to be raised above the ground – a ghostly sound, swishing as of feet amongst dry leaves, deepened by the gruntings of some deep sense satisfied. I crept forward till I made out that it was really formed of human figures whirling slowly round and round the lamp in what seemed to be a dance. And suddenly I stood still in horror. Every other figure of those dancers was a skeleton, and between every two skeletons danced a young girl in white, so that the whole swirling ring was formed alternately of skeletons and these grey-white girls. They took no notice of me, and I crept a little nearer still. Yes! these skeletons were the young men I had seen starting out of the houses as I passed, with the look of queer and awful hunger on their faces that now seemed to grin. The girls who danced between them had wan, pitiful beauty, and their eyes were turned to the skeletons whose long hands grasped theirs, as though begging them to return to flesh. Not one noticed me, so deeply were they all absorbed in their mystic dance. Then I saw what they were dancing round. Above their heads, below the greenish lamp, a dark thing was dangling. It swung and turned there like a joint of meat roasting before a fire – the fully dressed body of an elderly man. The green lamplight glinted on his grey hair, and on his bloated features when the face came athwart the light. It swung slowly from left to right, and the dancers as slowly whirled from right to left, always meeting that revolving face, as though to enjoy the sight of it. What did it mean – what were they doing? these sad shapes rustling round the obscene thing suspended there! What strange and awful rite was I watching by the ghostly phosphorescence of that lamp? If those hungry skeletons and wan-grey girls haunted and amazed me, much more haunting and gruesome was that dead face up there with the impress still on it of bloated life; how it gripped and horrified me, with its dead fishy eyes and its neck thick-rolled with flabby flesh, turning and turning on its invisible spit to the sound of feet swishing in dead leaves, and those grunting sighs. What was this ghostly revenge on the gibbeted figure which yet had a look of cold and fattened power? Who was it they had caught and swung up there, like some dead crow, to sway in the winds of heaven? What awful crime towards these skeleton dancers and pale maidens could this elderly man be expiating?

And I remembered with a shudder how those young men had looked at me as I passed, and suddenly it came to me: I was watching the execution of MY generation. There it swung, gibbeted by the youths and maidens whom, through its evil courses, it had murdered. And seized with panic I ran forward up the street straight through the fabric of my dream, that swayed and rustled to left and right of me.

John Galsworthy was born in Surrey in 1867. Trained as a barrister, Galsworthy travelled in the 1890s for his family shipping firm and met Joseph Conrad, whose close friend he became. Conrad encouraged him to write. In 1906, Galsworthy published *The Man of Property*, the first volume of *The Forsyte Saga*, his best-known work which chronicles the suffocating morality of an upper-middle-class family. During the war, Galsworthy worked as a hospital orderly in northern France. This powerful story is a homage to the generation of men who died in the war. It is taken from his short story collection *Forsytes, Pendyces and Others*, which was published posthumously in 1935. Throughout his life Galsworthy campaigned for prison reform, women's rights, animal welfare and the abolition of censorship. In 1932, he was awarded the Nobel Prize for Literature. He died six weeks later in London.

ERICH MARIA REMARQUE

SWEET DREAMS THOUGH THE GUNS ARE BOOMING

from *All Quiet on the Western Front*

translated by Brian Murdoch

W HEN ROLL CALL IS OVER Kat says to me, 'How do you fancy roast goose?'

'Not a bad idea,' I reply.

We climb on to a munitions convoy. The ride costs us two cigarettes. Kat has taken careful note of the place. The shed belongs to the head-quarters of some regiment. I decide that I will fetch the goose, and I get instructions on how to do it. The shed is behind the wall, and only barred with a wooden peg.

Kat cradles his hands for me, I put my foot in and scramble up over the wall. Meanwhile Kat keeps a look-out.

I wait for a few moments to let my eyes get used to the dark, then pick out where the shed is. I creep towards it very quietly, grope for the peg, take it out and open the door.

I can make out two white shapes. Two geese. That's a nuisance; if you grab one, the other one will make a racket. So it'll have to be both of them – it should work, if I'm quick.

I make a jump for them. I get one of them straight away, then a couple of seconds later the other one. I bang their heads against the wall like a madman, trying to stun them. But I obviously don't use enough force. The beasts hiss and beat out all round them with their wings and

· 533 ·

their feet. I fight on grimly, but my God, geese are strong! They tug at me and I stumble this way and that. In the dark these white things have become terrifying, my arms have sprouted wings and I'm almost afraid that I'll take off into the skies, just as if I had a couple of observation balloons in my hands.

And then the noise starts; one of them has got some air into his throat and sounds off like an alarm clock. Before I can do anything about it I hear noises coming towards me from outside, something shoves me and I'm lying on the ground listening to angry growling. A dog. I look to one side, and he makes for my throat. I lie still at once and pull my chin down into my collar.

It's a bull mastiff. After an eternity it draws its head back and sits down beside me. But whenever I try to move, it growls. I think for a moment. The only thing I can do is try and get hold of my service revolver. At all events I have to get out of here before anyone comes. Inch by inch I move my hand along.

I feel as if this is all going on for hours. Every time I make a slight movement there is a threatening growl; I lie still and try again. The minute I get hold of my gun, my hand starts to tremble. I press down against the ground and think it out: pull the gun out, shoot before he can get at me, and get the hell out as quickly as possible.

I take a deep breath and calm myself. Then I hold my breath, jerk up the revolver, there is a shot and the mastiff lurches aside, howling, I make it to the door of the shed and tumble over one of the geese, which was flapping out of the way.

I make a grab while I'm still running, hurl it with a great swing over the wall and start to scramble up myself. I'm not quite over the wall when the mastiff, which has come to itself again, is there and jumping up at me. I drop down quickly. Ten paces away from me stands Kat with the goose in his arms. As soon as he sees me, we run for it.

At last we can get our breath back. The goose is dead, Kat saw to that in a moment. We want to roast it straight away, before anyone realizes what has happened. I fetch pots and some wood from the huts, and we crawl into a small, deserted shed that we know about and which is useful for things like this. We put up a thick covering to block the only window hole. There is a makeshift cooker there – an iron plate lying across some bricks. We light a fire.

Kat plucks and draws the goose. We put the feathers carefully to one side. We want to use them to stuff two small pillows, with the motto 'Sweet Dreams though the Guns are Booming' on them.

The barrage from the front can be heard as a dull humming all around our hideout. Firelight flickers on our faces, shadows dance on the walls. Airmen drop bombs. At one point we hear muffled screaming. One of the huts must have been hit.

Aircraft roar. The *ratatat* of the machine-guns gets louder. But our light can't be seen from anywhere outside.

And so we sit facing one another, Kat and I, two soldiers in shabby battledress, roasting a goose in the middle of the night. We don't talk much, but we have a greater and more gentle consideration for each other than I should think even lovers do. We are two human beings, two tiny sparks of life; outside there is just the night, and all around us, death. We are sitting right at the edge of all that, in danger but secure, goose fat runs over our fingers, our hearts are close to one another, and time and place merge into one – the brightnesses and shadows of our emotions come and go in the flickering light of a gentle fire. What does he know about me? What do I know about him? Before the war we wouldn't have had a single thought in common – and now here we are, sitting with a goose roasting in front of us, aware of our existence and so close to each other that we can't even talk about it.

It takes a long time to roast a goose, even when it is young, and there is plenty of fat. And so we take turns. One does the basting, while the other gets a bit of sleep. Gradually there is a wonderful smell all around us.

The noises from outside all merge into one another, become a dream which disappears from the waking memory. Half asleep, I watch Kat as he lifts and lowers the basting spoon. I love him; his shoulders, his angular, slightly stooped frame – and then I see woods and stars behind him, and a kindly voice says words to me that bring me peace, me, an ordinary soldier with his big boots and his webbing, and his pack, who is making his tiny way under the sky's great vault along the road that lies before him, who forgets things quickly and who isn't even depressed much any more, but who just goes onwards under the great night sky.

A little soldier and a kindly voice, and if anyone were to caress him, he probably wouldn't understand the gesture any more, that soldier with the big boots and a heart that has been buried alive, a soldier who marches because he is wearing marching boots and who has forgotten everything except marching. Aren't those things flowers, over there on the horizon, in a landscape that is so calm and quiet that the soldier could weep? Are those not images that he has not exactly lost, because he never had them to lose, confusing images, but nevertheless of things that can no longer be his? Are those not his twenty years of life?

Is my face wet, and where am I? Kat is standing in front of me, his gigantic distorted shadow falls across me like home. He says something softly, smiles and goes back to the fire.

Then he says, 'It's ready.'

'OK, Kat.'

I shake myself. The golden-brown roast is glowing in the middle of the room. We get out our folding forks and pocket-knives and carve ourselves off a leg each. We eat it with army-issue bread that we dip into the gravy. We eat slowly and enjoy it to the full.

'Like it, Kat?'

'Great. How about you?'

'Great, Kat.'

We are brothers, pressing one another to take the best pieces. When we have finished I smoke a cigarette and Kat has a cigar. There is a lot left over.

'Kat, how about us taking a bit over to Kropp and Tjaden?'

'Right,' he says. We cut off a chunk and wrap it up carefully in newspaper. We were planning to take the rest back to our billets, but Kat laughs and just says, 'Tjaden.'

I agree that we'll have to take it all. So we make our way to the hen-run prison to wake up the pair of them. Before we go we pack away the feathers.

Kropp and Tjaden think we are a mirage. Then they get stuck in. Tjaden is gnawing away, holding a wing with both hands as if he were playing a mouth organ. He slurps the gravy out of the pot and smacks his lips. 'I'll never forget you for this.'

We walk back to the huts. There is the great sky again, and the stars, and the first streaks of dawn, and I am walking beneath that sky, a soldier with big boots and a full belly, a little soldier in the early morning – and beside me walks Kat, angular and slightly stooping, my pal.

The silhouettes of the huts loom over us in the dawn light like a black and welcome sleep.

ERICH MARIA REMARQUE

THE DEAD MAN'S ROOM

from *All Quiet on the Western Front*

translated by Brian Murdoch

W E OFTEN GET VOLUNTEER AUXILIARY NURSES from the Red Cross. They are well meaning, but they can be a bit on the clumsy side. When they re-make our beds they often hurt us, and then they are so shaken that they hurt us even more.

The nuns are more reliable. They know how to get hold of us, but we would really prefer them to be more cheerful. Some of them do have a good sense of humour, it's true, and those are great. There is no one who wouldn't do anything in the world for Sister Tina, a wonderful nurse, who cheers up the whole wing, even when we can only see her from a distance. And there are a few more like her. We'd go through hell and high water for them. We really can't complain – you get treated like a civilian by the nuns here. On the other hand, when you think of the garrison hospitals, then you really start to worry.

Franz Waechter doesn't regain his strength. One day he is taken out and doesn't come back. Josef Hamacher knows what has happened. 'We won't see him again. He's been taken to the Dead Man's Room.'

'What Dead Man's Room?'

'You know, the Dying Room—'

'What's that?'

'The small room at the corner of this wing. Anybody who is about to snuff it gets taken there. There are two beds. It's called the Dying Room all over the hospital.'

'But why do they do that?'

'So they don't have so much work afterwards. It's easier, too, because it's right by the entrance to the mortuary. Maybe they want to make sure that nobody dies on the wards, and do it so as not to upset the others. They can keep an eye on a man better, too, if he is in there on his own.'

'What about the man himself?'

Josef shrugs. 'Usually he is past noticing much any more.'

'Does everyone know about this?'

'Anyone who has been here for a while finds out, of course.'

★

That afternoon Franz Waechter's bed is made up again. After a couple of days they come and take the new man away. Josef indicates with his hand where he is going. We watch a good few more come and go.

Relatives often come and sit by the beds crying, or talking softly and shyly. One old lady is very reluctant to leave, but she can't stay there all night, of course. She comes back very early on the following morning, but not quite early enough; because when she goes up to the bed there is already somebody new in it. She has to go to the mortuary. She gives us the apples that she had brought with her.

Little Peter is getting worse, too. His temperature chart looks bad, and one day a flat hospital trolley is put beside his bed. 'Where am I going?' he asks.

'To have your dressings done.'

They lift him on to the trolley. But the nurse makes the mistake of taking his battledress tunic from its hook and putting it on the trolley with him, so that she doesn't have to make two journeys. Peter realizes at once what is going on and tries to roll off the trolley. 'I'm staying here!'

They hold him down. He cries out weakly with his damaged lung, 'I don't want to go to the Dying Room.'

'But we're going to the dressing ward.'

'Then why do you need my tunic?' He can't speak any more. Hoarse and agitated, he whispers, 'Want to stay here.'

They don't answer, and move him out. By the door he tries to sit up. His head of black curls is bobbing, his eyes are full of tears. 'I'll be back! I'll be back!' he shouts.

The door closes. We are all rather worked up, but nobody says anything. Eventually Josef says, 'Plenty of them have said that. But once you are in there you never last.'

★

They operate on me and I puke for two whole days. My bones don't seem to want to knit properly, says the doctor's clerk. There's another man whose bones grow together badly and he has to have them broken again. It's all pretty wretched.

Our latest additions include two recruits who have flat feet. When he is doing his rounds the chief surgeon finds this out and stops, delighted. 'We'll get rid of that problem,' he tells them. 'We'll just do a little operation and you'll both have healthy feet. Take their names, nurse.'

Once he has left, Josef – who knows everything – gives them a warning. 'Whatever you do, don't let him operate on you. That business is the old man's medical hobby-horse. He's dead keen on anyone he can get hold of to work on. He'll operate on you for flat feet, and sure enough, when he's finished you won't have flat feet any more. Instead you'll have club feet and you'll be on crutches for the rest of your days.'

'What can we do?' asks one of them.

'Just say no. You're here to have your bullet wounds treated, not your flat feet. Think about it. Now you can still walk, but just let the old man get you under the knife and you're cripples. He's after guinea pigs for his experiments, and the war is a good time for him, just like it is for all the doctors. Have a look around the ward downstairs; there are at least a dozen men hobbling about after he's operated on them. A good few of them have been here since 1914 or 15 – for years. Not a single one of them can walk better than he could before, and for nearly all of them it's worse, most of them have to have their legs in plaster. Every six months he catches up with them and breaks the bones again, and every time that's supposed to do the trick. You be careful – he's not allowed to do it if you refuse.'

'What the hell,' says one of the two men wearily, 'better your feet than your head. Who knows what you'll get when you're back at the front. I don't care what they do to me, so long as I get sent home. Having a club foot's better than being dead.'

The other one, a young man like us, doesn't want to. The next morning the old man has them brought down and argues with them and bullies them for so long that they both agree after all. What else can they do? They are just the poor bloody infantry and he's top brass. They are brought back chloroformed and with plaster casts on.

★

Albert is in a bad way. They take him away and amputate. The whole leg from the upper thigh downwards is taken off. Now he hardly ever speaks. Once he says that he will shoot himself the minute he can lay his hands on a revolver.

A new hospital transport train arrives. Our room gets two blinded soldiers. One of them is very young, a musician. The nurses never use knives when they feed him; he's already grabbed one once out of a nurse's hand. In spite of these precautions, something still happens. The sister who is feeding him one evening is called away, and leaves the plate and the fork on the side table while she is gone. He gropes across for the fork, gets hold of it and rams it with all his force into his chest, then grabs a shoe and hammers on the shaft as hard as he can. We shout for help and it takes three men to get the fork out. The blunt prongs had gone in a long way. He swears at us all night, so that none of us can sleep. In the morning he has a screaming fit.

Again there are empty beds. One day follows another, days filled with pain and fear, with groans and with the death rattle. Even having a Dying Room is no use any more because it isn't enough; men die during the night in our room. Things just go faster than the nurses can spot.

One day, though, our door is flung open, a hospital trolley is rolled in, and there sits Peter on his stretcher, pale, thin, upright and triumphant, with his tangle of black curls. Sister Tina pushes the trolley over to his old bed with a broad smile on her face. He's come back from the Dying Room. We had assumed he was long since dead.

He looks at us. 'What about that, then?'
And even Josef has to admit that it is a new one on him.

★

After a while a few of us are allowed out of bed. I am given a pair of crutches, too, so that I can hobble about. But I don't use them much; I can't bear the way Albert looks at me when I walk across the ward. His eyes follow me with such a strange look in them. Because of that I often try to slip out into the corridor – I can move more freely there.

On the floor below us there are men with stomach and spinal wounds, men with head wounds and men with both legs or arms amputated. In the right-hand wing are men with wounds in the jaw, men who have been gassed and men wounded in the nose, ears or throat. In the left-hand wing are those who have been blinded and men who have been hit in the lungs or in the pelvis, in one of the joints, in the kidneys, in the testicles or in the stomach. It is only here that you realize all the different places where a man can be hit.

Two men die of tetanus. Their skin becomes pale, their limbs stiffen, and at the end only their eyes remain alive – for a long time. With many of the wounded, the damaged limb has been hoisted up into the air on a kind of gallows; underneath the wound itself there is a dish for the pus to drip into. The basins are emptied every two or three hours. Other men are in traction, with heavy weights pulling down at the end of the bed. I see wounds in the gut which are permanently full of matter. The doctor's clerk shows me X-rays of hips, knees and shoulders that have been shattered completely.

It is impossible to grasp the fact that there are human faces above these torn bodies, faces in which life goes on from day to day. And on top of it all, this is just one single military hospital, just one – there are hundreds of thousands of them in Germany, hundreds of thousands of them in France, hundreds of thousands of them in Russia. How pointless all human thoughts, words and deeds must be, if things like this are possible! Everything must have been fraudulent and pointless if thousands of years of civilization weren't even able to prevent this river of blood, couldn't stop these torture chambers existing in their hundreds of thousands. Only a military hospital can really show you what war is.

I am young, I am twenty years of age; but I know nothing of life except despair, death, fear, and the combination of completely mindless superficiality with an abyss of suffering. I see people being driven against one another, and silently, uncomprehendingly, foolishly, obediently and innocently killing one another. I see the best brains in the world inventing weapons and words to make the whole process that much more sophisticated and long-lasting. And watching this with me are all my contemporaries, here and on the other side, all over the world – my whole generation is experiencing this with me. What would our fathers do if one day we rose up and confronted them, and called them to account? What do they expect from us when a time comes in which there is no more war? For years our occupation has been killing – that was the first experience we had. Our knowledge of life is limited to death. What will happen afterwards? And what can possibly become of us?

*

The oldest man in our room is Lewandowski. He is forty, and has been in the hospital for ten months already with a serious stomach wound. Only in recent weeks has he made enough progress to be able to limp around a little, bent double.

For the past few days he has been very excited. His wife has written to him from the little place away in Poland where she lives, that she has managed to get enough money together to pay for the journey to come and visit him.

She is on her way and might turn up any day. Lewandowski has lost his appetite, and even gives away sausage with red cabbage when he has only eaten a couple of mouthfuls. He is forever going round the room with his letter, and all of us have read it a dozen times already, the postmark has been inspected God knows how often, and there are so many grease stains and fingermarks on it that the writing can barely be deciphered any more. The inevitable happens: Lewandowski gets a fever and has to go back into bed.

He hasn't seen his wife for two years. She had a baby after he left, and she's bringing it with her. But Lewandowski has something quite different on his mind. He had been hoping to get permission to leave the hospital when his old woman came, for obvious reasons; it's all very nice to see someone, but when you get your wife back after such a long time you want something else altogether, if at all possible.

Lewandowski has talked about all this for hours with us, because there are no secrets in the army. Nobody bothers about it, anyway. Those of us who are already allowed out have told him about a few perfect places in the town, gardens and parks where nobody would disturb him. One man even knew of a small room.

But what use is all that now? Lewandowski is confined to bed and miserable. All the joy will go out of his life if he has to miss out on this. We tell him not to worry and promise that we will sort the whole business out somehow.

His wife appears the next afternoon, a little crumpled thing with anxious, darting eyes, like a bird's, wearing a kind of mantilla with frills and bands. God alone knows where she can have inherited the thing.

She murmurs something quietly, and waits shyly by the door. She is shocked to find that there are six of us in the room.

'Come on, Marya,' says Lewandowski, swallowing his Adam's apple dangerously, 'you can come on in, nobody's going to hurt you.'

She walks round the room and shakes hands with each one of us. Then she shows us the baby, which in the meantime has dirtied its nappy. She has a large, beaded bag with her and she takes a clean nappy out of it and neatly changes the child. This gets her over any initial embarrassment, and the two start to talk to each other.

Lewandowski is extremely fidgety and keeps looking across at us miserably with his bulging round eyes.

The time is right. The doctor has done his rounds, and at most a nurse might stick her head into the room. One of us goes outside again nevertheless – to make sure. He comes back in and nods. 'No sign of man nor beast. Just tell her, Johann, and then get on with it!'

The two of them talk in their own language. The wife looks up, blushing a little and embarrassed. We grin amiably and make dismissive gestures – what is there to worry about? To hell with the proprieties, they were made for different times. Here in bed is Johann Lewandowski the carpenter, a soldier who has been crippled by a bullet, and there is his wife – who knows when he will see her again, he wants to have her and he shall have her, and that's that.

Two men stand guard at the door to intercept and occupy any nurses that might happen to come past. They reckon to keep watch for about a quarter of an hour.

Lewandowski can only lie on one side, so someone props a couple of pillows against his back. Albert gets the baby to hold, then we all turn round a bit, and the black mantilla disappears under the covers while we play a noisy and vigorous game of cards.

Everything is fine. I'm holding a damn good hand with all the high cards in clubs which has just about beaten everyone. With all this going on we have almost forgotten Lewandowski. After a time the baby begins to howl, although Albert is rocking it backwards and forwards despairingly. There is a bit of rustling and crackling and when we glance up, as if we were just doing so casually, we see that the child has the bottle in its mouth and is already back with its mother. It all worked.

We now feel like one big family, the woman is bright and cheerful, and Lewandowski lies there sweating and beaming.

He unpacks the beaded bag, and out come a couple of good sausages. Lewandowski takes the knife as if it were a bunch of flowers and saws the meat into chunks. He makes a sweeping gesture of invitation towards us all, and his little crumpled wife moves from one of us to the next, and laughs, and shares out the meat – she looks positively pretty as she does so. We call her 'mother' and she likes that, and plumps our pillows up for us.

★

After a few weeks I have to go to physiotherapy every morning. There they strap up my leg and exercise it. My arm has long since healed.

New hospital transport trains arrive from the front. The bandages are not made out of cloth any more, they are just white crêpe paper. There is too much of a shortage of proper bandage material out there.

Albert's stump heals well. The wound has practically closed. In a few weeks' time he will be sent to be fitted for an artificial leg. He still doesn't talk a lot, and he's much more serious than he was before. Often he breaks off in mid-conversation and just stares into the distance. If he hadn't been with the rest of us he'd have put an end to it long ago.

But now he is over the worst. Sometimes he even watches while we play cards.

I'm given convalescent leave.

My mother doesn't want to let me go again. She is so weak. It is all even worse than last time.

Then I'm recalled by my regiment, and go back to the front. Leaving my friend Albert Kropp is hard. But in the army you get used to things like that.

ERICH MARIA REMARQUE

HE FELL IN OCTOBER

from *All Quiet on the Western Front*

translated by Brian Murdoch

T'S AUTUMN. There are not many of the old lot left. I am the last one
of the seven from our class still here.

Everyone is talking about peace or an armistice. Everyone is waiting.
If there is another disappointment, they will collapse, the hopes are too
strong, they can no longer be pushed aside without exploding. If there
is no peace, then there will be a revolution.

I have been given fourteen days' rest because I swallowed a bit of
gas. I sit all day in a little garden in the sunshine. There will soon be an
armistice, I believe in it too, now. Then we shall go home.

My thoughts stop there and I can't push them on any further. What
attracts me so strongly and awaits me are raw feelings – lust for life,
desire for home, the blood itself, the intoxication of escaping. But these
aren't exactly goals.

If we had come back in 1916 we could have unleashed a storm out
of the pain and intensity of our experiences. If we go back now we shall
be weary, broken-down, burnt-out, rootless and devoid of hope. We shall
no longer be able to cope.

No one will understand us – because in front of us there is a generation of men who did, it is true, share the years out here with us, but who
already had a bed and a job and who are going back to their old positions, where they will forget all about the war – and behind us, a new

generation is growing up, one like we used to be, and that generation will be strangers to us and will push us aside. We are superfluous even to ourselves, we shall grow older, a few will adapt, others will make adjustments, and many of us will not know what to do – the years will trickle away, and eventually we shall perish.

But perhaps all these thoughts of mine are just melancholy and confusion, which will be blown away like dust when I am standing underneath the poplars once again, and listening to the rustle of their leaves. It cannot have vanished entirely, that tenderness that troubles our blood, the uncertainty, the worry, all the things to come, the thousand faces of the future, the music of dreams and books, the rustling and the idea of women. All this cannot have collapsed in the shelling, the despair and the army brothels.

The trees here glow bright and gold, the rowan berries are red against the leaves, white country roads run on towards the horizon, and the canteens are all buzzing like beehives with rumours of peace.

I stand up.

I am very calm. Let the months come, and the years, they'll take nothing more from me, they *can* take nothing more from me. I am so alone and so devoid of any hope that I can confront them without fear. Life, which carried me through these years, is still there in my hands and in my eyes. Whether or not I have mastered it, I do not know. But as long as life is there it will make its own way, whether my conscious self likes it or not.

★

He fell in October 1918, on a day that was so still and quiet along the entire front line that the army despatches restricted themselves to the single sentence: that there was nothing new to report on the western front.

He had sunk forwards and was lying on the ground as if asleep. When they turned him over, you could see that he could not have suffered long – his face wore an expression that was so composed that it looked as if he were almost happy that it had turned out that way.

⌒

Erich Maria Remarque was born in Osnabruck, Germany, in 1898. He was conscripted into the German Army in 1915 and transferred to the Western Front. In combat in July 1917 he received multiple shrapnel wounds and was repatriated to a military hospital. *All Quiet on the Western Front* was written in 1927 but not published till 1929 as Remarque was not immediately able to find a publisher. The book was banned by the Nazis in 1933 and, along with his works, burned in public. That year Remarque and his wife fled to Porto Ronco in Switzerland. During the Second World War, the Nazis arrested his sister, Elfriede Scholz. She was beheaded in December 1943. The Court President declared at the trial: 'Your brother is unfortunately beyond our reach – you, however, will not escape us.' The Remarques spent the war in the United States and returned to Porto Ronco in 1948. He died there in 1970.

All Quiet was an instant success: in its first eighteen months in print it sold 2.5 million copies in twenty-five languages. The film adaptation directed by Lewis Milestone won the Oscar for Best Picture in 1930. The book is a sympathetic portrayal of male camaraderie; it conveys the soldiers' ability to steal moments of pleasure on the front. It is also the moving declaration of a lost generation.

PERMISSIONS

Every endeavour has been made to locate the copyright holders to the texts included here. Please could any copyright holders we were unable to locate get in touch with Serpent's Tail.

★

Extracts from Vera Brittain's *Testament of Youth* are included by permission of Mark Bostridge and Timothy Brittain-Catlin, literary executors for the Vera Brittain Estate; Mulk Raj Anand *Across the Black Waters* © Oriental Paperbacks; Siegfried Sassoon *Memoirs of an Infantry Officer* © Faber and Faber; Mary Borden *The Forbidden Zone* © Patrick Aylmer; Gabriel Chevallier *Fear* © Le Dilettante; Emilio Lussu *A Soldier on the Southern Front* © Giovanni Lussu; Wyndham Lewis *Blasting and Bombardiering* © Wyndham Lewis Memorial Trust; Richard Aldington *Death of a Hero* © Penguin Books; Stratis Myrivilis *Life in the Tomb* © Quartet Books; Raymond Escholier *Mahmadou Fofana* © Françoise Escholier-Achard; Robert Musil *The Blackbird*, translation from the German by Peter Wortsman, from *Posthumous Papers of a Living Author* by Robert Musil © Archipelago Books; Liviu Rebreanu *The Forest of the Hanged* © Peter Owen Books; Jaroslav Hašek *The Good Soldier Švejk* trans. © Cecil Parrott; Miroslav Krleža *The Croatian God Mars* ©HDP Croatian Writers' Society; Viktor Shklovsky *A Sentimental Journey* © Cornell